I0820018

ПРИКЛЮЧЕНИЯ ШЕРЛОКА ХОЛМСА

АРТУР КОНАН ДОЙЛ

Приключения Шерлока Холмса

АРТУР КОНАН ДОЙЛ

Иллюстрации Sidney Paget (1860–1908)

В книгу вошли широко известные рассказы о Шерлоке Холмсе: «Скандал в Богемии», «Союз рыжих», «Установление личности», «Тайна Боскомской долины», «Пять зернышек апельсина», «Человек с рассеченной губой», «Голубой карбункул», «Пестрая лента», «Палец инженера», «Знатный холостяк», «Берилловая диадема», «Медные буки». С иллюстрациями Сидни Паже к первому изданию книги в 1892 году.

ISBN: 978-1-7637479-8-2

СКАНДАЛ В БОГЕМИИ

I

Для Шерлока Холмса она всегда оставалась «Этой Женщиной». Я редко слышал, чтобы он называл ее каким-либо другим именем. В его глазах она затмевала всех представительниц своего пола. Не то чтобы он испытывал к Ирэн Адлер какое-либо чувство, близкое к любви. Все чувства, и особенно любовь, были ненавистны его холодному, точному, но удивительно уравновешенному уму. По-моему, он был самой совершенной мыслящей и наблюдающей машиной, какую когда-либо видел мир; но в качестве влюбленного он оказался бы не на своем месте. Он всегда говорил о нежных чувствах не иначе, как с презрительной насмешкой, с издевкой. Нежные чувства были в его глазах великолепным объектом для наблюдения, превосходным средством сорвать покров с человеческих побуждений и дел. Но для изощренного мыслителя допустить такое вторжение чувства в свой утонченный и великолепно налаженный внутренний мир означало бы внести туда смятение, которое свело бы на нет все завоевания его мысли. Песчинка, попавшая в чувствительный инструмент, или трещина в одной из его могучих линз — вот что такое была бы любовь для такого человека, как Холмс. И все же для него

существовала одна женщина, и этой женщиной была покойная Иран Адлер, особа весьма и весьма сомнительной репутации.

За последнее время я редко виделся с Холмсом — моя женитьба отдалила нас друг от друга. Моего личного безоблачного счастья и чисто семейных интересов, которые возникают у человека, когда он впервые становится господином собственного домашнего очага, было достаточно, чтобы поглотить все мое внимание. Между тем Холмс, ненавидевший своей цыганской душой всякую форму светской жизни, оставался жить в нашей квартире на Бейкер-стрит, окруженный грудами своих старых книг, чередуя недели увлечения кокаином с приступами честолюбия, дремотное состояние наркомана — с дикой энергией, присущей его натуре.

Как и прежде, он был глубоко увлечен расследованием преступлений. Он отдавал свои огромные способности и необычайный дар наблюдательности поискам нитей к выяснению тех тайн, которые официальной полицией были признаны непостижимыми. Время от времени до меня доходили смутные слухи о его делах: о том, что его вызывали в Одессу в связи с убийством Трепова, о том, что ему удалось пролить свет на загадочную трагедию братьев Аткинсон в Тринкомали, и, наконец, о поручении голландского королевского дома, выполненном им исключительно тонко и удачно.

Однако, помимо этих сведений о его деятельности, которые я так же, как и все читатели, черпал из газет, я мало знал о моем прежнем друге и товарище.

Однажды ночью — это было 20 марта 1888 года — я возвращался от пациента (так как теперь я вновь занялся частной практикой), и мой путь привел меня на Бейкер-стрит. Когда я проходил мимо хорошо знакомой двери, которая в моем уме навсегда связана с воспоминанием о времени моего сватовства и с мрачными событиями «Этюда в багровых тонах», меня охватило острое желание вновь увидеть Холмса и узнать, над какими проблемами нынче работает его замечательный ум. Его окна были ярко освещены, и, посмотрев вверх, я увидел его высокую, худощавую фигуру, которая дважды темным силуэтом промелькнула на опущенной шторе. Он

быстро, стремительно ходил по комнате, низко опустив голову и заложив за спину руки. Мне, знавшему все его настроения и привычки, его ходьба из угла в угол и весь его внешний облик говорили о многом. Он вновь принялся за работу. Он стряхнул с себя навеянные наркотиками туманные грезы и распутывал нити какой-то новой загадки. Я позвонил, и меня проводили в комнату, которая когда-то была отчасти и моей.

Он встретил меня без восторженных излияний. Таким излияниям он предавался чрезвычайно редко, но, мне кажется, был рад моему приходу. Почти без слов, он приветливым жестом пригласил меня сесть, подвинул ко мне коробку сигар и указал на погребец, где хранилось вино. Затем он встал перед камином и оглядел меня своим особым, проницательным взглядом.

Then he stood before fire

— Семейная жизнь вам на пользу, — заметил он. — Я думаю, Уотсон, что с тех пор, как я вас видел, вы пополнели на семь с половиной фунтов.

— На семь.

— Правда? Нет, нет, немного больше. Чуточку больше, уверяю вас. И снова практикуете, как я вижу. Вы мне не говорили, что собираетесь впрячься в работу.

— Так откуда же вы это знаете?

— Я вижу это, я делаю выводы. Например, откуда я знаю, что вы недавно сильно промокли и что ваша горничная большая неряха?

— Дорогой Холмс, — сказал я, — это уж чересчур. Вас несомненно сожгли бы на костре, если бы вы жили несколько веков назад. Правда, что в четверг мне пришлось быть за городом и я вернулся домой весь испачканный, но ведь я переменил костюм, так что от дождя не осталось следов. Что касается Мэри Джен, она и в самом деле неисправима, и жена уже предупредила, что хочет уволить ее. И все же я не понимаю, как вы догадались об этом.

Холмс тихо рассмеялся и потер свои длинные нервные руки.

— Проще простого! — сказал он. — Мои глаза уведомляют меня, что с внутренней стороны вашего левого башмака, как раз там, куда падает свет, на коже видны шесть почти параллельных царапин. Очевидно, царапины были сделаны кем-то, кто очень небрежно обтирал края подошвы, чтобы удалить засохшую грязь. Отсюда я, как видите, делаю двойной вывод, что вы выходили в дурную погоду и что у вас очень скверный образчик лондонской прислуги. А что касается вашей практики, — если в мою комнату входит джентльмен, пропахший йодоформом, если у него на указательном пальце правой руки черное пятно от азотной кислоты, а на цилиндре — шишка, указывающая, куда он запрятал свой стетоскоп, я должен быть совершенным глупцом, чтобы не признать в нем деятельного представителя врачебного мира.

Я не мог удержаться от смеха, слушая, с какой легкостью он объяснил мне путь своих умозаключений.

— Когда вы раскрываете свои соображения, — заметил я, — все кажется мне смехотворно простым, я и сам без труда мог бы все это сообразить. А в каждом новом случае я совершенно ошеломлен, пока вы не объясните мне ход ваших мыслей. Между тем я думаю, что зрение у меня не хуже вашего.

— Совершенно верно, — ответил Холмс, закуривая папиросу и вытягиваясь в кресле. — Вы смотрите, но вы не наблюдаете, а это большая разница. Например, вы часто видели ступеньки, ведущие из прихожей в эту комнату?

— Часто.

— Как часто?

— Ну, несколько сот раз!

— Отлично. Сколько же там ступенек?

— Сколько? Не обратил внимания.

— Вот-вот, не обратили внимания. А между тем вы видели! В этом вся суть. Ну, а я знаю, что ступенек — семнадцать, потому что я и видел, и наблюдал. Кстати, вы ведь интересуетесь теми небольшими проблемами, в разрешении которых заключается мое ремесло, и даже были добры описать два-три из моих маленьких опытов. Поэтому вас может, пожалуй, заинтересовать вот это письмо.

Он бросил мне листок толстой розовой почтовой бумаги, валявшийся на столе.

— Получено только что, — сказал он. — Прочитайте-ка вслух.

Письмо было без даты, без подписи и без адреса.

«Сегодня вечером, без четверти восемь, — говорилось в записке, — к Вам придет джентльмен, который хочет получить у Вас консультацию по очень важному делу. Услуги, оказанные Вами недавно одному из королевских семейств Европы, показали, что Вам можно доверять дела чрезвычайной важности. Такой отзыв о Вас мы со всех сторон получали. Будьте дома в этот час и не подумайте ничего плохого, если Ваш посетитель будет в маске».

— Это в самом деле таинственно, — заметил я. — Как вы думаете, что все это значит?

— У меня пока нет никаких данных. Теоретизировать, не имея данных, опасно. Незаметно для себя человек начинает подтасовывать факты, чтобы подогнать их к своей теории, вместо того чтобы обосновывать теорию фактами. Но сама записка! Какие вы можете сделать выводы из записки?

I carefully examined the writing

Я тщательно осмотрел письмо и бумагу, на которой оно было написано.

— Написавший это письмо, по-видимому, располагает средствами, — заметил я, пытаясь подражать приемам моего друга. — Такая бумага стоит не меньше полкроны за пачку. Очень уж она прочная и плотная.

— Диковинная — самое подходящее слово, — заметил Холмс. — И это не английская бумага. Посмотрите ее на свет.

Я так и сделал и увидел на бумаге водяные знаки: большое «E» и маленькое «g», затем «P» и большое «G» с маленьким «t».

— Какой вывод вы можете из этого сделать? — спросил Холмс.

— Это несомненно имя фабриканта или, скорее, его монограмма.

— Вот и ошиблись! Большое «G» с маленьким «t» — это сокращение «Gesellschaft», что по-немецки означает «компания». Это обычное сокращение, как наше «K°». «P», конечно, означает «Papier», бумага. Расшифруем теперь «E». Заглянем в иностранный географический справочник… — Он достал с полки тяжелый фолиант в коричневом переплете. — Eglow, Eglonitz… Вот мы и нашли: Egeria. Это местность, где говорят по-немецки, в Богемии, недалеко от

Карлсбада.[1] Место смерти Валленштейна,[2] славится многочисленными стекольными заводами и бумажными фабриками… Ха-ха, мой мальчик, какой вы из этого делаете вывод? — Глаза его сверкнули торжеством, и он выпустил из своей трубки большое синее облако.

— Бумага изготовлена в Богемии, — сказал я.

— Именно. А человек, написавший записку, немец. Вы замечаете странное построение фразы: «Такой отзыв о вас мы со всех сторон получали»? Француз или русский не мог бы так написать. Только немцы так бесцеремонно обращаются со своими глаголами. Следовательно, остается только узнать, что нужно этому немцу, который пишет на богемской бумаге и предпочитает носить маску, лишь бы не показывать своего лица… Вот и он сам, если я не ошибаюсь. Он разрешит все наши сомнения.

Мы услышали резкий стук лошадиных копыт и визг колес, скользнувших вдоль ближайшей обочины. Вскоре затем кто-то с силой дернул звонок.

Холмс присвистнул.

— Судя по звуку, парный экипаж… Да, — продолжал он, выглянув в окно, — изящная маленькая карета и пара рысаков… по сто пятьдесят гиней каждый. Так или иначе, но это дело пахнет деньгами, Уотсон.

— Я думаю, что мне лучше уйти, Холмс?

— Нет, нет, оставайтесь! Что я стану делать без моего биографа? Дело обещает быть интересным. Будет жаль, если вы пропустите его.

— Но ваш клиент…

— Ничего, ничего. Мне может понадобиться ваша помощь, и ему тоже… Ну, вот он идет. Садитесь в это кресло, доктор, и будьте очень внимательны.

---

[1] Карлсбад (Карловы Вары) — курорт в Чехословакии.

[2] Валленштейн — немецкий полководец XVII века.

Медленные, тяжелые шаги, которые мы слышали на лестнице и в коридоре, затихли перед самой нашей дверью. Затем раздался громкий и властный стук.

— Войдите! — сказал Холмс.

A man entered

Вошел человек ростом едва ли меньше шести футов и шести дюймов,[1] геркулесовского сложения. Он был одет роскошно, но эту роскошь сочли бы в Англии вульгарной. Рукава и отвороты его двубортного пальто были оторочены тяжелыми полосами каракуля; темно-синий плащ, накинутый на плечи, был подбит огненно-красным шелком и застегнут на шее пряжкой из сверкающего берилла. Сапоги, доходящие до половины икр и обшитые сверху дорогим коричневым мехом, дополняли то впечатление варварской пышности, которое производил весь его облик. В руке он держал широкополую шляпу, а верхняя часть его лица была закрыта черной маской, опускавшейся ниже скул. Эту маску, походившую на забрало, он,

[1] Шесть футов и шесть дюймов — приблизительно 1 метр 90 сантиметров.

очевидно, только что надел, потому что, когда он вошел, рука его была еще поднята. Судя по нижней части лица, это был человек сильной воли: толстая выпяченная губа и длинный прямой подбородок говорили о решительности, переходящей в упрямство.

— Вы получили мою записку? — спросил он низким, грубым голосом с сильным немецким акцентом. — Я сообщал, что приду к вам. — Он смотрел то на одного из нас, то на другого, видимо не зная, к кому обратиться.

— Садитесь, пожалуйста. — сказал Холмс. — Это мой друг и товарищ, доктор Уотсон. Он так добр, что иногда помогает мне в моей работе. С кем имею честь говорить?

— Вы можете считать, что я граф фон Крамм, богемский дворянин. Полагаю, что этот джентльмен, ваш друг, — человек, достойный полного доверия, и я могу посвятить его в дело чрезвычайной важности? Если это не так, я предпочел бы беседовать с вами наедине.

Я встал, чтобы уйти, но Холмс схватил меня за руку и толкнул обратно в кресло:

— Говорите либо с нами обоими, либо не говорите. В присутствии этого джентльмена вы можете сказать все, что сказали бы мне с глазу на глаз.

Граф пожал широкими плечами.

— В таком случае я должен прежде всего взять с вас обоих слово, что дело, о котором я вам сейчас расскажу, останется в тайне два года. По прошествии двух лет это не будет иметь значения. В настоящее время я могу, не преувеличивая, сказать: вся эта история настолько серьезна, что может отразиться на судьбах Европы.

— Даю слово, — сказал Холмс.

— И я.

— Простите мне эту маску, — продолжал странный посетитель. — Августейшее лицо, по поручению которого я действую, пожелало, чтобы его доверенный остался для вас неизвестен, и я

должен признаться, что титул, которым я себя назвал, не совсем точен.

— Это я заметил, — сухо сказал Холмс.

— Обстоятельства очень щекотливые, и необходимо принять все меры, чтобы из-за них не разросся огромный скандал, который мог бы сильно скомпрометировать одну из царствующих династий Европы. Говоря проще, дело связано с царствующим домом Ормштейнов, королей Богемии.

— Так я и думал, — пробормотал Холмс, поудобнее располагаясь в кресле и закрывая глаза.

Посетитель с явным удивлением посмотрел на лениво развалившегося, равнодушного человека, которого ему, несомненно, описали как самого проницательного и самого энергичного из всех европейских сыщиков. Холмс медленно открыл глаза и нетерпеливо посмотрел на своего тяжеловесного клиента.

— Если ваше величество соблаговолите посвятить нас в свое дело, — заметил он, — мне легче будет дать вам совет.

Посетитель вскочил со стула и принялся шагать по комнате в сильном возбуждении. Затем с жестом отчаяния он сорвал с лица маску и швырнул ее на пол.

He tore the mask from his face

— Вы правы, — воскликнул он, — я король! Зачем мне пытаться скрывать это?

— Действительно, зачем? Ваше величество еще не начали говорить, как я уже знал, что передо мной Вильгельм Готтсрейх Сигизмунд фон Ормштейн, великий князь Кассель-Фельштейнский и наследственный король Богемии.

— Но вы понимаете, — сказал наш странный посетитель, снова усевшись и поводя рукой по высокому белому лбу, — вы понимаете, что я не привык лично заниматься такими делами! Однако вопрос настолько щекотлив, что я не мог доверить его кому-нибудь из полицейских агентов, не рискуя оказаться в его власти. Я приехал из Праги инкогнито специально затем, чтобы обратиться к вам за советом.

— Пожалуйста, обращайтесь, — сказал Холмс, снова закрывая глаза.

— Факты вкратце таковы: лет пять назад, во время продолжительного пребывания в Варшаве, я познакомился с хорошо известной авантюристкой Ирэн Адлер. Это имя вам, несомненно, знакомо?

— Будьте любезны, доктор, посмотрите в моей картотеке, — пробормотал Холмс, не открывая глаз.

Много лет назад он завел систему регистрации разных фактов, касавшихся людей и вещей, так что трудно было назвать лицо или предмет, о которых он не мог бы сразу дать сведения. В данном случае я нашел биографию Ирэн Адлер между биографией еврейского раввина и биографией одного начальника штаба, написавшего труд о глубоководных рыбах.

— Покажите-ка, — сказал Холмс. — Гм! Родилась в Нью-Джерси в 1858 году. Контральто, гм… Ла Скала, так-так!.. Примадонна императорской оперы в Варшаве, да! Покинула оперную сцену, ха! Проживает в Лондоне… совершенно верно! Ваше величество, насколько я понимаю, попали в сети к этой молодой особе, писали ей компрометирующие письма и теперь желали бы вернуть эти письма.

— Совершенно верно. Но каким образом?

— Вы тайно женились на ней?

— Нет.

— Никаких документов или свидетельств?

— Никаких.

— В таком случае, я вас не понимаю, ваше величество. Если эта молодая женщина захочет использовать письма для шантажа или других целей, как она докажет их подлинность?

— Мой почерк.

— Пустяки! Подлог.

— Моя личная почтовая бумага.

— Украдена.

— Моя личная печать.

— Подделка.

— Моя фотография.

— Куплена.

— Но мы сфотографированы вместе!

— О-о, вот это очень плохо! Ваше величество действительно допустили большую оплошность.

— Я был без ума от Ирэн.

— Вы серьезно себя скомпрометировали.

— Тогда я был всего лишь кронпринцем. Я был молод. Мне и теперь только тридцать.

— Фотографию необходимо во что бы то ни стало вернуть.

— Мы пытались, но нам не удалось.

— Ваше величество должны пойти на издержки: фотографию надо купить.

— Ирэн не желает ее продавать.

— Тогда ее надо выкрасть.

— Было сделано пять попыток. Я дважды нанимал взломщиков, и они перерыли весь ее дом. Раз, когда она путешествовала, мы

обыскали ее багаж. Дважды ее заманивали в ловушку. Мы не добились никаких результатов.

— Никаких?

— Абсолютно никаких.

Холмс засмеялся.

— Ничего себе задачка! — сказал он.

— Но для меня это очень серьезная задача! — с упреком возразил король.

— Да, действительно. А что она намеревается сделать с фотографией?

— Погубить меня.

— Но каким образом?

— Я собираюсь жениться.

— Об этом я слышал.

— На Клотильде Лотман фон Саксен-Менинген. Быть может, вы знаете строгие принципы этой семьи. Сама Клотильда — воплощенная чистота. Малейшая тень сомнения относительно моего прошлого привела бы к разрыву.

— А Ирэн Адлер?

— Она грозит, что пошлет фотоснимок родителям моей невесты. И пошлет, непременно пошлет! Вы ее не знаете. У нее железный характер. Да, да, лицо обаятельной женщины, а душа жестокого мужчины. Она ни перед чем не остановится, лишь бы не дать мне жениться на другой.

— Вы уверены, что она еще не отправила фотографию вашей невесте?

— Уверен.

— Почему?

— Она сказала, что пошлет фотографию в день моей официальной помолвки. А это будет в ближайший понедельник.

— О, у нас остается три дня! — сказал Холмс, зевая. — И это очень приятно, потому что сейчас мне надо заняться кое-какими

важными делами. Ваше величество, конечно, останетесь пока что в Лондоне?

— Конечно. Вы можете найти меня в гостинице Лэнгхэм под именем графа фон Крамма.

— В таком случае, я пришлю вам записочку — сообщу, как продвигается дело.

— Очень прошу вас. Я так волнуюсь!

— Ну, а как насчет денег?

— Тратьте, сколько найдете нужным. Вам предоставляется полная свобода действий.

— Абсолютно?

— О, я готов отдать за эту фотографию любую из провинций моего королевства!

— А на текущие расходы?

Король достал из-за плаща тяжелый кожаный мешочек и положил его на стол.

— Здесь триста фунтов золотом и семьсот ассигнациями, — сказал он.

Холмс написал расписку на страничке своей записной книжки и вручил королю.

— Адрес мадемуазель? — спросил он.

— Брайони-лодж, Серпантайн-авеню, Сент-Джонсвуд.

Холмс записал.

— И еще один вопрос, — сказал он. — Фотография была кабинетного размера?

— Да, кабинетного.

— А теперь доброй ночи, ваше величество, к я надеюсь, что скоро у нас будут хорошие вести... Доброй ночи, Уотсон, — добавил он, когда колеса королевского экипажа застучали по мостовой. — Будьте любезны зайти завтра в три часа, я бы хотел потолковать с вами об этом деле.

II

Ровно в три часа я был на Бейкер-стрит, но Холмс еще не вернулся. Экономка сообщила мне, что он вышел из дому в начале девятого. Я уселся у камина с намерением дождаться его, сколько бы мне ни пришлось ждать. Я глубоко заинтересовался его расследованием, хотя оно было лишено причудливых и мрачных черт, присущих тем двум преступлениям, о которых я рассказал в другом месте. Но своеобразные особенности этого случая и высокое положение клиента придавали делу необычный характер. Если даже оставить в стороне самое содержание исследования, которое производил мой друг, — как удачно, с каким мастерством он сразу овладел всей ситуацией и какая строгая, неопровержимая логика была в его умозаключениях! Мне доставляло истинное удовольствие следить за быстрыми, ловкими приемами, с помощью которых он разгадывал самые запутанные тайны. Я настолько привык к его неизменным триумфам, что самая возможность неудачи не укладывалась у меня в голове.

A drunken-looked groom

Было около четырех часов, когда дверь отворилась и в комнату вошел подвыпивший грум, [1] с бакенбардами, с растрепанной шевелюрой, с воспаленным лицом, одетый бедно и вульгарно. Как ни привык я к удивительной способности моего друга менять свой облик, мне пришлось трижды вглядеться, прежде чем я удостоверился, что это действительно Холмс. Кивнув мне на ходу, он исчез в своей спальне, откуда появился через пять минут в темном костюме, корректный, как всегда. Сунув руки в карманы, он протянул ноги к пылающему камину и несколько минут весело смеялся.

— Чудесно! — воскликнул он, затем закашлялся и снова расхохотался, да так, что под конец обессилел и в полном изнеможении откинулся на спинку кресла.

— В чем дело?

— Смешно, невероятно смешно! Уверен, что вы никогда не угадаете, как я провел это утро и что я в конце концов сделал.

— Не могу себе представить. Полагаю, что вы наблюдали за привычками или, может быть, за домом мисс Ирэн Адлер.

— Совершенно верно, но последствия были довольно необычайные… Однако расскажу по порядку. В начале девятого я вышел из дому под видом безработного грума. Существует удивительная симпатия, своего рода содружество между всеми, кто имеет дело с лошадьми. Станьте грумом, и вы узнаете все, что вам надо. Я быстро нашел Брайони-лодж. Это крохотная шикарная двухэтажная вилла; она выходит на улицу, позади нее сад. Массивный замок на садовой калитке. С правой стороны большая гостиная, хорошо обставленная, с высокими окнами, почти до полу, и с нелепыми английскими оконными затворами, которые мог бы открыть и ребенок. За домом ничего особенного, кроме того, что к окну галереи можно добраться с крыши каретного сарая. Я обошел

[1] Грум — конюх.

этот сарай со всех сторон и рассмотрел его очень внимательно, но ничего интересного не заметил. Затем я пошел вдоль улицы и увидел, как я и ожидал, в переулке, примыкающем к стене сада, конюшню. Я помог конюхам чистить лошадей и получил за это два пенса, стакан водки, два пакета табаку и вдоволь сведений о мисс Адлер, а также и о других местных жителях. Местные жители меня не интересовали нисколько, но я был вынужден выслушать их биографии.

— А что вы узнали об Ирэн Адлер? — спросил я.

— О, она вскружила головы всем мужчинам в этой части города. Она самое прелестное существо из всех, носящих дамскую шляпку на этой планете. Так говорят в один голос все серпантайнские конюхи. Она живет тихо, выступает иногда на концертах, ежедневно в пять часов дня выезжает кататься и ровно в семь возвращается к обеду. Редко выезжает в другое время, кроме тех случаев, когда она поет. Только один мужчина посещает ее — только один, но зато очень часто. Брюнет, красавец, прекрасно одевается, бывает у нее ежедневно, а порой и по два раза в день. Его зовут мистер Годфри Нортон из Темпла.[1] Видите, как выгодно войти в доверие к кучерам! Они его возили домой от серпантайнских конюшен раз двадцать и все о нем знают. Выслушав то, что они мне рассказывали, я снова стал прогуливаться взад и вперед вблизи Брайони-лодж и обдумывать дальнейшие действия.

Этот Годфри Нортон, очевидно, играет существенную роль во всем деле. Он юрист. Это звучит зловеще. Что их связывает и какова причина его частых посещений? Кто она: его клиентка? Его друг? Его возлюбленная? Если она его клиентка, то, вероятно, отдала ему на хранение ту фотографию. Если же возлюбленная — едва ли. От решения этого вопроса зависит, продолжать ли мне работу в Брайони-лодж или обратить внимание на квартиру того джентльмена в Темпле. Этот вопрос очень щекотлив и расширяет поле моих розысков... Боюсь, Уотсон, что надоедаю вам этими подробностями, но, чтобы вы поняли всю ситуацию, я должен открыть вам мои мелкие затруднения.

---

[1] Темпл — лондонский квартал, где сосредоточены конторы юристов.

— Я внимательно слежу за вашим рассказом, — ответил я.

— Я все еще взвешивал в уме это дело, когда к Брайони-лодж подкатил изящный экипаж и из него выскочил какой-то джентльмен, необычайно красивый, усатый, смуглый, с орлиным носом. Очевидно, это и был тот субъект, о котором я слышал. По-видимому, он очень спешил и был крайне взволнован. Приказав кучеру ждать, он пробежал мимо горничной, открывшей ему дверь, с видом человека, который чувствует себя в этом доме хозяином.

Он пробыл там около получаса, и мне было видно через окно гостиной, как он ходит взад и вперед по комнате, возбужденно толкует о чем-то и размахивает руками. Ее я не видел. Но вот он вышел на улицу, еще более взволнованный. Подойдя к экипажу, он вынул из кармана золотые часы и озабоченно посмотрел на них. «Гоните, как дьявол! — крикнул он кучеру. — Сначала к Гроссу и Хенке на Риджент-стрит, а затем к церкви святой Моники на Эджвер-роуд. Полгинеи, если доедете за двадцать минут!»

Они умчались, а я как раз соображал, не последовать ли мне за ними, как вдруг к дому подкатило прелестное маленькое ландо.[1] Пальто на кучере было полузастегнуто, узел галстука торчал под самым ухом, а ремни упряжи выскочили из пряжек. Кучер едва успел остановить лошадей, как Ирэн выпорхнула из дверей виллы и вскочила в ландо. Я видел ее лишь одно мгновение, но а этого было довольно: очень миловидная женщина с таким лицом, в которое мужчины влюбляются до смерти. «Церковь святой Моники, Джон! — крикнула она. — Полгинеи, если доедете за двадцать минут!»

Это был случай, которого нельзя было упустить, Уотсон. Я уже начал раздумывать, что лучше: бежать за ней вслед или прицепиться к задку ландо, как вдруг на улице показался кэб. Кучер дважды посмотрел на такого неказистого седока, но я вскочил прежде, чем он успел что-либо возразить. «Церковь святой Моники, — сказал я, — и полгинеи, если вы доедете за двадцать минут!» Было без двадцати

---

[1] Ландо — открытая коляска, запряженная парой лошадей.

пяти минут двенадцать, и, конечно, нетрудно было догадаться, в чем дело.

Мой кэб мчался стрелой. Не думаю, чтобы когда-нибудь я ехал быстрее, но экипаж и ландо со взмыленными лошадьми уже стояли у входа в церковь. Я рассчитался с кучером и взбежал по ступеням. В церкви не было ни души, кроме тех, за кем я следовал, да священника, который, по-видимому, обращался к ним с какими-то упреками. Все трое стояли перед алтарем. Я стал бродить по боковому приделу, как праздношатающийся, случайно зашедший в церковь. Внезапно, к моему изумлению, те трое обернулись ко мне, и Годфри Нортон со всех ног бросился в мою сторону.

«Слава богу! — закричал он. — Вас-то нам и нужно. Идемте! Идемте!»

«В чем дело?» — спросил я.

«Идите, идите, добрый человек, всего три минуты!»

Меня чуть не силой потащили к алтарю, и, еще не успев опомниться, я бормотал ответы, которые мне шептали в ухо, клялся в том, чего совершенно не знал, и вообще помогал бракосочетанию Ирэн Адлер, девицы, с Годфри Нортоном, холостяком.

Все это совершилось в одну минуту, и вот джентльмен благодарит меня с одной стороны, леди — с другой, а священник так и сияет улыбкой. Это было самое нелепое положение, в каком я когда-либо находился; воспоминание о нем и заставило меня сейчас хохотать. По-видимому, у них не были выполнены какие-то формальности, и священник наотрез отказался совершить обряд бракосочетания, если не будет свидетеля. Мое удачное появление в церкви избавило жениха от необходимости бежать на улицу в поисках первого встречного. Невеста дала мне гинею, и я собираюсь носить эту монету на часовой цепочке как память о своем приключении.

I found myself mumbling responses

— Дело приняло весьма неожиданный оборот, — сказал я. — Что же будет дальше?

— Ну, я понял, что мои планы под серьезной угрозой. Похоже было на то, что молодожены собираются немедленно уехать, и потому с моей стороны требовались быстрые и энергичные действия. Однако у дверей церкви они расстались: он уехал в Темпл, она — к себе домой. «Я поеду кататься в парк, как всегда, в пять часов», — сказала она, прощаясь с ним. Больше я ничего не слыхал. Они разъехались в разные стороны, а я вернулся, чтобы взяться за свои приготовления.

— В чем они заключаются?

— Немного холодного мяса и стакан пива, — ответил Холмс, дергая колокольчик. — Я был слишком занят и совершенно забыл о еде. Вероятно, сегодня вечером у меня будет еще больше хлопот. Кстати, доктор, мне понадобится ваше содействие.

— Буду очень рад.

— Вы не боитесь нарушать законы?

— Ничуть.

— И опасность ареста вас не пугает?

— Ради хорошего дела готов и на это.

— О, дело великолепное!

— В таком случае, я к вашим услугам.

— Я был уверен, что могу на вас положиться.

— Но что вы задумали?

— Когда миссис Тернер принесет ужин, я вам все объясню... Теперь, — сказал он, жадно накидываясь на скромную пищу, приготовленную экономкой, — я должен во время еды обсудить с вами все дело, потому что времени у меня осталось мало. Сейчас без малого пять часов. Через два часа мы должны быть на месте. Мисс Ирэн или, скорее, миссис, возвращается со своей прогулки в семь часов. Мы должны быть у Брайони-лодж, чтобы встретить ее.

— Что же дальше?

— А это предоставьте мне. Я уже подготовил то, что должно произойти. Я настаиваю только на одном: что бы ни случилось— не вмешивайтесь. Вы понимаете?

— Я должен быть нейтрален?

— Вот именно. Не делать ничего. Вероятно, получится небольшая неприятность. Не вмешивайтесь. Кончится тем, что меня отнесут в дом. Через четыре или пять минут откроют окно гостиной. Вы должны стать поближе к этому открытому окну.

— Хорошо.

— Вы должны наблюдать за мною, потому что я буду у вас на виду.

— Хорошо.

— И когда я подниму руку — вот так, — вы бросите в комнату то, что я вам дам для этой цели, и в то же время закричите: «Пожар!» Вы меня понимаете?

— Вполне.

— Тут ничего нет опасного, — сказал он, вынимая из кармана сверток в форме сигары. — Это обыкновенная дымовая ракета, снабженная с обоих концов капсюлем, чтобы она сама собою воспламенялась. Вся ваша работа сводится к этому. Когда вы закричите «Пожар!», ваш крик будет подхвачен множеством людей,

после чего вы можете дойти до конца улицы, а я нагоню вас через десять минут. Надеюсь, вы поняли?

— Я должен оставаться нейтральным, подойти поближе к окну, наблюдать за вами и по вашему сигналу бросить в окно этот предмет, затем поднять крик о пожаре и ожидать вас на углу улицы.

— Совершенно верно.

— Можете на меня положиться.

— Ну, и отлично. Пожалуй, мне пора уже начать подготовку к новой роли, которую придется сегодня играть.

A simple-minded clergyman

Он скрылся в спальне и через несколько минут появился в виде любезного, простоватого священника. Его широкополая черная шляпа, мешковатые брюки, белый галстук, привлекательная улыбка и общее выражение благожелательного любопытства были бесподобны. Дело не только в том, что Холмс переменил костюм. Выражение его лица, манеры, самая душа, казалось, изменялись при каждой новой роли, которую ему приходилось играть. Сцена потеряла в его лице

прекрасного актера, а наука — тонкого мыслителя, когда он стал специалистом по расследованию преступлений.

В четверть седьмого мы вышли из дому, и до назначенного часа оставалось десять минут, когда мы оказались на Серпантайн-авеню. Уже смеркалось, на улице только что зажглись фонари, и мы принялись расхаживать мимо Брайони-лодж, поджидая возвращения его обитателей. Дом был как раз такой, каким я его себе представлял по краткому описанию Шерлока Холмса, но местность оказалась далеко не такой безлюдной, как я ожидал. Наоборот: эта маленькая, тихая улица на окраине города буквально кишела народом. На одном углу курили и смеялись какие-то оборванцы, тут же был точильщик со своим колесом, два гвардейца, флиртовавших с нянькой, и несколько хорошо одетых молодых людей, расхаживавших взад и вперед с сигарами во рту.

— Видите ли, — заметил Холмс, когда мы бродили перед домом, — эта свадьба значительно упрощает все дело. Теперь фотография становится обоюдоострым оружием. Возможно, что Иран так же не хочется, чтобы фотографию увидел мистер Годфри Нортон, как не хочется нашему клиенту, чтобы она попалась на глаза его принцессе. Вопрос теперь в том, где мы найдем фотографию.

— Действительно, где?

— Совершенно невероятно, чтобы Ирэн носила ее при себе. Фотография кабинетного формата слишком велика, и ее не спрятать под женским платьем. Ирэн знает, что король способен заманить ее куда-нибудь и обыскать. Две попытки такого рода уже были сделаны. Значит, мы можем быть уверены, что с собой она фотографию не носит.

— Ну, а где же она ее хранит?

— У своего банкира или у своего адвоката. Возможно и то и другое, но я сомневаюсь и в том и в другом. Женщины по своей природе склонны к таинственности и любят окружать себя секретами. Зачем ей посвящать в свой секрет кого-нибудь другого? Она могла положиться на собственное умение хранить вещи, но вряд ли у нее была уверенность, что деловой человек, если она вверит ему свою

тайну, сможет устоять против политического или какого-нибудь иного влияния. Кроме того, вспомните, что она решила пустить в ход фотоснимок в ближайшие дни. Для этого нужно держать его под рукой. Фотоснимок должен быть в ее собственном доме.

— Но два раза взломщики перерыли дом.

— Чепуха! Они не знали, как надо искать.

— А как вы будете искать?

— Я не буду искать.

— А как же иначе?

— Я сделаю так, что Ирэн покажет его мне сама.

— Она откажется.

— В том-то и дело, что ей это не удастся... Но, я слышу, стучат колеса. Это ее карета. Теперь в точности выполняйте мои указания.

В эту минуту свет боковых фонарей кареты показался на повороте, нарядное маленькое ландо подкатило к дверям Брайони-лодж. Когда экипаж остановился, один из бродяг, стоявших на углу, бросился открывать дверцы в надежде заработать медяк, но его оттолкнул другой бродяга, подбежавший с тем же намерением. Завязалась жестокая драка. Масла в огонь подлили оба гвардейца, ставшие на сторону одного из бродяг, и точильщик, который с такой же горячностью принялся защищать другого. В одно мгновение леди, вышедшая из экипажа, оказалась в свалке разгоряченных, дерущихся людей, которые дико лупили друг друга кулаками и палками. Холмс бросился в толпу, чтобы защитить леди. Но, пробившись к ней, он вдруг испустил крик и упал на землю с залитым кровью лицом. Когда он упал, солдаты бросились бежать в одну сторону, оборванцы — в другую. Несколько прохожих более приличного вида, не принимавших участия в потасовке, подбежали, чтобы защитить леди и оказать помощь раненому. Ирэн Адлер, как я буду по-прежнему ее называть, взбежала по ступенькам, но остановилась на площадке и стала смотреть на улицу; ее великолепная фигура выделялась на фоне освещенной гостиной.

He gave a cry and dropped

— Бедный джентльмен сильно ранен? — спросила она.

— Он умер, — ответило несколько голосов.

— Нет, нет, он еще жив! — крикнул кто-то. — Но он умрет раньше, чем вы его довезете до больницы.

— Вот смелый человек! — сказала какая-то женщина. — Если бы не он, они отобрали бы у леди и кошелек и часы. Их тут целая шайка и очень опасная. А-а, он стал дышать!

— Ему нельзя лежать на улице... Вы позволите перенести его в дом, мадам?

— Конечно! Перенесите его в гостиную. Там удобный диван. Сюда, пожалуйста!

Медленно и торжественно Холмса внесли в Брайони-лодж и уложили в гостиной, между тем как я все еще наблюдал за происходившим со своего поста у окна. Лампы были зажжены, но шторы не были опущены, так что я мог видеть Холмса, лежащего на диване. Не знаю, упрекала ли его совесть за то, что он играл такую роль, — я же ни разу в жизни не испытывал более глубокого стыда, чем в те минуты, когда эта прелестная женщина, в заговоре против которой я участвовал, ухаживала с такой добротой и лаской за раненым. И все же было бы черной изменой, если бы я не выполнил поручения Холмса. С тяжелым сердцем я достал из-под моего пальто

дымовую ракету. «В конце концов, — подумал я, — мы не причиняем ей вреда, мы только мешаем ей повредить другому человеку».

Холмс приподнялся на диване, и я увидел, что он делает движения, как человек, которому не хватает воздуха. Служанка бросилась к окну и широко распахнула его. В то же мгновение Холмс поднял руку; по этому сигналу я бросил в комнату ракету и крикнул: «Пожар!» Едва это слово успело слететь с моих уст, как его подхватила вся толпа. Хорошо и плохо одетые джентльмены, конюхи и служанки — все завопили в один голос: «Пожар!» Густые облака дыма клубились в комнате и вырывались через открытое окно. Я видел, как там, за окном, мечутся люди; мгновением позже послышался голос Холмса, уверявшего, что это ложная тревога.

Проталкиваясь сквозь толпу, я добрался до угла улицы. Через десять минут, к моей радости, меня догнал Холмс, взял под руку, и мы покинули место бурных событий. Некоторое время он шел быстро и не проронил ни единого слова, пока мы не свернули в одну из тихих улиц, ведущих на Эджвер-роуд.

— Вы очень ловко это проделали, доктор, — заметил Холмс.

— Как нельзя лучше. Все в порядке.

— Достали фотографию?

— Я знаю, где она спрятана.

— А как вы узнали?

— Ирэн мне сама показала, как я вам предсказывал.

— Я все же ничего не понимаю.

— Я не делаю из этого никакой тайны, — сказал он, смеясь. — Все было очень просто. Вы, наверно, догадались, что все эти зеваки на улице были моими сообщниками. Все они были наняты мною.

— Об этом-то я догадался.

— В руке у меня было немного влажной красной краски. Когда началась свалка, я бросился вперед, упал, прижал руку к лицу и предстал окровавленный... Старый прием.

— Это я тоже смекнул...

— Они вносят меня в дом. Ирэн Адлер вынуждена принять меня, что ей остается делать? Я попадаю в гостиную, в ту самую комнату, которая была у меня на подозрении. Фотография где-то поблизости, либо в гостиной, либо в спальне. Я твердо решил выяснить, где именно. Меня укладывают на кушетку, я притворяюсь, что мне не хватает воздуха. Они вынуждены открыть окно, и вы получаете возможность сделать свое дело.

— А что вы от этого выиграли?

— Очень много. Когда женщина думает, что у нее в доме пожар, инстинкт заставляет ее спасать то, что ей всего дороже. Это самый властный импульс, и я не раз извлекал из него пользу. В случае дарлингтоновского скандала я использовал его, также и в деле с арнсворским дворцом. Замужняя женщина спасает ребенка, незамужняя — шкатулку с драгоценностями. Теперь мне ясно, что для нашей леди в доме нет ничего дороже того, что мы ищем. Она бросилась спасать именно это. Пожарная тревога была отлично разыграна. Дыма и крика было достаточно, чтобы потрясти стальные нервы. Ирэн поступила точно так, как я ждал. Фотография находится в тайничке, за выдвижной дощечкой, как раз над шнурком от звонка. Ирэн в одно мгновение очутилась там, и я даже увидел краешек фотографии, когда она наполовину вытащила ее. Когда же я закричал, что это ложная тревога, Ирэн положила фотографию обратно, глянула мельком на ракету, выбежала из комнаты, и после этого я ее не видел. Я встал и, извинившись, выскользнул из дома. Мне хотелось сразу достать фотографию, но в комнату вошел кучер и начал зорко следить за мною, так что мне поневоле пришлось отложить свой налет до другого раза. Излишняя поспешность может погубить все.

— Ну, а дальше? — спросил я.

— Практически наши розыски закончены. Завтра я приду к Ирэн Адлер с королем и с вами, если вы пожелаете нас сопровождать. Нас попросят подождать в гостиной, но весьма вероятно, что, выйдя к нам, леди не найдет ни нас, ни фотографии. Возможно, что его величеству будет приятно своими собственными руками достать фотографию.

— А когда вы отправитесь туда?

— В восемь часов утра. Она еще будет в постели, так что нам обеспечена полная свобода действий. Кроме того, надо действовать быстро, потому что брак может полностью изменить ее быт и ее привычки. Я должен немедленно послать королю телеграмму.

«Good-night, Mister Herlock Holmes»

Мы дошли до Бейкер-стрит и остановились у дверей нашего дома. Холмс искал в карманах свой ключ, когда какой-то прохожий сказал:

— Доброй ночи, мистер Шерлок Холмс!

На панели в это время было несколько человек, но приветствие, по-видимому, исходило от проходившего мимо стройного юноши в длинном пальто.

— Я где-то уже слышал этот голос, — сказал Холмс, оглядывая скудно освещенную улицу, — но не понимаю, черт возьми, кто бы это мог быть.

III

Эту ночь я спал на Бейкер-стрит. Мы сидели утром за кофе с гренками, когда в комнату стремительно вошел король Богемии.

— Вы действительно добыли фотографию? — воскликнул он, обнимая Шерлока Холмса за плечи и весело глядя ему в лицо.

— Нет еще.

— Но вы надеетесь ее достать?

— Надеюсь.

— В таком случае, идемте! Я сгораю от нетерпения.

— Нам нужна карета.

— Мой экипаж у дверей.

— Это упрощает дело.

Мы сошли вниз и снова направились к Брайони-лодж.

— Ирэн Адлер вышла замуж, — заметил Холмс.

— Замуж? Когда?

— Вчера.

— За кого?

— За английского адвоката, по имени Нортон.

— Но она, конечно, не любит его?

— Надеюсь, что любит.

— Почему вы надеетесь?

— Потому что это избавит ваше величество от всех будущих неприятностей. Если леди любит своего мужа, значит, она не любит ваше величество, и тогда у нее нет основания мешать планам вашего величества.

— Верно, верно. И все же… О, как я хотел бы, чтобы она была одного ранга со мною! Какая бы это была королева!

Он погрузился в угрюмое молчание, которого не прерывал, пока мы не выехали на Серпантайн-авеню.

Двери виллы Брайони-лодж были открыты, и на лестнице стояла пожилая женщина. Она с какой-то странной иронией смотрела на нас, пока мы выходили из экипажа.

— Мистер Шерлок Холмс? — спросила она.

— Да, я Шерлок Холмс, — ответил мой друг, смотря на нее вопрошающим и удивленным взглядом.

— Так и есть! Моя хозяйка предупредила меня, что вы, вероятно, зайдете. Сегодня утром, в пять часов пятнадцать минут, она уехала со своим мужем на континент с Черингкросского вокзала.

— Что?! — Шерлок Холмс отшатнулся назад, бледный от огорчения и неожиданности. — Вы хотите сказать, что она покинула Англию?

— Да. Навсегда.

— А бумаги? — хрипло спросил король. — Все потеряно!

— Посмотрим! — Холмс быстро прошел мимо служанки и бросился в гостиную.

Мы с королем следовали за ним. Вся мебель в комнате была беспорядочно сдвинута, полки стояли пустые, ящики были раскрыты — видно, хозяйка второпях рылась в них, перед тем как пуститься в бегство.

Холмс бросился к шнурку звонка, отодвинул маленькую выдвижную планку и, засунув в тайничок руку, вытащил фотографию и письмо. Это была фотография Ирэн Адлер в вечернем платье, а на письме была надпись: «Мистеру Шерлоку Холмсу. Вручить ему, когда он придет».

Мой друг разорвал конверт, и мы все трое принялись читать письмо. Оно было датировано минувшей ночью, и вот что было в нем написано:

«Дорогой мистер Шерлок Холмс, вы действительно великолепно все это разыграли. На первых порах я отнеслась к вам с доверием. До пожарной тревоги у меня не было никаких подозрений. Но затем, когда я поняла, как выдала себя, я не могла не задуматься. Уже несколько месяцев назад меня предупредили, что если король решит

прибегнуть к агенту, он, конечно, обратится к вам. Мне дали ваш адрес. И все же вы заставили меня открыть то, что вы хотели узнать. Несмотря на мои подозрения, я не хотела дурно думать о таком милом, добром, старом священнике... Но вы знаете, я сама была актрисой. Мужской костюм для меня не новость. Я часто пользуюсь той свободой, которую он дает. Я послала кучера Джона следить за вами, а сама побежала наверх, надела мой костюм для прогулок, как я его называю, и спустилась вниз, как раз когда вы уходили. Я следовала за вами до ваших дверей и убедилась, что мною действительно интересуется знаменитый Шерлок Холмс. Затем я довольно неосторожно пожелала вам доброй ночи и поехала в Темпл, к мужу.

Мы решили, что, поскольку нас преследует такой сильный противник, лучшим спасением будет бегство. И вот, явившись завтра, вы найдете гнездо опустевшим. Что касается фотографии, то ваш клиент может быть спокоен: я люблю человека, который лучше его. Человек этот любит меня. Король может делать все, что ему угодно, не опасаясь препятствий со стороны той, кому он причинил столько зла. Я сохраняю у себя фотографию только ради моей безопасности, ради того, чтобы у меня осталось оружие, которое защитит меня в будущем от любых враждебных шагов короля. Я оставляю здесь другую фотографию, которую ему, может быть, будет приятно сохранить у себя, и остаюсь, дорогой мистер Шерлок Холмс,

преданная вам

Ирэн Нортон, урожденная Адлер».

— Что за женщина, о, что за женщина! — воскликнул король Богемии, когда мы все трое прочитали это послание. — Разве я не говорил вам, что она находчива, умна и предприимчива? Разве она не была бы восхитительной королевой? Разве не жаль, что она не одного ранга со мной?

— Насколько я узнал эту леди, мне кажется, что она действительно совсем другого уровня, чем ваше величество, — холодно сказал Холмс. — Я сожалею, что не мог довести дело вашего величества до более удачного завершения.

— Наоборот, дорогой сэр! — воскликнул король. — Большей удачи не может быть. Я знаю, что ее слово нерушимо. Фотография теперь так же безопасна, как если бы она была сожжена.

— Я рад слышать это от вашего величества.

— Я бесконечно обязан вам. Пожалуйста, скажите мне, как я могу вознаградить вас? Это кольцо…

Он снял с пальца изумрудное кольцо и поднес его на ладони Холмсу.

— У вашего величества есть нечто еще более ценное для меня, — сказал Холмс.

— Вам стоит только указать.

— Эта фотография.

Король посмотрел на него с изумлением.

— Фотография Ирэн?! — воскликнул он. — Пожалуйста, если она вам нужна.

— Благодарю, ваше величество. В таком случае, с этим делом покончено. Имею честь пожелать вам всего лучшего.

«This photograph!»

Холмс поклонился и, не замечая руки, протянутой ему королем, вместе со мною отправился домой.

Вот рассказ о том, как в королевстве Богемии чуть было не разразился очень громкий скандал и как хитроумные планы мистера Шерлока Холмса были разрушены мудростью женщины. Холмс вечно подшучивал над женским умом, но за последнее время я уже не слышу его издевательств. И когда он говорит об Ирэн Адлер или вспоминает ее фотографию, то всегда произносит, как почетный титул: «Эта Женщина».

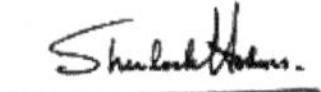

СОЮЗ РЫЖИХ

Это было осенью прошлого года. У Шерлока Холмса сидел какой-то пожилой джентльмен, очень полный, огненно-рыжий. Я хотел было войти, но увидел, что оба они увлечены разговором, и поспешил удалиться. Однако Холмс втащил меня в комнату и закрыл за мной дверь.

— Вы пришли как нельзя более кстати, мой дорогой Уотсон, — приветливо проговорил он.

— Я боялся вам помешать. Мне показалось, что вы заняты.

— Да, я занят. И даже очень.

— Не лучше ли мне подождать в другой комнате?

— Нет, нет... Мистер Уилсон, — сказал он, обращаясь к толстяку, — этот джентльмен не раз оказывал мне дружескую помощь во многих моих наиболее удачных исследованиях. Не сомневаюсь, что и в вашем деле он будет мне очень полезен.

Mr. Jabez Wilson

Толстяк привстал со стула и кивнул мне головой; его маленькие, заплывшие жиром глазки пытливо оглядели меня.

— Садитесь сюда, на диван, — сказал Холмс.

Он опустился в кресло и, как всегда в минуты задумчивости, сложил концы пальцев обеих рук вместе.

— Я знаю, мой дорогой Уотсон, — сказал он, — что вы разделяете мою любовь ко всему необычному, ко всему, что нарушает однообразие нашей будничной жизни. Если бы у вас не было этой любви к необыкновенным событиям, вы не стали бы с таким энтузиазмом записывать скромные мои приключения... причем по совести должен сказать, что иные из ваших рассказов изображают мою деятельность в несколько приукрашенном виде.

— Право же, ваши приключения всегда казались мне такими интересными, — возразил я.

— Не далее, как вчера, я, помнится, говорил вам, что самая смелая фантазия не в силах представить себе тех необычайных и диковинных случаев, какие встречаются в обыденной жизни.

— Я тогда же ответил вам, что позволяю себе усомниться в правильности вашего мнения.

— И тем не менее, доктор, вам придется признать, что я прав, ибо в противном случае я обрушу на вас такое множество удивительных фактов, что вы будете вынуждены согласиться со мной. Вот хотя бы та история, которую мне сейчас рассказал мистер Джабез Уилсон. Обстановка, где она произошла, совершенно заурядная и будничная, а между тем мне сдается, что за всю свою жизнь я не слыхал более чудесной истории... Будьте добры, мистер Уилсон, повторите свой рассказ. Я прошу вас об этом не только для того, чтобы мой друг, доктор Уотсон, выслушал рассказ с начала до конца, но и для того, чтобы мне самому не упустить ни малейшей подробности. Обычно, едва мне начинают рассказывать какой-нибудь случай, тысячи подобных же случаев возникают в моей памяти. Но на этот раз я вынужден признать, что ничего похожего я никогда не слыхал.

Толстый клиент с некоторой гордостью выпятил грудь, вытащил из внутреннего кармана пальто грязную, скомканную газету и разложил ее у себя на коленях. Пока он, вытянув шею, пробегал глазами столбцы объявлений, я внимательно разглядывал его и пытался, подражая Шерлоку Холмсу, угадать по его одежде и внешности, кто он такой.

К сожалению, мои наблюдения не дали почти никаких результатов. Сразу можно было заметить, что наш посетитель — самый заурядный мелкий лавочник, самодовольный, тупой и медлительный. Брюки у него были мешковатые, серые, в клетку. Его не слишком опрятный черный сюртук был расстегнут, а на темном жилете красовалась массивная цепь накладного золота, на которой в качестве брелока болтался просверленный насквозь четырехугольный кусочек какого-то металла. Его поношенный цилиндр и выцветшее бурое пальто со сморщенным бархатным воротником были брошены тут же на стуле. Одним словом, сколько я ни разглядывал этого человека, я не видел в нем ничего примечательного, кроме пламенно-рыжих волос. Было ясно, что он крайне озадачен каким-то неприятным событием.

От проницательного взора Шерлока Холмса не ускользнуло мое занятие.

— Конечно, для всякого ясно, — сказал он с улыбкой, — что наш гость одно время занимался физическим трудом, что он нюхает табак, что он франкмасон,[1] что он был в Китае и что за последние месяцы ему приходилось много писать. Кроме этих очевидных фактов, я не мог отгадать ничего.

Мистер Джабез Уилсон вскочил с кресла и, не отрывая указательного пальца от газеты, уставился на моего приятеля.

— Каким образом, мистер Холмс, могли вы все это узнать? — спросил он. — Откуда вы знаете, например, что я занимался

---

[1] Франкмасоны (сокр. — масоны) — члены тайного религиозно-философского общества.

физическим трудом? Да, действительно, я начал свою карьеру корабельным плотником.

— Ваши руки рассказали мне об этом, мой дорогой сэр. Ваша правая рука больше левой. Вы работали ею, и мускулы на ней сильнее развиты.

— А нюханье табаку? А франкмасонство?

— О франкмасонстве догадаться нетрудно, так как вы, вопреки строгому уставу вашего общества, носите запонку с изображением дуги и окружности.[1]

— Ах да! Я и забыл про нее… Но как вы отгадали, что мне приходилось много писать?

— О чем ином может свидетельствовать ваш лоснящийся правый рукав и протертое до гладкости сукно на левом рукаве возле локтя!

— А Китай?

— Только в Китае могла быть вытатуирована та рыбка, что красуется на вашем правом запястье. Я изучил татуировки, и мне приходилось даже писать о них научные статьи. Обычай окрашивать рыбью чешую нежно-розовым цветом свойствен одному лишь Китаю. Увидев китайскую монетку на цепочке ваших часов, я окончательно убедился, что вы были в Китае.

Мистер Джабез Уилсон громко расхохотался.

— Вот оно что! — сказал он. — Я сначала подумал, что вы бог знает какими мудреными способами отгадываете, а, оказывается, это так просто.

— Я думаю, Уотсон, — сказал Холмс, — что совершил ошибку, объяснив, каким образом я пришел к моим выводам. Как вам известно, «Omne ignotum pro magnifico",[2] и моей скромной славе грозит

---

[1] Дуга и окружность — масонские знаки. Прежде они были тайными, но современные масоны, нарушая старинный устав, нередко носят их на брелоках и запонках.

[2] «Все неведомое кажется нам великолепным» (лат.)

крушение, если я буду так откровенен... Вы нашли объявление, мистер Уилсон ?

— Нашел, — ответил тот, держа толстый красный палец в центре газетного столбца. — Вот оно. С этого все и началось. Прочтите его сами, сэр.

Я взял газету и прочел:

Союз Рыжих во исполнение завещания покойного Иезекин Хопкинса из Лебанона, Пенсильвания (США).

Открыта новая вакансия для члена Союза. Предлагается жалованье четыре фунта стерлингов в неделю за чисто номинальную работу. Каждый рыжий не моложе двадцати одного года, находящийся в здравом уме и трезвой памяти, может оказаться пригодным для этой работы. Обращаться лично к Дункану Россу в понедельник, в одиннадцать часов, в контору Союза, Флитстрит, Попс-корт, 7.

— Что это, черт побери, может означать? — воскликнул я, дважды прочитав необычайное объявление.

Холмс беззвучно засмеялся и весь как-то съежился в кресле, а это служило верным признаком, что он испытывает немалое удовольствие.

— Не слишком заурядное объявление, как по-вашему, а? — сказал он. — Ну, мистер Уилсон, продолжайте вашу повесть и расскажите нам о себе, о своем доме и о том, какую роль сыграло это объявление в вашей жизни. А вы, доктор, запишите, пожалуйста, что это за газета и от какого числа.

— «Утренняя хроника». 27 апреля 1890 года. Ровно два месяца назад.

— Отлично. Продолжайте, мистер Уилсон.

— Как я вам уже говорил, мистер Шерлок Холмс, — сказал Джабез Уилсон, вытирая лоб, — у меня есть маленькая ссудная касса на Сэкс-Кобург-сквер, неподалеку от Сити. Дело у меня и прежде шло неважно, а за последние два года доходов с него хватало только на то, чтобы кое-как сводить концы с концами. Когда-то я держал двух

помощников, но теперь у меня только один; мне трудно было бы платить и ему, но он согласился работать на половинном жалованье, чтобы иметь возможность изучить мое дело.

«What on earth does this mean?»

— Как зовут этого услужливого юношу? — спросил Шерлок Холмс.

— Его зовут Винсент Сполдинг, и он далеко не юноша. Трудно сказать, сколько ему лет. Более расторопного помощника мне не сыскать. Я отлично понимаю, что он вполне мог бы обойтись без меня и зарабатывать вдвое больше. Но, в конце концов, раз он доволен, зачем же я стану внушать ему мысли, которые нанесут ущерб моим интересам?

— В самом деле, зачем? Вам, я вижу, очень повезло: у вас есть помощник, которому вы платите гораздо меньше, чем платят за такую же работу другие. Не часто встречаются в наше время такие бескорыстные служащие.

— О, у моего помощника есть свои недостатки! — сказал мистер Уилсон. — Я никогда не встречал человека, который так страстно увлекался бы фотографией. Щелкает аппаратом, когда нужно работать, а потом ныряет в погреб, как кролик в нору, и проявляет пластинки. Это его главный недостаток. Но в остальном он хороший работник.

— Надеюсь, он и теперь еще служит у вас?

— Да, сэр. Он да девчонка четырнадцати лет, которая кое-как стряпает и подметает полы. Больше никого у меня нет, я вдовец и к тому же бездетный. Мы трое живем очень тихо, сэр, поддерживаем огонь в очаге и платим по счетам — вот и все наши заслуги... Это объявление выбило нас из колеи, — продолжал мистер Уилсон. — Сегодня исполнилось как раз восемь недель с того Дня, когда Сполдинг вошел в контору с этой газетой в руке и сказал: «Хотел бы я, мистер Уилсон, чтобы господь создал меня рыжим».

«Почему?» — спрашиваю я.

«Да вот, — говорит он, — открылась новая вакансия в Союзе рыжих. Тому, кто займет ее, она даст недурные доходы. Там, похоже, больше вакансий, чем кандидатов, и душеприказчики ломают себе голову, не зная, что делать с деньгами. Если бы волосы мои способны были изменить свой цвет, я непременно воспользовался бы этим выгодным местом».

«Что это за Союз рыжих?» — спросил я. — Видите ли, мистер Холмс, я большой домосед, и так как мне не приходится бегать за клиентами, клиенты сами приходят ко мне, я иногда по целым неделям не переступаю порога. Вот почему я мало знаю о том, что делается на свете, и всегда рад услышать что-нибудь новенькое...

«Неужели вы никогда не слыхали о Союзе рыжих?» — спросил Сполдинг, широко раскрыв глаза.

«Никогда».

The League has a vacancy.

«Это очень меня удивляет, так как вы один из тех, что имеет право занять вакансию».

«А много ли это может дать?» — спросил я.

«Около двухсот фунтов стерлингов в год, не больше, но работа пустяковая и притом такая, что не мешает человеку заниматься любым другим делом».

«Расскажите мне все, что вы знаете об этом Союзе», — сказал я.

«Как вы видите сами, — ответил Сполдинг, показывая мне объявление, — в Союзе рыжих имеется вакантное место, а вот и адрес, по которому вы можете обратиться за справкой, если хотите узнать все подробности. Насколько мне известно, этот Союз был основан американским миллионером Иезекией Хопкинсом, большим чудаком. Он сам был огненно-рыжий и сочувствовал всем рыжим на свете. Умирая, он оставил своим душеприказчикам огромную сумму и завещал употребить ее на облегчение участи тех, у кого волосы ярко-рыжего цвета. Мне говорили, что этим счастливцам платят превосходное жалованье, а работы не требуют с них почти никакой».

«Но ведь рыжих миллионы, — сказал я, — и каждый пожелает занять это вакантное место».

«Не так много, как вам кажется, — ответил он. — Объявление, как видите, обращено только к лондонцам и притом лишь ко

взрослым. Этот американец родился в Лондоне, прожил здесь свою юность и хотел облагодетельствовать свой родной город. Кроме того, насколько я слышал, в Союз рыжих не имеет смысла обращаться тем лицам, у которых волосы светло-рыжие или темно-рыжие, — там требуются люди с волосами яркого, ослепительного, огненно-рыжего цвета. Если вы хотите воспользоваться этим предложением, мистер Уилсон, вам нужно только пройтись до конторы Союза рыжих. Но имеет ли для вас смысл отвлекаться от вашего основного занятия ради нескольких сот фунтов?..»

Как вы сами изволите видеть, джентльмены, у меня настоящие ярко-рыжие волосы огненно-красного оттенка, и мне казалось, что, если дело дойдет до состязания рыжих, у меня, пожалуй, будет шанс занять освободившуюся вакансию. Винсент Сполдинг, как человек весьма сведущий в этом деле, мог принести мне большую пользу, поэтому я распорядился закрыть ставни на весь день и велел ему сопровождать меня в помещение Союза. Он очень обрадовался, что сегодня ему не придется работать, и мы, закрыв контору, отправилось по адресу, указанному в объявлении.

Я увидел зрелище, мистер Холмс, какого мне никогда больше не придется увидеть! С севера, с юга, с востока и с запада все люди, в волосах которых был хоть малейший оттенок рыжего цвета, устремились в Сити. Вся Флит-стрит была забита рыжими, а Попс-корт был похож на тачку разносчика, торгующего апельсинами. Никогда я не думал, что в Англии столько рыжих. Здесь были все оттенки рыжего цвета: соломенный, лимонный, оранжевый, кирпичный, оттенок ирландских сеттеров, оттенок желчи, оттенок глины; но, как и указал Сполдинг, голов настоящего — живого, яркого, огненного цвета тут было очень немного. Все же, увидев такую толпу, я пришел в отчаяние. Сполдинг не растерялся. Не знаю, как это ему удалось, но он проталкивался и протискивался с таким усердием, что сумел провести меня сквозь толпу, и мы очутились на лестнице, ведущей в контору. По лестнице двигался двойной людской поток: одни поднимались, полные приятных надежд, другие спускались в унынии. Мы протискались вперед и скоро очутились в конторе…

— Замечательно интересная с вами случилась история! — сказал Холмс, когда его клиент замолчал, чтобы освежить свою память понюшкой табаку. — Пожалуйста, продолжайте.

— В конторе не было ничего, кроме пары деревянных стульев и простого соснового стола, за которым сидел маленький человечек, еще более рыжий, чем я. Он обменивался несколькими словами с каждым из кандидатов; по мере того как они подходили к столу, и в каждом обнаруживал какой-нибудь недостаток. Видимо, занять эту вакансию было не так-то просто. Однако, когда мы, в свою очередь, подошли к столу, маленький человечек встретил меня гораздо приветливее, чем остальных кандидатов, и, едва мы вошли, запер двери, чтобы побеседовать с нами без посторонних.

«Это мистер Джабез Уилсон, — сказал мой помощник. — Он хотел бы занять вакансию в Союзе».

«И он вполне достоин того, чтобы занять ее, — ответил человечек. — Давно не случалось мне видеть такие прекрасные волосы!»

Он отступил на шаг, склонил голову набок и глядел на мои волосы так долго, что мне стало неловко. Затем внезапно кинулся вперед, схватил мою руку и горячо поздравил меня.

He congratulated me warmly.

«Было бы несправедливостью с моей стороны медлить, — сказал он. — Однако, надеюсь, вы простите меня, если я приму некоторые меры предосторожности». Он вцепился в мои волосы обеими руками и дернул так, что я взвыл от боли.

«У вас на глазах слезы, — сказал он, отпуская меня. — Значит, все в порядке. Извините, нам приходится быть осторожными, потому что нас дважды обманули с помощью париков и один раз — с помощью краски. Я мог бы рассказать вам о таких бесчестных проделках, которые внушили бы вам отвращение к людям».

Он подошел к окну и крикнул во все горло, что вакансия уже занята. Стон разочарования донесся снизу, толпа расползлась по разным направлениям, и скоро во всей этой местности не осталось ни одного рыжего, кроме меня и того человека, который меня нанимал.

«Меня зовут мистер Дункан Росс, — сказал он, — и я тоже получаю пенсию из того фонда, который оставил нам наш великодушный благодетель. Вы женаты, мистер Уилсон? У вас есть семья?»

Я ответил, что я бездетный вдовец. На лице у него появилось выражение скорби.

«Боже мой! — мрачно сказал он. — Да ведь это серьезнейшее препятствие! Как мне грустно, что вы не женаты! Фонд был создан для размножения и распространения рыжих, а не только для поддержания их жизни. Какое несчастье, что вы оказались холостяком!»

При этих словах мое лицо вытянулось, мистер Холмс, так как я стал опасаться, что меня не возьмут; но, подумав, он заявил, что все обойдется:

«Ради всякого другого мы не стали бы отступать от правил, но человеку с такими волосами можно пойти навстречу. Когда вы могли бы приступить к выполнению ваших новых обязанностей?»

«Это несколько затруднительно, так как я занят в другом деле», — сказал я.

«Не беспокойтесь об этом, мистер Уилсон! — сказал Винсент Сполдинг. — С той работой я справлюсь и без вас».

«В какие часы я буду занят?» — спросил я.

«От десяти до двух».

Так как в ссудных кассах главная работа происходит по вечерам, мистер Холмс, особенно по четвергам и по пятницам, накануне получки, я решил, что недурно будет заработать кое-что в утренние часы. Тем более, что помощник мой — человек надежный и вполне может меня заменить, если нужно.

«Эти часы мне подходят, — сказал я. — А какое вы платите жалованье?»

«Четыре фунта в неделю».

«А в чем заключается работа?».

«Работа чисто номинальная».

«Что вы называете чисто номинальной работой?»

«Все назначенное для работы время вам придется находиться в нашей конторе или, по крайней мере, в здании, где помещается наша контора. Если вы хоть раз уйдете в рабочие часы, вы потеряете службу навсегда. Завещатель особенно настаивает на точном выполнении этого пункта. Будет считаться, что вы не исполнили наших требований, если вы хоть раз покинете контору в часы работы».

«Если речь идет всего о четырех часах в сутки, мне, конечно, и в голову не придет покидать контору», — сказал я.

«Это очень важно, — настаивал мистер Дункан Росс. — Потом мы никаких извинений и слушать не станем. Никакие болезни, никакие дела не будут служить оправданием. Вы должны находиться в конторе — или вы теряете службу».

«А в чем все-таки заключается работа?»

«Вам придется переписывать „Британскую энциклопедию“. Первый том — в этом шкафу. Чернила, перья, бумагу и промокашку вы достанете сами; мы же даем вам стол и стул. Можете ли вы приступить к работе завтра?»

«Конечно», — ответил я.

«В таком случае, до свиданья, мистер Джабез Уилсон. Позвольте мне еще раз поздравить вас с тем, что вам удалось получить такое хорошее место».

Он кивнул мне. Я вышел из комнаты и отправился домой вместе с помощником, радуясь своей необыкновенной удаче. Весь день я размышлял об этом происшествии и к вечеру несколько упал духом, так как мне стало казаться, что все это дело — просто мошенничество, хотя мне никак не удавалось отгадать, в чем может заключаться цель подобной затеи. Казалось невероятным, что существует такое завещание и что люди согласны платить такие большие деньги за переписку «Британской энциклопедии». Винсент Сполдинг изо всех сил старался подбодрить меня, но, ложась спать, я твердо решил отказаться от этого дела. Однако утром мне пришло в голову, что следует хотя бы сходить туда на всякий случай. Купив на пенни чернил, захватив гусиное перо и семь больших листов бумаги, я отправился в Попс-корт. К моему удивлению, там все было в порядке. Я очень обрадовался. Стол был уже приготовлен для моей работы, и мистер Дункан Росс ждал меня. Он велел мне начать с буквы «А» и вышел; однако время от времени он возвращался в контору, чтобы посмотреть, работаю ли я. В два часа он попрощался со мной, похвалил меня за то, что я успел так много переписать, и запер за мной дверь конторы.

Так шло изо дня в день, мистер Холмс. В субботу мой хозяин выложил передо мной на стол четыре золотых соверена — плату за неделю. Так прошла и вторая неделя и третья. Каждое утро я приходил туда ровно к десяти и ровно в два уходил. Мало-помалу мистер Дункан Росс начал заходить в контору только по утрам, а со временем и вовсе перестал туда наведываться. Тем не менее я, понятно, не осмеливался выйти из комнаты даже на минуту, так как не мог быть уверен, что он не придет, и не хотел рисковать такой выгодной службой.

Прошло восемь недель; я переписал статьи об Аббатах, об Артиллерии, об Архитектуре, об Аттике и надеялся в скором времени

перейти к букве «Б». У меня ушло очень много бумаги, и написанное мною уже едва помещалось на полке. Но вдруг все разом кончилось.

— Кончилось?

— Да, сэр. Сегодня утром. Я пошел на работу, как всегда, к десяти часам, но дверь оказалась запертой на замок, а к двери был прибит гвоздиком клочок картона. Вот он, читайте сами.

Он протянул нам картон величиною с листок блокнота. На картоне было написано:

СОЮЗ РЫЖИХ РАСПУЩЕН 9 ОКТЯБРЯ 1890 ГОДА

Мы с Шерлоком Холмсом долго разглядывали и краткую эту записку и унылое лицо Джабеза Уилсона; наконец смешная сторона происшествия заслонила от нас все остальное: не удержавшись, мы захохотали.

The door was shut and locked.

— Не вижу здесь ничего смешного! — крикнул наш клиент, вскочив с кресла и покраснев до корней своих жгучих волос. — Если вы, вместо того чтобы помочь мне, собираетесь смеяться надо мной, я обращусь за помощью к кому-нибудь другому!

— Нет, нет! — воскликнул Холмс, снова усаживая его в кресло. — С вашим делом я не расстанусь ни за что на свете. Оно буквально

освежает мне душу своей новизной. Но в нем, простите меня, все же есть что-то забавное... Что же предприняли вы, найдя эту записку на дверях?

— Я был потрясен, сэр. Я не знал, что делать. Я обошел соседние конторы, но там никто ничего не знал. Наконец, я отправился к хозяину дома, живущему в нижнем этаже, и спросил его, не может ли он сказать мне, что случилось с Союзом рыжих. Он ответил, что никогда не слыхал о такой организации. Тогда я спросил его, кто такой мистер Дункан Росс. Он ответил, что это имя он слышит впервые.

«Я говорю, — сказал я, — о джентльмене, который снимал у вас квартиру номер четыре».

«О рыжем?»

«Да».

«Его зовут Уильям Моррис. Он юрист, снимал у меня помещение временно — его постоянная контора была в ремонте. Вчера выехал».

«Где его можно найти?»

«В его постоянной конторе. Он оставил свой адрес. Вот: Кинг-Эдуард-стрит, 17, близ собора святого Павла».

Я отправился по этому адресу, мистер Холмс, но там оказалась протезная мастерская; в ней никто никогда не слыхал ни о мистере Уильяме Моррисе, ни о мистере Дункане Россе.

— Что же вы предприняли тогда? — спросил Холмс.

— Я вернулся домой на Сэкс-Кобург-сквер и посоветовался со своим помощником. Он ничем не мог мне помочь. Он сказал, что следует подождать и что, вероятно, мне сообщат что-нибудь по почте. Но меня это не устраивает, мистер Холмс. Я не хочу уступать такое отличное место без боя, и, так как я слыхал, что вы даете советы бедным людям, попавшим в трудное положение, я отправился прямо к вам.

— И правильно поступили, — сказал Холмс. — Ваш случай — замечательный случай, и я счастлив, что имею возможность заняться

им. Выслушав вас, я прихожу к заключению, что дело это гораздо серьезнее, чем может показаться с первого взгляда.

— Уж чего серьезнее! — сказал мистер Джабез Уилсон. — Я лишился четырех фунтов в неделю.

— Если говорить о вас лично, — сказал Холмс, — вряд ли вы можете жаловаться на этот необычайный Союз. Напротив, вы, насколько я понимаю, стали благодаря ему богаче фунтов на тридцать, не говоря уже о том, что вы приобрели глубокие познания о предметах, начинающихся на букву «А». Так что, в сущности, вы ничего не потеряли.

— Не спорю, все это так, сэр. Но мне хотелось бы разыскать их, узнать, кто они такие и чего ради они сыграли со мной эту шутку, если только это была шутка. Забава обошлась им довольно дорого: они заплатили за нее тридцать два фунта.

— Мы попытаемся все это выяснить. Но сначала разрешите мне задать вам несколько вопросов, мистер Уилсон. Давно ли служит у вас этот помощник... тот, что показал вам объявление?

— К тому времени он служил у меня около месяца.

— Где вы нашли его?

— Он явился ко мне по моему объявлению в газете.

— Только он один откликнулся на ваше объявление?

— Нет, откликнулось человек десять.

— Почему вы выбрали именно его?

— Потому что он разбитной и дешевый.

— Вас прельстила возможность платить ему половинное жалованье?

— Да.

— Каков он из себя, этот Винсент Сполдинг?

— Маленький, коренастый, очень живой. Ни одного волоска на лице, хотя ему уже под тридцать. На лбу у него белое пятнышко от ожога кислотой.

Холмс выпрямился. Он был очень взволнован.

— Я так и думал! — сказал он. — А вы не замечали у него в ушах дырочек для серег?

— Заметил, сэр. Он объяснил мне, что уши ему проколола какая-то цыганка, когда он был маленький.

— Гм! — произнес Холмс и откинулся на спинку кресла в глубоком раздумье. — Он до сих пор у вас?

— О да, сэр, я только что видел его.

— Он хорошо справлялся с вашими делами, когда вас не было дома?

— Не могу пожаловаться, сэр. Впрочем, по утрам в моей ссудной кассе почти нечего делать.

— Довольно, мистер Уилсон. Через день или два я буду иметь удовольствие сообщить вам, что я думаю об этом происшествии. Сегодня суббота… Надеюсь, в понедельник мы всё уже будем знать.

— Ну, Уотсон, — сказал Холмс, когда наш посетитель ушел, — что вы обо всем этом думаете?

— Ничего не думаю, — ответил я откровенно. — Дело это представляется мне совершенно таинственным.

— Общее правило таково, — сказал Холмс, — чем страннее случай, тем меньше в нем оказывается таинственного. Как раз заурядные, бесцветные преступления разгадать труднее всего, подобно тому как труднее всего разыскать в толпе человека с заурядными чертами лица. Но с этим случаем нужно покончить как можно скорее.

— Что вы собираетесь делать? — спросил я.

— Курить, — ответил он. — Эта задача как раз на три трубки, и я прошу вас минут десять не разговаривать со мной.

He curled himself up in his chair.

Он скрючился в кресле, подняв худые колени к ястребиному носу, и долго сидел в такой позе, закрыв глаза и выставив вперед черную глиняную трубку, похожую на клюв какой-то странной птицы. Я пришел к заключению, что он заснул, и сам уже начал дремать, как вдруг он вскочил с видом человека, принявшего твердое решение, и положил свою трубку на камин.

— Сарасате[1] играет сегодня в Сент-Джемс холле, — сказал он. — Что вы думаете об этом, Уотсон? Могут ваши пациенты обойтись без вас в течение нескольких часов?

— Сегодня я свободен. Моя практика отнимает у меня не слишком много времени.

— В таком случае, надевайте шляпу и идем. Раньше всего мне нужно в Сити. Где-нибудь по дороге закусим.

Мы доехали в метро до Олдерсгэйта, оттуда прошли пешком до Сэкс-Кобург-сквер, где совершились все те события, о которых нам рассказывали утром. Сэкс-Кобург-сквер — маленькая сонная площадь

[1] Сарасате (1844-1908) — знаменитый испанский скрипач и композитор.

No label was affixed to identify it as evidence. Elliot was familiar with the labels she was talking about.

Bat Girl used her thumbnail to spread out the photos. Small labels were affixed to the bottom left corner and read #1 of 26, #2 of 26, etc. "These are labeled correctly. But they aren't considered evidence, more part of the case file. I'm not sure about the rest of the stuff, but I doubt any of this is real evidence."

"Why do you sound unsure?" the athlete asked.

Bat Girl shrugged. "Whoever put this here could've removed the evidence tags. If that's the case and we get caught with these, it'll look like we stole them. And that's a felony."

2

Seema Choudhury knew she should have stayed away. Her mother always said curiosity killed the cat, and this time Seema's curiosity could literally make her one dead pussy. What if the note sender was the killer? Dead was not a look she wanted to sport. Her mother would be so disappointed. She could hear her now, harping about how Seema took for granted all the things her parents had given her, how they'd sacrificed so much from the moment they immigrated from India. *And Seema goes and gets killed.* Or worse, thrown in jail.

And yet she desperately wanted to inspect every single item in the evidence box. She grabbed her bat, twisting it in her hands as she wrestled with the options.

"Neither of you touch another thing," Professor Snyder said. "I'll call the police. We'll tell them what happened, and this problem will fix itself."

Professor Snyder moved toward Seema and the journalism student—what had the professor called her? Seema scrolled through her memory index. Elliot. An odd name for

a girl who looked like a more-fitting name would be Barbie or Tiffany or something, with her long, straight blond hair and big blue eyes. She was beauty queen pretty, even with her permanent scowl. She looked like she came from money too.

Elliot nodded. "Yeah, we could call the police. That's probably the right thing to do." But she continued to hold the lid to the box and stare hungrily inside.

The longing on Elliot's face was precisely how Seema felt. The Jaime Sullivan murder had intrigued her. Scared her, to be honest. She did carry a bat around most places, after all. The night Jaime had been murdered had been an eventful one for Seema. Since that night, she kept the bat near her at all times.

Time was taking its toll on Jaime's case. One day Jaime's death was all the news. and the next, students were bitching about the restrictions and how unfair it was they were paying for what happened to a girl who went and got herself killed. As if Jaime's fate could never have been theirs. They were more worried about their civil liberties or perceived injustice rather than an actual heinous crime.

The audacity was stunning, really. Infuriating. A killer was free. Why was no one incensed about that? Assholes, all of them.

Seema said, mostly to Elliot, "The professor's right. Giving this back to the cops is the right thing to do. Like I said, getting caught with this and knowingly not turning it back in to the police is a felony served through prison time. No thanks. I can't let anything get in my way of getting into law school." She looked around the room to see who agreed. They were a motley crew and certainly not in her sphere of people she hung with on campus. Outside of this event, she believed it to be unlikely their paths would ever cross again.

"Right, right, so we give it back. I'm down with that. I mean, I'm not crazy about being in the room right now with this shit. Felony, you say?" the guy in the school jersey said. His basketball tucked under his arm, he tugged at the collar of his jersey. "My mama told me to take the scholarship out here, said I needed to get out of Memphis and away from trouble. I'm thinkin' trouble just found me here."

Seema wrung her hands around the bat's neck. "It pisses me off that someone put us in this position. Good thing I'm here to tell you the legal repercussions of this." She pointed the bat at the box. "I noticed cameras at the entrance and in the hallway that can probably prove we weren't the ones to bring it in."

Elliot looked to the professor. "We need to see if there's a video or a log. Maybe we can figure out who delivered this *gift*."

Professor Snyder nodded. "I'm sure the police will do that. As this young lady said, taking property from an evidence room is a big deal."

Elliot cleared her throat. "What do we do after we turn this in? Walk away from here and pretend we never got a letter? Do we cross our fingers and hope the police solve Jaime Sullivan's murder?"

Seema didn't like the idea of any murder going unsolved, but she had to be practical. She shrugged. "Why do we think we can solve it?"

The sports dude chuckled. "Someone thought we could. Someone thought we would do a better job than the cops." His tone was very matter of fact.

Professor Snyder took the lid from Elliot and settled it back on the box. "You know, that's a curious thing. This letter. Why do you suppose you were picked for this?" She

leaned against the desk, her back to the box of Jaime's personal items, blocking it. She crossed her arms.

Elliot shrugged. "How do we know we were hand-picked? What if everyone on campus got the letter and we are the only ones who came?"

The dowdy girl dressed in baggy sweats and a gaudy hat shook her head. "I asked the girls on my dorm floor. I was the only one who got a letter."

"I asked too. I mean, I didn't just show them the letter, but I asked if anyone in the locker room got a weird letter about Jaime Sullivan, and no one fessed up," Jock Boy said.

"Would you fess up?" Seema asked.

"Hell yeah, I would. Because this is some freaky shit, this letter."

Elliot tapped her finger to her chin. "But we can't assume we were the only ones to get it. We were just the only ones to show up."

"I'm regretting that now," Ugly-Sweatpants Girl said.

Seema narrowed her eyes. "What did you think was going to happen when you got here?"

"I don't know. I didn't expect the actual box of evidence. I didn't expect anyone to say we could be charged with a felony. I thought maybe we'd sit around and talk about what happened and ... and..."

"Speculate? Hypothesize? M-m-me too." This from the tall, gangly dork who'd joined them at the last minute. He blushed as he spoke and didn't look any of them in the eye.

Professor Snyder put up her hand, her way of getting their attention. "Was the letter addressed?"

Elliot was first to answer. "Mine had only my name. No address. No return address. No postage, yet it was in my mailbox."

Professor Snyder looked at everyone. "Was that the same for each of you?"

They all nodded.

She crossed her arms over her chest. "I don't like this. The more I learn about this letter, the more certain I am that we should turn over this box and all walk away. Nothing good can come from this."

Elliot nodded. "It's odd, that's for sure. But maybe all of us here have something in common?"

Seema asked, "Like what? We've already established that we don't know each other." She tapped her bat on the ground. "I'm Seema Choudhury. I'm a senior. Prelaw. And I didn't know Jaime."

"I'm Elliot Long." Elliot pointed to herself. "Since I have access to the building, I'm sure you all have put together that I'm a journalism major, a junior. I didn't know Jaime Sullivan either." She pointed to the jock. "I think you and I have something in common. My brother played baseball for the university as well. Nathan Long."

Jock Boy nodded. "Yeah, I knew him. That's what I meant when I said I knew who you were." He didn't smile or look at Elliot as people do when they realized they had a mutual acquaintance.

Elliot would not meet anyone's gaze.

Seema found both of their behaviors odd. Especially since Nathan Long had been a star on campus and was one in the baseball world. He'd gone straight to the major leagues on a fat contract. Seema didn't even like sports, and she knew that.

Jock Boy said, "I'm Trey Smith-Coleman. Senior. Communications."

The group looked at the tall guy. He appeared

disheveled. His hair was curly and in need of a haircut, or at the least, a comb needed to sneak up on him. A worn army-green backpack was over one shoulder, duct tape on all the corners of the bag.

"I'm... I'm... um... Teddy Galloway. I went... I am... um..." He searched for words.

Or perhaps the right words? Seema didn't know, but waiting for him to spit it out was excruciating. "You're what? A senior? What? How about your major?"

"Premed," Teddy said. "Accelerated program. But I—"

"Did you know Jaime? She was in nursing school," Sweatpants Girl asked.

Teddy shook his head. "Maybe I, uh, saw her around, but I, um ... no. I don't think I knew her."

Sweatpants Girl was last to go. "I'm Hillary. Hillary Redding." She looked at Seema. "I went to the same high school as Jaime. She was two years ahead of me. But I didn't really know her. She was nice to me though."

"You knew her more than the rest of us," Elliot said.

Hillary gave a one-shoulder shrug.

Professor Snyder cleared her throat. "There doesn't appear to be any rhyme or reason as to why you five are here." She reached across her desk and picked up the phone. "I'm calling security. Let's wrap this up and get home before curfew."

Seema glanced at her watch. It was already nine thirty. She hated the late hour of the meeting, but maybe that was all part of the plan?

Professor Snyder pressed a few buttons and waited. She gave them each a thin smile. Moments later she hung up the phone. "They aren't answering. I'm going to walk to the security office. Everyone wait here, okay?"

No one argued or demanded to leave.

The room was quiet, the only sound the fading squeaks of Professor Snyder's Birkenstocks.

"I guess this is it, then," Elliot said.

"How do we continue anyway without the evidence box? Where would we even start?" Seema asked.

Elliot raised a brow. "Well, maybe they'd let us check the video feed to see who dropped off the box, and we could track that person down."

"As if." Seema rolled her eyes. "Are you saying you're still interested in pursuing this?"

"No." Elliot tapped her chin with one finger. She sighed. "Maybe. To be honest, Jaime Sullivan's death seems to always be on my mind. I think now I'm going to have even more difficulty not pursuing this. And maybe I could find out who dropped off the box from the professor."

Seema narrowed her eyes. It was as though Elliot could read Seema's thoughts. She pointed to the box. "If we don't turn this in, if we touch it, look through it, and it's part of the evidence, then we're compromising the official investigation. If they do end up charging someone, our actions tonight could be what sets a killer free."

Hillary said, "But the letter said it was a cold case. I think that means they aren't going to charge anyone anytime soon."

Seema rolled her eyes. "Do you not watch the news? They caught the Golden State Killer decades after he committed his crimes. And preserving the DNA for all those years helped with the conviction."

Elliot said, "They lost some to heat and poor storage but kept a lot. I saw a story where the survivors and family members of the victims were weeping with relief because of

that conviction. I'd hate to be the reason Jaime Sullivan's family never gets closure."

Hillary said, "She didn't have family. Not that I know of. Just her mom, and well, she was ... wasted most of the time. She didn't even arrange Jaime's funeral. A counselor from our high school did it."

"You didn't know her, but you know about her mom?" Seema asked.

Hillary nodded. "My dad's a fisherman, and he would say how her mom was always down at the bars at the docks. I know more than once her mom was hospitalized from an OD. Jaime would live with our counselor during those times."

Elliot put her attention fully on Hillary. "This is the same counselor who took care of the funeral?"

"Yes," Hillary said.

Elliot looked at Seema. "She has no one advocating for her. No family to hound the police. Except maybe this counselor. Who could have sent the letters."

Hillary shook her head. "He lives three and a half hours from here, and why give any of you a letter?"

Even though her clothes were gaudy, the girl called Hillary had a point.

Elliot said, "So Jaime's murder continues to go unsolved."

Trey said, "I heard once there was something stupid like two hundred and fifty thousand cold cases. And about six thousand gets added each year. Odds like that ain't good."

Seema tsked to get their attention. "We can't. You all do know what I mean when I say felony, right?"

"But what if this isn't evidence? What if it's random

things someone who lived at her dorm took from her place?" Elliot proposed.

Seema said, "Then their stupid ass should come forward. They should be here right now."

Elliot shrugged one shoulder. "Maybe they're too scared to come forward."

Hillary rubbed her hands up and down her arms. "But we wouldn't be messing anything up if we took it, right?"

Seema flipped her hand, palm up. "Who knows. Besides, how would you explain these items if you were caught with them? These aren't photos Jaime took. They're *crime scene* photos. No one would believe the story about tonight."

Teddy inhaled a stuttered breath, showing what likely everyone else felt too.

Trey said, "So don't get caught."

Elliot looked around the room. "I'm not ready to walk away. I want time to look at all these items."

"What are you going to do? Take a few things before the professor gets back?" Seema asked.

"If anyone wants deniability, they need to walk out right now." Elliot jabbed her finger toward the office door. "If you stay, we have to swear to each other right here and now that this stays between us. No narcs. If you're in, you're in. If you want out, there's the door."

Teddy slumped back against the wall. He stuck a hand in his mop of hair. "Oh, jeez. This isn't good. No good. I... I... I..."

"In or out, Teddy?" Elliot asked firmly. She stuck her hand out, palm down. She wanted an old-school hand huddle to seal the deal. "Decide right now."

Trey snorted and looked Elliot directly in the eye. "Jeez, your family is trouble."

Seema stuck her hand on top of Elliot's. "We make a pact that whatever we do stays in this group. We can't tell anyone. We can only trust each other."

"Trust complete strangers. Yeah, right." But Trey stuck his hand on top of the other two. "I'm in. My mama will kill me if she finds out."

"I'm not sure what I can contribute," Hillary said.

"So then walk out right now," Seema challenged.

Hillary stuck her hand on top of the others while glaring at Seema. Under her breath she muttered something about rudeness. The group turned to Teddy.

"Oh, jeez." He tugged at his hair, his eyes closed.

"Decision time, Teddy. Come on. Tick tick." Seema didn't mince words. Indecisive people annoyed the hell out of her, and if Teddy put his hand on theirs, she knew he was going to be a thorn in her side.

He looked at them through a small slit in one eye. "Okay, okay." He gulped convulsively. He put a shaky hand on top of the others.

"Ugh, your hand's all sweaty," Hillary said.

"On the count of three, everyone swear that everything stays in this group. We protect each other," Elliot said. "One, two, three."

"I swear," they all said in unison as they looked around, scrutinizing each other.

Seema clasped her hands together. "Welcome to the Campus Murder Club. We are officially in business. Teddy, give me your backpack. We need to put as much evidence as we can in it before the professor comes back."

3

"Why not use her messenger bag?" Teddy pointed to Elliot's bag.

"Because she's too obvious." Seema wiggled her hand with urgency. "Give it."

Reluctantly, Teddy shrugged off his backpack and handed it to Elliot. Seema had already removed the lid from the box and was ready to pour the entire contents into the backpack.

"No," Elliot said quickly and a bit too loudly. "We have to leave some stuff or Professor Snyder will know something's up." She paused to listen for noise outside the office. Hearing nothing worrisome she continued but lowered her voice. "If the box was empty when we looked inside, then we would have said something."

Seema snapped and pointed a finger at Elliot. "Good thinking. What should we take?"

"Is there a property list or something that'll tell us what's in there?" Trey asked. He was standing at the door keeping

watch, occasionally spinning the basketball on his index finger.

"I don't even want to know how you know there's a list," Hillary said.

Trey gave her a weird look. "TV. How do you not know this? Wha'chu watch on TV?"

"I know from listening to true crime podcasts," Elliot said. Which wasn't entirely the truth, but knowing Trey knew her brother unnerved Elliot. That meant he likely knew her story, and she was hoping not to share that with the others. Not that they couldn't Google her and learn whatever they wanted to know.

Trey studied her for a moment. But he didn't say anything, only returned his attention to the door and the hallway beyond.

"My dad is a lawyer in Seattle," Seema said. "I learned to read looking at property lists." She dug into the box and came up empty-handed. "No list."

Elliot investigated the box contents. "Um, I'm not sure what we should leave behind." She showed the box to Teddy.

He told the others what was in the box. He pointed to the journal and newspaper clippings. "Take those." His voice was low and trembled slightly.

Elliot swallowed hard. Thinking about those items, the story they might tell, the secrets they might reveal, made her light-headed.

Elliot unzipped the pack and spread the opening wide. Inside was the Andy Weir novel *The Martian*, a handful of unused latex gloves, and an *Anatomy for Med Students* textbook. The image on the cover was a partially dissected torso. And not an illustration. Elliot grimaced and shot Teddy a

quick look. He wiped a line of sweat from his brow with the sleeve of his shirt.

"Med student books are disgusting," she said.

"I find them fascinating," he said.

"Come on, let's get on with this," Seema said.

Elliot gestured for her to start.

"Wait," Teddy said. "Wear gloves."

Elliot pulled out four gloves and handed two to Seema.

After putting them on, Seema tossed the items to Elliot, who pushed them into the backpack. Everything else stayed in the box.

Seema pulled out the photos.

"Leave those," Trey said. "They're marked like they're evidence. Use your camera to take pics. Do the same with the dates."

Seema and Elliot spread out the photos and index cards with the dates and took pictures. Elliot turned them over to make sure they weren't missing anything.

Seema restacked everything and put them in the box. Once it was all sorted, Seema peered into the box. "I think this is good. We left the photos and the mail." She glanced at Teddy. "This will give us a good start."

"I think she's coming," Trey whispered.

Seema fumbled with putting the lid back on the box. Elliot zipped the pack and tossed it to Teddy. They stuffed their gloves in their pants pockets.

"Maybe someone else could wear this," Teddy mumbled.

Elliot shook her head. "Professor Snyder will notice. She was an investigative journalist for years with a focus on personal crimes. She'll notice right away. Put your back to the wall."

"And for fuck's sake, can you try to stop sweating? You look like you've gone for a run in the rain," Seema said.

If possible, Teddy's face paled further. He adjusted the pack over his shoulder and shuffled backward to the wall.

He was going to give them away, and then they would be in trouble. This was beyond being in the same room with the evidence box. This was officially tampering with evidence.

"Hey," Hillary said, pointing to the box. "Is there anything in there?" She gestured to the manila envelope with the bolded words CAMPUS MURDER CLUB Case #1 scrolled across it in bold print.

Elliot reached for the envelope.

"Wait," Trey said. "Use the glove or something. It's cool for your prints to be on the lid but not the envelope."

"Good call," Hillary said.

Trey grunted and said under his breath, "Don't hear that often. Or at all."

"Careful," Seema said to Elliot. "Try not to remove it."

Elliot sighed. "The opening is up against the box. I have to remove part of the envelope from the box to open it." She'd pulled her shirtsleeve down to cover her hand and paused as she looked at Seema and the group. "Unless anyone has any other ideas?"

No one chimed in.

"Hurry," Trey said. "I hear her shoes."

Elliot tugged on the end of the envelope; it gave way, bringing a layer of the box with it. "Get tape." She gestured to the dispenser on the professor's desk. Elliot opened the envelope's flap and pulled out a single sheet of paper. She handed it to Hillary.

"Tuck it up your shirt or something," Seema said as she folded over a strip of tape into a loop, sticky on all sides.

"Put it on the box where the layer came off," Elliot whispered.

The squeaking of Professor Snyder's cork soles on the floor was getting louder. A second set of shoes, the steps heavier and producing more of a steady thud, was in sync with Professor Snyder's pace.

She was getting close, and she was bringing security with her.

Seema did as Elliot said, and Elliot pressed the envelope back in place. She tucked the gloves in her pocket and jumped back from the box. Seema hurried to a spot next to Hillary, who'd folded the paper and stuck it in her back pocket. Trey scurried to the spot next to Teddy, where he'd been before.

"Breathe, man," he told Teddy.

"Easy for you to say. I feel like I got a bomb stuck to my back," Teddy whispered.

The door swung open, and Professor Snyder entered with a campus security guard.

She pointed to the box. "There it is." She faced the group. "Officer Timmons will stay with us until the police get here. He's been tasked with watching the box. They will want to take statements from all of us."

"How soon will they get here?" Seema asked.

"About thirty minutes, they said."

"Okay, so do we have to wait in here until they come, or can we go back to the lobby?" Elliot asked.

"I suppose the lobby will work. Don't leave the building."

Seema touched her stomach. "Is there a vending machine? I'm starved."

Elliot straightened. "Yeah, in the student lounge. Come on, I'll show you." She moved to the door.

Seema followed. She grabbed Teddy's arm. "You're the one who mentioned popcorn. I'm guessing you're hungry too. Let's see what they have." She tugged him out with her.

Teddy mumbled, "I didn't say anything about—"

"Shh," Seema whispered.

"Snacks sound good," Trey said. "Wait for me."

Elliot looked over her shoulder to find the entire group following her. Professor Snyder stood in the doorway watching them.

"The lounge is right around the corner," Elliot said, probably a little too loudly and cheerfully.

She turned the corner and waited for Seema and Teddy to catch up. She pulled her messenger bag off. Once they turned the corner, she grabbed Teddy's backpack and handed him her bag.

"Give me this. I'm going to empty it. If they search your bag, then we're sunk."

Seema asked, "Where are you going to put it?"

"I have a locked storage cabinet two floors up. I keep stuff there for my podcast. I'll take it there for now."

Trey said, "Elevator gonna be too loud."

Elliot pointed to an exit sign. "I'll take the stairs."

"Make it fast," Seema said.

Elliot took off for the stairs, the backpack slung over her shoulder. The others went into the lounge.

She dashed up the two flights, skipping steps every chance she could, knowing time was her enemy. She reached the studio and swiped her keycard, jerking the door open the instant it unlatched. It took her less than two minutes to get

into her storage cabinet, put the evidence inside, and get back to the stairs. She flew down them, stumbling the last four steps and nearly falling, catching herself by gripping the rail. This didn't stop her as her feet went out from under her, and she landed on her backside. The steps caught her across the calves, the impact like being clobbered with a lead pipe. But she didn't stop to rub them or anything. She couldn't take a chance that the cops wouldn't come sooner. In her experience, police were notoriously bad at keeping time and their word.

She paused at the stairwell door and eased it open, looking for the professor, cops, or campus security.

Trey was in the hallway, outside the lounge. He gave her a chin nod in acknowledgment and a thumbs-up. The coast was clear. She fast walked to him, and he held the door open to the lounge.

Inside, she tossed Teddy his backpack. He checked the interior and gave her a tight smile. Surprisingly, he still seemed overly nervous.

"Teddy, when they question you, are you going to be okay?" Seema asked.

"I can explain this." He gestured to himself. "I'll be okay. Now that my backpack is good."

She cut her eyes to Elliot's. Uncertainty was written across the other girl's face.

"I still have the letter," Hillary said. "You don't think they'll search us, do you?"

They looked at each other, all of them searching for the answer. Elliot's gaze landed on Seema.

She sighed. "I think they could. Especially when they think the box might be missing stuff. They'll question us tonight and again later. I'm sure."

"Man, why a second time?" Trey groaned.

Seema said, "Because they won't be sure things are missing tonight. But if this is evidence, then they'll be sure things are missing later, and that's why they'll come back."

"We'll need someplace to keep this stuff," Elliot said.

"Not it," Trey said. "I ain't taking that shit home."

Elliot rolled her eyes. "I meant someplace neutral. That means none of us can have it in places we use often, like your locker in the gym, Trey, or our rooms."

"Where would that be?" Hillary asked.

Elliot shrugged.

"One problem at a time," Seema said. "Hillary, let me see the paper."

Hillary pulled it out of her pocket and handed it over.

Seema unfolded it. Typed on the sheet were two lines.

The first said: **Get what you can, you won't have this opportunity for long**.

The second was a hyperlink. **www.allthingsforum.-com/truecrimesleuth/join**

Elliot took a picture of the paper, refolded it, then stuck it under one of the couch cushions.

"Is it safe there?" Hillary asked.

Elliot grimaced. "Probably not, but it's not like the couches are cleaned. Did you see how much food was under there? It's gross. But it's all we got." She thought about pinning it under several flyers on the student corkboard, but that felt riskier.

Teddy moved to the snack machine. "They have popcorn here." He chuckled.

Elliot smiled. "Never mind that. I need caffeine."

"Ugh, me too," Seema said.

They gathered around the coffee vending machine and

made their purchases. They settled into the couches to wait. Trey took the seat next to Elliot. He set the basketball between them. She side-eyed him. He had the cutest dimples she'd ever seen. Gawd, she hated that she thought a dumb jock was a hottie. Why was she always attracted to the athletes? She really needed a new type.

Seema said, "When they question us, stick to the truth. We talked about taking stuff out of the box but didn't. Teddy, the questions are all semantics. If they asked you if you took anything from the box, you say no because you didn't. Elliot and I did. Got it?"

Teddy nodded. "Got it."

Professor Snyder opened the door. "Police are here. They want to interview each of you separately. Anyone want to go first?"

There were no takers.

"Okay, then Elliot, let's start with you. Apparently, you already know Detective Madden."

Elliot groaned. There were very few people in the world Elliot despised. Officer Gene Madden topped the list.

4

After Elliot left to be questioned, the others waited in uncomfortable silence. Trey spun his ball while tapping his foot in nervous anticipation. Seema continued to sigh with exasperation. No one talked, which heightened Hillary's already-tense nerves. She picked at her short fingernails and wondered if the campus cop posted outside the door was listening in.

The student lounge door swung open, causing everyone to jump. Professor Snyder entered. Elliot was not with her.

"Any volunteers to go next?" she asked and gestured to the hallway behind her.

"Where's Elliot?" Seema asked.

"She went home." Professor Snyder's cold expression stopped any further questions.

But Hillary could see the confusion she felt on the others faces. What had happened during Elliot's interview that she had to go directly home? Assuming the professor was telling the truth.

Hillary glanced at her watch. Forty minutes from the

time Elliot left to when the professor came back. If the interviews were going to take even half as long, the last person to be interviewed would be there past midnight. Hillary was ready to go home. Heck, she wished she hadn't come.

That wasn't true either. She was sort of glad she came. But she was scared. She just wasn't sure what she feared.

"I'll go." Hillary shot to her feet. If she sat there any longer with her thoughts, she'd probably go nuts. Or worse, crack under scrutiny. She might have stuck her hand on top of the others and committed to the pact, but what did that really mean? Nothing. People broke their word all the time. Even Hillary's mom, when she up and left fourteen years ago.

"Bring your stuff with you," Professor Snyder said.

Her stuff? She hadn't come with anything. Hillary paused. Did she mean the note that had been taped on the box? But how could the professor know she had it?

She glanced at the others, wondering what to do. Seema caught her eye and gave a slight head shake. Hillary blew out a slow breath. She'd almost gotten them all busted. She'd have to be on her toes for this interview. Not get tripped up. She didn't want to blow it. She wasn't ready to walk away from this. Whatever it was.

"I don't have anything," Hillary said. She followed the professor out.

Professor Snyder stopped at her office door, her hand on the knob. "Don't be nervous, Hillary. Just tell the truth."

Hillary nodded. "Easy peasy."

Professor Snyder swung open the door, and standing inside was a tall, well-built, light-skinned Black man with a close-cut, military-style haircut. He was closer in age to Hillary than Professor Snyder. Late twenties, easily.

He crossed his arms, leaned against the desk, and frowned down at her. "Take a seat, please."

Hillary's palms began to sweat, and she wiped them on her jeans. She sat in one of the professor's office chairs. The two chairs had been pushed back closer to the wall to allow the officer room for his current posture. Probably done on purpose to intimidate her. Lord, she hated that. Often people thought short, chubby girls were pushovers. And maybe she was to a degree. But having always been on the fringe of everything, never brought into the fold, and always afraid she'd look pathetic or stupid, Hillary had developed a protective wall. She put it up now.

She crossed her ankles instead of her arms, having read somewhere that this seemed more casual. She pushed back her ball cap so he could see more of her face.

"I'm Detective Madden. I have just a few questions for you, and then campus security will escort you home. What's your full name?"

"Hillary Redding."

"Tell me what brought you here, Hillary?"

"Professor Snyder. She asked for a volunteer, and that's me."

Madden's lips thinned, probably already irritated with her. But if he was going to be vague, she was too.

"I meant, what brought you here to the Thompson Journalism Building tonight?"

Hillary made an "Oh" face. "The letter I got. It told me to be here today at nine. So I came."

Madden held up the letter. Probably Elliot's copy. "This is what you got?"

"Yeah."

"Do you have your copy on you?"

Hillary shook her head. "I took a picture of it in case I needed it but left the original at home."

"So you came here alone because of a letter about a murder. Did you think that might not be safe?"

"That's why I told my RA, and I emailed a photo of the letter to my roommate. She knew I was coming here too. And I have a stun gun." From her front pocket, Hillary pulled out a palm sized, black plastic square with a red button.

"You do know there are restrictions with those."

Hillary nodded. "That's why it's been in my pocket, and no one knew about it. Only extreme circumstances. Like maybe facing a killer."

"If you thought a killer was going to be here, why did you come?"

Hillary shook her head. "I didn't think a killer would be *here*. I thought there might be one on the walk home."

"What did you think you would find here tonight?"

Hillary gave a short laugh. "I thought maybe it would be a bunch of students gathered around, rehashing everything. Like on a podcast or something but not a podcast. Just students talking about it. I certainly didn't expect a box of whatever it is in there. Is that real evidence?" She wanted to know if they had indeed committed a felony.

"Why do you ask? If this is evidence and you all handled it, I hope you understand the legal implications such as—"

Hillary waved her hand dismissively. "Yeah, I know."

"Let's get back to why you came here tonight. You came because you wanted to talk about Jaime Sullivan's death?" He raised a brow in interest.

"I went to high school with her. She's the first person I knew who's died." So far, all truth. This was easy.

"Were you friends?"

Hillary shook her head. She didn't have many friends ... any, really. Sure, she knew people. She talked to people, but she never had sleepovers. She never went to parties. She didn't even have social media for fear that no one would *friend* her. "No, we didn't run in the same crowds. I mostly saw her at school."

Jaime had friends. For having such a crappy home life, the universe had granted Jaime Sullivan comfort by giving her the friendship of the entire student body and the majority of the teachers too. Jaime Sullivan made friends wherever she went. Such was the reality of pretty girls.

"Okay, so you came tonight thinking you might meet some people and sit around talking about Jaime's case."

"Yep."

Madden continued, "You come into the professor's office and see the box. Tell me what happens then."

"We talked about looking at what was in the box."

"Anyone take anything out?"

Hillary shook her head. "Elliot took off the lid and looked in, but no one took anything out."

"Nothing was taken from the box?"

Hillary nodded. "Nothing."

"Do you know what was in the box?"

She shook her head. "I didn't look inside, and Professor Snyder put the lid back on before she left to get security."

Madden eased onto Professor Snyder's desk. He stuffed his hands in his front pockets. "Tell me what happened when the professor left."

Hillary looked up at the ceiling, like she was trying to remember how it played out, even though she could clearly see it fresh in her mind. Plus, she wasn't sure how Elliot or the others would answer these questions,

so again, she tried to stick as close to the truth as possible.

"Um, at first we stood there all silent. It was awkward, and I would have left had the professor not said to stay put. I think it was Seema who said it was a good thing we weren't touching the stuff in the box because if it was evidence, and if the cops did find Jaime's killer and we jacked up the evidence, then that person could get away with it."

"Do you know how this box came to be here?"

Hillary shook her head. "No. It's kinda creepy though. And it doesn't make the police department look good if evidence can be taken from your building and show up here. And the letter said that you all hadn't been able to solve the crime, which was why we were sent the letter."

"And you all think you can solve it?" His lips quirked into a half smirk.

Hillary rolled her eyes. "As if. But it was tempting. And with the box sitting there ready for us to look at what was inside, well, you get it. You see, right? How hard it was to ignore the box?" One thing she'd learned over the years with her many interviews with counselors and child welfare was knowing she needed to tell the person something they wanted to hear, to put them at ease. Madden was no different. But Hillary worried she was painting herself into a corner and would mess up if the interview didn't end soon. She jiggled her foot in a poor attempt to steady her nerves.

"Are you saying you opened it and took stuff from it?" Madden leaned in.

Hillary leaned back. "No, Seema said that would be a felony, and no one wants to go to jail. But we talked about it. For a second, we considered it. That's how close we came to breaking the law. How scary is that?"

"And no one took anything from the box. Not you, not Elliot? No one."

Hillary sighed with exasperation. "Yeah, that's what I just said."

Madden glanced at her jiggling foot. "You seem nervous."

She glanced at her foot, too, and stopped jiggling it. "Yeah, I'm being interviewed by the cops. Shouldn't I be nervous?"

Madden studied her. "How do you know Elliot Long?"

"I don't. I just met her today."

"Had you wanted to meet her before today?"

Hillary didn't understand the question and thought Madden was trying to confuse her. "I didn't know Elliot before today, so I didn't want to meet her before today either. Because I didn't even know she existed."

Madden leaned back and crossed his arms. "You didn't read about her in the paper?"

Hillary shook her head in confusion. "No. I don't read the paper."

"So you didn't concoct this whole gathering as a way to meet Elliot Long?"

"Why would we be here if this is because of Elliot?" Hillary straightened her shoulders, her nervousness replaced with curiosity.

"That's what I'm trying to establish, a connection to Elliot."

"Who I didn't know existed until tonight. And I don't know the others, either, if that's your next question. It's not like I went through the student directory and randomly picked people. Because one, I didn't send this letter, and two, I didn't plant that box." She looked

at Madden like he was a nutter. His questions were weird.

"Are you a true crime fan? Like to listen to gory podcasts and read all the books?"

Hillary picked at her thumbnail. "I like to watch Hallmark Channel mysteries. Anything else is too gory. I don't do well with gore. My dad's a fisherman, and I get sick to my stomach when he cleans fish. It's gross." She grimaced remembering the time she threw up on the dock after watching a fisherman clean a swordfish.

Madden sighed and stood. "You can go. Campus security will escort you home. As you are aware, the campus at night isn't the safest." He stepped closer. "But make note, Hillary. This isn't over. A detective will be out to interview you again. Stealing property from the police department is a felony. A big one."

"Good thing I didn't take anything, then."

"Someone will pay for this. You better be telling the truth. We're done for tonight, but I have a feeling our paths will cross again. This murder club thing, it's over. Go back to your dorm, put your head in the books, and focus on school."

Hillary swallowed with apprehension. The police couldn't make them not have the club, right?

"Do you understand?"

"Yes, sir."

"Good." He patted her shoulder. "Don't worry about these people or Jaime Sullivan. That's for us to handle."

"Only you aren't handling it," Hillary mumbled as she turned toward the door to leave.

"Hillary?"

She turned back.

Madden met her gaze. "This business is not for a group

of students to take on. There's a killer out there. And if this letter is for real, did you consider for a moment that you might be the next target? All of you might be targeted?"

Hillary felt like an idiot. A scared one. Because not for a second had she thought that at all. What would a killer want with her?

5

Elliot pressed the elevator button and waited for the doors to close.

"Are you sure it's okay to be in here?" Hillary asked as they rode the elevator up to the third floor. They had gathered again the next evening at the Thompson Journalism building at nine p.m. Elliot had met them at the door to let each of them in.

"I have a podcast to edit and put out this week, so I'm usually here on Friday nights anyway," Elliot said.

"Not much of a social life, huh?" Trey had left his basketball at home. Along with his good mood.

"And just what did *you* cancel to be here tonight?" Elliot spat out the words.

He held up his hands in defense. "I wasn't sayin' I had plans. Just reflecting on you not having 'em. But I guess you don't date much these days anyway. Not after what happened to your last boyfriend."

Tension filled the small, enclosed space as Trey and Elliot stared at each other. Elliot's eyes narrowed. "Just say

what you want to say." She held her breath, hoping he'd say nothing. It wasn't that she didn't think the group would find out. She wasn't ready for the stares and endless questions just yet.

He stood ramrod straight. "I did say it. I ain't trying to pick a fight. Or hell, maybe I am." He ran a hand down his face, wiping away his frustration. "I wasn't sure I'd see y'all again. I wasn't sure I wanted to. Then Seema showed up at the gym and was all whispers and coded messages and shit. And I got excited. Probably an adrenaline junkie, like Mama says."

Seema chuckled. "I said tonight, nine. Same place. Be there. Not sure what there was to decipher."

Teddy and Hillary chuckled.

"What? Worried about not being included? Why pick on me? I am not in charge of this group." Elliot's temper was rising.

Trey huffed. "You're the only one I know. Well, I don't know ya, but you know what I mean. One degree of separation and all that. Plus, I know about ya."

Elliot felt, more than saw, the others' heads swivel to her.

She looked at the others, then glanced away and mumbled, "I guess you could say I was a victim of a crime. Well, my entire family was actually." Just once she would have liked to be part of something where her past wasn't always the elephant in the room.

Seema said, "I know about you too. I Googled you."

Hillary smacked herself in the forehead. "Dang it! I meant to do that. Just tell us what's going on. That cop asked me how I knew you. Asked if I'd seen you on the news."

"Asked me the same," Teddy said. "I forgot to Google as well."

The elevator chimed, and the doors slid open. Elliot gestured for the others to precede her.

"Listen, what happened to me is hard to talk about. Detective Madden was one of the officers who handled my case. I've been dealing with him for over two years, and it's not been easy. But right now, can we focus on why we're here? Because what happened to me has nothing to do with Jaime Sullivan." She glanced at everyone, afraid they'd pull out their phones and search, afraid this would all come to a screeching halt. To Seema and Trey, she said, "Wouldn't you agree?"

"I suppose," said Seema, her voice low and filled with something—pity?

The room was exceptionally quiet. Hillary's hands covered her mouth. Teddy wiped his brow with his forearm.

Trey said, "It might though. That cop seemed to think you were the center of all this."

Then Seema said, "I can't find a purpose for why we would all be here because of you. Are you sure you didn't know Jaime Sullivan? Did she have anything to do with your family's case?"

Elliot shook her head. "I asked myself those same questions last night, and I can't find a link."

"I'll stop bringing it up," Trey said. He moved to a random door and turned the handle.

His words took the steam out of her. "That's not where we're going." Elliot pointed to the door behind her on the right. "That's where the stuff is."

"I didn't come here for you anyway," Seema said. "I came for Jaime. Your shit makes no difference to me." She gestured to the door. "Are you going to unlock it?"

Elliot smiled. Seema was rough around the edges, but

Elliot could appreciate that. She slid her ID through the key strip and pushed it open when the lock disengaged.

Trey entered, followed by Seema.

"How did you know where to find me?" Hillary asked before entering.

Elliot said, "I used my investigative journalism skills. I looked you up in the directory. Saw you lived in Hammond Hall and went over there. I assumed you had a morning class, as most sophomores do. You were coming out as I was coming up, so I followed you to class. Good timing actually."

Hillary smiled and went into the room.

Teddy stopped at the door as well. He met Elliot's gaze. "I got my issues. Too many to worry about yours. So don't sweat it." He smiled. It was hard not to notice the light sheen of perspiration on his forehead.

"No pun intended," Elliot said.

"Oh no. I meant it." He chuckled and went into the room.

Elliot followed and let the door close behind her. From her messenger bag, Elliot pulled out the note they'd tucked under the couch cushions.

"After I was done with my interview, a campus cop was supposed to take me home, but there were some kids splashing in the clock tower fountain that he went off to take care of. I made like I was going home but circled back. While you all were being interviewed, I came in the back door and came up here. I made copies of everything. I also printed out the pictures I took with my phone." She tapped the first line on paper. "*Get what you can, you won't have long*. This bugged me. I'm not sure what it means, but I wanted to have backups of everything."

"Wait," Teddy said. "When did you get the paper? I was

the last to be interviewed, and I didn't get out of here until after midnight."

"I came to school at seven a.m. and collected this bad boy." Elliot held the paper in the air.

"Let's see the stuff," Seema said.

Elliot unlocked the cabinet and let the door swing open. She took a step back.

"What's wrong?" Hillary asked.

"The stuff is all gone." She pulled out a manila folder. "This is copies of everything, but the journal and news clippings are all gone."

Everyone took a step closer and looked into the empty cabinet.

"I put the originals in a grocery bag just in case I had to open the cabinet when someone else was around. I didn't want anyone to see it. But that's gone. Just the copies of everything are in here."

Seema took the envelope and opened it. She pulled out the wad of papers and spread them out on the table. "But all of these are copies of what was in the journal and the newspaper clippings?"

Elliot glanced over the pages then nodded. "Looks like it." She pointed to the pictures and dates. "Yeah, I printed these out last."

Seema began to sort the items into stacks, journal pages, newspaper clippings, photos. When Teddy joined and started doing the same, she stopped and went back to the cabinet, inspecting the lock and surrounding areas.

"It doesn't look like it was broken into. It's weird, but it's not like we need the originals anymore."

The others had joined Teddy and were sorting through the photocopies.

"Weird for sure," Hillary said. "Do you think the person who left us the box took the stuff?"

Everyone stopped what they were doing and looked at each other.

"That would mean we're being watched," Trey said.

Hillary visibly shivered.

"You aren't having second thoughts, are you, Hillary?" Seema asked.

Hillary took off her ball cap and put it on backward. "No, it just gave me the creeps is all."

Trey tapped the second line of the note. "Elliot, did you try this link?" He met her gaze.

"I checked it out last night. It's a link to an online forum and a group in that forum."

"What kinda group?" Seema asked.

"True crime. I assume we're supposed to join the group," Elliot said.

"Do you think whoever orchestrated this is in the group?" Hillary asked.

Elliot nodded. "I do. Yeah. Because I joined and get this..." She reached into her messenger bag and took out her laptop. Instead of connecting to the school Wi-Fi, she used her phone as a hotspot. "I think I'm a little paranoid, but I don't want to leave such an obvious trail."

She opened the group *True Crime Solvers* and showed the others.

"Here's the freaky part." She clicked on a few icons, and a private chat opened. "I got this no more than five minutes after I joined the group."

The private message read:

Welcome, Elliot. I'm glad you found your way here. It will be

our little secret that you might have committed a crime to get here. But then again, so did I. I hope you aren't going to be alone in this journey because, if so, then I should state that you will truly be alone. This is a group effort. Not a club of one. I look forward to the others joining. When they do, and only when they do, you will learn more about this case. The officer you spoke with last night will be back. Now's the time to scramble to get ahead.

"Dude, it's like I can hear the crazy laugh from TV shows at the end of that. That's creepy as shit." Trey backed away from the laptop. "I ain't joining. No way, man."

"I don't think any of us have a choice if we want to do this and do it right," Elliot said. The private message freaked her out, too, and she was glad to have shared it.

"Well, we can't join now," Seema said. "We can't use the building's Wi-Fi."

"You could hotspot like me," Elliot offered. "I checked, and there are two towers close by, so even if the police pulled my phone records, they can't pinpoint that I was in the building, only on campus."

"But Wi-Fi is all over campus. Won't they ask why we didn't just use that?" Hillary said.

"Yeah, but community Wi-Fi is notoriously bad for security. So if they ask, then I say maybe I was checking my bank account or something, where I wanted more security. That's why I used my hotspot," Elliot said.

Teddy pointed to the screen. "How did this person know you joined? Is this the username you gave?"

"Yeah, I was going for something totally not me."

Teddy gave a crooked smile. "SciFiDude. I would totally pick that name."

Elliot laughed. "Sorry, it's taken. But seriously. How did he know it was me?"

Seema asked, "Why do you think it's a he?"

Elliot hadn't thought about this anonymous person's gender. "I was using he generically."

"We should call this person *the killer*," Hillary said.

"Only we don't know they're the killer for sure," Seema added.

Elliot tossed up her hands in frustration. "Okay, let's call this person the messenger. Now can anyone tell me how the messenger knew it was me joining the group?"

Trey pulled out a chair and plopped into it. "Did you use your real name when you joined the site? Or an email related to you?"

"Yeah, I gave an old email I don't use often. I thought I was being clever with using a fake name, birthdate, and username."

"So your messenger is probably on admin. Or hacked into the forum, but I'd bet part of admin. I've had this happen on gamer sites. They see all your info. So they know the real deal on who's signing into the groups." Trey spun in the chair, doing two rounds before stopping.

"Well, that might be a good thing. Maybe we can find out who all the admins for the site are," Seema said.

Trey snorted. "Good luck. Remember, the messenger took items from this case that belonged to the po-po. I'm guessing he's not so careless on this site." He was now doing quick side-to-side swivels.

"Let's be positive and hope he did make a mistake,"

Hillary said as she pulled out her phone. "I'm signing up now."

Seema caught Elliot's eye and did an eye roll. "Wait, maybe we should create a joint email account and all join with that?"

Elliot shook her head. "You'll need an email to join, and it will recognize the address and say you have an account."

"Then maybe we should make very similar email accounts," Seema said.

"Why, if he's going to know it's us anyway?" Teddy asked.

Hillary, who'd been typing on her phone, paused. "You know that cop last night said something that gave me the creeps."

Trey was nodding. "He said lots to creep me out."

Teddy said, "Did he tell you we might be targets? Because he said maybe we were the targets. That maybe Jaime's case was a ruse to bring us together."

Trey froze. "Yeah, that's scary shit right there. Why would we be the targets? We didn't know Jaime."

Elliot shook her head. "Detective Madden is a douchebag. He would use scare tactics to get people to do what he wants. And he's a liar. He literally gets all choked up when he has to tell the truth."

Seema held up a hand. "Detective Madden aside, what he was saying was that it's possible that whoever started this has a vendetta toward each of us and is using Jaime Sullivan as a ruse. We can't forget that."

6

Seema's matter-of-fact statement that the messenger orchestrated the situation because of an ulterior motive toward each of them made everyone in the room pause. Silence floated around them. Then their focus shifted to Elliot.

She understood why they would look to her to be the impetus—it was easier to wrap the mind around her being the target than each of them. Besides, there was no denying she'd been singled out to a degree. She felt like a target.

Teddy cleared his throat. "Let's break this concern apart into two. First, what one person could have an agenda toward each of us? For a moment, Detective Madden's scare tactic worked. But statistically speaking, what are the odds that we've all forged a grievance with this individual? They're slim, that's for sure."

"What if it's a bunch of people? What if it's a club of killers like we're a club of sleuths?" Hillary said. She was dressed in loose-fitting jeans, a baggy T-shirt and hoodie. She nervously played with the zipper of the hoodie.

"I suppose anything is possible," Teddy said.

Seema was suspiciously quiet.

"And the second part?" Hillary asked.

"Why a grievance against Elliot?" Teddy's eyes met hers. Pity wasn't in his expression; it was sympathy, and she oh-so-very-much appreciated that.

Elliot slumped into a chair. She would have to address the elephant. "Me being the target? It's possible, I suppose. After my ... after..." She waved her hands in the air as if trying to conjure the words or the strength to say them. "After—"

"After your parents were murdered?" Trey finished, his voice low and soft.

Hillary gasped. Teddy pulled up a chair and sank into it.

Elliot blew out a slow, shaky breath. "Yeah, after that, I got a lot of threats. Detective Madden said it was normal. I suppose I could ask him for the list of people who've threatened me."

Seema nodded. "We should look at the list, just in case."

The room was quiet as the others absorbed what they'd just learned. Elliot stared at a burnt-out lightbulb on the ceiling.

"No one was convicted of your parents' murder, correct?" Seema asked.

Elliot shook her head. "The police think they know who did it, but they don't have enough evidence to charge them. The guys are already in prison for thirty years."

"Essentially, the murder of your parents is a cold case though, right?" Seema asked.

Elliot's answer was the slightest nod of her head.

Seema crossed her arms. "That could be the link. Or the

reason why you were picked for this. You can't solve the one cold case that means everything to you, so you solve others."

"Sounds like a movie made for TV." Elliot laughed awkwardly.

Hillary was the only one to smile.

Trey caught Elliot's eye, probably wondering if she was going to fill in more of the blanks, but she couldn't. She was too busy grappling with the possibility that whoever had orchestrated the Campus Murder Club might have done it to get to her and roped in four innocent people in the process. She wouldn't be able to cope should something happen to any of them because of her. She'd lose her mind for sure. She buried her head in her hands as the thought of it all overwhelmed her, and she needed to gather her composure.

Trey said, "Does anyone else have anything as tragic in their past?"

Hillary shook her head. "It's just me and my dad. My mom ran off when I was little."

Teddy wiped a hand down his face. "I've been lucky. No such type of tragedy in my past."

"Nothing so personal for me," Seema said. "A boy in my high school went missing our senior year. That's all I can think of."

Trey shook his head. "Nothing in comparison. I've had bad shit happen but nothing like an unsolved murder."

Elliot pressed her palm to her temples, pushing against the threatening headache. "If anyone wants to back out of this club now, they can. I would totally understand. I like to think Detective Madden was simply trying to scare us. I mean, he does think everyone but him is inept, so the idea that students might actually solve a crime the police couldn't

won't sit well with him. But knowing I'm being watched, well, it's scary." She gestured to the locker.

Seema reached across the table and picked up a stack of papers. "Here's what I think. I think you might be the link but not in a scary way. You were the obvious person to watch because everything went down here, in the journalism building. Our actions were predictable. In hindsight, maybe one of us should have taken the stuff from the building. But because we didn't have as much time, we left it here."

Teddy nodded with vigor. "Yeah, the probability of us taking the stuff out of the building was likely slim. It's a safe gamble to focus on you, Elliot. The fact that you've been a victim of a crime might just be a coincidence."

Elliot didn't believe in coincidences, but she appreciated the lifeline Teddy was throwing her.

Seema said, "I think we start going through all this stuff. We make a timeline and suspect list. And we keep our minds open to the fact that there could be a possible hidden agenda."

"Sounds good," Trey said. "I know this'll sound weird, but if anyone gets a weird-ass feeling, something nagging at them but can't explain it, you tell us. It don't have to make sense."

"Instinct," Elliot said.

"Instincts don't lie. Instinct has kept me out of trouble hundreds of times." Trey tapped his gut. "I've gotten real good at listening to it."

"You know," Elliot said as she stood, "even if this person does have an ulterior motive, even if all this has to do with my parents' deaths, I still want to know who killed Jaime Sullivan."

"Agreed," Seema said.

Elliot pulled a stack of papers toward her and started flipping through them, stopping to pull out a single sheet. "Look at this newspaper article. It's about Jaime's high school's tribute after she died. Students flocked to the campus with posters, flowers, and pictures to create a memorial. But that's not what got my attention. It's what the counselor said. He, a Mr. Bruce Lightner, said that despite all the hardships Jaime had as a young child and a young adult, she defied the odds. From poverty to homelessness to a mother who struggled with addiction, Jaime knew she was going to be a statistic. She chose to be the statistic opposite of what everyone expected." She handed the page to Seema. Hillary moved to stand next to her to look at the page.

"As someone who has always lived in the shadow of her older brother, I can relate to Jaime always living in the shadow of her trauma." She waved her hand dismissively. "Yes, I know Nathan being a superstar athlete is not even remotely close to the same as what Jaime lived with. I'm just saying that I know what the weight of a shadow feels like. And mine was not even a fraction as heavy as hers. I relate to her. And here we are six months after her death, and she's almost forgotten. What I'm saying is, I don't care about anyone's ulterior motive. I care about Jaime Sullivan getting peace. Getting justice."

Seema handed the photocopied article to Teddy.

Elliot said, "There are tons of articles about all the good deeds she'd done."

Hillary flipped through the pages. "She was always volunteering somewhere. Always helping out. I'm ashamed to admit that I sometimes hated her for it. She was too perfect."

"Likely compensating for all her childhood shit," Seema

said. She waved the copied article in the air. "This counselor. Bruce Lightner, he's the same one who paid for Jaime's funeral?"

Hillary nodded. "Yeah, she lived at his place sometimes."

Seema crossed her arms. "For me, he's suspect number one. What's his real motive with Jaime? I want that question answered. Maybe he brought the box."

Hillary reared back. "I hope you're not implying that Mr. Lightner was doing something ... something awful to Jaime. He's a grandpa, for Pete's sake."

Seema shrugged. "Even grandpas can be pedophiles."

Hillary covered her mouth in horror.

Trey began to swivel in his seat. "Maybe he's a dirty old man. Wouldn't be the first time."

Hillary closed her eyes, hands still over her mouth. "Just shut up," she said between her fingers. "I really like him."

Elliot took out a notebook and pencil and flipped to the first page. On the top she wrote *SUSPECTS*. On the line below that, she wrote *Bruce Lightner*.

"Elliot, can we make more copies of these?" Seema asked.

Elliot gave her a thumbs-up then made a note about more copies in her notebook.

Teddy made a suggestion. "Let's divide this stuff between us. Take it home, read through it. Make notes of anything that stands out to you. We can meet up again in a few days and compare notes. Sound good?"

"Solid," Trey said. "I want the journal. Ain't never had the chance to read a chick's journal before. I feel honored." He stopped swiveling long enough to give a mock bow in his chair.

"Are we meeting here?" Hillary asked.

Elliot shook her head. "The building is super busy during the earlier part of the week. We need to find someplace else."

"How about the medical quad?" Teddy offered. The medical quad was a two-acre outdoor area where students and school medical staff often ate their lunches and hung out. On one end, the quad connected to the back side of the four-story medical building. On the other end, the quad connected to the student rec center. It wouldn't be out of the norm for any of them to be at the quad. Besides, the views of the mountains and the fountains scattered throughout the quad gave the place a peaceful vibe. The quad was across campus from the journalism building, but when Elliot was on that side, she often made a point of going there because it was such a nice place.

"Okay, Monday. What time?" Elliot asked as she gathered all the papers in preparation to make copies.

They worked out the time, Elliot made the copies, and they said goodbye at the front of the journalism building, each going their own way. Each with something of Jaime's in their bags.

Elliot unlocked her bike, hurriedly stuffing the chain into her bag. A branch broke behind her, and she spun around to find nothing. A second branch broke to her left, and Elliot reached into her bag and grasped her pepper spray, flicking the safety off. "Who's there?"

What an idiotic thing to say. As if someone with nefarious intentions was going to answer back. A third branch broke, this time farther away as if the person was moving away from her, not toward. A flash of white caught her atten-

tion at grass level. But as fast as she'd seen it, the flash was gone. For a moment, she wondered if she was imagining it. But not willing to spend the time investigating, Elliot jumped on her bike and pedaled quickly away in the opposite direction, toward home.

7

The following Monday, they met at the quad after the lunch rush. It was the only time during the day that everyone was free. Meeting up at night worked, but Hillary was glad to be talking about Jaime Sullivan's murder in the sunlight. The after-hours meetings—granted, only two so far—with their macabre subject matter were wearing on her nerves. She didn't want to tell the others that though. Especially Seema, with her sharp tongue and heartless attitude. If she knew Hillary didn't like the nighttime meetings, Hillary would never hear the end of it. Seema was always harping on Teddy about his stammer or his sweating, or she was rolling her eyes at something Trey said. Hillary's preference would easily become one more thing for Seema to bitch about.

Hillary found Teddy's uncertainty sweet. As a person who was uncertain about every stinking thing, she related. Of course, ever since she'd started her anonymous hip-hop dance page on Instagram and YouTube, Hillary had devel-

oped a little backbone. Or maybe she should call it courage or self-esteem. Weren't they all the same?

Yeah, Seema probably looked at Hillary and saw a dumpy sophomore with the baggy Billie Eilish fashion sense. Heck, they all probably looked at Hillary and saw that. But Hillary Redding's truth, her secret that put a smile on her face was knowing the baggy sweats and hoodies she wore were all paid for by sponsors, and the affiliate income she made was paying for school. Hillary hadn't made the grades for a scholarship, and she wasn't about to tie herself down with debt. She didn't want to graduate with a butt ton of student loans.

And there was something wonderful and empowering about having hundreds of thousands of likes on her profile. Maybe Teddy could do something similar. Not hip-hop, of course, but maybe science minded.

Hillary Redding had no social media for fear of no one liking or friending her. @QueenDancer didn't care if people liked her. She just danced to let it all go, and the likes came pouring in. Hillary's only complaint was how hard it was to tap into @QueenDancer's courage as Hillary Redding. *Old habits die hard*, she supposed.

Seema plopped onto the bench beside Hillary at the square table for eight and smiled. If that was what the curling up on half her lip was.

"How was your reading?" she asked.

Hillary returned the smile, only hers was the real deal. "Yeah, interesting. I had the diary or ... journal. Whatever."

"Me too," Elliot said, sitting across from them.

Trey sat next to her. Teddy took a seat between the two groups.

"Do you know who OB is?" Elliot asked Hillary. "Jaime only refers to people by initials."

"Oliver Bridges. He and Jaime dated off and on. His dad is a fisherman like mine."

Seema opened her computer and then a document, where she added Oliver's name. "Where is he, do you know?"

Hillary shook her head. "Oliver didn't go to college. Or last I heard, he didn't. He had been living in Seattle and was driving long-haul semis. But a while ago, he was in a bad accident and hasn't been able to drive. I was talking to my dad last night, and he said Oliver kinda lost it after Jaime died and hasn't been around. I checked his social media, and he hasn't posted since the day of her funeral."

"Who all read the journal?" Teddy asked.

Elliot said, "Hillary, Trey, and I read the journal. Seema, you looked at the articles. And Teddy, you reviewed the photos."

He nodded. "I'd love to see the autopsy report because my notes are mere speculation. Though likely accurate. Her injuries weren't atypical nor unusual." He reached into his worn backpack and pulled out a composition-style notebook that looked just as worn as the pack. Small strips of silver duct tape bound the fraying corners of the notebook. "From online searches, I began to draft a twenty-four-hour timeline of Jaime's death."

Teddy flipped open the book to reveal small all-caps printing along a line. He swiveled the book so the others could see it.

Elliot cleared her throat while she reached into her messenger bag. She smiled at Teddy as she pulled out a large square of heavy-looking paper. "I did something similar.

Mine's forty-eight hours. I would love to combine what you have with mine." She unfolded the square to reveal two legal-sized sheets taped together at the ends. Along the center was a straight black line.

Elliot pointed to the writing above the line. "This marks events happening around Jaime. What others have reported —from what I read online as well— and what is below the line are Jaime's actual events that we know of."

Hillary leaned in to look at Elliot's timeline. Above the line were several marks with notes. Below the line were eight. Clocked out at end of shift, left building, arrived at dorm, scooter seen in parking lot, didn't show up for shift, reported missing for work, when her body was found, and estimated time of death.

Teddy's version looked similar to Elliot's.

"Hmm," Trey said. "Looks like y'all have the same info." He looked at the others. "Which means we don't know shit."

Seema sighed and crossed her arms. "What we know gives us a place to start."

Trey gave her an irritated look. "I didn't say we didn't have that. I just said we don't know shit."

Irritation crackled between the two. Hillary was relieved when Elliot cleared her throat to get their attention.

She said, "I agree with Trey. Not only do I think we don't know much, but this is all secondhand reports. The police could have left out information intentionally."

The group was quiet.

"I do have something that might be a clue," Elliot said.

The others sat up. She had their full attention.

"I was looking at the cards with the dates. I plugged them into a search browser, and nothing obvious caught my attention, so I went personal. I keep a digital planner. I

plugged the dates into my planner to see what would pop up on those dates, thinking maybe I was somewhere. Nothing did."

Trey's shoulders sank.

Seema scowled. "Were you going somewhere with this?"

Elliot held up a finger. "I broadened my search. One month before Jaime was killed." Elliot pointed to the index card with the September date. "I wrote an article for the school website on campus safety and students who didn't have cars. I interviewed Jaime. The article ran on this date." She tapped the card. "She said the worst thing about having a scooter and not a car was rainy days. So I had met Jaime. I interviewed her. I looked up my notes from that day, and I said she was nice and easy to talk to. We bonded over not having cars."

Intrigued, Hillary asked, "Could the other dates be articles too?"

Elliot shook her head. "There are seven cards. There are five of us. Maybe one specific date is significant to each of us like this one was to me?"

"That's everyone's homework," Seema said. "It's going to take some time for me to dig through my stuff to check dates."

Teddy tapped a finger on the table. "I don't know if I'm going to find anything. I have some days that I can't really account for. I don't keep a planner."

Elliot said, "Do what you can, Teddy. In the meantime, did everyone join the forum?" She looked around the group.

Hillary had. The others nodded that they had as well.

"No DMs?"

Everyone shook their heads.

Elliot tapped her finger to her chin. "Weird. I expected a

clue or something. He said we all had to join, we did, and I expected *something*."

Seema said, "Give it some time. While we wait, we can work this too." She tapped the timeline. "We know that on Friday, Jaime had a morning pharmacology lab from nine to eleven. She was seen entering her dorm before noon. From there she was seen leaving her dorm in her work scrubs at three forty. Her work shift started at four. I did a test-drive from her dorm to the nursing home, and it's twelve minutes when hitting all the lights."

Hillary felt like she had something to add. "Jaime talks a lot in her journal about how she wasn't enjoying being a CNA."

"Certified nursing assistant," Elliot said. "In case anyone didn't know that." But she ducked her head in possible embarrassment because the news had labored on about Jaime being a CNA and working third shift. A dum-dum who never paid attention would be the only excuse for someone who didn't know.

Hillary smirked and continued. "She wrote that a few nurses and doctors liked to use CNAs for scapegoats. Things like not properly securing patients who had precautions. She said typically the nurses who abused CNAs were lazy, and they didn't last long, but the doctors did, and she found that discouraging."

Seema moved her finger to one notch over on the timeline. "We're going to assume that she clocked in at four and then clocked out again at 12:30 a.m. when her shift ended. We can amend this if we learn differently. She wasn't seen alive again. One article remarked how Jaime had the same routine every weekend. Another student in Jaime's dorm said you could set your clock by Jaime and her weekend

schedule. So that opens the aspect of someone stalking her, of them using her predictability against her."

Trey shook his head. "She worked every weekend. That doesn't sound fun at all."

Elliot smiled. "You have a thing about nightlife, don't you?" Her words weren't accusatory.

Trey leaned back from the table, looking relaxed. "I have a thing about fun. I like to have fun. I like to laugh. I think people don't do enough laughing or having fun."

He had a point, Hillary thought.

Teddy said, "I certainly don't laugh enough."

Elliot stared off in the distance. "I stopped having fun when my parents were killed." She snapped her attention back to Trey. "You're right. People don't laugh enough, or they seem to put fun off. Jaime worked three of the four weekends, so at least she took one weekend for fun."

"We hope," Seema said.

"One weekend is better than nothin'," Trey added. "Girl was a die-hard worker, giving up her weekends like that."

Elliot tapped her chin. "I thought about that. Jaime's dorm is a private dorm and all females. Even if she's on scholarship, most of the expense of that dorm isn't covered, but it's cheaper than getting an apartment."

Hillary sighed. "And theoretically safer than an apartment."

Seema groaned. "Guess not."

Elliot continued. "Jaime had a single room. That's the most expensive. She didn't have a car, just a scooter."

"The scooter was found at a bar in downtown Vancouver. The guy who was arrested for stealing the scooter, Howie Middleman, said he found the scooter in the parking lot of Jaime's employment with the lights on and the key in

the ignition. She didn't take it home the night she was killed," Teddy said. "And the scooter hadn't been disabled or anything because Mr. Middleman said it started right up, and he rode it to the bar, fifteen minutes away. The paper I read said he didn't know Jaime, and he swears he never saw her. He wasn't arrested for her murder."

"Which means the police didn't have enough to charge him," Seema added.

"How does she end up at her dorm without her scooter? And her scooter end up across town? Why doesn't she take her scooter home?" Hillary asked.

"Maybe it was raining?" Elliot said.

"Maybe she caught a ride with someone?" Trey offered.

"But leave her key in the ignition?" Hillary shook her head. "It doesn't make sense."

"Maybe it was a booty call and a damn fine one at that. Maybe she got all distracted," Trey offered as levity. Because the truth was, they didn't know, and nothing reminded them more that they were out of their elements than a lack of information.

"Okay, maybe." Elliot glanced at Hillary. "But I didn't get that from the journal. Did you? And other than this Oliver dude, it doesn't seem she was dating anyone?"

Hillary answered. "Yeah, from what I read, she wasn't looking to get tied down to anyone. She had a few dates here and there, and like I said, she and Oliver were off-again, on-again."

"She was seeing him even in college?" Seema asked.

Hillary shrugged one shoulder. "That's my take, though less in college than in high school. Elliot?"

"Yeah, if I'm reading between the lines, I get the feeling they were each other's comfort food, but that they were

moving in different directions. I also didn't pick up on any new love interest. And like Trey said, she was too busy on the weekends. All work."

Trey shook his head. "Not exactly what I said. All I meant was the girl didn't have any days off. But I'm thinkin' she had some fun. Did you two not notice the grocery lists she had in her journal?"

Elliot reached for the journal pages. "Yeah, but it seemed like any other list."

Trey raised a brow and looked at Hillary. "Nothing stood out?"

She said, "There were a few things I didn't know but nothing weird."

Trey rolled his eyes. "I'm guessing YCare isn't something either of you are familiar with?"

Both Hillary and Elliot shook their heads.

Seema chuckled.

Trey said, "YCare is a hoo hah hoodie. A baby blocker. Canceling out what the Y deposits."

Hillary was confused.

Her face must have shown it because Seema laughed, then said, "It's a female condom."

Excitedly, Elliot whipped out the journal pages and thumbed madly through them. "Ugh, I wish we had the journal before this one. We only have two months to go from." She pulled out four pages. "Over the course of the last two months, she put YCare on four grocery orders."

Teddy asked, "How often did she order groceries?"

Trey smiled. "Every two weeks, it looks like. Jaime was hittin' it. Good for her."

Seema said, "Now we have to figure out who, if not this Oliver dude."

Teddy tapped the timeline. “Jaime was supposed to show up for her shift at four on Saturday. She didn’t. According to the reports I read, the girl who lives across the hall from her knocked on her door, and when Jaime didn’t answer, she got the RA involved. The RA is the one who found her. And that’s where we are with what we have.”

Seema nodded. “I think we should split up again and talk to people. Like the Lightner character. Hillary is our way in with him. We’ll do that together. She’ll need someone unbiased at that meeting. Someone who might see him for what he may really be. But also the girl who lived across the hall from Jaime, the one who got the RA involved.”

“Lindsay Volmer,” Elliot said. “And I want to go to where Jaime worked and talk to some people there.”

“I’ll go with you,” Trey said. When the others looked surprised, he put his palms up in mock defense. “What’s the big deal? I just don’t want to read any more. I’d rather do something with action.”

“Hillary will call Lightner and see if he’ll video chat with us. I don’t want to drive out to the other side of the state, but I will if I have to,” Seema said.

“Do I get a say in any of this?” Hillary asked.

Seema gestured to her, indicating she should go ahead with her complaint.

Hillary sighed in frustration. “All right, I’ll call Mr. Lightner.”

“Let me know if he won’t meet online, and I can drive out there with you if you have to go,” Elliot offered.

“I’ll read the journal,” Teddy said. “I’ll see if any of the medical school’s professors knows the medical examiner. Maybe I can find an in that way.”

Hillary almost fell out of her seat when Seema smiled at Teddy.

"Great idea," she said and clapped him on the shoulder.

Hillary, about to question Seema's kindness, stopped when her phone rang. She glanced at the screen. "It's the police." She looked at the others, a knot of fear coiled in her stomach.

"Answer it," Seema barked.

With shaky hands Hillary answered the call. "Hello?"

"Hillary Redding?"

"Yes."

"This is Detective Madden. We met four nights ago at the journalism building."

Hillary looked at the others as she said, "Yes, I remember you, Detective Madden."

Elliot's shoulders dropped.

"We would like you to come into the station for a few more questions. At your earliest convenience, of course. How does today work?"

"Um, I have a class in a little bit. I don't have a car, and I don't know where the station is."

"How about we meet at the campus security office? That should be more convenient for you. When does your class start?"

"Four." Hillary wanted to kick herself. Why was she being so compliant? If Seema was on the phone, she bet Seema would make the cop wait.

"Great. How about you head here now. We'll see you at the campus security office in thirty minutes. Thanks, Hillary." He ended the call.

She gulped and looked at the others. Before anyone

could say anything, Elliot's phone rang. She showed the others her screen. It was the police.

"Looks like our second meeting with the cops is about to happen," Seema said.

Teddy gulped.

Trey wiped a hand down his face. "And for a second there, I let my guard down."

Seema wagged her finger. "Never let your guard down."

"Never," said Elliot as she pressed the button to answer the call.

8

Each person in the dance-with-danger-death-club got a call from Madden. Trey didn't want to admit it unnerved him. Offering to tag along with Elliot turned out to be a bonus. He didn't want to go alone to the station, and he figured Elliot was an old pro at being around cops. Any nervousness he might have would be overshadowed by her sour attitude. Where Trey was from, the cops weren't always the good guys they were supposed to be. Or heck, maybe they were, but the streets of Memphis weren't nice to anyone.

The main reason he wanted to tag along with someone was because he didn't want to do more reading. It wasn't that he couldn't read; it was that he hated it. He was a listen-to-the-book or podcast guy. Yeah, he thought the journal and stuff they found in the box were helpful, but they weren't gonna get anywhere fast with what they had. They needed to talk to people, and talking to people was Trey's jam. Growing up in Memphis was like attending the school of hard knocks on a daily basis, for life. Or for as long as a man

stayed there. Trey had attended a good neighborhood school with lots of mamas and grandmamas minding the kids. But he'd learned real quick to tell the difference between the bullshitters and the sincere. Bullshitters always had tells that weren't accounted for by nerves.

That was why Trey wanted to get out there and get face time. He wanted to find the liars and the lovers and uncover the legit story. And tagging along with Elliot Long wasn't bad either. She was cute for a tight-ass, no-sense-of-humor white girl. But if he'd lost his people in a brutal homicide and had an older brother who was a ginormous douchebag like Nathan Long, he'd probably be the same. Hell, he'd probably be beating the shit out of anyone and everything just to deal with the heaviness of it all.

"Should we come up with a plan?" Trey asked, rubbing his hands together as they walked out of the quad to the parking lot.

"You know you don't have to come with me?" Elliot gave him a puzzled look.

"I know. But I think it'll be good for both of us to get the vibe and compare notes. Besides, you have a bike. I have a car. It'll be faster if I drive. You don't want to be late to the cop shop."

"Like I care," she said bitterly. "I don't live to make Detective Madden's life easier."

Trey quirked a brow, surprised at her tone. "I'm not saying you should, but my mama always says you can catch more flies with honey than vinegar. Ever try that with him?" He hurried to explain. "Not judging, only wonderin' if he's the kind who needs to be flattered."

Elliot shook her head. "I don't know what Madden needs. At first, I was compliant and did everything the

cops said to do. But I realized they were coddling me, not telling me anything. Had I not gone bitchy, I'd still be popping in the station on Wednesdays asking for the latest updates and being told there's nothing. At least this way, I don't feel like I'm being patted on the head and sent on my way."

Trey wanted to ask her if that was all Madden had done that she found so unforgivable, but Elliot needed time to open up, and he could wait.

They reached the parking lot, and Trey gestured to a bright-blue Honda Civic. He followed her to the passenger side and opened her door. She jumped back in surprise.

"Hey, my mama raised a gentleman." He smiled wide.

She smiled back. "Yeah, I guess so." She got in, and when he joined her, she said, "You know my mom used to say the same thing. About vinegar and honey. She used to say it to Nathan more than me. I really miss her."

She looked ahead, staring at something out the front windshield. Trey couldn't imagine not having his mama around, and he didn't know what to say, so he started the car and let the moment rest between them.

Her phone chimed with a text. Elliot glanced at it and groaned.

"Cops again?"

"Worse, my brother's agent. The guy is so smarmy." Elliot flicked the screen to read the text. "I guess I should be glad he texts instead of calls. A person can only avoid a call so many times."

"Bill Rodgers is your brother's agent, right?"

Elliot nodded. "You know him? Is he trying to recruit you? Because I'm sorry if so. I don't mean to be so rude."

Trey snort laughed. "Nah, you couldn't pay me to have

Rodgers as my name, image, likeness, advisor, or my agent. He's a D-hole. What's he want?"

She read the text. "My brother's team will be in Seattle for a game next week, and they want me to come. He'll have tickets and will call. As if."

Trey navigated through traffic. "You going?"

"Hard pass. Thanks, but no thanks." Elliot cleared her throat. "I get the feeling you don't like my brother."

Trey turned on the radio. Elliot turned it off.

"Seriously, you can tell me," she said.

"It's not that I don't like him. I wasn't close enough to him to like or dislike. He was two years ahead of me and the superstar."

"And?"

"And nothing. He talked a lot of trash, and I talked it back."

Elliot chuckled. "One of the few to talk back. I bet that didn't go over well."

"A few punches and it's water under the bridge. Well, for most guys it is."

"With Nathan, punches don't matter. You either helped his star shine, or he cut you out, trying to dim your star in the process," Elliot finished.

Trey kept his eyes on the road. "Yeah, something like that. So, he was like that at home too?"

Elliot turned on the radio. She mumbled, "At home he was built up to be the superstar. No real lessons in humility, that's for sure. My parents created a monster. And since their death he's consumed himself with baseball."

Trey tried to picture what life would be like without Mama and how he and his kid brother, Titan, would handle it. One thing he was sure as hell certain of, he'd hold tight to

Titan, and they'd go through the journey together. He cut his eyes to Elliot. She was going it alone. That made him sad, but he was smart enough to not show her that. She was the kinda girl who kept her anger close and would get pissed at pity.

"We're going to the nursing home, right?"

"Yeah, it's on Highway 99 in Salmon Creek. Near the hospital."

Trey pointed his car in that direction. "What's the plan?"

She shrugged. "I thought I'd ask to speak with anyone who worked with Jaime and ask that person a lot of questions."

"Assuming they'd want to answer them."

She crossed her fingers and waved them in the air.

"And the plan if we can't find someone to chat?"

Elliot shook her head. "I don't think like that. Defeatist talk. We'll find someone."

Jaime had worked in a skilled nursing and rehabilitation facility that was attached to the hospital yet ran as a separate entity. More part of the medical complex than the hospital itself. Based on the information from the website, Elliot shared with Trey that the patients were all ages from eighteen and older with various medical issues.

"Guess that would be good experience for a person about to graduate nursing school," Trey said.

"Yeah, and would likely help with getting directly hired because they look to hire internally first."

They pulled into the parking lot. Trey glanced at his watch. "We have two hours before we have to be at the station to see Madden."

Elliot huffed before getting out of the car. She beelined for the front entrance.

"We're just gonna walk in the front doors and do what?"

"Ask the first person we see if they knew Jaime." She pushed her shoulders back straighter and marched ahead.

Her plan needed work. He surveyed the area. The building itself was two stories. To the side a walled-off area appeared to be an outside eating and hangout space for staff. He'd noticed resident space had been clearly marked around the property. Other than that, the place had the fortress vibe.

Trey let Elliot lead the way. Beyond the sliding double doors of the entrance sat a receptionist at a large, curved desk, blocking them from going any farther.

"Good afternoon. How can I help you?" She was an older woman, likely someone's grandma. She had that sweet tone and kind smile. If she was anything like the grandmamas Trey knew, they didn't have a chance in hell of getting past her.

"Um, ah ...we're here to see..." Elliot gestured to the space beyond the receptionist.

"Do you have a family member here to see? A friend?" The receptionist waited patiently for Elliot to answer.

Elliot glanced at Trey, but he didn't have anything to offer. He knew a dead end when he saw one.

"You're on," he whispered. "Good luck."

Elliot sighed. "My name is Elliot Long. I'm a journalism student at the university. I have a podcast." She gestured to Trey. "We have a podcast. We'd like to talk to a few people who knew Jaime Sullivan."

The receptionist shook her head.

Elliot continued in a rush. "Not about what happened. But a human-interest piece. Who she was as a person. It's been six months, and we don't want people to forget her. We

don't want people to remember her as just a girl who had something terrible happen to her."

Briefly Trey wondered if Elliot might be pulling from her own experience.

The receptionist gave Elliot a kind smile. "That's very sweet, but I can't let you back there. And any media requests must be run through administration. Why don't you leave your name and number, and I'll turn it over to them." She pushed a pad of paper and pen forward.

Elliot shifted in frustration, and Trey stepped forward.

"We'd appreciate that, ma'am." He gestured for Elliot to leave her information. "We know this is a delicate situation, and we respect that. From all our research, Jaime Sullivan seemed like a nice girl. A real pull-herself-up-by-the-boot-straps kinda chick ... um girl. We'd like her story to be one of inspiration despite the tragedy."

The receptionist was nodding repeatedly. "She typically came in when I was getting ready to leave, but she always had a kind word to say and always asked about my family."

"Yes, ma'am, that's what others are saying too. That's what we want to tell our peers on campus." He leaned in toward the receptionist and lowered his voice. "You know how college kids can be, a little self-centered. We want to remind them that now is when to be kind, to be giving, to make change. Later sometimes doesn't come."

Misty eyed, the receptionist dabbed the side of her index finger under one eye. "I'll make sure to press upon the administration to give you a call. That's a story I'd love to read."

Trey gave her a broad smile. "And if they might talk to her closest friend... What's her name?" He gestured to Elliot,

who jumped into action. She pulled out her notebook and began flipping pages, as if looking for a name.

The receptionist said, "I don't know who Jaime was close with here. Like I said she was coming in as I was leaving, but I often saw her with one of the nurses. Lucas."

Elliot tapped her paper. "Yep, that's the name I have here. Thanks so much."

Trey smiled at the receptionist. "We appreciate your time. Thanks again." He gestured to the picture on her desk, the one he'd caught sight of when he'd moved closer. "Good-looking family. Those your kids?"

She laughed and waved him off. "Dear heavens no, those are my grandkids. Why do you think I'm smiling so big in the picture? Grandkids are easier, fun, and a blessing."

Trey laughed. "My grandmama says something similar, and when my brother and I misbehave, she tells us we're supposed to bring her joy, not heartache, and to knock it off. She's the best."

"Do you see her often?"

Trey shook his head. "She's back in Memphis. I'm going home this summer, and she's the first stop I'm gonna make." He leaned in conspiratorially. "She makes the best oatmeal raisin cookies."

The receptionist laughed. "Cookies are my specialty too."

"As my mama would say, 'They fill my cup.'"

The receptionist pressed her hands to her heart and beamed at him.

"Well, we've taken enough of your time. Thanks again." He patted the counter twice and pushed away.

The receptionist said, "If you want to find Lucas, he

sometimes works the second shift or third. You could catch him at four p.m. or midnight."

"Thank you," Trey said and elbowed Elliot.

She jumped into action. "Yes, thank you so much. Have a great day."

They waved and exited the building.

Outside, Elliot looked at Trey in awe. "You were amazing in there. I don't even know how you got a name out of her. So smart." She pulled him away from the view of the door and to a bench on the side of the entrance. She plopped down.

He tugged at his shirt collar, embarrassment making his neck hot. Praise on the ball field was one thing. He knew he had talent. Praise for being clever was not something he was used to. He rubbed his hand over the back of his neck.

Elliot gestured for him to sit. "We're gonna wait to see if Lucas shows up. It's three thirty, not a long wait."

"We have to be at the cop shop at four."

Elliot flipped her hand in a dismissive wave. "They'll wait."

Trey shook his head. "What are you gonna do? Ask everyone coming in if their name is Lucas?"

"Maybe. Do you have a better idea?"

His brows rose. "Yeah, I do. It looks like behind that wall over there is an employee break space. I thought maybe I'd toss you over the wall and you could talk to a few more employees. Maybe get some info about Jaime *and* a description of Lucas."

9

Elliot leaned against the six-and-a-half-foot brick wall and shook her head. Why should she be the one to fly in the air? "How about I give you a boost instead?"

Trey chuckled. "I outweigh you. I don't think you can lift me."

"I don't have to lift. I just have to..." She laced her fingers together and, with palms up, acted like she was tossing an imaginary person upward.

Trey stuck his hands in his pockets. "Okay, sure. What questions you want me to ask? How you want me to go through this 'interview'?" He did air quotes.

Elliot pressed her lips together in resignation. "All right, you boost me." Based on what had happened earlier, he'd probably be more successful than her. But pride wouldn't let her concede. Not to him. Not to anyone.

Trey winked. "Knew you'd see it my way." He laced his fingers together and waited for her to step onto his combined palms.

She dropped her messenger bag, squared her shoulders, blew out a breath, and placed one hand on each of his shoulders. "Don't toss me over, just lift."

"I supposed you don't know this, but I've done this before with my brother. I know how to boost someone up and not over. It's up to you to grab the top and get up there."

She looked at him with suspicion.

"Don't go making up stories about me in your head. My mama hides candy at the top of her closet. It's how we'd get some without being obvious. Titan can snatch a bag off the shelf and put it back in its place while in midair."

Elliot grinned. "Ready?"

"On the count of three. One, two, three!"

She stepped onto his palms and put her trust in him. Doing so was a strange and unnerving sensation. But she figured if she couldn't trust him to not pole vault her over a wall, they were in trouble as team members. Plus, knowing Trey wasn't awed by her brother made her like him more. Stupid as that may have been.

With Trey's boost, Elliot went up high enough to get a glimpse over the wall. She caught the ledge coming down, scraping her palms and forearms as she collided with the wall and slid down slightly. She planted her feet against the wall to add traction and stability. Gripping the ledge with all her strength and using her leg muscles, she scaled the wall like Spiderman. She slid a couple of times but eventually managed to pull herself up to sit on the ledge.

Trey hooted with pride and shook a fist in the air.

She surveyed the employee space. Three round tables with chairs, a smoker's trash can with an ashtray, and one bench.

She looked down at Trey. "No one."

"What? I heard people talking."

"I guess they went inside. It's empty."

"Drop over and go through the door. Maybe you'll find someone then?"

Elliot gave it a moment's consideration. "Wait, someone's coming." Through the glass door, a woman was looking at her.

The door from the building opened, and a middle-aged woman in blue scrubs stuck her head out. "Can I help you?"

Elliot smiled. "Yeah, I was looking for someone who might talk to me about Jaime Sullivan. I heard she had a friend here named Lucas?"

The lady glanced into the building, then back at Elliot. "Lucas isn't here yet. And not many people on this shift knew Jaime. She always worked later. But listen, my boss saw you and called security. You better scram."

Elliot gave her a thumbs-up. "Thanks for the heads-up. Oh, wait. Lucas. Can you tell me what he looks like?"

The lady nodded. "Tall, dark hair, good-looking kid. Wears the ugliest shoes. Nikes with gold stripes. Now go!"

Elliot thanked her again and looked back at Trey. "Security's coming."

He stepped away but put out his hands in case she needed help when she dropped from the ledge. She pushed off and dropped, landing on her feet, using her hands to push off the earth and stay upright.

"I landed like an Avenger," she said with a grin.

Trey grabbed her bag. "Come on, Black Widow, let's go."

He dragged her around the side of the wall, away from the front door and hopefully security. He continued to pull

her behind him, zigzagging through the copse of trees that surrounded the medical complex until they were in the parking lot. Elliot glanced behind her and realized that Trey had navigated them to a spot that made it look like they couldn't have been the ones scaling the wall. In fact, closer to the property was another couple, a tad older than her and Trey, if she had to guess. They were walking into the parking lot, and the security guard was rushing toward them. Likely mistaking them as the wall scalers simply because of proximity.

"That was clever," she told Trey.

"Street skills. Come on, let's get out of here before he gets wise and calls the cops. We already have their attention. We don't want this on their radar too."

"Good point." Elliot took her messenger bag and draped it across her body. From inside the bag, she took out a ball cap. "This might help too." She tucked her hair through the back to make a ponytail and adjusted the hat to cover her face.

Trey gestured to the hat and smiled. "You carry that around?" He gestured for her to head toward his car.

"No, not until I met Hillary and thought about how nondescript the hat makes her."

"It's covered in jewels," he said in disagreement. "That's pretty obvious."

"Sure, until I ask you what color hair she has, and you can't tell me. All she has to do is take off the hat, and she's a different person."

Trey paused and studied Elliot. "I wonder if Hillary knows that."

Elliot shrugged in response, her attention snagged on a

tall guy wearing scrubs. He was putting a gym bag in his trunk. He had dark hair and was cute, she supposed. College aged. Could he be Lucas? Elliot moved around a few cars to look at his shoes. Sure enough he was wearing Nikes with a gold swoosh.

Elliot whispered to Trey. "I think that's Lucas."

They jogged the two lanes ahead to catch him.

"Hey, excuse me," Elliot called.

The guy slammed his trunk and faced her with an expectant look on his face.

"Do I know you?" He kept a hand on his car, as if it might offer something as a weapon should he need it.

She ran up to him. "Hi, I'm Elliot Long. You're Lucas, right?"

He took a step back but nodded.

"I'm working on a story about Jaime Sullivan, and I was told you might be able to tell me more about her. It's a human-interest piece. Not about her murder but about her." She breathed out the last word and sucked in a breath. She wasn't winded per se. It was more as though the excitement of getting actual information was leaving her breathless.

"I don't want to talk about Jaime." He pushed from the car and turned toward the building.

"C'mon, man, just five minutes," Trey called.

"Five minutes doesn't seem to be enough time to do a respectable human-interest story," Lucas said, cutting through the cars.

"Okay, I lied about that. Trey and I are part of a group of people trying to find Jaime's killer."

Lucas stopped and turned to study them. "No way. What are you? Wannabe cops or something?"

Elliot shook her head. "We're..."

"Citizen sleuths," Trey said, refusing to look at Elliot when she cut her eyes to him. "Students who care. The cops aren't doing shit, man, and if you really were her friend, that should piss you off. Unless you did it, of course."

Elliot gasped. Stupidly, she hadn't given that possibility its due. She snaked her hand into her bag, looking for anything that could be used as a possible weapon.

Lucas came toward them. His brows were furrowed, his lips pressed thin. He puffed out an exasperated sigh before saying, "It does piss me off. No one even cared when she didn't show up for work. I'm the one who noticed. I'm the one who pointed it out."

"I'm sorry for your loss," Elliot said. She pulled her hand from her bag. "From what I've read about Jaime, what I've learned, she seemed like a nice person. Too nice to be forgotten like this."

Trey leaned against a car. "Listen, man, we get this is painful for you. And cold catching you in the parking lot before work isn't very nice of us. But anything you can tell us about Jaime, about that day, we'd appreciate it. We don't have a lot."

Elliot almost snickered. They had nothing, really, but she kept her composure because whether Lucas knew it or not, he had all the control.

"If you don't want to talk to us, could you tell us anyone who might be willing?" Elliot asked.

Lucas ran a hand through his hair. "The night she died I worked the seven p.m. to seven a.m. shift. I was here all night. I have an alibi."

"You saw her when she left that night?" Elliot asked. "Was she upset or worried or anything?"

He shook his head. "She was herself. We made plans to have dinner together the next day. We both had big tests coming up and planned to quiz each other. Not for the same class. I'm working toward being a nurse practitioner."

Trey said, "You said you planned to have dinner, but she was working, I thought?"

Lucas fidgeted with his smartwatch, spinning the dial. "She was working. I was gonna bring in food for dinner, and we would quiz each other over her dinner break."

"Which was what time?" Elliot asked.

"She liked to take her first break after eight."

Elliot ran through their conversation, trying to connect pieces. "Her shift started at four, right?"

"Yep."

"She was found after six?" Elliot asked.

Lucas nodded.

"I can't get these pieces to connect." Elliot made like she was putting two things together.

"I came in a little after five to ask her what she wanted me to pick up for dinner. She wasn't here, and she hadn't called in. The charge nurse is a cranky bitch, and when I asked if she'd called Jaime to see what was up, she told me she didn't have time to track down slackers."

Trey said, "I didn't get the slacker vibe from what I read about Jaime."

Lucas crossed his arms. "She wasn't. But she was gonna graduate soon, and that threatened some of the other nurses here. Jaime was gonna be a kick-ass nurse. She cared about her patients."

"You come in, Jaime's not here, and no one called to check on her?"

Lucas crossed his arms, as if to block out the bad memories.

Elliot continued. "Did you call Jaime?"

He briefly closed his eyes and grimaced. "She didn't answer. My girlfriend lives in the same dorm, so I called her and asked her to go to Jaime's room. She did. She knocked. No answer. She got the RA involved. That's who found Jaime."

"Your girlfriend is Lindsay Volmer?" Elliot asked, recalling the name from the group's conversation earlier.

"Yeah."

"And that's how you found out?" Trey asked, shaking his head sadly.

He wiped a hand down his face. "My girlfriend called back, freaking out. Screaming 'She's dead, she's dead,' and at first, I thought it was some sort of mistake. A bad joke or something. But it was real."

Elliot lowered her voice. "And the night before, when she left work. Did she leave with anyone? Meet up with anyone?"

There was a sadness about him when he shook his head. "No, she said, 'See ya tomorrow' and left."

"And the person of interest they brought in, Howie Middleman, he wasn't waiting for her here?" Trey asked.

"Nope, she didn't mention anyone waiting for her, and I didn't see anyone outside the door. She had her scooter key in hand and was talking about how excited she was to sleep in."

Trey asked, "Did she ever have anyone waiting for her when she got off?"

"Not that I ever saw. Jaime was focused on school and

doing well. She had applied to the same nurse practitioner program I'm in and was going for a coveted scholarship. She needed nothing but A's to even be considered. Because of that, she wasn't much of a party person. Sometimes after a hard shift, some of us would go down the street for a drink. She never came."

Elliot tapped her chin and glanced at Trey. "So how did her scooter end up at the bar in Vancouver? Do you think her scooter was taken from campus? Middleman had been drinking so maybe he took it from campus or lied?"

Lucas harrumphed. "I've wondered the same."

Elliot asked, "Was it raining when she left?"

"Yeah, the cops think she caught a ride because of the rain. I dunno."

Elliot tapped her chin. "Are there any cameras for the parking lot?"

"Nope, cops suggested the facility get some, but they're too cheap to staff that because someone has to monitor and maintain them."

"Any ideas of who she might have caught a ride with?" Trey asked.

Lucas's voice was raspy with emotion. "I don't think even the police have any ideas."

Elliot looked at Trey. "Seems like someone should try to find out." To Lucas, she said, "Is there anyone else we could talk with who might know? Who was the nurse she worked with on the day shift? I'm assuming you guys worked together often."

"Yeah, no matter the shift we tended to overlap some. Aaron Simmons was the nurse working seven a.m. to seven p.m. He left several hours before her. Kim Bath is another

nurse she worked frequently with. She wasn't working that night."

"You know if either are working today?" Trey asked.

Lucas shook his head. "Kim was a traveler. She's moved on to a different state or something." He scanned the parking lot. "Aaron's car isn't here, so he's not working here today."

10

Elliot's body hummed in the seat as Trey navigated the streets taking them to the police station.

"We've got some leads! We've got leads!" She clenched her hands in excitement and pounded on the dash.

"Easy there, Sherlock Holmes. It's one lead, and what does it even mean?"

"I think she was taken from the parking lot. I think she met up with someone who she was using those condoms with. They went out for a bit. He dropped her off at her scooter. Someone grabbed her."

"Someone grabbed her and took her back to her dorm?" Trey shook his head in uncertainty.

"Okay, it's got some holes. I just think the parking lot is the key to what happened."

"I hate to say this, but I bet we probably would have learned this from the messenger."

"But we didn't get it from the messenger, and this means we don't need him. That's why I am so excited. And, really, I think maybe we should go about this without any help

from the messenger. Maybe whatever he feeds us will be skewed and limit our perspective. Like we don't want to see the same things the police saw. We need to see everything fresh. You see what I'm saying?" She was talking a mile a minute.

"*Si*," said Trey and chuckled.

"I'm sorry, for the first time since we started this, I actually believe we might be able to do this."

"You didn't think we could do this when we all stuck our hands on each other's and made a pact?" Trey cut his eyes to her.

"I was hopeful. But this makes me more than hopeful. This is confidence. We need to talk to more people. We need to make the timeline tight. We can do this, Trey. I truly believe we can."

Obviously, her excitement wasn't contagious because his smile was barely a lift on one side of his mouth.

"I hope you're right. Don't go getting nuts on me. Next thing you'll suggest is that we wait in the parking lot at midnight and see what Jaime saw."

Elliot raised her brows in consideration.

"It was a joke. It's a bad idea." He shook his head.

His stupid reticence was definitely contagious. Elliot sank back into the seat. "You're such a buzzkill. Wanna tell me why?"

He sighed and sped through a yellow light. "You know that saying 'You don't know what you don't know'?"

"I've heard it before, sure."

"Yeah, well, there's a whole lot I don't know about this case. But I know that I don't know. I know there's information out there, and I don't have it. Shit, I can't help feeling like we're behind the eight ball in this game and that what

we *need* to know is purposefully being kept from us. Know what I mean?"

"Yeah, I think so. Like we're purposefully being fed info and purposefully being kept in the dark." She tapped her chin. "What if I poked the bear?"

He pulled into the police station and whipped his little car into a spot, throwing the gearshift into park. "Whadya mean 'poke the bear'? Sounds like a stupid idea."

She rolled her eyes. "I didn't figure you for a chicken."

He pointed a finger close to her nose. "Don't call me a chicken."

Her lips twitched. "All I meant by poking the bear was that I'd PM the messenger and tell him we all joined and are ready to take this to the next level." She shrugged one shoulder casually.

Trey nodded a few times, as if with each nod he was working her idea over and deciding if he liked it or not. "Yeah, that might be a good idea."

Elliot whipped out her phone and tapped the screen a few times, pulling up the forum. She entered the private message page and placed the phone on her knee. She blew on her palms and rubbed her hands together, gleefully smiling at Trey as she did so.

She said, "Time to poke the bear." Her fingers flew across the screen, and moments later she hit Send. "Okay, done."

"What did you say, specifically?"

"I pointed out that we had all joined and were hoping to hear from him by now, and I said that I couldn't help but wonder if he was jerking us around and probably knew even less than what we did about Jaime's death. And I might have said that I wondered if the cops were right that he was some

weirdo with a vendetta." She gave him a wide smile. "I challenged him. I said give us something real. Something specific that the reason we were sent the letter was to help solve Jaime's case."

Trey closed his eyes as if gathering strength. "That's not what you said you were going to say earlier." He opened his eyes and glared at her. "What if he *is* a psycho with a vendetta?"

"Well, better we know it now, right? Come on, we're late. I see Madden at the door, and he knows we're here." She opened the door and went out, leaving Trey to follow her.

He caught up with her, making his car beep by engaging the lock on his key fob. "You know, I can't figure you out. One moment, I think you're cautious. The next, I'm tossing you up a wall, and you're challenging a nameless, faceless person. I don't know how I feel about all this."

"I suppose your first reaction not being fear is a good sign." She smiled. "I have fear all the time. I think I'm so used to it, my barometer might be broken."

They climbed the four steps to the police station. Madden opened the door for them.

"Cutting it close," he said.

"We're right on time," Elliot countered.

Madden smiled. "I didn't realize you two were friends."

"Well, we are," Elliot said. "I didn't realize you kept a list of all my friends. Is that on a drive somewhere I can update? I'd hate for you to have misinformation. And also, I'm gonna need the list of people who've threatened me. Can I get that?"

Madden shook his head and followed them into the station. "Why do you want to know that stuff? It's just crazy

people, and according to what you reported last, you haven't had a threat in six months."

"Maybe I'm taking your words of caution last Thursday seriously? I'm not kidding when I say I want a list. Can you email it to me?"

Madden said, "I can. Jeff Harmon is the detective who wants to meet with you. He's in charge of the Jaime Sullivan case. I believe you know Detective Harmon, Elliot."

Elliot groaned. To Trey, she said, "Harmon is the detective in charge of my parents' case as well. Looks like he's oh for two. I wonder if Harmon is the kiss of death to a case, inevitably making them cold. I dislike him way more than I dislike Madden." She jerked her thumb in the direction of the officer.

Madden cleared his throat and gestured for them to follow. He led them to a hallway with a row of doors. "These are the interview rooms. Obviously, you won't be interviewed together." He gestured to the first door. "Elliot, if you want to wait here. Trey, you're in the room next door."

Elliot paused at the door. "I think I want a lawyer. Don't you think I should have a lawyer, Madden?"

"If you comply and answer a few questions, you'll be out of here in minutes. If you want to wait for a lawyer and stonewall us at every move, this will turn into a long night. You aren't under arrest. It's just questions about the box of stuff. There's no need to be difficult," Madden snapped.

"Hey," Trey said sharply. "Maybe consider for a moment that every time she sees you, every time she comes here, she is reminded of what's happened to her. Reminded of the fact that the police have done jack all and still can't show her the decency of respect or compassion for her loss. If it was me, man, I'd have fuckin' lost my shit by now. Hell, I'd probably

be in jail for my actions. Personally, I think she's showing impressive restraint." Trey opened a door and stepped inside the interviewee's room. His voice carried out the door. "Ah man, this place smells like old tacos and a fart."

Elliot's heart swelled with appreciation. No one, *no one*, had ever understood her like Trey.

Madden hung his head. A rare dogged expression marked his face. "If you'd feel more comfortable with your lawyer or maybe having this chat outside, let me know."

Ignoring him. Elliot stepped into the interview room. She took a seat at the table and waited. Moments later, she heard the door to Trey's room open, but she couldn't hear the conversation.

Madden came into her room with a cold bottle of water. "Harmon decided to talk with Trey first. I brought you this in case you were thirsty."

"Thank you."

Madden paused at the door. "Listen, Harmon's feathers are ruffled because the pictures were from his case file."

"What about the other stuff?"

"What other stuff?"

Elliot almost said the journal and newspaper articles but caught herself. "Wasn't there mail and things like that in the box?"

Madden sighed. "Apparently, those were taken from her apartment after the police were done collecting evidence, likely when whoever packed up her place. The other stuff wasn't listed on any evidence sheet."

"So whoever sent us that box doesn't have any more information than the rest of us citizens. And what was in the box was stuff the cops deemed unnecessary to the case." Elliot had to disagree. She believed the journal to be filled

with important information. Look what they'd learned from it so far.

"With the exception of the pictures." Madden stepped from the room and closed the door.

Ten minutes later, Elliot was still waiting. She decided not to pull out her phone for fear she was being watched behind the one-way mirror. Instead, she pulled out a notebook and drew faces, caricatures. She itched to write down her thoughts but stuck to the activity she knew would piss Harmon off. She drew a round face with excessive jowls and a round pig nose.

When Detective Harmon blew into the room, he did so by pushing the door open with such force it bounced off the wall and caused her to jump. She slammed her notebook closed.

"Hand it over, let me see what you wrote." Harmon was middle-aged and as wide as he was tall. He was round faced and bald-headed, and without fail, both his tie and shirt would inevitably sport a stain of some sort. Today it looked to be mustard.

"You know I don't have to," Elliot said. "But because you asked so nicely..." She held up the page with the faces. She pointed to the one with the pig nose. "Gosh, this kinda looks like you. Whoops." She put the notebook in her messenger bag. "Let's get this over with."

"I see you haven't gotten any kinder." Harmon grunted as he sat in the chair across from her.

"I see you're still hoping the two guys in prison you like for my parents' murder haven't confessed, and you're still hoping they will, so you don't have to do any real detective work and find the actual killer."

For the last two years, Harmon's single-minded focus

was on the cat burglar team that had blazed a path down the I-5 corridor, stealing from rich. Only problem was they'd never killed before, and just because Elliot's parents' home had been burglarized after they'd been shot execution style, it didn't mean the crime had been committed by the two cat burglars. Any person with a brain could see the only similarity was that several thousand dollars in jewelry and art had been stolen.

"The facts line up, Miss Long."

"If the facts lined up, why haven't you charged them?" This was the merry-go-round conversation they had once a month.

"Because we need more."

She smiled. "Like I said, you're banking on hope. But you shit in one hand, put hope in the other, see which one fills up first. And that's what you got, Detective. Shit. Now ask your questions so I can get out of here."

He narrowed his eyes. "Last time you were here"—he flipped open a small notepad he'd taken from his pocket — "just three weeks ago, you sat at my desk."

"I sat on the chair in front of your desk."

"Did you or did you not go through my files and steal those picture of Jaime Sullivan?"

Elliot's mouth dropped open. She hadn't seen a direct accusation coming. "What? No, of course not. How could I have possibly done that? Your desk is surrounded by other cop desks. Surely, someone would have seen me being nosy."

"Are you trying to create this club to get back at me?"

Incredulous, Elliot snorted. "Detective Harmon, I have far more to do than spend my time trying to get back at you. That will be taken care of by karma. I didn't create this club. I didn't take the pictures. I was sent a letter like the others,

and in fact, Detective Madden said that this whole thing could have been created to get to me. I'm sure you remember how many threats I got after my parents were murdered."

Harmon sniffed. "And your boyfriend. Mostly people were upset because your boyfriend got shot too."

Elliot pressed her lips together and stared at the table, her hands clasped in her lap. The guilt she carried from Bryce being shot was suffocating. There was no point in reminding Harmon that she and Bryce had broken up weeks before. That she'd limited their interactions, and it wasn't her fault that Bryce had been at her house when the murders happened. The realization that had she been home, she would likely be dead was never far from her thoughts.

Elliot blinked back tears.

"What else was in the box?"

Elliot shook her head. "Everything you got was what we got."

"And you have no idea who started this?"

"No."

"If I find out you are involved, that you took those pictures, that this is some sick game you're playing, I will do exactly what Bryce Zimmerman's mom wants me to do and that's to throw you in jail and throw away the key. You understand me?"

"Are you threatening me, Detective? Because if you are, I'll happily call my lawyer down so you can make this official. Fingerprint the box. Fingerprint the stuff. You won't find my fingerprints anywhere on it other than the lid because I have nothing to do with this."

He wagged his finger.

Elliot stood. "You don't scare me. Contrary to what you might think, Detective. It's not my fault your skills were

called into question. Mrs. Zimmerman's the one who filed the lawsuit against the department. You forget she sued me as well. Weirdly, I'm as frustrated as she is with how you handled my family's case and continue to handle it. But that's not why we're here. Or is it? If you have any further questions for me, email."

She marched to the door. It swung open before she could grab the handle. Madden had been watching and waiting.

"Trey is in the lobby waiting for you." He gestured to the front.

Trey was looking at his phone when she came into the room. He jumped up, his eyes asking a million questions as he searched her face.

She shook her head.

Madden opened the front door for them.

They stepped into the sun, and Elliot pulled in a deep breath.

Madden called her name. She looked over her shoulder at him.

"I'm sorry. That was unnecessary," he said.

But she had no words and instead turned and continued to Trey's car. Once they were both in and the doors closed, Elliot held up her hand. "I don't want to talk about it."

"Me either," Trey said. He held up his phone. "The messenger wrote back."

Elliot took the phone and saw the message that had been sent to everyone.

It read: *I said everyone must join. You are missing an essential member.*

11

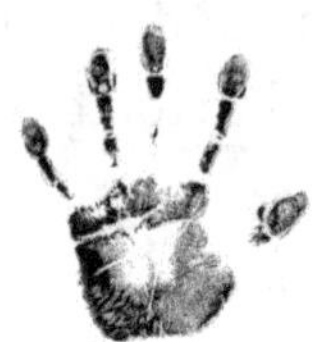

The hour was late. The day had been long. It was hard to believe she was still on the same Monday when they'd met at the quad for lunch. The day had been exciting, invigorating, scary, and ... something else. But also ... long. Oh, so long. And the day wasn't over yet.

Elliot glanced at her watch. She'd been going strong for sixteen hours now. And though it was ten at night, to Elliot it felt like three in the morning. She made her way to the medical school's quad, saw Seema at one of the outdoor tables, headed that way, and plopped onto one of the bench seats. She threw her messenger bag on the table, then laid her head down on the bag.

The night was chilly, and both Elliot and Seema were wearing hoodies. Elliot hoped the rain would hold off as they had nowhere inside to meet that was nearby. She supposed they could all go back to her apartment, but for some reason, she wasn't ready to have them in her personal space. They could go to the student center, but doing so felt ... careless? Elliot wasn't sure, only that it felt wrong for some reason.

"Are you tired or just dejected?" Seema asked.

From her messenger-bag pillow, Elliot looked up at her. "I know we just saw each other earlier today at lunch, but I feel like an entire week has passed instead of ... what's it been ... ten hours? Are you not exhausted?"

Seema shook her head and, from under the table, pulled out an energy drink. "My life force."

Elliot nodded to the energy drink. "Are you worried about having too much caffeine?" Her mother used to harp on about how bad energy drinks were.

Seema arched a single brow. "No, because I'm already addicted, and there are worse things to get addicted to."

"True." Elliot appreciated Seema's perspective about life. "I got the list of people who threatened me in the past. Madden sent it in an email earlier."

Seema wiggled her fingers indicating she wanted to see it. Making sure the email was pulled up, Elliot handed over her phone. "It's two pages."

"I want to see if I know any names." Seema took the phone and began her scroll.

The sound of someone running toward them had Elliot looking over her shoulder.

Trey was headed their way. He skidded to a stop at their table and flung himself on the bench across from them. "Damn, y'all, I wasn't sure I was gonna make it. I had to stay late at practice because, you know. I was late getting there, and I couldn't really tell my coach I was at the cop shop without having to come up with a legit-sounding reason or the truth. When practice ended, I needed a shower and food."

The breeze carried his cologne, or maybe his aftershave,

across to her. She liked it. Not overpowering but subtle. Yet strong enough to catch a person's attention.

"Here comes Teddy," Trey said and jerked his chin in the direction behind Elliot. She didn't bother looking, taking his word, her focus on Seema. She handed back Elliot's phone with a shake of her head.

"Hopefully, Glitter Girl shows up so we can get down to business. I still have a test to study for." Seema looked around for Hillary.

Trey gestured behind Seema. "I think that's her coming. The light's catching something and making that person sparkly."

"Sounds like her." Seema's tone had a slight derisive note.

"What's that?" Trey gestured to Elliot's phone.

"The list of people who threatened me. Madden emailed it." Elliot handed him the phone.

Moments later, the two joined the group. Hillary was tricked out in a bejeweled hat and a hoodie with colored sequins running along the path of the zipper.

"Wow, what a day," she said and slid into the seat next to Elliot. "I'd say today was very interesting."

"Anyone else have an *interesting* day?" Seema mocked.

"Ell and I did," Trey said, looking up from the phone. "I mean, interesting is a good way to describe it, don't ya think?" He looked at Elliot.

Elliot snapped her fingers and pointed to Hillary. "Interesting. I was looking for another word to describe today. Interesting." The more Elliot thought about it, the more the word fit. "I'd say today was invigorating, frustrating, exciting, and yeah ... interesting."

Seema huffed. She probably hadn't been expecting anyone to agree with Hillary.

"Hey," Trey said. "I play ball with this guy." He turned the phone so Elliot could see the screen. "He's a real piece of work."

She read the name. Elijah Peters. She knew him. He was a student at the university as well. She glanced at Trey. "I hadn't looked at the list yet. But Elijah, well, he idolized Nathan and Bryce." She covered her face with her hands. "I should have looked at this list a long time ago."

"I don't recognize the name," Seema said.

"Me either," said Teddy and Hillary.

"We should add him to our list of things to do. Each of us should check him out to see if we recognize him. Maybe we've had an altercation and don't know it. Maybe his face is familiar, not his name," Seema suggested.

"What is the name?" Hillary asked.

"Elijah Peters. He's a senior, and if you just come to practice, you can see him. I don't know what he's studying other than douchebaggery." Trey handed Elliot back her phone.

Elliot said, "Quick question before we jump into what we learned. What did you think of the message from the messenger?"

"What message?" Seema asked.

"You didn't see it?" Elliot was caught off guard. She looked to Hillary and Teddy, who were shaking their heads.

"I messaged the messenger today." Elliot glanced at Trey to see if he would tell them that what she'd done was instigate the messenger, but he kept mum. "I asked him why we hadn't heard from him. I told him we'd all joined and were ready to go forward."

Trey slapped his hand on the table. "Get this shit, he said not everyone has joined." He pointed a finger at each of them. "Which one of you is lying about joining?"

The others sat back, offended.

"I joined." Seema aimed a finger back at Trey. "So shut your mouth." She looked at Hillary.

Hillary clasped a hand to her chest. "You think it's me? You just wait a second. I joined too." She whipped out her phone and pulled the forum up. "See." She shoved it first in Seema's face, then Trey's.

Everyone looked at Teddy. He shook his head. "It's not me. I joined too." He fumbled with his bag and eventually pulled out his cell phone. It was powered off, and the others waited for him to turn it on.

Seema sighed loudly and crossed her arms. Apparently, no amount of frustration or impatience could make Teddy move any faster. He moved at his own pace.

Eventually, the phone booted up, and he touched the app, opening up the forum. He shoved the phone at Trey. "See, I'm a member."

"Maybe it's you, Trey, that's not a member," Seema said.

"Aw shit." Trey slapped his forehead. "You're right, Seema. All this time I forgot to do it. And here I was accusing you all. I'm such an asshole."

Elliot smiled at his sarcasm. She waved her hand before them to bring their attention back to her. When they'd stopped bickering, she put a hand on Trey's arm and faced him. "I was thinking about this. There are seven index cards with dates. There are only five of us. What if we're missing two people?"

Seema groaned.

Elliot continued her focus on Trey as she tried to push

back against the nagging feeling she was missing something. "I sent the message right before we went into the police station. When I came out of the interview room, Madden was waiting for me. He said you were in the lobby." She raised her voice excitedly. "And you were chomping at the bit to tell me about the message. Remember?"

He nodded.

She glanced at her phone. "Why do you and I have the message and not the others? I just checked the time stamp. The messenger sent the message while I was being interviewed by Harmon. Is it a coincidence that he included you, or did he know we were together?"

"That confirms that he's watching you," Teddy said.

"Maybe he's watching Trey," Seema said.

"Or..." Trey said. "He picked us to watch because we were together and you all were separate."

Hillary looked over her shoulder, searching the quad grounds. "That's so creepy."

Seema chugged from her energy drink then tossed the empty into a nearby trash can. She tipped her head toward Elliot. "Sorry, my money is on you. He's watching you. He picked the journalism building, your professor. That's how your stuff got taken from the locker. You're the link."

Elliot closed her eyes and tried to calm her racing heart. She did as her therapist had taught her. *Breathe in with one count, out with the next.* She said, "I don't get why I would be the link. Maybe we should stop this right now. Or if you want, I can step out of the club."

"We could do that." Seema looked to the others. "Anyone want to quit now? It's still early."

No one said anything.

"Until we know more," Trey said, "no more nighttime

trips on your bike. I'll take you places if you need to go somewhere. Like tonight. I'll run you home."

Elliot shook her head, ready to put up a fight.

Teddy placed a hand on her shoulder. "He's right. We need to dig further into your list and research the people. Then we can reassess. For all we know, you could be up against a cop or something. Better to be safe than sorry."

Hillary grimaced. "That cop Harmon was jonesing to blame everything on you. This could be all his doing."

Trey said, "Since you brought up that Harmon asshole, did you learn that none of what we took was evidence? So that's good. No felony there."

"Harmon accused me of stealing the photos of Jaime from his desk. They were in *his* case file." Elliot explained her relationship with Harmon. How acrimonious it had gotten over the past two years.

Teddy said, "He wanted to nail you with those photos. Kept trying to get me to confess to his delusion. Tried to scare me and said I'd end up like Bryce Zimmerman. I don't know who that is."

Elliot rubbed her palm against the outside corner of her eye. "He played baseball with my brother, would have graduated the same year. Was supposed to sign a big contract to play ball. We dated for a while. Not long, maybe six months." She glanced at Trey, maybe for reassurance, or for signs of something more ... disgust? Judgment? She wasn't sure.

"Bryce had come to the house ... the day my parents were killed. We got into an argument in the driveway. I told him to leave several times. We'd broken up, and I had no interest in getting back together." She paused to steady her nerves. The memories were fresh in her mind's eye, the most vivid of

nightmares. "He was cursed with the same thing my brother has, a planet-sized ego. Bryce couldn't accept that I didn't want to date him anymore. Anyway, we're fighting in the driveway, and he refused to leave. So I did. I got in my car and drove off."

She looked up at the dark sky. No stars to be seen as the medical quad's lamps blocked them out.

Elliot blinked several times and said to the others the one thing she'd only told one other person, her therapist. "I had to leave. The space felt suffocating. I felt unsafe, and the urge to run was overwhelming."

Trey's quiet voice broke her fugue. "You thought Bryce might hurt you?"

Elliot nodded. "I suspected he and Nathan might have dabbled with performance-enhancing drugs. His fuse was short. His strength was astonishing. I had no defense. So I left." She glanced at each of the others in turn. "I tell you this because it was shortly after I left that whoever killed my parents arrived. Bryce was still there. He was also shot. But he survived. Bryce's mom sued me and the police department. Her suit against me was dismissed. But the one against the cops and Harmon dragged on and was eventually settled out of court. See, Bryce was found in my room, naked. My guess is that he decided to wait for me there, still refusing to believe we were over. But those scene photos had also been in Harmon's case file, and they'd been leaked to the media. Harmon thought I'd taken them to destroy his career."

"Did you?" Hillary asked.

"Oh my god, Hillary," Seema exclaimed.

Elliot put up a hand. "It's okay. It's a fair question." She turned to Hillary. "No, I didn't. But this is why Harmon is gunning for me. Why he's asking you the questions he is."

Hillary held up a hand. "Sorry, I know this is naïve sounding, but weren't your parents in the house?"

Elliot said, "It's not like our bedrooms were close or anything. It was a big house. But my parents were killed in the kitchen. Whoever did it searched the house after and found Bryce."

Hillary shuddered. "To think people wanted to buy those pictures."

Seema tapped a finger on the table in repetition. "It's a cold world, Hillary. Back to the messenger. So you sent a message to the messenger, and he said that not everyone had joined. Who do you think that is? If this is about you, could it be someone related to your case?"

Elliot shrugged. "Like who? Madden? If Harmon is behind this, why would he want to get another cop involved?"

Teddy said, "To ruin him. And you at the same time."

Elliot shook her head in confusion. "But why bring you four in?"

"That's what we have to figure out," Teddy said.

The group sat in silence a few beats before Trey said, "Elliot and I spoke with one of Jaime's coworkers. He gave us a new lead. A nurse she worked with named Aaron Simmons. Elliot and I are going to track him down." He filled the others in on their conversation with Lucas.

The energy among the group changed from uncertain to excited.

Seema rubbed her hands together eagerly. "It feels so good to have a lead."

Elliot leaned forward excitedly. "I know, right?"

Teddy slapped his hands on the table. "The professor. The obvious person is the professor."

"What are you talking about?" Seema said. "What about the professor?"

"I think the messenger wants her to be our mentor, our guide in this. I bet she has to join. She got a phone call with instructions to go to the building. Probably from the same person who sent us our notes. The box of stuff was left on *her* desk. She's an established and ethical investigative journalist who has the skills to help us solve this. I bet she's one of the people who need to join."

Elliot put a hand to her heart and laughed. "I thought you were saying Professor Snyder was the killer or the messenger or something."

"Sorry. I'm still stuck on the unanswered question. The member or members who haven't joined," Teddy said.

Elliot tapped her chin. "Only she didn't have any interest in joining us. She did the opposite. She shut us down."

Teddy nodded. "That's her ethics. Maybe the messenger expected that. Maybe the stuff in the box wasn't real evidence because he knew she'd not go for that. You know, it's one thing to slip a reporter a copy of documents that incriminates someone, it's something else to slip them the real deal."

"You ain't shittin'," Trey said. "I think Teddy's on to something here."

Seema shook her head. "That's all based on a lot of assumptions. A lot."

Teddy countered, "You got anything better?"

Seema shook her head. "No, I don't. It's an assumption, or it's plausible."

Hillary said, "So we're gonna go ask the professor to join our group?" She sounded incredulous.

"Not it," Trey said, putting his finger on his nose. The universal telltale sign that something smelled.

Elliot laughed. "Trey's right. I don't think we can ask her. She'll know we lied to both her and Madden. We could be asking for trouble if we do that."

"What if we keep that part out?" Seema asked. "Just tell her we got another message to join this group and that the messenger said we didn't have all the members, and we think he means her."

Elliot said, "Then we'll always be waiting for him to inadvertently narc us out." Elliot met Seema's gaze and raised a brow. "But I think I know a work-around. I have an idea."

"You think we should make up an email and impersonate her," Seema answered.

Elliot looked embarrassed. "What do you think?"

No one could come up with any solid argument against it. Not that any of them thought it was a good idea. They created an email account for Professor Snyder and joined the group in the forum. Then they waited.

While doing so they made plans to find Aaron Simmons.

Hillary and Seema told the group they'd scheduled a Zoom with the counselor.

"Well, Hillary scheduled it," Seema said.

Hillary sat up a tad straighter. Probably pleased with Seema's unexpected acknowledgment. "It was easy. Back to the professor. What if she's not the missing member?"

Elliot put her palms up in question. "Then we go it alone. Trey and I found out some good stuff today. Maybe we don't need the messenger?" She posed it as a question because she needed reassurance.

"Maybe," Teddy said. They began to pack up to leave.

"Hey, what was your good news?" Trey asked him.

Teddy eased into a smile. "I might have found a way into the ME's office. Getting inside might be easier than we think."

The others brightened.

"How so?" Seema asked.

Teddy waved her off. "I don't want to jinx it. I'll let you know in a few days."

Elliot turned to Hillary. "You said you had an interesting day. Anything to do with the case?"

Hillary slapped herself on the forehead, almost knocking off her hat. "Holy crap, I can't believe I almost forgot to tell you. When I was leaving the campus police station, I ran into this kid in the lobby. He followed me out and stopped me. Said he heard them asking me about Jaime Sullivan and you, Elliot. Asked me what was going on. I told him nothing." She looked at Seema. "I said I didn't know him, and why would I tell him anything. He said because he was interested in the Jaime Sullivan murder too. Said the anniversary was sitting heavy with him. Said he felt like he needed to do something about it." She snapped her fingers. "Hey, maybe he's our missing member if it's not the professor. Maybe he got a letter, too, but never showed up."

Elliot thought back to the noises in the woods, the flash of white between the trees.

"Did he give you his name?" Elliot asked.

"Joe. Joe Lennox. He's another journalism student."

Elliot plopped onto the bench and let her messenger bag slip to the ground.

"I guess you know him," Trey said.

"Joe is a senior. Seniors have a capstone project they have to do as part of their final. And initially I had thought

that maybe Joe was behind all this. That this was his senior project."

Trey moved closer to Elliot. "You sayin' you think this dude could be the messenger?"

Elliot did a half nod and shoulder shrug. "Yes. I mean no. Not anymore. Doubtful. When we met that first night, I briefly entertained the idea that this might be some sort of sociology project or a journalism student's project. And I thought Joe would be the likely candidate to come up with it."

Seema huffed angrily. "Well, that information would have been handy on day one. You should have said something."

"Hell yeah, you should have," Trey said.

Elliot shook her head. "I dismissed it when Professor Snyder said she got that phone call. For a senior project the student needs a teacher to sign off on it and monitor it."

Seema crossed her arms. "Maybe he went rogue. Maybe it's not for his project but some other agenda he has."

Trey clapped his hands together in determination. "Time to meet this Joe dude. We need to have some words."

12

Trey pressed the toes of his right foot into the dirt and ground them against the earth, leaning forward to test his weight. He tapped his bat against the ground and assumed his swinging position.

He was going to swing high and hard. Nail that sumbitch.

The light on the pitching machine blinked faster, the prompt that the ball was going to launch in three, two, one.

Crack!

Trey knocked the ball into left field. He tapped the bat again and got into the position, waiting for the light.

Crack!

The ball shot out in the same direction as the previous one.

Trey shifted his position ever so slightly, turned his hips, put his weight on his front leg, and waited for the light.

Crack.

The ball went deep into right field.

"You're looking good, Trey. Right on target. Glad to see

you out here this evening getting some extra practice in. Thought maybe you were getting tired of baseball."

"Not me, Coach. Never." Trey kept his eyes on the light. He was always on target, but tonight he was on target with deep balls. Because tonight he was burning up his frustration by putting faces on the balls and whacking them as hard as he could. The messenger. The Joe dude. He didn't know what either looked like, but he could imagine. Catching up with Journalism Joe was harder than they thought. Tuesday had been a bust—they were in classes when he was free—and today he skipped so they hadn't been able to corner him. Two nights had passed since they'd learned about Joe, and Trey felt like time was slipping through his fingers like grains of sand.

Trey wanted to stake out the journalism building, but Elliot wouldn't let him, so there he was. Taking his frustration out on a ball.

Shit, this murder club was distracting him too much. Eating up too much time. If Mama found out Trey was prioritizing the club over class, and right under practice and games, she'd clock him upside the head and ask him what the hell was wrong with him. He couldn't afford to let his grades go any lower than they were. He was barely above the acceptable GPA to keep his scholarship as it was. Never mind his dad's reaction. His dad's quiet disappointment was worse than getting slapped upside the head. If he was smart, he'd quit the murder club. But no one had ever called him smart. And besides, he didn't wanna quit.

"I'm not a quitter," he mumbled.

"What was that?" Coach asked.

"Nuthin', Coach. Just the rantings of an idiot."

Crack!

His goal was deep midfield, and that was where the ball went.

"Well, look sharp, looks like you have company."

Trey looked over his shoulder toward his coach and saw Elliot and Seema. Elliot gave him a small wave.

A ball whizzed by his head.

Shit! He moved to the power box and shut the machine off then took off his helmet. He left the cage, chucking his bat and helmet next to his bat bag, which was sitting on the ground.

"What's up?"

A few of his teammates in other cages paused to check out Elliot and Seema. Or maybe to just to look at Elliot. If the guys were anyone else other than her brother's former teammates, he'd know they were looking at her because of how pretty she was. But these guys were her brother's old teammates, so they looked at her like she was some freak in a cage. The girl who had everything and nothing. A famous brother and dead parents. The haunting of a horrific crime. Not a lot of guys had liked her brother. Or her boyfriend. But on teams, there was a brotherhood, an unspoken code, and because there was a conspiracy theory that Elliot had something to do with Zimmerman getting shot, that she might not be an innocent victim, that made her *persona non grata*.

Elliot and Seema approached.

Elliot said in a low voice, "Joe is in the journalism building. He looks like he's going to be there awhile. We thought we'd confront him and thought we'd see if you wanted to come."

"Hell yeah, I do. What if he leaves before we get there?"

"Hillary is watching. She volunteered to stay. Said since

he approached her before, she could use that to stall him," Seema said.

Trey nodded in approval. He took off his gloves, then moved to pack everything in his duffel. "Let's go have a chat with Joe." He zipped the bag and stood, gesturing for the girls to precede him.

"Evil bitch," one dude said from a batting cage.

Trey ignored him. So did Seema and Elliot.

The idiot continued. "Hey, Trey, I thought you came out here to stay out of trouble. And that girl is trouble all day long. Hang with her, and you'll get yourself shot."

The player was Elijah Peters. His adoration for Nathan Long and Bryce Zimmerman continued to this day. Could he be behind this all?

He met Seema's eyes and jerked his head toward the idiot. "He look familiar to you?"

She studied the guy. Made direct eye contact and scanned him up and down.

"What are you looking at, sweetheart?" Elijah asked her.

"Oh, you wish," she told him. To Trey she said, "Nope, never seen him. I'd remember someone that gross."

Trey turned to his teammate. "Shut your mouth hole, Elijah. You're letting all the stupid out." Trey didn't bother to make eye contact; he slung the insult over his shoulder.

Elijah stammered. "What, you ... stupid? I'm not the one who needs a math tutor. For algebra."

Trey didn't say anything, though the words stung. He hated that he needed tutors. That school wasn't as easy for him as it seemed to be for others.

Another player in a different batting cage mumbled, "Shut up, man. Algebra's hard."

Trey smiled. He waited until they were away from the batting cages to ask the girls, "How we gettin' there?"

Elliot pointed to Seema. "She drove me. Is your car here?"

Trey shook his head.

Seema gestured to a white Subaru Forester. "Guess I'm driving."

As they were getting into the car, Elliot said, "I don't think Elijah is our messenger. I don't think he's smart enough to be covert. He likes attention, and he's too impulsive. When Seema looked at him, he showed no sign of recognition."

They made it to the journalism building and were parked in seven minutes flat. Normally, with the lights and one-way road, the trip would take ten, but Seema didn't seem to care about rules like red lights and such. Trey admired the girl for her in-your-face personality. With Seema, a person always knew where they stood.

"What about Teddy?" Trey asked.

"He can't come," Seema answered. "Said he had something to take care of."

Hillary was sitting on a bench outside the building. She wasn't wearing her typical ball cap but was in the sloppy hoodie and baggy jeans. She gave an energetic wave when she saw them.

"Been quiet, Hillary?" Elliot asked.

Hillary joined them. "Unless he went out the back, he's still in there."

Elliot waved for them to follow her. "Let's go see if Joe's our messenger or our missing member."

Elliot swiped her ID, then led them into the building and

headed straight for the elevators. "The fourth floor is the library and study floor. That's where he is."

They rode up in silence. Right before the arrival bell chimed, Hillary asked, "What if he's neither?"

"What?" Trey asked. "Neither what?"

"What if he's not the messenger or someone who got the letter? Do we tell him about the club?"

Trey shook his head. "We have to play it tight." If Joe was neither, they were back to square one.

"Ugh, I left my bat in the car," Seema said while giving her hands a quick wringing.

"You ain't gonna need it," Trey said.

"I know that," Seema snapped. "But I'm getting complacent. What happens if I'm alone and I forget it?" She gave Trey her angry-bitch face. It was a lot like her resting-bitch face, but her nostrils flared, and her brows had a deeper slant.

"Jeez, what happened to you where you need a bat at all times?" he asked.

"Nothing," she said and crossed her arms.

Elliot cleared her throat and gestured for them to exit the elevator. "Okay, so I have to try to find out if he's the messenger and using Jaime Sullivan's death for his senior project or if he got a letter, all without letting him know we're part of a club. Should be easy." She rolled her eyes.

"I got faith in you, Ell," Trey said. "If need be, we can play this like we did at the nursing home. Just give me a look." He'd take over and do all the talking, but as he saw it, they were in Elliot's house, and she should lead the convo. Until she handed it over.

She nodded in understanding, then led them halfway

down the hallway to a set of double doors. She pulled open one door and exposed a large library-style room.

The area was empty except for one student. A tall blond dude sat at a long table, stretched out to the point his legs were poking out from the other side of the table. From the way he was dressed, Mr. GQ was headed out for a photo shoot or something. He wore a button-down shirt, crisp jeans, and perfectly gelled hair. Joe had books and notebooks spread out around him and a laptop open.

Trey knew guys like Joe. Journalism Joe was just another Elijah Peters. A cling-on first, the sort who looked for others to make their big break for them, their hard work coming in second. Joe probably had aspirations of doing the nightly news or something. Or maybe writing the next best true crime bestseller. Joe was the sort to make money off others' misfortunes. Trey knew he shouldn't judge a person by their cover, but it wasn't the cover that bugged Trey... It was the empty pages behind the cover, the ones written in invisible ink so no one would know the truth. That duplicity was what bugged Trey. He'd take the Seemas of the world any day over people like Joe.

Elliot gestured in Joe's direction so they would all know who he was. She marched ahead, and when she arrived at his side, she flung her messenger bag on the table and took a seat.

"Hey, Joe," she greeted him.

Trey liked how she wasn't afraid of anything.

Joe's upper lip curled slightly as he straightened. "What do you want?"

Trey took it all in. Interesting. From the way Joe sat back, he saw Elliot as a threat.

"I heard you met my friend, Hillary." Elliot gestured to Hillary.

Hillary waved. Seema rested a hip on the side of the table, leaning on her left hand toward Joe. Trey went for the seat to Joe's left.

Joe glanced at Hillary then rolled his eyes. He pulled out a notebook and started flipping through it, as if to say he wasn't curious at all about their sudden appearance. "I didn't know you were friends. And so what if I did meet her? Why would you and the Scooby-Doo gang have a problem with that?"

Elliot sat back and crossed her arms. "I actually don't have a problem with you meeting Hillary. But something weird has happened to me—well, to all of us—and I'm kinda wondering if you had something to do with it."

Joe paused his page flipping. "Weird, how?"

Elliot shook her head. "You first. Tell me why you were at the campus cop shop that day. And why you chased after my friend Hillary here." She waved to Hillary.

"Nah, you first. You have my full attention."

He and Elliot stared at each other. Like some kind of showdown, neither willing to break eye contact. Elliot's eyes didn't even water. Much less blink or waver.

Joe tossed down his pen like he was frustrated, glanced at Trey over his shoulder, then moved his chair to the right. To Elliot, he said, "I was there following up on a story. I overheard them talking and thought I'd see if I could get more info out of Sparkle Pants there." He pointed to Hillary.

Hillary gasped and ran her hands down the top of her pants, making the rhinestones on the side seams twinkle.

Joe continued, "As an investigative journalist, I am always looking for a story. I thought maybe she had one. I still kinda think she does, considering the way you all have come in here and are overreacting to one conversation."

The room went quiet for two short beats as Elliot and Joe studied each other some more.

Joe broke the silence. "Now it's your turn. I'm waiting. What do you mean by weird? You got a stalker? Because it's not me. I wasn't stalking her. Or you." He looked around the group. "Or any of you."

Elliot's brows went up. "That's an odd thing to say. No one said anything about stalking. I said something weird. I didn't say stalking. Weird, like anonymous emails."

Joe sat back and crossed his arms. "You all have the same stalker? What'd you do? Witness something? Participate in a group dare that went wrong? Got some kinda secret do-or-die pact or something?" He looked around the group, stopping at Elliot. "You've got to be the unluckiest person I know. First your family, now this."

Trey leaned close to Joe. "Don't, man. That's uncool." He kept his voice low and slightly threatening.

Elliot cleared her throat. "You told Hillary that you were interested in the Jaime Sullivan case. We'd like to know how curious you are."

"What's that mean?"

Elliot rolled her eyes. "It means I'm wondering if you're digging into Jaime Sullivan's murder. Maybe using it as your senior project?"

Joe gave a derisive laugh. "Wouldn't you like to know what my senior project is."

Elliot threw up her hands in frustration. "Doofus, I'm a year behind you. It's not like I'm going to steal your idea. Besides, you should have already put in the proposal by now. Who's the faculty supervisor for your project?"

Joe wagged his finger in Elliot's face. "Nope, not going to

tell you. What does any of this have to do with Jaime Sullivan or my senior project?" He looked to the group.

Seema tapped the wood in front of Joe. "Do you know who I am?"

He studied her. "No, should I? Because I get the feeling I shouldn't." He glared at Seema.

She stared hard at Joe until he looked away, then turned to Elliot and Trey. "I think he's telling the truth."

Trey tapped Joe on the shoulder to get his attention. "Hey, man, you said something about stalking. Not a word to be said casually, if you ask me. We're acting like weirdos"—Trey made air quotes—"because some anonymous dude asked us to join this true crime forum. Any chance you're a member?"

Joe looked at him like he'd lost his mind. "You're here because you got an anonymous request to join a forum? Ever heard of spam? You all should learn the difference."

Trey kept his face devoid of any emotion. "True Crime Solvers is the name. You a member?"

Joe shook his head. "Never heard of it."

"Prove it," Seema said. "Give me your phone."

Joe stared at her like she'd lost *her* mind. "I'm not gonna give you my phone." He reached for his phone, and for a beat, Trey thought he was caught. That they'd made Joe nervous enough and he was about to crack.

Instead, Joe held up the phone to his face to unlock it then turned it to show the screen to Seema. "Here, look. See any icons for that app?"

Seema swiped the screen a few times then, when she was done, looked at Trey and shook her head.

"You guys are crazy," Joe said.

Trey slapped a hand on the table. "No, man. We're cautious. It wasn't spam. It was legit."

"And you thought I sent it?" Joe looked around the group. "This email was about Jaime Sullivan, right? I'm guessing you got scared and went to the campus police about it." He pointed to Hillary.

Elliot met Trey's gaze. He knew her well enough now to know she wasn't correcting Joe on purpose. Let him think it was an email. If he slipped up and called it a letter, then they would know he was lying. Of course that wouldn't tell them if he was the sender or a recipient.

"You told me you were interested in the Jaime Sullivan story," Hillary said.

Joe waved a dismissive hand. "That's because I heard the cops ask you about it. But I did some more digging, and there's nothing to the story. It's dead. No suspects. And the one person of interest they had is dead too. The whole thing is dead, dead, dead." He slapped the notebook against the table and pointed to Elliot. "You think there's a story there, go for it. But I can promise you, there isn't. I love that you're wasting your time on stupid shit. Your story is this email, *maybe*. Could just be a prank. You can keep that tidbit about the email being a story if you want. I gave it to you for free."

Elliot leaned forward. "What did you say?"

Seema leaned forward as well. Trey gripped the back of Joe's chair.

"I was implying that you're clueless as a journalist if you're chasing the Jaime Sullivan story. You aren't a worthy competitor. You know that, right?"

"I'm not talking about that, you idiot. I'm asking about the person of interest being dead," Elliot said.

"Yeah, I asked my source at the real cop shop about the

case, and he told me that the dude who found her scooter and took it pub hopping was found a few months back, dead. Dead in a tent on the side of the street in some homeless camp. Overdose."

The room was quiet.

"Is that significant? Do you know something about Jaime Sullivan that I don't?" Joe asked.

Elliot shook her head. "No. Someone on this true crime forum is sending us messages about Jaime Sullivan. I agree with you that the story can't go anywhere. It's played. But I'd like to know who the person is."

"I'm flattered that you thought it might be me." He smiled. "Yeah, it's clever. Like me. But I don't chase dead ends."

Trey said, "We thought it was a cruel prank, and I'd really like to meet this prankster and have words with him." Trey rubbed his fist.

Joe put up both hands in defense. "It's not me, man. I swear."

Elliot pushed back from the table. "If I find out—"

"It's not me," Joe insisted.

Trey stood and, after a last look at Joe, gestured for the others to head out. Trey trailed behind them, not saying goodbye, looking back, or anything.

In the elevator, after the doors had closed, Seema asked, "Do you think it worked?"

"What worked? What happened there?" Hillary asked. "I'm lost."

Trey explained, "Joe's not our guy. Just an opportunist. He started to smell a story, and Elliot tried to throw him off the trail."

Elliot filled in the blanks. "Right now, he thinks we're

being pranked. He thinks Jaime's case is closed. Too cold to be reopened. But if he knows how we all came together, he'll start sniffing around and could cause trouble. I tried to play it off like we were being pranked because that's something he can relate to. He'd prank people in a heartbeat. Hopefully, he'll write this off as a weird night and leave us alone."

"The last thing we need is investigative journalist Joe dogging us. I bet he'd out us on the student website in a heartbeat," Trey said.

Elliot couldn't agree more. "Faster than a heartbeat."

13

Three days ago, Seema had sent her sharply worded message to the messenger—and nothing. No response whatsoever. Did this mean it wasn't the professor who was left to join the forum? Or did the messenger know that the professor hadn't really joined?

Frustrated to her breaking point, Seema had sent a second message last night on the forum. She straight up told him what she was feeling, and she looped the others in on the message as well.

Her note read:

All this cryptic bullshit is exhausting. Just tell us who needs to join if it's not Professor Snyder. Because not doing so tells me this is nothing but a game for you. Which is why I will find out who you are, and when I do, I will learn of your intentions. If they are anything other than finding Jaime Sullivan's murderer, I will sue you until I own everything of yours, including your teeth. So you can go ahead and tell us who needs to join and who you are, so we can get on with this.

So far there had been no response. Zero.

"Clearly he knows we made up the email, and it's not actually the professor who joined," Hillary said.

"How could he know?" Seema asked.

Hillary leaned forward and lowered her voice. "The same way he knew Trey and Elliot were together. He's watching us. Maybe we're bugged. Maybe he *hears* us. I searched for bugs on the Internet, and they are tiny and hard to detect. It's a possibility."

Seema grunted in response, frustrated with the lack of information and concerned there might be truth to Hillary's words. If this person, the messenger, actually violated their privacy by bugging them, Seema was going to come undone. Just thinking about it sent a shiver down her spine. The queasiness of dread filled her stomach. She did not do fear. No, not her. She did control, and this feeling of being out of control was the catalyst for her simmering rage. She was beginning to despise the goddamn messenger.

"Maybe the professor is the messenger," Teddy said. The group gave that some serious thought. But if the professor was the messenger, why the ruse and the need for anonymity?

Seema struggled to buy Teddy's theory but couldn't envision the professor playing the two roles. The parts didn't line up. Seema repeatedly wrung the neck of the bat lying across her lap, working out her anger.

They were meeting at the medical quad again. It was lunchtime, and everyone was shoving in their food before their next class—or, in Seema's case, her online interview of the school counselor Bruce Lightner. They were going back to Seema's dorm room to do the interview. Seema was determined to not get wooed by this counselor.

"So, Elliot," Seema said, bringing up her other suspicion, "how's Joe been?"

Elliot rolled her eyes. "Nothing's changed. If he did have anything to do with this club or is now interested, then he's playing it close. I saw Professor Snyder today, and she acted normally too. If she's the messenger, she's good at playing it off. She hasn't even brought up that night in her office."

Teddy pulled a notebook from his backpack. "I did some digging on Howie Middleman, the guy who took the scooter."

Seema had filled Teddy in on what they'd learned during their confrontation with Joe.

Teddy continued, "There's nothing in the paper about him specifically, not even an article about his body being found. I think they wrote him off because he was homeless, so it didn't make the news. I tried to find any living relative and have come up short. I'll keep digging."

Seema found being a member of the Campus Murder Club challenging, which she liked, and maddening, which she despised. They'd take one step forward and two steps back.

"So there's a possibility Joe might have lied about that," Seema said. "We need an in with the cops too."

Everyone looked at Elliot.

She shook her head. "Nope. No way. I can't go make nice with Madden or any of them; they'd be suspicious from minute one."

"You're trying to be an investigative reporter. Maybe you should repair that bridge, so you'll have some connections when you graduate," Seema pointed out. She wanted Elliot to be as riled up as she was. Enough so she would put her grievances aside and go get them some clues. Dammit!

"I plan to move far, far away and start fresh," Elliot said.

Seema didn't believe her. She narrowed her eyes and pressed Elliot more. "Why haven't you moved away before now?"

Elliot adjusted in her seat, pushing her bento box of sushi away. "Well, I was enrolled here, for one. I was waiting to see if they would catch the guys and close my parents' case, for another."

Seema gave Elliot her best lawyer face, a look that said, *Give me a break.* "But when you graduate, you're okay to move away even if they haven't closed the case and, according to you, likely won't ever close the case."

Elliot wrapped her arms around herself. "Maybe between now and then something will change. But I'm not going to make nice with anyone at the police department. I can't do it. One of you all can do that."

"We need the messenger," Hillary said. "He started this, and he had to have planned to give us info."

"No, we don't," Elliot said. "We just need to find another way to get the information. Teddy, didn't you say you were working on something?"

He nodded. "It's not for sure yet. As soon as it is I'll let you know. It could help us a lot. I'm paranoid about jinxing us, so I'm not going to share just yet." He pointed to Elliot's sushi. "You done with that?"

She pushed the bento toward him. "Anyone have time to look at their calendars to see if they can make sense of the dates?"

Both Hillary and Seema shook their heads. Teddy just shrugged.

Elliot studied Trey, who was staring at his burger like it was the most interesting piece of food he'd ever seen.

"Trey?" He had Elliot's undivided attention.

He was looking everywhere but at her.

"Well, you're not obvious at all," Seema said. "Might as well spill."

Trey groaned and balled up the remains of his burger in the wrapper then tossed it in the trash can several feet away. He gave Elliot an apologetic look. "Remember when we were going to the skilled nursing and Nathan's agent texted you?"

"Yeah." Elliot waited for him to continue.

"Well, it brought up some old memories. From back when Nathan was here. Then that day you and Seema came to get me at the batting cages and Peters was there being an asswipe."

Elliot could only nod as she waited, hands gripping the edge of her seat under the table.

"I was in bed that night thinking about Joe and Elijah and how they're alike, and then I thought about the time Nathan and I threw fists at each other and how Peters lied to the coach about how I started it, and I was pissed. Your brother was mad because I was getting the headlines for the game, not him. He had a shitty game, and he came at me. But like always, your brother got away with murder, and I got blamed. I hated him for it. I hated everyone who supported him. And I had a name, image, likeness rep at that time who told me it would be best for me to apologize to your brother to make things look good. I refused and dropped my agent. I haven't had one since."

"And this happened on one of those dates?" Elliot's voice was low.

Trey said, "I think so. It was the night he pitched a game

where the team had four home runs. Statistically, his worst game ever, early in the season. Do you remember it?"

Elliot pulled out her phone to look through the dates. "It was early in the season, right? It was before my parents were killed. So, two years ago."

"Yeah, I think so."

Elliot paused on the date in February. She opened another browser and searched for the dates of the school's baseball team games. One of them fell on the same date as the date on the index card. Elliot cross-checked the game with the stats just to make sure that Trey's recollection was correct.

She looked up from her phone. "Holy crap, that matches a date."

Seema slapped her hand on the table. "Was Jaime there?"

Trey looked at each of them. "I can't be sure. But there were some nursing students there who helped patch me up. One of the coaches took your brother to the hospital." Trey smiled with pride.

"If Jaime was there, that's three of us who have had an interaction with her," Hillary said.

"But that doesn't make sense. Tons of kids here have had interactions with her," Elliot said.

"It's likely used to keep us engaged in the case," Teddy said. "Three of you have had positive interactions with Jaime. That makes it more personal for you."

"Okay," Seema continued. "I kinda think a girl getting killed in her dorm room made it personal for me, but whatever."

Hillary laughed. "I agree."

"Let's all keep working on the dates," Teddy said. "We

can hypothesize that each of these interactions are positive, but we only have two of the seven figured out. It doesn't pay to assume."

"Let's call it," Seema said. "Hillary and I are meeting with Lightner in a little bit. What are you all up to?"

Elliot said, "Trey and I are going to follow up with this Aaron dude from Jaime's work. I reached out to Lindsay Volmer; she's Lucas's girlfriend. He called her about Jaime's absence, remember? And she was the one to get the RA. Haven't heard from her yet."

Seema pressed a few buttons on her phone. "I'm free tomorrow morning if anyone wants to go with me to hang out at the dorm." They needed to get the case moving forward. Seema had the sense that things were stalling out. Maybe it was because the messenger hadn't been in touch and they had no real direction. They were dependent on hard work and luck. Lots of luck.

Elliot volunteered. "I have nothing tomorrow as well."

"I can come," Trey added.

Elliot asked, "I thought you had a midmorning class."

He smirked. "I'll skip."

Elliot shook her head. "Nope. Besides, it might be better if it's girl to girl. We'll grab you if we think it'll help."

Trey looked pissed. "Man, if I want to skip—"

Elliot cut him off. "No. No one skips. We can't let this consume us. We can't let this become the main focus. School is number one. After my parents were killed, all I wanted to do was find the killer. The urge took over my life. I slacked on the podcast. I slacked on my assignments, my classes. I've spent a year trying to catch up. I have those same urges here. But we'll solve this case, and when we do, we still have to have something else in our lives. We still have to be preparing

to be a lawyer or a doctor or an athlete or…" She paused and looked at Hillary. "I don't know what you're studying."

Hillary smiled. "Me either. I'll let you know when I know."

Seema didn't know what that was like, not having a plan. Hillary's lack of direction irritated the hell out of her. It was as if Hillary was letting life happen to her instead of happening to life.

Seema glanced at her watch. "Well, we need to be going. It's a ten-minute walk to my sorority house."

They separated after making plans to meet again. Elliot let everyone know she would be staying late at the journalism building tonight and Friday if they needed her. She and Seema made plans to connect in the morning.

Seema and Hillary walked in silence to Seema's sorority house. Seema had to give Hillary credit for not filling in the space with random chatter. Seema totally thought she would.

As they approached the stairs to the front door, Hillary paused. Seema turned to face her. "What's up?"

Hillary stared at the large white front door with the Alpha Zeta symbol painted in black. "I've never been inside a sorority or a fraternity, for that matter."

Seema rolled her eyes. "Well, they aren't going to eat you or anything. It's like any place with too many women. Fun, exhausting, bitchy, and home. You should consider rushing for one."

Hillary laughed in surprise. "I'm not sorority material."

Seema opened the door. "Most of us aren't, but you make a good teammate. You'd do well."

She knew she caught Hillary off guard, and she secretly

liked that. The girl had a sad story, to be sure. And though that wouldn't garner any pity from Seema, Hillary's resiliency was something Seema could appreciate. Hillary just needed a little faith in herself. And a better wardrobe.

Seema led the way to her room and gestured for Hillary to make herself comfortable in the chair next to her desk, though Hillary was distracted by the room's decoration. In this space, Seema let her heritage show. Bright colors with whispery fabrics adorned the walls, the bed, and the windows, though navy blue and rose gold were the primary tones.

Seema flipped open her laptop and put in the Zoom information, starting the meeting. They were a few minutes early, but moments later, Mr. Lightner was in the virtual waiting room.

Seema gestured for Hillary to sit close enough so he could see her, and then she clicked the button that moved him from the waiting room to the virtual conference room.

Bruce Lightner was easily in his sixties, his hair gray and thinning, his face round and happy. He wore round glasses with wire rims and looked like the type who could play Santa at a party, if given the right beard.

Hillary waved. "Hi, Mr. Lightner. This is my ... uh, friend, Seema. She and I are working together on a project, and we were hoping you could help us."

He smiled. "It's good to see you, Hillary, and to see you doing well. I'm very proud of you. And it's nice to meet you, Seema. Are you a sophomore as well?"

Seema shook her head. "Senior, prelaw." She recognized her error as soon as the words left her mouth. "Our project spans two classes—same teacher, different lesson."

Lightner nodded like he understood. “And this project is about Jaime?”

Elliot had told them that she’d been telling others she was doing a human-interest piece on Jaime. Hillary and Seema agreed to go in that same vein.

Hillary said, “Yeah, the class is sociology, and we want to show how Jaime had overcome a lot of odds. We decided to use her as a subject because her case has been basically forgotten here on campus.”

Seema huffed. “It’s pathetic how quickly everyone forgets.”

Lightner smiled. “Not by those who loved her. Jaime was a special person, an old soul. Sometimes I forget that she’s gone. You know, I’ve never been one to declare something as unfair, but Jaime’s life being cut short was unfair to her. She deserved so much more.” He dabbed a finger at the corner of his eye.

Seema studied him. His words felt practiced, like maybe he’d said them a lot. “We know the basics. Jaime was working to be a nurse, with ambition to go to grad school. She worked hard and studied hard, and she was very driven for her goals. But was there anything specific that drove her toward nursing?”

Mr. Lightner looked up in thought. “Maybe it was because she’d been a caregiver most her life. Research shows that people who have that role in their home life tend to seek it out in their professional life as well. She was very empathetic for a person who justifiably could have been bitter and angry.”

“Do you know why she was able to be so positive?” Seema asked. “This is for our project. It would be nice if we

could narrow it down to something. Counseling? Her formative years being stable?"

Lightner shook his head. "Maybe just the kindness of strangers? Or the kindness of her community, I should say. Because nothing in her life was stable. I like to think that because she was embraced and not shunned, that made a difference. Society has a way of looking in the opposite direction when children or even adults are struggling. Especially when addiction is at the root." He shook his head sadly. "Her poor mother never caught a break."

Seema straightened. The past tense of his sentence caught her attention. "How is her mother?"

Lightner stared at the camera. "You don't know?"

Both girls shook their heads.

"She overdosed a day after the funeral. This one, she didn't survive."

Hillary clasped her hand over her mouth.

"That's awful," Seema said. "That a mother could be so selfish. Just awful."

Lightner continued, "Maybe she wanted to die. Burying her only child wrecked her. I brought her to campus to help her clean out Jaime's dorm. She didn't handle it very well. Maybe the combination of the two was too much."

"You helped her clean out Jaime's dorm?" Seema asked. "That's nice. I'm sure it wasn't easy for you."

He shook his head. "The police had left it in quite the state. Crime scene tape, the room a mess, the struggle apparent. We donated almost everything. Her mom was living in a shelter, so she didn't have the room to take anything. I think all she took was a stuffed animal. I have a few things here, in a box." He gestured over his shoulder with his thumb. "Pic-

tures and her awards. Some journals. Things I didn't think could be donated or thrown away. I guess I was having a hard time letting go too. I'm not sure what I'll do with the stuff."

"No reason why you have to decide now," Hillary said. "You know, I have a friend in the journalism department. She was saying she might do a human-interest story on Jaime. Maybe she could use some of the stuff for her article. If you're okay with that, maybe hang on to it for a while longer."

He looked up as if he was trying to compose himself. "The tragedy of it all weighs heavily on me. I'll do what I can to help."

Hillary asked a few more questions that were what she and Seema considered irrelevant. Questions they hoped made their project sound authentic.

"Mr. Lightner," Seema said, "I know this project is about Jaime and defying the odds of her childhood, but may I ask you a personal question? I don't want to be rude."

Hillary looked at her in question, worried.

Lightner nodded.

"Why did you take such an interest?"

He half smiled. "It was my wife who started it. She was Jaime's kindergarten teacher. Then again, a few years later as her second-grade teacher. She'll tell you she saw a bright child who lived with hard circumstances and a government system that was so broken it was actually part of the problem. She made it her mission to help kids like Jaime out. There have been a handful over the years. When Jaime moved to middle school and high school, my wife handed the baton to me." He sucked in a heavy breath. "You know, when you volunteer at soup kitchens or shelters, you get a fix for that day. But when you help someone beat the odds every

day, their rewards are your rewards, and it's very fulfilling. That's why we became foster parents. To help Jaime and others like her. Selfishly, it made us feel like we were doing something valuable."

Hillary smiled. "Mrs. Lightner was my second-grade teacher too. You both have made positive impressions on lots of kids, myself included."

He smiled. "You're bright and curious, Hillary. That can take you far. You just have to have faith in yourself."

"Thank you," Hillary said, ducking her head in embarrassment.

Seema needed to ask Lightner where he was on the day Jaime died, but she struggled to find a less obnoxious way to do so without just blurting it out. "The day Jaime died, by chance did you talk to her? Was she worried about anything? Anyone? I know this isn't any of my business, but this whole situation makes no sense."

Lightner said, "She called earlier that day. It was my birthday, and we were having a big party. She apologized for not coming. Said she couldn't shift her hours and had a big test to study for and the bus schedule to get here was terrible. She'd have spent more time on the bus than actually here. In hindsight, had she made it to the party, she would probably still be alive."

"We can't know that," Seema said. "My dad's a lawyer, and the one thing he harps on about is that dwelling on the what-ifs is a waste of energy and not a healthy habit."

Lightner sighed heavily. "Just hard to do."

"But doable."

Hillary said, "Mr. Lightner, have you seen Oliver?"

"Occasionally. He's been busy with rehab. Sometimes he puts fresh flowers on Jaime's grave. Well, I assume it's him.

But I know he's struggling too. Has a lot of anger. We meet and have coffee sometimes. He misses her. We all do."

They wrapped up the conversation with a few more benign questions, then thanked the counselor for his time. He offered to meet them again if they had more questions. Seema ended the connection and closed the laptop. Hillary had her phone out. She showed it to Seema.

"Look, here is Mr. Lightner's daughter's Facebook page. It shows him at the party. The clock behind the bar gives us a time stamp and him an alibi. There's no way he could have gotten here in time to kill her. I knew he was innocent. I knew he was a good guy." She closed her eyes in relief. "Thank the Lord. I couldn't have taken it if he was a bad guy."

Seema scrolled through the pictures. "You're right. He wasn't able to get here in time to be our killer. And look, Jaime posted on one of the pictures. Too bad we can't see what time that was."

Hillary opened her eyes to read the post.

"He may not be our killer, Hillary, but he could be our messenger. He is in possession of Jaime's belongings, and he cleaned out her dorm room."

Hillary shook her head. "How would he get into the journalism building? And why pick you or Teddy or Trey? That doesn't make sense."

Seema waved her finger in the air. "It doesn't make sense now. But it might once we have all the facts."

Hillary crossed her arms. "I don't think he's the messenger but I'm okay if he is. He's a nice guy and not the least bit scary."

"You're scared of the messenger?" Seema asked.

"You aren't? It would be a huge relief if it *was* Mr. Lightner. Huge."

Seema had to agree with Hillary. If one were to look at people superficially. But Lightner was too good to be true, and Seema would bet cold, hard cash that he had a few skeletons in his closet.

Question was, did they have anything to do with Jaime and the Campus Murder Club?

14

Elliot lingered at the medical quad. Seema and Hillary were off to meet online with the counselor. Teddy was being very mysterious about his outing to somewhere unknown, plying everyone with promises to tell everything when he could. Superstition was powerful for Teddy, which was weird considering he was a science guy.

She caught sight of Trey's back as he hustled toward the sports complex. After grabbing her messenger bag off the table, she sprinted to catch up with him.

"Hey." Elliot fell into stride with him. "You have practice or a class this afternoon?"

"I have practice in half an hour. Classes are done for the day. *Mom.*"

Elliot let that go. "Any tests?"

He shook his head. "Why you nagging me about school?"

Elliot grimaced. He was more irritated than she thought. "Sorry. I'll try to stop. I wanted to know if you want to go back to Jaime's work tonight and see if either Lucas or Aaron were there. I have questions for both of them. I did some

online searching for Aaron, and his Facebook stuff is private."

Trey put out his fist for a pound. "I'll pick you up around five thirty."

She bumped her fist against his and smiled. They separated, and Elliot went to the journalism building for her class. She needed to know if Professor Snyder was the messenger or their missing member. Enough was enough.

She arrived early enough that only a handful of students had trickled in. Elliot approached Professor Snyder as she set up her lectern.

"Good afternoon, Professor," Elliot said, searching for an entry point to the question she wanted ask. It wasn't like she could come right out and ask, "Care to join a true crime forum?"

"Hello, Elliot. How are you?"

Elliot shrugged. "Well. You?"

"Same. What can I help you with?"

Um," Elliot shifted her messenger bag to her other shoulder. "I was wondering if ... um..."

Professor Snyder watched Elliot with patience, her reading glasses low on her nose.

"Um ... about the other night."

Professor Snyder stopped her setup. She took off her readers and placed them on the lectern before giving Elliot her full attention. "I'm surprised it's taken you this long to approach me about that night."

"Well, I wasn't sure if you wanted to talk about it. The entire evening was very weird. Anyway, I was wondering if maybe you've had any more anonymous calls or emails or something."

Professor Snyder's brows rose. "Are you saying that this

person, whoever did this, has contacted you again?"

Elliot wasn't sure how much of the truth she should divulge. Professor Snyder's reticence on the initial night couldn't be misinterpreted. An invitation to join the club would go over like a lead balloon.

"I'm saying it's hard to walk away from what was shared that night. To know that case and so many others are just put on the shelf and essentially forgotten."

Professor Snyder took a step closer and lowered her voice. "Elliot, I know you didn't start out in journalism. That your parents' case going unsolved has led you in this direction. I was a lot like you when I was first starting out. A champion for truth and justice. I very much understand your struggle to walk away from that letter and the box. But let me say this: in all my decades of being a journalist, rarely was I able to do something the police couldn't."

"There was that college by Seattle that helped solve a cold case. It's not impossible."

"No, it's just rare. That was one case in how many? There will always be outliers. And yes, you all could have been an outlier. But you don't have the support of the police. You aren't running a program or doing a study like that college was. That's why I wasn't interested in pursuing that information from the other night any further."

Elliot absorbed what the professor was saying, trying not to feel dejected by their situation. The professor had made some good points.

"Thanks, Professor." She smiled then moved away, intending to find a seat. She paused and turned back. "One last question."

"Of course," Professor Snyder slid her readers on her nose, then picked up some papers, preparing to move on.

"Did you always know your sources?"

"Yes, eventually, but mostly yes immediately. The ability to offer anonymity is a powerful tool a journalist has." Professor Snyder looked at Elliot over her readers, the look reminding Elliot that, as a student, she did not have such privilege.

Elliot smiled. "Thank you." She moved to find a seat, thinking about her last question.

Three rows up, Elliot was about to pass Joe, who unfortunately was also in the Media Ethics class. Joe stuck an arm out to block her from moving.

"Weirdo with the weirdo friends, where are you going? Aren't you a suck-up-from-the-front-row girl?"

"You used weirdo twice, dumbass. Maybe work on broadening your vocabulary instead of spending time wondering why I'm sitting back here, staring at the back of your dumb head."

"You should get used to that, staring at the back of my dumb head, because I'm always going to be one step ahead of you."

Elliot gave him her *as if* look and pushed his arm out of the way. "I doubt that, but good news, at least we agree on one thing."

He gave her a puzzled look.

"That your head is dumb." She pushed past him and found a seat three rows behind him, picking one that gave her a perfect shot at the back of his dumb head.

* * *

Elliot was watching out her window for Trey. When she saw his car pull into the apartment parking lot, she bolted. She

was down the stairs and headed toward his car no sooner than he'd parked and gotten out.

"Girl, I can come get ya."

She waved him off. "I know. But I'm excited to get going. I was watching for you from my window." She headed to the passenger side of his car. He met her there and opened the door.

He shook his head. "You need a life."

She stopped short. Her eyes didn't meet his. "Yeah, I know."

"Shit," he mumbled. "If you need a life, then I need one, too, because the team was going out for wings after practice, and I turned that opportunity down to come here. I *wanted* to do this more. And this could be a dead end. Wings are never a dead end. Wings and sports on TV are a good time."

Elliot laughed and slid into the seat. "Thanks for not bailing on me." She knew Trey felt bad about telling her that she needed a life. Even though he was right. She did. Two years of grieving had taken precedence over anything else. This murder club was literally the first thing she'd found interest in outside of school and hounding the police. "And you're right. I do need a life. But one thing at a time for me. The fact that I'm not hanging out at the journalism building every day for all hours is a huge step for me."

Trey slapped his hands together. "Well then, let's go out there and solve us a murder."

As they drove to the nursing home, Elliot told Trey about her exchanges with Joe and Professor Snyder.

"Don't you think it's strange she's never asked me about last week? I mean, not even a hint that it happened until I approached her today."

"It is strange," Trey said. "But may be nothing. And we

need something."

Elliot agreed. "Hopefully, Seema and Hillary found out something today. And hopefully, we will, too, and whatever Teddy has going on could lead to something ... something big. I keep saying this, but maybe we don't need the messenger."

"Maybe, but I'd like to know who else was invited. Wouldn't you?"

"Of course, but I can't control that. I can only control me."

Elliot's phone chimed with a text message, and she glanced at the screen. Her brother's agent again, nagging her about going to the game in Seattle. She ignored the text, glad she had her Read Receipts off.

"You speak with Nathan lots?"

Elliot shook her head. "He checks in occasionally but mostly to see if I'm watching his game. If I tell him I'll watch, he'll call and want to talk about how he pitched. Like I care."

"Do you like baseball?"

Elliot gave his question thought. "I don't know. It's always been in my life. It was baseball all the time. Even when I didn't want to go, I had to be at the ball field. From the time I was little, while Nathan was pitching, I had to go. I finally convinced my parents I was old enough to be left alone, which was when I was sixteen, by the way." She waved her hand dismissively. "But that's not the point. I'd be all in on Nathan if he even cared a lick for me. If he even asked me what was going on with my life. After our parents were killed, he just went about splitting everything down the middle, per their wills, and went off into the fame-and-glory sunset."

Trey pulled into the skilled nursing center's parking lot.

"Hey, look!" Elliot pointed. "There's Lucas. I was afraid you were gonna have to toss me up the wall again." She smiled at Trey. "And I was prepared to do it."

Trey whipped into the nearest spot. Elliot was out the door before he could turn the car off.

She jogged toward Lucas, calling his name.

He turned to her, and confusion, then recognition crossed his face.

"Hey, I'm Elliot. Remember me?" she said even though she knew he did. "I'm catching you in the parking lot again." She caught up to him and slapped him on the side of the arm as if they were old friends. "I promise to stop catching you like this."

Lucas smiled. "No worries." To Trey, he gave a chin nod. "What up, man? Saw you play the other night. Looking good."

Trey and Lucas shook hands. "Thanks. You go to the games often?"

"When I get the chance."

"Next time, let me know. We can grab some food after or something."

Elliot cleared her throat. "We're lucky to catch you out here."

Lucas's expression said the opposite. He looked irritated, in fact. "I forgot my study notes. I was just grabbing them from the car."

"We won't keep you long. I'm hoping you could help us get in touch with Aaron Simmons. I've left a few messages for him here, but he hasn't returned my call. Any chance he's working tonight?"

Lucas shrugged. "Probably, but not here."

"I don't understand," Elliot said.

"I'm only part-time with the hospital, so I pick up extra hours by working for a contract company. Aaron works solely for the contract company, as far as I know."

Elliot asked, "If I call them, will they tell me where he is?"

Lucas shook his head. "But we have an app where we request hours and stuff. I can look and see if he's on the schedule somewhere." He pulled out his phone and tapped on the screen.

"Was Jaime working for them too?"

Lucas nodded. "She had the same deal. Only a part-time employee here. She went through the contract company when she wanted more hours. But mostly that was her filling in at the hospital because she didn't have transportation to go farther."

Trey pointed to the hospital next to the skilled nursing home. "That hospital?"

Again, Lucas nodded. "It's stupid, really. They can't keep staff and won't hire us full-time because they're so cheap, so they keep us part-time to not pay benefits. It's cheaper for them to pay a contract company than employ people full-time."

"I bet that makes for a lot of turnover," Elliot said.

Lucas agreed. "For sure."

"So Jaime didn't work at any other facility? Like Aaron or you do?" Trey asked.

Lucas glanced up from his phone. "Every once in a while. If Aaron or I were working there, too, and we could take her. But she didn't like it. She was a creature of habit, and she hated taking favors from people, rides. It made sense, though, because our shifts didn't line up." He flipped the phone to face Elliot and Trey. "Aaron is working at Moun-

tain View tonight. He gets off at seven." He glanced at his watch. "You can wait him out and catch him when he leaves."

Lucas gave a brief description of Aaron and the car he drove. Elliot wrote it down in her notebook. On a separate page she wrote her number then ripped off the paper and handed it to Lucas.

"Listen, sometimes we get together and talk about what happened to Jaime. If you ever want to join us, you're welcome to. That's my number. Just text me."

Lucas took the paper, glanced at it, then folded it and put it in his scrubs back pocket. "Thanks."

They said their goodbyes, and once back in the car, Trey said, "Did you just invite him into the club?"

Elliot shook her head. "I invited him to hang out with us. We need to get to know him. He knew Jaime, and we have nothing on him. Nothing. We can't eliminate him or move him up higher on our list."

"Which is why I invited him to hang out after a game." Trey smiled.

"We're both nuts. We both might have invited a killer into our lives."

Trey chuckled. "Where I'm from, the streets are hard. I'm guessin' Lucas isn't the first killer I've met."

Elliot grimaced, thinking of her parents. "I wonder if we can all say that."

They rode in silence the ten minutes to the other facility. They drove through the parking lot and parked by Aaron's new Bronco.

"What's the plan? Wait to catch him in the parking lot? I mean, it's been working but... it's going to be more than an hour before he gets off."

Elliot drummed her fingers on the dash. "Why don't we try to walk in?"

Trey shrugged, then pushed open his door. "Can't hurt."

They entered the building through sliding doors. Unlike the other facility, no receptionist sat in the middle of the long hallway. A standing signpost said all visitors must check in at the front office with an arrow pointing to a door and a window. Only the window's blinds were shut. A Closed sign hung in the window.

Elliot looked at Trey and smiled. Luck was seemingly on their side. They continued to the end of the hallway, which required a right or left turn.

"The path is before us. We must choose correctly," Trey said in a game-show-host voice.

A sign was fixed on the wall before them. To the left was the rehab department, with its wing of beds, the gym, cafeteria, and recreation and art room. To the right were two additional wings, coded by colors: blue and green. Both wings were labeled Long-term.

"I think we should go right, but then where?"

"And all we got is a vague description," Trey said.

"We could split up," Elliot suggested halfheartedly.

But at that moment, from the left, Bryce Zimmerman came around the corner. His mother was pushing his wheelchair.

Elliot gasped in surprise.

Bryce took one look at her and did what he'd always done since the shooting when he saw her.

He began screaming and flinging his body around in distress.

Essentially, he freaked out.

A

Nurse

Lives Here

15

Elliot turned on her heel and began a speed walk toward the exit.

Trey watched everything unfold at mock speed. For the first time in a long time, he didn't know what to do, how to react. He felt helpless.

"What are you doing here? You aren't supposed to be near Bryce!" Mrs. Zimmerman yelled. She looked caught between soothing Bryce and attacking Elliot.

"How was I supposed to know you were here?" Elliot called over her shoulder, above the cacophony of noise Bryce was making.

Trey was surprised she didn't simply run out. He wanted to. The noise was awful and painful. A guttural cry paired with the clanging of Bryce's wheelchair as he flung his body back and forth. As if he was trying to reach Elliot, to grab her. Hurt her, probably.

The anti-tippers of Bryce's wheelchair clashed with the floor with a high-pitched clang. The noise paired with his howling sounded as if someone was murdering a chicken.

Mrs. Zimmerman ran to her son, whispering and cooing in an attempt to quiet him.

But Bryce's stare was deadlocked on Elliot, and the farther she moved away, the louder he got.

A male nurse ran around the corner and grabbed the back of Bryce's chair, swiveling him around, back toward the rehab wing. He pushed Bryce out of sight, though the noise continued.

Trey followed Elliot, who'd made it outside. Adjacent to the parking lot was a small sitting area with tables and benches. She headed in that direction, the waning light casting the space into shadows. She made it to a bench and collapsed on it, her shoulders slumped. He caught up with her and pretended not to see the tears on her face as he took the seat next to her. She would hate that.

Instead, he said, "When I was in third grade one of the kids from the neighborhood got hit by a car while we were playing baseball in an empty field. He ran into the road to chase a ball. He was never the same. His mom blamed all of us. It sure was hard to see her afterward. My mama said we had something like survivor's guilt because it wasn't us that got hit. 'Course, this kid's mom didn't scream at us when she saw us. Just gave us sad looks. Does Bryce always do that?"

Elliot used her palm to wipe away her tears. "Every time. I get it. I do. That's why I try to stay away, even before she had a restraining order issued on me." She let out a shaky breath. "She thinks I shot him."

Trey reared back. "You gotta be fuckin' kidding me."

Elliot shook her head. "I was in my car driving around when my parents were killed and Bryce was shot. I went through Starbucks about twenty minutes before, which makes the window of opportunity pretty narrow, according to my

lawyer. But that's not the same as a solid alibi. And besides, he was there because of me, so in a way I did do this to him."

"You know that's bullshit thinkin', right?" He recited one of his dad's favorite sayings.

Elliot sucked in a deep breath.

"Bullshit thinking is when you take on the blame that belongs to someone else. Bryce could have left. A bad person could have not gone and done what he did to your family. You ain't to blame. No matter what his mom or those haters say."

"You sound like my therapist."

"Well, your therapist is right." He pointed to the far parking lot where Mrs. Zimmerman was loading Bryce into a wheelchair-accessible minivan. The nurse who had intervened was helping them. "Look, they're leaving. As I see it, we have two choices. We can leave, too, or we can stay and try to meet this Aaron dude."

"As much as I want to go home, I think we should stay."

Trey stood and held out a hand. "Come on, then. Let's go." She gave him her hand, and he pulled her to a stand. "Girl, the worst has already happened. The rest is just noise."

She leapt forward and pulled him into a hug. Surprising the heck out of him.

"Thank you for saying that."

He hugged her back, wondering when was the last time she'd been hugged.

When they separated, he gestured with his head to the building, asking if she was ready.

She nodded.

Together they walked back into the building. They got to

the junction where they'd stood before when the nurse who'd helped the Zimmermans came from the rehab wing.

Trey gave him a chin nod. "Hey, man, thanks for your help back there."

The nurse stuck a key card back into the pocket on his shirt. "She sure doesn't like you." His gaze was on Elliot.

"I know," she said. "And neither does Bryce."

The nurse gave her a look of pity. "I guess. He seemed desperate to get to you. His mom says he's being assessed for a communication device, and she hopes once he gets it that he"—the nurse cleared his throat—"well, she's hoping he'll be able to say who did this to him."

"I'd like that too. Do they think he'll get it soon?" Elliot asked.

The nurse said, "Dunno. Apparently, the assessment happened today. Motor and language have to come together for a device to work, and that seems to be the two main areas affected."

If Bryce could talk ... if he could name his shooter... Elliot couldn't even imagine what that would mean for herself, her brother, and justice for her parents and Bryce.

The nurse was tall and lanky with floppy brown hair. His name tag read *A. Simmons*.

Trey pointed to the nameplate on his chest. "You're Aaron."

The nurse looked slightly surprised. "I am."

"We're actually here to see you," Elliot said. She stuck out her hand. "I'm Elliot Long. I left a few messages for you at the other nursing home."

Aaron snapped his fingers. "Right, right. You wanted to talk to me about Jaime Sullivan. Sorry I haven't had a chance

to return calls. And to be honest, I'm not sure I want to talk about Jaime."

Trey stuck out his hand. "Trey Smith-Coleman. I get what you're saying. It's not fun to rehash hard shit. But we'd sure appreciate a few minutes of your time."

Elliot added, "We're doing a human-interest article on her for the campus paper. It's been six months since her murder, without an arrest. The case is cold and all but forgotten. We'd like to change that. Just remind people of who she was."

Aaron studied her then Trey while scratching his chin. "What do you want from me?"

"You knew her. We thought maybe you could give us some insight into her."

"Insight, like what? I only knew her from work."

"What was she like at work?" Elliot asked.

Aaron didn't even pause to give the question thought. "Better than most. She cared about the patients. She would have made a hell of a nurse. She had an eye for detail, a good sense of impending status changes with patients. It was kinda eerie how intuitive she was."

"What do you mean?" Trey asked. "Dumb that down for people like me who don't know jack about taking care of people."

"Jaime knew her patients well. If they were off behaviorally, she'd look at the chart and mention something to the charge nurse to keep an eye out for."

"I bet that didn't make her very popular," Trey said.

Aaron shook his head. "There were rumors that she was making people sick so she could be the hero and make them better, but they were started by jealous nurses who had a history of being lazy."

"Do you think any of these nurses could have killed Jaime?"

Aaron grimaced. "Sure, if Jaime had been poisoned or something like that. But because she was assaulted ... well, that seems unlikely. Besides, like I said, they were too lazy to put in the effort, and they were all females."

Elliot and Trey glanced at each other.

"How did you find me?" Aaron asked. He glanced at his watch.

"Lucas. We asked him if there was anyone else we could talk to. He suggested you."

Aaron crossed his arms, irritation skittering across his face.

"I guess she and Lucas were close?" Trey asked.

Aaron shrugged one shoulder. "I think he liked her more than she liked him. He would whine about his girlfriend a lot, and I think that annoyed Jaime. Did Lucas tell you we went to Jaime's funeral together?"

Elliot shook her head. "He didn't."

"Carpooled. His naggy girlfriend came too. She didn't seem to care for Jaime much. Said Jaime kept to herself in the dorm. Didn't really have a lot of friends. I think she knew her boyfriend had a crush on Jaime."

"She didn't like all the studying they did together?" Trey asked.

Aaron snort laughed. "Lucas wishes. From what I saw, they talked about class and tests, but I didn't see them study together. But then I wasn't around every single time."

"What was Jaime's funeral like?" Trey asked.

Aaron shook his head. "It was sad, man. Lots of people turned out. Her boyfriend was there, or that's what people said he was. He was wasted."

"Drunk?" Trey asked.

"Or overly medicated, but the dude had to be carried out. Crying and mumbling."

"What was he saying?" Elliot asked.

"No one could make it out. He was incoherent. Inconsolable. It was tragic."

"You saw her the night she died, right?" Elliot asked.

"Yeah, I guess. We worked together part of that day. I left before her, though."

"Weren't you both on the same shift?" Trey asked.

"No, nurses do seven to seven. CNAs have three shifts. She typically did second shift. She was there until midnight. I booked it out of there right after seven."

"Was there anyone waiting for her in the parking lot?"

Aaron's brows furrowed. "How is this a human-interest piece? You all sound like the cops. For what it's worth, my alibi checked out." He glanced at his watch again. "Listen. I have to get back."

Elliot was quick to respond, hoping to leave their meeting on a positive note. "Sorry, I think the mystery of what happened sometimes distracts me, but I think for the article that it's more about how a person can have something horrible happen to them without anyone being the wiser. Like in the case of Lucas's girlfriend... It literally happened across the hall from her." She looked at Trey. "The article should also remind us that Jaime had a lot of friends who miss her, and they are the final victims. They have no closure."

Trey nodded approvingly, going along with Elliot's ruse.

Aaron tipped his chin in agreement as well. "I'd love to read that. Can I get your number, and you let me know when it comes out?"

Elliot said, "Sure." She gave him her cell number.

He sent her a follow-up text. "Now you have mine too. If you have any other questions, then just fire off a text or something."

"Will do. Thanks for your time," Elliot said. "And for helping earlier."

"Yeah, we appreciate it," Trey said.

They said goodbye and went their separate ways.

Inside the car, Trey said, "You catch a glimpse of that watch? That's a Hamilton. Starts at a grand easily."

"No wedding ring, so he's probably single with money to spend on himself and no one else."

"What do you think about one of the other nurses as a suspect?"

Elliot put her head on the dashboard, thinking about all they'd learned. "It's possible. But they might have had to hire someone to do the deed. Because he was right. The assault rules female nurses out."

"But not men nurses. And if Jaime's killer was a hired gun, there ain't no way we're ever gonna find out who did this."

"Nope. But what are the odds?"

"He wasn't very kind about Lucas either," Trey added.

"You think?"

Trey shook his head. "How come you didn't come clean about the club like you did with Lucas?"

"I didn't with Lucas the first time either. Just being cautious, I guess." She chewed her lip. "I'm feeling like we're in over our heads."

Trey laughed. "You just now feeling that? I feel it all the time."

They drove toward campus.

"Do you think the others will want to meet? I think we should talk about everything, and I don't want to wait," Elliot said.

"You'll only know if you text them and ask."

Elliot pulled out her phone. "I have to get the podcast up tonight, but it shouldn't take me long to do it. It just needs a final look through, and then maybe we can meet at the journalism building?"

Before she could send a text out, one came in. From Seema. The message read:

Check the forum. Messenger responded.

"The messenger responded," she said.

"What's he say?" Trey asked, his attention going from the road to her.

She pulled up the app and went to the messages. She read it out loud. "I can't tell you who I am, for my protection and yours. And I'm not sure you'd help me if you knew. My intentions are the same as yours, to bring a killer to justice. My reasons are the same as yours and I have others that are personal. As for not telling you who is the remaining member, I set this challenge for the group because if you all can't figure that out, then how can you help me solve Jaime's murder? The players aren't as random as they seem. You want to quit. Then quit."

Elliot and Trey glanced at each other.

"I don't know what to think," she said.

She was about to text that thought to Seema when a second text came in. This one from Teddy. She read the message aloud again.

"Come to the hospital. Morgue. Back of the building."

She showed the phone to Trey. "It was sent to all of us."

Trey shook his head. "I sure hope that's genuinely from Teddy and not someone spoofing his number. But there's only one way to find out." Trey pulled into the center lane and turned the car back in the direction of the hospital.

Suddenly, for Elliot, it felt like the case was finally picking up steam. Elliot couldn't help thinking of that famous Sherlock Holmes quote.

The game is afoot.

16

They arrived at the back of the hospital where large black letters painted on the side of the building spelled MORGUE.

An arrow pointed the way to a two-vehicle docking bay with large double doors where the ambulances dropped off the bodies.

Elliot sat stiffly in her seat, trying to be in the moment and not in the past when she had come before.

Trey found a parking spot two yards from the docking bay but didn't immediately turn off the car. His car's headlights cast pale light over the large empty parking lot.

"It's kinda creepy," Trey said. "Even without the word Morgue so large there on the building."

Elliot swallowed. "I've been here before. Never from this side, though. And even in daylight, the place is creepy."

"Aw, shit," he said. "Maybe you shouldn't come."

She shook her head and pointed to where one of the double doors was opening. "Look, there's Teddy."

A car swung into the light, its headlights briefly shining

over Teddy and Trey's car before it pulled into a spot next to them. Seema.

She gave them a nod and, once situated, turned off her car.

Together, the three walked to where Teddy stood in one of the bays, the large garage door open.

"Where's Hillary?" he asked.

Seema shrugged. "No response. She's probably watching that new dance on TikTok from Dancing Queen. My sorority sisters were talking about it today, how it was dropping around now, and they all wanted to learn the new moves."

The disdain was clear in Seema's voice.

"What are you doing here, Teddy? And dressed in that jumpsuit?" Elliot pointed to a patch on the top left breast pocket. "Wait, do you work here?"

"What does that mean?" Trey asked. "Are you working on the ... you know?"

"Well, not yet. But I can and will. Essentially my job is to finish up on what the day shift didn't get done. You know, paperwork and prep stuff. Cleanup."

Seema chuffed. "Gross."

"How are you going to manage that with school? I read about how difficult the accelerated medical program is. Thirty percent wash out. Students have breakdowns because the demand and pace is strenuous, and that's being kind. I'm saying this because I'm worried, Teddy. I don't want this side hobby to mess any of us up." Elliot hated how motherly she sounded.

Teddy shuffled awkwardly. He ducked his head. "I'm one who washed out. Well, I'm not officially out. I'm supposed to restart this summer. If I'm stable and ready.

Currently, I have time for this, and it'll help us with the case. I thought you all would be stoked."

Trey put out a fist. "Dude, we're so stoked. You know Elliot is a worrier."

They pounded fists. A wide smile broke across Teddy's face.

"What do you mean, if you're stable?" Seema asked. "Is there something we should know?"

Teddy swallowed a few times before answering, his Adam's apple bobbing rapidly. "I have schizophrenia. Was diagnosed over a year ago. I've been stable on my meds for a while. Other than the excessive sweating, they seem to be working." He gave a wry smile.

Elliot stepped up and hugged Teddy. He bent down awkwardly as she was a good foot shorter than him. She now understood why he'd been so cautious about telling them about his opportunity. Why his science brain gave credit to superstition.

"I'm okay, Elliot."

"I know you are. I just wanted to give you a hug to let you know you aren't alone, and if you need someone, I can be that someone."

Teddy's arms tightened around her. They were a motley crew. All of them alone for some reason or other. Whether it be far from home, no home, or a personal struggle that made them alone, they weren't alone anymore. They had each other. Maybe that was why the messenger had brought them together. He said their selection hadn't been random.

For the first time in a long time, Elliot considered whether the messenger actually might be a friend instead of a possible foe.

Elliot and Teddy separated, smiling at each other.

"Not to be rude, but you could have told us all this in a text," Seema said. But the typical disdain that laced her voice wasn't present.

Teddy's smile spread. "Yeah, but in a text, I couldn't show you what I have access to." He gestured to the open space behind him. "Come see."

Elliot stared at the dark space behind him. Teddy nudged her, and when she returned her attention to him, he was holding a small jar of Vicks VaporRub.

"I picked this way because I'm guessing you came through the main entrance when you came for your parents. This shouldn't be too familiar. And if you put some of this in your nose, the smell will be different. So it's like tricking the brain to not relive the experience." He shrugged as if to say it was the best he had.

Elliot took the jar and spun the lid off. She dabbed the gel in her nose, instantly being able to breath better, eucalyptus the only scent she was getting. She handed it back to Teddy when she was done then squared her shoulders and, with a nod, followed them into the darkness. Small sparsely spaced fluorescent lights lit the way down the long hallways.

"I hope this is less creepy in daylight," Trey said.

"Not much," Teddy answered.

At the end of the hallway, they had one option. The morgue was straight ahead, and to access it, one had to go through the swinging double doors and enter the same room the deceased did when they got to the morgue. The body room. Teddy had left one of the double doors ajar, and a bright light from within flooded the hallway.

Teddy gestured for Elliot, Trey, and Seema to precede him. They went through the double doors to a large room, painted a sterile bluish-white, that was clean and devoid of

bodies. To the right were a row of three offices, each sporting a single window that looked out into the autopsy area where they were standing. The farthest office was accessed from the other side. Elliot knew that space held a couch and chair and was more a waiting room than an office. Straight ahead was the viewing window where two years ago, Elliot had stood on the other side and looked into this space to view her parents, and to the left of that was a larger office with double windows. In black vinyl letters, the name of the medical examiner was stuck to the glass.

To her left were the horizontal refrigerators. Elliot turned toward Teddy, giving him her sole focus. He gestured for them to follow him to the medical examiner's office. Teddy flicked a badge over a sensor at the door, and following a buzz and the lock releasing, he swung it open.

They all entered the office space.

"Are you going to get in trouble for having us here?" Elliot asked.

He shook his head. "There aren't any cameras. Isn't that sad? The ME said the hospital won't put them in place and wants her department to include them in its budget. The ME said it's the hospital's responsibility and she isn't going to use her budget on something the hospital should be providing. Besides, she barely has enough to run this department as it is."

Trey shook his head. "The more I hear about this place, the less I like it. If I ever have to go to the hospital, you all need to make sure I go somewhere else."

Elliot reminded Seema and Teddy about the hospital's policy to not hire full-time employees to keep expenses down and how Jaime had worked for the contract service to pick up more hours.

The space they'd entered was a large office with a desk on one side of the room and a small round table with four chairs on the other, as if meetings were held there.

When Elliot had come to identify her parents, she'd only ever seen the large space she'd just left and the office in the corner. After she confirmed her parents' identity, she'd turned and exited the morgue, escaping into a brightly lit hallway of the hospital where she'd emptied the contents of her stomach into a large trash can outside the door, likely placed there for that specific reason. Nathan had been training in the gym when the murders had happened. And he'd flat-out refused to go to the morgue, instead going to the ball field to practice. But because he'd been first to come home after the terrible event and walked into the grisly scene, he pretty much felt as if he had a free pass. As much as Elliot wanted to be mad at him for not being with her, she understood. On some level.

"Look at this." Teddy gestured to the laptop on the table. He moved to it and wiggled the mouse. Behind the table a large whiteboard came to life and projected Teddy's computer screen. He clicked on a widget, typed a few things, then pointed at the screen.

"This is Jaime's autopsy report."

"Get the fuck out," Seema said and plopped onto the couch. "I mean, I grasped that you would be able to get us some information by working here, but I didn't think on day one you would have this type of access."

Teddy grinned. "It's not day one, it's day three, and yeah, my professors like me. I have a high aptitude for medicine and the riddles that come with practicing medicine. I'm good at thinking outside the box. Well, I was better at it before this went crazy." He tapped his head. "I guess they shared that

with Dr. Frank—that's the ME—because when I asked if I could look at previous cases, study them, she asked me to start with the cold cases because fresh eyes on those were always welcome. The one silver lining about having my break is how much support I've had from family and the staff here." His gaze flicked to Elliot. "No one gave up on me even when I gave up on myself early on."

Elliot squeezed his arm. "I bet the ME wants you to go into her brand of medicine. Big brains like yours are always sought after."

Seema cleared her throat. "That's all fabulous." She pointed to Teddy. "You may be the next Sherlock and Elliot your Watson, but for now, could we please look at the file? The suspense is killing me."

The others chuckled and took a seat on the couch while Teddy clicked on some things. A diagram of the human body appeared with a paragraph next to it. "Jaime had sex before she died."

"We know that. She was assaulted."

Teddy shook his head. "There's no trauma"—he cleared his throat—"down there to indicate she was forced." He pointed to the body on the diagram.

"But that doesn't rule out that she was. Sometimes sexual assaults don't have obvious signs," Seema said, then added, "I learned this from my dad."

Teddy pointed to Seema. "True. But with multiple tests, including blue light and dyes, no abrasions, bruising, split-type lacerations, or tearing was seen. Plus, I'll explain one more element as to why we think she wasn't forced in a second. On her neck were several bruises."

"She was strangled, right?" Trey asked.

Teddy clicked on the computer. The screen shifted, and

photos popped up. "Yes, strangled. This is the side of Jaime's neck. See the pattern of bruises go down in a row, and they're light ... well, lighter than the others that are closer to the center of the neck. This row of bruises are from the four fingers gripping her neck. But when you move in more toward the center, you see contusions that are darker. That's the thumb and palm of the hand bruising as asphyxiation is happening."

Elliot stared at the photos. The bruising pattern was so obvious that she could see the placement of the hand. "This person had big hands."

Teddy tipped his head once. "We think about an eight-to-nine inch spread. So maybe over six feet."

"What's that bruise from?" Seema pointed to a brownish area that was in the lower right side of the frame.

Teddy clicked to the next photo. "Good eye, Seema. That's called an ecchymosis. It's a type of bruising. Let me explain the types—"

Seema interrupted. "Is it relevant?"

"Kinda. But I won't nerd out on the science of it. I'll stick just to the facts, ma'am."

Elliot chuckled. Teddy was in his element. This was the most confident and relaxed she'd seen him ... ever.

Teddy tapped the bruise slightly above the middle of Jaime's left collarbone. "That's a hickey, and because its coloration is similar in nature to the others, it was likely given around the same time. Give or take a few hours."

Trey leaned back against the sofa. "We knew she was hooking up with someone. She was getting female condoms."

"Which wasn't used here. A male condom was. We know this because of the spermicide left behind. I looked at the list of items in her room that we got from the messenger.

The box of female condoms was in her room, and only one had been taken. I cross-checked it with the grocery order. They'd been delivered that day. And the female condom pack isn't listed anywhere. So I am assuming it was used."

Seema sat forward. "Wait, so Jaime maybe used a female condom that day and then later had sex again and used a male condom?"

"Yeah, that's kinda how it looks. I mean, like I said, it's an assumption. "

"We need the list of itemized items in her backpack and purse." Elliot tapped her chin. Perhaps this was something the messenger could get them?

"Here's something else that I discovered." Teddy held up a finger and then exited the room. He came back with his backpack. From between the main pocket, he took out a wad of papers. "These are Jaime's journal pages." He stacked the pages on the desk neatly. "Come look at them."

The others gathered around the desk, looking down at the pages.

Teddy began to slowly spread them out side by side. "Do you see anything?

Elliot studied the pages hard, straining to see something, anything. "What are we looking for?"

Teddy pointed to the edge of the page, what would be the margin of the journal. "Look here. It's faint. Like maybe she wrote this lighter or something."

Everyone leaned in closer.

Elliot said, "It looks like ... it was cut off. So could those be letters or...?" She looked at another page. The marks were different.

At least half or slightly more of whatever Jaime had written had been cut off.

"I think it's initials and dates." Teddy reached into his backpack and pulled out his notebook.

He'd redrawn the marks several times in a column and attempted to finish the missing sections by making the marks into letters or numbers. Clearly, he'd gone down the alphabet and used zero through nine on each marking as a way to rule out errors.

Trey pointed to the series of numbers and letters. One in the center of the first column had been circled. "You think this page here"—he held up a copy of Jaime's journal page—"has the initials DH 9/17/21." He looked at Elliot. "I cross-checked them to our index card dates. They don't match."

Elliot, who had been reaching for her phone to do just that, let her hand fall to her side. "Bummer."

"Dude, you're genius," Seema said in awe.

"Yeah, I know. It comes with its burdens." He laughed.

"Could this be people she was sleeping with?" Trey asked.

Elliot looked at Teddy's notebook. "If Teddy's decoding was right and it is who she was sleeping with and the dates, there are six guys we need to find."

Seema sighed and slumped back onto the couch. "Like looking for a needle in a haystack."

17

Lying on her bed, Seema stared up at her bedroom ceiling, fixating on the swath of midday sunlight that ran across it. She was trying to sort through everything they'd learned. Speaking with the counselor yesterday hadn't given them anything to go off of. Everything Seema hypothesized was just that—a guess. Seema wanted to bring to the group something solid. Like the initials in the margins of the journal. Finding those could mean something big or could mean a million different things.

Seema repeatedly punched at the bed, each hit working through a frustration. Thankfully, she had no interest in going into the investigative side of law. She liked everything cut and dried.

She found the Campus Murder Club off-the-charts maddening. If asked, people who knew her would never believe she'd have joined a group the likes of the Campus Murder Club. But she had. Yeah, because she'd been overly curious. And yeah, angry that most of the student body had

moved on as if the death of another student hadn't happened or, worse, was insignificant.

But what Seema hadn't told the others, the real force driving Seema to find Jaime's killer, was the unanswered question.

Had Jaime's killer been the same person who'd mugged and assaulted Seema? Both events had happened on the same night. Seema's attacker had jumped her on her walk back to sorority row. Knocked her down, punched her in the face when she'd fought back, and cut her tiny cross-body purse from her body, stealing her cash, credit card, phone, and student ID. Then he'd grinded into her three times, gave her tit a viselike painful squeeze before jumping up, kicking her in the side, then running off in the direction of sorority row and the dorms where Jaime lived. Had Seema been murdered, would she have been as easily forgotten as Jaime?

Seema knew serial offenders escalated their behavior. One minute they were mugging people and grinding against them, and the next they were raping and killing. It was a story as old as time.

Seema sucked in a deep breath. Whenever she thought of that motherfucker, rage took over.

Grabbing her phone, she pulled up the campus police portal to check if there were any leads or arrests on her case. Not that her story was comparable to Elliot's, but the unresolved status of the case was something they had in common. She could only imagine how Elliot must have felt knowing a murderer was out there. Sometimes Seema could barely control her rage and almost wanted to come across her perp while she had her bat. Game on. Who would be the attacker then?

Pulling up her case showed that nothing more had been

done. She clicked over to see if the number of muggings and rapes on campus had gone up. They hadn't. Except that stat was misleading because they were up from last year, just not up for the month. She could not put to rest the worry that her attacker and Jaime's killer could be one and the same.

Last year, Seema worked at the campus student legal department, a place where students came for free counsel when they were having legal issues. On a whim, she pulled up the internal website, rolling her eyes at how the IT department dropped the ball because she still had access that should have been removed a year earlier when she left. The school's cyber security was just as pathetic as its campus police. She plugged Jaime's name in the search bar.

Seema was surprised to see a case pop up attached to Jaime's name. She pulled up the case report and read it. Jaime had come to student legal aid with a concern about identity theft and wanted to know about her options and ramifications of those options as it was her mother who had stolen her identity and used it to take out a few credit cards.

What caught Seema's eyes was the date of the report. It matched a date on one of their index cards. She scanned for the name of the person who had done the intake. Seema Choudhury.

But no matter how hard Seema tried, she could not recall the meeting at all.

Frustrated and somewhat ashamed of herself, she exited the portal and pulled up a messaging app, scrolling to Elliot's name. Seema was more determined than ever to make headway on Jaime's cold case.

Pick you up in forty-five? Let's go meet Lindsay Volmer.

Elliot's response came back seconds later: *I'll be ready.*

She included her address.

Seema liked the Barbie-faced journalist. When this was all over, staying in touch with Elliot was something Seema believed to be doable.

She rolled out of bed to get ready. Thirty minutes later, she grabbed her purse and bat and exited her room.

Today, they were going to find out more. Today would be one step forward and no steps backward.

Elliot was waiting in the parking lot when Seema swung in. She jumped into the passenger seat and buckled up.

"I hope she's there," Elliot said.

"If she's not, maybe we can talk to some others."

"I went through the journal pages again last night, looking for more initials and dates. I didn't find any. I mapped the dates and the only common denominator I could find was she wrote them on days when she worked."

Seema raised a brow as she cut across lanes and passed cars. "Do you think she was sleeping with someone at work?"

"Maybe. At this point I think anything is possible. What's the plan with Volmer?"

Seema cut across another lane and turned onto the main road for campus. A car honked in frustration. Seema shot the driver the bird. Had they not been driving so slowly, maybe Seema wouldn't have had to cut them off.

"I say we just get her to talk about that day."

"Sounds solid," Elliot said.

Seema filled Elliot in on what she had discovered earlier.

"Her mom stole her identity? That's awful. How much did she take?"

"Eight grand. No wonder Jaime worked a lot." Seema swung into the parking lot in front of the dorms and came to a rocking stop in a spot, her front tires bouncing off the curb.

Seema had to give Elliot credit. Not once had Elliot

grabbed the "Oh Shit" handle during the drive or commented about Seema's quick stops.

The sun was out, the temps in the high seventies, and several coeds were sitting on blankets in front of the dorms.

"Do we know what Volmer looks like?" Seema asked.

Elliot held up her phone. "I did some Internet searches and found these. They're from her high school, so they're a few years old. But it's a place to start." She thumbed through the three pictures she'd found. Lindsay as a cheerleader. Lindsay on homecoming court. Lindsay as a Keyette. The social club was associated with the Key Club, which was for boys and had the primary goal of serving others.

Seema asked, "How do you know for sure that's her?"

Elliot thumbed to a fourth picture. "The guy next to her is Lucas."

"Mr. and Mrs. Key Club." Seema made like she was barfing. "I don't know about your high school, but the Key Club at mine only worked to serve its own interest."

Elliot gave a wry smile. "Same. But I was still a member."

Seema snort laughed. "Me too. Come on, let's go find our Keyette sister."

Seema scanned the students on her side of the sidewalk that had spread out large blankets and were soaking up the sun. She watched Elliot do the same. The door to the dorm was ajar, held open by a book acting as a stopper.

"It's a clinical psychology textbook." Elliot pointed to the book. "Do you think that means anything?" Her half smile said she was joking.

But Seema couldn't resist. "Bats in the belfry?"

"Blow away the cobwebs?"

"Batshit crazy?"

"I'd like to think of this open door as an open invitation

and an opportunity." Elliot held open the door and gestured for Seema to enter.

"I like how you think."

The dorm entrance opened to a large foyer. One wall had mailboxes for each of the rooms. There was also a large bulletin board with several papers flapping slightly in the breeze. A few of the residents moved around them. No one seemed to care that strangers had entered their supposedly secure dorm.

"Do you think it's because we're girls, and if a guy were standing here, they'd at least acknowledge that?" Seema asked.

Elliot shrugged. "Maybe because it's daylight and the door is open. Look." She pointed to a door at the end of the foyer. "There's where the RA lives. Let's go talk to her."

Elliot was off before Seema could even form an opinion on if she liked the idea or not. Elliot rapped on the door.

With the given sunshine and temps, it was unlikely the RA would be in. If she had any kind of life, she wouldn't be.

The door swung open to reveal a tall girl who was likely Seema's age. She was as thin as a waif, with her long hair in two braids down the side. She wore John-Lennon-style specs and a Beatles T-shirt.

"Do I know you?" she asked and scanned the girls up and down.

From her pants pocket Elliot pulled out her student ID. "I'm Elliot Long. I'm a journalism student. This is Seema Choudhury. We know we're interrupting your Saturday, and we're sorry, but we'd love to talk to you about Jaime Sullivan. I'm doing a human-interest piece on her. It's been six months, and her case has gone nowhere."

"Zilch suspects. We're hoping by reminding people of her loss, maybe it'll reinvigorate the case," Seema added.

The RA didn't slam the door in their faces. She didn't immediately demand for them to get out. She simply continued to stare at them through those yellow-tinted glasses.

"Were you the one to find her?" Elliot lowered her voice. "I read that the RA and another resident opened the door. I'm so sorry you had to see something like that." There was no faking the sincerity of Elliot's words.

"It was awful. You see these shows on TV or listen to podcasts, and a part of you still thinks its fiction until you open a door and you see it for real."

Elliot squeezed the RA's arm. "I'm sorry. What's your name?"

"Kara."

"I'm sorry, Kara," Elliot said.

Kara put her hand over Elliot's. "Thanks. Weirdly, that helps."

Elliot smiled knowingly. "It's the small things. Do you think you can tell me what you saw when you opened the door?"

Kara heaved out a deep sigh and leaned against the frame of her door. "I knocked several times, and she didn't answer. I told Lindsay that Jaime probably wasn't in her room. Her scooter wasn't outside."

"How'd you know that?" Seema interrupted.

Kara grabbed a braid and began to twist it around her fingers. "I used to have a scooter too. We parked by each other. I got rid of my scooter."

"Ah," Seema said. "I get that."

"What made you open the door?

"I made her," a voice from behind Elliot and Seema said.

They turned to find Lindsay Volmer with her hands on her hips.

"Who are you?" she asked, looking between them.

Elliot gave the journalist human-interest spiel and added, "I met Lucas a few days ago. You can ask him about me."

Lindsay crossed her arms. "He mentioned you." She glanced at Kara before continuing. "I made her open the door because Lucas swore something was wrong. And he was right, wasn't he? Jaime never missed work or class. You could set your watch by her. Heck, she even had her groceries delivered around the same time. Many of the girls on our floor knew if we needed something, we could have her put it on her order. Clockwork."

"So Kara opens the door and...?" Seema prompted.

"And there's Jaime, laid out on the floor, eyes wide open, a very unflattering color of gray, her room is a mess, she's naked, and..." Lindsay's attempt to be candid about the scene was negated by the horror reflected on her face.

"And I started to scream. I backed out until I ran into Lindsay's door. That's when I thought to call the police," Kara said. "When I close my eyes, it's all I can see sometimes."

Seema looked to Lindsay.

"I closed the door and called Lucas." She swallowed hard. "I can't image ever feeling as helpless as I did that day."

Seema could. She wanted to say that they should try getting jumped and punched in the face. Try being the assaulted. But she kept those things to herself.

"After the police came, I stayed as far away from that

room as I could." Kara shook her head in resignation. "Just awful."

"For the human-interest story we know that Jaime was a dedicated student and hard worker. We'd like to know more about her. Was she dating anyone? Did she like to have fun? Because she appears to have been all work and no play."

Seema looked around the dorm. "How do you even have a boyfriend around here? I heard these all-girl private dorms were insanely strict."

Kara nodded adamantly. "We are, and we take our pledge seriously."

Lindsay groaned. "That stupid pledge is why my parents planted me here. Chastity, academics, excellence," she said the last three words in a high-pitched, nasally voice. "This is the no-fun dorm. The only way you're getting any action around here is if you are a lesbian because girls are welcome all hours, any hours."

Seema chuckled. "But come on, we all know there are ways around that."

Kara shook her head. "Nope, we have cameras at all the entrances and exits. Someone monitors them twenty-four seven."

"Yep, she's right," Lindsay said and rolled her eyes. "Even the screens have sensors. If they pop off, an alarm goes off. And when an alarm goes off, Olaf the big oaf comes running."

"Olaf?" Seema asked.

"That's what they call the security guards who monitor the video feeds and alarms," Kara answered.

"Where were they when Jaime was getting murdered?" Elliot asked.

Lindsay gave her a "no shit" look. "Seriously. I don't feel safe here at all anymore."

"Do you need me anymore?" Kara asked. "Because I have an exam I need to study for."

"If I think of any more questions, can I come back?" Elliot asked.

Kara gave a small shrug. "Sure, I guess." She gave a small wave, retreated back into her room, and kicked the door closed.

"It's a wonder she called the cops. She was hysterical," Lindsay said.

"If there are cameras at every door and on the screens, how did her killer get in?" Seema pointed to a set of couches, silently asking if Lindsay wanted to sit.

Lindsay rolled her eyes and moved to a couch. "It's common knowledge that all anyone has to do is put a fridge magnet over the sensors on the window to interrupt the trigger. I've never tried it, so I don't know. But the night security guard says it's not possible and the outside camera should have picked up someone coming up to the building and her window. But the camera doesn't show anything. So they ruled that out. I overheard the director and one of the guards say that Jaime came in by herself."

"And to get in, a person has to have a key or a keycard?" Elliot looked around for a keypad.

"It's coded to the student ID. My parents thought that would keep me and Lucas apart, but he has his own place, so I just go there. My parents are so naive."

Seema asked, "Why did they want to keep you apart?"

"Because we've been together since I was in ninth grade. They say they don't want to see me get tied down, that I should date and have different experiences. But really, it's

because Lucas isn't going to be a doctor or something that makes mega money. Their priorities are all jacked, and they worry about me." She shook her head in disbelief.

"High school sweethearts, that's kinda nice," Elliot said. "There's something comfortable about starting college with a built-in friend already."

Lindsay gave her the once-over. "You had your brother. He and Lucas graduated the same year. My parents always used to ask if I ever got to meet Nathan Long. They would have loved to see me with someone like him."

It was Elliot's turn to roll her eyes.

But Seema was the first to speak, hoping to reduce the sticky spot Elliot was in. When it came to talking about her brother, Elliot's feeling were always evident on her face. "From what I've heard about Nathan Long, just be glad you never did meet him. Sorry, Elliot, I know he's your brother and all but—"

"But Lucas seems like a nice-enough guy," Elliot finished.

"Yeah, he is. But we have been together. For. Ever. It's like we can predict each other's next move. We're boring." Lindsay flipped her long blonde hair from one shoulder to the other.

Elliot recalled what Aaron had said about Lucas being more interested in Jaime than she was in him. "I knew Jaime was trying to get into the same master's program as Lucas. He mentioned that he was helping her. Didn't that bug you?"

Lindsay shifted on the couch, her gaze directly on Elliot's. "Not really. We've spent the last few years on and off, seeing other people during the off time. He never once took Jaime out. They never saw each other outside of work."

She crossed her legs and found a strong interest in the ankle hem of her jeans. She toyed with the material. "And you know, I think Jaime kinda understood. She had a boyfriend from high school who sometimes came around. We once talked about how hard it was to break those old habits." She laughed. "Not that Lucas is a habit. Well, maybe he kinda is."

"Were you on or off when Jaime was killed? Just curious," Elliot said.

"Off. But off doesn't mean that we don't see each other. He's my best friend." She truly appeared as casual as she sounded. As if it was no big deal that her boyfriend was seeing the girl across the hall. "Complicated, I know."

"And Jaime and Oliver, her high school boyfriend? When was the last time he came around?" Elliot continued to probe.

Lindsay shook her head. "Mmm, maybe at the start of the school year? I seem to recall it being a pretty day, like this, and it being busy in the dorm with people moving in. I don't think I saw him after that. Well, except at the funeral. He was really broken up. Like messed up bad."

"Did you see the cops process the scene?" Seema asked, shifting gears.

Lindsay said, "Yeah, took about three days. Then her mom and this old guy came to pick up her belongings."

"This old guy, he was at the funeral, right?" Seema asked her.

"Yeah, Lighter or something."

"Lightner. He was Jaime's counselor in high school."

"Well, he was a wreck. Her mom just seemed to zone the whole thing out. But the counselor dude couldn't stop sobbing."

"He said they took some of her things back with them," Seema said.

"Yeah, journals, textbooks, pictures, a stuffed animal. But they donated her clothes and groceries and bedding and stuff."

"Journals!" Seema wanted to smack herself upside the head. Even Lightner had mentioned the notebooks, and she'd not put the stupid pieces together. Her eyes met Elliot's. "Journals with writing in the margins perhaps?"

"Yeah, paper. Anything Jaime scribbled on, they kept. How sad that paper is all they have left of her."

18

Lindsay Volmer had been a gift. They'd ended the conversation with Lindsay telling them a few cute stories about Jaime that could be used in the human-interest piece Elliot said she was writing. Ugh, she actually needed to do a human-interest story on Jaime just for credibility purposes.

She wondered if she could pitch the idea to the podcast crew, and maybe they would take that on. She'd happily produce it. She made a mental note to get crime statistics from the campus police.

They left Lindsay and headed back to Seema's car, not saying anything until they were behind the closed doors.

"Feel like going on a road trip?" Seema pulled out her phone.

"Are you thinking to Port Angeles?"

"And to the box of stuff Lightner carried out of Jaime's dorm room. He said they had Jaime's journals."

Elliot nodded in agreement. "After what Teddy found in

it, it would be silly for us to ignore those. Plus, we're not getting any help from the messenger. Who are you calling?"

Seema held up a finger. "Hey, Sparkle Pants, feel like making a visit to your hometown? I can pick you up in twenty."

Hillary.

Elliot crossed her fingers, hoping Hillary was agreeing to the impromptu trip.

"Great," Seema said. "See you then."

"Let's see if Teddy wants to go as well. Trey has a game, so he can't." Elliot texted Teddy and waited for a response. "I hope he has his phone on."

"You snooze, you lose."

Moments later a text came back. Elliot said, "He's in. He'll wait for us at the main campus entrance to pick him up."

Forty-five minutes later they were on the road to Port Angeles. Elliot filled the others in on their conversation with Lindsay. They looped Trey in through FaceTime.

The drive passed quickly as the club members spent the remainder of the trip talking about the case, reviewing what they knew, and going over Elliot's list of people who had made threats against her. Only Elijah Peters was a name they knew. The others were random weirdos with strong feelings about baseball and her brother.

Teddy had his notebook out and took copious notes, reviewing the suspect list and developing the means, motive, and opportunity for each person.

"Our top suspects are the people who worked with Jaime. Lucas and Aaron, and there's probably someone we don't even know about yet. They have means and opportunity. Motive is still questionable."

"I think it's safe to say any of our top suspects should be a man, based on the hand size and how she was killed. Don't you think, Teddy?" Seema asked.

"Yeah, I mean, unless we come across a stocky woman with great upper-body strength."

Elliot turned in her seat. "I guess it's possible Jaime had sex with someone, that person left, and the woman came in. They got into a fight, one thing led to another, and Jaime is dead."

Seema added, "It would explain how no one noticed anything strange. Like the night security. A woman coming and going at any hour wouldn't be out of the norm at Jaime's dorm."

Hillary snickered. "You rhymed. The norm at the dorm. Is there such thing as a norm at a dorm? Because now murder is the norm at the dorm. Mwahaha." She tossed her head back and gave the laugh a second time.

Elliot chuckled. "Feeling nervous about seeing the Lightners, aren't you?"

Hillary was about to laugh a third time but cut the laugh short. "How'd you know? They mean a lot to me. They were so nice to me growing up, and I hate lying to them."

"I could tell because I get a little punchy, too, when I'm nervous." Elliot gave her a smile.

"I've never seen you punchy," Hillary said.

"That's because my threshold for getting nervous is higher than yours. Spending endless hours with the cops will do that to a person." She pointed to herself. "Nerves of steel now. But Hillary, we aren't going to accuse the Lightners of anything."

"I might. He still seems pervy to me," Seema said.

Hillary groaned.

"I'm kidding, Hillary. Mostly. But Elliot's right. We're going there to ask for their help. If it makes you feel better, tell them about the club. Tell them what we're doing. We can apologize for the ruse the other day. If you think they'll understand."

Hillary shook her head. "We don't have to tell them. I'm just nervous you're going to accuse Mr. Lightner right in front of his wife, and then he'll have a heart attack or something awful, and I'll never be able to live with myself."

Seema laughed and looked at Hillary in the rearview mirror. "Accuse him of what? Being a pedophile? A murderer? The messenger? Would it make you feel better if I promised not to do any of those things? I mean, unless he hints at something, then I might ask him in a roundabout way. Trust me, my dad is a lawyer. I know how to use discretion when I want to. And because I know you're a mess back there, I will make sure to use it. Cool?"

Hillary smiled. "Yeah, cool. Thanks."

Elliot glanced at Teddy and raised her brows ever so slightly. It would seem the two members who butted heads the most had found common ground.

"Take the next exit," Hillary said. "Then the first right."

Seema followed her directions and drove them away from downtown into an older, more established neighborhood with tall, towering trees and large yards. The houses climbed rolling hills, and many had views of water and mountains. Hillary's directions led them down a long street.

"There." She pointed to a pretty blue house with white shutters with a long driveway and several gnomes surrounding the mailbox.

"Okay, well, the gnomes thing is kinda weird and creepy," Seema said.

"Mrs. Lightner makes kids who misbehave and are at risk for getting expelled paint the gnomes, and then she displays them here."

"There are eight," Teddy said.

"That's how many it took before kids who were having trouble were put on the gnome list. We called it gnome watch. If you got on gnome watch, you spent time with Mrs. Lightner, like an in-school suspension, and you had to pick out your gnome and talk about how you were going to paint it. Most of the time, the kids never got to the actual gnome painting before Mrs. Lightner got to the heart of the issue."

"And she displays them at her house?" Seema asked. "They look like she keeps them up. The paint hasn't faded."

Hillary said, "Some of the kids who did the gnomes come here and refresh their gnome. It's like a badge of honor. They were the ones who led the way to developing the program."

Seema pulled close to the house and put the car in park. She groaned. "You're making it hard not to like them."

"I know, right! That's why this is so distressing for me," Hillary said.

Seema put up a finger. "But let me remind you. The BTK killer—"

"We know! He had a Cub Scout group," Hillary finished.

"Let us not forget it and get blindsided by smoke and mirrors." Seema flung open her door and got out. The others followed. Seema led them to the front door, then stepped aside to let Hillary knock. Within seconds, the door swung open wide, and an older woman with a graying chin-length bob stood before them.

"Hillary!" She threw her arms wide, opening herself up for a hug. "What brings you here?"

Hillary stepped into her arms. "Hello, Mrs. Lightner. It's good to see you." When she moved away, she gestured to the three behind her. "These are my friends. This is Seema Choudhury, Teddy Galloway, and Elliot Long. We spoke to Mr. Lightner a few days about Jaime Sullivan, and he mentioned that he had some of her journals and things from her dorm. We were hoping maybe we could take a look at those?"

"Oh, of course. He did tell me you were doing a paper on Jaime. Had I known you were coming, I would have been more prepared."

Hillary cut her eyes to the others. "We should have called. I wasn't thinking." Her cheeks flushed pink with embarrassment.

"That's my fault," Seema said. "We were nearby working on a project for class, and I sprang it on Hillary."

"Oh, it's no big deal. Come in. Come in." Mrs. Lightner stepped aside and waved her hand in a grand gesture, ushering them into the house. When Elliot stepped up to the threshold, Mrs. Lightner put a hand on her shoulder.

"I know this is out of the blue, but I wanted to say that I am so sorry about your parents. I'm sure your mother would be proud of how you've handled yourself and how well you seem to be doing. You're strong and resilient, and that's a tribute to them."

Elliot's gaze went wide, and her eyes got misty. She hadn't expected to be recognized by Mrs. Lightner or for kind words to follow.

Would her mother be proud of her?

Sometimes Elliot wondered. In the days and months following the double murder, Elliot had been recognized—and often. Initially, people were kind and full of pity, many

saying things she was sure they regretted later. After their clumsy attempts to be sympathetic, curiosity always won out, and they'd say something like "So sorry for your loss. I can't imagine what it was like finding them. Was it awful?"

Mrs. Lightner gave her shoulder a squeeze. "I sure hope they find out who did that to your parents."

Elliot felt likewise to her very core, she so desperately wanted to know who was responsible for completely altering her life. "Me too."

Mrs. Lightner continued, "Maybe it's the mom in me, but I have a strong need to reach out to orphans. Though Jaime wasn't technically an orphan, her mother had abandoned her long ago for drugs. That's why your story struck a chord with me. And at first, I couldn't imagine what it was like not knowing, not having any answers to such a devastating event. Until now, of course."

And that was when Elliot saw the same thing in Mrs. Lightner's eyes that she'd seen in her own when she looked in the mirror—a hollowness, a void that another person had left. "Jaime's death being unsolved is unsettling for you."

Mrs. Lightner gave a half smile. "Sometimes it's painfully bothersome. And you, you're too young to be encumbered like that. I just want to wrap you in a hug." Instead, she put an arm around Elliot's shoulder and gave her a tight side hug.

It had been a long time since Elliot had felt such kindness. When the story about Bryce broke, the kindness of strangers evaporated. Some people went from offering condolences to shouting mean things and even going so far as to throw eggs at her.

Elliot turned into Mrs. Lightner. "I could use a hug, and I think you could too."

They clutched each other for several beats. For Elliot, the hug felt so good, like she was in her mom's arms again.

They slowly separated, and both Elliot and Mrs. Lightner swiped at their eyes.

"Here, let's go into the family room, and I can get you all some drinks." Mrs. Lightner swept past them and gestured for them to follow her.

Seema raised a brow and looked Elliot in the eye, silently asking her if she was okay. Elliot nodded.

Hillary stepped up close to Elliot. "See," she said. "They're amazing, aren't they?"

Elliot, working on the lump in her throat, squeezed Hillary's arm gently in response.

In the family room, Mrs. Lightner gestured for them to take a seat. "Let me go find Bruce." She vanished from the room.

"Wow, look at that," Seema said and pointed to a wall.

Elliot turned and took in the massive number of photos that hung on the wall. A time stamp of several lives.

Teddy stepped up to the pictures, moving to the corner where the images seemed to start. As if telling a story. Hillary moved next to him and pointed to a few.

"These people look familiar," Seema said.

"That's the Lightners' biological children. You saw them on that Facebook page."

"And the rest are students?" Teddy asked.

Hillary said, "Students and foster kids they took in."

"There must be over a hundred photos here," Seema said.

Hillary moved down the wall a few steps. "Here's Jaime in elementary school. She was getting an award for perfect attendance."

The others stepped up to look. Then Elliot moved to a different section. "Here she is again. Getting another award."

Hillary looked at the photo. "For debate. That's high school."

Seema asked, "Who are the others in the picture?"

Hillary pointed to the tall, brown-haired guy standing next to Jaime. "That's Oliver. He wasn't on the debate team. He was just there to support her."

"Is this you, Hillary?" Teddy asked.

Hillary leaned in, groaned at the image but nodded.

Elliot did the same. The picture was of Hillary around middle school. Acne. A bad haircut and a shirt that wasn't flattering her figure, a figure that was slow to let go of baby fat.

"I had that shirt, Hillary," Elliot said.

Hillary rolled her eyes. "My dad never bought me anything that was popular at that time but that shirt, and I never wanted that shirt. I knew it would look terrible on me."

"It looked terrible on everyone. It wasn't you. It was the shirt. I think the trend for that shirt had to be a prank the adults were playing on the kids," Elliot told her.

"Hi ho!" Mr. Lightner called from behind them. He was coming in from the sliding door that connected the family room to the outdoors. "What a pleasant surprise." In his arms was a large box, one that typically stored reams of paper.

Mrs. Lightner was right behind him. "Oh, I see you are admiring my wall of love. All those kids are treasures that have blessed our lives. We have been so lucky." She smiled at Mr. Lightner and then the others.

Elliot gave Hillary a smile. "They're talking about you," she mouthed.

Hillary's cheeks turned pink.

"I knew after we talked the other day that you two wouldn't be able to resist looking at this box." Mr. Lightner looked at Seema and Hillary. He set it on the coffee table then pulled off the lid. Instantly, the others surrounded the table and looked inside, much like they had on that first night that brought them together.

"Déjà vu," Teddy said under his breath. Seema chuckled.

"What do you think you're going to find in here?" Mr. Lightner asked. He stuck out his hand to Seema. "Bruce Lightner. It's nice to meet you in person, Ms. Choudhury."

Seema grinned and shook his hand. "The feeling is mutual. We appreciate you being so gracious about our unexpected visit."

"Oh, let me get those drinks," Mrs. Lightner said and flittered out of the room.

To Hillary, Mr. Lightner opened his arms for a hug. "Mrs. L is right. College does look good on you. We're very proud of you."

"Thank you." Hillary gestured to the box. "Do you think it would be okay if we borrowed some of the stuff from here?"

"This for your class?" He raised one brow.

Elliot stepped forward and thrust out her hand. "Hi, I'm Elliot Long. I'm a journalism major. When I found out about Seema and Hillary's class, I asked them if we might be able to look at the items. I'm doing an article and podcast about Jaime."

"Not that I'm complaining, but why the sudden interest? It's been six months since she died." He stuck his hands in the front pockets of his jeans.

"You may know about what happened to my family. For

something as violent as this to happen on campus would, of course, catch my attention. And because no one has been arrested in my parents' murder and no one had been arrested in Jaime's, well, I just struggle with that. I don't want people to forget." There was a lot of truth to her words. And by Elliot speaking up, Hillary didn't have to. Elliot could see why Hillary didn't want to lie to the Lightners.

Seema moved to stand by the box and rubbed her finger along the edge of the opening. "I was assaulted the night Jaime was murdered. I can't help but wonder if maybe that wasn't the same person. Or why I am alive and she isn't."

"*That's* why you carry the bat," Hillary said.

Seema gave a gallant shrug.

"What about you, young man?" Lightner asked Teddy.

Teddy had a slight sheen of perspiration on his forehead and used the sleeve of his shirt to wipe it away while saying, "I just came along for the ride and the company."

"He's also premed," Elliot said. "He knows lots of things we don't."

Mrs. Lightner came back into the room carrying a tray of glasses and several cans of carbonated drinks. "Who's thirsty?" She set the tray next to the box.

Hillary stepped up and took a can and glass of ice. "Thank you."

Seema and Elliot followed.

Mr. Lightner looked around at each of them. "You say this is for a class and for a podcast and article. You bunch aren't trying to be like the Scooby gang or something? Solving this crime on your own?"

Hillary, who'd been about to take a drink, paused and then lowered her glass. "Why would you ask that?"

"I just know how kids are. They think they can do anything they set their minds to."

Mrs. Lightner took a playful swat at Mr. Lightner, catching him on the arm. "Oh, Bruce. Just because you read about that citizen sleuth club at the University of Oregon doesn't mean that every college has one or that Hillary is part of such a club. And who cares if she is in such a group? This town is struggling. Oliver is struggling. We're struggling with this loss. Knowing what happened to Jaime would give us closure, and if the article Elliot is working on or the class project Hillary is working on happens to help them figure out who did this, then who would complain about that?"

"Not me," he said. To the group, he asked, "You want to take it all?"

"We'll return it," Seema said. "And we'll take good care of it."

Teddy reached into the box and pulled out a journal. He flipped it open and started scanning pages. "These are her older journals." He flipped through a few books. "They go back at least a year." He paused on a page and looked up, meeting Elliot's gaze. He gave her a slight nod.

Mr. Lightner reached into the box and took out another journal. He scanned a few pages. "I don't know what you think you'll find in those pages. We've both read them, looking for anything, something. Most of it is the ramblings of a college kid." He dropped the book back into the box.

"Most of it?" Teddy repeated.

"All of it," Mrs. Lightner said. "She talks about her classes. She complains about the people at work. She outlines what she wants after graduation. There's no smoking gun. Just a girl with dreams."

"Reading it felt like we were invading her privacy," Mr. Lightner said.

"Maybe if we read it, we will see something else since we didn't know her personally," Elliot said.

"I have a question," Seema said. "You mentioned that Oliver was having a hard time. Have you seen him lately? Since we talked?"

The Lightners looked at each other. "I haven't. Have you?" he asked his wife.

"No, but I ran into his mom at the grocery store. When I asked how he was doing, she acted like I was making a mountain our of a molehill. Kept saying he was great." She looked at the group. "You know he was in an accident a few months before Jaime died. He was hurt pretty bad and was having lots of back pain afterward."

Hillary said, "Yeah, I remember my dad mentioning something about that. Said driving the truck was going to be hard for him, and Dad thought he might end up on the boat like his dad after all."

"And that's what I asked about, and she just blew it off. Said he was doing fine, was still driving the truck, and all about how he and Taylor Meadows were dating."

Hillary choked on her drink. She put her glass on the table, got control of her coughing, then spat out with thick venom, "Taylor Meadows? She's awful! Why would he date her? She's like the opposite of Jaime."

Seema chuckled. "Tell us how you really feel."

Hillary looked contrite. "I'm sorry. That was mean. But she's such a terrible person. She made high school hell for me."

Mrs. Lightner squeezed Hillary's shoulder. "I have to

admit I was surprised too. But maybe they'll be good for each other. Maybe he'll teach her some patience."

"And kindness," Hillary mumbled. "Though if he's had it rough lately, I doubt she's been any good for him. I can't see her helping him heal or anything."

"Maybe we can help Oliver. Maybe he's struggling with no closure too. Let's hope we find something in this box that was overlooked. Can we please take it with us?" Elliot asked.

Mr. Lightner looked hesitant. "It's all we have."

Seema said, "We'll take good care of it. In fact, we'll make copies of what we can and bring everything back—"

"Next week, max. I have to come back to see my dad, and I'll return it then," Hillary said.

Teddy put the lid on the box. They made conversation for a few more minutes, and then the murder club members left but not before thanking the Lightners profusely. In the box they carried out to Seema's car were the initials of the men Jaime was intimate with—and likely the initials of her killer.

19

No one said anything once they were in the car. The Lightners stood on the porch and waved them off. Hillary sat with the box on her lap, her arms around it as if hugging and protecting the box at the same time.

Once Seema turned onto the street, Teddy said, "You can relax, Hillary. Nothing is going to happen to the box while we're in the car." He smiled and reached for the box. "We can set it on the floor."

She returned the smile. "I just feel responsible for this box. This means a lot to them, and I don't want to lose it, but I also can't wait to dig in because I think something big could be in here."

"I know there are initials in the margin," Teddy said. "I saw them when I flipped through the journal at the Lightners'."

Out of sight of their house, Seema pulled over to the side of the road. She turned to face the others. "Before we dig

into the box, which I want to say I am desperate to do, I think we need to make a pit stop first."

"Pit stop? I have a bad feeling about this," Hillary said.

"Any chance you can go on Facebook and see where Taylor is? Or Oliver?" Seema asked Hillary. "I think while we're here we should try to talk to Oliver. Maybe he knows something. He's very distraught. Maybe there's a reason for that."

"You mean other than his girlfriend being brutally murdered?" Teddy asked.

Hillary shook her head. "I don't have Facebook. And if I did, I certainly wouldn't be friends with Taylor. The last thing I care about are what all the mean people from high school are doing. No thanks."

Seema narrowed her eyes. And she went to speak but nothing came out.

"I think the fact that you don't have Facebook broke Seema," Elliot said.

Seema shook her head. "I think you're the only person I know who doesn't have Facebook. I mean, it's just a surprise. Like, I would never have thought you wouldn't have Facebook. How about TikTok?"

Hillary shook her head. Which was true. She didn't have a TikTok account. DancingQueen did. And an Instagram account as well. But not Facebook. Nope. Neither Hillary nor her alter ego were on Facebook.

Seema turned away and bent down. It took Hillary a moment to realize she was rummaging through her purse. She handed her unlocked phone to Hillary. "Go on my Facebook and see if Oliver or Taylor have public pages."

Hillary took the phone and typed in Oliver's name in the search. She found his account and scrolled through it. "It's

just lots of memes and stuff. He posted more frequently before Jaime died. Pictures of them. Pictures of places he'd been. I'm guessing this was all while he was driving the truck." She showed everyone the pictures on the screen. "But it looks like, after Jaime's death, he stopped posting. All the posts on his page are others tagging him, and they're memes and such."

"How about Taylor?" Elliot asked.

Hillary put Taylor's name in the search. "Ugh, just seeing her face makes me want to vomit. She made my life hell. And, of course, she posts everything all the time. I bet the girl farts and posts about how awesome it smells. And people believe her." Disgusted, she handed Seema her phone.

Teddy chuckled. "I don't have any social media. And I don't feel like I'm missing anything."

Hillary appreciated Teddy's support. "I could hug you."

Seema and Elliot leaned over the phone.

"Oh, yeah, she's a tool." Seema scrolled through the page. "Do you know where Oliver lives?"

Hillary nodded. "He's still living with his parents."

"Let's drive by and see if he's home." Seema put the car into drive.

Fifteen minutes later, they were back downtown and weaving through weather-beaten neighborhoods.

Elliot turned to Hillary. "What was that about Oliver working on the fishing boats?"

"His dad is a fisherman, has his own boat. My dad has worked for him sometimes. Oliver was very vocal about not being a fisherman. He was happy to pass down the 'family business' to his kid brother." She did air quotes. "But it

sounds like after his accident, he might not be able to drive long haul anymore."

"What kind of accident was it?" Teddy asked.

"I'm not sure. I've heard mixed stories, so I don't know what's truth and what's rumor. I asked my dad the other day, and he said one of the stories is that he fell asleep. Someone else said he heard Oliver was doping to stay awake and misjudged a turn. Whatever. But he overcorrected on a curve, I guess, and lost control and flipped the rig down the side of a hill into a river."

"Now I really want to meet him," Seema said. "Which street is his?"

"Two more, take a left."

Seema made the turn and slowed.

"It's the brown house halfway down on the left."

They drove by but didn't stop. There were no cars in the driveway or lights on in the house. The house gave the vibe of being empty.

"It's almost five," Elliot said. "Could they be coming home from work soon maybe?"

Seema went to the end of the street and did a three-point turn. When she got to Oliver's house, she pulled into the driveway and idled.

"Go to the door and knock," she said to Hillary.

"Are you crazy? I am not going to the door to knock. What if he's there? What do I say? This was your idea. You go to the door and knock."

Elliot opened her car door. "I'll go with you. I'll use my human-interest story."

Hillary groaned. "I do not want to be here. I want that on the record." She pushed open the door and forced herself out

of the car. She did not want to see these people. "I went far away to college for a reason."

"And yet you answered a message from a stranger about a girl you went to school with, and here you are. Tangled deep in something from your hometown," Elliot said.

"It's unlikely Jaime's death has anything to do with here and everything to do with someone back at school."

"So it seems."

"Besides, she was always nice to me," Hillary mumbled.

Together, they walked to the door. Elliot pressed the doorbell and then moved to stand next to Hillary. They waited. No sounds. No movement. Elliot rang the bell again.

"Looks like no one's home," Hillary said. She jerked her thumb toward the car and raised a brow, asking the silent question. Elliot gave a nod.

They walked back to the car. Hillary quickly slid into her seat. "Okay, he's not here. Can we go now? Can we go back to Vancouver?"

"Sure, but we should get something to eat before we make the long drive. Anyone else hungry?" Seema looked at the others.

"I am," Teddy said.

"I could eat," Elliot said as she pulled her seat belt across her body.

"Yeah, I guess I could too," Hillary said.

"Great," Seema said. She turned to look at Hillary. "Do you want to tell me the name of Taylor's family's restaurant?" She held up her phone. "I can use the app for directions."

Hillary dropped her head on the back of the seat. "Seriously? I stepped right into that. I thought we were doing a drive-through or something."

"Wouldn't fish or steak be a much better option than drive-through? What's the restaurant's name?"

Hillary closed her eyes and pointed outside the window. "Go to the top of the road. Take a right. Drive straight until you come to the water. It's the big restaurant on the left."

Seema chuckled and did as Hillary said. They arrived ten minutes later.

"If I'm lucky," Hillary said, "Taylor won't be working. Not that she'll even acknowledge that she knows me and tortured me for four years."

"Look at it this way," Teddy said. "It's not like you're walking in alone. You're walking in with three friends. You're not the same Hillary she went to high school with. You went off to college. She stayed here. Maybe you should pretend you don't know her."

Hillary shoulder nudged him. "Thanks. That means a lot."

"Give me an example of how mean she was," Elliot said. "Not because I'm questioning you but because it will give me a sense of who she is."

Hillary gave an exaggerated shrug. "Gee, where do I start." She looked out the window as she scrolled through her memories. "How about this. Every year, the school would do a color run and make everybody participate. We have to do, like, a million laps around the field, and every time you cross the finish line, they throw these paint bombs on you. It's a powder that gets everywhere. Why the school thought this would make running fun is beyond me. Anyway, Taylor, because she was a grade higher than me, got to toss the paint bombs. She would wait until I was super close and throw it in my face. You're supposed to aim for the chest and below. I would move to the other side or try to hide behind people,

but she made a point of getting me, and if she couldn't get my face, she'd aim for my butt. I was the only one with paint on their face and ass but nowhere else."

"She sounds like a real peach but not very imaginative," Seema said.

"Thank God," Hillary said.

"Vain," Elliot said to Seema.

"Petty," Seema added. "And attention-seeking. Uses mean-girl strategies to get compliance. Anything worse than that? Violent? Aggressive?" Seema caught Hillary's gaze in the rearview mirror.

"When someone spreads ugly rumors and lies about another person, that feels aggressive and violent," Hillary spat out.

Elliot turned in her seat. "Yes, it one hundred percent is both of those things. Why we're asking is because we want to know if she's capable of escalating. Could she have gone after Jaime over Oliver? Is jealousy our motive? And if we push her buttons, what will she do?"

Hillary groaned.

"Only one way to find out," Seema said. She whipped her Subaru into the parking lot that was already half-full of vehicles.

They made the way to the restaurant, Hillary dragging behind. Teddy dropped back and slung an arm around Hillary's shoulders.

Sure enough, at the hostess stand stood Taylor. Her hair was dyed platinum, her eye makeup was expertly applied, giving her a brooding look. Her clothes were tight and emphasized her assets. It was clear by Taylor's flirtatious manner with the crowd of men being seated before Hillary and her friends that Taylor used her figure to her benefit.

Hillary couldn't stand people like that, man or woman. Anyone with a great figure or who worked hard on their body should just let it speak for themselves. Humility went a long way, Hillary believed.

As Taylor returned to the hostess station, Teddy leaned to whisper in Hillary's ear, "Turn away from her. Act like we aren't here for her and you don't care who she is. Talk to me."

Hillary shifted so Taylor was in her periphery and Teddy was in her focus. "How did you get so smart about things of this nature?" It wasn't that Teddy was unattractive because he was a total hottie—if you could get past the sweatiness and nerves. Yet for the first time, she saw who he must have been before his diagnosis. Tall, broad shoulders, bright-green eyes, and a smile so beguiling Hillary had to stop herself from falling right then and there. She was getting sucked in by his kindness, seeking a brightness in response to Taylor's powerfully negative juju, which fairly radiated off her. Taylor's black energy was confusing Hillary. Teddy being kind did not a love relationship make. Hillary knew that. She was not the same Hillary from high school, who was desperate for any kindness from anyone and often mistook it for more than it was.

"You okay?" Teddy asked quietly. "You got a little pale there."

Hillary tried to shake off the angst she was feeling. "It's just all this is, like, digging up crap about myself I thought I left behind. Parts of me I don't want to revisit."

Teddy's smile was bittersweet. "I get that. I'm there right now. Only opposite. I'm missing who I used to be."

Hillary gently placed a hand on his upper arm. "I'm sorry, I didn't mean—"

"Nope, it's all good." He waved off the last of her sentence.

"Oh my God," Taylor's nasally voice echoed through the waiting area. "Is that a Vuitton Pochette Métis cross-body bag? I have never seen one of those in person."

Hillary shifted to watch the exchange. Seema glanced down at her bag and looked as if she was seeing the classic Vuitton bag covered in colored dots for the first time.

"Oh, this? Yeah, my dad got it for me last time he was in London. Like why he thought the dots would be something I'd like, I'll never know. I love the white bags, classic bags. But if I don't use it occasionally, my dad gets upset. Trust me, I learned this the hard way when he flipped out over a Burberry trench I *did not like*. Now, it's just easier to wear these ugly things around when I'm not worried about being seen, not that I'm too worried about that. I already posted on Insta that I was stuck with this thing. You have to own the narrative. Know what I'm saying?"

Hillary caught Teddy's eye and smiled. Seema was good. In one paragraph, she'd established that she was wealthy, spoke the same vapid girl-language Taylor did, and was of like minds with social climbing. One story from Hillary, and Seema had figured out Taylor. Hillary was impressed.

"Totally get it," Taylor said. "I love a cross-body bag. It helps accentuate certain traits I have." She stuck out her large chest.

Hillary rolled her eyes.

"Do we need a reservation?" Elliot asked.

The place was half-empty.

"Oh no. Not yet. You all are early enough. I can seat you. Just two or is he with you too?"

Hillary's mouth dropped in amazement. Even with her

back slightly to Taylor and Taylor's attention on Seema's stupid bag, Taylor could still negate Hillary's presence with one sentence.

Teddy grinned. "Four. We need a table for four." He pulled Hillary to his side, turning her to face Taylor.

Hillary glanced at Taylor and kept her expression neutral, trying to channel the confidence that @Dancing-Queen embodied. But it was hard when faced with issues she'd avoided rather than dealt with.

They had a second to survey each other before Elliot drew Taylor's attention. "I'm starving, and I heard this place has the best seafood."

Taylor turned to Elliot, a dismissive look on her face. This was what Hillary called her resting face. Perpetual bitch face.

Taylor studied Elliot. "Do we know each other? You seem very familiar to me."

Elliot put her finger to her chin. "Where do you go to college? Maybe from there?"

Seema turned to Hillary. "Is she rushing with you for the sorority?"

Hillary shook her head, fully on board with her friend's ruse. "Nope, she doesn't go to our school."

"No, I don't," Taylor said, ignoring Hillary, scrutinizing Elliot.

Which in turn made Hillary do so as well. Curious as to what Taylor might see. Why had Hillary never noticed how well-dressed Elliot was? The diamonds in her ears. The expensive leather messenger bag across her body. Elliot was blond and beautiful and poised. She looked like old money.

These were the people Hillary knew Taylor would suck up to. In that moment, Hillary stood taller. These were her

friends. Yeah, they'd come together in a weird twist of events, but she knew she could call on them if she needed.

"Well," Elliot said. "If you're a sports fan, you might know my brother, Nathan Long. He plays baseball—"

"Oh, yeah, I do know who he is. My boyfriend is a huge fan."

"Which means you also know about my family. So maybe where you know me from is the news."

Hillary didn't know how Elliot did it. How she talked about such a tragedy without breaking down into a mass of heartbreak.

"Yeah, that must be it. You're a celeb of sorts." Taylor pulled out four menus.

Hillary was disgusted. "You're kinda a celeb, too, Taylor."

Taylor looked down her nose at Hillary. "How so, dumpy?"

Seema opened her mouth to say something, but Teddy put a hand on her arm to stop her.

Hillary steadied her nerves through a deep breath. "Because, bimbette, you're dating Oliver Bridges, aren't you? I mean, Jaime's only been dead six months, and you're the new girlfriend of the guy whose high school sweetheart was murdered. I bet you use that as a line at parties."

Elliot acted surprised. "You're dating Oliver Bridges? I heard he's not holding it together well."

Taylor lifted her nose. "He's fine." She flipped her hair over her shoulder. "He wasn't doing well until we started dating, but he gets better every day. I guess he knew I'd be the life raft he needed." She gestured for them to follow her before she continued talking. "Maybe our common grief for losing Jaime is what brought us together, sure, but I think it

was meant to be anyway. We always had chemistry in high school, and then after Jaime died, it was like the universe wanted us to be together, kept pushing us into each other's path. He was always here, hanging out."

She stopped at a four-top table and set the menus down.

Seema took the seat next to Hillary. "I heard he drove a truck. That's got to be hard on a relationship." She patted Taylor's hand. "And listen, I get it. Some people are just going to always think it was a rebound thing, but I think two people hurting can come together and heal. That sounds like what you've got with Oliver."

Taylor preened. "You can ask him for yourself. He's at the bar. Like I said, he was always coming in. I saw it for the sign it was." She gestured over her shoulder to the bar area. It was closed, partly partitioned off with half walls made of old ship floors.

Sure enough, Oliver sat on a bar stool at the end of the bar, two empty glasses in front of him. His shoulders dropped as he stared down at the mahogany bar and not at the several TVs going on around him.

Hillary and Seema went to stand. Elliot put her hand out, stopping them. To Taylor, she said, "Do you mind if I go introduce myself to him?"

Taylor hesitated.

Seema said, "Don't worry. He's not her type. She likes the jocks."

Elliot opened her mouth as if to protest but then quickly closed it. "Yeah, it's a fault I wish I could change." She gave a gallant shrug. "But more, as someone who's lost a loved one, I like to reach out to others like me and just let them know they aren't alone. It's weird how powerful that can be from a stranger."

"Be my guest," Taylor said. "I have to get back to work." She gestured to the line of people at the hostess stand.

Taylor strolled off, not looking back.

Elliot put her bag on a chair. "I think I should go alone."

"You going to play the human-interest story?" Seema asked.

"I don't know. I think I'll play it by ear."

"Want me to sit on the other side to see if I can pick up anything?" Teddy asked. "Sometimes I'm a good observer of people."

Elliot paused. "Yeah, but wait about seven minutes before you show up. I don't want him to notice he's been flanked. Oh, and order me a Sprite, please."

She squared her shoulders and then made her way to the bar.

20

Elliot slid onto the stool next to Oliver but did not make eye contact. She watched him through the bar's mirror and her periphery, hoping he couldn't tell.

She sighed heavily, pushed back her hair, and sighed again. Then she dropped her messenger bag to the ground.

"What'll it be?" the bartender asked. "And your ID."

She wished she knew what Jaime had drunk. What a good opener that might be. Not that she could get it anyway. She was one year short of being legal.

She glanced at the large poster of the frozen margarita taped to part of the bar's back-wall mirror.

"Well, seeing as how I'm not legal, can I get a virgin strawberry margarita?" She pointed to the poster. "I can pretend I'm on an island far away from here." She spoke in an "oh, woe is me" tone.

The bartender gave a chin nod and strolled away to the blenders.

Elliot leaned slightly toward Oliver. "I'd actually like one loaded with alcohol. I've had the day from hell. I wrecked my car. And I use my car to do my job, so now I'll probably be out of a job. I'd ask how this day can get any worse, but I feel like that might be tempting fate. Know what I mean?"

For the first time, she looked at Oliver and made eye contact.

Holy smokes. He looked rough. He sported three days' growth, and his hair was mussed. His eyes were bloodshot, and Elliot wondered how long he'd been sitting at the bar. Considering they opened at four, it was likely Oliver started to get his drink on a few hours before that.

He looked down at her and reared back slightly, as if trying to get her in better focus, then bobbed his head and looked at her chest, giving up on her facial features, most likely.

"I wrecked my rig," he said. "Hurt my lower back so badly I need daily medication to cope with the pain." He raised his beer bottle in a mock salute.

"Yikes, that sounds awful. But I suppose your silver lining would be, if you were on the job, at least you have workers comp."

Oliver took a long pull of his beer. Elliot noticed his T-shirt was sweat-stained around the neck and underarm.

"Nope, was off the clock. Fell asleep at the wheel driving home trying to keep a date with my girlfriend."

Elliot grimaced. "Oh no. I bet she feels awful."

He shrugged lazily. "Maybe she did at first, but she never approved of this." He tipped the bottle again, then spun it around between his palms. "And that's all she could see."

Elliot didn't know how to respond. Taylor didn't strike

her as a girl who cared that he was a drinker. He was, after all, drinking in her family restaurant. So she must not care that much.

The bartender returned with Elliot's margarita, and she thanked him, for the drink and the interruption of the conversation, which allowed her not to respond.

"Is there anything they can do about your back?" Elliot pulled the margarita close and sipped from the straw.

"Rehab and things like that. Maybe surgery. But I need to work more than twenty hours a week for insurance, and I can't sit longer than a few hours at a time. Makes working long haul hard. Know what I mean?" Oliver asked.

For the first time, Elliot noticed his words were slightly slurred. He pushed the empty beer bottle to the side and signaled to the bartender for another.

If Elliot was reading the bartender's expression correctly, he wasn't very happy about the request.

"Slow it down a little, man," the bartender said while delivering the beer.

"It's not like I'm driving," Oliver replied sarcastically.

"Yeah, but she's on till closing, and that's five hours away." The bartender glanced toward the front of the building.

Elliot turned in that direction and saw Taylor at the hostess stand.

"Whatever," Oliver said and started working on the beer.

"Wait, your girlfriend works here?" Elliot asked as the bartender walked away. "I guess you all worked out the drinking thing."

He tossed back half the beer then set it on the bar, wiping his mouth with the back of the hand. "That's my new girlfriend. My old girlfriend is dead."

He said it so matter-of-factly, Elliot gasped. She hadn't expected his blunt manner.

"I'm sorry," she said.

"Me too. More than you will ever know," he said quietly then snagged his beer and finished it off.

"Can I ask what happened? I know that's a nosy question but well ... I guess I should introduce myself." She held out her hand. "I'm Elliot Long. You might not know my name, but you'll know my brother's name, and then you'll know my story. I'm Nathan Long's sister."

She hadn't known how she was going to get Oliver to open up about Jaime, and she wasn't keen on the ruse, but she was in it now, so she stayed the course.

Oliver shifted in his seat to face her, his mouth slack. "Seriously? My girlfriend used to go to the same school as Nathan Long, and when I'd go see her, I'd catch some of his games or watch him on the practice field. He's awesome."

Elliot faked a smile. "Yeah, lots of people think so. Baseball thinks so too, apparently. So, your girlfriend..." She jerked her thumb in Taylor's direction. "Not that one. Your old girlfriend went to Southern Washington University? Because I do too."

"Do you get free tickets to all of Nathan's games?" Oliver stood and stretched his back.

Elliot tried to looked bummed out. "He's in California, and I never go down there, so I have never asked about the game tickets, to be honest." Never mind the incessant texts she'd been getting from his agent trying to get her to go to the Seattle game next week.

Oliver's brows went up. "I'd be down there all the time." He swayed slightly and put his hand on the bar to steady

himself. “I’d probably become a roadie or something for the team. I love baseball. Played it in high school.”

Elliot saw a trip down memory lane happening and decided to cut it off at the pass. “Well, after our parents were murdered, things between Nathan and I are ... well, it’s weird. Loss like that has a toll. Losing someone is hard. Losing someone to a violent crime seems worse somehow. I’m sure you know what I mean. You’ve been through it.”

Oliver stilled. He’d been arching his back for a stretch, but he eased out of the arch, his eyes narrowing in on her. “I never said my girlfriend died of a—what did you call it?—a violent crime.”

Instantly, Elliot knew she’d made a misstep. “Ah ... well, I go to Southern Washington, and I just assumed.” She didn’t know what to say.

“Who are you? What do you want?”

“I’m Elliot Long, and Nathan is my brother.” She tried the topic he’d liked the most first. He took a step closer, and she could smell the sweat and beer on him.

“Yeah, but who are you, and what do you want from me?” His brown eyes darkened.

“I just want to ask you a few questions about Jaime, please.” She made her request quietly, hoping if she stayed calm and low key, he would too.

Oliver exploded. “You’re a reporter, aren’t you?” His voice boomed throughout the restaurant.

“Not really but kinda. I’m a journalism student—”

“Who wants to make their name off a dead girl and my grief. Get out of here. Get out of my sight. You’re disgusting!”

Oliver stepped closer, and Elliot slid out of her chair on the opposite side, putting it between them. But that

didn't stop him. He leaned across the chair and spit in her face.

Elliot had not been expecting that reaction. She closed her eyes and tried to steady her racing heart, slowly bringing her sleeve up to wipe her face.

"Get out of here!" Oliver screamed. "Get out of my face before I punch you in yours!" He shoved her in the shoulder, sending her backward.

Elliot stumbled back and nearly fell. She caught herself on the chair next to her. Seema rushed into the picture and helped her. Teddy stood between her and Oliver.

"Come on, let's get out of here," Seema said and handed Elliot her messenger bag.

"Step back," Teddy said. "I'm not a small woman you can push down. And I'm certifiably unbalanced, so step back."

He and Oliver were engaged in a stare down, both posturing and looking ready to fight.

Seema threw an arm around Elliot and hustled her out of the restaurant. Hillary backed her car out of the parking spot, then pulled up to the restaurant in a squeal of tires. She jumped out and moved to open the back door for Elliot. After Elliot slid into the seat, Hillary handed her a pack of wipes.

"I keep these in my backpack. Thought maybe you might want them."

"Yes, please," Elliot said, ripping into the pack. Though she'd wiped the spit off her face, she could still emotionally feel it stinging her.

Teddy walked out with a swagger. He looked untouched.

"You get shotgun," Hillary said. She rushed to the other back door and climbed in.

Seconds later, they were on the road headed out of Port Angeles.

"Can we please get drive-through?" Teddy asked. "I'm starving."

21

On the drive back, Teddy picked up a journal, ready to tear into it.

"Anyone need to decompress about what just happened before I start going through these journals?" He stuffed two fries in his mouth at the same time.

"That was insane," Hillary said. "I've never seen Oliver like that."

Elliot had wiped her face several times with handfuls of wipes and yet she still kept—subconsciously, he bet—brushing her sleeve over the spit spot.

"Thanks for intervening, Teddy." Elliot gave him a grateful smile.

He returned her smile. "It's not for me to judge, but that guy is dealing with some serious demons. Are you okay?"

"I will be. I'm more grossed out than anything." Elliot laughed.

Seema burst out laughing. "Yeah, I never saw that coming. So gross."

They laughed about it some more, breaking the ugliness that had come with the attack.

Teddy flipped open the journal, excited by what he saw. "It's all here," he said and grabbed a handful of fries. "The initials are as clear as day, and I'd like to point out that I had guessed at the initials correctly."

He reached into his backpack and pulled out a worn-looking composition book and flipped to pages where he'd glued Xeroxed copies of the edges of Jaime's journal. He showed Hillary and Elliot the journal and his book. "Look, we aren't guessing anymore."

Elliot turned in the seat to face them, excitement on her face. "But if we had to guess, at least we now know your deductions were spot-on. Maybe that'll come in handy if we have to guess in the future."

He liked knowing his brain, although it sometimes had glitches, was still working top notch.

Elliot ran her finger down the margin of the journal. "When you did this, did you see a pattern? I've found three sets of initials in here." She flipped through several pages.

"No pattern, really. Not when she puts them in her journal and the initials don't repeat later. It's like when she writes them down, then she's one and done. We don't see it again. Except for one set of initials. DH was the first set she wrote, and they appear throughout the journal. He consistently shows up."

"Maybe that was her steady?" Hillary offered. "Maybe the others are one-night stands or brief flings? Maybe that's the frequency. Are Oliver's initials in the book? I don't remember him being mentioned."

Teddy shook his head. He'd spent hours trying to find a pattern.

Elliot added, "From what I remember, she never names anyone in her journal, including him."

Teddy said, "The only mention of anything or anyone specific is on her grocery list. That followed a pattern." He chuckled, though more from frustration than anything else.

"It's not very *Dear Journal* to have a journal but not talk about the guys you're hooking up with. Am I the only one who finds that weird?" Seema asked.

"I wouldn't know. I would never keep a journal, in case my brother or mother found it and used it against me. My brother, especially," Elliot said. "But maybe that's a paranoid mentality."

Hillary shook her head. "I'd never put anything in writing either."

Seema chuckled. "I confessed everything in my journal."

"You weren't worried about your parents finding it?" Hillary asked.

Seema shook her head. "I moved the hiding spot every week. Just in case. My mom wasn't very good about covering her tracks."

The others laughed.

Teddy turned one of Jaime's journals over in his hands, considering their purpose. "I found her journal more to be about keeping track of all the things she was juggling and less about the angst of her life. But maybe she too was afraid of who might read her journal, now that I think about it. Because she lived alone and didn't appear to have a relationship with her mom. So why not write everything down, and if she was afraid it would be read, then by whom?"

"Maybe she was just naturally paranoid about it, based on the hand life had dealt her," Hillary said.

"Trauma could be why," Elliot added.

"I'm with Teddy. I still think it's odd," Seema mumbled.

"Okay, so how many different initials are there?" Elliot asked.

Teddy flipped through the book in his hand then pulled a second out of the box and flipped through it. "Five. Over eight months, but I'll have an exact timeline when I go through the books. That's my best guess right now."

"This is exciting, yet I feel like I shouldn't be excited. I feel like we have the potential to get a lot of info," Hillary said. "But then I think that this will likely go nowhere. I mean, I'm sure the cops looked into all this."

Teddy watched Hillary chew her lower lip in worry. As he saw it, there were two types of people. First, those who took everything at face value. If someone reliable told them a house was haunted, they accepted that as truth. How else could weird events be explained?

Then there was the other type of people. They would look at the haunted house and find all the other possibilities, even go as far as farfetched ideas. Neither type of person was wrong, just different. Hillary was type one. The cops were type one. Heck, Teddy used to be that type too. Now he was type two because he knew deep in his bones the cops had missed something. They'd overlooked the obvious.

Elliot snorted. "Don't be so sure. It depends on the cop. Some of them like the path of least resistance, and they follow the obvious leads and try to shoehorn that into a believable case. Some are just unimaginative and do the same. At least that's my experience." Clearly, she felt like he did.

And not for the first time, Teddy was glad that an anonymous letter had brought them all together. This was exactly what he needed.

"Which one is Madden?" Seema asked. "Harmon was easy enough to figure out. My dad rips apart guys like him on the stand. He can smell them from a mile away."

Elliot chuckled. "I think I'd like your dad. Madden is hard. Because at first, I thought he was one of the good ones. The kind you read about in books and see on TV, the kind that hunts for clues and killers and never gives up." She sighed and shook her head. "But I was wrong. He's more like Harmon, only he can cloak it better. Which I find more dangerous. I don't trust him in the least."

"Can I ask a personal question?" This was from Hillary.

"I suppose, though I can't guarantee I'll answer it."

"That's cool," Hillary said. "Your brother. He's famous. Especially around here. I would have thought the cops would have fallen all over themselves to help him out."

Teddy didn't know Elliot's brother or his reputation. Sports were background noise for him. But he'd been curious about this as well.

Elliot smiled. "They did, and Nathan has bought into everything they've said. But he doesn't care to show up and ask about our parents' case. He's too busy, and he says he lets me do that because I'm good at it. But I think it boils down to him not caring. Me, on the other hand, I probably care too much. I probably pushed too hard. The whole thing about catching flies with honey instead of vinegar, but I can't find the honey when we're talking about who murdered my mom and dad."

"How can he not care?" Teddy asked. "I have unwavering support from my family, as I imagine he did with his sports pursuits. I am in this car today having a lucid conversation with friends because of my parents and siblings. I don't get it." Teddy couldn't even comprehend having to go

without his parents' support. Or worse, what he'd do if they were suddenly gone. The thought left him cold.

Elliot dug into her messenger bag and pulled out the hoodie she'd balled up. Unbuckling her seat belt, she pulled it on.

The temperature in the car wasn't overly cold. And outside was rainy, but spring was in the air with the sun peeking from behind the rain clouds.

"I can adjust the temp," Seema said. "I didn't realize it was so cold."

"It might just be me," Elliot said.

Whenever she talked about Nathan—or thought about him, for that matter—darkness enveloped her. Maybe it was sadness, grief because she'd lost him that awful day as well. No matter how hard he pretended nothing had changed.

Teddy faced her, waiting for a response. "If it's too personal..."

She waved him off. "My parents didn't want Nathan to take the contract. They didn't like his agent and didn't think he had Nathan's best interest at heart. Nathan had a few offers on the table, but this one was the biggest and came with the most expectations and demands. They built in crazy incentives that... I dunno ... maybe they could see how competitive Nathan was even with himself. With the right 'supplements', he can be a machine." She did air quotes around supplements. "My parents wanted him to look at the other deals. They called the agent a pusher and tried to get Nathan to see long term, but he was determined to take this deal, and because he was twenty there was nothing they could do about it. Of course, that didn't stop my dad from trying. Anyway, when they were murdered, Nathan and my parents were on the outs. Maybe that's how he copes with it?

I like to think he throws himself into baseball as a way to forget about how things ended between them."

Seema asked, "Your parents thought the agent was pushing performance-enhancing drugs?"

Elliot shrugged. "I guess. I was never looped in on the conversations."

There was a lull in the conversation. The heaviness of the topic made the air thick. Elliot searched for something new to say, something that would change the tone, but she was stuck thinking about her parents and Nathan. Hillary was the one who brought up the next topic.

She held up Seema's bat that had been rolling around the back seat's floorboard. "So now we know why you have this. Why didn't you say something the night we first met?"

"As if I was going to tell a bunch of strangers about being assaulted. It's not an easy thing to talk about. You should know what I mean." She looked at Elliot.

"I do," Elliot said. "But did you ever think that maybe that's why you were given the letter?"

"Yes, only because my assault happened on the night Jaime was murdered. I wondered if maybe I am someone who saw the killer?" Seema's voice was unnaturally hushed, uncertain. Which was unusual for the girl who did everything with intention and confidence.

"Where were you when it happened?" Teddy asked.

"Sorority row. About two blocks south of Jaime's dorm."

"Did he ... did he do ... you know ... terrible things?" Hillary asked.

Seema looked at her in the rearview mirror. "You mean other than punch me in the face, threaten to rape me, steal my money and confidence and sense of safety? No."

"I-I just meant that—" Hillary stammered.

"It's okay," Elliot said. "We know what you mean. It's not an easy question to ask." She leaned toward the front seat. "Do you think he was just there for the money, or what does your gut tell you? Because I know that if your gut tells you something more could have happened, it's even harder to process and deal."

Elliot noticed Seema stiffen. She adjusted the heat. Washington evenings were typically cooler until summertime. Spring only showed up during the day.

Seema cleared her throat. "Had we not been on the sidewalk, had some people not come out of one of the sororities, had I not fought like hell and got a couple of blows in, I think the whole situation would have been exponentially worse. I think this guy was more than a mugger. He escalated quickly. Frankly, I'm surprised there haven't been more campus incidents escalating in scale."

"Maybe there have, but they've been off campus. Maybe whoever killed Jaime went into the city after?" Teddy said.

"Maybe." Seema shivered.

Elliot felt it too. The chill of the scary possibility that something far more sinister was out there than a person who had killed once. How naïve of them to think otherwise. Maybe it was because the messenger had lured them in and weirdly given them the illusion of things being safer than they were. Maybe Madden was right, and they were in over their heads.

Elliot pulled the sides of her zip-up hoodie together and swallowed. She stared at the box of Jaime's effects.

"We'll be on campus in fifteen. Hillary, I'll take you home first," Seema said.

"I can walk from Hillary's," Teddy said.

Seema shook her head. "I think I'd feel better if I saw everyone safely home."

"I am not going to get a wink of sleep," Elliot said. "I'll be thinking about these journals all night."

"Me too," said Teddy. "I have already resigned myself to going through them tonight and sleeping all day tomorrow before my graveyard shift."

"Who is going to loop Trey in?" Hillary asked.

"You know, how about we go to the journalism building and make copies of all this so we can go all through it when we have time? I can call Trey to see if he will meet us there, and we can all fill him in," Elliot offered.

"I'm in," Seema said.

"Me too," Teddy added.

"Well, duh, that's a yes for me," said Hillary.

Elliot texted Trey and got an immediate response. "He'll be there. He's going to be stoked when he hears what we learned and sees what we got."

"This day has been full of surprises," Seema said.

22

A misty drizzle greeted the group on its return to campus. The moon was hidden behind a cloud, and paired with the mist, the night felt darker, more ominous. There would be no seeing someone in this mess unless they were close. Even the streetlights appeared dimmer.

Elliot directed Seema to pull into the shared parking lot between the journalism building and the fine arts building next door, where the staff parked. This gave the group easier access to the front door. Elliot would worry about any ticket they might get later. They all exited the car, with Teddy carrying Jaime's box. Hillary carried Seema's bat.

"I hate when it's this dark out," Hillary mumbled.

Elliot had to agree. No moon and the tall trees just made the night feel as if the darkness was swarming in. She shifted her thoughts by glancing at her phone. "Trey's walking over, so he'll be coming from that direction." She pointed to the woods adjacent to the journalism building.

"I bet he wouldn't have walked had he had the conversation we did in the car," Hillary mumbled.

Teddy chuckled. "Oh, I don't know. He might have. Trey's not afraid of much."

Elliot gave the others her card to get into the building. "I'll wait for Trey out here. You get the box inside."

"As if we're going to leave you out here all alone in the dark," Seema said. "Especially after the conversation we had earlier."

Everyone gave nervous laughs. Elliot glanced at the woods and thought about the time she'd seen something in the brush, a flash of white. When she knew someone had been out there. Seema's attacker, perhaps? Elliot had assumed the person's presence had to do with the letter they'd all gotten, but in truth, the woods cut across campus and came out at the dorms. They were an easy place to hide and logistically provided access to all parts of campus.

Yeah, she didn't want to be outside alone. "Let's split up, then two take the box inside, and someone wait with me."

"I'll stay," Hillary said and swung the bat.

"You sure? I don't mind staying," Teddy offered.

"Okay, you stay," Hillary said and handed him that bat. "I'm more scared than I thought." She smiled weakly.

Hillary took the box from Teddy and followed Seema to the building.

Elliot moved to where she would normally park her bike. She opened her mouth to tell Teddy about how she'd seen the flash of white in the woods on the first night they all met and how she'd seen it again a few times after that when a branch snapped in the dark blanket of trees.

Elliot waited for Trey to appear. She glanced over her

shoulder. Teddy was moving to sit on the bench fifteen yards away.

Trey didn't appear. Elliot strained to hear another sound, thinking maybe she imagined the first. She stared into the inky darkness of the forest.

She sucked in her breath when she caught a flash of white and heard the squishing of something padding across the wet ground.

Elliot whipped out her phone and texted Trey.

ELLIOT

There's someone in the woods, directly across from the bike rack.

TREY

Got a late start. I can circle that way and come up behind them maybe.

Be careful.

She thumbed down the screen and tapped the flashlight icon, pointing the sudden light toward the noise, aiming low to the ground.

Another rustle and a flash of white. Elliot gasped and nearly dropped her phone. Had she imagined it? Maybe the flash of white had been a reflection off something else? Trash like a crushed can or a reflection off a damp leaf?

She pointed the light up, eye level. "I know you're there," she said. "Just come out."

"Elliot?" Teddy asked.

Goose bumps ran up Elliot's arm. Instinct told her someone was staring at her, just like she was staring at them. Only she couldn't see them.

Elliot wanted to believe the person was there for the same reason she was, that the person in the woods was there because of Jaime, but how could they be? She hadn't known she was going to be there until twenty minutes ago. No, this person was someone who used the woods as a cloak. Who moved through the night with ease.

Elliot stepped toward the trees. "I know you're there. Just show yourself. I've seen you before, and I see you now."

"Elliot?" Teddy asked, coming up close. "What's going on?"

Her phone vibrated. She glanced at the text from Trey.

Where are they?

"If the bike rack is noon, they're at nine o'clock!" she yelled, hoping Trey would know what she meant. She didn't dare take her eyes off the area to text.

But that was when all hell broke loose. Whoever had been staring back at her took off. Branches and twigs snapped as the person ran through the woods, the sounds colliding with the stillness of the air and echoing.

"They're running toward the main road!" she yelled and took off into the trees. She could hear Teddy moving quickly behind her.

Elliot entered the dark woods within seconds, crashing through the branches without a second thought until it dawned on her that whoever she was chasing might be the person who assaulted Seema. They might be the person who killed Jaime.

"Elliot!" Trey hollered.

She knew he was telling her not to chase after the ghost

in the woods, but she wasn't going to let him go it alone. He needed someone to cover his six.

"They're at your nine o'clock!" she yelled after locking in Trey's location and the runner's. Trey was coming into the wood perpendicular to Elliot. The runner was straight in front of her.

In a blur of brush and a crunch of branches, Elliot sensed more than saw Trey surpass her and catch up to their mystery person. Her phone flashlight was not bright enough to show her more than a narrow slice of the trees before her.

The two went down in a cacophony of oomphs and grunts, the forest breaking their fall. Based on the sound of the twigs snapping, the mystery person was putting up a good fight.

"They might have a weapon," Teddy said as he blew past Elliot.

Teddy was wearing a headlamp, which cast a brighter, more expansive light and offered far more visibility than her phone. She stammered in her run, having not thought once about this person being armed. What if the runner had a knife? What if what she thought was the runner fighting back was instead Trey fighting for his life? But quickly, she caught herself and picked up her pace, following behind in Teddy's wake, letting his light lead the way.

"Trey!" she yelled.

Why hadn't she thought this through better? She mentally kicked herself for not telling the others and, as a team, coming up with a plan? It was unlikely this would be the last night this person would be in the woods. They'd been there so many other times before.

"Trey!" she yelled again and broke through a swatch of

branches to the space where Trey and the mystery person were on the ground.

Teddy had come to a stop and was watching the two on the ground, likely assessing the situation, his light swinging from side to side.

From what she could tell there was no weapon in sight.

Trey reared back, his right hand raised to throw a punch, when Elliot saw who he was straddling.

"Lucas!"

Trey socked him in the nose and pulled back his hand again to send another punch.

Lucas covered his face with his arms. "Stop, man!"

Elliot gave Lucas a quick once-over, moving her phone light over him, her mind not accepting that he had been the person in the woods all along. Her gaze paused at his white Nikes with the gold stripe. Yep, that was what she had seen. That had been the flash of color.

She wanted to slap herself upside the head for not putting the pieces together.

"I should punch you fifty times more," Trey said, his arm still cocked.

Lucas, still with his hands over his face, said, "Come on, man. Be cool."

Trey was on his knees, straddled across Lucas. "What the actual fuck, man?"

Lucas asked, "Can I remove my hands? Or are you planning on hitting me again?"

"It all depends on what you say." Trey stayed in his threatening position.

Elliot stepped closer and looked down at Lucas. "Yeah, let's hear it. And I don't wanna hear some BS about how you just happened to be in the woods today and saw me or some-

thing. Or that we invited you and you were checking it out because I know that's not true. You've been in these woods several times, and you were in the woods on day one."

Trey's head snapped toward Elliot. "Are you kidding me?"

He looked back at Lucas, who had let his hand relax a little and was peeking through his fingers.

Trey shook his head and reared back slightly. "Man, I want to hit you again. You've been playing us for fools."

"Where are you guys?" someone called from beyond the trees.

"Over here," Teddy said, pointing his light in the direction of the voice. "Can you see my light?"

"We see you. Don't move," came a disembodied voice from deep within the trees.

Trey looked at Elliot in confusion. "It's Seema and Hillary."

Moments later, the two joined the group, Hillary still clutching the box.

"What the hell is going on?" Seema asked, her phone flashlight going from face to face. "Who the hell is that guy?"

Teddy pointed to Elliot. "She just told us that this guy on the ground has been in the woods watching us from day one."

"Which day is day one, for clarity?" Seema asked, a sharpness to her tone.

"Yeah, Seema. It's what you're thinking. I saw a flash of his shoes the first night we met, the night we were told to meet here. I knew someone was in there." She pointed to Lucas's shoes.

Seema stepped close and pointed her light in Lucas's face. "And do we know this guy?"

"This is Lucas. He worked with Jaime. Trey and I talked to him at the nursing home. He's Lindsay Volmer's boyfriend."

Seema stepped even closer, the tip of her shoe pressing against Lucas's shoulder. "And why were you in the woods that night?"

Lucas dropped his hands. "I got a letter too."

Hillary gasped.

"And you showed up," Elliot said. "But you hid in the woods. Why?"

Lucas covered his eyes and sighed heavily. "I don't know. I just thought I wasn't ready to bring up Jaime, to relive everything, but I wanted her killer to be found. It's very confusing."

"She was your friend," Trey said. He dropped his arm, and he slid off Lucas. "She was your friend, and her murderer hasn't been caught." He stood and dusted off his pants.

"For all we know, you're her murderer," Seema said to Lucas.

Lucas's hands flew from his face as he jerked upright into a sitting position. He pointed a finger at her. "I did not kill Jaime."

"I feel like there's a but in there," Elliot said. She faced Teddy and Trey. "Don't you feel like he wanted to say but?"

Trey said, "Yep, feels like a big but."

Teddy offered his hand to Lucas and helped him up.

"I didn't want to join your group. I didn't want to rehash everything again, *but* I feel like I should do something. That night, man, I can't get it out of my head. I could've helped her. I should've given her a ride or something." His voice was nasally as he pressed his hands to his bleeding nose.

"What are you talking about?" Trey asked.

Lucas brushed a hand down his face, then groaned. "I think you might have broken my nose." That was when Elliot noticed the blood around his nose and mouth. His hands had hidden it earlier.

"Who cares?" Trey said. "What do you mean you should have done something?"

"That night. It was raining when she left. I should have made her call an Uber or something. Maybe if I'd taken her home, none of this would have happened."

"And how were you supposed to take her home if you were working?" Elliot asked.

"My dinner break was at one. I could have taken her home then, but she knew that Lindsay would get upset, so she didn't wait. What if she had waited? What if she had gotten home earlier? These are all the things I think about." His voice was tight as if he was talking around a lump. "These are all the things I think about all the time," he said quietly.

"Only she wasn't killed outside the dorm. She was killed in the safety of her own room. How would you have stopped that? How would you have ensured she was safe there?" This from Teddy.

Lucas scuffed a foot against the ground. "I don't know. But maybe anything different in her day would have changed the outcome."

To Elliot, Lucas was experiencing something akin to survivor's guilt. He was closely associated with a tragedy but not so close that he'd had a direct impact. "And then you got a letter in the mail, and you thought you would come check it out."

"If you felt so helpless, why not join the group?" Trey questioned.

"If I'd joined your group and we talked about Jaime's last day, you would know that I could've done more. That's why I chickened out. Well, that and Lindsay asked me to ignore the letter. She's scared."

"You know your reasoning is bullshit, man," Trey said. "Unless you killed her, what do you have to feel guilty about? That's why it's bullshit. Why are you holding on to something that somebody else did?"

Lucas ducked his head. "I wish I could bring her back." His voice was anguished and quiet.

Trey stepped up to him. "What I want to know is why—if you were so scared to join the group, if you weren't getting involved because your girlfriend didn't want you to—were you suddenly coming around trying to hang with me?" He turned to the others. "Lucas caught up with me after practice today and asked to hang out. We went out to dinner, and he was there when I got the text. That's how he knew to be in the woods. So I'm guessing he was trying to use me for information."

Lucas didn't deny it.

Seema cleared her throat. "Well, that says a lot. Whether we can trust you or not will be determined by your actions moving forward. But for now, you have something we want, and you're gonna give it to us."

"What's that?" Lucas asked.

"Information," Teddy said.

"And while he's at it, he's going to join the forum," Trey said, giving Lucas a shove on the shoulder. "Welcome to the Campus Murder Club."

"No," Lucas said with a shake of his head. "I don't think I can—"

Trey cut him off. "You don't have a choice anymore."

"I need a minute to think about this."

"Okay," Seema said. "Take one minute. Because that's all the time we had to make our decision too." She set her phone timer to sixty seconds.

"Can we move this into the building?" Hillary inclined her head toward the journalism building. "I don't want campus patrol to find us all standing out here."

"Time's up," Seema said.

Elliot pointed her light in the direction she wanted to go. "I can't wait to see what the messenger has to say now."

23

Teddy was not one to judge people on first impressions. He himself rarely gave a quality first impression because often people saw the sweating and his general unease first. Those were hard traits to look past. Teddy knew firsthand there was always a story behind another person's mannerisms and behavior, and he wanted to know Lucas's story.

He was clearly interested in Jaime's case but torn between a friend who was dead and could not confront him for his inactions and a living sorta-girlfriend who, as Seema described, was not afraid to state her mind.

Lucas was a guy caught in between and struggling with every step. Teddy could relate, though his situation involved different reasons.

They followed Elliot to the elevator and third floor, back to the same room where Elliot kept her locker. Trey continued to glare at Lucas.

Teddy took the box from Hillary, who then handed Lucas a napkin she had in her pocket.

"You have"—she gestured to the area around her nose and mouth—"you know, blood."

"I'll step into the bathroom—" Lucas started.

"No, you won't. We aren't letting you out of our sight. For all we know, you'll climb out a window or something to get out of here." Trey crossed his arms.

"You know where I work. You know my girlfriend and where I go to school. I'm not going to be hard to find if I were to run, which I'm not going to do."

Trey shook his head. "Nah, we got you on the hook, and we aren't letting you off until we're good and ready."

"I have wipes and stuff in my locker." Elliot opened the door and handed a package of wipes to Lucas. She gestured to the magnetized mirror inside the locker door.

Lucas returned Trey's glare then stepped up to the locker and began to clean his face. A thin stream of blood trickled out of his nose.

Teddy put the box on the table and stood next to Lucas, inspecting his nose. "We need to pack that. Stop the bleeding and realign it."

Lucas winced. "Yeah, but I don't have anything."

Teddy swung his backpack off his back and to the ground. He unzipped it with flourish and pulled out an emergency kit.

"Dude, when did you start carrying that?" Seema asked.

Teddy smiled. "After our first meeting at the medical quad. I wanted to be prepared in case something went wrong."

Trey chuckled. "I like that your version of something going wrong can be fixed with a first aid kit. That's my version of positive."

Seema pushed Trey on the shoulder and grinned. "And

my first thought on seeing the kit was, good, if something were to happen, he might be able to keep us alive until the EMTs arrive."

Others in the group laughed, breaking the thick tension surrounding them.

"You have a dark outlook, Seema Choudhury," Trey said but with a grin and a joking tone.

She pointed a finger at him. "And don't you forget it."

Teddy put on latex gloves and pulled out a pack of gauze. He offered Lucas a pair of gloves.

"You premed or something?" Lucas asked.

"Yeah, something like that. You want me to pack it or are you good? I can hand you what you need."

Lucas looked at his nose and the gauze. He gently pressed a finger to the bridge of his nose and winced. "I think I'm going to need help. Treating other people, easy. Treating myself, not so easy."

Teddy could relate. When he first started having signs of schizophrenia, he knew what it was but totally thought he could handle and treat it himself. He'd been wrong. He gestured for Seema to join them.

"I need you to hand me things, okay?"

She joined them and readied herself to assist.

He handed her the gloves that he'd pulled out for Lucas and put the gauze in her hands once she donned the gloves.

"Okay, tilt your head back," he directed Lucas, who complied. "Tell me about Jaime at work. Elliot and Trey said that she wasn't well liked by the nursing staff."

While Lucas talked, Teddy packed his nose, being as gentle as possible. Trey had whacked Lucas good.

"They would have liked her just fine if she'd just been any old CNA who did their job and went home. But Jaime

was about to finish nursing school and knew a lot. Her instincts for what people were experiencing were excellent. It didn't happen often, but she caught a few nursing mistakes, and on one occasion the doc was looking through the charts and reviewing treatment with the head nurse, who was making recommendations. Jaime interrupted and contradicted the nurse's recommendations. And of course, Jaime was right. Jaime believed—yow, that hurts!"

Teddy eased his fingers off Lucas's nose briefly. He was almost done but was at the part where he had to pack a little more, and the pressure would be uncomfortable. "Sorry. Almost done. You were saying? Jaime believed what?"

"Jaime believed that if you saw enough of the same, then you had to be extra vigilant to look for the outlier. And in this case, she thought the patient was an outlier. She said he was having complications he shouldn't have and suggested a different approach."

"And she was right?" Seema asked.

"Yeah, the guy was declining until Jaime intervened. Six weeks later, he was discharged to outpatient and made a full recovery."

"And Jaime did this more than once?"

"I know of two times."

Elliot joined the group. "Same nurse both times?"

"No."

"Two more pieces, and we're done," Teddy said. "Did Jaime ever talk about her social life? Did Lindsay ever say anything about Jaime's night life?"

"What do you mean?" Lucas asked. His eyes darted to those he could see.

Teddy gently pressed gauze up one side of Lucas's nose.

"We have Jaime's journal. We've read a few things in there that—"

"The girl was getting her game on. Getting condoms in her groceries every two weeks. Any idea who she was hooking up with?"

"She had a boyfriend from home. Maybe him?"

"No," Elliot said. "He was on the road some of those times, and then he was in an accident and recovering for another part. We think she was having casual meetups or something."

"All done," Teddy said. He stepped away and removed his gloves. He took the supplies from Seema and repacked them before tucking them in his backpack, purposefully keeping his actions casual. The vibe he got from Lucas was that he was protective of Jaime, though Teddy wasn't sure if that was because of their work history, his guilt, or something else. "Listen, we're only guessing about Jaime and her social life. Trying to put the random pieces we get together. But right now, it's the only thing that makes sense. And no one here cares if she was having casual hookups."

"Nah, if that's the case the girl is my hero," Trey said, pulling out a chair and tossing himself into it. He pointed a finger at Hillary. "Do not think I mean that I like her because I think she was getting around. I like the idea of it because she was having fun. She worked all the time. I want to know she had some laughs before she died. And I liked that she wasn't so sexually repressed that she couldn't enjoy herself." He nodded as if agreeing with himself. "Yeah, you get one life. Grab all the joy you can. Who cares what people say?"

Trey pulled out a second chair and kicked it toward Lucas, indicating he should sit.

Lucas took the chair and eased into it. "She never talked

about anything like that. I don't know who she was hooking up with. I know she still saw her old boyfriend. We sometimes talked about that. You know, how she and Oliver had dated most of high school, and it was hard just cutting that out. Same with Linds and me. I mean, Linds is one of my best friends. Even when she's not my girlfriend. Jaime and Oliver were kinda the same."

"Kinda?" Hillary asked. "I went to school with both of them. They were tight."

Lucas looked around the group, then sighed. "After his accident, he struggled to get off the pain meds. They fought about it a lot."

Elliot looked at Teddy. "Maybe that's when she started seeing other people. Maybe as a way to break the dependency, you know?"

Teddy reached into the box and pulled out her journal. He flipped to the front of the books. "Do the initials AD or DH mean anything?"

Lucas's brow furrowed. "No. I need context."

"Could they be other nursing students she hooked up with? Or do the nurses study with students pursuing other degrees, like premed or something?" Seema asked. "Any coworkers with those initials?"

Lucas pulled out his phone. "I have an app from the contract company we worked for. The coworkers are listed. I can check. But it's not all of them. There's also the staff at the facility."

Seema gestured for him to check. "What are the initials?"

"AD, DH, ML, SW, and RY," Teddy read.

Lucas flipped his finger over the screen, repeating the initials, and as he scrolled, Trey looked over his shoulder.

"I don't see any of those. Wait, here's one. Mark Lewis. But I don't think they ever worked together. He's on the other side of town. I'm looking at his history, and he's never worked at the facilities over here." Lucas looked at the group. "Sorry."

"Hey, while you have your phone out, you need to join this forum," Trey said and tapped him on the shoulder. "Do it now."

"Please," Elliot said.

Trey rolled his eyes.

"This the forum you accused me of being a member of when we met?"

"Yep," Trey said.

Elliot said, "Okay, we can rule out some of her colleagues. But I think we need to get a list of the nursing students. See if we can match any of the initials."

"How do we get a list?" Hillary asked. She was in a chair, her head on the table. "Can we ask the professor?"

"We're gonna ask the messenger," Trey said. "That asshole is gonna do some heavy lifting for once." He continued to walk Lucas through the membership-joining process.

When Lucas was done, he looked at Teddy. "Can I see those initials and dates? Maybe that will help."

Teddy pulled his chair next to Lucas's. "DH is the only one that keeps turning up. The rest show up only once. I can write out the dates for you."

Lucas looked through the journal. "I'll put the dates in my phone on the notes app."

"What are you thinking?" Teddy could see Lucas working out something. Lucas was seeing something they hadn't.

Lucas shook his head. "It's probably nothing."

"No, don't do that. We need to trust you, and starting out by withholding info is not how that's done."

Lucas was typing into his phone. "It's stupid and maybe way off base."

"Nothing is stupid or off base," Hillary said. "If I had to deal with the possibility that Mr. Lightner might have harmed Jaime, then you have to deal with whatever it is you think is stupid."

Lucas looked up. "Lightner. That's the counselor, right? He's a sweet old man."

"Exactly," Hillary said. "So tell us your stupid."

Lucas put his phone on his leg. "It's just something Jaime said once. About how some of the patients who died shouldn't have died."

Teddy sat back in understanding. "Maybe these are their initials?"

Lucas said, "Maybe." His phone chimed, and he glanced at the screen. "Oh shit."

Everyone in the room went on high alert. Hillary sat up.

"What?" Teddy asked.

"It's Lindsay. She wants to know where I am. She's at my place. What am I going to tell her? She's going to freak out."

The other phones in the room chimed. Teddy looked at Seema then Elliot. His phone was off, but he knew in his gut that had it been on, it would have chimed.

"It's from the messenger," Elliot said.

"What's he say?" Teddy asked.

Elliot read the message. "The truth is a puzzle, and the pieces are scattered. You must put them together to see the whole picture."

Lucas looked at his phone. The app to the forum they

had made him join was open. Things were moving way too fast. His whole point for being in the woods and hanging out with Trey was to try to find something out. He wanted to know what they were up to, but he certainly didn't want to be knee-deep in their citizen sleuth club. Doing so gave him a bad feeling. A ball of dread was now hunkered down in his stomach and raging.

Lucas pressed the red dot that indicated he had a message on the forum. The sender was anonymous. His message read: *You may be new to the game. The others have had a head start, but know the truth is waiting for you. If you have the courage to face it.*

24

"What the hell does that mean?" Seema asked, waving her phone in the air. "We have our final member, and all the messenger can say is we have to put the pieces together. Well, no shit, Sherlock."

"Just ask him," Trey said.

"I will." Elliot dropped into a chair, her focus on her screen. She was done with all the cryptic BS. Her thumbs flew across the screen. She spoke what she was typing. "Yeah, we know about putting pieces together. What is it you think we've been doing? We have the last member, and that's all you have for us? Is your message supposed to be motivational? Because it's not."

Seema's chuckle was derisive.

Elliot continued typing. "You started this. It's time you step up. We have no idea if what we've found is anything new or helpful. And sometimes I feel like this is a social experiment that has nothing to do with Jaime at all."

"I'm out," Seema said, her statement adding another twist to the events.

To threaten to call it quits after getting the last member and the journals made zero sense. And typing the threat had surprised Elliot, but she meant it. She couldn't stand to have two unsolved cases lingering over her, and if Lucas was telling the truth about Jaime and her lack of sexual encounters, then what the initials could mean was infinite. She typed "we're done" then hit the Send button.

If Seema felt like Elliot, overwhelmed and frustrated, then did the others?

"We've come so far." Hillary slumped in a chair.

"Have we?" Trey asked. He pointed to Lucas. "Maybe we smoked the killer out, but how can we prove it?"

Lucas tossed up his hands. "I. Did. Not. Kill. Jaime."

Elliot tossed her phone on the table. "Now we wait."

Teddy ran a sleeve over his forehead. "I don't think I'm ready to give up."

Elliot gave him a sad smile. "I'm sorry. What I did was unfair. I shouldn't have spoken for the group. You should—" But before she could continue, their phones chimed simultaneously. She looked at Trey, who was staring down at his phone.

He glanced up. "It's from him."

Seema cleared her throat and read, "Before I share what I have, I need to know who is in and who is out. Because if one of you is out, then the team is incomplete, and there is no point. Decide now. Move forward or stop. Stop, and it ends right now." She looked around the group and finished the last line. "You have five minutes."

"Five minutes. That's not long enough to decide!" Hillary exclaimed.

"It's a tactic. We are deciding based on our guts. Too much time, and we can find reason for any position we take," Elliot said.

"It's used in all sorts of places like marketing and interrogations. Behavior-based. Four minutes. What's it going to be, friends?" Seema asked.

"Is he teasing us by saying he has something to share? What if he has nothing?" Teddy asked.

"Then we walk," Elliot said. "I'll stay to find out. But if it's a ruse, then we are all out. Seema?"

Seema looked at her phone, then at Elliot. "Yeah, okay. Deal." She put her hand out, like she had that first night they met.

"Deal," Teddy said and put his hand over hers.

"Deal," Hillary said, doing the same.

Trey and Elliot followed. Trey gave Lucas a glare.

He stood and moved to the group. "Deal," he said and put his hand on top of theirs.

They held for a second then broke. Elliot sent a message: *We are all in so long as this relationship starts working both ways.*

They waited for a response.

"This is the person who sent the initial message?" Lucas asked, breaking the silence.

"Yeah," Trey said.

"And you all have no idea who it is?" He looked at each of them in turn.

They shook their heads.

Elliot cleared her throat. "We thought it was my journalism professor, Dr. Snyder, but... Well, I guess it still could be her. She received a call that first night, telling her to come here. We found a box in her office with some of Jaime's

effects. She told us to not touch it and went to get security. I've tried to talk to her about this case since then, and she blows me off. And I guess it just doesn't feel like it's her. Which is a stupid thing to say. Because I actually have no proof."

Lucas dipped his chin in understanding. "Who else do you think it could be?"

"Why don't you help us out, Mr. I-don't-want-to-be-involved? Who do you think it could be?" Trey asked.

Before Lucas could answer, the phones chimed.

"It's a download," Seema said.

Teddy moved to stand behind Elliot. She clicked on the link.

"Whoa," Seema said. "It's interview reports, the incident report, and notes that look to have come from a police file."

Elliot scrolled through the file too.

"Witness testimonies, phone records. Holy shit, this is the real deal." Seema's voice had gotten quieter.

"Could we get in trouble for this?" Hillary asked, looking at her screen.

"I don't think so. We didn't take it. This is no different than someone posting this online for the world to see. That person is in serious trouble if they get caught."

"Look here. Lucas's statement is in here," Trey said.

Lucas shrugged. "Read it. There's nothing in there I wouldn't tell you."

Elliot scrolled until she found Lucas's testimony. "Harmon was the detective who interviewed you?"

"The first time. Then he had another cop came back for another round."

Elliot studied Lucas. "What did you think of Harmon?"

"He's a tool, that's for sure. Tried to get me to confess

because I was the last person to see her. But my alibi is rock solid." He said the last part to Trey. "I was at work, need I remind you?"

Elliot moved her chair closer to Lucas. "What was she like that last night? Do you think she had a sense of something going wrong soon?"

Lucas met her gaze, appearing uncertain as to why she would ask that question.

She continued, "I think I knew things were going to go bad the day my parents died. It was one of those days, you know. My mom and Nathan had gotten into a fight, and he'd stormed out. I forgot I had a test in my science class and bombed it. My car had a flat tire, and I was late to a class while it got changed. Then Bryce showed up, and there was no reasoning with him. So I just left. I ran from everyone because the whole thing felt ... bad ... ominous."

Seema said, "I wonder though if that's not hindsight. Because we all have days like that, and nothing tragic happens."

Elliot let out a deep sigh. "Maybe."

"You left because Bryce was too forceful. You knew he was going to get aggressive," Seema said.

"That's what I told Harmon. And Madden."

"Because that's what you believed in the moment. Don't second-guess now. It's pointless." Seema gave Elliot's shoulder a squeeze.

"Madden, that was the other cop. Made me think of the computer game," Lucas said. He cleared his throat and looked up at the ceiling. "No, I don't think Jaime knew. She was pretty happy that night. She felt good about her upcoming test and her application." He gave a small smile as he reflected on that night six months ago. "She was talking

about when she got out of school, how she was thinking of taking a traveling job. Marking off all the states was a bucket list for her, I think."

"I think so too," Teddy said. "Look." He'd been flipping through a journal and showed them a page. It listed four states. Idaho, Washington, Oregon, and California. "She numbered them, and the number five spot is blank. She also listed nurse practitioner schools in other states on the previous page. Maybe as a backup in case she didn't get in here." He raised his brows in question.

Lucas looked away from the ceiling and to the book. "Yeah, she mentioned that, but I told her not to worry. She was going to get in here. She had this need to get away, though. A fresh start, I think."

"I get that," Elliot said.

He made eye contact with Elliot. "To answer your question. No, I don't think she did know. At least not when I saw her. I can't say how she felt after she left the building."

Elliot nodded and looked back at her screen. Speaking around the lump in her throat was difficult.

"Here's what I think we should do with all this info. We need to pick through it. Come up with a plan of attack. See if anything stands out. I'd split it up, but I think we all need to read everything."

Trey groaned. "I have two exams and a game this week."

"How about I read it and record an audio for you? You can listen to it while you're at practice and stuff," Teddy offered.

Trey stuck out his fist to bump. "For reals?"

Teddy smiled. "I read everything out loud. It's how I absorb it."

"Let's read what we can and meet back here in two days? That enough time?" Elliot asked. "Come at eight."

They had a plan. They had a whole set of new leads. Elliot was once again rejuvenated.

She texted the messenger: *We're on it.* Then she closed the app and walked out with the others.

25

Elliot sat on the floor in her apartment, poring over the pages of Jaime's journal and the downloads the messenger had sent. The other members of the Campus Murder Club had scattered over the weekend and were doing their own things, maybe even studying the same thing she was. Trey had a game, Hillary had a big test, and Teddy was working. Elliot had been stuck making up on assignments she'd let slide over the last few days. She'd decided to skip her morning class because she just couldn't wait a moment longer to go through what the messenger had sent.

Elliot set aside the journal and spread out the downloaded pages, ordering them in stacks. Suspect and witness interviews, cops' notes, and crime scene reports.

A quick glance at her watch told her she had forty minutes before she was meeting Trey, Seema, and Hillary at the bookstore to make copies of the journals.

She glanced back at the pile. The cops' notes were what

drew Elliot's attention. As she turned the pages, her heart began to race. The notes were familiar. Maybe it was the writing, the way the person scribbled on the page and used a combination of cursive and print. But Elliot's instincts told her there was more to it. The detective essentially had a template, a list of standard questions they tried to answer, almost like a checklist. That wasn't what Elliot found unusual. She was a fan of being organized and having systems. She read the comments next to the questions a few more times.

Condition of the crime scene: Was this mess the typical state of the residence, or was the crime scene disturbed?

Victim's last known activity: What was the victim doing before attacked? Did she let her attacker in? Engage in questionable behavior?

Inconsistencies with this case: If there are, what are they? And do they need to be further investigated? How did the person get in? Test magnet rumor.

Elliot set the pages down then looked up at the ceiling, took a deep breath, and tried to clear her mind of all the unimportant stuff so she could grab the thread of thought that was eluding her. She'd read this before, but she struggled to recall where.

A cold chill of realization ran down Elliot's spine. She picked herself up off the floor and went to her closet. Pushed against the back wall was a printer-paper box, only the contents were not reams of paper but copies of police notes Bryce's mother's lawyer had used in the court case against Elliot and the police department. Elliot pulled out the box and set it in the middle of the living room next to where she'd been sitting. After taking a deep breath, she flipped off the

lid and dug through the box until she found the notes. Harmon's notes. The first time she'd read them, she'd cried and thrown up. To think the people in charge of solving the crime of her parents' murder thought so little of her family.

Condition of the crime scene: Cold, sterile. Not a friendly place to be. Flaunting their riches. Clear false sense of security.

Victim's last known activity: Were they involved in any risky or questionable activities? Did they make any enemies due to their wealth?

Inconsistencies with this case: Given the victims' privileged backgrounds, were they involved in any shady dealings or unsavory behavior? Did they have any secrets that they were hiding? Daughter's story appears as just that—fiction. Focus on her.

Detective Jeff Harmon was the lead cop on Jaime's case. Okay, she knew that. He'd called her into the police station because he thought she'd taken stuff from his desk. Had Harmon known his notes and reports had been taken at the same time as the pictures? Elliot hoped that the messenger, assuming he'd been the one to take them, had put the originals back. But what if Harmon had noticed them missing?

Elliot held up the cop's notes from both investigations. His bias was so clear. He did not have empathy toward victims. He was the type of person who assumed the worst of all people, regardless. Elliot grabbed a pen from her nearby backpack and scratched out a note on one of the pages from the messenger. She wrote: *Who was the cop who investigated the homeless man's death?*

Elliot tapped her chin with the pen. Were they looking at a negligent cop? How many of his cases were left

unsolved? And even more baffling, how was this not an issue with the department? And furthermore, shame on Madden for letting his deadbeat partner get away with being a shitty cop.

Disgusted, she set the pages aside and pulled out her timeline. She'd added a thread of suspects and their timelines too. What was weird was everyone had an alibi. Lucas was at work and had several witnesses to corroborate that. Oliver said he was at home, and his parents confirmed that he hadn't been feeling well following an intensive outpatient appointment and had been sleeping off his aches and pains. The cops had pinged his cell phone, which showed his phone never left the area near his home. Howie Middleman, the homeless man who had taken Jaime's scooter, was at a downtown bar getting smashed. Video from street cameras proved this. Elliot flipped through the paperwork to read his witness statement. Howie stated he didn't even know who Jaime was and that he found the keys in the ignition of the scooter. Like the scooter was begging to be taken. So he took it.

Elliot was glad for the transcript, as it was opinion free. No comments in the margin from a biased person. Just the conversation as it happened. She reached into her backpack and pulled out a highlighter, ready to mark any portion that was news to her. For the most part, what the news reported was essentially the gist of the interview. She noticed that the pages were numbered. Page one of fifteen, etc., and because Elliot was a check and double-check person, she made sure each page was included. It was. She did the same for Oliver's and Lucas's interviews. It was on the last page of Lucas's interview that something caught her eye. The initials.

She scrolled through her memory, trying to recall a

person with those initials as she scanned the page looking to see how often the initials occurred and the first time Lucas mentioned them. He had never mentioned a CZ to them. On the bottom of page fourteen was the first mention. She read the lines.

> Lucas: "She was in a good mood. I'd given her a charm, a star. It was for good luck. She'd been feeling down about the master's program, and even though I assured her that she was a lock to get it, she didn't think so. I kept telling her one day she was going to get out of school and have a crap ton of money, and she could replace the CZ in the charm with real diamonds. I was trying to make her laugh."
>
> Harmon: "So you gave her a charm, hmm. Why? Did you like her?"
>
> Lucas: "Yeah, she was my friend. Had been for a few years now. I liked her a lot. But not like you're insinuating."
>
> Harmon: "What does your girlfriend think about you giving another girl a charm?".
>
> Lucas: "She wouldn't care."
>
> Harmon: "So she doesn't know."
>
> Lucas: "I just bought it yesterday on a whim, and I haven't seen Lindsay to tell her."
>
> Harmon: "You called her."
>
> Lucas: "Yeah, to have her check on Jaime. That's what started this whole thing. I didn't think to mention it as Lindsay was delivering her bad news."
>
> Harmon: "If you say so."

Elliot groaned. She despised Harmon.

But there was something in Lucas's interview. Or maybe it was simply that he'd never shared this. Could he and Jaime have been friends with benefits? Were his initials in her book?

Elliot highlighted what she'd just read. She was going to show the group and confront Lucas.

Her phone rang, and she glanced at the screen. Gene Madden.

Elliot answered the call with trepidation.

"Detective?"

"Elliot, I'm sorry to bother you, but I think you need to come down to the Salmon Creek Rehab and Nursing Facility. Bryce Zimmerman is here. He received his communication device yesterday and has been training on it. There's something you need to hear."

Elliot's heart sputtered, held in suspension as fear gripped her, then took off at a gallop. "I don't think I'm wanted down there, and my presence would not be a good idea."

"I'm here now. I'll be here with you. But you need to come down here now. I'm sending a patrol car for you."

The seriousness of his voice was like a cold splash of water. "Am I in trouble?"

"No, I just think you'll want to get here sooner rather than later, and your bike isn't the fastest mode of transportation. Patrol Officer Williams is picking you up. She should be there in five minutes."

Elliot didn't know what to say as her mind ran rampant with possibilities.

"Elliot?"

"Okay."

Madden had nothing more to say but breathed heavily

into the phone, a sign that he was worried. "Okay," he finally said and disconnected.

With shaking hands, Elliot packed the papers in her backpack and grabbed her keys. She went to the landing to wait for the police, forgetting all about her friends at the bookstore.

26

When Trey got to the campus bookstore, Hillary was already at one of the three copy machines. She had papers spread out at her feet. Whatever the copy machine produced Seema picked up and took to a table to sort or collate or whatever.

"Looks like I'm not needed here," Trey told them.

"I'm not needed here either," Seema said. "Hillary had this all sorted before I got here. And she won't let me put any money in the machine."

"You didn't ask us for gas money when we went to Port Angeles, so this is on me."

Hillary finished with a paper and moved to the side of the machine where Trey saw the box they'd gotten from the Lightners. She laid the paper gently in the box, spending a moment to adjust the items already in the box. Trey caught Seema's eye, a silent message passing between them. Hillary was taking the responsibility of caring for the box very seriously.

"I offered to drive Hillary back to Port Angeles today or

tomorrow to return the box. Thought maybe we could try to talk to Taylor or Oliver again. Hillary would read this out loud"—she swept her hand over all the papers —"and maybe we'll get lucky."

Trey gave them a thumbs-up. "Sounds solid. I wish I could go, but I have practice today and tomorrow. I gotta be fresh and on time. Coach has been dropping hints that he thinks my dedication isn't what it used to be. Gotta prove him wrong." He made like he was flexing his muscles.

"I think we have maybe an hour or slightly more of copying. Didn't Elliot say she was coming? Maybe we can all ride out today," Seema proposed. "You'll just have to wait and hear about it like last time." She pretended to flex her muscles.

Trey took out his phone. And checked for messages. Nothing. "I'm surprised she's not here." He fired off a text to her, expecting an immediate response but getting nothing instead.

One of the copy machines became free, and Seema jumped to claim it. "Trey, bring me that stack by Hillary's feet. I'll start copying that, and we'll be done even sooner."

Trey stepped up to the machines, tucking his phone in his front pocket. Hillary pointed to a pile, and he picked it up. He glanced at this page. "This is from a journal?"

Hillary looked at the pages he was holding. "Yeah, that's the first journal. I copied all three volumes first. Now I am copying all the copies."

He opened his mouth to ask a question, but she held up a hand to stop him.

"Yeah, I know I could have done all the copies at once, but I was trying to get the best copies because so much is written in the margins. Sometimes I had to try more than

once to capture the writing. Doing that in multiples of five felt wasteful to me."

"Six," Trey said.

"What?" Hillary asked.

"Lucas is number six. He should get a copy."

Hillary closed her eyes and groaned.

"Dammit," Seema said. "I forgot about him."

Trey handed her the papers. "I guess we can forget about him if we want, but if we want his help, maybe we should share."

Seema narrowed her eyes. "I'm not sure I like him."

"I liked him until yesterday," Trey said. "But that's because I feel played."

Hillary said, "Maybe you should trust your first instincts and give him the benefit of the doubt. I read his interview last night. The cop asked Lucas if there was something going on between him and Jaime because he'd given her a charm. Did you all read that?"

"Dammit," Seema said. "I started at the beginning, and his was not the first interview."

"I was waiting on Teddy's recordings of it," Trey said. "A charm?"

"Yeah, for a bracelet. A star. He said he gave it to her for good luck." She filled them in about Jaime's worries over nursing school.

Trey crossed his arms. "He never mentioned that little tidbit."

Hillary raised her brows. "He asked if I'd drop off his copies at work." She looked at Seema. "Can we do that before we head out of town? We can ask him about it."

"Yeah, sure. Give me a chance to get another feel for him."

"Nope. Nuh-uh. I can do it. I want to ask Lucas about it, and maybe we can also chat about what else he hasn't told us." Trey's brows furrowed.

"Okay," Hillary said. "You might get more flies with honey, if you know what I mean."

"Fuck that," Trey said.

Seema laughed. "Yeah, I'm with Trey on this one."

Trey rolled his head to stretch out the tension in his neck. "I can take Teddy's to him as well. He's working today. Got called in early because the regular examiner's assistant called in sick. He was weirdly excited about it." Trey made like he was cringing, though he was very happy for Teddy. Okay, it was a little cringy, working with the deceased. He was glad there were people like Teddy who liked that sort of thing.

They made small talk about the case as they copied and sorted.

"Anyone need prints of what the messenger sent?" Hillary held up a stack of papers. "I had them printed out so I could go through them. Scrolling on the phone doesn't always work for me."

Seema shook her head. "I annotate using an app called Kami."

Trey quirked a lazy smile. "I prefer them to be read to me."

"Dude." Seema chuckled. "I like to do both, read and be read to. Helps me catch things."

Hillary interrupted. "Well, we're done. I guess Elliot isn't going to make it." She had moved the box to a nearby table along with the packets of paper. She touched a stack. "These are for Lucas and Teddy. You sure you don't mind running them over to them? We could go with you."

Trey shook his head. "Nah, I got this. You all have three hours in the car. You should get going."

They separated at the door with promises to text the moment there was any news of anything.

Trey headed to his car with a stack of copies in his hand, wanting to wring the papers to relieve his tension.

Once in his car he texted Lucas.

Headed your way. Have journal copies

LUCAS

Cool, I'll meet you outside. Text me when U get here. I'm at the facility by the hospital.

Trey didn't respond. He was glad that he technically had one place to go. Teddy was at the hospital too. But before he pulled out of the parking lot, he texted Elliot:

Where are U? Okay? Did you see that Lucas gave Jaime a charm? Never told us that. I'm headed to see him now.

He stared at the screen and hoped for a response, though wasn't expecting one. She still hadn't responded to his earlier text. His phone vibrated in his hand.

ELLIOT

At the Salmon Creek rehab facility. With Madden. I'll fill you in later. Saw that about Lucas. Ask Teddy to send us a pic of it. It should be listed in her personal effects.

TREY

Need support?

ELLIOT

No. Thanks.

Trey's imagination came up with a thousand different scenarios about why Elliot would be at the rehab facility. The one common element to the scenarios was Bryce Zimmerman. This had to do with him. Well, to hell with her saying no. He was going to go anyway. Right after he got some info from Lucas and dropped off the packets.

When Trey arrived at the nursing and rehab facility attached to the hospital, he texted Lucas to tell him he was at the bench outside.

Lucas came out in minutes. "Hey, man," he said. His nose and eye were bruised and swollen.

Trey would decide later if he felt bad about that or not. He thrust the paper at him.

Lucas flipped through a few pages. "Perfect. I can maybe use the dates to narrow my search too."

"What do you know that you're not sharing?"

Lucas held up his hand. "I don't know anything yet. I'm just following a weird-ass thread from a conversation I had with Jaime a long time ago."

"Was this the same conversation you had with her when you gave her that charm?" Trey crossed his arms.

Lucas looked puzzled. "No, this conversation was a few months before she died. I feel like you might punch me in the nose again. Why?"

"You didn't think it was important to tell us about the charm?"

Lucas tossed up his hands in frustration. "When would I

do that? The first time I met you and Elliot, she said she was doing a human-interest piece on Jaime. Because it was relevant then? Or maybe it was when you were considering me her killer?"

"This makes you look super suspicious now." Trey raised a brow. "You could have mentioned this last night."

"Oh, sure. Hey guys, yeah, I'm your missing member, and by the way, I gave Jaime a charm the night she died. She was my friend, and she was worried about not getting into grad school, and I thought I'd do something nice for her. It doesn't seem relevant. I also bought her dinner a handful of times. She bought me dinner just as many times too. We split a funnel cake once. Should I tell you about that? Or how about the time we fell asleep watching *Clerks*, and I got kicked out of her dorm for it? That weird security guard in her building said he was going to turn me into campus police for breaking the house rules, even though we'd fallen asleep in the public space and were clearly not doing anything nefarious. But I guess I should have brought all those incidents up too. I don't see why a simple charm that hung on a simple silver bracelet that she already had is such a big deal."

"Were you sleeping with her? Are your initials in the margin?"

Lucas grunted in frustration. "I don't think those are the initials of hookups. Listen, I've gotta go. I was on a break, and it's over. Thanks for this." He waved the papers.

Trey watched him walk away, knowing he hadn't answered the question. But Lucas had made a point. The only significance of the charm was that he had given it to her the night she was murdered. They had a history together, and if someone dissected it enough, they could find tons of

situations they could shoehorn into a slightly plausible motive.

He left the nursing facility and headed to Teddy at the morgue. He entered through the front of the morgue because it was still normal business hours. Coming in this way offered a different presentation. The front office was set up like a waiting room, with the couch and chair. In the corner was a desk where Teddy sat banging two fingers maniacally on a desktop keyboard.

"Hey, man," Trey said. "You don't have to beat it into submission. You can go lighter on the keys." He tossed the copies on the desk.

Teddy grinned, pausing to flex his fingers. "Yeah, I just get so focused I don't realize it. Wanna hang around? I pulled the autopsy report from the homeless man. I was going to look over it again after reading the cop interview."

Trey snapped his fingers. "Elliot and Hillary said that they read Lucas's interview, and he gave Jaime a charm the night she died. A star or something. I just asked him about it, and he said it wasn't a big deal. They were friends, and that's hard for me to swallow because where I'm from if you give a girl jewelry, there's usually more to it unless the girl is your momma or granny or something. Know what I mean?"

"Maybe. I've never given a girl other than my mom jewelry."

"Me either, and that's my point. Anyway, Elliot wanted to know if you could get us a picture of it, the charm from the autopsy report. They photograph that stuff too?"

Teddy said. "We photograph everything. Yeah, hang on." He went back to hammering the keyboard, then switched to a mouse and scrolled. He squinted at the screen. "I'm not seeing a charm of any sort. Let me double-check the inven-

tory sheet." He did some more scrolling, then looked at Trey. "She did not come into the morgue with any jewelry except her earrings, which were"—he looked back at the screen—"gold studs shaped like seashells."

Trey leaned against the desk. "Is that weird? That it's not listed?"

"Let's check the crime sheet inventory. I'll let you know in a minute." He did some more clicking on the computer. "I put the docs on the cloud, so I just have to log in to my cloud and get them." More clicking and scrolling.

"Okay, here's the inventory. Was it a necklace?"

"Bracelet. Silver, Lucas said."

Teddy shook his head. "No jewelry was found at the scene other than in the small box she had on her dresser, and it's not inventoried there either. We can go through the pictures to double-check."

"Yeah," Trey said. "We should do that."

He texted Elliot to fill her in. Then he texted Lucas and asked for a picture because now more than ever he wanted a visual. Trey left out the part that the charm hadn't been found on Jaime at the time of her death.

27

Like Madden had promised, a patrol officer arrived to pick Elliot up five minutes after he called. Though she was in uniform, Officer Williams showed Elliot her badge and ID and explained why she was there, who had sent her, and where they were going. All measures to make Elliot feel comfortable, she knew, and likely something Madden had instructed her to do. She had to give him credit for his thoughtfulness, a trait she didn't often see with the cops she'd dealt with.

The ride to the rehab and nursing facility was shorter than she expected. Though logically, she knew this was typical when someone dreaded showing up somewhere, time usually tended to fly. Irony. Her stomach coiled nervously with apprehension. Elliot didn't know what to expect once she arrived. She secretly thought she might be arrested. For the first time since being shot, Bryce was going to have his say. And she could only imagine what he might say. If his behavior in the past—his overly extreme agitation every time he saw her—was any indication, she did not anticipate this

going well. The patrol car pulled up to the front entrance of the facility, a curved drive that allowed drop-offs right at the front doors. Madden was waiting for her and opened the door for her before she even reached for the handle. Dread skittered across her skin, leaving behind goose bumps.

"I'll be with you the whole time," he said.

Sounded like a warning to her. "What's this about? I know you said he's talking, but why can't you just tell me what he said?" She tried to keep the tremor from her voice.

Madden, dressed in a suit that looked to have been on his body for more than twenty-four hours, if she were to go by the creases, stuffed his hands in his pants pockets. "Telling you would be a lot easier, but I think this is something that you're gonna want to hear and see for yourself."

For the last year, Madden's partner, Harmon, had been gunning to blame Elliot for something, anything. She looked around, expecting him to be present, and when she saw he wasn't nearby gloating, she took that as a positive sign. Whether it was or not remained to be seen, but she needed something to cling to.

Madden continued, "Mrs. Zimmerman is here. She knows you're coming, and she's been warned to behave, or she'll be removed from the room."

Elliot didn't like the way that sounded because why would she need to be warned? Elliot hesitated and looked behind her toward the parking lot, wondering if she could just run. Had they been at the facility next to the hospital, she could run to Teddy at the morgue or just run anywhere. But this location felt more isolated. The entrance doors slid open, and Officer Williams entered. Elliot wondered what that meant too. She imagined Madden probably thought that having a female arrest Elliot was kinder than doing it

himself, should that be the ultimate goal of her presence. Clearly, they knew Elliot would consider running. Just as she had.

Madden paused at a set of double doors marked Rehab Gym. He grabbed the handle but didn't turn the knob right away. "I'd like to tell you that everything's going to be okay, but once you hear what Bryce has to say, I don't know if that's going to be the case."

Elliot swallowed hard. "Harmon has been wanting to put this on me since the day my parents died. If this is some trap or something, then just arrest me now. Or at the very least let me call my lawyer so he can be here too."

"Have you committed a crime?"

The question was subjective. Elliot had received some documents on Jaime Sullivan's case that could be considered problematic. But illegal? She wasn't sure. "I'm not answering any questions without my lawyer."

Madden's brows rose, and his lips twitched. "Fair enough. Let's go in. I'll be here the whole time," he repeated.

Elliot groaned. "I don't know if you know this or not, but that is not as comforting to me as you might think."

Madden opened the door and gestured for her to enter.

Inside the gym were three therapy mat tables. Mrs. Zimmerman was sitting on one next to Bryce, her face buried in her hands. A woman who looked to be in her midthirties was standing in front of Bryce and his chair, fidgeting with a device attached to his chair's tray.

When Bryce caught sight of Elliot, he began rocking in his chair and making loud vocalizations, like he normally did, but the therapist put a hand on his shoulder and prompted him to change his behavior by saying, "Bryce. Hey, Bryce, use your device to tell her what you want to say."

She turned to Elliot and gestured for her to come closer. Mrs. Zimmerman looked up from her hands and glared at Elliot.

Bryce looked between Elliot and the tablet-sized device attached to his wheelchair. He then glanced at his therapist, who gave him a thumbs-up as encouragement to start. She made a few slight adjustments to the device then gestured for him to go.

It took Elliot a few moments to notice the pattern. He would look at the device for a few seconds then look away. Then the device would beep.

"He is using his gaze to track to the letters or words that he wants," the therapist explained. The name tag pinned to her shirt read: Bethany Mills, Speech Language Pathologist.

Elliot watched in fascination. She started counting the seconds of how long Bryce would hold his gaze before moving to the next letter. She was impressed at how quickly he moved.

Bryce made the device beep twice and looked at her with a smug smile on his face.

"Hi, Elliot," the device said in a strikingly similar-sounding voice to Bryce's.

Elliot couldn't help but smile. A greeting wasn't what she was expecting, and she realized she enjoyed hearing his voice. It was far more pleasant than the screeching he made.

"Hi, Bryce." She realized that during all the times that she'd seen him in the past, she never said hello. A simple greeting had been overlooked. She never asked him how he was doing or feeling. She never said "I'm sorry," having always been too off-balance and unnerved by his screaming and rocking to attempt a civilized conversation.

Elliot gave Madden a questioning look, silently asking if this was what he'd brought her down here for.

He shook his head and turned his attention to Bryce. "Bryce, a little while ago I asked you a question. I asked you where you were when you were injured. Do you remember?"

Bryce bowed his head and moved his upper body forward slightly. She took this to be his "yes."

The speech therapist said to Elliot, "We established that this was his yes. Tell us where you were, Bryce, when you got shot."

Heat ran up Elliot's chest. He'd been in her room, naked in her bed, waiting for her.

Bryce's eyes danced across the machine, and seconds later, the machine responded with, "At Elliot's house."

"And what were you doing at Elliot's?" Madden asked.

Bryce immediately went back to his communication device. Seconds later, it said, "Fighting."

Elliot wanted to cry. Yeah, they'd been fighting. And she had no interest in reliving the past. It was awful. Terrible. The whole day had been a nightmare that she lived forever. Funny how that fight with him had been the worst part of the day until she'd returned home. Elliot backed up to one of the mat tables and dropped to sit, clinging precariously to the table's edge. She glanced at Mrs. Zimmerman, who was watching Elliot, her hands gripping her knees, her knuckles white.

Madden stepped closer to Bryce and put a hand on his shoulder. "I'm sorry to ask this again. If you don't want to talk about it, I understand, but can you tell us again who did this to you? Who shot you?"

Bryce looked to Elliot, and she could have sworn he

looked apologetic. He looked back at Madden and swayed in his seat.

"That's a no," the speech therapist told Elliot.

Madden said, "I think she needs to hear it from you. I can tell her, but ultimately, we will end up here. You and I both know she's a girl who needs the facts, and for her, seeing is believing."

Bryce sat back in his chair and studied Elliot. Not sure what he was looking for, she gave a single nod, signaling it was okay to tell her.

That must have been what he needed because he looked at his device and began his typing, the beats coming in a fast pattern.

She held her breath and tried to keep her mind from running through all the possibilities of what he might say.

The device gave two beeps then said, "Nathan."

Time paused as the name hung heavily in the air. Elliot tried to suck in some air, tried to remain calm, but her heart raced in her chest, making catching her breath difficult.

All her worst fears rose to the surface, and suddenly Elliot needed to run. To get as far away from Bryce's words and the possibility of their truth.

She leapt to her feet unable to focus on anything in her current surroundings but instead got flashes of her parents' faces, her brother's. That day when she came home to find the cops and emergency responders in her driveway, Nathan had been sitting inside an ambulance, looking shell-shocked and sick to his stomach.

Elliot spun, her knees knocking against the mat therapy table.

"Elliot?" Madden said from somewhere far away, his voice tinny and faint.

She put up one hand to shield herself from anything incoming as she used her other hand to guide her away from the mat table. Her world was swimming and off-kilter, making vision difficult.

In the haze she caught the flash of red and a few letters. EXIT. She stumbled toward that.

"Elliot?" Madden called from the distance.

She rushed as fast as she could toward the red blur, desperate to escape. She collided with a door, searching madly for the handle, finding it in seconds, and pushing her way out into the hallway.

The space was slightly dimmer, which to Elliot's shocked brain meant safety. Because in the dark she could hide. She stumbled down the hall, her hand dragging against the wall to help orient herself. She squeezed her eyes together in a pathetic attempt to regain control. Her breath was ragged and shallow, and she was sweaty and clammy at the same time.

She ran smack into someone and stumbled backward, further disoriented.

"I'm sorry," she mumbled, her shoulder pressed against the wall.

"Hey, are you okay?"

Hands gently grasped her shoulders and steadied her. "You look like you might be sick. Here." The guy led her to a chair and stuck what had to be a trash can in her hands. She sat with the can on her lap, and a second later ducked her head over the edge, losing the contents of her stomach to its depths.

Someone rubbed her back.

Elliot waited for more vomit to follow, only to realize that she was done and that slowly the world around her was

starting to right itself. As if upchucking had exorcised the poison that was killing her. Only she knew that not to be true.

She removed the can from her lap and put it on the floor.

"Here," said the guy who had helped her. He pressed a cold cloth in her hand. She wiped her mouth. He took the cloth and replaced it with a second fresh cold cloth. "Press that to your forehead."

She did as he instructed. She leaned back in the chair and closed her eyes.

In a soothing and calm voice, the guy said, "You're in shock. Do you like the beach?"

She murmured a yes.

"Picture the beach. As the waves come in, pull in a long, steady breath."

She did as he said, her heart beating like mad.

"Now, watch the wave go out and let your breath out with it. Nice and slow."

Again, she followed the commands, picturing the water moving on and off the shoreline, seeing her feet standing at the edge, and watching the flow.

Her heart began to slow as he repeated the steps, and she let him guide her. Slowly, reality flowed over her, and her racing heart began to slow. She opened her eyes to thank her rescuer.

The nurse, Aaron Simmons, was crouched in front of her. She met his gaze, and he smiled.

"Thank you," she said.

He squeezed her hand. "How do you feel?" He held out another hand to take the cloth.

"Like I'm no longer drowning." Elliot blinked back the tears.

"Can I get you anything?"

She shook her head.

"Are you here because of Jaime and your story? Did you learn something that upset you?"

She shook her head a second time. "Actually, that's going well. We've learned lots of things, and Lucas—you know him—he's been a real help. No, this is about Bryce Zimmerman. You remember him? You helped out the last time he saw me and started screaming."

Aaron rocked back on his heels. "Ah, Bryce. He got upset again when he saw you? I guess that would be hard to get used to."

She looked over his shoulder to where Madden was coming out of the rehab gym.

"No," she said. "The opposite, actually. Remember that device you said he was getting? Well, he has it, and he's had a lot to say."

Aaron squeezed her hand again. "I take it what he has to say isn't all that comforting. I'm sorry."

Madden approached. Aaron stood.

"Elliot?"

She looked up at Madden, and a tear rolled down her face. She couldn't bring herself to say what she was thinking. What she'd always been thinking.

Madden took the seat next to her. "You think Bryce is telling the truth, don't you?"

She looked at the floor, unable to hold back the flood of tears that had threatened to unleash the moment she heard Nathan's name. She stuck her palms to her cheeks and through her tears said, "Yeah, I think my brother killed our parents."

28

Lucas found an empty nurses' station in the blue wing. Many of the residents were at movie night, held in the commons located at the center of the facility. Like Lucas, the cleaning staff was taking advantage of the mostly empty wing and was cleaning the floors. The sterile smell of disinfectant lingered in the air.

Lucas didn't know what to make of the other members of the Campus Murder Club. And he couldn't help but wonder who had selected all of them and brought them together. He couldn't shake the nagging feeling that now that he was *outed*, so to speak, bad things were going to happen. Weirdly, he'd felt safer cloaked in the shadows of the trees and lying to Trey and Elliot. Well, maybe omitting facts was a more friendly term to describe withholding truths from Trey and Elliot. Omitting facts was easier for him to swallow.

Glancing around to check for nurses, all of whom seemed to have gone to movie night as well, Lucas took in a deep breath and logged on to the medical records system. Sure, he could have done this anywhere, but he didn't want

anyone to see what he was doing, to ask questions. Never mind that the company meticulously recorded who accessed which files and when, but Lucas didn't care. He didn't want to have to explain what he was doing to his coworkers. The chance the company would ask was slim.

Using the pages from Jaime's journal that Trey had dropped off as a guide, he used the search bar to type in one set of initials then groaned when he saw a few hundred names pop up. There was no filter to isolate for location, and the database was pulling names from the company's facilities nationwide.

He was stuck scrolling through old patient records, searching for initials that matched those scribbled in the margins of Jaime's journal from the two facilities where Jaime had worked. The work would be tedious.

The other members of the Campus Murder Club were convinced the initials belonged to men Jaime had slept with, but Lucas knew better. Jaime wasn't the type for one-night stands. She had been too focused on her studies and trying to get into the master's program to get involved in anything messy.

As he sifted through the digital archives, Lucas couldn't help but feel a sense of urgency. He needed to find something—anything—that would bring him closer to understanding what had happened to his friend. His brow furrowed as he tried to recall what Jaime had specifically confided in him about her suspicions, but the memories remained frustratingly elusive. He hadn't taken her seriously. Heck, she hadn't taken herself seriously, saying she was likely being paranoid because she'd seen far too many true crime movies of late.

His fingers beat a steady rhythm on the down arrow as

he scanned the pages for locations. He refused to give up. He owed it to Jaime to figure out the truth behind the mysterious initials. He was on the sixth page when he came across a familiar name.

"DM... Derrick Meanders," he muttered under his breath. He recalled a conversation he'd had with Jaime about Derrick, a young man who was a patient at the skilled nursing facility. Derrick had been recovering well from cancer surgery, which involved having parts of his tongue removed and rebuilt. With no family or support system, Lucas had done his best to be there for Derrick, forming a bond with the young man.

Lucas's heart raced. Derrick had been his patient at one time. Could this be it? He clicked on the patient's file and quickly skimmed through his medical history.

"Gotcha," he whispered, eyes glued to the screen as he reviewed the patient's information. Derrick had died unexpectedly of heart failure. Lucas recalled his surprise when he'd learned of the death the next day, coming into work. And the sorrow he'd felt knowing Derrick didn't have any family who would mourn his loss. Jaime had been surprised, too, mentioning then her crazy idea that Derrick's heart failure had been facilitated. Yet Lucas didn't see how this might be related to Jaime's murder.

He wrote Derrick's name in his pocket notebook with Derrick's date of birth and date of death and printed out a summary of his patient care. Then he cleared the search and put in another set of initials.

As Lucas delved deeper into the shadowy world of medical records, he couldn't help but feel a growing sense of unease. What if Jaime had done what he was doing now?

On a whim he got out of the patient files and went to the

employee records. The company was so large and top-heavy that people came and went, and yet their names were still showing as active employees. He was hoping that would be the case with Jaime. He scrolled through the employees until he found her name, then clicked it, thanking the gods of laziness that the company was a slow-moving cog when it came to its IT department.

When her name popped up, Lucas clicked on her caseload. Theoretically, that would show any and every patient she had been assigned to. Lucas was hoping to match initials that way.

He found two other sets of matching initials. He did the same for them as he had done for Derrick, noting their dates of birth and death, causes of death, and printing summary sheets.

Then he went back to the patient search, needing only two more names. As Lucas continued to delve into the records, he began to notice a pattern of unexpected deaths among patients with initials matching those in Jaime's journal. As the evidence piled up, his heart raced with a mix of excitement and fear.

"I'm going to need more." His hands shook as he clicked through file after file, printing page after page. "Jaime might have been on to something," Lucas muttered to himself as he stared at his computer screen. He could still hear the playful tone in her voice when she'd confided her suspicions to him and how he'd laughed it off, calling her paranoid.

"Maybe you're in the wrong profession. You should be a detective, Jaime," he had teased her, never taking her words seriously.

"Ha, maybe I am. With my nursing skills, my sharp sleuthing skills, and my experience handling people with

addiction, I would probably be a super cop," she had replied with a grin, but there was that glint of determination in her eyes that he couldn't quite forget.

Lucas's phone chimed, startling him so much he jumped up from the stool he'd been sitting on. He looked around and laughed. None of the custodial staff had noticed, thankfully. He pulled it from his breast pocket.

Lindsay: *Here with food. Where r u?*

Lucas: *Blue wing. Nurses' station.*

Lindsay had been there enough to know how to find him.

Five minutes later, she was walking down the dimly lit hallway toward him.

"What are you doing down here? I thought you had the rehab wing tonight."

The rehab wing was the red wing. He'd forgotten he'd told Lindsay his schedule.

"Just ... research. I wanted privacy," Lucas replied, minimizing the window on his computer screen.

"Research, huh? Is this for that Campus Murder Club?" She set two to-go containers from his favorite Chinese restaurant on the counter.

"You got upset when we talked about this last night. Are you sure you want to revisit the subject?" He pulled out a stool for her.

"Lucas, I saw what someone did to her. Have you forgotten that?" She plopped onto the stool. "I'm scared."

"I know. But I think I'm on to something here." He tapped the copied journal pages.

Lindsay picked them up. "This is the journal stuff you were telling me about?"

Lucas reached for the papers on the printer and showed her the first few pages. "Jaime might not have been paranoid

like I thought. She may have been right about something bad happening to patients here," he admitted, recounting his findings. "I've found patients with initials matching the ones she wrote down, and they all died unexpectedly."

Lindsay's eyes widened. "That's ... that's terrifying, Lucas. If someone is killing people here, then doesn't that make them a serial killer? This is big time."

"Yeah," he said, shaking his head. "When you say it like that, it's really scary. But if it is a serial killer, then they're preying on sick and helpless people. Not healthy, thriving people."

"That you know of. And we both took Psych 101. We know serial killers evolve, and their MOs can change. I don't like this at all. Maybe you should leave this be," Lindsay suggested hesitantly.

"Look at this," he replied, his voice a mix of excitement and trepidation. He spread the pages out before her. "I've been trying to find a connection between these patients—the ones Jaime wrote initials for. They all died unexpectedly, but there's no clear link between them. But they were people too. So if this person killed Jaime because she found out about them, then she was victim number six. That's six people, Linds. Six."

"Please, Lucas," she pleaded, her voice wavering slightly. "Let the police handle this. Don't get yourself mixed up in something that could hurt you."

"Only they aren't," he told her, frustration lacing his voice. "It's been six months, and nothing."

Lindsay bit her lip, looking between the papers and Lucas. "But what if they don't know about this stuff? What if they could do more, would do more if you shared this with the police?"

Lucas was scooping up some rice but paused. "You're right. I'll share this with the others tomorrow morning, then I'll take it to the police right afterward. We'll see what they do with it." He brought the loaded spork to his mouth.

Lindsay put her hand on his, reclaiming his attention. "Promise me. And promise me you won't do anything dangerous, okay?" Lindsay whispered, her eyes pleading. "You're my best friend. You know that, right?"

He squeezed her hand. "And you're mine. I promise to be careful," he replied, trying to sound reassuring. He put down his spork and wrapped her in a hug. Deep down, he had an inkling that whatever secrets lay beneath what he'd uncovered were bound to be more perilous than he could ever imagine.

He switched the subject while they ate. Asking about her classes and what big trip they wanted to take this summer on their annual kick-off-the-summer-season excursion. He was looking forward to the getaway. He'd stockpiled more than three weeks of time off. Lindsay always had great travel ideas.

They tossed around several locations, stuck on the prospect of using their passports. Lindsay stood and gathered their trash, the smile fading from her lips. She tapped the papers on the desk.

"Are you sure this is a good idea?"

He shook his head. "I'm not sure about anything anymore, except I am sure that I don't want to go to Canada. I want something tropical."

Lindsay rolled her eyes and smiled. She tossed the containers in the trash, then returned to where he sat at the computer.

She watched him pull up Jaime's caseload and click on a patient's name. "What are you looking for?"

"I'm looking to see if any of her other patients died the same way. I think I'm gonna have to go through this manually."

"Could these deaths just be a coincidence?" she asked hesitantly, her voice barely a whisper.

"Maybe," Lucas admitted, his fingers still tapping away, searching for the elusive thread that would tie everything together. "But I doubt it. I can't shake the feeling that Jaime was on to something."

"Well, you know how I feel about this. I won't nag." Lindsay squeezed his upper arm gently.

"Jaime was my friend, Linds," he said quietly, his eyes still fixed on the screen. "I can't just sit back and do nothing when there's a chance I could help find out what happened to her."

He glanced over at Lindsay. She looked so uncertain, terrified.

"What about Sam?" he asked her. "He's your friend. You wouldn't want to know what happened to him if he was suddenly murdered?"

Sam was a guy Lindsay had briefly dated in college while she and Lucas were on a break. Lucas secretly believed the only reason she and Sam hadn't worked out was because her parents liked him so much. That and she wasn't the easiest girl to get along with. But Lucas understood her idiosyncrasies. Her parents were not the easiest people to please.

Lindsay fidgeted with the hem of her shirt, her gaze flicking back and forth between Lucas and the computer screen. "Of course I would, but—" She stopped.

“But what?” He spun on the stool to face her. “Say what you’re really thinking.”

“But I never slept with Sam, and you and Jaime ... well, you did sleep together. And it wasn’t just once. I can’t help but wonder if she didn’t mean more to you than you’ve led me to believe.”

29

Following practice, Trey returned directly to the morgue. He didn't even take the time to change out of his practice gear other than to swap out his cleats for sneakers and change his shirt so he wasn't so rank.

Upon entering through the after-hours back door, he was hit with a wave of morgue scent—formaldehyde. The aroma hung heavily in the air. Trey associated it with the smell of death. The flickering fluorescent lights buzzing overhead just added to the creepy vibe. He was reminded of the scene in *Men in Black* where Will Smith meets an alien and gets a clue—and hits on the hot medical examiner.

There were no hot chicks in this morgue. Just Teddy. Who wasn't Trey's type.

"Check it out," Teddy said as Trey pushed through the double doors that took him straight into the autopsy room. Teddy had moved his work from the office, where earlier they'd been looking for mention of Jaime's charm, to the actual autopsy room. When Trey stepped into the large,

brightly lit space, it looked like a tree had barfed. Paper covered several of the metal tables.

"Ah ... Ted, you feeling okay?" Trey studied his friend. Sure, he was sweaty, but who wouldn't be under those lights? And sweaty was normal for Teddy. But he didn't look out of sorts, just focused. Seriously, intensely focused.

Teddy stepped back, closer to Trey, and surveyed the room. "I have looked at every piece of paper we have access to. Jaime's autopsy. The cops' notes. The inventory list from the crime scene. I looked at reports from those autopsied right after Jaime to see if maybe the charm got mixed up or something and listed under another person." He swept his arm to cover the width and breadth of the room. "Nothing." He stepped forward and scooped a thin pile of papers off the desk chair. "Only what Lucas said to the cop in the interview. And that cop, by the way, doesn't even try to find the charm, just notes that it hasn't been located. Don't you find that weird?"

Trey raised a brow. Weird. "Which part? Because right now, I'm finding a lot weird."

Teddy pulled out a banker's box and started collecting the papers and stacking them neatly in the box. "That the cop didn't even look for the charm. If the charm doesn't exist, then Lucas lied, but I can't figure out why he'd do that. Not having the charm causes him more problems than never mentioning the charm."

"Unless the cops find a receipt for it or something. Then he has to explain why he never mentioned a charm." Trey watched Teddy work meticulously while his brain churned. Trey wished he had a fraction of those brains Teddy had.

"Nah, I think it's weird the cops didn't follow up on the charm. I think it's a big deal."

"I think we're making the charm a big deal, and maybe it's not. It could have fallen off going into her dorm, or for all we know, she thought it was junk and chucked it. The options are many." Trey pointed to a pile of papers stacked offset, in a crisscross pattern. The stack was about a foot high from the floor. "You want these in the box?"

Teddy shook his head. "That's our work for tonight."

Trey looked back at the stack. "Dude, seriously?"

"Yeah, Lucas texted me a list of names to pull the autopsy reports, and that's what they are. We have to find the common link—or at least try to."

Trey groaned. He liked the sleuthing, just not the paperwork part of it.

"Do you mind calling Seema or Hillary and asking them if they have the charm in the box? I didn't see it, and I don't see it referenced in the journal, but I might have missed it. And I'm leaving no stone unturned."

"Before I do that, why don't we try to meet our first objective— get a picture of the charm?" Trey whipped out his phone, the dim screen casting a pale glow as he pulled up his texts. Lucas hadn't responded to his earlier request. He sent a reminder text.

They waited. Teddy watched him. Trey shrugged. "He could be with a patient or something. Not gonna lie, I want an immediate response. Kinda bothered that he didn't send it earlier."

"For sure. Why don't we spread these out and get set up while we wait?" Teddy pointed to the papers. "I was thinking we'd set them out by date of death." He picked up a sheet off the top and showed a line to Trey. "That's where you can find it. This is the first page of an autopsy report."

"Okay, I'll take the top half." He reached down and took several sections.

Teddy pointed to the tables. "We have four autopsy tables. Let's makes them months by quarters." He pointed to the far left and moved to the right, going back to front. "Q1, Q2, Q3, and Q4. If the date of death is on the quarter, put it on that table."

Trey glanced at his first sheet. It had an August date of death. Trey used his fingers to count to August to figure out the quarter. He was placing the first stack on Q3 when his phone chimed with a text.

Lucas had sent an image of a charm. Trey sent the image to everyone else on the team. Then he dialed up Hillary for a FaceTime; he knew Seema was driving. His fingers drummed against the cold metallic surface of the autopsy table as he considered the charm.

Teddy was right. The cops seemed not to have put a lot of effort into the case, and that bugged Trey. He wondered if that was why the messenger had reached out to them. He'd likely felt the same frustration Trey was feeling now. The same disenchantment with the system.

Hillary answered.

"Hey, guys," he greeted. "I don't know if you read Lucas's police report yet, but he mentioned he gave Jaime a charm. I just sent you a picture of it. We haven't found any reference to it besides his statement to the cops. Can you check her box for it? Teddy said he can't find where it was mentioned in the journal. Does anyone remember if it was?"

"Sure thing, Trey," Seema responded, with Hillary chiming in in agreement. The image on the phone bounced around as Hillary rustled through the box.

"When did he give her the charm?" Hillary asked.

"The night she died," Trey said.

Teddy came to stand nearby and waved to Hillary on the screen.

Hillary was looking between the box and the screen. "Then there won't be mention of it in her journal. She wrote in her journal on mornings. Her journal entries are always about the previous day. Since she was killed at night, she never got the chance to write about the charm the next day. That's why there's no mention of it! No charm in the box either," Hillary confirmed, disappointment coloring her words. "We'll keep looking, though."

"Damn," Trey muttered, rubbing his chin thoughtfully. "That makes sense, but it still doesn't explain where the charm is now."

"Weird, right?" Teddy said.

"Maybe." Trey was starting to let his imagination about the charm run away with all sorts of possibilities.

"What are you all doing?" Hillary asked.

"Lucas sent us a bunch of people to check out. We're doing that."

"Dead people?" Hillary looked horrified.

Teddy came close to the phone. "Dead people's autopsy reports, not the actual people."

Hillary blew out a breath, sounding relieved. "I don't know what I though—"

"Anyone heard from Elliot?" Seema asked.

"She texted and said she was doing something with Madden. I'm guessing it has to do with her parents' case. She said she'd reach out if she needed anything." Trey had the sudden urge to check in on Elliot. She'd been silent for a long time.

"If you learn anything, let us know," Seema said. "We're almost there."

"Will do, and you all do the same." Trey waved and disconnected. His gaze met Teddy's across the room. "The case of the missing good luck charm."

Teddy chuckled. "And the case of the absent friend."

Trey rubbed his hand down his face. There was no denying he was worried.

Teddy continued, "Elliot's going to be okay. She's smart and a good advocate for herself. She'll reach out if she needs help. For now, all we can do is focus on these autopsies."

"True that." Trey picked up his pile and worked on sorting the rest of the papers. He was ready to dive into the world of the deceased. His mind struck a thought. "Hey, did you check the homeless guy? What if the charm was with her scooter?"

Teddy said, "That was the first path I went on. It wasn't listed on the inventory of the scooter, and it wasn't listed in Howie Middleman's inventory of possession in his tent or on his person."

"Dang it," Trey said and went back to his papers.

When they were done, Teddy stood at the head of the table with a notepad, pencil, and highlighter. "We're gonna do this the old-fashioned way." He picked up the top paper off one stack and showed it to Trey. "I showed you this earlier. I think we start here. It'll give us cause of death and other info. I think we start looking for common threads. You want to read or write?" He waved the notepad.

"Write. I think you'll pick up on common things before me."

Teddy handed him the notepad and pencil then went to

gather all the top sheets. Trey stood at the end of a table and waited for Teddy to start.

"Okay," Teddy said. "Cause of death is where I'm starting. We have heart failure, myocardial infarction—that's a heart attack, overdose, heart failure, suicide." Teddy looked up at Trey and raised a brow. "That was unexpected. And the last is stroke."

Trey waited for Teddy to make a smart observation about these causes of death, but he didn't. He just continued to scan the page. "Everyone was between twenty-five and forty-five, mostly male but two females." He straightened and looked between the pages.

"What?" Trey asked. "What did you find?"

Teddy looked up. "None of these people had next of kin. The state buried them."

"Is that uncommon?" Trey wasn't sure.

"I really don't know. I'm going to research it."

"But maybe the connection is more that they were all residents at that facility?" Trey asked.

"Depends on what payor system the facility used. If they take state insurance or those with no insurance, that would explain some of the indigent care patients."

"Blah blah blah. I don't know what any of that means," Trey said.

"It means this could mean something or might mean nothing. Just like the charm." Teddy tossed the papers on the table.

"We sure are going nowhere fast," Trey said. "Let's keep going, and maybe we'll find something concrete."

Teddy's and Trey's phones chimed simultaneously. A text from Lucas to the team:

Meet up tomorrow 8 a.m. Want to show what I found.

TEDDY

Works for me.

TREY

I can be there.

HILLARY

Seema and I can try. Depends on when we get out of Port T.

Elliot did not respond, which only increased Trey's apprehension and his worry that something bad had happened to Elliot.

Teddy met Trey's gaze. "Why don't you go look for Elliot? Just do a welfare check. Maybe I'm just being jumpy because of all this, but I'd feel better if we had eyes on her."

"Agreed," Trey said.

"In the meantime, I'll keep digging. The more we know, the more we can share tomorrow too."

"True that." Trey set the notepad down.

It was then that both young men heard a faint noise in the distance—the unmistakable sound of footsteps echoing through the morgue's empty halls. Trey and Teddy exchanged a look, their hearts pounding in unison as they prepared themselves for whatever might come next.

30

"Dude! Think it's your boss?" Trey whispered urgently. He glanced nervously over his shoulder in the direction from where the noise had come. "Maybe I should hide or something. Don't want to get you into trouble for having me here."

Teddy hesitated, uncertain. The hour was getting late, and there was no reason anyone would be skulking around the morgue. If it was Dr. Franks, she would've just walked right in, no need for secrecy. Teddy found the ME to be a reasonable and intelligent woman. She wouldn't get upset about Trey's presence.

What unnerved Teddy was the slow shuffle of the gait of the person moving toward them. As if they were waiting after each step, waiting to see if their presence had become known. Whoever it was had entered from the ambulance bay where there was little camera coverage.

Finally, Teddy made a decision. "You wait in the office. Leave the light on. Anyone familiar with this department has to know someone is here, so hopefully, they'll think you are

that someone and supposed to be here. Unlike this person." Teddy jerked his thumb in the direction of the doors. "I don't think this person is supposed to be here. Or wants anyone to know they're here. And I want to know why."

"I ain't leaving you hanging," Trey insisted.

"I'm going to dim the lights and wait here, behind this table." He moved to get behind a rolling table that was pushed against the wall. "I'll use it as a weapon if I have to. You being out of sight will give us an advantage. They'll think you are me and probably leave you alone."

Trey hesitated. A second scuffle of a foot sliding against the floor came from outside the door. Whoever was out there paused as quickly as the sound had been made.

Teddy flicked his hand to the office then reached for the light switch, shutting off the bright overheads. "Sit at the desk or something, so they can see your shadow."

"Sit at the desk? Make me feel like a sitting duck," Trey whispered.

Teddy waved for him to go.

"Easy for you to say. You won't be the target. You're the surprise," Trey mumbled then bolted quietly for the office. He slipped inside without a sound. A few seconds later, he came back to the doorway holding the lid to an old metal trash can and scissors.

Teddy gave him a thumbs-up. Trey disappeared back into the office, and his shadow grew large as he moved toward the blind-covered window. He turned them slightly to block anyone's view from seeing in but threw some light in the big room, giving Teddy an advantage. He scanned the space for the darkest parts, tucked himself into one, and pulled a rolling table laden with surgical implements in front of him, ready to shove it at the intruder.

He made a mental note to thank Trey later for adjusting the blinds. The person coming in the morgue knew someone was there but didn't want anyone to know they were. Trey being in the office offered a false sense of security. Trey turning up the blinds provided just that.

With a deep breath to calm his hammering heart, Teddy waited, straining to listen. What seemed like an eternity passed before the soft creak of a door hinge pierced the silence. Adrenaline surged through Teddy's veins as he prepared for action, heart pounding in anticipation. Had Trey not come to help him, he'd be there alone, faced with no one to cover his six and likely caught off guard while he worked in the office.

If the person's intentions were nefarious.

Teddy had to think they were.

The tension was palpable, each second stretching into infinity as he waited for the intruder to reveal themselves.

Logically, Teddy knew what the Campus Murder Club was doing—looking into Jaime's case—could be dangerous. But he'd done the math to figure out the odds, and they weren't worrisome. Begrudgingly, he admitted something in that moment he'd refused to admit when he'd looked at the stats. That the unknown of one data point, the identity of the killer, and their unpredictability made his stats useless.

The double doors to the autopsy room creaked open, casting a thin sliver of light into the darkness. Teddy's grip tightened on the edge of the rolling table, his heart pounding in his ears. He sensed more than saw the tall, slender figure slip inside, pause briefly, then scurry toward the far office that belonged to Brian Lyman, the day shift assistant.

Adrenaline coursed through Teddy's veins. In one breath he decided to follow the intruder and was in motion.

Teddy crept quietly to the office and stood to the side of the office window. He wanted to verify who he believed to have come in. Though why Lyman felt the need to creep in was beyond Teddy.

He inched toward the ledge of the window, trying to peek in. He caught a glimpse of the tall man who was going through the desk drawers and pulling out handfuls of items haphazardly.

Teddy turned to get Trey's attention, only to find the athlete quietly padding toward him, a trash can lid in one hand, a pair of scissors in the other.

"Who is it?" Trey whispered. He did the same as Teddy by peeking in the window. "Is he stealing stuff? What the hell?"

"That's Brian Lyman. He's the ME's assistant, day shift. He's the one who called in sick today."

Trey looked back into the window, keeping to the shadows. "He don't look sick to me."

"Me either."

"And it looks like he's stealing stuff. What do you think about that?"

Teddy gestured for Trey to follow him. They moved to stand back by the ME's office and the rolling autopsy table. "He knows someone is supposed to be here, so why didn't he tell me he was here? I wouldn't have thought anything of it."

"He doesn't want you to know he's here."

"Precisely." Teddy pointed at Trey. "I say we give him a little scare like he gave us."

"And then we ask him what he's doing?"

"For sure." Teddy pointed to the light switch. "Feel like being a dead man?" He patted the table. "I'm thinking of

rolling you in front of his office door nice and slow. Spook him a little bit."

Trey handed Teddy his lid and scissors and climbed on the table. "I like how you think."

Once Trey was on the table, belly-up, Teddy draped the white sheet over him.

"Should I hold my breath?" Trey asked.

"No, just don't do any big breaths. He won't be looking. I'm going to roll you and then dash into the office. I'll watch through the blinds. Take these just in case." He put the scissors Trey had been carrying on the table next to Trey's hand.

"Well, I don't like that. Now I'm kinda spooked."

"I said just in case." Teddy looked between Trey and the office, worried Lyman would come out at any minute.

"Why does there even have to be a 'just in case'?" Trey said then pulled the sheet over his head.

Teddy made sure the brakes were unlocked and gave a slight shove, using enough momentum to send the table where he wanted it but not so much it would speed by the door. As an added bonus Teddy hadn't even thought about, one of the wheels squeaked. So as Trey and the table rolled toward Lyman's office, an eerie *squeak, squeak* filled the space.

Teddy chuckled as he dashed for the ME's office and tried to position himself so he could watch but not give anything away.

Trey and the table cruised past the office at a speed so slow but steady, it looked as if a ghost was pushing it. Or an invisible person.

A moment after Trey went past the office, Lyman came to stand in the doorway. He looked at the table then reached across the nearby wall toward the next office and flicked the

light switch. The autopsy room was flooded with light. Lyman looked around.

Teddy took that as his cue. He, too, moved to stand in the doorway, snagging a file folder off the desk as he went.

"Hey, what are you doing here? I didn't hear you come in," Teddy said.

"Uh, hey, Teddy," Lyman stammered, clearly caught off guard. "I was just grabbing some stuff I forgot at the office, man. Did you see that, the table that rolled by?"

Teddy laughed. "Tables don't roll on their own. You're losing it. Must be the fever or your cold or something playing tricks on you."

Lyman looked at Trey and the table. "Someone came in?"

Teddy nodded, and because he and Trey had been neck-deep in the files Lucas had sent, he went with what was on the top of his head. "Young guy from the skilled nursing here. I was trying to track down family, but looks like there isn't any. Poor guy. And to make things worse I forgot to put him on ice. Whoops." Teddy grimaced. "Don't tell the doc."

Lyman appeared to pale slightly. He studied the table more. "Did he, uh—" He cleared his throat a few times. "I mean, is he an organ donor?"

Teddy opened the folder and pretended to scan some papers that weren't inside. "Nope."

Lyman visibly relaxed. "Want me to help you get him in the freezer?"

"Nah, I got it." Teddy made his way to the table, looking into what he could see of Lyman's office as he passed. "Dude, are you quitting or something?" With his chin, he gestured to the box on Lyman's desk and the scattered mess of papers all around. "Because it looks like you're cleaning house. Consid-

ering that you're here when you called in sick." Teddy stood by the table and blocked Lyman's view of Trey's chest, just in case Trey did take a deep breath.

Lyman slumped against the doorjamb. "Listen, I called in because I had an interview for another job. And it's panning out."

"So you're just going to up and leave without notice?" Teddy didn't like guys who reneged on responsibility. Guys who took everything for granted. That Lyman could walk away from a job without so much as a "thank you very much" was despicable.

"Sure, why not?" Lyman sighed, casting a nervous glance toward the exit before continuing. "I've been thinking about quitting for a while now."

"And you come in after hours to get your stuff?"

"I was packing my stuff. So what? Tonight just felt like the right time to make a clean break."

Teddy eyed him suspiciously, taking note of Lyman's flushed cheeks and the way he avoided making eye contact. Something wasn't adding up, but Teddy couldn't quite put his finger on it.

"You better get going then." Teddy gestured to Lyman's office.

Lyman hesitated a moment, then scurried into his office, closing the door behind him. Teddy wheeled the table toward the freezers, working to keep his body in front of Trey in case Lyman was watching.

"It's gonna be cold for a minute," Teddy said in a hushed voice.

"Oh no, you ain't," Trey whispered. "You are not putting me in that freezer thing. No fucking way."

"Relax, I'm not. I'm just going to open the door and act

like I'm putting you in there. I need to see if he's watching us first, though."

Trey grumbled something about a prank gone too far.

Teddy moved to the freezer and opened the door, the entire time keeping his eyes on Lyman's window. From behind the blinds, Teddy could tell Lyman was moving around the room quickly. Teddy whipped the sheet off Trey. "Move! Go to the ME's office."

Trey sprang from the table and dashed to the office faster than light.

Teddy moved the table and slammed the freezer door. He wheeled the table to the cleaning station.

Lyman's door opened, and he flicked his office light off. He came into the large room.

"I can't ask you not to say anything, but I'd appreciate it if you wouldn't." Lyman was carrying a large banker's box. He moved to stand by the table where Teddy and Trey had spread out the reports of the autopsies Lucas had requested.

"It's an awkward position you're putting me in," Teddy said.

Lyman put his box on the table and stared at Teddy. "That's fair. I just ... it's just sometimes too much here. Like I was starting to think death was stalking me, that it was everywhere. Know what I mean?"

"I have schizophrenia, so yeah. I might have an understanding of what you're talking about." Teddy was typically a sympathetic person, but Brian Lyman rubbed him wrong, and he couldn't muster sympathy for him.

"What's all this?" Lyman asked as he flipped through a few pages, then scanned down the row of reports.

"Copies that have to be purged. Just making sure the digital versions are all online," Teddy said.

"Did you pull these?"

Something about Lyman's tone made Teddy uncomfortable. He'd once read a book about instinct and trusting it and currently his instinct was sending out alarms.

"No," he lied. "Why would I need reports?"

Lyman stared at him, holding one page in his hand. After several heartbeats, Lyman put the paper down and picked up his box. "I guess you wouldn't need them." With a nod of his head, Lyman turned on his heel and left the morgue.

Teddy waited several beats, straining to hear Lyman's footsteps move down the hall, half-expecting him to suddenly come back in. After waiting more than five minutes, he turned toward the office, and Trey was standing in the doorway.

"That dude is weird," Trey said. "Something was off about him."

"Maybe. Or maybe we're just super paranoid. But I figured something out," Teddy said.

"What's that?"

Teddy gestured to the papers on the table behind him. "What these autopsies have in common."

31

Seema and Hillary made it to Port Angeles before twilight. They discussed going to the restaurant to find Oliver or Taylor first, but Hillary was apprehensive about leaving the box alone in the car. She just had a bad feeling she couldn't shake.

Thankfully, Seema didn't give her a hard time about it. Just drove to the Lightners and even got out of the car with her.

"What?" Seema asked when she caught Hillary's puzzled look.

"I guess I thought maybe you'd just sit in the car with it idling. I know you're in a hurry to get to the restaurant."

"I still have enough time to say hi to the Lightners." Seema gestured for Hillary to precede her up the walk.

"You like them, don't you? Everyone likes them. It's okay. I'm glad you no longer think they're responsible." Hillary tried to keep the "I told you so" out of her voice.

"Don't get ahead of yourself. One thing I learned from my dad is there are always surprises around the corner."

But Hillary could tell Seema didn't believe the Lightners were going to turn out rotten.

Before they reached the door, Mrs. Lightner flung it open. "Hello, I saw you on the Ring camera, and I was surprised to see you so soon." She opened her arms to hug them both.

"We know how much Jaime's things mean to you all, and we wanted to return them sooner rather than later," Hillary said.

Mr. Lightner came out from behind his wife and took the box. "Did you find anything helpful?"

Mrs. Lightner ushered the girls inside.

Seema said, "We may have a few leads. A guy who worked with Jaime thinks he might be able to add context to a few things in the journal. We're meeting with him tomorrow morning."

"Can I get either of you a drink?" Mrs. Lightner offered.

"We're not staying long. Seema wants to go to Taylor's restaurant and talk to her or see if Oliver is there." Hillary plopped onto the couch.

"We can save you a trip then," Mr. Lightner said. "I just saw Taylor and Oliver down at the pavilion on the pier. Kami Shipley is having an engagement party there. I popped by for a bit. Just got home, in fact."

"So you think they're still down there?" Hillary asked.

"Yeah, the party was just getting started when I left. No one wants their guidance counselor around for a party. So I did my due diligence and left."

Hillary wagged her finger at Seema. "I am not crashing that party."

"We'll see." Seema gave her a coy smile.

Hillary rolled her eyes and, in doing so, caught the large

Texas star that was over the Lightners' fireplace. She'd paid it no attention the last time she was there. The star had resided there forever.

Hillary pointed to the star. "Do you know anything about a charm Jaime had? It was a star. Looked kinda like that but had large white Swarovski stones in the center?"

Mrs. Lightner shook her head.

Mr. Lightner paused and stared at Hillary.

"What?" she asked.

"I think I've seen something like that, but I'm trying to place where. I don't think it was Jaime's. I don't remember anything about a charm. She was very cautious with how she spent her money."

"It was a gift," Seema said. "And we didn't expect you to know anything about it. We were just hoping."

"A gift, hmm. From Oliver?" Mrs. Lightner's brows rose.

Hillary shook her head. "A coworker."

"That's interesting," Mrs. Lightner said.

"Why do you say that?" Seema asked, sitting next to Hillary on the couch.

"Because Jaime knew Oliver was very possessive. He's a very insecure person. Jaime knew this. He wants to achieve, wants to do right, but his pride can get in the way. I'm surprised she would take a gift from someone else."

Mr. Lightner snapped his fingers. "I got it. I think I saw something like what you're describing on a necklace. Oliver was wearing it. I thought it was a little feminine, but you know how guys will wear something from their girl. I assumed it was Taylor's."

Seema popped up. "Are you sure?"

"Well, not one hundred percent but at least seventy-

five," Mr. Lightner said. "What's the significance of this charm?"

Seema shook her head. "Maybe nothing, but it's missing from her stuff. It's not listed anywhere, and she could have lost it, but we thought we'd try to find it, just in case." She shared a knowing look with Hillary, who stood as well.

"I guess we're crashing a party," Hillary said with dread.

Seema laughed. "It'll be fun."

"Doubtful."

They thanked the Lightners, promised to fill them in if they learned anything, also promised to be careful, then made their way to Seema's car.

"Thanks for not telling them that if Oliver does have the charm, it means he could be Jaime's killer." Hillary pulled the seat belt over her.

"I couldn't do that to them. It's going to hurt soon enough." Seema started her Subaru. "Care to scroll through pictures again?" Looking specifically for the charm was going to be far easier than searching photos with no goal in mind.

"Good idea." Hillary plugged in directions to the pavilion on Seema's phone, then pulled out her phone and started with Facebook then moved to Instagram. She had better access there, as Taylor followed her @DancingQueen account. She was thumbing through several pictures on Taylor's account, all ones she'd seen before, when she found one of them at La Push Beach. Taylor had taken a selfie of herself and Oliver. His shirt was open, and something silver rested against his chest. It looked to be a chain of some sort. When Hillary zoomed in, she could tell it was a necklace. She followed the chain to the end, looking for a charm.

Hillary gasped. She closed Instagram and pulled up the text from Trey with the image Lucas had sent. Though what

she'd seen on Taylor's post hadn't been the clearest due to the zooming in, the shape was unmistakable.

Seema was glancing madly between Hillary and the road. "What? What did you find?"

Hillary looked at her. "The charm. He's wearing it on a necklace. It matches the picture from Lucas." Hillary thought her expression must looked as horrified as she felt because Seema immediately pulled the car over into a parking lot.

"Okay, let's think this through. How did Oliver get the charm?"

"You tell me because I only have one way in mind, and it's awful," Hillary said. "How could he do it?" Tears pooled in her eyes. "They were together for years. Who would he be without her? Jaime ... she ... she..." Hillary buried her face in her hands and let the tears flow.

"Maybe it was jealousy or an accident?"

Hillary looked up. "He strangled her."

"Crime of passion. Didn't he have an alibi?" Seema was scrolling through her phone.

Hillary used the hem of her shirt to dry her eyes while waiting, knowing Seema was checking into Oliver's alibi. "It says his mother is his alibi. She said he was in a lot of pain that night after therapy and went to bed early. She checked on him before turning in at eleven, and he was in bed. That would make it hard for him to be in Vancouver around the time of death. Maybe he could have done it if he left right after his mom checked on him. And drove like a maniac."

"Don't forget," Seema said. "My dad likes to hammer this point. It's about context. Did she go in the room and actually see him asleep in bed? Or did she look in, see a lump, and assume?"

Hillary grimaced and let her head drop on the back of the seat. "So what now? We can't just storm the party and demand he show us the charm. He'll run, I bet."

Seema said, "Yeah, we need to draw him out. If he is wearing the charm, we need to get him arrested. What if I ask him to meet me outside, and I start a scene? I could try to get him worked up. You saw how he reacted to Elliot. We could use that."

"What if he attacks you? Am I enough to stop him? Nope. That's not the best plan."

"Do you have any ideas?"

Hillary looked down at her phone with the Instagram page pulled up. "Yeah, I do actually."

She toggled to her account, then got out of the car. From her backpack in the back seat, she pulled out her bedazzled ball cap and stuck it on the ground next to her shoes. She snapped a picture and added the text: *Flash dance with me at Port Angeles Pier parking lot. 45 minutes. B there or B Square.*

She posted the photo and invite then looked across the parking lot at the large box store. She got in the car. "We need to go there. I need speakers."

"What are you doing?"

"I'm drawing them out. If we see he's wearing the charm, I'll cause a scene, and you'll call the police. If he's not wearing the charm—"

"We'll have to regroup. You're right. How are you going to draw them out?"

"You'll see."

Thirty-five minutes later, they were at the peer parking lot. A small group of people were gathering. Hillary scanned the crowd for Taylor, hoping she had notifications on and

had been alerted to the impromptu dance. She pulled her hair back into a ponytail and pulled the ball cap low over her eyes, hiding a large portion of her face. From her backpack she pulled out a new hoodie that had been sent to her from a sponsor. Hillary pulled it on and zipped it.

"Here, take a picture of me from the back with this hoodie." She handed Seema her phone.

"What the fuck is happening?" Seema asked, laughing slightly, though she did as Hillary asked.

Hillary posted the image to her account, Seema watching over her shoulder.

"Wait, you're Dancing Queen? You have, like, thousands of subscribers."

"Half a million to be exact, and I've been working on a new dance. One I think will work for this event."

"Holy shit," Seema said. "I'm impressed. I had you all wrong. I'm sorry."

"That's okay. Most people have me wrong at first. But this alter ego pays for college and is changing my life. And I like the anonymity."

Seema smiled. "What do you want me to do?"

"When I give you the signal, start the music. I'll start to dance. You look for Taylor and Oliver. She's a big fan. See if you can see the charm."

Seema chuckled. "Okay. She's going to shit her pants when she learns it's you." She wagged her brows. She reached into her trunk and pulled out her bat. "Just in case."

"Yeah, that part makes me sad." Hillary pulled the cap down lower and checked her watch. "Game time."

She handed Seema her phone with the song pulled up then took the speakers with her as she walked to the parking lot.

A few people screamed with excitement. Hillary kept her head down while she planted the speakers on opposite sides then moved to stand between them. She gave Seema a look to let her know she was ready. Seema pointed to a section of the crowd. Hillary glanced in that direction and saw Oliver and Taylor. She looked back at Seema, caught her eye, then nodded once. The signal to start the music.

Seconds later, Madonna's "Lucky Star" dance remix began to play, and Hillary started to dance. All her moves repeated, which was what made her so popular. She would do the sequence twice, and by then, most people could pick up on the moves. Tonight was no exception. By the third round of moves, people were joining her. They were laughing and cheering and singing along to the music.

Taylor dragged Oliver into the mix and was dancing not more than ten feet away. Hillary danced as Seema moved through the crowd, trying to do the moves occasionally so as to not stand out. Hillary's heart raced as she knew they would only have seconds when the song ended. At the last beat Hillary dipped and bowed. People cheered and chanted for more. Hillary looked up and saw Seema pointing at Oliver, poking him in the chest. His face was red, his hands fisted. Seema clutched the bat but didn't raise it. Hillary knew doing so would trigger Oliver more. Seema shifted the bat to her other hand, and that caught Oliver's attention. He grabbed for the bat, trying to wrench it from her. They struggled against each other.

Hillary called 911.

"What is your emergency?" the woman asked calmly.

In a feigned frightened and breathy voice, Hillary said, "I'm down at the pier, and there was a dancing flash mob, but things have gotten out of control. Two people just started

fighting, and one of them has a knife. Another has a bat. Please hurry." She made up the knife because she knew she needed something urgent to spur on the cops. Then Hillary pushed through the crowd, trying to get to Seema. Oliver was in her face. He had the bat in one hand and was pushing it into Seema's chest, while his other hand held her in place by gripping her arm tightly. Taylor was trying to calm him down. Seema was wincing in pain.

"Gun!" Hillary exclaimed. As expected, people screamed and scurried. When Oliver looked in her direction, surprised, Hillary launched herself at him. Using all the muscles in her legs, built up from dancing the last few years, she flew up in the air and spread her arms out wide like a sugar glider. When she came down, she took the three of them down with her in a heap of tangled limbs and cuss words.

32

Trey left the morgue at Teddy's behest, but he wasn't happy about it. He worried that twitchy Lyman guy might come back. Teddy had put some pieces together, and that other morgue dude's name was all over the paperwork. Trey knew desperate people did desperate things, and Lyman looked desperate. Nope, Trey didn't like it at all. But Teddy had proven crafty when Lyman had come the first time, and he was on heightened alert now.

The plan was for Trey to hurry and check on Elliot and then get back to the land of the dead. Yuck. If someone had told him he would go to college and spend the night in a morgue, he would have laughed himself witless. Yet there he was, hanging with the dead. Life was stranger than fiction.

He whipped his Honda into Elliot's apartment parking lot and was about to turn off the engine when he glanced at her apartment and saw the shadows of what he thought to be tall, beefy men moving around. All her lights were off, but they were using flashlights. He called Elliot's phone, but she

didn't answer. What if she was in there? He should try to find out. Yet he would need backup if she was, and Teddy couldn't leave the morgue. Lucas was at work, and Seema and Hillary were over three hours away.

Tapping his hands on his steering wheel, he recalled the last thing Elliot told him. She was with Madden.

Madden. Trey would go get his help, and maybe if he was lucky, Elliot would still be there.

Like a bat out of hell, Trey pulled out of the parking lot and drove the ten minutes to the police station, barely tapping the brakes. He found a spot close to the front door and jogged up to the door. The evening was over, and night had settled on the city. Trey did not want Elliot to go home alone and get ambushed by those intruders. Trey did not want Teddy to be alone. Trey felt overwhelmed. He didn't like the feeling at all. He flung the front glass door open and rushed in. Madden was standing there talking to another cop Trey didn't recognize.

"Whoa," Madden said. "What's wrong? Are you okay?"

Trey shifted nervously on his feet. "I was looking for Elliot Long. I was at her house, and there are some dudes in her apartment. They're moving around with flashlights. Looked suspicious as hell."

"Did you call it in?" Madden asked, his lips twitching.

Trey wanted to smack himself upside the head. "I didn't even think of that. I just came straight here."

"That's good. Less paperwork I have to do." He turned to the cop he was chatting with. "Excuse us for a second, Tom. Trey, come with me." He gestured for Trey to follow him.

"Did you hear what I said about Elliot's place?" Trey's worry was turning into frustration.

"I did, and I will let her explain everything. She's back here."

That shut Trey right up. He followed Madden to the back. The cop led him to the interview rooms and gestured to one with the door open.

"She's in there," Madden said.

Trey moved to look inside the door. Elliot was at the table sitting next to a tall woman in a business suit. Elliot had an assortment of Chinese takeout in front of her and was talking while the lady wrote on a yellow legal pad.

"Hey, Trey." Elliot waved vigorously. "What are you doing here?"

"I came to see you. I have things to tell you. I was at your house, and there were some dudes in your apartment. It's not safe to go there. What's going on here?" He looked from Elliot to Madden.

"Not safe yet," the woman said.

"Those guys are my protective detail." Elliot waved her hand as if she were trying to erase her words. "Let me back up. Earlier today, Madden called me and told me to come down to that same rehab center where you and I met that nurse, Aaron." She waited for Trey to acknowledge that he knew what she was talking about before she continued.

"Well, Bryce Zimmerman now has what is called an augmentative communication device. It's his voice. And when asked who shot him, he named my brother."

Trey's mouth dropped open. "The fuck? Really? That's crazy. I mean, your brother is an asshole, but a killer?"

Madden stepped up to the door. "Let's pause this a second. They're coming out of the interview room."

Everyone went silent. Trey, not knowing what was going on, looked from person to person. The door across the way

opened, and his teammate Elijah Peters came out. Two detectives followed. Elijah was red faced like he'd been crying. It wasn't until the two cops took Elijah out of the interview space and exited through another door that Madden spoke.

"He confessed that he can't recall if Nathan was at the gym that night. Just that he was supposed to be there. But it wasn't unlike Nathan to be at the weight room but not working out. Instead, he'd be in one of the small spaces with a girl. Elijah said he assumed that was where Nathan was. He doesn't believe Nathan could have done this, and he was adamant about Nathan being at the gym that night because he thought Nathan was being framed because he was going to be famous."

Elliot rolled her eyes.

Trey was stunned. "You mean Nathan really might have done this?"

Elliot blew out a slow breath. "I'm afraid so. You remember me telling you he and Bryce were trying steroids? He was just as mood swingy, and he was very angry with my parents because they didn't want him to take the big contract. They'd had a huge fight that morning, and my dad said they needed to talk some more. Nathan was furious. He said it was all decided, and Dad threatened to go over Nathan's head."

"Holy shit." Trey pulled out a chair and sank into it. He scrubbed his hands down his face.

"Right now, the police are trying to build a case, but my lawyer"—she gestured to the woman—"thinks I need to have protection. Apparently, Nathan has been tipped off. We don't know how. But he's coming to town. He has a game, remember? The cops are short staffed and stretched thin,

and you know how I feel about them." She gave Madden a look, but there was a hint of teasing in it. "Rebecca, my lawyer, knows a top-notch security expert in Seattle, and he's sent men down to set up a protection detail. Those are the people you saw in my apartment. They're checking my apartment out and will fortify it. Until then, I'm in a hotel, and I have a bodyguard from now on. I put one on the Zimmermans too. Bryce is not safe until Nathan is arrested."

Trey was stunned. He didn't really know what he expected when he'd come to the station, but it wasn't this. For a moment, he had forgotten they all had lives and histories outside the Campus Murder Club.

Elliot took the seat next to him and put her hand on his arm. "I'm sorry. I just threw a lot at you. And about someone you know."

Trey shook his head. "It's just been a night of curveballs, to be honest. And speaking of that I should get back to Teddy. You're busy here and clearly have a lot to do. Just let me know when you can hang."

"What's going on with the other thing? You've learned something, haven't you?"

Trey looked from the lawyer to Madden. "Not much. We're meeting with Lucas in the morning at the coffee shop off 99th. If you can make it. Early. Seven thirty."

Elliot went to say something, but her phone rang. "Sorry I didn't answer any of your calls. We were deep in dealing with things here." She glanced at the screen, then showed it to Trey. Hillary's name was listed. "But now I can get this one." She accepted the call and put the phone to her ear.

"Hey, how's it going?"

For a person who just learned her brother might be a killer, Elliot was handling it well. Yeah, she likely cried her

heart out—her red-rimmed eyes gave that away—but she was moving off shock and into anger, if Trey was reading her correctly.

"Wait, what? Say that again?" She held the phone away and pressed speaker.

Hillary's voice came through in a rush. "We've been arrested in Port Angeles. But don't worry, Seema called her dad. He's on his way to straighten it out. But I'm calling because Oliver was arrested too! He's wearing the star charm. If you go on Instagram to @DancingQueen, you'll see it all play out in video." Hillary laughed. "Sorry, I'm just so blown away with how things have turned out. We caught him, Elliot! We caught Jaime's killer!"

Elliot met Trey's gaze. Her mouth fell open. Madden stepped into the room.

"Are you sure?" Elliot asked.

"Oh yeah. He's singing like a canary. That's a saying, right? Anyway, you should tell that cop, the one who interviewed us the first night. He's the nicer of the two. But tell them to contact the PD out here."

"I'm speechless," Elliot said.

"We did it, Elliot. We did it! We caught him. He's saying how he drove down to Vancouver late that night and snuck in through her window. He's saying she was with some other guy—like on a date—and he saw her get dropped off. He said he confronted her, they fought, and he just lost control of himself. He's blaming the meds he was on. And he's crying like a big old crybaby. Seema said it's kinda sad."

"Do you need me to do anything? Are you both okay?"

"Oh yeah. But I have to go. You were my one call. Tell others, will you?"

"Sure. In fact, Trey is here, and he just heard the whole

thing, which is good because I think I'm so shocked I might forget what you told me."

"Well, watch the videos. You'll see it all!" She laughed again. "We'll be home in a few hours, I think. We'll let you know, and we can meet up."

"If you're back in town by seven thirty tomorrow, don't forget we're meeting Lucas at the coffee shop on Highway 99. We can celebrate," Trey said.

"You bet." There was some commotion happening through the phone. Hillary said, "I have to go. Others need to use the phone. See ya soon." Hillary didn't wait for a goodbye before disconnecting.

Trey didn't know what to say. A smile spread across his face.

Madden leaned over the table. "Wait a sec. Are you two telling me that night you got that box and I asked if you were going to pursue this and every one of you said no, that was a lie?"

Elliot smiled. "I'll have to ask my lawyer if I should answer that question."

"Does it matter?" Trey asked. "Hillary said Oliver confessed. And he was wearing the star charm. Jaime got that charm the night she died. How did he get it if he wasn't with her?"

Madden held up one finger. "That's a separate issue. I'm going to go call the Port Angeles police and find out what's going on. Then we're going to have a talk about you all and this club."

"Do you want to do all that before or after you watch the videos?" Elliot pulled up her Instagram account and found the account Hillary had mentioned.

Madden glared at her but waited for her to start the video.

Captured on video was an unbelievable act of bravery by Hillary.

"Dang, that girl can dance," Trey said more than once, his voice booming with pride. "And she's got some vertical jump skills. She's badass."

They'd done it. They'd found Jaime's killer.

33

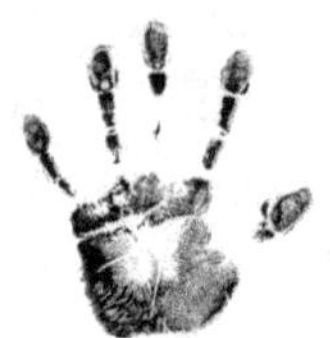

Lindsay slid the cup of Americano across the table to Lucas. "You're exhausted, so remind me again why we're here. If they caught Jaime's killer, then what's the point of this?"

"To celebrate? Besides, I think Jaime was on to something, and maybe we should see it through. I dunno. That could be adrenaline talking. The more I say this out loud, the more I think I should take these documents to the police and let it go." He tapped the folder on the table between them.

Lindsay threw up her hands in mock praise. "Hallelujah. Now you're saying all the words I want to hear."

He grabbed her hand and squeezed it. "You know I love you, right? You're my best friend."

She leaned across the table and kissed his cheek. "I know. I love you too. You're my best friend too."

"Mostly because your parents hate it though, right?"

"Nah, that was in the beginning, but you've grown on me. If they started liking you tomorrow, it wouldn't change

how I feel at all." She grinned, then dumped a pack of sugar in her coffee.

"Hey, I saw a great beach resort in Fiji I thought we might consider." He patted his pockets, looking for his phone. "Did I bring my phone in?"

Lindsay looked under the papers on the table. "You probably left it in the car. That's how tired you are."

"I couldn't sleep if I wanted to." The relief that came with knowing Jaime's killer had been apprehended made Lucas exuberant.

And that Oliver confessed and was in police custody gave Lucas a sense of closure he hadn't even known he needed. And to think, it was the charm he had given Jaime that was the nail in Oliver's coffin. Lucas couldn't help but think that was Jaime working from beyond the grave. Man, he missed her. She'd been a fling, sure. A way to see if he and Lindsay should be together. He knew not all high school sweethearts were meant to go the distance. But whatever their romantic future held, he knew Lindsay would be his friend forever. They had something special. Maybe he and Jaime would have had the same kind of long-lasting friendship, too, had she lived.

"I'm going to go to the car and get my phone. I want to show you this place."

"Let's look it up here." She put her phone on the table.

Lucas shook his head. "They don't have a website. One of the nurses told me about it and sent me pictures. It's private and small. It exists solely on word of mouth."

"It sounds amazing." She handed him the keys.

"Be right back." He stood and took a large sip of coffee. As he set his cup down, he winked, then dashed off.

He fast walked out of the coffee shop and onto the side-

walk. Traffic was picking up for the morning rush, and he caught a wave of baked bread and hot meat from the fast-food restaurant next door.

"Hey, Lucas," a voice called from behind him.

He glanced over his shoulder to find Teddy and Trey walking toward him and the coffee shop.

"Hey." He waved. "Lindsay is inside. I'm running to the car to grab my phone. I'll be right back."

Teddy waved a folder in the air. "Wait till you see what I found."

Lucas gave him a thumbs-up and a wide, happy grin. Today was a great day.

He looked both ways then dashed into the road to cross to the other side of the street where Lindsay had parallel parked.

He reached the car, jogged to the passenger side, and whipped open the door. Sure enough, his phone was there on the passenger's side floor. Snatching it up, he slammed the door then went back to the front of the car and checked for traffic, all while stuffing Lindsay's keys in his pocket.

All clear, he stepped into the road. He was halfway across when he heard the screeching of tires and turned to find a car hurtling toward him. The windows were dark, and he couldn't see the driver. For a second, Lucas froze, unsure which direction to run toward. He picked toward the coffee shop.

"Lucas!" Trey hollered.

Lucas sprinted as fast as he could, adrenaline running through his veins. But he couldn't get away from the car as it was swerving toward him instead of away.

Then, impact.

The car hit Lucas with full force, sending him flying.

The sound of bones cracking filled the air. The sickening thud of his body hitting the ground silenced everything else.

From far away, he heard Lindsay scream. He would know her voice anywhere.

His vision blurred, and his body shook as pain radiated through every inch of him.

He tried to move, to get up, to run, but his body refused to cooperate. He could feel the warm stickiness of his own blood seeping through his clothes, and he knew he was dying.

He closed his eyes for a second to regroup. When he opened them, Lindsay was beside him, tears streaming down her face. "Lucas, stay still. Help is on the way."

Teddy came into view. "Lucas, focus on me. Watch my face. I want you to just breathe, nice and steady. I got you." Teddy glanced up at someone standing above him, but Lucas couldn't see who it was. His vision was fading.

"I got pictures of the car." Trey knelt by Teddy. "We got you, Lucas. Everything is going to be okay. We got you."

Lucas tried to nod, but he couldn't move. When he heard the wail of the siren headed toward them, he knew everything was going to be okay.

* * *

Elliot rushed into the hospital and went up three floors to the surgery wing. She found her friends sitting in the waiting room. Hillary and Seema flanked Lindsay, who was sobbing into her shirt.

Elliot didn't know what to say. She took in the shattered expressions on her friends' faces and wanted to weep. Teddy stood and caught Elliot before she could reach the group. He

gestured for her to go back to the hallway, and he followed her out there.

They made sure to be out of Lindsay's sight and hearing.

"Dear lord, Teddy."

"It was awful. Trey and I watched it all. Lindsay too. It was clearly intentional."

"Then we need to go to the police."

"Trey is downstairs talking to a cop now. Trey got pictures. Hopefully, a license plate."

"Do we know anything?" Elliot pressed her palms to her cheeks, trying to stave off the tears. Her mind couldn't wrap around the fact that Lucas had been hit by a car and, if Teddy was right, on purpose.

"No, we probably won't until his parents get here. None of us are family. But it wasn't good. The car was traveling at high speed and didn't stop. He hit the ground hard. I think there are a lot of internal injuries." Teddy stuck his hands in his hair and tugged, stressed. "I can't stop seeing it."

The elevator chimed, and the doors slid open, drawing Teddy's and Elliot's attention. Trey stepped out. He caught sight of them and shuffled over. "Jeez, what a shitty day. Any word?" he asked Teddy.

Teddy shook his head. "What did the police say?"

"They were very thankful considering I have enough good photos to solve their crime."

"You got the license plate?" Teddy asked.

Trey nodded. He looked like he was being held together with duct tape and bubble gum.

Elliot, needing one herself, pulled Trey into a hug. "That was quick thinking."

"He shouldn't have been there. We should have canceled

once we knew Oliver confessed." Trey buried his face in her hair.

"I say stuff like that all the time. You can't do that. It doesn't make it better, and it will eat you up. Someone shouldn't have hit him with a car and left." Elliot rubbed his back.

They held each other for a moment, then broke apart.

"We should go back in there." Elliot gestured to the waiting room.

Teddy sighed with resignation and led the way.

When they entered, Lindsay stood. She looked at Trey. "What do you know?"

"They have a good lead. I got the license plate. They're tracking down the person now."

Lindsay gave his upper arm a soft squeeze, as if to say thanks. As if knowing that justice was on the job gave her peace of mind. She returned to twisting the hem of her shirt. "Hopefully, we'll hear something soon."

Trey stepped to her. "Listen, when you left in the ambulance, I went in the shop and got your stuff. It's in my car. When you're ready I can grab it."

Lindsay whispered, "Thank you." She went to sit back down but stood suddenly. "There was a folder. A manila folder. Did you grab that?"

Trey said, "Yes, and your purse."

Her eyes went wide. "I forgot about my purse."

"I'll go get it now." Trey went to leave.

"Wait," she called. "Grab the folder. Lucas wanted you all to see what was in the folder. And, by God, we are going to do what he wanted while he fights for his life."

"I'll go with you," Teddy said. He and Trey left.

"Can I get you something to drink, Lindsay? Water?" Elliot offered.

"That would be nice, thanks." Lindsay sat, looking a little lost and confused.

Elliot left to get drinks for everyone and came back at the same time Trey and Teddy did. Lindsay took the folder Trey handed her and opened it.

"Last night, Lucas went through the charts and found five patients matching the initials in Jaime's journal. The only thing they had in common was that they died unexpectedly of complications they shouldn't have had."

"And they had no family," Teddy pointed out. "But Trey and I found another link." He pulled a twice-folded manila folder from his back pocket. "This is what I was bringing to show Lucas. All these guys were organ donors. Only I didn't find them on the registry. And another thing in common was that Brian Lyman, the assistant for the medical examiner, was the one who did their paperwork and handled the organ donations. But I can't find where the organs went."

Trey jumped into the conversation. "Last night, Brian Lyman came to the morgue and cleaned out his desk. Told Teddy some lie about getting a new opportunity."

Seema asked, "Do you think it's possible he knew what Lucas found—and what you found, Teddy—and he's why we're here now?"

Teddy pressed two fingers to his temple and winced. "Yeah. He saw these papers out last night. I tried to play it off, and I didn't put the pieces together until after he left. So yeah, it's possible."

"Lucas thought..." Lindsay cleared her throat. "Well Lucas said Jaime believed someone was killing patients at the nursing home, and maybe she was right. And maybe it was

for the organs. Because they all died unexpectedly and from untraceable means."

"Holy shit," Trey said and sank into a chair. "Are we certain Oliver killed her?"

Hillary gave a sad smile. "He confessed. He was all broken up about it."

Seema snorted. "Broken up as much as a demented person could be. He was not in his right mind, sure. Drugged out, jealous, and feeling like a failure while she was succeeding. He made bad choices and not once made a good one, and she paid for them with her life."

Hillary put a hand up, asking them to pause. "Wait, there was something." She squinted as if trying to recall what it was. "Oliver said he saw someone drop Jaime off. A guy. He said she'd been out on a date. He saw a guy drop her off, and it fueled his growing rage. He went on a rant about how she dumped him, how she wouldn't help him with his pain, and that she was washing her hands of him."

"She wasn't on a date because she'd gotten off work earlier. But she and Lucas were fooling around," Lindsay said.

The room went quiet. Seema cleared her throat. Trey took a drink of his Coke.

Lindsay sighed. "It's okay. I knew about it. Lucas and I weren't together. I was dating some guy from my accounting class. He and Jaime weren't dating, per se. But they were sleeping together occasionally."

"That must have been awkward with her living across the hall," Elliot said.

"Actually, no. Jaime and I talked about it. I knew she needed to make a clean break from Oliver but didn't know how. Lucas needed to know I'm the perfect one for him, and

I needed to know the same." Her lip quivered, and a tear rolled down her face. "So we talked about it. My mom is a psychologist. I grew up talking about everything. I made Lucas do the same."

"Did they sleep together that night?" Seema asked.

Lindsay nodded. "That's why he wanted to join your group. He felt responsible. He felt like he should have walked her out or made sure she called an Uber."

"So it was because of the rain that she didn't take her scooter?" Elliot asked. "The camera shows it was there."

"I guess. Lucas said she never came back inside. If she'd called an Uber, she would have typically waited inside."

Seema said, "This makes sense then if we think she caught a ride with someone. A guy, if Oliver is to be believed. That person was already in the parking lot."

"It may not be important, but I'd like to know who that someone was," Trey said.

"Oh, I think it's important," Elliot said. She went to say more but stopped when Madden stepped into the room. He looked grief-stricken.

"Lindsay, Lucas's parents are here. They're down the hall, and the doctor is there. Let me take you to them."

Lindsay stood and wobbled slightly. With a gentle hand on her back, Madden guided her from the room.

Moments later, he returned. Everybody was still in place, looking at the files.

He cleared his throat. "I have the family's permission to share this with you. Lucas passed away a few minutes ago. His injuries were very severe, and he lost a lot of blood. The surgeons did what they could but were unable to save him."

34

Elliot and Trey sat in his car in her apartment building parking lot. Elliot stared up at her apartment.

"You don't have to do this, you know," she said as she fidgeted with the strap on her messenger bag.

"I know I don't have to. I want to. I don't think you should have to do this alone. It's been a freaking awful day already."

They'd left Seema and Hillary at the hospital to be with Lindsay. Teddy went back to the morgue to talk to the ME and to study the files more. The determined look on his face, to find an answer and bring justice to Lucas, had expressed what everyone was feeling.

Trey pointed to the bat resting between Elliot's legs. "Funny how Seema gave you that. I can't imagine she'd part with it so easily."

"Said it was good luck, and I'll take all I can right now." Elliot twisted her hand over the head of the bat. The irony

that she had been given a good luck bat while trying to trap her baseball player brother was not lost on her. She'd taken it mostly because Seema had demanded it.

Elliot would have preferred to stay with her friends, but Nathan's phone call, telling her he was in town and was coming to see her, had convinced Madden that now was the time to try to button everything up.

Elliot didn't think getting Nathan to confess would be that easy.

Madden's voice popped into her head, coming through on the earpiece he'd given to both her and Trey. "Okay, it's confirmed that Nathan has arrived and is leaving the airport. He should be here in twenty minutes."

"If he comes straight here," Elliot said. "He might go somewhere else."

"Like where?" Trey asked.

Elliot gave him a knowing look. "Hopefully, to where he keeps the gun he used. Hopefully, not to the Zimmermans."

"I bet he ditched the gun," Trey said. "But it would blow my mind if it was on campus right now and had been all along."

"Either way," Madden said, "we've got a tail on him. I'm going to ask one more time. Are you sure you don't want to wear a vest? I am very uncomfortable with this. I'd rather you have a vest on or not do this at all."

Elliot sighed. "If Nathan is the one who shot our parents and Bryce, he never once aimed for the chest." She turned to Trey. "Are you sure?"

He didn't hesitate. "Yep. Let's go."

Another voice came over the ear communication. "Elliot, this is Gavin. I'm in charge of your detail. Your apartment

has been swept. It's clean from any people—no bombs or traps. A delivery truck just entered from the back entrance. We'll watch him, but you should be good. We can hear everything. Just say 'help,' and we're ten seconds away."

Elliot didn't want to say that ten seconds to a bullet was more than enough time. But she knew a confrontation was inevitable, and if the cops could get enough on audio that would help with their prosecution, then she was game. The alternative—Nathan being free—was not one she liked.

Trey offered his fist to bump. "Let's do this."

She pounded her fist to his, then opened the door. He did the same and followed her up the walk to her building and to the stairs. Elliot looked around. Everything seemed good. Normal. She tried to breathe evenly and slowly to keep her heart steady.

At the turn in the stairway Trey's phone rang. She paused and waited while he took the phone out of his pocket.

"It's Teddy." He answered the call.

Elliot watched as he listened. She didn't like standing in the open, so she gestured that she was going into her apartment. Trey gave her a thumbs-up, his attention on the call.

Her door was at the top of the stairs, and Elliot was there turning the key and pushing it open within seconds. She left it cracked for Trey and set the bat to rest against the wall by the front door.

To anyone else her apartment looked slightly messy, like that of a busy college student. But Elliot could tell people had been in her space and had gone through everything. There was a disheveled look about the place. She slung her messenger bag on her couch and bent to pick up the stacks of paper she had been going through twenty-four hours ago, even though it felt like last week.

"Dude, you're not going to believe this. Teddy said—" Trey pushed his way into the apartment.

He didn't finish his sentence as a delivery man pushed in behind him, shoving Trey hard enough in the back that he stumbled toward Elliot. The man slammed the door closed.

"What the fuck?" Trey said as he caught his balance.

Elliot helped steady him.

"It's Aaron Simmons, one of the nurses who worked with Jaime," Elliot said more to Madden than Trey.

Madden said, "Gavin's men are almost to the door."

"No," said Elliot. She caught Trey's eye. "Wait."

"Why would I wait?" Aaron said as he whipped out a gun that he took turns pointing at them both. "I had a good thing going until you both started poking your nose into everything. Ruined my five-year plan."

"Your five-year plan?" Trey asked.

"Millions of dollars in my bank account and a life languishing on the beach. All because Jaime had to be a superstar nurse and you all had to try to find Jaime's killer. Human-interest story, my ass." Aaron was dressed in brown shorts, a T-shirt, and a ball cap pulled low. No wonder he had gotten away with being mistaken for a delivery driver. Elliot hardly recognized him.

"So why did you kill Brian Lyman? And Lucas? Why not start over in another state and keep adding to your account?" Trey moved to stand in front of Elliot.

"What?" Elliot asked, shocked. She'd heard the name Brian Lyman before, but with all that had happened, she couldn't place it.

Trey pointed at Aaron. "This piece of shit here was killing off patients in the nursing facility and sending them to his accomplice, Brian Lyman, who was the ME's assistant.

Lyman would forge paperwork saying they were organ donors and that the organs were earmarked. Which they were but for the black market."

"Is that what Teddy told you on the phone?" Elliot asked.

Trey kept his attention on Aaron. "Yeah, looks like Aaron here is clipping loose ends. Brian Lyman showed up in the morgue an hour ago from an overdose. Only he'd had a drug test at work a few days ago and was clean as a whistle. The staff is looking to prove it was homicide. Teddy said Lyman's death looks very much like Howie Middleman's death."

Add another victim to the list. But Aaron had messed up when he moved from homeless people or those with no family to those surrounded by people. And he underestimated Jaime's compassion for all mankind, homeless or not.

"Why?" Elliot asked. "Why would you hit Lucas?" She shook her head and blinked back the tears threatening to fall.

"I don't owe you anything," Aaron said.

"You're in my house, pointing a gun at me. I think you owe me a hell of a lot more than you think. Lucas was my friend. He didn't do anything to you."

"A gun? We're coming in," Gavin said.

"No!" Trey and Elliot said in unison.

"One minute," Elliot said. "Why are you here, Aaron?"

"Maybe he's a sore loser," Trey said.

"Maybe he needs to confess," Elliot said. "Maybe he needs to tell people why he did it."

"Shut up," Aaron raged.

"Looks like you aren't as clever as you think," Elliot said. "It's all come undone and left you exposed."

Aaron's hand was shaking as he pointed the gun at Elliot. His face twisted in anger. "You want to know why I did it?" Spittle flew from his mouth. "It's simple. I enjoyed it. Seeing the life drain out of their eyes, feeling the power that came with being the one who controls life and death. And the money, of course. It was a handsome reward for my efforts. These people were a drain on society. Taking up community and government resources that could be used for other people. And with the rest of us paying for what they can't. No, the scales aren't balanced, but what I did was balance them. And in their death, they gave back. They paid off their debt."

"With their life and their organs." Elliot felt a chill run down her spine at his words. She couldn't believe someone could be so callous and heartless. "You're sick," she said, her voice barely above a whisper. He was a serial killer.

Aaron chuckled. "Maybe I am. But it doesn't matter now. I'm done running, and I'm not going to jail. I'd rather go out on my own terms."

"You were the one who drove Jaime home that night, weren't you?" Elliot asked. "You were going to kill her too."

"I didn't have to. She saw her boyfriend there waiting for her, and I knew he was the jealous type. Plus, she smelled like sex. She and Lucas had gone at each other in one of the empty rooms at work. All I had to do was feed into his paranoia. She wouldn't let me walk her to the door. Getting him riled up was easy. I simply got out of my car and straightened my clothes. That dumbass's imagination did all the work. Problem solved. I got lucky there, kinda felt like the universe was telling me to keep up the good work. Now who wants to die first?" He raised the gun and aimed it at Elliot.

Trey sprang from where he was standing and tackled Aaron. The loud boom of the gun discharging echoed through the room. Trey fell to a heap on the floor but not before knocking the gun and Aaron to the ground.

Elliot lunged for the gun at the same time Aaron did. She landed on top of it, and Aaron landed on her.

Elliot's apartment door burst open. She expected to see Madden, but only Nathan was standing there.

Aaron lifted slightly then punched her in the side of the head.

Elliot was stunned. Unable to move. She felt like she'd been hit by a barbell. Aaron grabbed her by the shoulders and flipped her over, revealing the gun. Elliot saw stars and tried to fight back. She patted the ground madly, feeling for the weapon.

Aaron grabbed the gun by the barrel then straddled her. She knew then he was going to pistol-whip her to death. Aaron was escalating in his need for violence.

She caught a flash of her brother, a bat in his hand, and for a moment thought she was hallucinating. Having a flashback to before their lives fell apart.

Only when Nathan swung, Aaron went flying off her. Nathan roared and stepped over her, swinging at Aaron again. Then again.

"Freeze! Police!" boomed a voice.

Nathan froze. Seema's bat was positioned away from his body in what Elliot knew to be what batters called the follow-through. Nathan had followed through with his swing on Aaron.

He dropped the bat and sank to his knees, facing her. Eyes the same color as hers, the same as their mother's,

looked at her, pleading. “Please tell them I didn’t do it, Ellie. Tell them you know I couldn’t have hurt Mom and Dad.”

Elliot looked at her brother, who’d just saved her life, and tried to find the answer she knew they both wanted. That he was innocent. Only she knew she couldn’t because not once had he said he hadn’t done it.

35

The following day, everyone gathered around Trey's hospital bed, passing around a large box of pepperoni pizza—Trey's request.

"If we get caught with this in here, they're gonna kick us out," Hillary said.

Seema laughed. "No, they won't. They don't care anymore. He's cleared to eat, so eat he shall."

"How did your mom and dad take it?" Hillary asked Trey.

He had taken a bite of pizza, so he pointed to Teddy.

"I was there when Madden called," Teddy said. "They were freaked out. I could hear Trey's mom through the phone. She told Madden that if he did not call her every step of the way, she was going to have his head, and I believed her. I think Madden did too."

Trey laughed, then grimaced. "He's picking them up from the airport soon."

Elliot, having caught his expression, asked, "Are you in pain?"

"Only when I laugh," he told her, then took another bite.

"The doctor says the bullet went clean through the shoulder and didn't do any damage. Your athletic career is going to be unaffected," Teddy said.

"What did I miss while I was in surgery?" Trey asked.

"Well, not much since you weren't under long, but Hillary and I helped Lindsay pack. She's going to go home and finish the semester remotely. I can't blame her. Telling her they caught Aaron and that he will be charged with Lucas's death brought her some comfort, I hope."

Seema said, "All of you need to talk to someone to process what happened today. I'm serious when I say that."

"Did I tell you, Seema, that my brother used your bat to stop Aaron? I don't think you'll be getting it back anytime soon. Sorry. But it kinda was good luck for me." Elliot gave her hand a squeeze. "Thank you."

"We're all lucky to be sitting here right now. You know that, right?" Hillary asked.

"Yeah, I do," Teddy said. "It got me thinking about how short life is. About how there needs to be more people out there like Jaime looking out for the underprivileged. I think I want to go back to med school."

The group all hooted and hollered, giving him support and wishing him the best.

When the mood settled a bit, Elliot said, "I know we solved two crimes, but the price we paid for it... I'm not sure it was worth it. Remember when Hillary said she thought maybe we'd all sit around and talk about the case? In hindsight, that might have been what we should have done."

Teddy shook his head. "There is no understanding why what happened to Lucas happened. It doesn't make sense. Only a madman would find logic in his actions, but because

of Jaime and Lucas, we stopped a madman. Lots of people died because of him."

"Twenty-four people so far," said Madden, who had come in the room quietly.

"What?" Hillary asked.

"Twenty-four. That's currently the number of people Aaron Simmons murdered to take their organs. And we've only gone five years back so far."

Teddy shook his head with disgust. "That man took an oath."

"What's the word on the street, Detective?" Trey asked.

Madden glanced at his watch. "Your parents will be here in two hours. Aaron has been discharged from the hospital and is in custody, dealing with his concussion and broken arm, in a quiet, small cell with lots of privacy. We found the rental car he used when he hit Lucas, and the crime scene team is getting all the evidence off it now. He's going away for a very long time. He'll probably never be a free man again."

"Good," Elliot said. "I want him to rot in hell."

"We all do," Trey said.

"Your brother, on the other hand, has clammed up and has a lawyer. The opportunity to get him to incriminate himself was lost because of Aaron, but one of the cops interviewing him has a background in psychology, and she's hitting all the right buttons. His ego won't let him stay quiet for long. Until then, you keep the protective detail."

"Done." Elliot would have no problem with that, especially after seeing how her brother was in complete denial.

"I also talked to the Port Angeles police," Madden continued. "Regardless of Oliver's confession, you two will

be called to testify. If you have any questions about that, I can help. Just reach out."

Seema waved him off. "I've watched my dad prep hundreds of people. I got this, and since I'm going to convince Hillary to rush for my sorority and be my little sister, I can help her. But thanks for the offer."

"Oh, I'm rushing?" Hillary shook her head. "I don't think so. That's something Dancing Queen would do, not me."

"Girl, you are Dancing Queen," Seema said. "You need to accept that. We're going to have so much fun."

Hillary turned bright red. "You really think I can do it?"

"I so do," Seema said.

"I do too," Elliot echoed.

"Listen, one more thing," Madden said while crossing his arms. "This murder club, I'm serious, it has to stop. Investigations are dangerous, as you all found out. Promise me that if you get another request, you say no. Or bring it to me."

"Ha, trust us. We are done with all that," Trey said, pointing to his shoulder.

"Plus, you're, like, the only cool cop in town. If we had gotten stuck with Harmon this round, who knows what would have happened? There's no way he would have listened to us. Thanks for that, by the way," Elliot said.

Madden dipped his head once in acknowledgment of her thanks. "You should know Harmon has been put on administrative leave, and there is an internal affairs investigation. Turns out there are more than two of his cases that weren't properly investigated."

Elliot's mouth dropped open in surprise. She'd thought Harmon was made of Teflon. Nothing stuck to him.

Madden laughed. "Well, I have to run an errand before I

pick up Trey's parents. Try to stay out of trouble for the next few hours, at least." He winked. "I'll be back in a few."

No one said anything for several minutes after Madden left.

Then Teddy went to the door and looked out. "He's gone. Let's ask the question we all want to know. Has anyone reached out to the messenger? I haven't. Honestly, I didn't think about it until now."

Elliot and Trey shook their heads.

"We've been busy," Elliot said.

"Us too," Hillary said.

"I looked," Seema said. "There's no message. Nothing. I messaged him. I asked if he was pleased with the outcome. I also asked if he knew it was so dangerous, and if so, what the hell was wrong with him to have us look into this case? I told him Lucas's blood was on his hands. I was pretty angry. I mean, I still am. I think it's better for the messenger's safety that they remain anonymous."

"Except we knew the risks," Elliot said.

"Did we?" Seema asked.

Elliot looked at each of them. "Yeah, I kinda think we did. All of us except Teddy have had violence in our lives. All of us experienced unpredictability. We knew how life could change on a dime. Look at Lucas. Even he knew. He didn't want to join, because he knew it was dangerous, and he was right. We just refused to believe it could happen to us —again."

"We won't make that mistake a second time," Trey said.

"Is there going to be a second time?" Teddy asked. "Do you think the messenger will send us another case?"

"The real question is, would we take it if he did?" Hillary asked.

They all looked at each other. A smile played on Elliot's lips. "I'd like to say I would say no. And maybe I would, but I'm not one hundred percent convinced."

"Then let's hope he doesn't send one," Hillary said with a grin. "And even though we never found out what those other dates were related to, I'm okay letting those mysteries go cold."

Elliot chuckled. "I suspect those dates were all ones where each of us had an interaction with Jaime. A way to keep us interested in the case."

"Do you think it was one per person because there were seven dates? Lucas was member number six," Seema said.

"Maybe the professor was number seven," Teddy suggested.

They looked at each other. No one had a response.

Finally, Elliot broke the silence. "Yeah, I want the answers to those questions, but I think Hillary is right. I need to let these unanswered questions go. The important thing is two killers were caught."

"Maybe three." Trey gave her hand a squeeze. "Besides, ain't nobody got time to worry about loose threads."

Seema laughed. "Yeah, we have med school and law school and so much ahead of us. Who has the time?"

They all laughed. Because they all knew time could be made for something a person really wanted to do.

"Hand me the pizza box," Trey said.

"Speaking of time, what's everyone gonna do with all this extra time?" Teddy asked.

"I'm going to sleep," Seema said.

"I have dances to work on," Hillary said. "Can't pay for college when you don't have sponsorships."

"I'm going to ... oh, who am I kidding? I won't have

hardly any time once they charge my brother." Elliot shook her head in resignation.

"I'm gonna ask a girl out," Trey said. He looked at Elliot. "You think she could find the time to go on a date?"

She blushed and grinned. She'd wondered how he felt about her, if he was having the same feelings for her that she was for him.

"I think she'd definitely find the time for that," Elliot told him and squeezed his hand.

Only a few weeks ago, they hadn't known each other existed, and now, the five of them would forever be linked. Elliot couldn't ask for better people to have gone through this with.

* * *

Gene Madden parked outside the journalism building and made his way inside. He used the code Professor Snyder had given him. He found her sitting in her office, grading papers.

He knocked lightly on the door.

She looked pleased to see him and leapt to her feet. "Have you seen the kids?"

"Just came from the hospital. They're doing better, all things considered."

"That's a relief." She plopped back into her chair. "What a horrible thing to have happened. I feel so guilty."

"Good," Madden said. "Then you'll drop this stupid Campus Murder Club idea. No more cases, Lydia. I told you this wasn't a good idea."

"I'm not trying to be insensitive to what happened to that young man, but this group caught a serial killer and solved

Jaime's murder. And let's not forget, we got Harmon put on administrative leave. That's what you wanted, remember?"

"That kid paid with his life. Elliot and Trey almost did as well. Had Harmon done his job, maybe none of this would have been needed, and now that they're looking at all his cases, the club won't be needed. The professionals can handle it."

"You have to admit, they did a helluva good job. I feel bad thinking Lucas was the guilty party when he was clearly innocent. Who could have known this case had such deep layers?" Professor Snyder crossed her hands on her desk. The guilt had been heavy for her.

"Precisely why it stops here. One and done. Can I get your word on that, Lydia?"

The professor paused. "Crowdsourcing is the new way, Gene. Citizen sleuths aren't hampered by the law and rules and regulations like cops. Don't you see how important this is?"

Madden shook his head. "Now you're talking about a vigilante society, because if you ever want to bring someone to trial, those rules and regulations and laws you're so dismissive of are essential for a conviction. Give me your word, Lydia."

Professor Snyder sighed deeply and closed her eyes briefly. If the club ever did figure out the rest of the dates, they'd be on to another murder. Another cold case. And she'd be breaking her promise to Madden. In that moment, Professor Snyder accepted the risks.

When she opened her eyes, she met his gaze. "Okay, fine. I won't instigate any more gatherings of the Campus Murder Club."

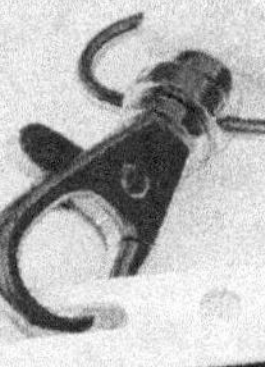
HOLD ON
LET ME
OVERTHIN
THIS
WHOSE IDEA WAS THIS ANYWAY
NURSES CALL THE SHOTS
NURSES DO IT BETTER

JAIME SULLIVAN
STUDENT NUMBER:
01355-73-1186
COLLEGE:
NURSING

A little about this book

Contains spoilers

I started this book a little into Covid closure. At that time things were going along the best they could considering a nationwide shutdown. We decided it would be a good time to adopt a dog. We were ready. We'd lost our terrier a few years earlier. We'd had him 15 years so his lost was deeply felt. But it was time to move on. We adopted Luke. He was a mix breed and full of energy. It wasn't always easy learning to live with a dog again. We'd gotten used to doing what we wanted to do when we wanted to do it and with a dog we had to be more purposeful. But he was such a good dog. He was worth it.

One day after the daily trip to the dog park we noticed a lump. And without going into all the details of poor veterinary care, difficulty getting appointments, and then exceptional compassionate veterinary care- it turned out the lump was cancer. Luke wasn't even 2 years old.

The cancer was aggressive. From diagnosis to when we had to let him go was 2 months. I'm very thankful to Laps Of Love who helped us during this awful period.

So to pay tribute to a really good dog- I made him a character in this book.

Both were loyal to the people they loved

Both were smart

Both were gone too soon

Open your phone's camera to scan the QR code and SAVE

Link will take you to KristiRoseBooks.com Buying from me means a deal for you.

Books by Kristi Rose

Samantha True Mysteries- These laugh out loud, action pack books take place in the Pacific Northwest. Join Samantha, an adult with dyslexia who's hid behind photography, on her adventures in her new life as a Private Investigator. A job she inherited when her new husband died unexpectedly and left behind a mess and another wife.

One Hit Wonder

All Bets Are Off

Best Laid Plans

Caught Off Guard

Two Time Loser

Dodged A Bullet

Audiobooks

* * *

The Cold Case Mystery Series:

Bone of Contention (Free at Prolific Works until October 2023)

* * *

PERFECT PLACE: A Liars Island Suspense

Perfect Place

Audiobook

* * *

The Wyoming Matchmaker Series- Whether marriage of convenience or star crossed lovers, everyone earns their happily ever after in this series.

The Cowboy Takes A Bride

The Cowboy's Make Believe Bride

The Cowboy's Runaway Bride

Book 4 Coming 2024

* * *

The No Strings Attached Series- A flirty, fun chick lit romance series

The Girl He Knows

The Girl He Wants

The Girl He Loves

Beach Town Love boxset

Audiobooks

* * *

The Meryton Brides Series- A wholesome romance series with a Pride and Prejudice theme

To Have and To Hold (Book 1)

With This Ring (Book 2)

I Do (Book 3)

Promise Me This (Book 4)

Marry Me, Matchmaker (Book 5)

community and then fire off an email and tell me 3 things about you!

Not ready to join? Email me below or follow me at one of the links below. Thanks for popping by!

You can connect with Kristi at any of the following:

www.kristirose.net

kristi@kristirose.net

Meet Kristi Rose

Hey! I'm Kristi. I write romances that will tug your heartstrings and laugh out loud mysteries. In all my stories you'll fall in love with the cast of characters, they'll become old, fun friends. **My one hope** is that I create stories that *satisfy any of your book cravings* and take you away from the rut of everyday life (sometimes it's a good rut).

When I'm not writing I'm spinning (riding a stationary bike), repurposing Happy Planners, or drinking a London Fog (hot tea with frothy milk).

I'm the mom of 2 and a milspouse (retired). We live in the Pacific Northwest and are under-prepared if one of the volcanoes erupts.

Here are 3 things about me:

- I lived on the outskirts of an active volcano (Mt.Etna)
- A spider bit me and it laid eggs in my arm (my kids don't know that story yet)
- I grew up in Central Florida and have skied in lakes with gators.

I'd love to get to know you better. Join my Read & Relax

Honeymoon Postponed (Book 6)

Matchmaker's Guidebook - FREE

* * *

The Second Chance Short Stories can be read alone and go as follows:

Second Chances

Once Again

Reason to Stay

He's the One

Kiss Me Again

or purchased in a bundle for a better discount.

The Coming Home Series: A Collection of 5 Second Chance Short Stories (Can be purchased individually).

Love Comes Home

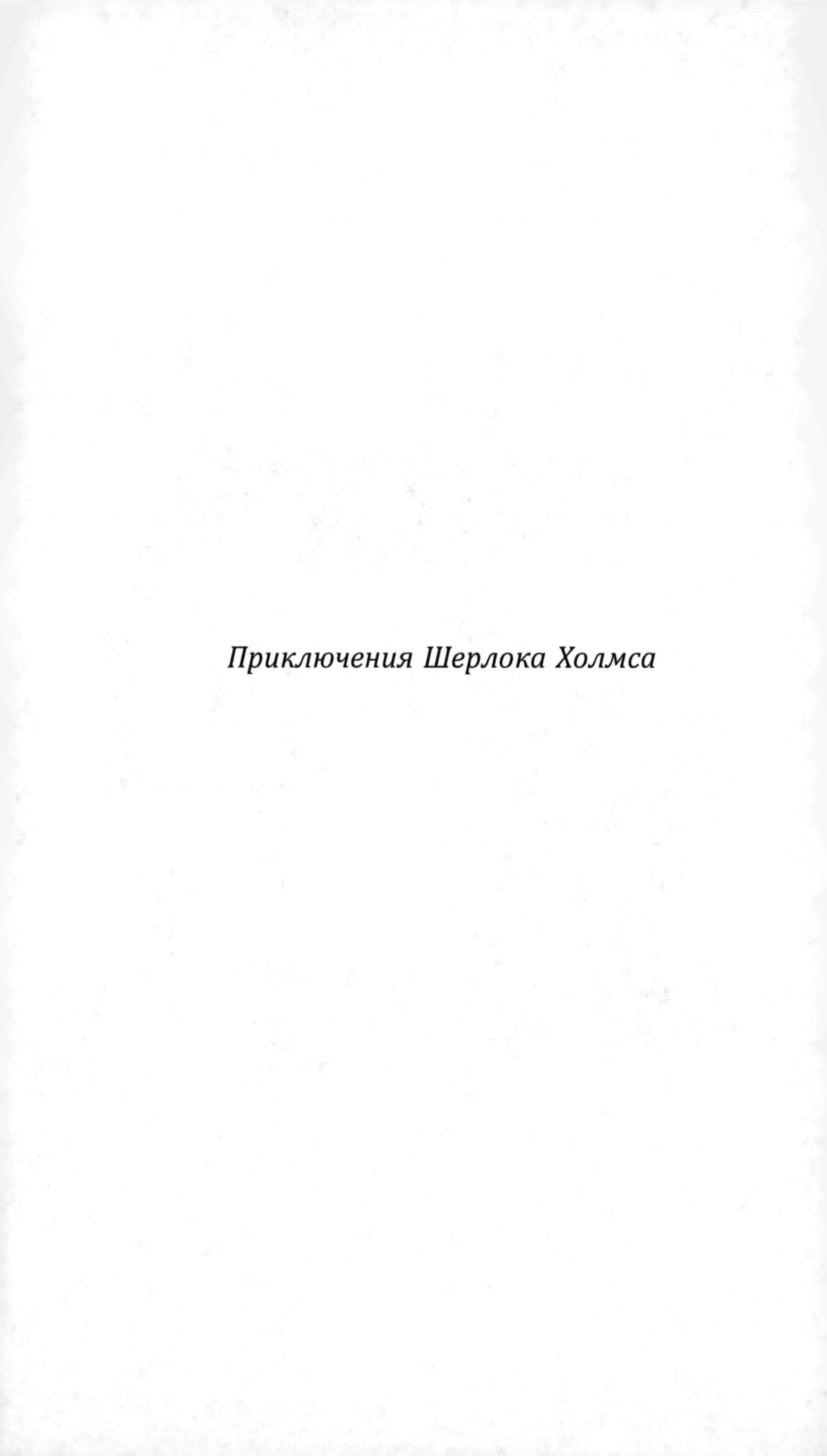

Приключения Шерлока Холмса

с жалкими претензиями на аристократический стиль. Четыре ряда грязноватых двухэтажных кирпичных домов глядят окнами на крохотный садик, заросший сорной травой, среди которой несколько блеклых лавровых кустов ведут тяжкую борьбу с насыщенным копотью воздухом. Три позолоченных шара и висящая на углу коричневая вывеска с надписью «Джабез Уилсон», выведенной белыми буквами, указывали, что здесь находится предприятие нашего рыжего клиента.

Шерлок Холмс остановился перед дверью, устремил на нее глаза, ярко блестевшие из-под полуприкрытых век. Затем он медленно прошелся по улице, потом возвратился к углу, внимательно вглядываясь в дома. Перед ссудной кассой он раза три с силой стукнул тростью по мостовой, затем подошел к двери и постучал. Дверь тотчас же распахнул расторопный, чисто выбритый молодой человек и попросил нас войти.

The door was instantly opened.

— Благодарю вас, — сказал Холмс. — Я хотел только спросить, как пройти отсюда на Стрэнд.

— Третий поворот направо, четвертый налево, — мгновенно ответил помощник мистера Уилсона и захлопнул дверь.

— Ловкий малый! — заметил Холмс, когда мы снова зашагали по улице. — Я считаю, что по ловкости он занимает четвертое место в Лондоне, а по храбрости, пожалуй, даже третье. Я о нем кое-что знаю.

— Видимо, — сказал я, — помощник мистера Уилсона играет немалую роль в этом Союзе рыжих. Уверен, вы спросили у него дорогу лишь затем, чтобы взглянуть на него.

— Не на него.

— На что же?

— На его колени.

— И что вы увидели?

— То, что ожидал увидеть.

— А зачем вы стучали по камням мостовой?

— Милейший доктор, сейчас время для наблюдений, а не для разговоров. Мы — разведчики в неприятельском лагере. Нам удалось кое-что узнать о Сэкс-Кобург-сквер. Теперь обследуем улицы, которые примыкают к ней с той стороны.

Разница между Сэкс-Кобург-сквер и тем, что мы увидели, когда свернули за угол, была столь же велика, как разница между картиной и ее оборотной стороной. За углом проходила одна из главных артерий города, соединяющая Сити с севером и западом. Эта большая улица была вся забита экипажами, движущимися двумя потоками вправо и влево, а на тротуарах чернели рои пешеходов. Глядя на ряды прекрасных магазинов и роскошных контор, трудно было представить себе, что позади этих самых домов находится такая убогая, безлюдная площадь.

— Позвольте мне вдоволь насмотреться, — сказал Холмс, остановившись на углу и внимательно разглядывая каждый дом один за другим. — Я хочу запомнить порядок зданий. Изучение Лондона — моя страсть… Сначала табачный магазин Мортимера, затем газетная лавчонка, затем кобургское отделение Городского и Пригородного банка, затем вегетарианский ресторан, затем каретное депо Макферлена. А там уже следующий квартал… Ну, доктор, наша работа окончена! Теперь мы можем немного поразвлечься: бутерброд, чашка кофе и — в страну скрипок, где все сладость, нега и гармония, где нет рыжих клиентов, досаждающих нам головоломками.

All afternoon he sat in the stalls.

Мой друг страстно увлекался музыкой; он был не только очень способный исполнитель, но и незаурядный композитор. Весь вечер просидел он в кресле, вполне счастливый, слегка двигая длинными тонкими пальцами в такт музыке; его мягко улыбающееся лицо, его влажные, затуманенные глаза ничем не напоминали о Холмсе-ищейке, о безжалостном хитроумном Холмсе, преследователе бандитов. Его удивительный характер слагался из двух начал. Мне часто приходило в голову, что его потрясающая своей точностью проницательность родилась в борьбе с поэтической задумчивостью, составлявшей основную черту этого человека. Он постоянно переходил от полнейшей расслабленности к необычайной энергии. Мне хорошо было известно, с каким бездумным спокойствием отдавался он по вечерам своим импровизациям и нотам. Но внезапно охотничья страсть охватывала его, свойственная ему блистательная сила мышления возрастала до степени интуиции, и люди, незнакомые с его методом, начинали думать, что перед ними не человек, а какое-то сверхъестественное существо. Наблюдая за ним в Сент-Джемс-холле и видя, с какой полнотой душа его отдается музыке, я чувствовал, что тем, за кем он охотится, будет плохо.

— Вы, доктор, собираетесь, конечно, идти домой, — сказал он, когда концерт кончился.

— Домой, понятно.

— А мне предстоит еще одно дело, которое отнимет у меня три-четыре часа. Это происшествие на Кобург-сквер — очень серьезная штука.

— Серьезная?

— Там готовится крупное преступление. У меня есть все основания думать, что мы еще успеем предотвратить его. Но все усложняется из-за того, что сегодня суббота. Вечером мне может понадобиться ваша помощь.

— В котором часу?

— Часов в десять, не раньше.

— Ровно в десять я буду на Бейкер-стрит.

— Отлично. Имейте в виду, доктор, что дело будет опасное. Суньте в карман свой армейский револьвер.

Он помахал мне рукой, круто повернулся и мгновенно исчез в толпе.

Я не считаю себя глупее других, но всегда, когда я имею дело с Шерлоком Холмсом, меня угнетает тяжелое сознание собственной тупости. Ведь вот я слышал то же самое, что слышал он, я видел то же самое, что видел он, однако, судя по его словам, он знает и понимает не только то, что случилось, но и то, что случится, мне же все это дело по-прежнему представляется непонятной нелепостью.

По дороге домой я снова припомнил и весь необычайный рассказ рыжего переписчика «Британской энциклопедии», и наше посещение Сэкс-Кобург-сквер, я те зловещие слова, которые Холмс сказал мне при прощании. Что означает эта ночная экспедиция и для чего нужно, чтобы я пришел вооруженным? Куда мы отправимся с ним и что предстоит нам делать? Холмс намекнул мне, что безбородый помощник владельца ссудной кассы весьма опасный человек, способный на большие преступления.

Я изо всех сил пытался разгадать эти загадки, но ничего у меня не вышло, и я решил ждать ночи, которая должна была разъяснить мне все.

В четверть десятого я вышел из дому и, пройдя по Гайд-парку, по Оксфорд-стрит, очутился на Бейкер-стрит. У подъезда стояли два кэба, и, войдя в прихожую, я услышал шум голосов. Я застал у Холмса двух человек. Холмс оживленно разговаривал с ними. Одного из них я знал — это был Питер Джонс, официальный агент полиции; другой был длинный, тощий, угрюмый мужчина в сверкающем цилиндре, в удручающе безукоризненном фраке.

— А, вот мы и в сборе! — сказал Холмс, застегивая матросскую куртку и беря с полки охотничий хлыст с тяжелой рукоятью. — Уотсон, вы, кажется, знакомы с мистером Джонсом из Скотленд-Ярда? Позвольте вас представить мистеру Мерриуэзеру. Мистер Мерриуэзер тоже примет участие в нашем ночном приключении.

— Как видите, доктор, мы с мистером Холмсом снова охотимся вместе, — сказал Джонс с обычным своим важным и снисходительным видом. — Наш друг — бесценный человек. Но в самом начале охоты ему нужна для преследования зверя помощь старого гончего пса.

— Боюсь, что мы подстрелим не зверя, а утку, — угрюмо сказал мистер Мерриуэзер.

— Можете вполне положиться на мистера Холмса, сэр, — покровительственно проговорил агент полиции. — У него свои собственные любимые методы, которые, позволю себе заметить, несколько отвлеченны и фантастичны, но тем не менее дают отличные результаты. Нужно признать, что бывали случаи, когда он оказывался прав, а официальная полиция ошибалась.

— Раз уж вы так говорите, мистер Джонс, значит, все в порядке, — снисходительно сказал незнакомец. — И все же, признаться, мне жаль, что сегодня не придется сыграть мою обычную партию в роббер. Это первый субботний вечер за двадцать семь лет, который я проведу без карт.

— В сегодняшней игре ставка покрупнее, чем в ваших карточных играх, — сказал Шерлок Холмс, — и самая игра увлекательнее. Ваша ставка, мистер Мерриуэзер, равна тридцати тысячам фунтов стерлингов. А ваша ставка, Джонс, — человек, которого вы давно хотите поймать.

— Джон Клей — убийца, вор, взломщик и мошенник, — сказал Джонс. — Он еще молод, мистер Мерриуэзер, но это искуснейший вор в стране: ни на кого другого я не надел бы наручников с такой охотой, как на него. Он замечательный человек, этот Джон Клей. Его дед был герцог, сам он учился в Итоне и в Оксфорде.[1] Мозг его так же изощрен, как его пальцы, и хотя мы на каждом шагу натыкаемся на его следы, он до сих пор остается неуловимым. На этой неделе он обворует кого-нибудь в Шотландии, а на следующей он уже собирает деньги на постройку детского приюта в Коррнуэлле. Я гоняюсь за ним уже несколько лет, а еще ни разу не видел его.

— Сегодня ночью я буду иметь удовольствие представить его вам. Мне тоже приходилось раза два натыкаться на подвиги мистера Джона Клея, и я вполне согласен с вами, что он искуснейший вор в стране... Уже одиннадцатый час, и нам пора двигаться в путь. Вы двое поезжайте в первом кэбе, а мы с Уотсоном поедем во втором.

Шерлок Холмс во время нашей долгой поездки был не слишком общителен: он сидел откинувшись и насвистывал мелодии, которые слышал сегодня на концерте. Мы колесили по бесконечной путанице освещенных газом улиц, пока наконец не добрались до Фаррингдон-стрит.

— Теперь мы совсем близко, — сказал мой приятель. — Мерриуэзер — директор банка и лично заинтересован во всем деле. Джонс тоже нам пригодится. Он славный малый, хотя ничего не

---

[1] В Итоне и Оксфорде находятся аристократические учебные заведения.

смыслит в своей профессии. Впрочем, у него есть одно несомненное достоинство: он отважен, как бульдог, и цепок, как рак. Если уж схватит кого-нибудь своей клешней, так не выпустит... Мы приехали. Вот и они.

Мы снова остановились на той же людной и оживленной улице, где были утром. Расплатившись с извозчиками и следуя за мистером Мерриуэзером, мы вошли в какой-то узкий коридор и юркнули в боковую дверцу, которую он отпер для нас. За дверцей оказался другой коридор, очень короткий. В конце коридора были массивные железные двери. Открыв эти двери, мы. спустились по каменным ступеням винтовой лестницы и подошли к еще одним дверям, столь же внушительным. Мистер Мерриуэзер остановился, чтобы зажечь фонарь, и повел нас по темному, пахнущему землей коридору. Миновав еще одну дверь, мы очутились в обширном склепе или погребе, заставленном корзинами и тяжелыми ящиками.

Mr. Merryweather stopped to light a lantern.

— Сверху проникнуть сюда не так-то легко, — заметит Холмс, подняв фонарь и оглядев потолок.

— Снизу тоже, — сказал мистер Мерриуэзер, стукнув тростью по плитам, которыми был выложен пол. — Черт побери, звук такой, будто там пустота! — воскликнул он с изумлением.

— Я вынужден просить вас не шуметь, — сердито сказал Холмс. — Из-за вас вся наша экспедиция может закончиться крахом. Будьте любезны, сядьте на один из этих ящиков и не мешайте.

Важный мистер Мерриуэзер с оскорбленным видом сел на корзину, а Холмс опустился на колени и с помощью фонаря и лупы принялся изучать щели между плитами. Через несколько секунд, удовлетворенный результатами своего исследования, он поднялся и спрятал лупу в карман.

— У нас впереди по крайней мере час, — заметил он, — так как они вряд ли примутся за дело прежде, чем почтенный владелец ссудной кассы заснет. А когда он заснет, они не станут терять ни минуты, потому что чем раньше они окончат работу, тем больше времени у них останется для бегства… Мы находимся, доктор, — как вы, без сомнения, уже догадались, — в подвалах отделения одного из богатейших лондонских банков. Мистер Мерриуэзер — председатель правления банка; он объяснит нам, что заставляет наиболее дерзких преступников именно в настоящее время с особым вниманием относиться к этим подвалам.

— Мы храним здесь наше французское золото, — шепотом сказал директор. — Мы уже имели ряд предупреждений, что будет совершена попытка похитить его.

— Ваше французское золото?

— Да. Несколько месяцев назад нам понадобились дополнительные средства, и мы заняли тридцать тысяч наполеондоров у банка Франции. Но нам даже не пришлось распаковывать эти деньги, и они до сих пор лежат в наших подвалах. Корзина, на которой я сижу, содержит две тысячи наполеондоров, уложенных между листами свинцовой бумаги. Редко в одном отделении банка хранят столько золота, сколько хранится у нас в настоящее время. Каким-то образом это стало известно многим, и это заставляет директоров беспокоиться.

— У них есть все основания для беспокойства, — заметил Холмс. — Ну, нам пора приготовиться. Я полагаю, что в течение ближайшего часа все будет кончено. Придется, мистер Мерриуэзер, закрыть этот фонарь чем-нибудь темным...

— И сидеть в темноте?

— Боюсь, что так. Я захватил колоду карт, чтобы вы могли сыграть свою партию в роббер, так как нас здесь четверо. Но я вижу, что приготовления врага зашли очень далеко и что оставить здесь свет было бы рискованно. Кроме того, нам нужно поменяться местами. Они смелые люди и, хотя мы нападем на них внезапно, могут причинить нам немало вреда, если мы не будем осторожны. Я стану за этой корзиной, а вы спрячьтесь за теми. Когда я направлю на грабителей свет, хватайте их. Если они начнут стрельбу, Уотсон, стреляйте в них без колебания.

Я положил свой заряженный револьвер на крышку деревянного ящика, а сам притаился за ящиком. Холмс накрыл фонарь и оставил нас в полнейшей тьме. Запах нагретого металла напоминал нам, что фонарь не погашен и что свет готов вспыхнуть в любое мгновение. Мои нервы, напряженные от ожидания, были подавлены этой внезапной тьмой, этой холодной сыростью подземелья.

— Для бегства у них есть только один путь — обратно, через дом на Сэкс-Кобург-сквер, — прошептал Холмс. — Надеюсь, вы сделали то, о чем я просил вас, Джонс?

— Инспектор и два офицера ждут их у парадного входа.

— Значит, мы заткнули все дыры. Теперь нам остается только молчать и ждать.

Как медленно тянулось время! В сущности, прошел всего час с четвертью, но мне казалось, что ночь уже кончилась и наверху рассветает. Ноги у меня устали и затекли, так как я боялся шевельнуться; нервы были натянуты. И вдруг внизу я заметил мерцание света.

Сначала это была слабая искра, мелькнувшая в просвете между плитами пола. Вскоре искра эта превратилась в желтую полоску.

Потом без всякого шума в полу возникло отверстие, и в самой середине освещенного пространства появилась рука — белая, женственная, — которая как будто пыталась нащупать какой-то предмет. В течение минуты эта рука с движущимися пальцами торчала из пола. Затем она исчезла так же внезапно, как возникла, и все опять погрузилось во тьму; лишь через узенькую щель между двумя плитами пробивался слабый свет.

«It's no use, John Clay»

Однако через мгновение одна из широких белых плит перевернулась с резким скрипом, и на ее месте оказалась глубокая квадратная яма, из которой хлынул свет фонаря. Над ямой появилось гладко выбритое мальчишеское лицо; неизвестный зорко глянул во все стороны: две руки уперлись в края отверстия; плечи поднялись из ямы, потом поднялось все туловище; колено уперлось в пол. Через секунду незнакомец уже во весь рост стоял на полу возле ямы и помогал влезть своему товарищу, такому же маленькому и гибкому, с бледным лицом и с вихрами ярко-рыжих волос.

— Все в порядке, — прошептал он. — Стамеска и мешки у тебя?.. Черт! Прыгай, Арчи, прыгай, а я уж за себя постою.

Шерлок Холмс схватил его за шиворот. Второй вор юркнул в нору; Джонс пытался его задержать, но, видимо, безуспешно: я услышал треск рвущейся материи. Свет блеснул на стволе револьвера, но Холмс охотничьим хлыстом стегнул своего пленника по руке, и револьвер со звоном упал на каменный пол.

— Бесполезно, Джон Клей, — сказал Холмс мягко. — Вы попались.

— Вижу, — ответил тот совершенно спокойно. — Но товарищу моему удалось ускользнуть, и вы поймали только фалду его пиджака.

— Три человека поджидают его за дверями, — сказал Холмс.

— Ах вот как! Чисто сработано! Поздравляю вас.

— А я — вас. Ваша выдумка насчет рыжих вполне оригинальна и удачна.

— Сейчас вы увидите своего приятеля, — сказал Джонс. — Он шибче умеет нырять в норы, чем я. А теперь я надену на вас наручники.

— Уберите свои грязные руки, пожалуйста! Не трогайте меня! — сказал ему наш пленник после того, как наручники были надеты. — Может быть, вам неизвестно, что во мне течет королевская кровь. Будьте же любезны, обращаясь ко мне, называть меня «сэр» и говорить мне «пожалуйста».

— Отлично, — сказал Джонс, усмехаясь. — Пожалуйста, сэр, поднимитесь наверх и соблаговолите сесть в кэб, который отвезет вашу светлость в полицию.

— Вот так-то лучше, — спокойно сказал Джон Клей.

Величаво кивнув нам головой, он безмятежно удалился под охраной сыщика.

— Мистер Холмс, — сказал Мерриуэзер, выводи нас из кладовой, — я, право, не знаю, как наш банк может отблагодарить вас за эту услугу. Вам удалось предотвратить крупнейшую кражу.

— У меня были свои собственные счеты с мистером Джоном Клеем, — сказал Холмс. — Расходы я на сегодняшнем деле понес небольшие, и ваш банк безусловно возместит их мне, хотя, в сущности, я уже вознагражден тем, что испытал единственное в своем роде приключение и услышал замечательную повесть о Союзе рыжих…

— Видите ли, Уотсон, — объяснил мне рано утром Шерлок Холмс, когда мы сидели с ним на Бейкер-стрит за стаканом виски с содовой, — мне с самого начала было ясно, что единственной целью этого фантастического объявления о Союзе рыжих и переписывания «Британской энциклопедии» может быть только удаление из дома не слишком умного владельца ссудной кассы на несколько часов ежедневно. Способ, который они выбрали, конечно, курьезен, однако благодаря этому способу они вполне добились своего. Весь этот план, без сомнения, был подсказан вдохновенному уму Клея цветом волос его сообщника. Четыре фунта в неделю служили для Уилсона приманкой, а что значит четыре фунта для них, если они рассчитывали получить тысячи! Они поместили в газете объявление; один мошенник снял временно контору, другой мошенник уговорил своего хозяина сходить туда, и оба вместе получили возможность каждое утро пользоваться его отсутствием. Чуть только я услышал, что помощник довольствуется половинным жалованьем, я понял, что для этого у него есть основательные причины.

— Но как вы отгадали их замысел?

— Предприятие нашего рыжего клиента — ничтожное, во всей его квартире нет ничего такого, ради чего стоило бы затевать столь сложную игру. Следовательно, они имели в виду нечто находящееся вне его квартиры. Что это может быть? Я вспомнил о страсти помощника к фотографии, о том, что он пользуется этой страстью, чтобы лазить зачем-то в погреб. Погреб! Вот другой конец запутанной нити. Я подробно расспросил Уилсона об этом таинственном помощнике и понял, что имею дело с одним из самых хладнокровных и дерзких преступников Лондона. Он что-то делает в погребе, что-то сложное, так как ему приходится работать там по нескольку часов каждый день в течение двух месяцев. Что же он может там делать? Только одно: рыть подкоп, ведущий в какое-нибудь другое здание. Пойдя к такому выводу, я захватил вас и отправился познакомиться с тем местом, где все это происходит. Вы были очень удивлены, когда я стукнул тростью по мостовой. А между тем я хотел узнать, куда прокладывается подкоп — перед фасадом или на задворках. Оказалось, что перед фасадом его не было. Я позвонил. Как я и ожидал, мне открыл помощник. У нас уже бывали с ним кое-какие стычки, но мы никогда не видали друг друга в лицо. Да и на этот раз я в лицо ему не посмотрел. Я хотел видеть его колени. Вы могли бы и сами заметить, как они у него были грязны, помяты, протерты. Они свидетельствовали о многих часах, проведенных за рытьем подкопа. Оставалось только выяснить, куда он вел свой подкоп. Я свернул за угол, увидел вывеску Городского и Пригородного банка и понял, что задача решена. Когда после концерта вы отправились домой, я поехал в Скотленд-Ярд, а оттуда к председателю правления банка.

— А как вы узнали, что они попытаются совершить ограбление именно этой ночью? — спросил я.

— Закрыв контору Союза рыжих, они тем самым давали понять, что больше не нуждаются в отсутствии мистера Джабеза Уилсона, — другими словами, их подкоп готов. Было ясно, что они постараются воспользоваться им поскорее, так как, во-первых, подкоп может быть обнаружен, а во-вторых, золото может быть перевезено в другое место. Суббота им особенно удобна, потому что она предоставляет им для бегства лишние сутки. На основании всех этих соображений я пришел к выводу, что попытка ограбления будет совершена ближайшей ночью.

— Ваши рассуждения прекрасны! — воскликнул я в непритворном восторге. — Вы создали такую длинную цепь, и каждое звено в ней безупречно.

Этот случай спас меня от угнетающей скуки, — проговорил Шерлок Холмс, зевая. — Увы, я чувствую, что скука снова начинает одолевать меня! Вся моя жизнь — сплошное усилие избегнуть тоскливого однообразия наших жизненных будней. Маленькие загадки, которые я порой разгадываю, помогают мне достигнуть этой цели.

— Вы истинный благодетель человечества, — сказал я.

Холмс пожал плечами:

— Пожалуй, я действительно приношу кое-какую пользу.

«L'homme c'est rien — I'oeuvre c'est tout",[1] как выразился Гюстав Флобер в письме к Жорж Санд.

---

[1] «Человек — ничто, дело — все» (фр.)

УСТАНОВЛЕНИЕ ЛИЧНОСТИ

— Мой дорогой друг, жизнь несравненно причудливее, чем все, что способно создать воображение человеческое, — сказал Шерлок Холмс, когда мы с ним сидели у камина в его квартире на Бейкер-стрит. — Нам и в голову не пришли бы многие вещи, которые в действительности представляют собою нечто совершенно банальное. Если бы мы с вами могли, взявшись за руки, вылететь из окна и, витая над этим огромным городом, приподнять крыши и заглянуть внутрь домов, то по сравнению с открывшимися нам необычайными совпадениями, замыслами, недоразумениями, непостижимыми событиями, которые, прокладывая себе путь сквозь многие поколения, приводят к совершенно невероятным результатам, вся изящная словесность с ее условностями и заранее предрешенными развязками показалась бы нам плоской и тривиальной.

— И все же вы меня не убедили, — отвечал я. — Дела, о которых мы читаем в газетах, как правило, представлены в достаточно откровенном и грубом виде. Натурализм в полицейских отчетах доведен до крайних пределов, но это отнюдь не значит, что они хоть сколько-нибудь привлекательны или художественны.

— Для того, чтобы добиться подлинно реалистического эффекта, необходим тщательный отбор, известная сдержанность, — заметил Холмс. — А этого как раз и не хватает в полицейских отчетах, где гораздо больше места отводится пошлым сентенциям мирового судьи, нежели подробностям, в которых для внимательного наблюдателя и содержится существо дела. Поверьте, нет ничего более неестественного, чем банальность.

Я улыбнулся и покачал головой.

— Понятно, почему вы так думаете. Разумеется, находясь в положении неофициального консультанта и помощника вконец запутавшихся в своих делах обитателей трех континентов, вы постоянно имеете дело со всевозможными странными и фантастическими явлениями. Но давайте устроим практическое испытание, посмотрим, например, что написано здесь, — сказал я, поднимая с полу утреннюю газету. — Возьмем первый попавшийся заголовок: «Жестокое обращение мужа с женой». Далее следует полстолбца текста, но я, и не читая, уверен, что все это хорошо знакомо. Здесь, без сомнения, фигурирует другая женщина, пьянство, колотушки, синяки, полная сочувствия сестра или квартирная хозяйка. Даже бульварный писака не смог бы придумать ничего грубее.

— Боюсь, что ваш пример неудачен, как и вся ваша аргументация, — сказал Холмс, заглядывая в газету. — Это — дело о разводе Дандеса, и случилось так, что я занимался выяснением некоторых мелких обстоятельств, связанных с ним. Муж был трезвенником, никакой другой женщины не было, а жалоба заключалась в том, что он взял привычку после еды вынимать искусственную челюсть и швырять ею в жену, что, согласитесь, едва ли придет в голову среднему новеллисту. Возьмите понюшку табаку, доктор, и признайтесь, что я положил вас на обе лопатки с вашим примером.

Он протянул мне старинную золотую табакерку с большим аметистом на крышке. Великолепие этой вещицы настолько не вязалось с простыми и скромными привычками моего друга, что я не мог удержаться от замечания по этому поводу.

— Да, я совсем забыл, что мы с вами уже несколько недель не виделись, — сказал он. — Это небольшой сувенир от короля Богемии в благодарность за мою помощь в деле с письмами Ирен Адлер.

— А кольцо? — спросил я, взглянув на великолепный бриллиант, блестевший у него на пальце.

— Подарок голландской королевской фамилии; но это дело настолько деликатное, что я не имею права довериться даже вам, хотя вы любезно взяли на себя труд описать некоторые из моих скромных достижений.

— А сейчас у вас есть на руках какие-нибудь дела? — с интересом спросил я.

— Штук десять — двенадцать, но ни одного интересного. То есть все они по-своему важные, но для меня интереса не представляют. Видите ли, я обнаружил, что именно незначительные дела дают простор для наблюдений, для тонкого анализа причин и следствий, которые единственно и составляют всю прелесть расследования. Крупные преступления, как правило, очень просты, ибо мотивы серьезных преступлений большею частью очевидны. А среди этих дел ничего интересного нет, если не считать одной весьма запутанной истории, происшедшей в Марселе. Не исключено, однако, что не пройдет и нескольких минут, как у меня будет дело позанятнее, ибо, мне кажется, я вижу одну из моих клиенток.

Говоря это, он встал с кресла и, подойдя к окну, смотрел на тихую, серую лондонскую улицу. Взглянув через его плечо, я увидел на противоположной стороне крупную женщину в тяжелом меховом боа, с большим мохнатым красным пером на кокетливо сдвинутой набок широкополой шляпе. Из-под этих пышных доспехов она нерешительно поглядывала на наши окна, то и дело порываясь вперед и нервно теребя застежку перчатки.

Внезапно, как пловец, бросающийся в воду, она кинулась через улицу, и мы услышали резкий звонок.

— Знакомые симптомы, — сказал Холмс, швыряя в камин окурок. — Нерешительность у дверей всегда свидетельствует о сердечных делах. Она хочет попросить совета, но боится: дело, очевидно, слишком щекотливое. Но и здесь бывают разные оттенки. Если женщину глубоко оскорбили, она уже не колеблется и, как правило, обрывает звонок. В данном случае тоже можно предположить любовную историю, однако эта девица не столько рассержена, сколько встревожена или огорчена. А вот и она. Сейчас все наши сомнения будут разрешены.

В эту минуту в дверь постучали, и мальчик в форменной куртке с пуговицами доложил о прибытии мисс Мэри Сазерлэнд, между тем как сама эта дама возвышалась позади его маленькой черней фигурки, словно торговый корабль в полной оснастке, идущий вслед за крохотным лоцманским ботом. Шерлок Холмс приветствовал гостью с присущей ему непринужденной учтивостью, затем закрыл дверь и, усадив ее в кресло, оглядел пристальным и вместе с тем характерным для него рассеянным взглядом.

Herlock Holmes welcomed her.

— Вы не находите, — сказал он, — что при вашей близорукости утомительно так много писать на машинке?

— Вначале я уставала, но теперь печатаю слепым методом, — ответила она. Затем, вдруг вникнув в смысл его слов, она вздрогнула и со страхом взглянула на Холмса. На ее широком добродушном лице выразилось крайнее изумление.

— Вы меня знаете, мистер Холмс? — воскликнула она. — Иначе откуда вам все это известно?

— Неважно, — засмеялся Холмс. — Все знать — моя профессия. Быть может, я приучился видеть то, чего другие не замечают. В противном случае, зачем вам было бы приходить ко мне за советом?

— Я пришла потому, что слышала о вас от миссис Этеридж, мужа которой вы так быстро отыскали, когда все, и даже полиция, считали его погибшим. О, мистер Холмс, если бы вы так же помогли и мне! Я не богата, но все же имею ренту в сто фунтов в год и, кроме того, зарабатываю перепиской на машинке, и я готова отдать все, только бы узнать, что сталось с мистером Госмером Эйнджелом.

— Почему вы так торопились бежать ко мне за советом? — спросил Шерлок Холмс, сложив кончики пальцев и глядя в потолок.

На простоватой физиономии мисс Мэри Сазерлэнд снова появился испуг.

— Да, я действительно прямо-таки вылетела из дома, — сказала она. — Меня разозлило равнодушие, с каким мистер Уиндибенк, то есть мой отец, отнесся к этому делу. Он не хотел идти ни в полицию, ни к вам, ничего не желает делать, только знает твердить, что ничего страшного не случилось, вот я и не вытерпела, кое-как оделась и прямо к вам.

— Ваш отец? — спросил Холмс. — Скорее, ваш отчим. Ведь у вас разные фамилии.

— Да, отчим. Я называю его отцом, хотя это смешно — он всего на пять лет и два месяца старше меня.

— А ваша матушка жива?

— О да, мама жива и здорова. Не очень-то я была довольна, когда она вышла замуж, и так скоро после смерти папы, причем он лет на пятнадцать ее моложе. У папы была паяльная мастерская на Тоттенхем-Корт-роуд — прибыльное дельце, и мама продолжала вести его с помощью старшего мастера мистера Харди. Но мистер Уиндибенк заставил ее продать мастерскую: ему, видите ли, не к лицу, — он коммивояжер по продаже вин. Они получили четыре тысячи семьсот фунтов вместе с процентами, хотя отец, будь он в живых, выручил бы гораздо больше.

Я думал, что Шерлоку Холмсу надоест этот бессвязный рассказ, но он, напротив, слушал с величайшим вниманием.

— И ваш личный доход идет с этой суммы? — спросил он.

— О нет, сэр! У меня свое состояние, мне оставил наследство дядя Нэд из Окленда. Капитал в новозеландских бумагах, четыре с половиной процента годовых. Всего две с половиною тысячи фунтов, но я могу получать только проценты.

— Все это очень интересно, — сказал Холмс. — Получая сто фунтов в год и прирабатывая сверх того, вы, конечно, имеете возможность путешествовать и позволять себе другие развлечения. Я считаю, что на доход в шестьдесят фунтов одинокая дама может жить вполне безбедно.

— Я могла бы обойтись меньшим, мистер Холмс, но вы ведь сами понимаете, что я не хочу быть обузой дома и, пока живу с ними, отдаю деньги в семью. Разумеется, это только временно. Мистер Уиндибенк каждый квартал получает мои проценты и отдает их маме, а я отлично живу перепиской на машинке. Два пенса за страницу, и частенько мне удается писать по пятнадцать — двадцать страниц в день.

— Вы очень ясно обрисовали мне все обстоятельства, — сказал Холмс. — Позвольте представить вам моего друга, доктора Уотсона; при нем вы можете говорить откровенно, как наедине со мною. А теперь, будьте любезны, расскажите подробно о ваших отношениях с мистером Госмером Эйнджелом.

Мисс Сазерлэнд покраснела и стала нервно теребить край своего жакета.

— Я познакомилась с ним на балу газопроводчиков. Папе всегда присылали билеты, а теперь они вспомнили о нас и прислали билеты маме. Мистер Уиндибенк не хотел, чтобы мы шли на бал. Он не хочет, чтобы мы где-нибудь бывали. А когда я завожу речь о каком-нибудь пикнике воскресной школы, он приходит в бешенство. Но на этот раз я решила пойти во что бы то ни стало, потому что какое он имеет право не пускать меня? Незачем водить компанию с подобными людьми, говорит он, а ведь там собираются все папины друзья. И еще он сказал, будто мне не в чем идти, когда у меня есть совсем еще не надеванное красное бархатное платье. Больше возражать ему было нечего, и он уехал во Францию по делам фирмы, а мы с мамой и мистером Харди, нашим бывшим мастером, пошли на бал. Там я и познакомилась с мистером Госмером Эйнджелом.

At the gasfitters' ball.

— Полагаю, что, вернувшись из Франции, мистер Уиндибенк был очень недоволен тем, что вы пошли на бал? — спросил Холмс.

— Нет, он ничуть не рассердился. Он засмеялся, пожал плечами и сказал: что женщине ни запрети, она все равно сделает посвоему.

— Понимаю. Значит, на балу газопроводчиков вы и познакомились с джентльменом по имени Госмер Эйнджел?

— Да, сэр. Я познакомилась с ним в тот вечер, а на следующий день он пришел справиться, благополучно ли мы добрались до дому, и после этого мы, то есть я два раза была с ним на прогулке, а затем вернулся отец, и мистер Госмер Эйнджел уже не мог нас навещать.

— Не мог? Почему?

— Видите ли, отец не любит гостей и вечно твердит, что женщина должна довольствоваться своим семейным кругом. А я на это говорила маме: да, женщина должна иметь свой собственный круг, но у меня-то его пока что нет!

— Ну, а мистер Госмер Эйнджел? Он не делал попыток с вами увидеться?

— Через неделю отец снова собирался во Францию, и Госмер написал мне, что до отъезда отца нам лучше не встречаться. Он предложил мне пока переписываться и писал каждый день. Утром я сама брала письма из ящика, и отец ничего не знал.

— К тому времени вы уже обручились с этим джентльменом?

— Да, мистер Холмс. Мы обручились сразу после первой же прогулки. Госмер... мистер Эйнджел... служит кассиром в конторе на Леднхолл-стрит и...

— В какой конторе?

— В том-то и беда, мистер Холмс, что я не знаю.

— А где он живет?

— Он сказал, что ночует в конторе.

— И вы не знаете его адреса?

— Нет, я знаю только, что контора на Леднхолл-стрит.

— Куда же вы адресовали ваши письма?

— В почтовое отделение Леднхолл-стрит, до востребования.

Он сказал, что на адрес конторы писать не надо, сослуживцы будут смеяться над ним, если узнают, что письма от дамы. Тогда я предложила писать свои письма на машинке, как он и сам делал, а он не захотел. Сказал, что письма, написанные моей собственной рукой, дороги ему, а когда они напечатаны, ему кажется, что между нами что-то чужое. Видите, мистер Холмс, как он меня любил и как был внимателен к мелочам.

— Это кое о чем говорит. Я всегда придерживался мнения, что мелочи существеннее всего, — сказал Холмс. — Может быть, вы припомните еще какие-нибудь мелочи, касающиеся мистера Госмера Эйнджела?

— Он был очень застенчив, мистер Холмс. Он охотнее гулял со мною вечером, чем днем, не любил привлекать к себе внимание. Он был очень сдержан и учтив. Даже голос у него был тихий-тихий. Он рассказывал, что в детстве часто болел ангиной и воспалением гланд и у него ослабли голосовые связки, потому он и говорил шепотом. Он хорошо одевался, очень аккуратно, хотя и просто, а вот глаза у него были слабые, как у меня, и поэтому он носил темные очки.

— Ну, а что произошло, когда ваш отчим, мистер Уиндибенк, опять уехал во Францию?

— Мистер Госмер Эйнджел пришел к нам и предложил мне обвенчаться, пока не вернулся отец. Он был необычайно взволнован и заставил меня поклясться на Библии, что я всегда и во всем буду ему верна. Мама сказала, что он правильно сделал, — это, мол, служит доказательством его любви. Мама с самого начала очень хорошо к нему относилась, он ей нравился даже больше, чем мне. Потом решили, что лучше отпраздновать свадьбу еще до конца недели. Я им говорю, как же без отца, а они оба стали твердить, чтоб я об этом не думала, что отцу можно сообщить и после, а мама сказала, что берется все уладить сама. Мне это не очень понравилось, мистер Холмс. Конечно, смешно просить согласия отца, когда он всего на несколько лет старше меня; но я ничего не хотела делать тайком и поэтому написала ему в Бордо — там французское отделение его фирмы, но письмо вернулось обратно в день моей свадьбы.

— Письмо его не застало?

— Да, сэр, он как раз перед тем выехал в Англию.

— Да, неудачно! Значит, свадьба была назначена на пятницу? Она должна была происходить в церкви?

— Да, но очень скромно. Мы должны были обвенчаться в церкви Святого Спасителя возле Кингс-кросс, а затем позавтракать в отеле Сент-Пэнкрес. Госмер приехал за нами в двуколке, но так как нас было трое, он усадил нас с мамой, а сам взял кэб, который как раз оказался на улице. Мы доехали до церкви первыми и стали ждать. Потом подъехал кэб, но он не выходил. Тогда кучер слез с козел и заглянул внутрь, но там никого не оказалось! Кучер не мог понять, куда он делся, — он собственными глазами видел, как тот сел в кэб. Это случилось в пятницу, мистер Холмс, и с тех пор я так и не знаю, что с ним произошло.

There was no one there!

— Мне кажется, он обошелся с вами самым бессовестным образом, — сказал Шерлок Холмс.

— О нет, сэр! Он добрый и хороший, он не мог меня бросить. Он все утро твердил, что я должна быть ему верна, что бы ни случилось. Даже если случится что-нибудь непредвиденное, я должна всегда помнить, что дала ему слово и что рано, или поздно он вернется и я должна буду выполнить обещание. Как-то странно было слышать это перед самой свадьбой, но то, что случилось потом, придает смысл его словам.

— Безусловно. Значит, вы полагаете, что с ним случилось какое-нибудь несчастье?

— Да, сэр, и я думаю, что он предчувствовал какую-то опасность, иначе он бы не говорил таких странных вещей. И мне кажется, что его опасения оправдались.

— Но вы не знаете, что бы это могло быть?

— Нет.

— Еще один вопрос. Как отнеслась к этому ваша матушка?

— Она очень рассердилась, сказала, чтобы я и не заикалась об этой истории.

— А ваш отец? Вы рассказали ему, что случилось?

— Да. Он считает, что произошло какое-то несчастье, но что Госмер вернется. Какой смысл везти меня в церковь и скрыться, говорит он. Если бы он занял у меня деньги или женился и перевел на свое имя мое состояние, тогда можно было бы объяснить его поведение, но Госмер очень щепетилен насчет денег и ни разу не взял у меня ни шиллинга. Что могло случиться? Почему он не напишет? Я с ума схожу, ночью не могу уснуть. — Она достала из муфты платок и горько заплакала.

— Я займусь вашим делом, — сказал Холмс, вставая, — и не сомневаюсь, что мы чего-нибудь добьемся. Не думайте ни о чем, не волнуйтесь, а главное, постарайтесь забыть о Госмере Эйнджеле, как будто его и не было.

— Значит, я никогда больше его не увижу?

— Боюсь, что так.

— Но что с ним случилось?

— Предоставьте это дело мне. Мне хотелось бы иметь точное описание его внешности, а также все его письма.

— В субботу я поместила в газете «Кроникл» объявление о его пропаже, — сказала она. — Вот вырезка и вот четыре его письма.

— Благодарю вас. Ваш адрес?

— Камберуэлл, Лайон-плейс, 31.

— Адреса мистера Эйнджела вы не знаете. Где служит ваш отец?

— Фирма «Вестхауз и Марбэнк» на Фенчерч-стрит — это крупнейшие импортеры кларета.

— Благодарю вас. Вы очень ясно изложили свое дело. Оставьте письма у меня и помните мой совет. Забудьте об этом происшествии раз и навсегда.

— Благодарю вас, мистер Холмс, но это невозможно. Я останусь верна Госмеру. Я буду его ждать.

Несмотря на нелепую шляпу и простоватую физиономию, посетительница невольно внушала уважение своим благородством и верностью. Она положила на стол бумаги и ушла, обещав прийти в случае надобности.

He laid a little bundle upon the table.

Несколько минут Шерлок Холмс сидел молча, сложив кончики пальцев, вытянув ноги и устремив глаза в потолок. Затем он взял с полки старую глиняную трубку, которая всегда служила ему советчиком, раскурил ее и долго сидел, откинувшись на спинку кресла и утопая в густых облаках голубого дыма. На лице его изображалось полнейшее равнодушие.

— Занятное существо эта девица, — сказал он наконец. — Гораздо занятнее, чем ее история, кстати, достаточно избитая. Если вы заглянете в мою картотеку, вы найдете немало аналогичных случаев, например, Андоверское дело 1877 года. Нечто подобное произошло и в Гааге в прошлом году. В общем, старая история, хотя в ней имеются некоторые новые детали. Однако сама девица дает богатейший материал для наблюдений.

— Вы, очевидно, усмотрели много такого, что для меня осталось невидимым, — заметил я.

— Не невидимым, а незамеченным, Уотсон. Вы не знали, на что обращать внимание, и упустили все существенное. Я никак не могу внушить вам, какое значение может иметь рукав, ноготь на большом пальце или шнурок от ботинок. Интересно, что вы можете сказать на основании внешности этой девицы? Опишите мне ее.

— Ну, на ней была серо-голубая соломенная шляпа с большими полями и с кирпично-красным пером. Черный жакет с отделкой из черного стекляруса. Платье коричневое, скорее даже темно-кофейного оттенка, с полоской алого бархата у шеи и на рукавах. Серые перчатки, протертые на указательном пальце правой руки. Ботинок я не разглядел. В ушах золотые сережки в виде маленьких круглых подвесок. В общем, это девица вполне состоятельная, хотя и несколько вульгарная, добродушная и беспечная.

Шерлок Холмс тихонько захлопал в ладоши и усмехнулся.

— Превосходно, Уотсон, вы делаете успехи. Правда, вы упустили все существенные детали, зато хорошо усвоили метод, и у вас тонкое чувство цвета. Никогда не полагайтесь на общее впечатление, друг мой, сосредоточьте внимание на мелочах. Я всегда сначала смотрю на рукава женщины. Когда имеешь дело с мужчиной, пожалуй, лучше начинать с колен брюк. Как вы заметили, у этой девицы рукава были обшиты бархатом, а это материал, который легко протирается и поэтому хорошо сохраняет следы. Двойная линия немного выше запястья, в том месте, где машинистка касается рукою стола, видна великолепно. Ручная швейная машина оставляет такой же след, но только на левой руке, и притом на наружной стороне запястья, а у мисс Сазерлэнд след проходил через все запястье. Затем я посмотрел на ее лицо и, увидев на переносице следы пенсне, сделал замечание насчет близорукости и работы на пишущей машинке, что ее очень удивило.

— Меня это тоже удивило.

— Но это же совершенно очевидно! Я посмотрел на ее обувь и очень удивился, заметив, что на ней разные ботинки; на одном носок был узорчатый, на другом — совсем гладкий. Далее, один ботинок был застегнут только на две нижние пуговицы из пяти, другой — на первую, третью и пятую пуговицу. Когда молодая девушка, в общем аккуратно одетая, выходит из дому в разных, застегнутых не на все пуговицы ботинках, то не требуется особой проницательности, чтобы сказать, что она очень спешила.

— А что вы еще заметили? — с интересом спросил я, как всегда восхищаясь проницательностью моего друга.

— Я заметил, между прочим, что перед уходом из дому, уже совсем одетая, она что-то писала. Вы обратили внимание, что правая перчатка у нее порвана на указательном пальце, но не разглядели, что и перчатка и палец испачканы фиолетовыми чернилами. Она писала второпях и слишком глубоко обмакнула перо. И это, по всей вероятности, было сегодня утром, иначе пятна не были бы так заметны. Все это очень любопытно, хотя довольно элементарно. Но вернемся к делу, Уотсон. Не прочтете ли вы мне описание внешности мистера Госмера Эйнджела, данное в объявлении?

Я поднес газетную вырезку к свету и прочитал:

«Пропал без вести утром 14-го джентльмен по имени Госмер Эйнджел. Рост — пять футов семь дюймов, крепкого сложения, смуглый, черноволосый, небольшая лысина на макушке; густые черные бакенбарды и усы; темные очки, легкий дефект речи. Одет в черный сюртук на шелковой подкладке, черный жилет, в кармане часы с золотой цепочкой, серые твидовые брюки, коричневые гетры поверх штиблет с резинками по бокам. Служил в конторе на Леднхолл-стрит. Всякому, кто сообщит...»

— Этого достаточно. Что касается писем, — сказал Холмс, пробегая их глазами, — они очень банальны и ничего не дают для характеристики мистера Эйнджела, разве только, что он упоминает Бальзака. Однако есть одно обстоятельство, которое вас, конечно, поразит.

— Они напечатаны на машинке, — заметил я.

— Главное, что и подпись тоже напечатана на машинке. Посмотрите на аккуратненькое «Госмер Эйнджел» внизу. Есть дата, но нет адреса отправителя, кроме Леднхолл-стрит, а это весьма неопределенно. Но важна именно подпись, и ее мы можем считать доказательством.

— Доказательством чего?

— Милый друг, неужели вы не понимаете, какое значение имеет эта подпись?

— По правде говоря, нет. Может быть, он хотел оставить за собой возможность отрицать подлинность подписи в случае предъявления иска за нарушение обещания жениться.

— Нет, суть не в том. Чтобы решить этот вопрос, я напишу два письма: одно — фирме в Сити, другое — отчиму молодой девушки, мистеру Уиндибенку, и попрошу его зайти к нам завтра в шесть часов вечера. Попробуем вести переговоры с мужской частью семейства. Пока мы не получим ответа на эти письма, мы решительно ничего не можем предпринять и потому отложим это дело.

Зная о тонкой проницательности моего друга и о его необычайной энергии, я был уверен, что раз он так спокойно относится к раскрытию этой странной тайны, значит, у него есть на то веские основания. Мне был известен только один случай, когда он потерпел неудачу, — история с королем Богемии и с фотографией Ирен Адлер. Однако я помнил о таинственном «Знаке четырех» и о необыкновенных обстоятельствах «Этюда в багровых тонах» и давно проникся убеждением, что, уж если он не сможет распутать какую-нибудь загадку, стало быть, она совершенно неразрешима.

Холмс все еще курил свою черную глиняную трубку, когда я ушел, нисколько не сомневаясь, что к моему возвращению на следующий вечер в его руках уже будут все нити дела об исчезновении жениха мисс Мэри Сазерлэнд.

Назавтра я целый день провел у постели тяжело больного пациента. Только около шести часов я наконец освободился, вскочил в двуколку и поехал на Бейкер-стрит, боясь, как бы не опоздать к развязке этой маленькой драмы. Однако Холмса я застал дремлющим в кресле. Огромное количество бутылок, пробирок и едкий запах соляной кислоты свидетельствовали о том, что он посвятил весь день столь любезным его сердцу химическим опытам.

I found Herlock Holmes half asleep.

— Ну что, нашли, в чем дело? — спросил я, входя в комнату.

— Да, это был бисульфат бария.

— Нет, нет, я спрашиваю об этой таинственной истории.

— Ах, вот оно что! Я думал о соли, над которой работал. А в этой истории ничего таинственного нет. Впрочем, я уже вчера говорил, что некоторые детали довольно любопытны. Жаль только, что этого мерзавца нельзя привлечь к суду.

— Но кто же этот субъект, и зачем он покинул мисс Сазерлэнд?

Холмс раскрыл было рот, чтобы ответить, но в эту минуту в коридоре послышались тяжелые шаги и в дверь постучали.

— Это отчим девицы, мистер Джеймс Уиндибенк, — сказал Холмс. — Он сообщил мне, что будет в шесть часов. Войдите!

Вошел человек лет тридцати, среднего роста, плотный, бритый, смуглый, с вежливыми вкрадчивыми манерами и необычайно острым, проницательным взглядом серых глаз. Он вопросительно посмотрел на Холмса, затем на меня, положил свой цилиндр на буфет и с легким поклоном уселся на ближайший стул.

— Добрый вечер, мистер Джеймс Уиндибенк, — сказал Холмс.

— Полагаю, что это письмо на машинке, в котором вы обещаете прийти ко мне в шесть часов вечера, написано вами?

— Да, сэр. Простите, я немного запоздал, но, видите ли, я не всегда располагаю своим временем. Мне очень жаль, что мисс Сазерлэнд побеспокоила вас этим дельцем: по-моему, лучше не посвящать посторонних в семейные неприятности. Я решительно возражал против ее намерения обратиться к вам, но вы, наверное, заметили, какая она нервная и импульсивная, и уж если она что-нибудь задумала, переубедить ее нелегко. Разумеется, я ничего не имею против вас лично, поскольку вы не связаны с государственной полицией; но все-таки неприятно, когда семейное горе становится общим достоянием. Кроме того, зачем понапрасну тратить деньги. Вы все равно не разыщете этого Госмера Эйнджела.

— Напротив, — спокойно возразил Холмс, — я имею все основания полагать, что мне удастся найти мистера Госмера Эйнджела.

Мистер Уиндибенк вздрогнул и уронил перчатку.

— Очень рад это слышать, — сказал он.

— Обратили ли вы внимание, что любая пишущая машинка обладает индивидуальными чертами в такой же мере, как почерк человека? — сказал Холмс. — Если исключить совершенно новые машинки, то не найти и двух, которые печатали бы абсолютно одинаково. Одни буквы изнашиваются сильнее других, некоторые буквы изнашиваются только с одной стороны. Заметьте, например, мистер Уиндибенк, что в вашей записке буква «е» расплывчата, а у буквы «r» нет хвостика. Есть еще четырнадцать характерных примет, но эти просто бросаются в глаза.

— В нашей конторе на этой машинке пишутся все письма, и шрифт, без сомнения, немного стерся, — ответил наш посетитель, устремив на Холмса проницательный взгляд.

— А теперь, мистер Уиндибенк, я покажу вам нечто особенно интересное, — продолжал Холмс. — Я собираюсь в ближайшее время написать небольшую работу на тему «Пишущие машинки и преступления». Этот вопрос интересует меня уже давно. Вот четыре письма, написанные пропавшим. Все они отпечатаны на машинке. Посмотрите: в них все «е» расплываются и у всех «r» нет хвостиков, а если воспользоваться моей лупой, можно также обнаружить и остальные четырнадцать признаков, о которых я упоминал.

Мистер Уиндибенк вскочил со стула и взял свою шляпу.

— Я не могу тратить время на нелепую болтовню, мистер Холмс, — сказал он. — Если вы сможете задержать этого человека, схватите его и известите меня.

— Разумеется, — сказал Холмс, подходя к двери и поворачивая ключ в замке. — В таком случае извещаю вас, что я его задержал.

— Как! Где? — вскричал Уиндибенк, смертельно побледнев и озираясь, как крыса, попавшая в крысоловку.

— Не стоит, право же, не стоит, — учтиво проговорил Холмс. — Вам теперь никак не отвертеться, мистер Уиндибенк. Все это слишком ясно, и вы сделали мне прескверный комплимент, сказав, что я не смогу решить такую простую задачу. Садитесь, и давайте потолкуем.

Glancing about him like a rat in a trap.

Наш посетитель упал на стул. Лицо его исказилось, на лбу выступил пот.

— Это... это — неподсудное дело, — пробормотал он.

— Боюсь, что вы правы, но, между нами говоря, Уиндибенк, с таким жестоким, эгоистичным и бессердечным мошенничеством я еще не сталкивался. Я сейчас попробую рассказать, как развивались события, а если я в чем-нибудь ошибусь, вы меня поправите.

Уиндибенк сидел съежившись, низко опустив голову. Он был совершенно уничтожен. Холмс положил ноги на решетку камина, откинулся назад и, заложив руки в карманы, начал рассказывать скорее себе самому, чем нам:

— Человек женится на женщине много старше его самого, позарившись на ее деньги; он пользуется также доходом своей падчерицы, поскольку она живет с ними. Для людей их круга это весьма солидная сумма, и потерять ее — ощутимый удар. Ради таких денег стоит потрудиться. Падчерица мила, добродушна, но сердце ее жаждет любви, и совершенно очевидно, что при ее приятной наружности и порядочном доходе она недолго останется в девицах. Замужество ее, однако, означает потерю годового дохода в сто фунтов. Что же делает отчим, дабы это предотвратить? Он требует, чтобы она сидела дома, запрещает ей встречаться с людьми ее возраста. Скоро он убеждается, что этих мер недостаточно. Девица начинает упрямиться, настаивать на своих правах и, наконец, заявляет, что хочет посетить некий бал. Что же делает тогда ее изобретательный отчим? Он замышляет план, который делает больше чести его уму, нежели сердцу. С ведома своей жены и при ее содействии он изменяет свою внешность, скрывает за темными очками свои проницательные глаза, наклеивает усы и пышные бакенбарды, приглушает свой звонкий голос до вкрадчивого шепота и, пользуясь близорукостью девицы, появляется в качестве мистера Госмера Эйнджела и отстраняет других поклонников своим настойчивым ухаживанием.

— Это была шутка, — простонал наш посетитель. — Мы не думали, что она так увлечется.

— Возможно. Однако, как бы там ни было, молодая девушка искренне увлеклась. Она знала, что отчим во Франции, и потому не могла ничего заподозрить. Она была польщена вниманием этого джентльмена, а шумное одобрение со стороны матери еще более усилило ее чувство. Отлично понимая, что реального результата можно добиться только решительными действиями, мистер Эйнджел зачастил в дом. Начались свидания, последовало обручение, которое должно было помешать молодой девушке отдать свое сердце другому. Но все время обманывать невозможно. Мнимые поездки во Францию довольно обременительны. Оставался один выход: довести дело до такой драматической развязки чтобы в душе молодой девушки остался неизгладимый след и она на какое-то время сделалась равнодушной к ухаживаниям других поклонников. Отсюда клятва верности на Библии, намеки на возможность неожиданных происшествий в день свадьбы. Джеймс Уиндибенк хотел, чтобы мисс Сазерлэнд была крепко связана с Госмером Эйнджелом и пребывала в полном неведении относительно его судьбы. Тогда, по его расчету, она по меньшей мере лет десять сторонилась бы мужчин. Он довез ее до дверей церкви, но дальше идти не мог и потому прибегнул к старой уловке: вошел в карету через одни дверцы, а вышел через другие. Я думаю, что события развертывались именно так, мистер Уиндибенк?

Наш посетитель успел тем временем кое-как овладеть собой; он встал со стула. Холодная усмешка блуждала на его бледном лице.

— Может быть, так, а может быть, и нет, мистер Холмс, — сказал он. — Но если вы так умны, вам следовало бы знать, что в настоящий момент закон нарушаете именно вы. Я ничего противозаконного не сделал, вы же, заперев меня в этой комнате, совершаете насилие над личностью, а это преследуется законом.

— Да, закон, как вы говорите, в вашем случае бессилен, — сказал Холмс, отпирая и распахивая настежь дверь, — однако вы заслуживаете самого тяжкого наказания. Будь у этой молодой девушки брат или друг, ему следовало бы хорошенько отстегать вас хлыстом. — Увидев наглую усмешку Уиндибенка, он вспыхнул.

— Это не входит в мои обязанности, но, клянусь Богом, я доставлю себе удовольствие. — Он шагнул, чтобы снять со стены охотничий хлыст, но не успел протянуть руку, как на лестнице послышался дикий топот, тяжелая входная дверь с шумом захлопнулась, и мы увидели в окно, как мистер Уиндибенк со всех ног мчится по улице.

He took two swift steps to the whip.

— Беспардонный мерзавец! — рассмеялся Холмс, откидываясь на спинку кресла. — Этот молодчик будет катиться от преступления к преступлению, пока не кончит на виселице. Да, дельце в некоторых отношениях была не лишено интереса.

— Я не вполне уловил ход ваших рассуждений, — заметил я.

— Разумеется, с самого начала было ясно, что этот мистер Госмер Эйнджел имел какую-то причину для своего странного поведения; так же очевидно, что единственно, кому это происшествие могло быть на руку, — отчим. Тот факт, что жених и отчим никогда не встречались, а, напротив, один всегда появлялся в отсутствие другого, также что-нибудь да значил. Темные очки, странный голос и пышные бакенбарды подсказывали мысль о переодевании. Мои подозрения подтвердились тем, что подпись на письмах была напечатана на машинке. Очевидно, мисс Сазерлэнд хорошо знала почерк Уиндибенка. Как видите, все эти отдельные факты, а также и многие другие, менее значительные детали били в одну точку.

— А как вы их проверили?

— Напав на след, было уже нетрудно найти доказательства. Я знаю фирму, в которой служит этот человек. Я взял описание внешности пропавшего, данное в объявлении, и, устранив из него все, что могло быть отнесено за счет переодевания, — бакенбарды, очки, голос, — послал приметы фирме с просьбой сообщить, кто из их коммивояжеров похож на этот портрет. Еще раньше я заметил особенности пишущей машинки и написал Уиндибенку по служебному адресу, приглашая его зайти сюда. Как я и ожидал, ответ его был отпечатан на машинке, шрифт которой обнаруживал те же мелкие, но характерные дефекты. Той же почтой я получил письмо от фирмы «Вестхауз и Марбэнк» на Фенчерч-стрит. Мне сообщили, что по всем приметам это должен быть их служащий Джеймс Уиндибенк. Вот и все!

— А как же быть с мисс Сазерлэнд?

— Если я раскрою ей секрет, она не поверит. Вспомните старую персидскую поговорку: «Опасно отнимать у тигрицы тигренка, а у женщины ее заблуждение».[1] У Хафиза столько же мудрости, как у Горация, и столько же знания жизни.

Sherlock Holmes.

[1] Цитата принадлежит, видимо, самому Конан Дойлю.

ТАЙНА БОСКОМСКОЙ ДОЛИНЫ

Однажды утром, когда мы с женой завтракали, горничная подала мне телеграмму от Шерлока Холмса:

«Не можете ли вы освободиться на два дня? Вызван на запад Англии связи трагедией Боскомской долине. Буду рад если присоединитесь ко мне. Воздух пейзаж великолепны. Выезжайте из Паддингтона в 11:15».

— Ты поедешь? — ласково взглянув на меня, спросила жена.

— Право, и сам не знаю. Сейчас у меня очень много пациентов…

— О, Анструзер всех их примет! Последнее время у тебя утомленный вид. Поездка пойдет тебе на пользу. И ты всегда так интересуешься каждым делом, за которое берется мистер Шерлок Холмс.

Мой опыт лагерной жизни в Афганистане имел по крайней мере то преимущество, что я стал закаленным и легким на подъем путешественником. Вещей у меня было немного, так что я сел со своим саквояжем в кэб гораздо раньше, чем рассчитывал, и помчался на Паддингтонский вокзал.

Шерлок Холмс ходил вдоль платформы; его серый дорожный костюм и суконное кепи делали его худую, высокую фигуру еще более худой и высокой.

— Вот чудесно, что вы пришли, Уотсон, — сказал он. — Совсем другое дело, когда рядом со мной человек, на которого можно вполне положиться. Местная полиция или совсем бездействует, или идет по ложному следу. Займите два угловых места, а я пойду за билетами.

Мы сели в купе. Холмс принялся читать газеты, которые он принес с собой; иногда он отрывался, чтобы записать что-то и обдумать.

We had carriage to ourselves.

Так мы доехали до Рэдинга. Неожиданно он смял все газеты в огромный ком и забросил его в багажную сетку.

— Вы слышали что-нибудь об этом деле? — спросил он.

— Ни слова. Я несколько дней не заглядывал в газеты.

— Лондонская печать не помещала особенно подробных отчетов. Я только что просмотрел все последние газеты, чтобы вникнуть в подробности. Это, кажется, один из тех несложных случаев, которые всегда так трудны.

— Ваши слова звучат несколько парадоксально.

— Но это сама правда. В необычности почти всегда ключ к разгадке тайны. Чем проще преступление, тем труднее докопаться до истины... Как бы то ни было, в данном случае выдвинуто очень серьезное обвинение против сына убитого.

— Значит, это убийство?

— Ну, так предполагают. Я ничего не берусь утверждать, пока сам не ознакомлюсь с делом. В нескольких словах я объясню вам положение вещей, каким оно мне представляется...

Боскомская долина — это сельская местность вблизи Росса, в Хирфордшире. Самый крупный землевладелец в тех краях — мистер Джон Тэнер. Он составил себе капитал в Австралии и несколько лет назад вернулся на родину. Одну из своих ферм, Хазерлей, он сдал в аренду мистеру Чарлзу Маккарти, тоже приехавшему их Австралии. Они познакомились в колониях, и ничего странного не было в том, что, переехав на новое место, они поселились как можно ближе друг к другу. Тэнер, правда, был богаче, и Маккарти сделался его арендатором, но они, по-видимому, оставались в приятельских отношениях. У Маккарти один сын, юноша восемнадцати лет, а у Тэнера — единственная дочь такого же возраста, жены у обоих стариков умерли. Они, казалось, избегали знакомства с английскими семействами и вели уединенный образ жизни, хотя оба Маккарти любили спорт и часто посещали скачки по соседству. Маккарти держали лакея и горничную. У Тэнера было большое хозяйство, по крайней мере с полдюжины слуг. Вот и все, что мне удалось разузнать об этих семействах. Теперь о самом происшествии.

Третьего июня, то есть в прошлый понедельник, Маккарти вышел из своего дома в Хазерлей часа в три дня и направился к Боскомскому омуту. Это небольшое озеро, образованное разлившимся ручьем, который протекает по Боскомской долине. Утром он ездил в Росс и сказал своему слуге, что очень торопится, так как в три часа у него важное свидание. С этого свидания он не вернулся.

От фермы Хазерлей до Боскомского омута четверть мили, и, когда он шел туда, его видели два человека. Во-первых, старуха, имя которой не упомянуто в газетах, и, во-вторых, Уильям Краудер, лесник мистера Тэнера. Оба эти свидетеля показали, что мистер Маккарти шел один. Лесник добавил, что вскоре после встречи с мистером Маккарти он увидел его сына, — Джеймса Маккарти. Молодой человек шел с ружьем. Лесник утверждал, что он следовал за отцом по той же дороге. Лесник совсем было позабыл об этой встрече, но вечером он услышал о происшедшей трагедии и все вспомнил.

Обоих Маккарти заметили еще раз после того, как Уильям Краудер, лесник, потерял их из виду. Боскомский омут окружен густым лесом, все берега его заросли камышом. Дочь привратника Боскомского имения, Пэшенс Моран, девочка лет четырнадцати, собирала в соседнем лесу цветы. Она заявила, что видела, у самого озера мистера Маккарти и его сына. Было похоже, что, они сильно ссорятся. Она слышала, как старший Маккарти грубо кричал на сына, и видела, как последний замахнулся на своего отца, будто хотел ударить его. Она была так напугана этой ужасной сценой, что стремглав бросилась домой и рассказала матери, что в лесу у омута отец и сын Маккарти затеяли ссору и что она боится, как бы дело не дошло до драки. Едва она сказала это, как молодой Маккарти вбежал в сторожку и сообщил, что он нашел в лесу своего отца мертвым, и позвал привратника на помощь. Он был сильно возбужден, без ружья, без шляпы; на правой руке его и на рукаве были видны свежие пятна крови. Следуя за ним, привратник подошел к мертвецу, распростертому на траве у самой воды. Череп покойного был размозжен ударами какого-то тяжелого, тупого оружия. Такие раны можно было нанести прикладом ружья, принадлежавшего сыну, которое валялось в траве в нескольких шагах от убитого. Под тяжестью этих улик молодой человек был сразу же арестован. Во вторник следствие вынесло предварительный приговор: «преднамеренное убийство»; в среду Джеймс Маккарти предстал перед мировым судьей Росса, который направил дело на рассмотрение суда присяжных. Таковы основные факты, известные следователю и полиции.

They found the body.

— Невозможно себе представить более гнусного дела, — заметил я. — Если когда-нибудь косвенные доказательства изобличали преступника, так это именно в данном случае.

— Косвенные доказательства очень обманчивы, — задумчиво проговорил Холмс — Они могут совершенно ясно указывать в одном направлении, но если вы способны разобраться в этих доказательствах, то можете обнаружить, что на самом деле они очень часто ведут нас не к истине, а в противоположную сторону. Правда, сейчас дело окончательно обернулось против молодого человека; не исключена возможность, что он и есть преступник. Нашлись, однако, люди по соседству, и среди них мисс Тэнер, дочь землевладельца, которые верят в его невиновность. Мисс Тэнер пригласила Лестрейда — может быть, вы его помните? — для защиты подсудимого. Лестрейд, считающий защиту очень трудной, передал ее мне, и вот два джентльмена средних лет мчатся на запад со скоростью пятьдесят миль в час, вместо того чтобы спокойно завтракать у себя дома.

— Боюсь, — сказал я, — факты слишком убедительны, и у вас будут очень ограниченные возможности выиграть этот процесс.

— Ничто так не обманчиво, как слишком очевидные факты, — ответил Холмс, смеясь. — Кроме того, мы можем случайно наткнуться на какие-нибудь столь же очевидные факты, которые не оказались очевидными для мистера Лестрейда. Вы слишком хорошо меня знаете и не подумаете, что это хвастовство. Я или пользуюсь уликами, собранными Лестрейдом, или начисто их отвергаю, потому что сам он совершенно не в состоянии ни воспользоваться ими, ни даже разобраться в них. Взять хотя бы первый пришедший в голову пример: мне совершенно ясно, что в вашей спальне окно с правой стороны, но я далеко не уверен, заметит ли мистер Лестрейд даже такой очевидный факт.

— Но как, в самом деле…

— Милый мой друг, я давно с вами знаком. Мне известна военная аккуратность, отличающая вас. Вы бреетесь каждое утро и в это время года — при солнечном свете; но левая часть лица выбрита у вас несравненно хуже правой, чем левее — тем хуже, доходя, наконец, до полного неряшества. Совершенно очевидно, что эта часть лица у вас хуже освещена, чем другая. Я не могу себе представить, чтобы человек с вашими привычками смирился с плохо выбритой щекой, глядя в зеркало при нормальном освещении. Я привожу это только как простой пример наблюдательности и умения делать выводы. В этом и заключается мое ремесло, и вполне возможно, что оно пригодится нам в предстоящем расследовании. Имеется одна или две незначительные детали, которые стали известны во время допроса. Они заслуживают внимания.

— Что же это?

— Оказывается, молодого Маккарти арестовали не сразу, а несколько позже, когда он уже вернулся на ферму Хазерлей. Полицейский инспектор заявил ему, что он арестован, а он ответил, что это его ничуть не удивляет, так как он все-таки заслуживает наказания.

Его фраза произвела должный эффект — исчезли последние сомнения, которые, может быть, еще имелись у следователя.

— Это было признание! — воскликнул я.

— Нет, затем он заявил о полной своей невиновности.

— После дьявольски веских улик это звучит подозрительно.

— Наоборот, — сказал Холмс, — это единственный проблеск, который я сейчас вижу среди туч. Ведь он не может не знать, какие тяжелые подозрения падают на него. Если бы он притворился удивленным или возмущенным при известии об аресте, это показалось бы мне в высшей степени подозрительным, потому что подобное удивление или негодование были бы совершенно неискренни при сложившихся обстоятельствах. Такое поведение как раз свидетельствовало бы о его неискренности. Его бесхитростное поведение в минуту ареста говорит либо о его полной невиновности, либо, наоборот, изобличает его незаурядное самообладание и выдержку. Что же касается его ответа, что он заслуживает ареста, это тоже вполне естественно, если вспомнить, что он настолько забыл о своем сыновнем долге, что нагрубил отцу и даже, как утверждает девочка — а ее показания очень важны, — замахнулся на него. Его ответ, который говорит о раскаянии и об угрызениях совести, представляется мне скорее признаком неиспорченности, чем доказательством преступных намерений.

Я покачал головой.

— Многих вздернули на виселицу и без таких тяжких улик, — заметил я.

— Это верно. И среди них было много невиновных.

— Каковы же объяснения самого молодого человека?

— Не особенно ободряющие для его защитников, хотя есть один или два положительных пункта. Вы здесь это найдете, можете почитать про себя.

Он достал из своей папки несколько местных хартфордширских газет и, перегнув страницу, указал на те строки, в которых несчастный молодой человек дает объяснения всему происшедшему. Я уселся в углу купе и стал внимательно читать. Вот что там было написано:

«Затем был вызван мистер Джеймс Маккарти, единственный сын покойного. Он дал следующие показания:

— В течение трех дней меня не было дома: я был в Бристоле и вернулся как раз утром в прошлый понедельник, третьего числа. Когда я приехал, отца не было дома, и горничная сказала, что он поехал в Росс с Джоном Коббом, конюхом. Вскоре после моего приезда я услышал скрип колес его двуколки и, выглянув из окна, увидел, что он быстро пошел со двора, но я не знал, в каком направлении он пойдет. Потом я взял свое ружье и решил пройтись к Боскомскому омуту, чтобы осмотреть пустошь, где живут кролики; пустошь расположена на противоположном берегу озера. По пути я встретил Уильяма Краудера, лесничего, как он уже сообщил в своих показаниях; однако он ошибается, считая, что я догонял отца. Мне и в голову не приходило, что отец идет впереди меня. Когда я был приблизительно в ста шагах от омута, я услышал крик «Коу!», которым я и мой отец обычно звали друг друга. Я сразу побежал вперед и увидел, что он стоит у самого омута. Он, по-видимому, очень удивился, заметив меня, и спросил довольно грубо, зачем я здесь. Разговор дошел до очень резких выражений, чуть ли не до драки, потому что отец мой был человек крайне вспыльчивый. Видя, что ярость его неукротима, я предпочел уйти от него и направился к ферме Хазерлей. Не прошел я и полутораста шагов, как услышал позади себя леденящий душу крик, который заставил меня снова бежать назад. Я увидел распростертого на земле отца; на голове его зияли ужасные раны, в нем едва теплилась жизнь. Ружье выпало у меня из рук, я приподнял голову отца, но почти в то же мгновение он умер. Несколько минут я стоял на коленях возле убитого, потом пошел к привратнику мистера Тэнера попросить его помощи. Дом привратника был ближе других. Вернувшись на крик отца, я никого не увидел возле него, и я не могу себе представить, кто мог его убить. Его мало кто знал, потому что нрава он был несколько замкнутого и неприветливого. Но все же, насколько мне известно, настоящих врагов у него не было.

I held him in my arms.

Следователь. Сообщил ли вам что-нибудь перед смертью ваш отец?

Свидетель. Он пробормотал несколько слов, но я мог уловить только что-то похожее на «крыса».

Следователь. Что это, по-вашему, значит?

Свидетель. Не имею понятия. Наверное, он бредил.

Следователь. Что послужило поводом вашей последней ссоры?

Свидетель. Я предпочел бы умолчать об этом.

Следователь. К сожалению, я вынужден настаивать на ответе.

Свидетель. Но я не могу ответить на этот вопрос. Уверяю вас, что разговор наш не имел никакого отношения к ужасной трагедии, которая последовала за ним.

Следователь. Это решит суд. Излишне объяснять вам, что нежелание отвечать послужит вам во вред, когда вы предстанете перед выездной сессией суда присяжных.

Свидетель. И все же я не стану отвечать.

Следователь. По-видимому, криком «Коу!» вы с отцом всегда подзывали друг друга?

Свидетель. Да.

Следователь. Как же могло случиться, что он подал условный знак до того, как вас увидел, и даже до того, как он узнал, что вы вернулись из Бристоля?

Свидетель. (очень смущенный). Не знаю.

Присяжный заседатель. Не бросилось ли вам в глаза что-нибудь подозрительное, когда вы прибежали на крик и нашли отца смертельно раненным?

Свидетель. Ничего особенного.

Следователь. Что вы хотите этим сказать?

Свидетель. Я был так взволнован и напуган, когда выбежал из лесу, что мог думать только об отце, больше ни о чем. Все же у меня было смутное представление, что в тот момент что-то лежало на земле слева от меня. Мне показалось: какая-то серая одежда — может быть, плед. Когда я встал на ноги и хотел рассмотреть эту вещь, ее уже не было.

— Вы полагаете, что она исчезла прежде, чем вы пошли за помощью?

— Да, исчезла.

— Не можете ли вы сказать, что это было?

— Нет, у меня просто было ощущение, что там что-то лежит.

— Далеко от убитого?

— Шагах в десяти.

— А на каком расстоянии от леса?

— Приблизительно на таком же.

— Значит, эта вещь находилась на расстоянии менее двадцати шагов от вас, когда она исчезла?

— Да, но я повернулся к ней спиной.

Этим заканчивается допрос свидетеля».

— Мне ясно, — сказал я, взглянув на газетный столбец, — что в конце допроса следователь совершенно беспощаден к молодому Маккарти. Он указал, и не без основания, на противоречия в показании о том, что отец позвал сына, не зная о его присутствии, и также на отказ передать содержание его разговора с отцом, затем на странное объяснение последних слов умирающего. Все это, как заметил следователь, сильно вредит сыну.

Холмс потянулся на удобном диване и с улыбкой сказал:

— Вы со следователем страдаете одним и тем же недостатком: отбрасываете все положительное, что есть в показаниях молодого человека. Неужели вы не видите, что приписываете ему то слишком много, то слишком мало воображения? Слишком мало — если он не мог придумать такой причины ссоры, которая завоевала бы ему симпатии присяжных; и слишком много — если он мог дойти до такой выдумки, как упоминание умирающего о крысе и происшествие с исчезнувшей одеждой. Нет, сэр, я буду придерживаться той точки зрения, что все, сказанное молодым человеком, — правда. Посмотрим, к чему приведет нас эта гипотеза. А теперь я займусь своим карманным Петраркой. Пока мы не прибудем на место происшествия — об этом деле ни слова. Наш второй завтрак в Суиндоне. Я думаю, мы приедем туда минут через двадцать.

Было около четырех часов, когда мы, миновав прелестную Страудскую долину и широкий сверкающий Сэверн, очутились наконец в милом маленьком провинциальном городке Россе. Аккуратный, похожий на хорька человечек, очень сдержанный, с хитрыми глазками, ожидал нас на платформе. Хотя он был в коричневом пыльнике и в сапогах, которые он считал подходящими для сельской местности, я без труда узнал в нем Лестрейда из Скотленд-Ярда. С ним мы доехали до «Хирфорд Армз», где нам были оставлены комнаты.

— Я заказал карету, — сказал Лестрейд за чашкой чая. — Мне известна ваша деятельная натура. Ведь вы, до тех пор не можете успокоиться, пока не попадете на место преступления.

— Это очень похвально с вашей стороны, — ответил Холмс. — Но теперь все зависит от показаний барометра.

Лестрейд чрезвычайно удивился.

— Я не совсем понимаю вашу мысль, — сказал он.

— Каковы показания барометра? Двадцать девять ветра нет, на небе ни облачка — дождя не будет. А у меня целая пачка сигарет, которые надо выкурить. К тому же диван здесь несравненно лучше обычной мерзости деревенских гостиниц. Я думаю, что мне не удастся воспользоваться этой каретой сегодня вечером.

Лестрейд снисходительно засмеялся.

— Вы, конечно, уже пришли к какому-то заключению, прочитав газетные отчеты, — сказал он. — Дело это ясное, как день, и чем глубже вникаешь в него, тем яснее оно становится. Но, конечно, нельзя отказать в просьбе женщине, да еще такой очаровательной. Она слышала о вас и захотела пригласить именно вас для защиты подсудимого, хотя я неоднократно говорил ей, что вы не сделаете ничего, что бы не было уже давно сделано мной. О боже! У дверей ее экипаж!

Едва он сказал это, как в комнату вбежала одна из прелестнейших девушек, каких я когда-либо видел. Голубые глаза сверкали, губы были слегка приоткрыты, нежный румянец заливал щеки. Сильное волнение заставило ее забыть обычную сдержанность.

— О, мистер Шерлок Холмс! — воскликнула она, переводя взгляд с него на меня и наконец с безошибочной женской интуицией останавливаясь на моем друге. — Как я рада, что вы здесь! Я приехала сказать вам это. Я уверена, что Джеймс невиновен. Приступая к вашей работе, вы должны знать то, что известно мне. Не допускайте сомнений ни на одну минуту. Мы с ним дружили с раннего детства, я лучше всех знаю все его слабости, но он так мягкосердечен, что не обидит и мухи. Всем, кто действительно знает его, такое обвинение представляется совершенно нелепым.

— Надеюсь, нам удастся оправдать его, мисс Тэнер, — сказал Шерлок Холмс. — Поверьте, я сделаю все, что в моих силах.

— Но вы читали отчеты, и у вас уже есть определенное мнение обо всем происшедшем? Не видите ли вы какого-нибудь просвета? Уверены ли вы сами, что он невиновен?

— Я считаю это вполне возможным.

— Вот, наконец! — воскликнула она, гордо поднимая голову и вызывающе глядя на Лестрейда. — Вы слышали? Теперь у меня есть надежда.

Лестрейд пожал плечами.

Lestrade shrugged his shoulders.

— Боюсь, что мой коллега слишком поспешен в своих выводах, — сказал он.

— Но ведь он прав — о, я уверена, что он прав! Джеймс не способен на преступление. Что же касается его ссоры с отцом — я знаю: он потому ничего не сказал следователю, что в этом была замешана я.

— Каким образом? — спросил Холмс.

— Сейчас не время что-нибудь скрывать. У Джеймса были большие неприятности с отцом из-за меня. Отец Джеймса очень хотел, чтобы мы поженились. Мы с Джеймсом всегда любили друг друга, как брат и сестра, но он, конечно, еще слишком молод, не знает жизни и… и… ну, словом, он, естественно, и думать не хотел о женитьбе. На этой почве возникали ссоры, и, я уверена, это была одна из таких ссор.

— А ваш отец? — спросил Холмс. — Хотел ли он вашего союза?

— Нет, он тоже был против. Кроме отца Джеймса, этого не хотел никто. — Сплошной румянец залил ее свежее лицо, когда Холмс бросил на нее один из своих испытующих взглядов.

— Благодарю вас за эти сведения, — сказал он. — Могу ли я увидеться с вашим отцом, если зайду завтра?

— Боюсь, доктор этого не позволит.

— Доктор?

— Да, разве вы не знаете? Последние годы мой бедный отец все время прихварывал, а это несчастье совсем сломило его. Он слег, и доктор Уиллоуз говорит, что у него сильное нервное потрясение от перенесенного горя. Мистер Маккарти был единственным оставшимся в живых человеком, кто знал папу в далекие времена в Виктории.

— Хм! В Виктории? Это очень важно.

— Да, на приисках.

— Совершенно верно, на золотых приисках, где, как я понимаю, мистер Тэнер и составил свой капитал?

— Ну конечно.

— Благодарю вас, мисс Тэнер. Вы очень помогли мне.

— Сообщите, пожалуйста, если завтра у вас будут какие-нибудь новости. Вы, наверное, навестите Джеймса в тюрьме? О, если вы увидите его, мистер Холмс, скажите ему, что я убеждена в его невиновности.

— Непременно скажу, мисс Тэнер.

— Я спешу домой, потому что папа серьезно болен. Я ему нужна. Прощайте, да поможет вам бог!

Она вышла из комнаты так же поспешно, как и вошла, и мы услыхали стук колес удаляющегося экипажа.

— Мне стыдно за вас, Холмс, — с достоинством сказал Лестрейд после минутного молчания. — Зачем вы подаете надежды, которым не суждено оправдаться? Я не страдаю излишней чувствительностью, но считаю, что вы поступили жестоко.

— Кажется, я вижу путь к спасению Джеймса Маккарти, — сказал Холмс. — У вас есть ордер на посещение тюрьмы?

— Да, но только для нас двоих.

— В таком случае, я изменяю свое решение не выходить из дома. Мы поспеем в Хирфорд, чтобы увидеть заключенного сегодня вечером?

— Вполне.

— Тогда поедем! Уотсон, боюсь, вам будет скучно, но часа через два я вернусь.

Я проводил их до станции, прошелся по улицам городка, наконец вернулся в гостиницу, прилег на кушетку и начал читать бульварный роман. Однако сюжет повествования был слишком плоским по сравнению с ужасной трагедией, открывающейся перед нами. Я заметил, что мысли мои все время возвращаются от книги к действительности, поэтому я швырнул книжку в другой конец комнаты и погрузился в размышления о событиях истекшего дня. Если предположить, что показания этого несчастного молодого человека абсолютно правдивы, то что же за дьявольщина, что за непредвиденное и невероятное бедствие могло произойти в тот промежуток времени, когда он отошел от своего отца, а потом прибежал на его крики? Это было нечто ужасное, кошмарное. Что же это могло быть? Пожалуй, мне, как врачу, дело станет яснее, если я познакомлюсь с характером повреждений. Я позвонил и потребовал последние номера местных газет, содержащие все материалы следствия слово в слово.

I tried to interest myself in a yellow-backed novel.

В показаниях хирурга устанавливалось, что третья задняя теменная кость и левая часть затылочной кости размозжены сильным ударом тупого орудия. Я нащупал это место на своей собственной голове. Несомненно, такой удар может быть нанесен только сзади. Это в некоторой степени снимало подозрение с обвиняемого, так как во время ссоры его видели стоящим лицом к лицу с покойным. Но этому нельзя придавать большого значения, потому что отец мог отвернуться, перед тем как его ударили. Однако нужно сообщить Холмсу и об этом. Затем очень странным представилось мне упоминание о крысе. Что это значит? Во всяком случае, не бред. Человек, умирающий от внезапного удара, никогда не бредит. Нет, вероятно, он пытался объяснить, как он встретил свою смерть. Что же он хотел сказать? Я долго пытался найти какое-нибудь подходящее объяснение. Вспомнил и случай с этой серой одеждой, которую заметил молодой Маккарти. Если так было на самом деле, значит, убийца потерял что-то, когда убегал — наверно, пальто, — и у него хватило наглости вернуться и взять его за спиной у сына, в двадцати шагах от него, когда тот опустился на колени возле убитого. Какое сплетение таинственного и невероятного в этом происшествии!

Меня не удивило мнение Лестрейда, но я верил в дальновидность Холмса и не терял надежды: мне казалось, что каждая новая деталь укрепляет его уверенность в невиновности молодого Маккарти.

Когда вернулся Холмс, было уже совсем поздно. Он был один, так как Лестрейд остановился в городе.

— Барометр все еще не падает, — заметил он, садясь. — Только бы не было дождя, пока мы доберемся до места происшествия! Ведь человек должен вложить в такое славное дело все силы ума и сердца. По правде сказать, я не хотел приниматься за работу, когда был утомлен длинной дорогой. Я виделся с молодым Маккарти.

— Что же вы от него узнали?

— Ничего.

— Дело не стало яснее?

— Ничуть. Я был склонен думать, что ему известно имя преступника и что он скрывает его. Но теперь я убежден — для него это такая же загадка, как и для всех остальных. Молодой Маккарти не особенно умен, но очень миловиден, и мне показалось, что он человек неиспорченный.

— Я не одобряю его вкуса, — заметил я, — если это действительно правда, что он не хотел жениться на такой очаровательной молодой девушке, как мисс Тэнер.

— О, под всем этим кроется пренеприятная история! Он страстно, безумно любит ее. Но как вы думаете, что он сделал года два назад, когда она была еще в пансионе, а сам он был совсем подростком? Этот идиот попался в лапы одной бристольской буфетчице и зарегистрировал свой брак с нею. Об этом никто не подозревает, но можете себе представить, какое было для него мучение слушать упреки, что он не делает того, за что он сам отдал бы полжизни! Вот это-то отчаяние и охватило его, когда он простер руки к небу в ответ на требование отца сделать предложение мисс Тэнер. С другой стороны, у него не было возможности защищаться, и отец его, который, как все утверждают, был человек крутого нрава, выгнал бы его из дому навеки, если бы узнал всю правду. Это со своей женой-буфетчицей юноша провел в Бристоле последние три дня, а его отец не знал, где он был. Запомните это обстоятельство, это очень важно. Однако не было бы счастья — несчастье помогло. Буфетчица, узнав из газет, что ее мужа обвиняют в тяжелом преступлении и, вероятно, скоро повесят, сразу же его бросила и призналась ему в письме, что у нее уже давно есть другой законный муж, который живет в Бермудских доках, и что с мистером Джеймсом Маккарти ее на самом деле ничто не связывает. Я думаю, это известие искупило все страдания молодого Маккарти.

— Но если он невиновен, кто же тогда убийца?

— Да, кто убийца? Я бы обратил ваше внимание на следующие два обстоятельства. Первое: покойный должен был с кем-то встретиться у омута, и этот человек не мог быть его сыном, потому что сын уехал и не было известно, когда он вернется. Второе: отец кричал «Коу!» еще до того, как он узнал о возвращении сына. Это основные пункты, которые предрешают исход процесса... А теперь давайте поговорим о творчестве Джорджа Мередита,[1] если вам угодно, и оставим все второстепенные дела до завтра.

Как и предсказывал Холмс, дождя не было; утро выдалось яркое и безоблачное. В девять часов за нами в карете приехал Лестрейд, и мы отправились на ферму Хазерлейи к Боскомскому омуту.

— Серьезные известия, — сказал Лестрейд. — Говорят, что мистер Тэнер из Холла так плох, что долго не протянет.

— Вероятно, он очень стар? — спросил Холмс.

— Около шестидесяти, но он потерял в колониях здоровье и уже очень давно серьезно болеет. Тут большую роль сыграло это дело. Он был старым другом Маккарти и, добавлю, его истинным благодетелем. Как мне стало известно, он даже не брал с него арендной платы за ферму Хазерлей.

— Вот как! Это очень интересно! — воскликнул Холмс.

— О да. И он помогал ему всевозможными другими способами. Здесь все говорят о том, что мистер Тэнер был очень добр к покойному.

— Да что вы! А вам не показалось несколько необычным, что этот Маккарти, человек очень небогатый, был так обязан мистеру Тэнеру и все же поговаривал о женитьбе своего сына на дочери Тэнера, наследнице всего состояния? Да еще таким уверенным тоном, будто стоило только сделать предложение — и все будет в порядке! Это чрезвычайно странно. Ведь вам известно, что Тэнер и слышать не хотел об их браке. Его дочь сама рассказала об этом. Не можете ли вы сделать из всего сказанного какие-нибудь выводы методом дедукции?

— Мы занимались дедукцией и логическими выводами, — сказал Лестрейд, подмигивая мне. — Знаете ли, Холмс, если в дальнейшем

---

[1] Джордж Мередит (1828-1909) — известный английский писатель.

так же орудовать фактами, можно очень легко удалиться от истины в мир догадок и фантазий.

— Что правда, то правда, — сдержанно ответил Холмс. — Вы очень плохо пользуетесь фактами.

— Как бы то ни было, я подтвердил один факт, который оказался очень трудным для вашего понимания, — раздраженно возразил Лестрейд.

— То есть, что…

— Что Маккарти-старший встретил свою смерть от руки Маккарти-младшего и что все теории, отрицающие этот факт, — просто лунные блики.

— Ну, лунные-то блики гораздо ярче тумана! — смеясь, ответил Холмс. — Если я не ошибаюсь, слева от нас ферма Хазерлей.

— Она самая.

Это было широко раскинувшееся комфортабельное двухэтажное, крытое шифером здание с большими желтыми пятнами лишайника на сером фасаде. Опущенные шторы на окнах и трубы, из которых не шел дым, придавали дому угрюмый вид, будто кошмарное преступление всей своей тяжестью легло на эти стены.

Мы позвонили у двери, и горничная, по требованию Холмса, показала нам ботинки, в которых был ее хозяин, когда его убили, и обувь сына, которую он надевал в тот день. Холмс тщательно измерил всю обувь в семи или восьми местах, затем попросил провести нас во двор, откуда мы пошли по извилистой тропинке, ведущей к Боскомскому омуту.

The maid showed us the boots.

Шерлок Холмс весь преображался, когда шел по горячему следу. Люди, знающие бесстрастного мыслителя с Бейкер-стрит, ни за что не узнали бы его в этот момент. Он мрачнел, лицо его покрывалось румянцем, брови вытягивались в две жесткие черные линии, из-под них стальным блеском сверкали глаза. Голова его опускалась, плечи сутулились, губы плотно сжимались, на мускулистой шее вздувались вены. Его ноздри расширялись, как у охотника, захваченного азартом преследования. Он настолько был поглощен стоящей перед ним задачей, что на вопросы, обращенные к нему, или вовсе ничего не отвечал, или нетерпеливо огрызался в ответ.

Безмолвно и быстро шел он по тропинке, пролегавшей через лес и луга к Боскомскому омуту. Это глухое, болотистое место, как и вся долина. На тропинке около нее, где растет низкая трава, было видно множество следов. Холмс то спешил, то останавливался, один раз круто повернул и сделал по лужайке несколько шагов назад. Лестрейд и я следовали за ним, сыщик с видом безразличным и пренебрежительным, в то время как я наблюдал за моим другом с большим интересом, потому что был убежден, что каждое его действие ведет к благополучному завершению дела.

Боскомский омут — небольшое, шириной ярдов[1] в пятьдесят, пространство воды, окруженное зарослями камыша и расположенное

[1] Ярд — около 0,9 метра.

на границе фермы Хазерлей и парка богача мистера Тэнера. Над лесом, подступающим к дальнему берегу, видны красные остроконечные башенки, возвышающиеся над жилищем богатого землевладельца.

Со стороны Хазерлей лес очень густой; только узкая полоска влажной травы шагов в двадцать шириной отделяет последние деревья от камышей, окаймляющих озеро. Лестрейд точно указал, где нашли тело; а земля действительно была такая сырая, что я мог ясно увидеть место, где упал убитый. Что же касается Холмса, то по его энергичному лицу и напряженному взгляду я видел, что он многое разглядел на затоптанной траве. Он метался, как гончая, напавшая на след, а потом обратился к нашему спутнику.

— Что вы здесь делали? — спросил он.

— Я прочесал граблями всю лужайку. Я искал какое-нибудь оружие или другие улики. Но как вам удалось…

— Ну, хватит, у меня нет времени! Вы выворачиваете левую ногу, и следы этой вашей левой ноги видны повсюду. Вас мог бы выследить даже крот. А здесь, в камышах, следы исчезают. О, как было бы все просто, если бы я пришел сюда до того, как это стадо буйволов все здесь вытоптало! Здесь стояли те, кто пришел из сторожки, они затоптали все следы вокруг убитого на шесть или семь футов.[1]

Он достал лупу, лег на непромокаемый плащ, чтобы было лучше видно, и разговаривал более с самим собой, чем с нами.

— Вот следы молодого Маккарти. Он проходил здесь дважды и один раз бежал так быстро, что следы каблуков почти не видны, а остальная часть подошвы отпечаталась четко. Это подтверждает его показания. Он побежал, когда увидел отца лежащим на земле. Далее, здесь следы ног отца, когда он ходил взад и вперед. Что же это? След от приклада, на который опирался сын, когда стоял и слушал отца. А это? Ха-ха, что же это такое? Кто-то подкрадывался на цыпочках! К тому же это квадратные, совершенно необычные ботинки. Он пришел,

[1] Фут — около 0,3 метра.

ушел и снова вернулся — на этот раз, конечно, за своим пальто. Но откуда он пришел?

Холмс бегал туда и сюда, иногда теряя след, иногда вновь натыкаясь на него, пока мы не очутились у самого леса, в тени очень большой, старой березы. Холмс нашел его следы за этим деревом и снова лег на живот. Раздался радостный возглас. Холмс долго оставался неподвижным, переворачивал опавшие листья и сухие сучья, собрал в конверт что-то похожее на пыль и осмотрел сквозь лупу землю, а также, сколько мог достать, и кору дерева. Камень с неровными краями лежал среди мха; он поднял и осмотрел его. Затем он пошел по тропинке до самой дороги, где следы терялись.

For a long time he remained there.

— Этот камень представляет большой интерес, — заметил он, возвращаясь к своему обычному тону. — Серый дом справа — должно быть, сторожка. Я зайду к Морану, чтобы сказать ему два слова и написать коротенькую записку. После этого мы еще успеем добраться до гостиницы, ко второму завтраку. Вы идите к карете, я присоединюсь к вам.

Минут через десять мы уже ехали к Россу. В руках у Холмса все еще был камень, который он поднял в лесу.

— Это может заинтересовать вас, Лестрейд, — сказал он, протягивая ему камень. — Вот чем было совершено убийство.

— Я не вижу на нем никаких следов.

— Их нет.

— Тогда как же вы это узнали?

— Под ним росла трава. Он пролежал там всего лишь несколько дней. Нигде вокруг не было видно места, откуда он взят. Это имеет прямое отношение к убийству. Следов какого-нибудь другого оружия нет.

— А убийца?

— Это высокий человек, левша, он хромает на правую ногу, носит охотничьи сапоги на толстой подошве и серое пальто, курит индийские сигары с мундштуком, в кармане у него тупой перочинный нож. Есть еще несколько примет, но и этого достаточно, чтобы помочь нам в наших поисках.

Лестрейд засмеялся.

— К сожалению, я до сих пор остаюсь скептиком, — сказал он. — Ваши теории очень хороши, но мы должны иметь дело с твердолобыми британскими присяжными.

— Ну, это мы увидим, — ответил спокойно Холмс. — У вас одни методы, у меня другие... Кстати, я, может быть, сегодня с вечерним поездом вернусь в Лондон.

— И оставите ваше дело незаконченным?

— Нет, законченным.

— Но как же тайна?

— Она разгадана.

— Кто же преступник?

— Джентльмен, которого я описал.

— Но кто он?

— Это можно очень легко узнать. Здесь не так уж много жителей.

Лестрейд пожал плечами.

— Я человек действия, — сказал он, — и никак не могу заниматься поисками джентльмена, о котором известно только, что он хромоногий левша. Я бы стал посмешищем всего Скотленд-Ярда.

— Хорошо, — спокойно ответил Холмс. — Я предоставил вам все возможности для разгадки этой тайны. Я ведь ничего не утаил от вас, и вы сами могли разгадать таинственное преступление. Вот мы и приехали. Прощайте. Перед отъездом я вам напишу.

Оставив Лестрейда возле его двери, мы направились к нашему отелю, где нас уже ждал завтрак.

Холмс молчал, погруженный в свои мысли. Лицо его было мрачно, как у человека, который попал в затруднительное положение.

— Вот послушайте, Уотсон, — сказал он, когда убрали со стола. — Садитесь в это кресло, и я изложу перед вами то немногое, что мне известно. Я не знаю, что мне делать. Я бы хотел получить от вас совет. Закуривайте, а я сейчас начну.

— Пожалуйста.

— Ну вот, при изучении этого дела нас поразили два пункта в рассказе молодого Маккарти, хотя меня они настроили в его пользу, а вас восстановили против него. Во-первых, то, что отец закричал «Коу» до того, как увидел своего сына. Во-вторых, что умирающий упомянул только о крысе. Понимаете, он пробормотал несколько слов, но сын уловил лишь одно. Наше расследование должно начаться с этих двух пунктов. Предположим, что все, сказанное юношей, — абсолютная правда.

— А что такое «коу»?

— Очевидно, он звал не своего сына. Он думал, что сын в Бристоле. Сын совершенно случайно услышал этот зов. Этим Криком «Коу!» он звал того, кто назначил ему свидание. Но «коу» — австралийское слово, оно в ходу только между австралийцами. Это веское доказательство, что человек, которого Маккарти надеялся встретить у Боскомского омута, бывал в Австралии.

— Ну, а крыса?

Шерлок Холмс достал из кармана сложенный лист бумаги, расправил его на столе.

— Это карта штата Виктория, — сказал он. — Я телеграфировал прошлой ночью в Бристоль, чтобы мне ее прислали. — Он закрыл ладонью часть карты. — Прочтите, — попросил он.

— *Arat*,[1] — прочитал я.

— А теперь? — Он поднял руку.

— *Ballarat*.

— Совершенно верно. Это и есть слово, произнесенное умирающим, но сын уловил только последние два слога. Он пытался назвать имя убийцы. Итак, Балларэт.

— Это потрясающе! — воскликнул я.

— Это вне всяких сомнений. А теперь, как видите, круг сужается. Наличие у преступника серого одеяния было третьим пунктом. Исчезает полная неизвестность, и появляется некий австралиец из Балларэта в сером пальто.

— И в самом деле!

— К тому же он местный житель, потому что возле омута, кроме фермы и усадьбы, ничего нет, и посторонний вряд ли забредет туда.

— Конечно.

— Затем наша сегодняшняя экспедиция. Исследуя почву, я обнаружил незначительные улики, о которых и рассказал этому тупоумному Лестрейду. Это касалось установления личности преступника.

— Но как вы их обнаружили?

— Вам известен мой метод. Он базируется на сопоставлении всех незначительных улик.

— О его росте вы, разумеется, могли приблизительно судить по длине шага. О его обуви также можно было догадаться по следам.

— Да, это была необыкновенная обувь.

— А то, что он хромой?

— Следы его правой ноги не так отчетливы, как следы левой. На правую ногу приходится меньше веса Почему? Потому что он прихрамывал — он хромой.

— А то, что он левша?

---

[1] A rat (а рэт) — по-английски значит «крыса».

— Вы сами были поражены характером повреждений, описанных хирургом. Удар был внезапно нанесен сзади, но с левой стороны. Кто же это мог сделать, как не левша? Во время разговора отца с сыном он стоял за деревом. Он даже курил там. Я нашел пепел и благодаря моему знанию различных сортов табака установил, что он курил индийскую сигару. Я, как вам известно, немного занимался этим вопросом и написал небольшую монографию о пепле ста сорока различных сортов трубочного, сигарного и папиросного табака. Обнаружив пепел сигары, я оглядел все вокруг и нашел место, куда он ее бросил. То была индийская сигара, изготовленная в Роттердаме.

He had stood behind that tree.

— А мундштук?

— Я увидел, что он не брал ее в рот. Следовательно, он курит с мундштуком. Кончик был обрезан, а не откушен, но срез был неровный, поэтому я решил, что нож у него тупой.

— Холмс, — сказал я, — вы опутали преступника сетью, из которой он не сможет вырваться, и вы спасли жизнь ни в чем не повинному юноше, вы просто сняли петлю с его шеи. Я вижу, где сходятся все ваши улики. Имя убийцы…

— Мистер Джон Тэнер, — доложил официант, открывая дверь в нашу гостиную и впуская посетителя.

«Mr. John Turner», said the waiter.

У вошедшего была странная, совершенно необычная фигура. Замедленная, прихрамывающая походка и опущенные плечи делали его дряхлым, в то время как его жесткое, резко очерченное, грубое лицо и огромные конечности говорили о том, что он наделен необыкновенной физической силой. Его спутанная борода, седеющие волосы и всклокоченные, нависшие над глазами брови придавали ему гордый и властный вид. Но лицо его было пепельно-серым, а губы и ноздри имели синеватый оттенок. Я с первого взгляда понял, что он страдает какой-то неизлечимой, хронической болезнью.

— Присядьте, пожалуйста, на диван, — мягко предложил Холмс. — Вы получили мою записку?

— Да, ее принес привратник. Вы пишете, что хотите видеть меня, дабы избежать скандала.

— Я думаю, будет много толков, если я выступлю в суде.

— Зачем я вам понадобился?

Тэнер посмотрел на моего приятеля. В усталых главах его было столько отчаяния, будто он уже получил ответ на свой вопрос.

— Да, — промолвил Холмс, отвечая более на взгляд его, чем на слова. — Это так. Мне все известно о Маккарти.

Старик закрыл лицо руками.

— Помоги мне, господи! — воскликнул он. — Но я бы не допустил гибели молодого человека! Даю вам слово, что я открыл бы всю правду, если бы дело дошло до выездной сессии суда присяжных…

— Рад это слышать, — сурово сказал Холмс.

— Я бы уже давно все открыл, если бы не моя дорогая девочка. Это разбило бы ее сердце, она не пережила бы моего ареста.

— Можно и не доводить дело до ареста, — ответил Холмс.

— Неужели?

— Я неофициальное лицо. Поскольку меня пригласила ваша дочь, я действую в ее интересах. Вы сами понимаете, что молодой Маккарти должен быть освобожден.

— Я скоро умру, — сказал старый Тэнер. — Я уже много лет страдаю диабетом. Мой доктор сомневается, протяну я месяц или нет. Все-таки мне легче будет умереть под своей собственной крышей, чем в тюрьме.

Холмс встал, подошел к письменному столу, взял перо и бумагу.

— Рассказывайте все, как было, — предложил он, — а я вкратце запишу. Вы это подпишете, а Уотсон засвидетельствует. Я представлю ваше признание только в случае крайней необходимости, если нужно будет спасать Маккарти. В противном случае обещаю вам не прибегать к этой мере.

— Хорошо, — ответил старик. — Скорее всего я не доживу до выездной сессии суда, так что меня это мало волнует. Я хотел бы только избавить Алису от такого удара. А теперь я все вам расскажу… Тянулось это долго, но рассказать я могу очень быстро… Вы не знали покойного Маккарти. Это был сущий дьявол, уверяю вас. Упаси вас бог от клещей такого человека! Я был в его тисках последние двадцать лет, он совершенно отравил мне жизнь.

Сначала я расскажу вам, как я очутился в его власти. Это произошло в начале шестидесятых годов на золотых приисках. Я тогда был совсем молодым человеком, безрассудным и горячим, готовым на любое дело. Я попал в плохую компанию, начал выпивать. На участке моем не оказалось ни крупинки золота — я стал бродяжничать и сделался, как у вас говорится, рыцарем большой дороги. Нас было шестеро, мы вели дикую, привольную жизнь, совершали время от времени налеты на станцию, останавливали фургоны на дорогах к приискам. Меня называли Балларэтским Черным Джеком. Моих ребят до сих пор помнят в колониях как банду Балларэта.

Однажды из Балларэта в Мельбурн под охраной конвоя отправили золото. Мы устроили засаду. Золото охраняли шесть конвоиров, нас тоже было шесть человек. Произошла жаркая схватка. Первым залпом мы уложили четырех. Но когда мы взяли добычу, нас осталось только трое. Я приставил дуло пистолета к голове кучера — это и был Маккарти. Господи, лучше бы я убил его тогда! Но я пощадил его, хотя и заметил, что он смотрит на меня своими маленькими злыми глазками, будто хочет запомнить черты моего лица. Мы завладели золотом, стали богатыми людьми и приехали в Англию, никем не заподозренные. Здесь я навсегда расстался со своими бывшими приятелями и начал спокойную, обеспеченную жизнь.

Я купил это имение, которое как раз продавалось в то время, и старался принести хотя бы небольшую пользу своими деньгами, чтобы как-то искупить прошлое. К тому же я женился, и хотя жена моя умерла молодой, она оставила мне милую маленькую Алису. Даже когда Алиса была совсем крошкой, ее ручонки удерживали меня на праведном пути, как ничто в мире. Словом, я навсегда покончил с прошлым. Все шло великолепно, пока я не попался в руки Маккарти…

Я поехал в город по денежным делам и на Риджент-стрит встретил Маккарти. На нем не было ни приличного пальто, ни обуви.

«Вот мы и встретились, Джек, — сказал он, прикасаясь к моей руке. — Теперь уж мы с вами больше не расстанемся. Я не один: у меня есть сынишка, и вы должны о нас позаботиться. В противном случае, вы знаете: Англия прекрасная страна, где чтут законы. Кроме того, везде есть полисмены».

Вот он и поселился со своим сыном на западе, и я не мог от них отделаться; они бесплатно живут на моей земле. У меня не было ни покоя, ни отдыха, ни забвения. Куда бы я ни шел, я везде натыкался на его хитрую, ухмыляющуюся физиономию. Когда Алиса подросла, стало еще хуже, так как он заметил, что для меня страшнее всякой полиции, если о моем прошлом узнает дочь. Что бы он ни захотел, он получал по первому требованию, будь то земля, постройка или деньги, пока он не потребовал невозможного. Он потребовал Алису. Сын его, видите ли, подрос, моя дочь — тоже, и, так как о моей болезни всем было известно, ему представилось, что это великолепный шанс для его сына завладеть всем моим состоянием. Но на этот раз я был тверд. Я и мысли не мог допустить, что его проклятый род соединится с моим.

Нельзя сказать, чтобы мне не нравился его сын, но в жилах юноши текла кровь его отца, этого было достаточно. Я все же стоял на своем. Маккарти, выведенный из себя, стал угрожать.

Мы должны были встретиться у омута, на полпути между нашими домами, чтобы поговорить обо всем. Когда я пришел на условленное место, я увидел, что он толкует о чем-то с сыном. Я закурил и ждал за деревом, пока он останется один. Но по мере того как я вслушивался в его слова, во мне закипала горечь и злоба, я не мог больше этого вынести. Он принуждал сына жениться на моей дочери, ничуть не заботясь о том, как она отнесется к этому, будто речь шла об уличной девчонке.

Я чуть с ума не сошел, когда подумал, что все, чем я дорожу, может очутиться во власти такого человека. Не лучше ли разбить эти оковы? Я уже умирающий, доведенный до отчаяния человек. Хотя рассудок мой ясен и силы не покинули меня, я понимал, что моя жизнь кончена. Но мое имя и моя дочь! Я спасу и то и другое, если заставлю Маккарти держать язык за зубами... Я его убил, мистер Холмс... Я бы убил его снова. Я большой грешник, но разве жизнь, полная страданий, не искупает вины? Я все терпел, но мысль, что моя дочь попадет в ту же западню, была невыносимы. Я убил его без угрызения совести, будто это была отвратительная ядовитая тварь. На крик прибежал его сын, но я успел спрятаться в лесу, хотя мне пришлось вернуться за пальто, которое я обронил... Это чистая правда, джентльмены, все служилось именно так.

— Что же, не мне судить вас, — промолвил Холмс, когда старик подписал свои показания. — Думаю, нам не придется представлять эти сведения в суд.

— Я вам полностью доверяю, сэр! Но что вы хотите предпринять?

— Принимая во внимание ваше здоровье — ничего. Вы сами знаете, что скоро предстанете перед судом, который выше земного суда. Я сохраню ваше признание, мне придется воспользоваться им, если Маккарти будет осужден. Если же он будет оправдан — ни один смертный, будете вы живы или нет, не узнает о вашей тайне, все это останется между нами.

— Тогда прощайте, — торжественно сказал старик. — Когда настанет ваш смертный час, вам будет легче при мысли о том, какое успокоение вы внесли в мою душу.

Шатаясь и дрожа всем своим гигантским телом, он медленно вышел из комнаты, прихрамывая на правую ногу.

— Бедные мы, бедные! — после долгой паузы воскликнул Холмс. — Почему судьба играет такими жалкими, беспомощными созданиями, как мы?

«Farewell, then», said the old man.

Выездная сессия суда присяжных оправдала Джеймса Маккарти под давлением многочисленных доказательств, представленных Холмсом. Старый Тэнер прожил месяцев семь после нашего свидания, сейчас его уже нет в живых. Есть все основания полагать, что Джеймс и Алиса могут спокойно жить в счастливом браке, не думая больше о черных тучах, которые омрачали их прошлое.

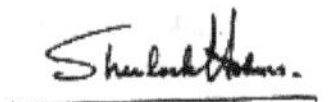

ПЯТЬ ЗЕРНЫШЕК АПЕЛЬСИНА

Когда я просматриваю мои заметки о Шерлоке Холмсе за годы от 1882 до 1890, я нахожу так много удивительно интересных дел, что просто не знаю, какие выбрать. Однако одни из них уже известны публике из газет, а другие не дают возможности показать во всем блеске те своеобразные качества, которыми мой друг обладал в такой высокой степени. Все же одно из этих дел было так замечательно по своим подробностям и так неожиданно по результатам, что мне хотелось бы рассказать о нем, хотя с ним связаны такие обстоятельства, которые, по всей вероятности, никогда не будут полностью выяснены.

1887 год принес длинный ряд более или менее интересных дел. Все они записаны мною. Среди них — рассказ о «Парадол-чэмбер», Обществе Нищих-любителей, которое имело роскошный клуб в подвальном этаже большого мебельного магазина; отчет о фактах, связанных с гибелью британского судна «Софи Эндерсон»; рассказ о странных приключениях Грайса Петерсона на острове Юффа и, наконец, записки, относящиеся к Кемберуэльскому делу об отравлении. В последнем деле Шерлоку Холмсу удалось путем исследования механизма часов, найденных на убитом, доказать, что часы были заведены за два часа до смерти и поэтому покойный лег спать в пределах этого времени, — вывод, который помог обнаружить преступника.

Все эти дела я, может быть, опишу когда-нибудь позже, но ни одно из них не обладает такими своеобразными чертами, как те необычайные события, которые я намерен сейчас изложить.

Был конец сентября, и осенние бури свирепствовали с неслыханной яростью. Целый день завывал ветер, и дождь барабанил в окна так, что даже здесь, в самом сердце огромного Лондона, мы невольно отрывались на миг от привычного течения жизни и ощущали присутствие грозных сил разбушевавшейся стихии. К вечеру буря разыгралась сильнее; ветер в трубе плакал и всхлипывал, как ребенок.

Шерлок Холмс был мрачен. Он расположился у камина и приводил в порядок свою картотеку преступлений, а я, сидя против него, так углубился в чтение прелестных морских рассказов Кларка Рассела, что завывание бури слилось в моем сознании с текстом, а шум дождя стал казаться мне рокотом морских волн.

Моя жена гостила у тетки, и я на несколько дней устроился в нашей старой квартире на Бейкер-стрит.

— Послушайте, — сказал я, взглянув на Холмса, — это звонок. Кто же может прийти сегодня? Кто-нибудь из ваших друзей?

— Кроме вас, у меня нет друзей, — ответил Холмс. — А гости ко мне не ходят.

— Может быть, клиент?

— Если так, то дело должно быть очень серьезное. Что другое заставит человека выйти на улицу в такой день и в такой час? Но скорее всего это какая-нибудь кумушка, приятельница нашей квартирной хозяйки.

Однако Холмс ошибся, потому что послышались шаги в прихожей и стук в нашу дверь.

Холмс протянул свою длинную руку и повернул лампу от себя так, чтобы осветить пустое кресло, предназначенное для посетителя.

— Войдите! — сказал он.

Вошел молодой человек лет двадцати двух, изящно одетый, с некоторой изысканностью в манерах. Зонт, с которого бежала вода, и блестевший от дождя длинный непромокаемый плащ свидетельствовали об ужасной погоде. Вошедший тревожно огляделся, и при свете лампы я увидел, что лицо его бледно, а глаза полны беспокойства, как у человека, внезапно охваченного большой тревогой.

He looked about him anxiously.

— Я должен перед вами извиниться, — произнес он, поднося к глазам золотой лорнет. — Надеюсь, вы не сочтете меня навязчивым… Боюсь, что я принес в вашу уютную комнату некоторые следы бури и дождя.

— Дайте мне ваш плащ и зонт, — сказал Холмс. — Они могут повисеть здесь, на крючке, и быстро высохнут. Я вижу, вы приехали с юго-запада.

— Да, из Хоршема.

— Смесь глины и мела на носках ваших ботинок очень характерна для этих мест.

— Я пришел к вам за советом.

— Его легко получить.

— И за помощью.

— А вот это не всегда так легко.

— Я слышал о вас, мистер Холмс. Я слышал от майора Прендергаста, как вы спасли его от скандала в клубе Тэнкервилл.

— А-а, помню. Он был ложно обвинен в нечистой карточной игре.

— Он сказал мне, что вы можете во всем разобраться.

— Он чересчур много мне приписывает.

— По его словам, вы никогда не знали поражений.

— Я потерпел поражение четыре раза. Три раза меня побеждали мужчины и один раз женщина.

— Но что это значит в сравнении с числом ваших успехов!

— Да, обычно у меня бывают удачи.

— В таком случае, вы добьетесь успеха и в моем деле.

— Прошу вас придвинуть ваше кресло к камину в сообщить мне подробности дела.

— Дело мое необыкновенное.

— Обыкновенные дела ко мне не попадают. Я высшая апелляционная инстанция.

— И все же, сэр, я сомневаюсь, чтобы вам приходилось за все время вашей деятельности слышать о таких непостижимых и таинственных происшествиях, как те, которые произошли в моей семье.

— Вы меня очень заинтересовали, — сказал Холмс. — Пожалуйста, сообщите нам для начала основные факты, а потом я расспрошу вас о тех деталях, которые покажутся мне наиболее существенными.

Молодой человек придвинул кресло и протянул мокрые ноги к пылающему камину.

— Меня зовут Джон Опеншоу, — сказал он. — Но, насколько я понимаю, мои личные дела мало связаны с этими ужасными событиями. Это какое-то наследственное дело, и поэтому, чтобы дать вам представление о фактах, я должен вернуться к самому началу всей истории...

У моего деда было два сына: мой дядя, Элиас, и мой отец, Джозеф. Мой отец владел небольшой фабрикой в Ковентри. Ему удалось расширить ее, когда началось производство велосипедов. Отец изобрел особо прочные шины «Опеншоу», и его предприятие пошло очень успешно, так что когда отец в конце концов продал свою фирму, он удалился на покой вполне обеспеченным человеком.

Мой дядя Элиас в молодые годы эмигрировал в Америку и стал плантатором во Флориде, где, как говорили, дела его шли очень хорошо. Во времена войны[1] он сражался в армии Джексона, а затем под командованием Гуда и достиг чина полковника. Когда Ли сложил оружие,[2] мой дядя возвратился на свою плантацию, где прожил три или четыре года. В 1869 или 1870 году он вернулся в Европу и арендовал небольшое поместье в Сассексе, вблизи Хоршема. В Соединенных Штатах он нажил большой капитал и покинул Америку, так как питал отвращение к неграм и был недоволен республиканским правительством, освободившим их от рабства.

Дядя был странный человек — жестокий и вспыльчивый. При всякой вспышке гнева он изрыгал страшные ругательства. Жил он одиноко и чуждался людей. Сомневаюсь, чтобы в течение всех лет, прожитых под Хоршемом, он хоть раз побывал в городе. У него был сад, лужайки вокруг дома, и там он прогуливался, хотя часто неделями не покидал своей комнаты. Он много пил и много курил, но избегал общения с людьми и не знался даже с собственным братом. А ко мне он, пожалуй, даже привязался, хотя впервые мы увиделись, когда мне было около двенадцати лет. Это произошло в 1878 году. К

---

[1] Гражданская война Южных и Северных штатов (1861 1865), окончившаяся победой северян над рабовладельческим Югом.

[2] Генерал Ли командовал Южной армией.

Джексон и Гуд — генералы этой армии.

тому времени дядя уже восемь или девять лет прожил в Англии. Он уговорил моего отца, чтобы я переселился к нему, и был ко мне по-своему очень добр. В трезвом виде он любил играть со мной в кости и в шашки. Он доверил мне все дела с прислугой, с торговцами, так что к шестнадцати годам я стал полным хозяином в доме. У меня хранились все ключи, мне позволялось ходить куда угодно и делать все что вздумается при одном условии: не нарушать уединения дяди. Но было все же одно странное исключение: на чердаке находилась комната, постоянно запертая, куда дядя не разрешал заходить ни мне, ни кому-либо другому. Из мальчишеского любопытства я заглядывал в замочную скважину, но ни разу не увидел ничего, кроме старых сундуков и узлов.

Однажды — это было в марте 1883 года — на столе перед прибором дяди оказалось письмо с иностранной маркой. Дядя почти никогда не получал писем, потому что покупки он всегда оплачивал наличными, а друзей у него не было.

«Из Индии, — сказал он, беря письмо. — Почтовая марка Пондишерри! Что это может быть?»

Дядя поспешно разорвал конверт; из него выпало пять сухих зернышек апельсина, которые выкатились на его тарелку. Я было рассмеялся, но улыбка застыла у меня на губах, когда я взглянул на дядю. Его нижняя губа отвисла, глаза выкатились из орбит, лицо стало серым; он смотрел на конверт, который продолжал держать в дрожащей руке.

«К.К.К.»! — воскликнул он. — Боже мой, боже мой! Вот расплата за мои грехи!»

«Что это, дядя?» — спросил я.

«Смерть», — сказал он, встал из-за стола и ушел в свою комнату, оставив меня в недоумении и ужасе.

Я взял конверт и увидел, что на внутренней его стороне красными чернилами была три раза написана буква «К». В конверте не было ничего, кроме пяти сухих зернышек апельсина. Почему дядю охватил такой ужас?

Я вышел из-за стола и взбежал по лестнице наверх. Навстречу мне спускался дядя. В одной руке у него был старый, заржавевший ключ, по-видимому, от чердачного помещения, а в другой — небольшая шкатулка из латуни.

«Пусть они делают что хотят, я все-таки им не сдамся! — проговорил он с проклятием. — Скажи Мэри, чтобы затопила камин в моей комнате и пошла за Фордхэмом, хоршемским юристом».

Я сделал все, как он велел. Когда приехал юрист, меня позвали в комнату дяди. Пламя ярко пылало, а на решетке камина толстым слоем лежал пепел, по-видимому, от сожженной бумаги. Рядом стояла открытая пустая шкатулка. Взглянув на нее, я невольно вздрогнул, так как заметил на внутренней стороне крышки тройное «К» — точно такое же, какое я сегодня утром видел на конверте.

«Я хочу, Джон, — сказал дядя, — чтобы ты был свидетелем при составлении завещания. Я оставляю свое поместье моему брату, твоему отцу, от которого оно, несомненно, перейдет к тебе. Если ты сможешь мирно пользоваться им, тем лучше. Если же ты убедишься, что это невозможно, то последуй моему совету, мой мальчик, и отдай поместье своему злейшему врагу. Мне очень грустно, что приходится оставлять тебе такое наследство, но я не знаю, какой оборот примут дела. Будь любезен, подпиши бумагу в том месте, какое тебе укажет мистер Фордхэм».

Я подписал бумагу, как мне было указано, и юрист взял ее с собой.

Этот странный случай произвел на меня, как вы понимаете, очень глубокое впечатление, и я все время думал о нем, не находи объяснений. Я не мог отделаться от смутного чувства страха, хотя оно притуплялось по мере того, как шли недели и ничто не нарушало привычного течения жизни. Правда, я заметил перемену в моем дяде. Он пил больше прежнего и стал еще более нелюдимым. Большую часть времени он проводил, запершись в своей комнате. Но иногда в каком-то пьяном бреду он выбегал из дому, слонялся по саду с револьвером в руке и кричал, что никого не боится, и не даст ни человеку, ни дьяволу зарезать себя, как овцу. Однако когда эти горячечные припадки проходили, он сразу бежал домой и запирался в комнате на ключ и на засовы, как человек, охваченный непреодолимым страхом. Во время таких припадков его лицо даже в холодные дни блестело от пота, как будто он только что вышел из бани.

Чтобы покончить с этим, мистер Холмс, и не злоупотреблять вашим терпением, скажу только, что однажды настала ночь, когда он совершил одну из своих пьяных вылазок, после которой уже не вернулся. Мы отправились на розыски. Он лежал ничком в маленьком, заросшем тиной пруду, расположенном в глубине нашего сада. На теле не было никаких признаков насилия, а воды в пруду было не больше двух футов. Поэтому суд присяжных, принимая во внимание чудачества дяди, признал причиной смерти самоубийство. Но я, знавший, как его пугала самая мысль о смерти, не мог убедить себя, что он добровольно расстался с жизнью. Как бы то ни было, дело на этом и кончилось, и мой отец вступил во владение поместьем и четырнадцатью тысячами фунтов, которые лежат на его текущем счете в банке…

We found him face downward in a little green-scummed pool.

— Позвольте, — прервал его Холмс. — Ваше сообщение, как я вижу, одно из самых интересных, какие я когда-либо слышал.

Укажите мне дату получения вашим дядей письма и дату его предполагаемого самоубийства.

— Письмо пришло десятого марта 1883 года. Он погиб через семь недель, в ночь на второе мая.

— Благодарю вас. Пожалуйста, продолжайте.

— Когда отец вступил во владения хоршемской усадьбой, он по моему настоянию произвел тщательный осмотр чердачного помещения, которое всегда было заперто. Мы нашли там латунную шкатулку. Все ее содержимое было уничтожено. Ко внутренней стороне крышки была приклеена бумажная этикетка с тремя буквами «К» и подписью внизу; «Письма, записи, расписки и реестр». Как мы полагаем, эти слова указывали на характер бумаг, уничтоженных полковником Опеншоу. Кроме этого, на чердаке не было ничего существенного, если не считать огромного количества разбросанных бумаг и записных книжек, касавшихся жизни дяди в Америке. Некоторые из них относились ко времени войны и свидетельствовали о том, что дядя хорошо выполнял свой долг и заслужил репутацию храброго солдата. Другие бумаги относились к эпохе преобразования Южных штатов и по большей части касались политических вопросов, так как дядя, очевидно, играл большую роль в оппозиции.

Так вот, в начале 84 года отец поселился в Хоршеме, и все шло у нас как нельзя лучше до 85 года. Четвертого января, когда мы все сидели за завтраком, отец внезапно вскрикнул от изумления. В одной руке он держал только что вскрытый конверт, а на протянутой ладони другой руки — пять сухих зернышек апельсина. Он всегда смеялся над тем, что он называл «небылицами насчет полковника», а теперь и сам испугался, когда получил такое же послание.

«What on earth does this mean?»

«Что бы это могло значить, Джон?» — пробормотал он.

Мое сердце окаменело.

«Это К.К.К.», — ответил я.

Отец заглянул внутрь конверта.

«Да, здесь те же буквы. Но что это написано под ними?»

«Положите бумаги на солнечные часы», — прочитал я, взглянув ему через плечо.

«Какие бумаги? Какие солнечные часы?» — спросил он.

«Солнечные часы в саду, других здесь нет. Но бумаги, должно быть, те, которые уничтожены».

«Черт возьми! — сказал он. — Мы живем в цивилизованной стране и не можем принимать всерьез такую чушь. Откуда это письмо?»

«Из Данди», — ответил я, взглянув на почтовый штемпель.

«Чья-нибудь нелепая шутка, — сказал он. — Какое мне дело до солнечных часов и бумаг? Нечего и обращать внимания на этакий вздор!»

«Я бы сообщил полиции», — сказал я.

«Чтобы меня высмеяли? И не подумаю».

«Тогда позвольте мне это сделать».

«Ни в коем случае. Я не хочу поднимать шум из-за таких пустяков».

Уговаривать отца было бы напрасным трудом, потому что он был очень упрям. А меня охватили тяжелые предчувствия.

На третий день после получения письма отец поехал навестить своего старого друга, майора Фрибоди, который командует одним из фортов Портсдаун-Хилла. Я был рад, что он уехал, так как мне казалось, что вне дома он дальше от опасности. Однако я ошибся. На второй день после его отъезда я получил от майора телеграмму, в которой он умолял меня немедленно приехать. Отец упал в один из глубоких меловых карьеров, которыми изобилует местность, и лежал без чувств, с раздробленным черепом. Я поспешил к нему, но он умер, не приходя в сознание. По-видимому, он возвращался из Фэрхема в сумерки. А так как местность ему незнакома и меловые шахты не огорожены, суд присяжных, не колеблясь, вынес решение: «Смерть от несчастного случая».

Я тщательно изучил все факты, связанные с его смертью, но не мог обнаружить ничего, что наводило бы на мысль об убийстве. Не было признаков насилия, не было никаких следов на земле, не было ограбления, не было посторонних лиц на дорогах. И все же излишне говорить вам, что я не находил покоя и был почти уверен, что отец мой попал в расставленные кем то сети.

При таких трагических обстоятельствах я вступил в права наследства. Вы спросите меня, почему я не отказался от него? Отвечу вам: я был убежден, что наши несчастья каким-то образом связаны с давними событиями в жизни моего дяди и что опасность будет мне угрожать одинаково в любом доме.

Мой бедный отец скончался в январе 85 года; с тех пор прошло два года и восемь месяцев. Все это время я мирно прожил в Хоршеме и начал уже надеяться, что это проклятье не тяготеет больше над нашей семьей, что оно рассеялось после гибели старшего поколения. Однако я слишком рано успокоился. Вчера утром меня постиг удар в той же самой форме, в какой он постиг моего отца...

Молодой человек достал из кармана смятый конверт и, повернувшись к столу, высыпал на скатерть пять маленьких сухих зернышек апельсина.

He shook out five little dried orange pips.

— Вот конверт, — продолжал он. — Почтовый штемпель — Лондон, Восточный район. Внутри те же самые слова, которые были в письме, полученном моим отцом; «К. К. К.», а затем: «Положите бумаги на солнечные часы».

— Что вы сделали? — спросил Холмс.

— Ничего.

— Ничего?

— По правде говоря, — он опустил лицо на тонкие белые руки, — я почувствовал себя беспомощным, как жалкий кролик, к которому приближается змея. По-видимому, я во власти какой-то непреодолимой и неумолимой силы, от которой не могут спасти никакие предосторожности.

— Что вы! Что вы! — воскликнул Шерлок Холмс. — Вы должны действовать, иначе вы погибнете. Только энергия может спасти вас. Теперь не время предаваться отчаянию.

— Я был в полиции.

— Ну, и?..

— Но там с улыбкой выслушали мой рассказ. Я убежден, что инспектор считает эти письма чьей-то шуткой, а смерть моих родных, как и установил суд присяжных, — несчастным случаем, никак не связанным с этими предупреждениями.

Холмс потряс в воздухе сжатыми кулаками.

— Невероятная тупость! — воскликнул он.

— Все же ко мне прикомандировали полицейского, который все время дежурит в моем доме.

— Он пришел с вами сейчас?

— Нет, ему приказано находиться при доме.

Холмс снова потряс в воздухе кулаками.

— Зачем вы пришли ко мне? — спросил он. — И главное, почему вы не пришли ко мне сразу?

— Я не знал. Только сегодня я говорил о моих опасениях с майором Прендергастом, и он посоветовал мне обратиться к вам.

— Ведь уже два дня, как вы получили письмо. Вам следовало начать действовать раньше. У вас нет, я полагаю, других данных, кроме тех, которые вы мне сообщили? Нет каких-либо наводящих подробностей, которые могли бы вам помочь?

— Есть одна вещь, — сказал Джон Опеншоу. Он пошарил в кармане пальто и, вынув кусок выцветшей синей бумаги, положил его на стол. — Мне помнится, — сказал он, — что в день, когда дядя жег бумаги, маленькие несгоревшие полоски, лежавшие среди пепла, были такого же цвета. Этот лист я нашел на полу дядиной комнаты и склонен думать, что это одна из бумаг, которая случайно отлетела от остальных и таким образом избежала уничтожения. Кроме упоминания зернышек, я не вижу в этой бумаге ничего, что могло бы нам помочь. Я думаю, что это страница дневника. Почерк, несомненно, дядин.

Холмс повернул лампу, и мы оба нагнулись над листом бумаги, неровные края которого свидетельствовали о том, что лист был вырван из книги. Наверху была надпись: «Март 1869 года», а внизу следующие загадочные заметки:

4-го. Гудзон явился. Прежняя платформа.

7-го. Посланы зернышки Мак-Коули, Парамору и Джону Свейну из Сент-Августина.

9-го. Мак-Коули убрался.

10-го. Джон Свейн убрался.

12-го. Посетили Парамора. Все в порядке.

— Благодарю вас, — сказал Холмс, складывая бумагу и возвращая ее нашему посетителю. — Теперь вы не должны терять ни минуты. Мы даже не можем тратить время на обсуждение того, что вы мне сообщили. Вы должны немедленно вернуться домой и действовать.

— Что я должен делать?

— Есть только одно дело, и оно должно быть выполнено немедленно. Вы должны положить бумагу, которую только что нам показали, в латунную шкатулку, описанную вами. Вы должны приложить записку и в ней сообщить, что все остальные бумаги были сожжены вашим дядей и остался только этот лист. Вы должны заявить это словами, внушающими доверие. Написав такое письмо, немедленно поставьте шкатулку на диск солнечных часов, как вам указано. Вы понимаете?

— Вполне понимаю.

— Не думайте в настоящее время о мести или о чем-либо подобном. Я полагаю, что этого мы могли бы добиться законным путем, но ведь нам еще предстоит сплести свою сеть, тогда как их сеть уже сплетена. Прежде всего надо отстранить непосредственную опасность, угрожающую вам. А затем уже выяснить это таинственное дело и наказать виновных.

— Благодарю вас, — сказал молодой человек, вставая и надевая плащ. — Вы вернули мне жизнь и надежду. Я поступлю так, как вы мне советуете.

— Не теряйте ни минуты. И главное, берегите себя, так как не может быть сомнения, что вам угрожает весьма реальная и большая опасность. Каким путем вы думаете вернуться домой?

— Поездом, с вокзала Ватерлоо.

— Еще нет девяти часов. На улицах будет очень людно, так что, я надеюсь, вы будете в безопасности. И все же вы должны очень остерегаться врагов.

— Я вооружен.

— Это хорошо. Завтра я примусь за ваше дело.

— Значит, я увижу вас в Хоршеме?

— Нет, секрет вашего дела — в Лондоне, и здесь я буду его искать.

— В таком случае, я приду к вам через день или два и сообщу все, что будет выяснено насчет шкатулки и бумаг. Я в точности выполню все ваши советы.

Он пожал нам руки и простился.

Ветер по-прежнему завывал и дождь стучал в окна. Казалось, этот странный рассказ навеян обезумевшей стихией, занесен к нам, как морская трава заносится бурей, и теперь снова поглощен ею.

Холмс сидел некоторое время молча, опустив голову и устремив взгляд на красное пламя камина. Затем он закурил трубку и, откинувшись на спинку кресла, стал следить за синими кольцами дыма, которые нагоняли друг друга под потолком.

His eyes bent upon the red glow of the fire.

— Я думаю, Уотсон, — заметил он наконец, — что в нашей практике не было более опасного и фантастического дела.

— Но вы составили себе определенное представление о характере этих опасностей? — спросил я.

— Здесь не может быть сомнения относительно их характера, — ответил он.

— Но в чем дело? Кто этот К. К. К. и почему он преследует несчастную семью?

Шерлок Холмс закрыл глаза и, опершись на подлокотники кресла, соединил концы пальцев.

— Истинный мыслитель, — заметил он, — увидев один-единственный факт во всей полноте, может вывести из него не только всю цепь событий, приведших к нему, но также и все последствия, вытекающие из него. Как Кювье[1] мог правильно описать целое животное на основании одной кости, так и наблюдатель, основательно изучивший одно звено в серии событий, должен быть в состоянии точно установить все остальные звенья — и

[1] Кювье (1769-1832) — знаменитый французский ученый, положивший начало палеонтологии (наука об ископаемых животных).

предшествующие, и последующие. Но чтобы довести искусство мышления до высшей точки, необходимо, чтобы мыслитель мог использовать все установленные факты, а для этого ему нужны самые обширные познания. Если мне не изменяет память, вы в ранние дни нашей дружбы очень точно определили границы моих знаний.

— Да, — ответил я, смеясь, — это был необыкновенный документ. Я помню, что философия, астрономия и политика стояли под знаком нуля. Познание в ботанике — колеблющиеся, в геологии — глубокие, поскольку дело касается пятен грязи из любого района в пределах пятидесяти миль вокруг Лондона; в химии — эксцентрические; в анатомии — разрозненные; в области уголовной литературы и судебных отчетов — исключительные: при этом скрипач, боксер, владеет шпагой, юрист, отравляет себя кокаином и табаком. Таковы были главнейшие пункты моего анализа.

Холмс усмехнулся при последних словах.

— Что ж, я говорю сейчас, как говорил и тогда, что человек должен обставить чердачок своего мозга всем, что ему, вероятно, понадобится, а остальные знания он должен сложить в чулан при своей библиотеке, откуда может достать их в случае надобности. Для такого дела, какое было предложено нам сегодня вечером, мы, конечно, должны мобилизовать все доступные нам ресурсы. Дайте мне, пожалуйста, том на букву «К» из Американкой энциклопедии. Он стоит на полке, которая рядом с вами. Благодарю вас. Теперь обсудим все обстоятельства и посмотрим, какой можно сделать из них вывод. Начать мы должны с предположения, что у полковника Опеншоу были весьма серьезные причины, заставившие его покинуть Америку. В его годы люди не склонны нарушать все свои привычки и добровольно отказываться от прелестного климата Флориды ради уединенной жизни в английском провинциальном городке. Его крайнее пристрастие к уединению в Англии подсказывает мысль, что он боялся кого-то или чего-то. Поэтому мы можем принять как рабочую гипотезу, что то был страх перед кем-то или чем-то, что заставило его покинуть Америку. О том, чего именно он боялся, мы можем судить только на основании зловещих писем, которые получали он и его наследники. Вы заметили почтовые штемпели этих писем?

— Первое было из Пондишерри, второе — из Данди и третье — из Лондона.

— Из Восточного Лондона! Какой вы можете сделать отсюда вывод?

— Это все океанские порты. По-видимому, писавший находился на борту корабля.

— Великолепно! У нас уже есть ключ. Вероятно, весьма вероятно, что писавший письма находился на борту корабля. А теперь посмотрим на это дело с другой стороны. В случае с Пондишерри прошло семь недель между угрозой и ее выполнением. В случае с Данди между угрозой и выполнением прошло всего три-четыре дня. Это вас наводит на какую-нибудь мысль?

— Большее расстояние, которое надо было в первом случае преодолеть.

— Но ведь письмо тоже должно было пройти большое расстояние.

— Тогда я не понимаю, в чем дело.

— Есть основание предполагать, что судно, на котором находится этот человек — или, может быть, их несколько, — парусное судно. Похоже на то, что они всегда посылали свои странные предупреждения или знаки перед тем, как отправиться на выполнение своего дела. Вы видите, как быстро дело последовало за предупреждением, посланным из Данди. Если бы они ехали из Пондишерри пароходом, они прибыли бы почти одновременно с письмом. Но прошло семь недель. Я думаю, что семь недель представляют разницу между скоростью почтового парохода, доставившего письмо, и скоростью парусника, доставившего автора письма.

— Это возможно.

— Это более чем возможно. Это вероятно. Теперь вы видите смертельную опасность в нашем последнем деле и понимаете, почему я настаивал, чтобы молодой Опеншоу был осторожен. Удар всегда настигал к концу срока, который нужен был отправителям письма, чтобы пройти расстояние на паруснике. Но ведь это письмо послано из Лондона, и поэтому мы не можем рассчитывать на отсрочку!

— Боже мой! — воскликнул я. — Что значит это беспощадное преследование?

— Очевидно, бумаги, увезенные Опеншоу, представляют жизненный интерес для человека или людей, находящихся на паруснике. Полагаю, что там не один человек. Один человек не мог бы совершить два убийства таким образом, чтобы ввести в заблуждение судебное следствие. В этом должно было участвовать несколько человек, притом изобретательных и решительных. Свои бумаги они решили получить, в чьих бы руках те ни находились. Таким образом, вы видите что «К. К. К.» перестают быть инициалами человека, а становятся знаком целого общества.

— Но какого общества?

— Вы никогда не слышали о Ку-клукс-клане? — сказал Шерлок Холмс, нагибаясь и понижая голос.

— Никогда не слышал.

Холмс перелистал страницы тома, лежавшего у него на коленях:

— Вот что здесь говорится:

«Ку-Клукс-Клан — название, происходящее от сходства со звуком взводимого затвора винтовки. Это ужасное тайное общество было создано бывшими солдатами Южной армии после гражданской войны и быстро образовало местные отделения в различных штатах, главным образом в Теннесси, в Луизиане, в обеих Каролинах, в Джорджии и Флориде. Это общество использовало свои силы в политических целях, главным образом для того, чтобы терроризировать негритянских избирателей, а также для убийства или изгнания из страны тех, кто противился его взглядам. Их преступлениям обычно предшествовало предупреждение, посылаемое намеченному лицу в фантастической, но широко известной форме: в некоторых частях страны — дубовые листья, в других — семена дыни или зернышки апельсина. Получив это предупреждение, человек должен был либо открыто отречься от прежних взглядов, либо покинуть страну. Если он не обращал внимания на предупреждение, его неизменно постигала смерть, обычно странная и непредвиденная. Общество было так хорошо организовано и его методы были настолько продуманны, что едва ли известен хоть один случай, когда человеку удалось безнаказанно пренебречь предупреждением или когда были раскрыты виновники злодеяния. Несколько лет организация процветала, несмотря на усилия правительства Соединенных Штатов и прогрессивных кругов Юга. В 1869 году движение неожиданно прекратилось, хотя отдельные вспышки расовой ненависти наблюдались и позже...»

— Заметьте, — сказал Холмс, откладывая том энциклопедии, — что внезапное прекращение деятельности общества совпало с отъездом из Америки Опеншоу, когда он увез с собой бумаги этой организации. Весьма возможно, что тут налицо и причина и следствие. Не приходится удивляться, что за молодым Опеншоу и его семьей следят беспощадные люди. Вы понимаете, что эта опись и дневники могут опорочить виднейших деятелей Юга и что многие не заснут спокойно, пока эти бумаги не будут у них в руках?

— Значит, страница, которую мы видели...

— Такая, какую можно было ожидать. Если мне не изменяет память, там было написано: «Посланы зернышки А. Б. В.» — то есть послали им предупреждение. Затем последовательно идут записи, что А и Б убрались, то есть покинули страну, и что В навестили. Боюсь, это плохо кончилось для В. Я думаю, доктор, нам удастся пролить некоторый свет на это темное дело. А тем временем единственное спасение для молодого Опеншоу — действовать так, как я ему посоветовал. Сегодня ничего больше мы не можем ни сказать, ни сделать... Передайте мне мою скрипку, и попытаемся на полчаса забыть отвратительную погоду и еще более отвратительные поступки людей.

К утру буря стихла, и солнце тускло светило сквозь туманный покров, нависший над Лондоном. Шерлок Холмс уже завтракал, когда я спустился вниз.

— Извините, что я начал без вас, — сказал он. — Я предвижу, что мне придется много поработать по делу молодого Опеншоу.

— Какие шаги вы собираетесь предпринять? — спросил я.

— Это в значительной степени зависит от результатов моих первых расследований. Может быть, мне придется еще съездить в Хоршем.

— Вы не собираетесь прежде всего поехать туда?

— Нет, я начну с Сити. Позвоните, и служанка принесет нам кофе.

В ожидании кофе я взял со стола газету и стал бегло просматривать ее. Я увидел заголовок, от которого у меня похолодело сердце.

— Холмс, — воскликнул я, — вы опоздали!

— А-а! — сказал он, отставляя чашку. — Я опасался, что так и будет. Как это произошло?

Он говорил спокойно, но я видел, что он глубоко взволнован.

«Holmes,» I cried, «you are too late.»

Мне бросилось в глаза имя Опеншоу и заголовок: «Трагедия у моста Ватерлоо». Вот что было написано:

«Вчера между девятью и десятью вечера констебль Кук, дежуривший у моста Ватерлоо, услышал крик о помощи и всплеск воды. Однако ночь была очень темная, бушевала буря, так что, несмотря на смелые попытки нескольких прохожих, оказалось невозможным спасти тонувшего. Был дан сигнал тревоги, и с помощью речной полиции тело удалось найти. Это был молодой джентльмен, имя которого, как видно по конверту, найденному в его кармане, Джон Опеншоу, проживавший вблизи Хоршема. Предполагают, что он спешил к последнему поезду, отходившему со станции Ватерлоо, и что в спешке при исключительной темноте сбился с дороги и шагнул через край одной из маленьких пристаней речного пароходства. На теле не было обнаружено следов насилия, и не может быть сомнения в том, что покойный оказался жертвой несчастного случая; это должно заставить власти обратить внимание на состояние речных пристаней».

Несколько минут мы сидели молча. Я никогда не видел Холмса таким угнетенным.

— Это наносит удар моему самолюбию, — сказал он наконец. — Бесспорно, самолюбие мелкое чувство, но с этим ничего не поделаешь. Теперь это становится для меня личным делом, и если бог пошлет мне здоровье, я выловлю всю банду. Он пришел ко мне за помощью, и я же послал его на смерть!

Он вскочил со стула, зашагал по комнате с пылающим румянцем на бледном лице, нервно сжимая и разжимая свои длинные, тонкие пальцы.

— Хитрые дьяволы! — выкрикнул он наконец. — Как им удалось заманить его туда, вниз, к реке? Набережная не лежит по дороге к станции. На мосту, конечно, даже в такую ночь было слишком людно. Ну, Уотсон, посмотрим, кто в конечном счете победит. Сейчас я пойду!

— В полицию?

— Нет, я сам буду полицией. Я сплету паутину, и пусть тогда полиция ловит в нее мух, но не раньше.

Весь день я был занят своей медицинской практикой и вернулся на Бейкер-стрит поздно вечером. Шерлок Холмс еще не приходил. Было почти десять часов, когда он вошел, бледный и усталый. Он подошел к буфету и, отломив кусок хлеба, стал жадно жевать его, запивая большими глотками воды.

— Проголодались? — заметил я.

— Умираю от голода. Совершенно забыл поесть. С утреннего завтрака у меня не было во рту ни крошки.

— Ничего?

— Ни крошки. Мне некогда было об этом думать.

— А как ваши успехи?

— Хороши.

— Вы нашли ключ?

— Они у меня в руках. Молодой Опеншоу недолго останется неотмщенным. Знаете, Уотсон, поставим на них их собственное дьявольское клеймо! Разве это плохо придумано?

— Что вы хотите сказать?

Он взял из буфета апельсин, разделил его на дольки и выдавил на стол зернышки. Из них он взял пять и положил в конверт. На внутренней стороне конверта он написал: «Ш.Х. за Д.О.». Затем он запечатал конверт и адресовал его: «Капитану Джеймсу Келгуну, парусник „Одинокая звезда". Саванна, Джорджия».

— Письмо будет ждать Келгуна, когда он войдет в порт, — сказал Холмс, тихо смеясь. — Это ему обеспечит бессонную ночь. Я уверен, что он сочтет письмо вестником той же судьбы, какая постигла Опеншоу.

— А кто этот капитан Келгун?

— Вожак всей шайки. Я доберусь и до других, но он будет первым.

— Как вы его обнаружили?

Он достал из кармана большой лист бумаги, сплошь исписанный датами и именами.

— Я провел весь день над ллойдовскими журналами и связками старых бумаг, прослеживая дальнейшую судьбу каждого корабля, прибывавшего в Пондишерри в январе и феврале 83 года. За эти месяцы было отмечено тридцать шесть судов значительного водоизмещения; из них одно судно, «Одинокая звезда», сразу привлекло мое внимание, так как местом отправления указан был

Лондон, между тем «Одинокая звезда» — это прозвище одного из штатов Америки.

— Кажется, Техаса.

— Я не был в этом уверен, не уверен и сейчас. Но я знал, что это судно должно быть американского происхождения.

— И что же?

— Я просмотрел записи прихода и ухода судов в Данди, и, когда я обнаружил, что парусник «Одинокая звезда» был там в январе 85 года, мои подозрения обратились в уверенность. Тогда я навел справки относительно судов, находящихся в настоящее время в Лондонском порту.

— И что же?

— «Одинокая звезда» прибыла сюда на прошлой неделе. Я спустился к докам Альберта и узнал, что сегодня утром с ранним приливом «Одинокая звезда» ушла вниз по реке, чтобы последовать обратно в Саванну. Я телеграфировал в Гревзенд и узнал, что «Одинокая звезда» прошла там недавно, и так как ветер восточный, я не сомневаюсь, что она уже миновала Гудуин и находится недалеко от острова Уайт.

— Что же вы теперь сделаете?

— О, Келгун теперь в моих руках! Он и два матроса, как я узнал, — единственные американцы на корабле. Все остальные финны и немцы. Я знаю также, что прошлую ночь все трое провели не на судне. Это мне сказал грузчик, который работал на погрузке «Одинокой звезды». Прежде чем парусник достигнет Саванны, почтовый пароход доставит мое письмо, а телеграф сообщит полиции в Саванне, что эти три джентльмена крайне нужны здесь в связи с обвинением их в убийстве.

Однако в самых лучших человеческих планах всегда оказывается какая-нибудь трещина, и убийцам Джона Опеншоу не суждено было получить зернышки апельсина, которые показали бы им, что другой человек, такой же хитрый и решительный, как они, напал на их след.

В том году равноденственные штормы были очень продолжительны и жестоки. Мы долго ждали из Саванны вестей об «Одинокой звезде», но так и не дождались. Наконец мы узнали, что где-то далеко, в Атлантике, видели разбитую корму корабля, залитую волной; на ней были вырезаны буквы «О. З.». Это все, что суждено было нам узнать о судьбе «Одинокой звезды».

ЧЕЛОВЕК С РАССЕЧЕННОЙ ГУБОЙ

Айза Уитни приучился курить опий. Еще в колледже, прочитав книгу де Куинси, в которой описываются сны и ощущения курильщика опия, он начал подмешивать опий к своему табаку, чтобы пережить то, что пережил этот писатель. Как и многие другие, он скоро убедился, что начать курить гораздо легче, чем бросить, и в продолжение многих лет был рабом своей страсти, внушая сожаление и ужас всем своим друзьям. Я так и вижу перед собой его желтое, одутловатое лицо, его глаза с набрякшими веками и сузившимися зрачками, его тело, бессильно лежащее в кресле, — жалкие развалины человека.

Однажды вечером, в июне 1889 года, как раз в то время, когда начинаешь уже зевать и посматривать на часы, в квартире моей раздался звонок. Я выпрямился в кресле, а жена, опустив свое шитье на колени, недовольно поморщилась.

— Пациент! — сказала она. — Тебе придется идти к больному.

Я вздохнул, потому что незадолго до этого вернулся домой после целого дня утомительной работы.

Мы услышали шум отворяемой двери и чьи-то торопливые шаги в коридоре. Дверь нашей комнаты распахнулась, и вошла дама в темном платье, с черной вуалью на лице.

— Извините, что я ворвалась так поздно, — начала она и вдруг, потеряв самообладание, бросилась к моей жене, обняла ее и зарыдала у нее на плече. — Ох, у меня такое горе! — воскликнула она. — Мне так нужна помощь!

— Да ведь это Кэт Уитни, — сказала жена, приподняв ее вуаль. — Как ты испугала меня, Кэт! Мне и в голову не пришло, что это ты.

— Я обращаюсь к тебе, потому что не знаю, что делать.

Это было обычным явлением. Люди, с которыми случалась беда, устремлялись к моей жене, как птицы к маяку.

— И правильно поступила. Садись поудобнее, выпей вина с водой и рассказывай, что случилось. Может быть, ты хочешь, чтобы я отправила Джеймса спать?

— О нет, нет! От доктора я тоже жду совета и помощи. Дело идет об Айзе. Вот уже два дня, как его нет дома. Я так боюсь за него!

Не в первый раз беседовала она с нами о своем несчастном муже — со мной как с доктором, а с женой как со своей старой школьной подругой. Мы утешали и успокаивали ее как могли. Знает ли она, где находится ее муж? Нельзя ли съездить за ним и привезти его домой?

Оказалось, что это вполне возможно. Ей было известно, что за последнее время он обычно курил опий в притоне, который находился на одной из восточных улиц Сити. До сих пор его оргии всегда ограничивались одним днем и к вечеру он возвращался домой в полном изнеможении, совершенно разбитый, но на этот раз он отсутствует уже сорок восемь часов и, конечно, лежит там среди всяких подозрительных личностей, вдыхая яд или отсыпаясь после курения. Она была убеждена, что он находился именно там, в «Золотом самородке» на Эппер-Суондем-лейн. Но что она может сделать? Как может она, молодая, застенчивая, робкая женщина, войти в такое место и вырвать своего мужа из толпы подонков?

Не пойти ли нам с ней вместе? Впрочем, зачем ей идти? Я лечил Айзу Уитни и, как доктор, мог повлиять на него. Без нее мне будет легче справиться с ним. Я дал ей слово, что в течение ближайших двух часов усажу ее мужа в кэб и отправлю домой, если он действительно находится в «Золотом самородке».

Через десять минут, покинув уютную гостиную, я уже мчался в экипаже на восток. Я знал, что мне предстоит довольно необычное дело, но в действительности оно оказалось еще более странным, чем я ожидал.

Сначала все шло хорошо. Эппер-Суондем-лейн — грязный переулок, расположенный позади высоких верфей, которые тянутся на восток вдоль северного берега реки, вплоть до Лондонского моста. Притон, который я разыскивал, находился в подвале между грязной лавкой и кабаком; в эту черную дыру, как в пещеру, вели крутые ступени. Посередине каждой ступеньки образовалась ложбинка — такое множество пьяных ног спускалось и поднималось по ним.

Приказав кэбу подождать, я спустился вниз. При свете мигающей керосиновой лампочки, висевшей над дверью, я отыскал щеколду и вошел в длинную низкую комнату, полную густого коричневого дыма; вдоль стен тянулись деревянные нары, как на баке эмигрантского корабля.

Сквозь мрак я не без труда разглядел безжизненные тела, лежащие в странных, фантастических позах: со сгорбленными плечами, с поднятыми коленями, с запрокинутыми головами, с торчащими вверх подбородками. То там, то тут замечал я темные, потухшие глаза, бессмысленно уставившиеся на меня. Среди тьмы вспыхивали крохотные красные огоньки, тускневшие по мере того, как уменьшалось количество яда в маленьких металлических трубках. Большинство лежали молча, но иные бормотали что-то себе под нос, а иные вели беседы странными низкими монотонными голосами, то возбуждаясь и торопясь, то внезапно смолкая, причем никто не слушал своего собеседника — всякий был поглощен лишь собственными мыслями. В самом дальнем конце подвала стояла маленькая жаровня с пылающими углями, возле которой на трехногом стуле сидел высокий, худой старик, опустив подбородок на кулаки, положив локти на колени и неподвижно глядя в огонь.

Как только я вошел, ко мне кинулся смуглый малаец, протянул мне трубку, порцию опия и показал свободное место на нарах.

— Спасибо, я не могу здесь остаться, — сказал я. — Здесь находится мой друг, мистер Айза Уитни. Мне нужно поговорить с ним.

Справа от меня что-то шевельнулось, я услышал чье-то восклицание и, вглядевшись во тьму, увидел Уитни, который пристально смотрел на меня, бледный, угрюмый и какой-то встрепанный.

— Боже, да это Уотсон! — проговорил он.

Он находился в состоянии самой плачевной реакции после опьянения.

— Который теперь час, Уотсон?

— Скоро одиннадцать.

— А какой нынче день?

— Пятница, девятнадцатое июня.

— Неужели? А я думал, что еще среда. Нет, сегодня среда. Признайтесь, что вы пошутили. И что вам за охота пугать человека!

Он закрыл лицо ладонями и зарыдал.

— Говорю вам, что сегодня пятница. Ваша жена ждет вас уже два дня. Право, вам должно быть стыдно!

— Я и стыжусь. Но вы что-то путаете, Уотсон, я здесь всего несколько часов. Три трубки... четыре трубки... забыл сколько! Но я поеду с вами домой. Я не хочу, чтобы Кэт волновалась... Бедная маленькая Кэт! Дайте мне руку. Есть у вас кэб?

— Есть. Ждет у дверей.

— В таком случае, я уеду сейчас же. Но я им должен. Узнайте, сколько я должен, Уотсон. Я совсем размяк и ослабел. Нет сил даже расплатиться.

Staring into the fire.

По узкому проходу между двумя рядами спящих, задерживая дыхание, чтобы не вдыхать одуряющих паров ядовитого зелья, я отправился разыскивать хозяина. Поровнявшись с высоким стариком, сидевшим у жаровни, я почувствовал, что меня кто-то дергает за пиджак, и услышал шепот:

— Пройдите мимо меня, а потом оглянитесь.

Эти слова я расслышал вполне отчетливо. Их мог произнести только находившийся рядом со мной старик. Однако у него попрежнему был такой вид, будто он погружен в себя и ничего кругом не замечает. Он сидел тощий, сморщенный, согбенный под тяжестью лет; трубка с опием висела у него между колен, словно вывалившись из его обессиленных пальцев. Я сделал два шага вперед и оглянулся. Мне понадобилось все мое самообладание, чтобы не вскрикнуть от удивления. Он повернулся так, что лица его не мог видеть никто, кроме меня. Спина его выпрямилась, морщины разгладились, в тусклых глазах появился их обычный блеск. Возле огня сидел, посмеиваясь над моим удивлением, не кто иной, как Шерлок Холмс. Он сделал мне украдкой знак, чтобы я подошел к нему, и опять превратился в дрожащего старика с отвислой губой.

«Holmes!» I whispered.

— Холмс! — прошептал я. — Что делаете вы в этом притоне?

— Говорите как можно тише, — прошептал он, — у меня превосходный слух. Если вы избавитесь от вашего ошалелого друга, я буду счастлив немного побеседовать с вами.

— Меня за дверью ждет кэб.

— Так отправьте вашего друга домой одного в этом кэбе. Вы можете за него не бояться, так как он слишком слаб, чтобы впутаться в какой-нибудь скандал. Будет лучше всего, если вы пошлете с кучером записку вашей жене, что вы встретили меня и остались со мной. Подождите меня на улице, я выйду через пять минут.

Трудно отказать Шерлоку Холмсу: его требования всегда так определенны и точны и выражены таким повелительным тоном. К тому же я чувствовал, что, как только я усажу Уитни в кэб, я уже выполню все свои обязательства по отношению к нему и мне уже ничто не помешает принять участие в одном из тех необычайных приключений, которые составляли повседневную практику моего знаменитого друга.

Помогать Шерлоку Холмсу в его изысканиях было для меня наивысшим счастьем. Поэтому я тотчас же написал записку жене, заплатил за Уитни, усадил его в кэб и стал терпеливо ждать неподалеку от дома. Кэб сразу же скрылся во мраке. Через несколько минут из курильни вышел старик, и я зашагал за ним по улице. Два квартала он прошел не разгибая спины и неуверенно шаркая старческими ногами. Потом торопливо оглянулся, выпрямился и от души захохотал. Предо мною был Шерлок Холмс.

— Вероятно, Уотсон, — оказал он, — вы вообразили, что я пристрастился к курению опия.

— По правде сказать, я действительно был удивлен, когда увидел вас в этой трущобе.

— И все же я удивился еще больше, чем вы, когда увидел в этой трущобе вас.

— Я искал там друга.

— А я — врага.

— Врага?

— Да. Короче говоря, Уотсон, я занят чрезвычайно любопытным делом и надеялся узнать кое-что из бессвязной болтовни очумелых курильщиков опия. Прежде мне это иногда удавалось. Если бы меня узнали в той трущобе, жизнь моя не стоила бы медяка, так как я уже бывал там не раз и негодяй ласкар, хозяин притона, поклялся расправиться со мною. На задворках этого дома, возле верфи святого Павла, есть потайная дверца, которая могла бы порассказать много диковинных историй о том, что выбрасывают через нее в черные, безлунные ночи.

— Неужели трупы?

— Да, Уотсон, трупы. Мы с вами были бы миллионерами, если бы получили по тысяче фунтов за каждого несчастного, убитого в этом притоне. Это самая страшная ловушка на всем берегу реки, и я опасаюсь, что Невилл Сент-Клер, попавший в нее, никогда не вернется домой. Но мы тоже устроим ловушку.

Шерлок Холмс сунул два пальца в рот и резко свистнул. Тотчас же издалека донесся такой же свист, а затем мы услышали грохот колес и стук копыт.

— Ну что же, Уотсон, — сказал Холмс, когда из темноты вынырнула двуколка с двумя фонарями, бросавшими яркие полосы света, — поедете вы со мною?

— Если буду вам полезен…

— Верный товарищ всегда полезен. В моей комнате в «Кедрах» имеются две кровати.

— В «Кедрах»?

— Да. Так называется дом мистера Сент-Клера. Я буду жить в его доме, пока не распутаю это дело.

— Где же этот дом?

— В Кенте, неподалеку от Ли. Нам нужно проехать семь миль.

— Ничего не понимаю.

— Вполне естественно. Сейчас я вам все объясню. Садитесь… Хорошо, Джон, вы нам больше не нужны. Вот вам полкроны. Ждите меня завтра часов в одиннадцать. Дайте мне вожжи. Прощайте.

Он хлестнул лошадь, и мы понеслись по бесконечным темным, пустынным улицам и наконец очутились на каком-то широком мосту, под которым медленно текли мутные воды реки. За мостом были такие же улицы с кирпичными домами; тишина этих улиц нарушалась только тяжелыми размеренными шагами полицейских да песнями и криками запоздалых гуляк.

He flicked the horse with his whip.

Черные тучи медленно ползли по небу, и в разрывах между ними то там, то здесь тускло мерцали звезды. Холмс молча правил лошадью, в глубокой задумчивости опустив голову на грудь, а я сидел рядом с ним, стараясь отгадать, что занимает его мысли, и не смея прервать его раздумье. Мы проехали несколько миль и уже пересекали пояс пригородных вилл, когда он наконец очнулся, передернул плечами и закурил трубку.

— Вы наделены великим талантом молчания, Уотсон, — сказал он. — Благодаря этой способности вы незаменимый товарищ. Однако сейчас мне нужен человек, с которым я мог бы поболтать, чтобы разогнать неприятные мысли. Представления не имею, что я скажу этой маленькой милой женщине, когда она встретит меня на пороге.

— Вы забываете, что я ничего не знаю.

— У меня как раз хватит времени рассказать вам все, пока мы доедем до Ли. Дело кажется до смешного простым, а между тем я не знаю, как за него взяться. Нитей много, но ни за одну из них я не могу ухватиться как следует. Я расскажу вам все, Уотсон, и, быть может, вам удастся найти хоть искру света в окружающем мраке.

— Рассказывайте.

— Несколько лет назад — точнее, в мае 1884 года — в Ли появился джентльмен по имени Невилл Сент-Клер, который, видимо, имел много денег. Он снял большую виллу, разбил вокруг нее прекрасный сад и зажил на широкую ногу, по-барски. Мало-помалу он подружился с соседями и в 1887 году женился на дочери местного пивовара, от которой теперь имеет уже двоих детей. Определенных занятий у него нет, но он прянимает участие в нескольких коммерческих предприятиях и обычно каждое утро ездит в город, возвращаясь оттуда с поездом 5.14. Мистеру Сент-Клеру теперь тридцать семь лет. Живет он скромно; он хороший муж и любящий отец; люди, встречавшиеся с ним, отзываются о нем превосходно. Могу еще прибавить, что долгов у него всего восемьдесят восемь фунтов десять шиллингов, а в банке на его текущем счету двести двадцать фунтов стерлингов. Следовательно, нет оснований предполагать какие-нибудь денежные затруднения.

В прошлый понедельник мистер Невилл Сент-Клер отправился в город раньше обычного, сказав перед отъездом, что у него два важных дела и что он привезет своему сынишке коробку с кубиками. Случайно в тот же самый понедельник, вскоре после его отъезда, жена его получила телеграмму, что на ее имя в Эбердинском пароходном обществе получена небольшая, но весьма ценная посылка, которую она ожидала уже давно. Если вы хорошо знаете Лондон, вам известно, что контора этого пароходного общества помещается на Фресно-стрит, которая упирается в Эппер-Суондем-лейн, где вы нашли меня сегодня вечером. Миссис Сеит-Клер позавтракала, отправилась в город, сделала кое-какие покупки, заехала в кантору общества, получила там свою посылку и в четыре часа тридцать пять минут шла по Суондем-лейн, направляясь к вокзалу... До сих пор вам все ясно, не правда ли?

— Конечно, здесь нет ничего непонятного.

— Если помните, в понедельник было очень жарко, и миссис Сент-Клер шла медленно, поглядывая, нет ли где кэба, так как ей очень не понравился район города, в котором она очутилась. И вот, идя по Суондем-лейп, она внезапно услышала крик и вся похолодела, увидев своего мужа, который смотрел на нее из окна второго этажа какого-то дома и, как ей показалось, жестами звал ее к себе. Окно было раскрыто, и она ясно разглядела лицо мужа, показавшееся ей чрезвычайно взволнованным. Он протянул к ней обе руки и вдруг исчез так внезапно, будто его насильно оттащили от окна. Однако ее зоркий женский взгляд успел заметить, что, хотя он одет в тот же черный пиджак, в котором он уехал из дому, на нем нет ни воротничка, ни галстука.

Уверенная, что с мужем случилась беда, она сбежала вниз по ступенькам (дом был тот самый, в котором помещается трущоба, где вы нашли меня нынче вечером) и, пробежав через переднюю комнату, попыталась подняться по лестнице, ведущей в верхние этажи. Но у лестницы она наткнулась на негодяя Ласкара, о котором я вам сейчас говорил. Ласкар с помощью своего подручного выставил ее на улицу. У него есть подручный, датчанин. Обезумев от ужаса, она побежала по улице и, к счастью, на Фресно-стрит встретила полицейских, которые совершали обход во главе с инспектором.

At the foot of the stairs she met this Lascar scoundrel.

Инспектор с двумя констеблями последовал за миссис Сент-Клер, и, несмотря на упорное сопротивление хозяина, им удалось проникнуть в ту комнату, в окне которой она видела мужа. Но здесь его не оказалось. Во всем этаже не нашли никого, кроме какого-то калеки отвратительной внешности, который, видимо, там и живет. И он и ласкар упорно клялись, что тут никого больше не было. Они так решительно все отрицали, что инспектор стал было уже сомневаться, не ошиблась ли миссис Сент-Клер, как вдруг она с криком кинулась к небольшому деревянному ящичку, стоявшему на столе, и сорвала с него крышку. Из ящичка посыпались детские кубики. То была игрушка, которую ее муж обещал привезти из города.

Эта находка и внезапное смущение калеки убедили инспектора в серьезности дела. Комнаты были тщательно обысканы, и обыск привел к открытию гнусного преступления.

Убранство этой квартиры, конечно, убогое. Передняя комната представляет собою что-то вроде гостиной, а рядом с ней помещается небольшая спальня, окно которой выходит на задворки одной из верфей. Между верфью и окном спальни есть узкий канал, который высыхает во время отлива, а во время прилива наполняется водой на четыре с половиной фута. Окно в спальне широкое и открывается снизу.

При осмотре были обнаружены на подоконнике следы крови; несколько кровавых пятен нашли также и на деревянном полу. За шторой в передней комнате удалось обнаружить всю одежду мистера Невилла Сент-Клера. Не было только его пиджака. Его ботинки, его носки, его шляпа, его часы — все оказалось тут. На одежде не нашли никаких следов насилия. Но сам мистер Невилл Сент-Клер бесследно исчез. Исчезнуть он мог только через окно, и зловещие кровавые пятна на подоконнике ясно указывали, что вряд ли ему удалось спастись вплавь, тем более что в тот час, когда совершалась трагедия, прилив достиг наивысшего уровня.

Теперь обратимся к негодяям, на которых падает подозрение. Ласкар известен как человек с темным прошлым, но из рассказа миссис Сент-Клер мы знаем, что через несколько мгновений после появления ее мужа в окне он находился внизу, и, следовательно, его можно считать лишь соучастником преступления. Он отрицает всякую свою причастность к этому делу. По его словам, у него нет ни малейшего представления о том, чем вообще занимается его жилец,

Хью Бун. Появление в комнате одежды пропавшего джентльмена — для него полнейшая загадка.

Вот все, что известно о хозяине-ласкаре. Теперь обратимся к угрюмому калеке, который живет во втором этаже над притоном и безусловно является последним человеком, видевшим Невилла Сент-Клера. Его зовут Хью Бун, и его безобразное лицо хорошо знает всякий, кому приходится часто бывать в Сити. Он профессиональный нищий; впрочем, для того чтобы обойти полицейские правила, он делает вид, будто продает восковые спички.

He is a professional beggar.

Как вы, вероятно, не раз замечали, на левой стороне Трэд-Нидл-стрит есть ниша. В этой нише сидит калека, поджав ноги и разложив у себя на коленях несколько спичечных коробков; вид его вызывает сострадание, и дождь милостыни так и льется в грязную кожаную кепку, которая лежит перед ним на мостовой. Я не раз наблюдал за ним, еще не предполагая, что нам когда-нибудь придется познакомиться с ним, как с преступником, и всегда удивлялся тому, какую обильную жатву он собирает в самое короткое время. У него такая незаурядная внешность, что никто не может пройти мимо, не обратив на него внимания. Оранжево-рыжие волосы, бледное лицо, изуродованное чудовищным шрамом, нижний конец которого рассек надвое верхнюю губу, бульдожий подбородок и проницательные темные глаза, цвет которых представляет такой резкий контраст с цветом его волос, — все это выделяет его из серой толпы попрошаек. У него всегда наготове едкая шутка для каждого, кто, проходя мимо, попытается задеть его насмешливым словом.

Таков обитатель верхнего этажа этой подозрительней курильни… После него никто уже не видел джентльмена, которого мы разыскиваем.

— Но ведь он калека! — сказал я. — Как мог он один совладать с сильным, мускулистым молодым человеком?

— У него искалечена только нога, и он слегка прихрамывает на ходу, вообще же он здоровяк и силач. Вы, Уотсон, как медик, конечно, знаете, что часто слабость одной конечности возмещается необычайной силой других.

— Пожалуйста, рассказывайте дальше.

— При виде крови на подоконнике миссис Сент-Клер стало дурно, и ее отправили домой в сопровождении полицейского, тем более что для дальнейшего расследования ее присутствие не было необходимо. Инспектор Бартон, принявший на себя ведение этого дела, тщательно обыскал весь притон, но не нашел ничего нового. Сделали ошибку: не арестовали Буна в первую же минуту и тем самым предоставили ему возможность в течение нескольких минут обменяться двумя-тремя словами со своим другом, ласкаром. Однако ошибка эта была скоро исправлена: Буна схватили и обыскали. Но обыск не дал никаких улик против него. Правда, на правом рукаве его рубашки оказались следы крови, но он показал полицейским свой безымянный палец, на котором был порез возле самого ногтя, и прибавил, что следы крови на подоконнике, вероятно, являются следствием того же пореза, так как он подходил к окну, когда у него из пальца шла кровь. Он упорно утверждал, что никогда не видел мистера Сент-Клера, и клялся, что присутствие одежды этого джентльмена у него в комнате — такая же тайна для него, как и для полиции. А когда ему передали, что миссис Сент-Клер видела своего мужа в окне его комнаты, он сказал, что это ей либо почудилось в припадке безумия, либо просто приснилось. Буна отвели в участок. Он громко протестовал. Инспектор остался поджидать отлива, надеясь обнаружить на дне капала какие-нибудь новые улики. И действительно, в липкой грязи, на самом дне, нашли кое-что, но совсем не то, что они с таким страхом ожидали найти. Когда отхлынула вода, они обнаружили в канале не самого Невилла Сент-Клера, а лишь пиджак Невилла Сент-Клера. И как вы думаете, что они нашли в карманах пиджака?

— Представить себе не могу.

— Я и не думаю, чтобы вы могли угадать. Все карманы были набиты монетами в пенни и в полпенни — четыреста двадцать одно пенни и двести семьдесят полпенни. Неудивительно, что отлив не унес пиджака. А вот труп — дело другое. Между домом и верфью очень сильное течение. Вполне допустимо, что труп был унесен в реку, в то время как тяжеловесный пиджак остался на дне.

— Но, если не ошибаюсь, всю остальную одежду нашли в комнате. Неужели на трупе был один лишь пиджак?

— Нет, сэр, но этому можно найти объяснение. Предположим, что Бун выбросил Невилла Сент-Клера через окно и этого никто не видел. Что стал бы он делать дальше? Естественно, что первым долгом он попытался бы избавиться от одежды, которая могла его выдать. Он берет пиджак, хочет выбросить его за окно, но тут ему приходит в голову, что пиджак не потонет, а поплывет. Он страшно торопится, ибо слышит суматоху на лестнице, слышит, как жена Сент-Клера требует, чтобы ее пустили к мужу, да вдобавок, быть может, его сообщник ласкар предупреждает его о приближении полиции. Нельзя терять ни минуты. Он кидается в укромный угол, где спрятаны плоды его нищенства, и набивает карманы пиджака первыми попавшимися под руку монетами. Затем он выбрасывает пиджак и хочет выбросить остальные вещи, но слышит шум шагов на лестнице и перед появлением полиции едва успевает захлопнуть окно.

He stuffs all the coins into the pockets.

— Это правдоподобно.

— Примем это как рабочую гипотезу, за неимением лучшего... Бун, как я вам уже говорил, был арестован и приведен в участок. Прежняя его жизнь, в сущности, безупречна. Правда, в продолжение многих лет он был известен как профессиональный нищий, но жил спокойно и ни в чем дурном замечен не был.

Вот в каком положении находится все это дело в настоящее время. Как видите, по-прежнему остаются нерешенными вопросы о том, что делал Невилл Сент-Клер в этой курильне опия, что там с ним случилось, где он теперь и какое отношение имеет Хью Бун к его исчезновению. Должен признаться, что не помню случая в моей практике, который на первый взгляд казался бы таким простым и был бы в действительности таким трудным.

Пока Шерлок Холмс рассказывал мне подробности этих удивительных происшествий, мы миновали предместье огромного города, оставили позади последние дома и покатили по дороге, с обеих сторон которой тянулись деревенские плетни. Как раз к тому времени, как мы очутились в деревне, весь его рассказ был закончен. Кое-где в окнах мерцали огни.

— Мы въезжаем в Ли, — сказал мой приятель. — За время нашего небольшого путешествия мы побывали в трех графствах Англии: выехали из Миддлсекса, пересекли угол Сэрри и приехали в Кент. Видите те огоньки между деревьями? Это «Кедры». Там возле лампы сидит женщина, настороженный слух которой несомненно уже уловил стук копыт нашей лошади.

— Отчего, ведя это дело, вы живете тут, а не на Бейкер-стрит? — спросил я.

— Оттого, что многое приходится расследовать здесь… Миссис Сент-Клер любезно предоставила в мое распоряжение две комнаты, и можете быть уверены, что она будет рада оказать гостеприимство моему другу, помогающему мне в моих розысках. О, как тяжело мне встречаться с ней, Уотсон, пока я не могу сообщить ей ничего нового о ее муже! Приехали! Тпру!..

Мы остановились перед большой виллой, окруженной садом. Передав лошадь выбежавшему нам навстречу конюху, мы с Холмсом пошли к дому по узенькой дорожке, посыпанной гравием. При нашем приближении дверь распахнулась, и у порога появилась маленькая белокурая женщина в светлом шелковом платье с отделкой из пышного розового шифона. Одной рукой она держалась за дверь, а другую подняла в нетерпении; нагнувшись вперед, полураскрыв губы, жадно глядя на нас, она, казалось, всем своим обликом спрашивала, что нового мы ей привезли.

— Ну? — громко спросила она.

Заметив, что нас двое, она радостно вскрикнула, но крик этот превратился в стон, когда товарищ мой покачал головой и пожал плечами.

— Узнали что-нибудь хорошее?

— Нет.

— А дурное?

— Тоже нет.

— И то слава богу. Но входите же. У вас был трудный день, вы, наверно, устали.

— Это мой друг, доктор Уотсон. Он был чрезвычайно полезен мне во многих моих расследованиях, и, по счастливой случайности, мне удалось привезти его сюда, чтобы воспользоваться его помощью в наших поисках.

— Рада вас видеть, — сказал она, приветливо пожимая мне руку. — Боюсь, что вам покажется у нас неуютно. Ведь вы знаете, какой удар внезапно обрушился на нашу семью…

— Сударыня, — сказал я, — я отставной солдат, привыкший к походной жизни, но, право, если бы даже я не был солдатом, вам не в чем было бы извиняться передо мною. Буду счастлив, если мне удастся принести пользу вам или моему другу.

— Мистер Шерлок Холмс, — сказала она, вводя нас в ярко освещенную столовую, где нас поджидал холодный ужин, — я хочу задать вам несколько откровенных вопросов и прошу вас ответить на них так же прямо и откровенно.

— Извольте, сударыня.

— Не щадите моих чувств. Со мной не бывает ни истерик, ни обмороков. Я хочу знать ваше настоящее, подлинное мнение.

— О чем?

— Верите ли вы в глубине души, что Невилл жив?

Шерлок Холмс, видимо, был смущен этим вопросом.

— Говорите откровенно, — повторила она, стоя на ковре и пристально глядя Холмсу в лицо.

— Говоря откровенно, сударыня, не верю.

— Вы думаете, что он умер?

— Да, думаю.

— Убит?

— Я этого не утверждаю.

— В какой же день он умер?

— В понедельник.

— В таком случае, мистер Холмс, будьте любезны объяснить мне, каким образом я могла получить от него сегодня это письмо?

«Frankly, now!» she repeated.

Шерлок Холмс вскочил с кресла, словно его ударило электрическим током.

— Что? — закричал он.

— Да, сегодня.

Она улыбалась, держа в руке листок бумаги.

— Можно прочитать?

— Пожалуйста.

Он выхватил письмо у нее из рук, разложил его на столе, разгладил и принялся внимательно рассматривать. Я поднялся с кресла и стал смотреть через его плечо. Конверт был простой, конторский; на конверте стоял почтовый штемпель Гревзенда; на штемпеле — сегодняшнее или, вернее, вчерашнее число, так как полночь уже миновала.

— Грубый почерк, — пробормотал Холмс. — Уверен, что это почерк не вашего мужа, сударыня.

— Да, на конверте чужой почерк, но внутри — почерк моего мужа.

— Человеку, который надписывал конверт, пришлось наводить справки о вашем адресе.

— Откуда вы это знаете?

— Имя на конверте, как видите, выделяется своей чернотой, потому что чернила, которыми оно написано, высохли сами собою. Адрес же бледноват, потому что к нему прикладывали пресс-папье. Если бы надпись на конверте была сделана сразу и если бы ее всю высушили пресс-папье, все слова были бы одинаково серы. Этот человек написал на конверте сперва только ваше имя и лишь спустя некоторое время приписал к нему адрес, из чего можно заключить, что адрес не был ему вначале известен. Конечно, это пустяк, но в моей профессии нет ничего важнее пустяков. Дайте мне взглянуть на письмо… Ага! Туда было что-то вложено.

— Да, там было кольцо. Его кольцо с печатью.

— А вы уверены, что это почерк вашего мужа?

— Один из его почерков.

— Один из его почерков?

— Его почерк, когда он пишет второпях. Обычно он пишет совсем иначе, но и этот его почерк мне хорошо знаком.

— «Дорогая, не волнуйся. Все кончится хорошо. Произошла ошибка, на исправление которой требуется некоторое время. Жди терпеливо. Невилл»… Написано карандашом на листке, вырванном из блокнота. Гм! Отправлено сегодня из Гревзенда человеком, у которого большой палец чем-то выпачкан. Ха! Если не ошибаюсь, человек, заклеивавший конверт, жует табак… Вы убеждены, сударыня, что это почерк вашего мужа?

— Убеждена. Это письмо написал Невилл.

— Оно отправлено сегодня из Гревзенда. Что ж, миссис Сент-Клер, тучи рассеиваются, хотя я не могу сказать, что опасность уже миновала.

— Однако он жив, мистер Холмс!

— Если только это не ловкая подделка, чтобы направить нас на ложный след. Кольцо, в конце концов, ничего не доказывает. Кольцо могли отнять у него.

— Но это его, его, его почерк!

— Хорошо. Но что, если письмо написано в понедельник, а послано только сегодня?

— Это возможно.

— А за этот срок многое могло произойти.

— О, не отнимайте у меня моей радости, мистер Холмс! Я знаю, что с ним ничего не случилось. Мы с ним настолько близки, что я непременно почувствовала бы, если бы он попал в настоящую беду. За день до того, как он исчез, он порезал себе нечаянно палец. Я была в столовой, он — в спальне, и я сразу побежала к нему, чувствуя, что с ним случилась беда. Неужели вы думаете, что я не знала бы о его смерти, если даже такой пустяк способен повлиять на меня!

— Я человек опытный и знаю, что женское непосредственное чутье может быть иногда ценнее всяких логических выводов. И это письмо, конечно, служит важным указанием, что вы правы. Однако, если мистер Сент-Клер жив, если он может писать вам письма, отчего же он не с вами?

— Не знаю. И представить себе не могу.

— В понедельник, уезжая, он ни о чем вас не предупреждал?

— Нет.

— И вы очень удивились, увидев его на Суондем-лейн?

— Очень.

— Окно было открыто?

— Да.

— Он мог бы окликнуть вас из окна?

— Да.

— Между тем, насколько я понял, у него вырвалось только бессвязное восклицание?

— Да.

— Вы подумали, что он зовет вас на помощь?

— Да. Он махнул мне руками.

— Но, быть может, он вскрикнул от неожиданности. Он мог всплеснуть руками от изумления, что видит вас.

— Возможно.

— И вам показалось, что его оттащили от окна?

— Он исчез так внезапно...

— Он мог просто отскочить от окна. Вы никого больше не видели в комнате?

— Никого. Но ведь этот отвратительный нищий сам признался, что Невилл был там. А лаокар стоял внизу, у лестницы.

— Совершенно верно. Насколько вы могли разглядеть, ваш муж был одет, как всегда?

— Но на нем не было ни воротничка, ни галстука. Я отчетливо видела его голую шею.

— Он когда-нибудь говорил с вами о Суондем-лейн?

— Никогда.

— А вы никогда не замечали каких-нибудь признаков, указывающих на то, что он курит опий?

— Никогда.

— Благодарю вас, миссис Сент-Клер. Это основные пункты, о которых я хотел знать всё. Теперь мы поужинаем и пойдем отдохнуть, так как весьма возможно, что завтра нам предстоит много хлопот.

В наше распоряжение была предоставлена просторная, удобная комната с двумя кроватями, и я сразу улегся, так как ночные похождения утомили меня. Но Шерлок Холмс, когда у него была какая-нибудь нерешенная задача, мог не спать по целым суткам и даже неделям, обдумывая ее, сопоставляя факты, рассматривая ее с разных точек зрения до тех пор, пока ему не удавалось либо разрешить ее, либо убедиться, что он находится на ложном пути. Я скоро понял, что он готовится просидеть без сна всю ночь. Он снял пиджак и жилет, надел синий просторный халат и принялся собирать в одну кучу подушки с кровати, с кушетки и с кресел. Из этих подушек он соорудил себе нечто вроде восточного дивана и взгромоздился на него, поджав ноги и положив перед собой пачку табаку и коробок спичек. При тусклом свете лампы я видел, как он сидит там в облаках голубого дыма, со старой трубкой во рту, рассеянно устремив глаза в потолок, безмолвный, неподвижный, и свет озаряет резкие орлиные черты его лица.

Так сидел он, когда я засыпал, и так сидел он, когда я при блеске утреннего солнца открыл глаза, разбуженный его внезапным восклицанием. Трубка все еще торчала у него изо рта, дым все еще вился кверху, комната была полна табачного тумана, а от пачки табаку, которую я видел вечером, уже ничего не осталось.

The pipe was still between his lips.

— Проснулись, Уотсон? — спросил он.

— Да.

— Хотите прокатиться?

— С удовольствием.

— Так одевайтесь. В доме еще все спят, но я знаю, где ночует конюх, и сейчас у нас будет коляска.

При этих словах он усмехнулся; глаза его блестели, и он нисколько не был похож на того мрачного мыслителя, которого я видел ночью.

Одеваясь, я взглянул на часы. Неудивительно, что в доме все еще спали: было двадцать пять минут пятого. Едва я успел одеться, как вошел Холмс и сказал, что конюх уже запряг лошадь.

— Хочу проверить одну свою версию, — сказал он, надевая ботинки. — Вы, Уотсон, видите перед собой одного из величайших глупцов, какие только существуют в Европе! Я был слеп, как крот. Мне следовало бы дать такого тумака, чтобы я полетел отсюда до Черинг-кросса! Но теперь я, кажется, нашел ключ к этой загадке.

— Где же он, ваш ключ? — спросил я, улыбаясь.

— В ванной, — ответил Холмс. — Нет, я не шучу, — продолжал он, заметив мой недоверчивый взгляд. — Я уже был в ванной, взял его и спрятал вот сюда, в чемоданчик. Поедем, друг мой, и посмотрим, подойдет ли этот ключ к замку.

Мы спустились с лестницы, стараясь ступать как можно тише. На дворе уже ярко сияло утреннее солнце У ворот нас поджидала коляска; конюх держал под уздцы запряженную лошадь.

Мы вскочили в экипаж и быстро покатили по лондонской дороге. Изредка мы обгоняли телеги, которые везли в столицу овощи, но на виллах кругом все было тихо — все спало, как в заколдованном городе.

— В некоторых отношениях это совершенно исключительное дело, — сказал Холмс, пуская лошадь галопом. — Сознаюсь, я был слеп, как крот, но лучше поумнеть поздно, чем никогда.

Мы въехали в город со стороны Сэрри. В окнах уже начали появляться заспанные лица только что проснувшихся людей. Мы переехали через реку по мосту Ватерлоо, свернули направо по Веллингтон-стрит и очутились на Бау-стрит. Шерлока Холмса хорошо знали в полицейском управлении, и, когда мы подъехали, два констебля отдали ему честь. Один из них взял лошадь под уздцы, а другой повел нас внутрь здания.

— Кто дежурный? — спросил Холмс.

— Инспектор Брэдстрит, сэр.

Из вымощенного каменными плитами коридора навстречу нам вышел высокий грузный полицейский в полной форме.

— А, Брэдстрит! Как поживаете? Я хочу поговорить с вами, Брэдстрит.

— Пожалуйста, мистер Холмс. Зайдите ко мне, в мою комнату.

Комната была похожа на контору: на столе огромная книга для записей, на стене телефон.

Инспектор сел за стол:

— Чем могу служить, мистер Холмс?

— Я хочу расспросить вас о том нищем, который замешан в деле исчезновения мистера Невилла Сент-Клера.

— Его арестовали и привезли сюда для допроса.

— Я знаю. Он здесь?

— В камере.

— Не буйствует?

— Нет, ведет себя тихо. Но как он грязен, этот негодяй!

— Грязен?

— Да. Еле-еле заставили его вымыть руки, а лицо у него черное, как у медника. Вот пусть только кончится следствие, а там уж ему не избежать тюремной ванны! Если бы вы на него посмотрели, вы согласились бы со мною.

— Я очень хотел бы на него посмотреть.

— Правда? Это нетрудно устроить. Идите за мной.

Чемоданчик свой можете оставить здесь.

— Нет, я захвачу его с собой.

— Хорошо. Пожалуйте сюда.

Он открыл запертую дверь, спустился по винтовой лестнице и привел нас в коридор с выбеленными стенами. Справа и слева шла вереница дверей.

— Его камера — третья справа, — сказал инспектор. — Вот здесь.

Он осторожно отодвинул дощечку в верхней части двери и глянул в отверстие.

— Спит, — сказал он. — Вы можете хорошенько его рассмотреть.

Мы оба приникли к решетке. Арестант крепко спал, медленно и тяжело дыша. Лицо его было обращено к нам. Это был мужчина среднего роста, одетый, как и подобает людям его профессии, очень скверно: сквозь прорехи порванного пиджака торчали лохмотья цветной рубахи. Он был действительно необычайно грязен, но даже толстый слой грязи, покрывавший лицо, не мог скрыть его отталкивающего безобразия. Широкий шрам шел от глаза к подбородку, и сквозь щель, прорубленную к верхней губе, постоянным оскалом торчали три зуба. Клок ярчайших рыжих волос падал на лоб и на глаза.

— Красавец, не правда ли? — сказал инспектор.

— Ему необходимо помыться, — заметил Холмс. — Я уже и раньше об этом догадывался и захватил с собой весь инструмент.

Он раскрыл чемоданчик и, к нашему изумлению, вынул из него большую губку.

He took out a very large bath-sponge.

— Хе-хе, да вы шутник! — засмеялся инспектор.

— Будьте любезны, откройте нам тихонько дверь, и мы живо придадим ему более приличный вид.

— Ладно, — оказал инспектор. — А то он и в самом деле позорит нашу тюрьму.

Инспектор открыл дверь, и мы втроем бесшумно вошли в камеру. Арестант шевельнулся, но сразу же заснул еще крепче. Холмс подошел к рукомойнику, намочил свою губку и дважды с силой провел ею по лицу арестанта.

— Позвольте мне представить вас мистеру Невиллу Сент-Клеру из Ли, в графстве Кент! — воскликнул Холмс.

Никогда в жизни не видел я ничего подобного. Лицо сползло с арестанта, как кора с дерева. Исчез грубый темный загар. Исчез ужасный шрам, пересекавший все лицо наискосок. Исчезла разрезанная губа. Исчез отталкивающий оскал зубов. Рыжие лохматые волосы исчезли от одного взмаха руки Холмса, и мы увидели бледного, грустного, изящного человека с черными волосами и нежной кожей, который, сидя в постели, протирал глаза и с недоумением глядел на нас, еще не вполне очнувшись от сна. Внезапно он понял все, вскрикнул и зарылся головой в подушку.

He broke into a scream.

— Боже, — закричал инспектор, — да ведь это и есть пропавший! Я знаю его, я видел фотографию!

Арестант повернулся к нам с безнадежным видом человека, решившего не противиться судьбе.

— Будь что будет! — сказал он. — За что вы меня держите здесь?

— За убийство мистера Невилла Сент... Тьфу! В убийстве вас теперь обвинить невозможно. Вас могли бы обвинить, пожалуй, только в попытке совершить самоубийство, — сказал инспектор, усмехаясь. — Я двадцать семь лет служу в полиции, но ничего подобного не видел.

— Раз я мистер Невилл Сент-Клер, то, значит, преступления совершено не было и, следовательно, я арестован незаконно.

— Преступления нет, но сделана большая ошибка, — сказал Холмс. — Вы напрасно не доверились жене.

— Дело не в жене, а в детях, — пылко сказал арестант. — Я не хотел, чтобы они стыдились отца. Боже, какой позор! Что мне делать?

Шерлок Холмс сел рядом с ним на койку и ласково похлопал его по плечу.

— Если вы позволите разбираться в вашем деле суду, вам, конечно, не избежать огласки, — оказал он. — Но если вам удастся убедить полицию, что за вами нет никакой вины, газеты ничего не узнают. Инспектор Брэдстрит может записать ваши показания и передать их надлежащим властям, и дело до суда не дойдет.

— О, как я вам благодарен! — вскричал арестант. — Я охотно перенес бы заточение, даже смертную казнь, лишь бы не опозорить детей раскрытием моей несчастной тайны! Вы первые услышите мою историю…

Отец мой был учителем в Честерфилде, и я получил там превосходное образование. В юности я много путешествовал, работал на сцене и, наконец, стал репортером одной вечерней лондонской газеты. Однажды моему редактору понадобилась серия очерков о нищенстве в столице, и я вызвался написать их. С этого и начались все мои приключения. Чтобы добыть необходимые для моих очерков факты, я решил переодеться нищим и стал попрошайничать. Когда я был еще актером, я славился умением гримироваться. Теперь это умение пригодилось. Я раскрасил себе лицо, а для того чтобы вызывать побольше жалости, намалевал на лице шрам и с помощью пластыря телесного цвета изуродовал себе губу, слегка приподняв ее. Затем, надев лохмотья и рыжий парик, я сел в самом оживленном месте Сити и принялся под видом продажи спичек просить милостыню. Семь часов я просидел не вставая, а вечером, вернувшись домой, к величайшему своему изумлению, обнаружил, что набрал двадцать шесть шиллингов и четыре пенса.

Я написал очерки и позабыл обо всей этой истории. Но вот, некоторое время спустя, мне предъявили вексель, по которому я поручился уплатить за приятеля двадцать пять фунтов. Я понятия не имел, где достать эти деньги, и вдруг мне в голову пришла отличная мысль. Упросив кредитора подождать две недели, я взял на работе отпуск и провел его в Сити, прося милостыню. За десять дней я собрал необходимую сумму и уплатил долг. Теперь вообразите себе, легко ли работать за два фунта в неделю, когда знаешь, что эти два фунта ты можешь получить в один день, выпачкав себе лицо, положив кепку на землю и ровно ничего не делая?

Долго длилась борьба между моей гордостью в стремлением к наживе, но страсть к деньгам в конце концов победила. Я бросил работу и стал все дни проводить на давно облюбованном мною углу, вызывая жалость своим уродливым видом и набивая карманы медяками.

Только один человек был посвящен в мою тайну — владелец низкопробного притона на Суондем-лейн, в котором я поселился. Каждое утро я выходил оттуда в виде жалкого нищего, и каждый вечер я превращался там в хорошо одетого господина, я щедро платил этому ласкару за его комнаты, так как был уверен, что он никому ни при каких обстоятельствах не выдаст моей тайны.

Вскоре я стал откладывать крупные суммы денег. Вряд ли в Лондоне есть хоть один нищий, зарабатывающий по семисот фунтов в год, а я зарабатывал и больше. Я навострился шуткой парировать замечания прохожих и скоро прославился на все Сити. Поток пенсов вперемешку с серебром сыпался на меня непрестанно, и я считал неудачными дни, когда получал меньше двух фунтов. Чем богаче я становился, тем шире я жил. Я снял дом за городом, я женился, и никто не подозревал, чем я занимаюсь в действительности. Моя милая жена знает, что у меня есть какие-то дела в Сити. Но какого рода эти дела, она не имеет ни малейшего представления.

В прошлый понедельник, закончив работу, я переодевался у себя в комнате, как вдруг, выглянув в окно, увидел, к своему ужасу, что жена моя стоит на улице и смотрит прямо на меня. Я вскрикнул от изумления, поднял руки, чтобы закрыть лицо, и кинулся к моему соучастнику ласкару, умоляя его никого ко мне не пускать. Я слышал внизу голос жены, но я знал, что подняться она не сможет. Я быстро разделся, натянул на себя нищенские лохмотья, парик и разрисовал лицо. Даже жена не могла бы узнать меня в этом виде.

Но затем мне пришло в голову, что комнату мою могут обыскать и тогда моя одежда выдаст меня. Я распахнул окно, причем второпях задел раненый палец (я поранил себе палец утром в спальне), и из ранки опять потекла кровь. Потом я схватил пиджак, набитый медяками, которые я только что переложил туда из своей нищенской сумы, швырнул его в окно, и он исчез в Темзе. Я собирался швырнуть туда и остальную одежду, но тут ко мне ворвались полицейские и через несколько минут, вместо того чтобы быть изобличенным как мистер Невилл Сент-Клер, я оказался арестованным как его убийца.

Больше мне нечего прибавить. Желая сохранить грим на лице, я отказывался от умывания. Зная, что жена будет очень тревожиться обо мне, я тайком от полицейских снял с пальца кольцо и передал его ласкару вместе с наскоро нацарапанной запиской, в которой я сообщал ей, что мне не угрожает никакая опасность.

— Она только вчера получила эту записку, — сказал Холмс.

— О боже! Какую неделю она провела!

— За ласкаром следила полиция, — сказал инспектор Брэдстрит, — и ему, видимо, никак не удавалось отправить записку незаметно. Он, вероятно, передал ее какому-нибудь матросу, завсегдатаю своего притона, а тот в течение нескольких дней все забывал опустить ее в ящик.

— Так это, без сомнения и было, — подтвердил Холмс. — Но неужели вас никогда не привлекали к суду за нищенство?

— Много раз. Но что значит для меня незначительный штраф!

— Однако теперь вам придется оставить свое ремесло, — сказал Брэдстрит. — Если вы хотите, чтобы полиция замяла эту историю, Хью Бун должен исчезнуть.

— Я уже поклялся себе в этом самой торжественной клятвой, какую только может дать человек.

— В таком случае, все будет забыто, — сказал Брэдстрит. — Но если вас заметят опять, мы уже не станем скрывать ничего... Мы очень признательны вам, мистер Холмс, за то, что вы раскрыли это дело. Хотел бы я знать, каким образом вы достигаете подобных результатов.

— На этот раз, — отозвался мой друг, — мне понадобилось посидеть на пяти подушках и выкурить полфунта табаку... Мне кажется, Уотсон, что, если мы сейчас поедем на Бейкер-стрит, мы поспеем как раз к завтраку.

ГОЛУБОЙ КАРБУНКУЛ

На третий день Рождества зашел я к Шерлоку Холмсу, чтобы поздравить его с праздником. Он лежал на кушетке в красном халате; по правую руку от него была подставка для трубок, а по левую — груда помятых утренних газет которые он, видимо, только что просматривал. Рядом с кушеткой стоял стул, на его спинке висела сильно поношенная, потерявшая вид фетровая шляпа. Холмс, должно быть очень внимательно изучал эту шляпу, так как тут же на сиденье стула лежали пинцет и лупа.

A very seedy hard-felt hat.

— Вы заняты? — сказал я. — Я вам не помешал?

— Нисколько, — ответил он. — Я рад, что у меня есть друг, с которым я могу обсудить результаты некоторых моих изысканий.

Дельце весьма заурядное, но с этой вещью, — он ткнул большим пальцем в сторону шляпы, — связаны кое-какие любопытные и даже поучительные события.

Я уселся в кресло и стал греть руки у камина, где потрескивал огонь. Был сильный мороз; окна покрылись плотными ледяными узорами.

— Хотя эта шляпа кажется очень невзрачной, она, должно быть, связана с какой-нибудь кровавой историей, — заметил я.

— Очевидно, она послужит ключом к разгадке страшной тайны, и благодаря ей вам удастся изобличить и наказать преступника.

— Нет, — засмеялся Шерлок Холмс, — тут не преступление, а мелкий, смешной эпизод, который всегда может произойти там, где четыре миллиона человек толкутся на площади в несколько квадратных миль. В таком колоссальном человеческом улье возможны любые комбинации событий и фактов, возникает масса незначительных, но загадочных и странных происшествий, хотя ничего преступного в них нет. Нам уже приходилось сталкиваться с подобными случаями.

— Еще бы! — воскликнул я. — Из последних шести эпизодов, которыми я пополнил свои записки, три не содержат ничего беззаконного.

— Совершенно верно. Вы имеете в виду мои попытки обнаружить бумаги Ирен Адлер, интересный случай с мисс Мэри Сазерлэнд и приключения человека с рассеченной губой. Не сомневаюсь, что и это дело окажется столь же невинным. Вы знаете Питерсона, посыльного?

— Да.

— Этот трофей принадлежит ему.

— Это его шляпа?

— Нет, он нашел ее. Владелец ее неизвестен. Я прошу вас рассматривать эту шляпу не как старую рухлядь, а как предмет, таящий в себе серьезную задачу... Однако прежде всего, как эта шляпа попала сюда. Она появилась в первый день Рождества вместе с отличным жирным гусем, который в данный момент наверняка жарится у Питерсона в кухне. Произошло это так. На Рождество, в четыре часа утра, Питерсон, человек, как вы знаете, благородный и честный, возвращался с пирушки домой по улице Тоттенхем-Корт-роуд. При свете газового фонаря он заметил, что перед ним, слегка пошатываясь, идет какой-то субъект и несет на плече белоснежного гуся. На углу Гудж-стрит к незнакомцу пристали хулиганы. Один из них сбил с него шляпу, а незнакомец, отбиваясь, размахнулся палкой и попал в витрину магазина, оказавшуюся у него за спиной. Питерсон кинулся вперед, чтобы защитить его, но тот, испуганный тем, что разбил стекло, увидев бегущего к нему человека, бросил гуся, помчался со всех ног и исчез в лабиринте небольших переулков, лежащих позади Тоттенхем-Корт-роуд. Питерсон был в форме, и это, должно быть, больше всего и напугало беглеца. Хулиганы тоже разбежались, и посыльный остался один на поле битвы, оказавшись обладателем этой помятой шляпы и превосходного рождественского гуся…

The roughs had flet at the appearance of Peterson.

— …которого Питерсон, конечно, возвратил незнакомцу?

— В том-то и загвоздка, дорогой друг. Правда, на карточке, привязанной к левой лапке гуся, было написано: «Для миссис Генри Бейкер», а на подкладке шляпы можно разобрать инициалы «Г. Б.». Но в Лондоне живет несколько тысяч Бейкеров и несколько сот Генри

Бейкеров, так что нелегко вернуть потерянную собственность одному из них.

— Что же сделал Питерсон?

— Зная, что меня занимает решение даже самых ничтожных загадок, он попросту принес мне и гуся и шляпу. Гуся мы продержали вплоть до сегодняшнего утра, когда стало ясно, что, несмотря на мороз, его все же лучше незамедлительно съесть. Питерсон унес гуся, и с гусем произошло то, к чему он уготован судьбой, а у меня осталась шляпа незнакомца, потерявшего свой рождественский ужин.

— Он не помещал объявления в газете?

— Нет.

— Как же вы узнаете, кто он?

— Только путем размышлений.

— Размышлений над этой шляпой?

— Конечно.

— Вы шутите! Что можно извлечь из этого старого рваного фетра?

— Вот лупа. Попробуйте применить мой метод. Что вы можете сказать о человеке, которому принадлежала эта шляпа?

Я взял рваную шляпу и уныло повертел ее в руках. Самая обыкновенная черная круглая шляпа, жесткая, сильно поношенная. Шелковая подкладка, некогда красная, теперь выцвела. Фабричную марку мне обнаружить не удалось, но, как и сказал Холмс, внутри сбоку виднелись инициалы «Г. Б.». На полях я заметил петельку для придерживавшей шляпу резинки, но самой резинки не оказалось. Вообще шляпа была мятая, грязная, покрытая пятнами. Впрочем, заметны были попытки замазать эти пятна чернилами.

— Я ничего в ней не вижу, — сказал я, возвращая шляпу Шерлоку Холмсу.

— Нет, Уотсон, видите, но не даете себе труда поразмыслить над тем, что видите. Вы слишком робки в своих логических выводах.

— Тогда, пожалуйста, скажите, какие же выводы делаете вы?

Холмс взял шляпу в руки и стал пристально разглядывать ее проницательным взглядом, свойственным ему одному.

— Конечно, не все достаточно ясно, — заметил он, — но кое-что можно установить наверняка, а кое-что предположить с разумной долей вероятия. Совершенно очевидно, например, что владелец ее — человек большого ума и что три года назад у него были изрядные деньги, а теперь настали черные дни. Он всегда был предусмотрителен и заботился о завтрашнем дне, но мало-помалу опустился, благосостояние его упало, и мы вправе предположить, что он пристрастился к какому-нибудь пороку, — быть может, к пьянству. По-видимому, из-за этого и жена его разлюбила…

— Дорогой Холмс…

— Но в какой-то степени он еще сохранил свое достоинство, — продолжал Холмс, не обращая внимания на мое восклицание. — Он ведет сидячий образ жизни, редко выходит из дому, совершенно не занимается спортом. Этот человек средних лет, у него седые волосы, он мажет их помадой и недавно подстригся. Вдобавок я почти уверен, что в доме у него нет газового освещения.

— Вы, конечно, шутите, Холмс.

— Ничуть. Неужели даже теперь, когда я все рассказал, вы не понимаете, как я узнал об этом?

— Считайте меня идиотом, но должен признаться, что я не в состоянии уследить за ходом ваших мыслей. Например, откуда вы взяли, что он умен?

Вместо ответа Холмс нахлобучил шляпу себе на голову. Шляпа закрыла его лоб и уперлась в переносицу.

— Видите, какой размер! — сказал он. — Не может же быть совершенно пустым такой большой череп.

— Ну, а откуда вы взяли, что он обеднел?

— Этой шляпе три года. Тогда были модными плоские поля, загнутые по краям. Шляпа лучшего качества. Взгляните-ка на эту шелковую ленту, на превосходную подкладку. Если три года назад человек был в состоянии купить столь дорогую шляпу и с тех пор не покупал ни одной, значит, дела у него пошатнулись.

— Ну ладно, в этом, пожалуй, вы правы. Но откуда вы могли узнать, что он человек предусмотрительный, а в настоящее время переживает душевный упадок?

— Предусмотрительность — вот она, — сказал он, показывая на петельку от шляпной резинки. — Резинки не продают вместе со шляпой, их нужно покупать отдельно. Раз этот человек купил резинку и велел прикрепить к шляпе, значит, он заботился о том, чтобы уберечь ее от ветра. Но когда резинка оторвалась, а он не стал прилаживать новую, это значит, что он перестал следить за своей наружностью, опустился. Однако, с другой стороны, он пытался замазать чернилами пятна на шляпе, то есть не окончательно потерял чувство собственного достоинства.

— Все это очень похоже на правду.

— Что он человек средних лет, что у него седина, что он недавно стригся, что он помадит волосы — все станет ясным, если внимательно посмотреть на нижнюю часть подкладки в шляпе. В лупу видны приставшие к подкладке волосы, аккуратно срезанные ножницами парикмахера и пахнущие помадой. Заметьте, что пыль на шляпе не уличная — серая и жесткая, а домашняя — бурая, пушистая. Значит, шляпа большей частью висела дома. А следы влажности на внутренней ее стороне говорят о том, как быстро потеет ее владелец, потому что не привык много двигаться.

— А как вы узнали, что его разлюбила жена?

— Шляпа не чищена несколько недель. Мой дорогой Уотсон, если бы я увидел, что ваша шляпа не чищена хотя бы неделю и вам позволяют выходить в таком виде, у меня появилось бы опасение, что вы имели несчастье утратить расположение вашей супруги.

— А может быть, он холостяк?

— Нет, он нес гуся именно для того, чтобы задобрить жену. Вспомните карточку, привязанную к лапке птицы.

— У вас на все готов ответ. Но откуда вы знаете, что у него в доме нет газа?

— Одно-два сальных пятна на шляпе — случайность. Но когда я вижу их не меньше пяти, я не сомневаюсь, что человеку часто приходится пользоваться сальной свечой, может быть, он поднимается ночью по лестнице, держа в одной руке шляпу, а в другой оплывшую свечу. Во всяком случае, от газа не бывает сальных пятен... Вы согласны со мною?

— Да, все это очень остроумно, — смеясь, сказал я. — Но, как вы сами сказали, тут еще нет преступления. Никто не пострадал — разве что человек, потерявший гуся, — значит, вы ломали себе голову зря.

Шерлок Холмс раскрыл было рот для ответа, но в это мгновение дверь распахнулась, и в комнату влетел Питерсон; щеки у него буквально пылали от волнения.

— Гусь-то, гусь, мистер Холмс! — задыхаясь, прокричал он.

— Ну? Что с ним такое? Ожил он, что ли, и вылетел в кухонное окно? — Холмс повернулся на кушетке, чтобы лучше всмотреться в возбужденное лицо Питерсона.

— Посмотрите, сэр! Посмотрите, что жена нашла у него в зобу!

Питерсон протянул руку, и на ладони его мы увидели ярко сверкающий голубой камень чуть поменьше горошины. Камень был такой чистой воды, что светился на темной ладони, точно электрическая искра. Холмс присвистнул и опустился на кущетку.

«See what my wife found in its crop!»

— Честной слово, Питерсон, вы нашли сокровище! Надеюсь, вы понимаете, что это такое?

— Алмаз, сэр! Драгоценный камень! Он режет стекло, словно масло!

— Не просто драгоценный камень — это тот самый камень, который...

— Неужели голубой карбункул графини Моркар? — воскликнул я.

— Конечно! Узнаю камень по описаниям, последнее время я каждый день вижу объявления о его пропаже в «Таймс». Камень этот единственный в своем роде, и можно только догадываться о его настоящей цене. Награда в тысячу фунтов, которую предлагают нашедшему, едва ли составляет двадцатую долю его стоимости.

— Тысяча фунтов! О, Боже!

Посыльный бухнулся в кресло, изумленно тараща на нас глаза.

— Награда наградой, но у меня есть основания думать, — сказал Холмс, — что по некоторым соображениям графиня отдаст половину всех своих богатств, только бы вернуть этот камень.

— Если память мне не изменяет, он пропал в гостинице «Космополитен», — заметил я.

— Совершенно верно, двадцать второго декабря, ровно пять дней назад. В краже этого камня обвинен Джон Хорнер, паяльщик. Улики против него так серьезны, что дело направлено в суд. Кажется, у меня есть об этом деле газетный отчет.

Шерлок Холмс долго рылся в газетах, наконец вытащил одну, разгладил ее, сложил пополам и прочитал следующее:

«КРАЖА ДРАГОЦЕННОСТЕЙ В ОТЕЛЕ „КОСМОПОЛИТЕН“

Джон Хорнер, 26 лет, обвиняется в том, что 22 сего месяца похитил у графини Моркар из шкатулки драгоценный камень, известный под названием «Голубой карбункул». Джеймс Райдер, служащий отеля, показал, что в день кражи Хорнер припаивал расшатанный прут каминной решетки в комнате графини Моркар. Некоторое время Райдер находился в комнате с Хорнером, но потом его куда-то вызвали. Возвратившись, он увидел, что Хорнер исчез, бюро взломано и маленький сафьяновый футляр, в котором, как выяснилось впоследствии, графиня имела обыкновение держать дагоценный камень, валялся пустой на туалетном столике. Райдер сейчас же сообщил в полицию, и в тот же вечер Хорнер был арестован, но камня не нашли ни при нем, ни у него дома. Кэтрин Кьюсек, горничная графини, показала, что, услышав отчаянный крик Райдера, она вбежала в комнату и тоже увидела пустой футляр. Полицейский инспектор Бродстрит из округа «Б» сообщил, что Хорнер отчаянно сопротивлялся при аресте и горячо доказывал свою невиновность. Поскольку стало известно, что арестованный и прежде судился за кражу, судья отказался разбирать дело и передал его суду присяжных. Хорнер, все время высказывавший признаки сильнейшего волнения, упал в обморок и был вынесен из зала суда».

— Гм! Вот и все, что дает нам полицейский суд, — задумчиво сказал Холмс, откладывая газету. — Наша задача теперь — выяснить, каким образом из футляра графини камень попал в гусиный зоб. Видите, Уотсон, наши скромные размышления оказались не такими уж незначительными. Итак, вот камень. Этот камень был в гусе, а гусь у мистера Генри Бейкера, у того самого обладателя старой шляпы, которого я пытался охарактеризовать, чем и нагнал на вас невыносимую скуку. Что ж, теперь мы должны серьезно заняться розысками этого джентльмена и установить, какую роль он играл в таинственном происшествии. Прежде всего испробуем самый простой способ: напечатаем объявление во всех вечерних газетах. Если таким путем не достигнем цели, прибегнем к иным методам.

— Что вы напишете в объявлении?

— Дайте мне карандаш и клочок бумаги. «На углу Гуджстрит найдены гусь и черная фетровая шляпа. Мистер Генри Бейкер может получить их сегодня на Бейкер-стрит, 221-б, в 6.30 вечера». Коротко и ясно.

— Весьма. Но заметит ли он объявление?

— Конечно. Он просматривает теперь все газеты: человек он бедный, и рождественский гусь для него целое состояние. Он до такой степени был напуган, услышав звон разбитого стекла и увидев бегущего Питерсона, что кинулся бежать, не думая ни о чем. Но потом он, конечно, пожалел, что испугался и бросил гуся. В газете мы упоминаем его имя, и любой знакомый обратит его внимание на нашу публикацию... Так вот, Питерсон, бегите в бюро объявлений, чтобы они поместили эти строки в вечерних газетах.

— В каких, сэр?

— В «Глоб», «Стар», «Пэлл-Мэлл», «Сент-Джеймс газетт», «Ивнинг ньюс стандард», «Эхо» — во всех, какие придут вам на ум.

— Слушаю, сэр! А как быть с камнем?

— Ах да! Камень я пока оставлю у себя. Благодарю вас. А на обратном пути, Питерсон, купите гуся и принесите его мне. Мы ведь должны дать этому джентльмену гуся взамен того, которым в настоящее время угощается ваша семья.

Посыльный ушел, а Холмс взял камень и стал рассматривать его на свет.

— Славный камешек! — сказал он. — Взгляните, как он сверкает и искрится. Как и всякий драгоценный камень, он притягивает к себе преступников, словно магнит. Вот уж подлинно ловушка сатаны. В больших старых камнях каждая грань может рассказать о какомнибудь кровавом злодеянии. Этому камню нет еще и двадцати лет. Его нашли на берегу реки Амоу, в Южном Китае, и замечателен он тем, что имеет все свойства карбункула, кроме одного: он не рубиново-красный, а голубой. Несмотря на его молодость, с ним уже связано много ужасных историй. Из-за сорока граней кристаллического углерода многих ограбили, кого-то облили серной кислотой, было два убийства и одно самоубийство. Кто бы сказал, что такая красивая безделушка ведет людей в тюрьму и на виселицу! Я запру камень в свой несгораемый шкаф и напишу графине, что он у нас.

— Как вы считаете, Хорнер не виновен?

— Не знаю.

— А Генри Бейкер замешан в это дело?

— Вернее всего, Генри Бейкер здесь ни при чем. Я думаю, ему и в голову не пришло, что, будь этот гусь из чистого золота, он и то стоил бы дешевле. Все очень скоро прояснится, если Генри Бейкер откликнется на наше объявление.

— А до тех пор вы ничего не хотите предпринять?

— Ничего.

— В таком случае я навещу своих пациентов, а вечером снова приду сюда. Я хочу знать, чем окончится это запутанное дело.

— Буду рад вас видеть. Я обедаю в семь. Кажется, к обеду будет куропатка. Кстати, в связи с недавними событиями не попросить ли миссис Хадсон тщательно осмотреть ее зоб?

Я немного задержался, и было уже больше половины седьмого, когда я снова попал на Бейкер-стрит. Подойдя к дому Холмса, я увидел, что в ярком полукруге света, падавшем из окна над дверью, стоит высокий мужчина в шотландской шапочке и в наглухо застегнутом до подбородка сюртуке. Как раз в тот момент, когда я подошел, дверь отперли, и мы одновременно вошли к Шерлоку Холмсу.

— Если не ошибаюсь, мистер Генри Бейкер? — сказал Холмс, поднимаясь с кресла и встречая посетителя с тем непринужденным радушным видом, который он так умело напускал на себя. — Пожалуйста, присаживайтесь поближе к огню, мистер Бейкер. Вечер сегодня холодный, а мне кажется, лето вы переносите лучше, чем зиму… Уотсон, вы пришли как раз вовремя… Это ваша шляпа, мистер Бейкер?

— Да, сэр, это, несомненно, моя шляпа.

Бейкер был крупный, сутулый человек с большой головой, с широким умным лицом и остроконечной каштановой бородкой. Красноватые пятна на носу и щеках и легкое дрожание протянутой руки подтверждали догадку Холмса о его наклонностях. На нем был порыжелый сюртук, застегнутый на все пуговицы, а на тощих запястьях, торчащих из рукавов, не было видно манжет. Он говорил глухо и отрывисто, старательно подбирая слова, и производил впечатление человека интеллигентного, но сильно помятого жизнью.

— У нас уже несколько дней хранится ваша шляпа и ваш гусь, — сказал Холмс. — Мы ждали, что вы дадите в газете объявление о пропаже. Не понимаю, почему вы этого не сделали.

Наш посетитель смущенно усмехнулся.

— У меня не так много шиллингов, как бывало когда-то, — сказал он. — Я был уверен, что хулиганы, напавшие на меня унесли с собой и шляпу, и птицу, и не хотел тратить деньги по-пустому.

— Вполне естественно. Между прочим, нам ведь пришлось съесть вашего гуся.

— Съесть? — Наш посетитель в волнении поднялся со стула.

— Да ведь он все равно испортился бы, — продолжал Холмс. — Но я полагаю, что вон та птица на буфете, совершенно свежая и того же веса, заменит вам вашего гуся.

— О, конечно, конечно! — ответил мистер Бейкер, облегченно вздохнув.

— Правда, у нас от вашей птицы остались перья, лапки и зоб, так что, если захотите…

Бейкер от души расхохотался.

— Разве только на память о моем приключении, — сказал он. — Право, не знаю, на что мне могут пригодиться disjecta membra[1]

[1] Останки (лат.)

моего покойного знакомца! Нет, сэр, с вашего разрешения я лучше ограничусь тем превосходным гусем, которого я вижу на буфете.

Шерлок Холмс многозначительно посмотрел на меня и чуть заметно пожал плечами.

— Итак, вот ваша шляпа и ваш гусь, — сказал он. — Кстати, не скажете ли мне, где вы достали того гуся? Я кое-что смыслю в птице и, признаться, редко видывал столь откормленный экземпляр.

— Охотно, сэр, — сказал Бейкер, встав и сунув под мышку своего нового гуся. — Наша небольшая компания посещает трактир «Альфа», близ Британского музея, мы, понимаете ли, проводим в музее целый день. А в этом году хозяин трактира Уиндигейт, отличный человек, основал «гусиный клуб». Каждый из нас выплачивает по нескольку пенсов в неделю и к Рождеству получает гуся. Я целиком выплатил свою долю, ну а остальное вам известно. Весьма обязан вам, сэр, — ведь неудобно солидному человеку в моем возрасте носить шотландскую шапочку.

Он поклонился нам с комически торжественным видом и ушел.

He bowed solemnly to both of us.

— С Генри Бейкером покончено, — сказал Холмс, закрывая за ним дверь. — Совершенно очевидно, что он понятия не имеет о драгоценном камне. Вы очень голодны, Уотсон?

— Не особенно.

— Тогда я предлагаю превратить обед в ужин и немедленно отправиться по горячим следам.

— Я готов.

Был морозный вечер, и нам пришлось надеть пальто и обмотать себе шею шарфом. Звезды холодно сияли на безоблачном, ясном небе, и пар от дыхания прохожих был похож на дымки от пистолетных выстрелов. Четко и гулко раздавались по улицам наши шаги. Мы шли по Уимпол-стрит, Харли-стрит, через Уитмор-стрит, вышли на Оксфорд-стрит и через четверть часа были в Блумсбери, возле трактира «Альфа», скромного заведения на углу одной из улиц, ведущих к Холборну. Холмс вошел в бар и заказал две кружки пива краснощекому трактирщику в белом переднике.

— У вас, надо полагать, превосходное пиво, если оно не хуже ваших гусей, — сказал Холмс.

— Моих гусей? — Трактирщик, казалось, был изумлен.

— Да. Полчаса назад я беседовал с мистером Генри Бейкером, членом вашего «гусиного клуба».

— А, понимаю. Но видите ли, сэр, гуси-то ведь не мои.

— В самом деле? А чьи же?

— Я купил две дюжины гусей у одного торговца в Ковент-Гарден.

— Да ну? Я знаю кое-кого из них. У кого же вы купили?

— Его зовут Брекинридж.

— Нет, Брекинриджа я не знаю. Ну, за ваше здоровье, хозяин, и за процветание вашего заведения! Доброй ночи!

— А теперь к мистеру Брекинриджу, — сказал Холмс, выходя на мороз и застегивая пальто. — Не забудьте, Уотсон, что на одном конце нашей цепи всего только безобидный гусь, зато к другому ее концу прикован человек, которому грозит не меньше семи лет каторги, если мы не докажем его невиновность. Возможно, впрочем, что наши розыски обнаружат, что виноват именно он, но, во всяком случае, в наших руках нить, ускользнувшая от полиции и случайно попавшая к нам. Дойдем же до конца этой нити, как бы печален этот конец ни был. Итак, поворот на юг, и шагом марш!

Мы пересекли Холборн, пошли по Энделл-стрит и через какие-то трущобы вышли на Ковентгарденский рынок. На одной из самых больших лавок было написано: «Брекинридж». Хозяин лавки, человек с лошадиным лицом и холеными бакенбардами, помогал мальчику запирать ставни.

— Добрый вечер! Каков морозец, а? — сказал Холмс.

Торговец кивнул головой, бросив вопросительный взгляд на моего друга.

— Гуси, видно, распроданы? — продолжал Холмс, указывая на пустой мраморный прилавок.

— Завтра утром можете купить хоть пятьсот штук.

— Завтра они мне ни к чему.

— Вон в той лавке, где горит свет, кое-что осталось.

— Да? Но меня направили к вам.

— Кто же?

— Хозяин «Альфы».

— А! Я отослал ему две дюжины.

— Отличные были гуси! Откуда вы их достали?

К моему удивлению, вопрос этот привел торговца в бешенство.

— А ну-ка, мистер, — сказал он, поднимая голову и упирая руки в бока, — к чему вы клоните? Говорите прямо.

— Я говорю достаточно прямо. Мне хотелось бы знать, кто продал вам тех гусей, которых вы поставляете в «Альфу».

— Вот и не скажу.

— Не скажете — и не надо. Велика важность! Чего вы кипятитесь из-за таких пустяков?

— Кипячусь? Небось, на моем месте и вы кипятились бы, если бы к вам так приставали! Я плачу хорошие деньги за хороший товар, и, казалось бы, дело с концом. Так нет: «где гуси?», «у кого вы купили гусей?», «кому вы продали гусей?» Можно подумать, что на этих гусях свет клином сошелся, когда послушаешь, какой из-за них подняли шум!

— Какое мне дело до других, которые пристают к вам с расспросами! — небрежно сказал Холмс. — Не хотите говорить — не надо. Но я понимаю толк в птице и держал пари на пять фунтов стерлингов, что гусь, которого я ел, выкормлен в деревне.

— Вот и пропали ваши фунты! Гусь-то городской! — выпалил торговец.

— Быть не может.

— А я говорю, городской!

— Ни за что не поверю!

— Уж не думаете ли вы, что смыслите в этом деле больше меня? Я ведь этим делом занимаюсь чуть не с пеленок. Говорю вам, все гуси, проданные в «Альфу», выкормлены в городе.

— И не пытайтесь меня убедить в этом.

— Хотите пари?

— Это значило бы попросту взять у вас деньги. Я уверен, что прав. Но у меня при себе есть соверен, и я готов поставить его, чтобы проучить вас за упрямство.

Торговец ухмыльнулся.

— Принеси-ка мне книги, Билл, — сказал он.

Мальчишка принес две книги: одну тоненькую, а другую большую, засаленную, и положил их на прилавок под лампой.

— Ну-с, мистер Спорщик, — сказал торговец, — я считал, что сегодня распродал всех гусей, но, ей-ей, Бог занес ко мне в лавку еще одного. Видите эту книжку?

— Ну и что же?

— Это список тех, у кого я покупаю товар. Видите? Вот здесь, на этой странице, имена деревенских поставщиков, а цифра после каждой фамилии обозначает страницу в гроссбухе, где ведутся их счета. А эту страницу, исписанную красными чернилами, видите? Это список моих городских поставщиков. Взгляните-ка на третью фамилию. Прочтите ее вслух.

«Just read it out to me.»

— «Миссис Окшотт, Брикстон-роуд, 117, страница 249», — прочел Холмс.

— Совершенно правильно. Теперь откройте 249-ю страницу в гроссбухе.

Холмс открыл указанную страницу: «Миссис Окшотт, Брикстон-роуд, 117 — поставщица дичи и яиц».

— А что гласит последняя запись?

— «Декабрь, двадцать второго. Двадцать четыре гуся по семь шиллингов шесть пенсов».

— Правильно. Запомните это. А внизу?

— «Проданы мистеру Уиндигейту, „Альфа“, по двенадцать шиллингов».

— Ну, что вы теперь скажете?

Шерлок Холмс, казалось, был глубоко огорчен. Вынув соверен из кармана, он бросил его на прилавок, повернулся и вышел молча, с расстроенным видом. Однако, пройдя несколько шагов, он остановился под фонарем и рассмеялся своим особенным — веселым и беззвучным — смехом.

— Если у человека такие бакенбарды и такой красный платок в кармане, у него можно выудить все что угодно, предложив ему пари, — сказал он. — Я утверждаю, что и за сто фунтов мне не удалось бы получить у него такие подробные сведения, какие я получил, побившись с ним об заклад. Итак, Уотсон, мне кажется, что мы почти у цели. Единственное, что нам осталось решить, — пойдем ли мы к этой миссис Окшотт сейчас или отложим наше посещение до утра. Из слов того грубияна ясно, что этим делом интересуется еще кто-то и я…

Громкий шум, донесшийся внезапно из лавки, которую мы только что покинули, не дал Холмсу договорить. Обернувшись, мы увидели в желтом свете качающейся лампы какого-то невысокого, краснолицого человека. Брекинридж, стоя в дверях лавки, яростно потрясал перед ним кулаками.

— Хватит с меня и вас и ваших гусей! — орал Брекинридж. — Проваливайте вы все к дьяволу! Если вы еще раз сунетесь ко мне с дурацкими расспросами, я спущу цепную собаку. Приведите сюда миссис Окшотт, ей я отвечу. А вы то тут при чем? Ваших, что ли, я купил гусей!

— Нет, но все же один из них мой, — захныкал человек.

— Ну и спрашивайте его тогда у миссис Окшотт!

— Она мне велела узнать у вас.

— Спрашивайте хоть у прусского короля! С меня хватит! Убирайтесь отсюда! — Он яростно бросился вперед, и человечек быстро исчез во мраке.

— Ага, нам, кажется, не придется идти на Брикстон-роуд, — прошептал Холмс. — Пойдем посмотрим, не пригодится ли нам этот субъект.

Пробираясь между кучками ротозеев, бродящих вокруг освещенных ларьков, мой друг быстро нагнал человечка и положил ему руку на плечо. Тот порывисто обернулся, и при свете газового фонаря я увидел, как сильно он побледнел.

— Кто вы такой? Что вам надо? — спросил он дрожащим голосом.

— Извините меня, — мягко сказал Холмс, — но я случайно слышал, что вы спрашивали у этого торговца. Я думаю, что могу быть вам полезен.

— Вы? Кто вы такой? Откуда вы знаете, что мне нужно?

— Меня зовут Шерлок Холмс. Моя профессия — знать то, чего не знают другие.

— О том, что мне нужно, вы ничего не можете знать.

— Прошу прощения, но я знаю все. Вы пытаетесь установить, куда попали гуси, проданные миссис Окшотт с Брикстон-роуд торговцу Брекинриджу, который, в свою очередь, продал их мистеру Уиндигейту, владельцу «Альфы», а тот передал «гусиному клубу», членом которого является Генри Бейкер.

— Сэр, вы-то мне и нужны! — вскричал человек, протягивая дрожащие руки. — Я просто не могу выразить, как все это важно для меня!

«You are the very man.»

Шерлок Холмс остановил проезжавшего извозчика.

— В таком случае лучше разговаривать в уютной комнате, чем тут, на ветреной рыночной площади, — сказал он. — Но прежде чем отправиться в путь, скажите, пожалуйста, кому я имею удовольствие оказывать посильную помощь?

Человечек заколебался на мгновение.

— Меня зовут Джон Робинсон, — сказал он, отводя глаза.

— Нет, мне нужно настоящее имя, — ласково сказал Холмс. — Гораздо удобнее иметь дело с человеком, который действует под своим настоящим именем.

Бледные щеки незнакомца загорелись румянцем.

— В таком случае, — сказал он, — мое имя — Джеймс Райдер.

— Так я и думал. Вы служите в отеле «Космополитен». Садитесь, пожалуйста, в кэб, и вскоре я расскажу вам все, что вы пожелаете узнать.

Маленький человечек не двигался с места. Он смотрел то на Холмса, то на меня с надеждой и испугом: он не знал, ждет ли его беда или удача. Наконец он сел в экипаж, и через полчаса мы были в гостиной на Бейкер-стрит.

Дорогой никто не произнес ни слова. Но спутник наш так учащенно дышал, так крепко сжимал и разжимал ладони, что было ясно, в каком нервном возбуждении он пребывает.

— Ну, вот мы и дома! — весело сказал Холмс. — Что может быть лучше пылающего камина в такую погоду! Вы, кажется, озябли, мистер Райдер. Садитесь, пожалуйста, в плетеное кресло. Я только надену домашние туфли, и мы сейчас же займемся вашим делом. Ну вот, готово! Так вы хотите знать, что стало с теми гусями?

— Да, сэр.

— Пожалуй, вернее, с тем гусем? Мне кажется, вас интересовал лишь один из них — белый, с черной полосой на хвосте…

Райдер затрепетал от волнения.

— О, сэр! — вскричал он. — Вы можете сказать, где находится этот гусь?

— Он был здесь.

— Здесь?

— Да, и оказался необыкновенным гусем. Не удивительно, что вы заинтересовались им. После своей кончины он снес яичко — прелестное, сверкающее голубое яичко. Оно здесь, в моей коллекции.

Наш посетитель, шатаясь, поднялся с места и правой рукой ухватился за каминную полку. Холмс открыл несгораемый шкаф и вытащил оттуда голубой карбункул, сверкавший, словно звезда, холодным, ярким, переливчатым блеском. Райдер стоял с искаженным лицом, не зная, потребовать ли камень себе или отказаться от него.

— Игра проиграна, Райдер, — спокойно сказал Шерлок Холмс. — Держитесь крепче на ногах, не то упадете в огонь. Помогите ему сесть, Уотсон. Он еще не умеет хладнокровно мошенничать. Дайте ему глоток бренди. Так! Теперь он хоть немного похож на человека. Ну и жалкая же личность!

Райдер едва держался на ногах, но водка вызвала у него на щеках слабый румянец, и он сел, испуганно глядя на своего обличителя.

— Я знаю почти все, у меня в руках почти все улики, и вы не многое сможете добавить. И все-таки рассказывайте, чтобы в деле не оставалось ни малейшей неясности. Откуда вы узнали, Райдер, о голубом карбункуле графини Моркар?

— Мне сказала о нем Кэтрин Кьюсек, — ответил тот дрожащим голосом.

— Знаю, горничная ее сиятельства. И искушение легко завладеть богатством оказалось сильнее вас, как это неоднократно бывало и с более достойными людьми. И вы не особенно выбирали средства для достижения своей цели. Мне кажется, Райдер, из вас получится порядочный негодяй! Вы знали, что этот паяльщик Хорнер был уже уличен в воровстве и что подозрения раньше всего падут на него. Что же вы сделали? Вы сломали прут каминной решетки в комнате графини — вы и ваша сообщница Кьюсек — и устроили так, что именно Хорнера послали сделать ремонт. Когда Хорнер ушел, вы взяли камень из футляра, подняли тревогу, и бедняга был арестован. После этого…

«Have mercy!» he shrieked.

Тут Райдер внезапно сполз на ковер и обеими руками обхватил колени моего друга.

— Ради Бога, сжальтесь надо мной! — закричал он. — Подумайте о моем отце, о моей матери. Это убьет их! Я никогда не воровал, никогда! Это не повторится, клянусь вам! Я поклянусь вам на Библии! О, не доводите этого дела до суда! Ради Христа, не доводите дела до суда!

— Ступайте на место, — сурово сказал Холмс. — Сейчас вы готовы ползать на коленях. А что вы думали, когда отправляли беднягу Хорнера на скамью подсудимых за преступление, в котором он не повинен?

— Я могу скрыться, мистер Холмс! Я уеду из Англии, сэр! Тогда обвинение против него отпадет…

— Гм, мы еще потолкуем об этом. А пока послушаем, что же действительно случилось после воровства. Каким образом камень попал в гуся, и как этот гусь попал на рынок? Говорите правду, ибо для вас правда — единственный путь к спасению.

Райдер повел языком по пересохшим губам.

— Я расскажу всю правду, — сказал он. — Когда арестовали Хорнера, я решил, что мне лучше унести камень на случай, если полиции придет в голову обыскать меня и мою комнату. В гостинице не было подходящего места, чтобы спрятать камень. Я вышел, будто бы по служебному делу, и отправился к своей сестре. Она замужем за неким Окшоттом, живет на Брикстон-роуд и занимается тем, что откармливает домашнюю птицу, для рынка. Каждый встречный казался мне полицейским или сыщиком, и, несмотря на холодный ветер, пот градом струился у меня по лбу. Сестра спросила, почему я так бледен, не случилось ли чего. Я сказал, что меня взволновала кража драгоценности в нашем отеле. Потом я прошел на задний двор, закурил трубку и стал раздумывать, что бы предпринять.

Есть у меня приятель по имени Модели, который сбился с пути и только что отбыл срок наказания в Пентонвиллской тюрьме. Мы встретились с ним, разговорились, и он рассказал мне, как воры сбывают краденое. Я понимал, что он меня не выдаст, так как я сам знал за ним кое-какие грехи, и потому решил идти прямо к нему в Килберн и посвятить его в свою тайну. Он научил бы меня, как превратить этот камень в деньги. Но как добраться туда? Я вспомнил о тех терзаниях, которые пережил по пути из гостиницы. Каждую минуту меня могли схватить, обыскать и найти камень в моем жилетном кармане. Я стоял, прислонившись к стене, рассеянно глядя на гусей, которые, переваливаясь, бродили у моих ног, и внезапно мне пришла в голову мысль, как обмануть самого ловкого сыщика в мире…

Несколько недель назад сестра обещала, что к Рождеству я получу от нее отборнейшего гуся в подарок, а она слово держит. И я решил взять гуся сейчас же и в нем пронести камень. Во дворе был какой-то сарай, я загнал за него огромного, очень хорошего гуся, белого, с полосатым хвостом. Потом поймал его, раскрыл ему клюв и как можно глубже засунул камень ему в глотку. Гусь глотнул, и я ощутил рукою, как камень прошел в зоб. Но гусь бился и хлопал крыльями, и сестра вышла узнать в чем дело. Я повернулся, чтобы ответить, и негодный гусь вырвался у меня из рук и смешался со стадом.

«Что ты делал с птицей, Джеймс?» — спросила сестра.

«Да вот ты обещала подарить мне гуся к Рождеству. Я и пробовал, какой из них пожирнее».

«О, мы уже отобрали для тебя гуся, — сказала она, — мы так и называли его: „Гусь Джеймса“. Вон тот, большой, белый. Гусей всего двадцать шесть, из них один тебе, а две дюжины на продажу».

«Спасибо, Мэгги, — сказал я. — Но если тебе все равно, дай мне того, которого я поймал».

«Твой тяжелее по крайне мере фунта на три, и мы специально откармливали его».

«Ничего, мне хочется именно этого, я бы сейчас и взял его с собой».

«Твое дело, — сказала сестра обиженно. — Какого же ты хочешь взять?»

«Вон того белого, с черной полосой на хвосте... Вон он, в середине стада».

«Пожалуйста, режь его и бери!»

Я так и сделал, мистер Холмс, и понес птицу в Килберн. Я рассказал своему приятелю обо всем — он из тех, с которыми можно говорить без стеснения. Он хохотал до упаду, потом мы взяли нож и разрезали гуся. У меня остановилось сердце, когда я увидел, что произошла ужасная ошибка, и камня нет. Я бросил гуся, пустился бегом к сестре. Влетел на задний двор — гусей там не было.

«Где гуси, Мэгги?» — крикнул я.

«Отправила торговцу».

«Какому торговцу?»

«Брекинриджу на Ковент-Гарден».

«А был среди них один с полосатым хвостом — такой же, какого я взял?» — спросил я.

«Да, Джеймс, ведь было два гуся с полосатыми хвостами, я вечно путала их».

Тут, конечно, я понял все и со всех ног помчался к этому самому Брекинриджу. Но он уже распродал гусей и не хотел сказать кому. Вы слышали сами, как он со мной разговаривал. Сестра думает, что я сошел с ума. Порой мне самому кажется, что я сумасшедший. И вот... теперь я презренный вор, хотя даже не прикоснулся к богатству, ради которого погубил себя. Боже, помоги мне! Боже, помоги! — Он закрыл лицо руками и судорожно зарыдал.

He burst into convulsive sobbing.

Потом наступило долгое молчание, лишь слышны были тяжелые вздохи Райдера, да мой друг мерно постукивал пальцами по столу. Вдруг Шерлок Холмс встал и распахнул настежь дверь.

— Убирайтесь! — проговорил он.

— Что? Сэр, да благословит вас небо!

— Ни слова! Убирайтесь отсюда!

Повторять не пришлось. На лестнице загрохотали стремительные шаги, внизу хлопнула дверь, и с улицы донесся быстрый топот.

— В конце концов, Уотсон, — сказал Холмс, протягивая руку к глиняной трубке, — я работаю отнюдь не затем, чтобы исправлять промахи нашей полиции. Если бы Хорнеру грозила опасность, тогда другое дело. Но Райдер не станет показывать против него, и обвинение рухнет. Возможно, я укрываю мошенника, но зато спасаю его душу. С этим молодцом ничего подобного не повторится, — он слишком напуган. Упеките его сейчас в тюрьму, и он не развяжется с ней всю жизнь. Кроме того, нынче праздники, надо прощать грехи. Случай столкнул нас со странной и забавной загадкой, и решить ее — само по себе награда. Если вы будете любезны и позволите, мы немедленно займемся новым «исследованием», в котором опять-таки фигурирует птица: ведь к обеду у нас куропатка.

ПЕСТРАЯ ЛЕНТА

Просматривая свои записи о приключениях Шерлока Холмса, — а таких записей, которые я вел на протяжении последних восьми лет, у меня больше семидесяти, — я нахожу в них немало трагических случаев, есть среди них и забавные, есть и причудливые, но нет ни одного заурядного: работая из любви к своему искусству, а не ради денег, Холмс никогда не брался за расследование обыкновенных, будничных дел, его всегда привлекали только такие дела, в которых есть что-нибудь необычайное, а порою даже фантастическое.

Особенно причудливым кажется мне дело хорошо известной в Суррее семьи Ройлоттов из Сток-Морона. Мы с Холмсом, два холостяка, жил тогда вместе на Бейкер-стрит. Вероятно, я бы и раньше опубликовал свои записи, но я дал слово держать это дело в тайне и освободился от своего слова лишь месяц назад, после безвременной кончины той женщины, которой оно было дано. Пожалуй, будет небесполезно представить это дело в истинном свете, потому что молва приписывала смерть доктора Гримеби Ройлотта еще более ужасным обстоятельствам, чем те, которые были в действительности.

Проснувшись в одно апрельское утро 1883 года, я увидел, что Шерлок Холмс стоит у моей кровати. Одет он был не по-домашнему. Обычно он поднимался с постели поздно, но теперь часы на камине показывали лишь четверть восьмого. Я посмотрел на него с удивлением и даже несколько укоризненно. Сам я был верен своим привычкам.

— Весьма сожалею, что разбудил вас, Уотсон, — сказал он. — Но такой уж сегодня день. Разбудили миссис Хадсон, она — меня, а я — вас.

— Что же такое? Пожар?

— Нет, клиентка. Приехала какая-то девушка, она ужасно взволнована и непременно желает повидаться со мной. Она ждет в приемной. А уж если молодая дама решается в столь ранний час путешествовать по улицам столицы и поднимать с постели незнакомого человека, я полагаю, она хочет сообщить что-то очень важное. Дело может оказаться интересным, и вам, конечно, хотелось бы услышать эту историю с самого первого слова. Вот я и решил предоставить вам эту возможность.

— Буду счастлив услышать такую историю.

Я не хотел большего наслаждения, как следовать за Холмсом во время его профессиональных занятий и любоваться его стремительной мыслью. Порой казалось, что он решает предлагаемые ему загадки не разумом, а каким-то вдохновенным чутьем, но на самом деле все его выводы были основаны на точной и строгой логике.

Я быстро оделся, и через несколько минут мы спустились в гостиную. Дама, одетая в черное, с густой вуалью на лице, поднялась при нашем появлении.

— Доброе утро, сударыня, — сказал Холмс приветливо. — Меня зовут Шерлок Холмс. Это мой близкий друг и помощник, доктор Уотсон, с которым вы можете быть столь же откровенны, как и со мной. Ага! Как хорошо, что миссис Хадсон догадалась затопить камин. Я вижу, вы очень продрогли. Присаживайтесь поближе к огню и разрешите предложить вам чашку кофе.

— Не холод заставляет меня дрожать, мистер Холмс, — тихо сказала женщина, подсаживаясь к камину.

— А что же?

— Страх, мистер Холмс, ужас!

С этими словами она подняла вуаль, и мы увидели, как она возбуждена, какое у нее посеревшее, осунувшееся лицо. В ее глазах был испуг, словно у затравленного зверя. Ей было не больше тридцати лет, но в волосах уже блестела седина, и выглядела она усталой и измученной.

She raised her veil.

Шерлок Холмс окинул ее своим быстрым всепонимающим взглядом.

— Вам нечего бояться, — сказал он, ласково погладив ее по руке. — Я уверен, что нам удастся уладить все неприятности... Вы, я вижу, приехали утренним поездом.

— Разве вы меня знаете?

— Нет, но я заметил в вашей левой перчатке обратный билет. Вы сегодня рано встали, а потом, направляясь на станцию, долго тряслись в двуколке по скверной дороге.

Дама резко вздрогнула и в замешательстве взглянула на Холмса.

— Здесь нет никакого чуда, сударыня, — сказал он, улыбнувшись. — Левый рукав вашего жакета по крайней мере в семи местах забрызган грязью. Пятна совершенно свежие. Так обрызгаться можно только в двуколке, сидя слева от кучера.

— Все так и было, — сказала она. — Около шести часов я выбралась из дому, в двадцать минут седьмого была в Летерхеде и с первым поездом приехала в Лондон, на вокзал Ватерлоо… Сэр, я больше не вынесу этого, я сойду с ума! У меня нет никого, к кому я могла бы обратиться. Есть, впрочем, один человек, который принимает во мне участие, но чем он мне может помочь, бедняга? Я слышала о вас, мистер Холмс, слышала от миссис Фаринтош, которой вы помогли в минуту горя. Она дала мне ваш адрес. О сэр, помогите и мне или по крайней мере попытайтесь пролить хоть немного света в тот непроницаемый мрак, который окружает меня! Я не в состоянии отблагодарить вас сейчас за ваши услуги, но через месяц-полтора я буду замужем, тогда у меня будет право распоряжаться своими доходами, и вы увидите, что я умею быть благодарной.

Холмс подошел к конторке, открыл ее, достал оттуда записную книжку.

— Фаринтош… — сказал он. — Ах да, я вспоминаю этот случай. Он связан с тиарой из опалов. По-моему, это было еще до нашего знакомства, Уотсон. Могу вас уверить, сударыня, что я буду счастлив отнестись к вашему делу с таким же усердием, с каким отнесся к делу вашей приятельницы. А вознаграждения мне никакого не нужно, так как моя работа и служит мне вознаграждением. Конечно, у меня будут кое-какие расходы, и их вы можете возместить, когда вам будет угодно. А теперь попрошу вас сообщить нам подробности вашего дела, чтобы мы могли иметь свое суждение о нем.

— Увы! — ответила девушка. — Ужас моего положения заключается в том, что мои страхи так неопределенны и смутны, а подозрения основываются на таких мелочах, казалось бы, не имеющих никакого значения, что даже тот, к кому я имею право обратиться за советом и помощью, считает все мои рассказы бреднями нервной женщины. Он не говорит мне ничего, но я читаю это в его успокоительных словах и уклончивых взглядах. Я слышала, мистер Холмс, что вы, как никто, разбираетесь во всяких порочных наклонностях человеческого сердца и можете посоветовать, что мне делать среди окружающих меня опасностей.

— Я весь внимание, сударыня.

— Меня зовут Элен Стоунер. Я живу в доме моего отчима, Ройлотта. Он является последним отпрыском одной из старейших саксонских фамилий в Англии, Ройлоттов из Сток-Морона, у западной границы Суррея.

Холмс кивнул головой.

— Мне знакомо это имя, — сказал он.

— Было время, когда семья Ройлоттов была одной из самых богатых в Англии. На севере владения Ройлоттов простирались до Беркшира, а на западе — до Хапшира. Но в прошлом столетии четыре поколения подряд проматывали семейное состояние, пока наконец один из наследников, страстный игрок, окончательно не разорил семью во времена регентства. От прежних поместий остались лишь несколько акров земли да старинный дом, построенный лет двести назад и грозящий рухнуть под бременем закладных. Последний помещик из этого рода влачил в своем доме жалкое существование нищего аристократа. Но его единственный сын, мой отчим, поняв, что надо как-то приспособиться к новому положению вещей, взял взаймы у какого-то родственника необходимую сумму денег, поступил в университет, окончил его с дипломом врача и уехал в Калькутту, где благодаря своему искусству и выдержке вскоре приобрел широкую практику. Но вот в доме у него случилась кража, и Ройлотт в припадке бешенства избил до смерти туземца-дворецкого. С трудом избежав смертной казни, он долгое время томился в тюрьме, а потом возвратился в Англию угрюмым и разочарованным человеком.

В Индии доктор Ройлотт женился на моей матери, миссис Стоунер, молодой вдове генерал-майора артиллерии. Мы были близнецы — я и моя сестра Джулия, и, когда наша мать выходила замуж за доктора, нам едва минуло два года. Она обладала порядочным состоянием, дававшим ей не меньше тысячи фунтов дохода в год. По ее завещанию, это состояние переходило к доктору Ройлотту, поскольку мы жили вместе. Но если мы выйдем замуж, каждой из нас должна быть выделена определенная сумма годового дохода. Вскоре после нашего возвращения в Англию наша мать умерла — она погибла восемь лет назад во время железнодорожной катастрофы при Кру.

После ее смерти доктор Ройлотт оставил свои попытки обосноваться в Лондоне и наладить там медицинскую практику и вместе с нами поселился в родовом поместье в Сток-Морон. Состояния нашей матери вполне хватало на то, чтобы удовлетворять наши потребности, и, казалось, ничто не должно было мешать нашему счастью.

Но странная перемена произошла с моим отчимом. Вместо того, чтобы подружиться с соседями, которые вначале обрадовались, что Ройлотт из Сток-Морона вернулся в родовое гнездо, он заперся в усадьбе и очень редко выходил из дому, а если и выходил, то всякий раз затевал безобразную ссору с первым же человеком, который попадался ему на пути. Бешеная вспыльчивость, доходящая до исступления, передавалась по мужской линии всем представителям этого рода, а у моего отчима она, вероятно, еще более усилилась благодаря долгому пребыванию в тропиках. Много было у него яростных столкновений с соседями, два раза дело кончалось полицейским участком. Он сделался грозой всего селения... Нужно сказать, что он человек невероятной физической силы, и, так как в припадке гнева совершенно не владеет собой, люди при встрече с ним буквально шарахались в сторону.

На прошлой неделе он швырнул в реку местного кузнеца, и, чтобы откупиться от публичного скандала, мне пришлось отдать все деньги, какие я могла собрать. Единственные друзья его — кочующие цыгане, он позволяет этим бродягам раскидывать шатры на небольшом, заросшем ежевикой клочке земли, составляющем все его родовое поместье, и порой кочует вместе с ними, по целым неделям не возвращаясь домой. Еще есть у него страсть к животным, которых присылает ему из Индии один знакомый, и в настоящее время по его владениям свободно разгуливают гепард и павиан, наводя на жителей почти такой же страх, как и он сам.

«He hurled the blacksmith over a parapet.»

Из моих слов вы можете заключить, что мы с сестрой жили не слишком-то весело. Никто не хотел идти к нам в услужение, и долгое время всю домашнюю работу мы исполняли сами. Сестре было всего тридцать лет, когда она умерла, а у нее уже начинала пробиваться седина, такая же, как у меня.

— Так ваша сестра умерла?

— Она умерла ровно два года назад, и как раз о ее смерти я и хочу рассказать вам. Вы сами понимаете, что при таком образе жизни мы почти не встречались с людьми нашего возраста и нашего круга. Правда, у нас есть незамужняя тетка, сестра нашей матери, мисс Гонория Уэстфайл, она живет близ Харроу, и время от времени нас отпускали погостить у нее. Два года назад моя сестра Джулия проводила у нее Рождество. Там она встретилась с отставным майором флота, и он сделался ее женихом. Вернувшись домой, она рассказала о своей помолвке нашему отчиму. Отчим не возражал против ее замужества, но за две недели до свадьбы случилось ужасное событие, лишившее меня единственной подруги…

Шерлок Холмс сидел в кресле, откинувшись назад и положив голову на длинную подушку. Глаза его были закрыты. Теперь он приподнял веки и взглянул на посетительницу.

— Прошу вас рассказывать, не пропуская ни одной подробности, — сказал он.

— Мне легко быть точной, потому что все события тех ужасных дней врезались в мою память... Как я уже говорила, наш дом очень стар, и только одно крыло пригодно для жилья. В нижнем этаже размещаются спальни, гостиные находятся в центре. В первой спальне спит доктор Ройлотт, во второй спала моя сестра, а в третьей — я. Спальни не сообщаются между собой, но все они имеют выход в один коридор. Достаточно ли ясно я рассказываю?

— Да, вполне.

Окна всех трех спален выходят на лужайку. В ту роковую ночь доктор Ройлотт рано удалился в свою комнату, но мы знали, что он еще не лег, так как сестру мою долго беспокоил запах крепких индийских сигар, которые он имел привычку курить. Сестра не выносила этого запаха и пришла в мою комнату, где мы просидели некоторое время, болтая о ее предстоящем замужестве. В одиннадцать часов она поднялась и хотела уйти, но у дверей остановилась и спросила меня:

«Скажи, Элен, не кажется ли тебе, будто кто-то свистит по ночам?»

«Нет», — сказала я.

«Надеюсь, что ты не свистишь во сне?»

«Конечно, нет. А в чем дело?»

«В последнее время, часа в три ночи, мне ясно слышится тихий, отчетливый свист. Я сплю очень чутко, и свист будит меня. Не могу понять, откуда он доносится, — быть может, из соседней комнаты, быть может, с лужайки. Я давно уже хотела спросить у тебя, слыхала ли ты его».

«Нет, не слыхала. Может, свистят эти мерзкие цыгане?»

«Очень возможно. Однако, если бы свист доносился с лужайки, ты тоже слышала бы его».

«Я сплю гораздо крепче тебя».

«Впрочем, все это пустяки», — улыбнулась сестра, закрыла мою дверь, и спустя несколько мгновений я услышала, как щелкнул ключ в ее двери.

— Вот как! — сказал Холмс. — Вы на ночь всегда запираетесь на ключ?

— Всегда.

— А почему?

— Я, кажется, уже упомянула, что у доктора жили гепард и павиан. Мы чувствовали себя в безопасности лишь тогда, когда дверь была закрыта на ключ.

— Понимаю. Прошу продолжать.

— Ночью я не могла уснуть. Смутное ощущение какого-то неотвратимого несчастья охватило меня. Мы близнецы, а вы знаете, какими тонкими узами связаны столь родственные души. Ночь была жуткая: выл ветер, дождь барабанил в окна. И вдруг среди грохота бури раздался дикий вопль. То кричала моя сестра. Я спрыгнула с кровати и, накинув большой платок, выскочила в коридор. Когда я открыла дверь, мне показалось, что я слышу тихий свист, вроде того, о котором мне рассказывала сестра, а затем что-то звякнуло, словно на землю упал тяжелый металлический предмет. Подбежав к комнате сестры, я увидела, что дверь тихонько колышется взад и вперед. Я остановилась, пораженная ужасом, не понимая, что происходит. При свете лампы, горевшей в коридоре, я увидела свою сестру, которая появилась в дверях, шатаясь, как пьяная, с белым от ужаса лицом, протягивая вперед руки, словно моля о помощи. Бросившись к ней, я обняла ее, но в это мгновение колени сестры подогнулись, и она рухнула наземь. Она корчилась, словно от нестерпимой боли, руки и ноги ее сводило судорогой. Сначала мне показалось, что она меня не узнает, но когда я склонилась над ней, она вдруг вскрикнула... О, я никогда не забуду ее страшного голоса.

«Боже мой, Элен! — кричала она. — Лента! Пестрая лента!»

Она пыталась еще что-то сказать, указывая пальцем в сторону комнаты доктора, но новый приступ судорог оборвал ее слова. Я выскочила и, громко крича, побежала за отчимом. Он уже спешил мне навстречу в ночном халате. Сестра была без сознания, когда он приблизился к ней. Он влил ей в рот коньяку и тотчас же послал за деревенским врачом, но все усилия спасти ее были напрасны, и она скончалась, не приходя в сознание. Таков был ужасный конец моей любимой сестры…

Her face blanched with terror.

— Позвольте спросить, — сказал Холмс. — Вы уверены, что слышали свист и лязг металла? Могли бы вы показать это под присягой?

— Об этом спрашивал меня и следователь. Мне кажется, что я слышала эти звуки, однако меня могли ввести в заблуждение и завывание бури и потрескивания старого дома.

— Ваша сестра была одета?

— Нет, она выбежала в одной ночной рубашке. В правой руке у нее была обгорелая спичка, а в левой спичечная коробка.

— Значит, она чиркнула спичкой и стала осматриваться, когда что-то испугало ее. Очень важная подробность. А к каким выводам пришел следователь?

— Он тщательно изучил все обстоятельства — ведь буйный характер доктора Ройлотта был известен всей округе, но ему так и не удалось найти мало-мальски удовлетворительную причину смерти моей сестры. Я показала на следствии, что дверь ее комнаты была заперта изнутри, а окна защищены снаружи старинными ставнями с широкими железными засовами. Стены были подвергнуты самому внимательному изучению, но они повсюду оказались очень прочными. Осмотр пола тоже не дал никаких результатов. Каминная труба широка, но ее перекрывают целых четыре вьюшки. Итак, нельзя сомневаться, что сестра во время постигшей ее катастрофы была совершенно одна. Никаких следов насилия обнаружить не удалось.

— А как насчет яда?

— Врачи исследовали ее, но не нашли ничего, что указывало бы на отравление.

— Что же, по-вашему, было причиной смерти?

— Мне кажется, она умерла от ужаса и нервного потрясения. Но я не представляю себе, кто мог бы ее так напугать.

— А цыгане были в то время в усадьбе?

— Да, цыгане почти всегда живут у нас.

— А что, по-вашему, могли означать ее слова о ленте, о пестрой ленте?

— Иногда мне казалось, что слова эти были сказаны просто в бреду, а иногда — что они относятся к цыганам. Но почему лента пестрая? Возможно, что пестрые платки, которые носят цыганки, внушили ей этот странный эпитет.

Холмс покачал головой: видимо, объяснение не удовлетворяло его.

— Это дело темное, — сказал он. — Прошу вас, продолжайте.

— С тех пор прошло два года, и жизнь моя была еще более одинокой, чем раньше. Но месяц назад один близкий мне человек, которого я знаю много лет, сделал мне предложение. Его зовут Армитедж, Пэрси Армитедж, он второй сын мистера Армитеджа из Крейнуотера, близ Рединга. Мой отчим не возражал против нашего брака, и этой весной мы должны обвенчаться. Два дня назад в западном крыле нашего дома начались кое-какие переделки. Была пробита стена моей спальни, и мне пришлось перебраться в ту комнату, где скончалась сестра, и спать на той самой кровати, на которой спала она. Можете себе представить мой ужас, когда прошлой ночью, лежа без сна и размышляя о ее трагической смерти, я внезапно услышала в тишине тот самый тихий свист, который был предвестником гибели сестры. Я вскочила, зажгла лампу, но в комнате никого не было. Снова лечь я не могла — я была слишком взволнована, поэтому я оделась и, чуть рассвело, выскользнула из дому, взяла двуколку в гостинице «Корона», которая находится напротив нас, поехала в Летерхед, а оттуда сюда — с одной только мыслью повидать вас и спросить у вас совета.

— Вы очень умно поступили, — сказал мой друг. — Но все ли вы рассказали мне?

— Да, все.

— Нет, не все, мисс Ройлотт: вы щадите и выгораживаете своего отчима.

— Я не понимаю вас...

Вместо ответа Холмс откинул черную кружевную отделку на рукаве нашей посетительницы. Пять багровых пятен — следы пяти пальцев — ясно виднелись на белом запястье.

— Да, с вами обошлись жестоко, — сказал Холмс.

Девушка густо покраснела и поспешила опустить кружева.

— Отчим — суровый человек, — сказала она. — Он очень силен, и, возможно, сам не замечает своей силы.

Наступило долгое молчание. Холмс сидел, подперев руками подбородок и глядя на потрескивавший в камине огонь.

— Сложное дело, — сказал он наконец. — Мне хотелось бы выяснить еще тысячу подробностей, прежде чем решить, как действовать. А между тем нельзя терять ни минуты. Послушайте, если бы мы сегодня же приехали в Сток-Морон, удалось бы нам осмотреть эти комнаты, но так, чтобы ваш отчим ничего не узнал.

— Он как раз говорил мне, что собирается ехать сегодня в город по каким-то важным делам. Возможно, что его не будет весь день, и тогда никто вам не помешает. У нас есть экономка, но она стара и глупа, и я легко могу удалить ее.

— Превосходно. Вы ничего не имеете против поездки, Уотсон?

— Ровно ничего.

— Тогда мы приедем оба. А что вы сами собираетесь делать?

— У меня в городе есть кое-какие дела. Но я вернусь двенадцатичасовым поездом, чтобы быть на месте к вашему приезду.

— Ждите нас вскоре после полудня. У меня здесь тоже есть кое-какие дела. Может быть вы останетесь и позавтракаете с нами?

— Нет, мне надо идти! Теперь, когда я рассказала вам о своем горе, у меня просто камень свалился с души. Я буду рада снова увидеться с вами.

Она опустила на лицо черную густую вуаль и вышла из комнаты.

— Так что же вы обо всем этом думаете, Уотсон? — спросил Шерлок Холмс, откидываясь на спинку кресла.

— По-моему, это в высшей степени темное и грязное дело.

— Достаточно грязное и достаточно темное.

— Но если наша гостья права, утверждая, что пол и стены в комнате крепки, так что через двери, окна и каминную трубу невозможно туда проникнуть, значит, ее сестра в минуту своей таинственной смерти была совершенно одна…

— В таком случае, что означают эти ночные свисты и странные слова умирающей?

— Представить себе не могу.

— Если сопоставить факты: ночные свисты, цыгане, с которыми у этого старого доктора такие близкие отношения, намеки умирающей на какую-то ленту и, наконец, тот факт, что мисс Элен Стоунер слышала металлический лязг, который мог издавать железный засов от ставни… если вспомнить к тому же, что доктор заинтересован в предотвращении замужества своей падчерицы, — я полагаю, что мы напали на верные следы, которые помогут нам разгадать это таинственное происшествие.

— Но тогда при чем здесь цыгане?

— Понятия не имею.

— У меня все-таки есть множество возражений…

— Да и у меня тоже, и поэтому мы сегодня едем в Сток-Морон. Я хочу проверить все на месте. Не обернулись бы кое-какие обстоятельства самым роковым образом. Может быть их удастся прояснить. Черт возьми, что это значит?

Так воскликнул мой друг, потому что дверь внезапно широко распахнулась, и в комнату ввалился какой-то субъект колоссального роста. Его костюм представлял собою странную смесь: черный цилиндр и длинный сюртук указывали на профессию врача, а по высоким гетрам и охотничьему хлысту в руках его можно было принять за сельского жителя. Он был так высок, что шляпой задевал верхнюю перекладину нашей двери, и так широк в плечах, что едва протискивался в дверь. Его толстое, желтое от загара лицо со следами всех пороков было перерезано тысячью морщин, а глубоко сидящие, злобно сверкающие глаза и длинный, тонкий, костлявый нос придавали ему сходство со старой хищной птицей.

«Which of you is Holmes?»

Он переводил взгляд то на Шерлока Холмса, то на меня.

— Который из вас Холмс? — промолвил наконец посетитель.

— Это мое имя, сэр, — спокойно ответил мой друг. — Но я не знаю вашего.

— Я доктор Гримеби Ройлотт из Сток-Морона.

— Очень рад. Садитесь, пожалуйста, доктор, — любезно сказал Шерлок Холмс.

— Не стану я садиться! Здесь была моя падчерица. Я выследил ее. Что она говорила вам?

— Что-то не по сезону холодная погода нынче, — сказал Холмс.

— Что она говорила вам? — злобно закричал старик.

— Впрочем, я слышал, крокусы будут отлично цвести, — невозмутимо продолжал мой приятель.

— Ага, вы хотите отделаться от меня! — сказал наш гость, делая шаг вперед и размахивая охотничьим хлыстом. — Знаю я вас, подлеца. Я уже и прежде слышал про вас. Вы любите совать нос в чужие дела.

Мой друг улыбнулся.

— Вы проныра!

Холмс улыбнулся еще шире.

— Полицейская ищейка!

Холмс от души расхохотался.

— Вы удивительно приятный собеседник, — сказал он. — Выходя отсюда, закройте дверь, а то, право же, сильно сквозит.

— Я выйду только тогда, когда выскажусь. Не вздумайте вмешиваться в мои дела. Я знаю, что мисс Стоунер была здесь, я следил за ней! Горе тому, кто станет у меня на пути! Глядите!

Он быстро подошел к камину, взял кочергу и согнул ее своими огромными загорелыми руками.

— Смотрите, не попадайтесь мне в лапы! — прорычал он, швырнув искривленную кочергу в камин и вышел из комнаты.

— Какой любезный господин! — смеясь, сказал Холмс. — Я не такой великан, но если бы он не ушел, мне пришлось бы доказать ему, что мои лапы ничуть не слабее его лап.

С этими словами он поднял стальную кочергу и одним быстрым движением распрямил ее.

— Какая наглость смешивать меня с сыщиками из полиции! Что ж, благодаря этому происшествию наши исследования стали еще интереснее. Надеюсь, что наша приятельница не пострадает от того, что так необдуманно позволила этой скотине выследить себя. Сейчас, Уотсон, мы позавтракаем, а затем я отправлюсь к юристам и наведу у них несколько справок.

Было уже около часа, когда Холмс возвратился домой. В руке у него был лист синей бумаги, весь исписанный заметками и цифрами.

— Я видел завещание покойной жены доктора, — сказал он. — Чтобы точнее разобраться в нем, мне пришлось справиться о нынешней стоимости ценных бумаг, в которых помещено состояние покойной. В год смерти общий доход ее составлял почти тысячу фунтов стерлингов, но с тех пор в связи с падением цен на сельскохозяйственные продукты, уменьшился до семисот пятидесяти фунтов стерлингов. Выйдя замуж, каждая дочь имеет право на ежегодный доход в двести пятьдесят фунтов стерлингов. Следовательно, если бы обе дочери вышли замуж, наш красавец получал бы только жалкие крохи. Его доходы значительно уменьшились бы и в том случае, если бы замуж вышла лишь одна из дочерей. Я не напрасно потратил утро, так как получил ясные доказательства, что у отчима были весьма веские основания препятствовать замужеству падчериц. Обстоятельства слишком серьезны, Уотсон, и нельзя терять ни минуты, тем более что старик уже знает, как мы интересуемся его делами. Если вы готовы, надо поскорей вызвать кэб и ехать на вокзал. Буду вам чрезвычайно признателен, если вы сунете в карман револьвер. Револьвер — превосходный аргумент для джентльмена, который может завязать узлом стальную кочергу. Револьвер да зубная щетка — вот и все, что нам понадобится.

На вокзале Ватерлоо нам посчастливилось сразу попасть на поезд. Приехав в Летерхед, мы в гостинице возле станции взяли двуколку и проехали миль пять живописными дорогами Суррея. Был чудный солнечный день, и лишь несколько перистых облаков плыло по небу. На деревьях и на живой изгороди возле дорог только что распустились зеленые почки, и воздух был напоен восхитительным запахом влажной земли.

Странным казался мне контраст между сладостным пробуждением весны и ужасным делом, из-за которого мы прибыли сюда. Мой приятель сидел впереди, скрестив руки, надвинув шляпу на глаза, опустив подбородок на грудь, погруженный в глубокие думы. Внезапно он поднял голову, хлопнул меня по плечу и указал куда-то вдаль.

— Посмотрите!

Обширный парк раскинулся по склону холма, переходя в густую рощу на вершине; из-за веток виднелись очертания высокой крыши и шпиль старинного помещичьего дома.

— Сток-Морон? — спросил Шерлок Холмс.

— Да, сэр, это дом Гримеби Ройлотта, — ответил возница.

— Видите, вон там строят, — сказал Холмс. — Нам нужно попасть туда.

— Мы едем к деревне, — сказал возница, указывая на крыши, видневшиеся в некотором отдалении слева. — Но если вы хотите скорей попасть к дому, вам лучше перелезть здесь через забор, а потом пройти полями по тропинке. По той тропинке, где идет эта леди.

— А эта леди как будто мисс Стоунер, — сказал Холмс, заслоняя глаза от солнца. — Да, мы лучше пойдем по тропинке, как вы советуете.

We got off, paid our fare.

Мы вышли из двуколки, расплатились, и экипаж покатил обратно в Летерхед.

— Пусть этот малый думает, что мы архитекторы, — сказал Холмс, когда мы лезли через забор, — тогда наш приезд не вызовет особых толков. Добрый день, мисс Стоунер! Видите, мы сдержали свое слово!

Наша утренняя посетительница радостно спешила нам навстречу.

— Я с таким нетерпением ждала вас! — воскликнула дна, горячо пожимая нам руки. — Все устроилось чудесно: доктор Ройлотт уехал в город и вряд ли возвратится раньше вечера.

— Мы имели удовольствие познакомиться с доктором, — сказал Холмс и в двух словах рассказал о том, что произошло.

Мисс Стоунер побледнела.

— Боже мой! — воскликнула она. — Значит, он шел за мной следом!

— Похоже на то.

— Он так хитер, что я никогда не чувствую себя в безопасности. Что он скажет, когда возвратится?

— Придется ему быть осторожнее, потому что здесь может найтись кое-кто похитрее его. На ночь запритесь от него на ключ. Если он будет буйствовать, мы увезем вас к вашей тетке в Харроу... Ну, а теперь надо как можно лучше использовать время, и потому проводите нас, пожалуйста, в те комнаты, которые мы должны обследовать.

Дом был из серого, покрытого лишайником камня и имел два полукруглых крыла, распростертых, словно клешни у краба, по обеим сторонам высокой центральной части. В одном из этих крыльев окна были выбиты и заколочены досками; крыша местами провалилась. Центральная часть казалась почти столь же разрушенной, зато правое крыло было сравнительно недавно отделано, и по шторам на окнах, по голубоватым дымкам, которые вились из труб, видно было, что живут именно здесь. У крайней стены были воздвигнуты леса, начаты кое-какие работы. Но ни одного каменщика не было видно.

Холмс стал медленно расхаживать по нерасчищенной лужайке, внимательно глядя на окна.

— Насколько я понимаю, тут комната, в которой вы жили прежде. Среднее окно — из комнаты вашей сестры, а третье окно, то, что поближе к главному зданию, — из комнаты доктора Ройлотта…

— Совершенно правильно. Но теперь я живу в средней комнате.

— Понимаю, из-за ремонта. Кстати, как-то незаметно, чтобы эта стена нуждалась в столь неотложном ремонте.

— Совсем не нуждается. Я думаю, это просто предлог, чтобы убрать меня из моей комнаты.

— Весьма вероятно. Итак, вдоль противоположной стены тянется коридор, куда выходят двери всех трех комнат. В коридоре, без сомнения, есть окна?

— Да, но очень маленькие. Пролезть сквозь них невозможно.

— Так как вы обе запирались на ключ, то из коридора попасть к вам в комнаты нельзя. Будьте любезны, пройдите в свою комнату и закройте ставни.

Мисс Стоунер исполнила его просьбу. Холмс предварительно осмотрев окно, употребил все усилия, чтобы открыть ставни снаружи, но безуспешно: не было ни одной щелки, сквозь которую можно было бы просунуть хоть лезвие ножа, чтобы поднять засов. При помощи лупы он осмотрел петли, но они были из твердого железа и крепко вделаны в массивную стену.

— Гм! — проговорил он, в раздумье почесывая подбородок.

— Моя первоначальная гипотеза не подтверждается фактами. Когда ставни закрыты, в эти окна не влезть… Ладно, посмотрим, не удастся ли нам выяснить что-нибудь, осмотрев комнаты изнутри.

Маленькая боковая дверь открывалась в выбеленный известкой коридор, в который выходили двери всех трех спален. Холмс не счел нужным осматривать третью комнату, и мы сразу прошли во вторую, где теперь спала мисс Стоунер и где умерла ее сестра. Это была просто обставленная комнатка с низким потолком и с широким камином, одним из тех, которые встречаются в старинных деревенских домах. В одном углу стоял комод; другой угол занимала узкая кровать, покрытая белым одеялом; слева от окна находился туалетный столик. Убранство комнаты довершали два плетеных стула да квадратный коврик посередине. Панели на стенах были из темного, источенного червями дуба, такие древние и выцветшие, что казалось, их не меняли со времени постройки дома.

Холмс взял стул и молча уселся в углу. Глаза его внимательно скользили вверх и вниз по стенам, бегали вокруг комнаты, изучая и осматривая каждую мелочь.

— Куда проведен этот звонок? — спросил он наконец указывая на висевший над кроватью толстый шнур от звонка, кисточка которого лежала на подушке.

— В комнату прислуги.

— Он как будто новее всех прочих вещей.

— Да, он проведен всего несколько лет назад.

— Вероятно, ваша сестра просила об этом?

— Нет, она никогда им не пользовалась. Мы всегда все делали сами.

— Действительно, здесь этот звонок — лишняя роскошь. Вы меня извините, если я задержу вас на несколько минут: мне хочется хорошенько осмотреть пол.

С лупой в руках он ползал на четвереньках взад и вперед по полу, пристально исследуя каждую трещину в половицах. Также тщательно он осмотрел и панели на стенах. Потом подошел к кровати, внимательно оглядел ее и всю стену снизу доверху. Потом взял шнур от звонка и дернул его.

— Да ведь звонок поддельный! — сказал он.

— Он не звонит?

— Он даже не соединен с проволокой. Любопытно! Видите, он привязан к крючку как раз над тем маленьким отверстием для вентилятора.

— Как странно! Я и не заметила этого.

— Очень странно... — бормотал Холмс, дергая шнур. — В этой комнате многое обращает на себя внимание. Например, каким нужно быть безумным строителем, чтобы вывести вентилятор в соседнюю комнату, когда его с такой же легкостью можно было вывести наружу!

— Все это сделано тоже очень недавно, — сказала Элен.

— Примерно в одно время со звонком, — заметил Холмс.

— Да, как раз в то время здесь произвели кое-какие переделки.

— Интересные переделки: звонки, которые не звонят, и вентиляторы, которые не вентилируют. С вашего позволения, мисс Стоунер, мы перенесем наши исследования в другие комнаты.

Комната доктора Гримеби Ройлотта была больше, чем комната его падчерицы, но обставлена так же просто. Походная кровать, небольшая деревянная полка, уставленная книгами, преимущественно техническими, кресло рядом с кроватью, простой плетеный стул у стены, круглый стол и большой железный несгораемый шкаф — вот и все, что бросалось в глаза при входе в комнату. Холмс медленно похаживал вокруг, с живейшим интересом исследуя каждую вещь.

— Что здесь? — спросил он, стукнув по несгораемому шкафу.

— Деловые бумаги моего отчима.

— Ого! Значит, вы заглядывали в этот шкаф?

— Только раз, несколько лет назад. Я помню, там была кипа бумаг.

— А нет ли в нем, например, кошки?

— Нет. Что за странная мысль!

— А вот посмотрите!

«Well, look at this.»

Он снял со шкафа маленькое блюдце с молоком.

— Нет, кошек мы не держим. Но зато у нас есть гепард и павиан.

— Ах, да! Гепард, конечно, всего только большая кошка, но сомневаюсь, что такое маленькое блюдце молока может насытить этого зверя. Да, в этом надо разобраться.

Он присел на корточки перед стулом и принялся с глубоким вниманием изучать сиденье.

— Благодарю вас, все ясно, — сказал он, поднимаясь и кладя лупу в карман. — Ага, вот еще кое-что весьма интересное!

Внимание его привлекла небольшая собачья плеть, висевшая в углу кровати. Конец ее был завязан петлей.

— Что вы об этом думаете, Уотсон?

— По-моему, самая обыкновенная плеть. Не понимаю, для чего понадобилось завязывать на ней петлю.

— Не такая уж обыкновенная… Ах, сколько зла на свете, и хуже всего, когда злые дела совершает умный человек!.. Ну, с меня достаточно, мисс, я узнал все, что мне нужно, а теперь с вашего разрешения мы пройдемся по лужайке.

Я никогда не видел Холмса таким угрюмым и насупленным. Некоторое время мы расхаживали взад и вперед в глубоком молчании, и ни я, ни мисс Стоунер не прерывали течения его мыслей, пока он сам не очнулся от задумчивости.

— Очень важно, мисс Стоунер, чтобы вы в точности следовали моим советам, — сказал он.

— Я исполню все беспрекословно.

— Обстоятельства слишком серьезны, и колебаться нельзя. От вашего полного повиновения зависит ваша жизнь.

— Я целиком полагаюсь на вас.

— Во-первых, мы оба — мой друг и я — должны провести ночь в вашей комнате.

Мисс Стоунер и я взглянули на него с изумлением.

— Это необходимо. Я вам объясню. Что это там, в той стороне? Вероятно, деревенская гостиница?

— Да, там «Корона».

— Очень хорошо. Оттуда видны ваши окна?

— Конечно.

— Когда ваш отчим вернется, скажите, что у вас болит голова, уйдите в свою комнату и запритесь на ключ. Услышав, что он пошел спать, вы снимете засов, откроете ставни вашего окна и поставите на подоконник лампу; эта лампа будет для нас сигналом. Тогда, захватив с собой все, что пожелаете, вы перейдете в свою бывшую комнату. Я убежден, что, несмотря на ремонт, вы можете один раз переночевать в ней.

— Безусловно.

— Остальное предоставьте нам.

— Но что же вы собираетесь сделать?

— Мы проведем ночь в вашей комнате и выясним причину шума, напугавшего вас.

— Мне кажется, мистер Холмс, что вы уже пришли к какому-то выводу, — сказала мисс Стоунер, дотрагиваясь до рукава моего друга.

— Быть может, да.

— Тогда, ради всего святого, скажите хотя бы, отчего умерла моя сестра?

— Прежде чем ответить, я хотел бы собрать более точные улики.

— Тогда скажите по крайней мере, верно ли мое предположение, что она умерла от внезапного испуга?

— Нет, неверно: я полагаю, что причина ее смерти была более вещественна... А теперь, мисс Стоунер, мы должны покинуть вас, потому что, если мистер Ройлотт вернется и застанет нас, вся поездка окажется совершенно напрасной. До свидания! Будьте мужественны, сделайте все, что я сказал, и не сомневайтесь, что мы быстро устраним грозящую вам опасность.

«Good-bye, and be brave.»

Мы с Шерлоком Холмсом без всяких затруднений сняли номер в гостинице «Корона». Номер наш находился в верхнем этаже, и из окна видны были ворота парка и обитаемое крыло сток-моронского дома. В сумерках мы видели, как мимо проехал доктор Гримеби Ройлотт; его грузное тело вздымалось горой рядом с тощей фигурой мальчишки, правившего экипажем. Мальчишке не сразу удалось открыть тяжелые железные ворота, и мы слышали, как рычал на него доктор, и видели, с какой яростью он потрясал кулаками. Экипаж въехал в ворота, и через несколько минут сквозь деревья замелькал свет от лампы, зажженной в одной из гостиных. Мы сидели в потемках, не зажигая огня.

— Право, не знаю, — сказал Холмс, — брать ли вас сегодня ночью с собой! Дело-то очень опасное.

— А я могу быть полезен вам?

— Ваша помощь может оказаться неоценимой.

— Тогда я непременно пойду.

— Спасибо.

— Вы говорите об опасности. Очевидно, вы видели в этих комнатах что-то такое, чего не видел я.

— Нет, я видел то же, что и вы, но сделал другие выводы.

— Я не заметил в комнате ничего примечательного, кроме шнура от звонка, но, признаюсь, не способен понять, для какой цели он может служить.

— А на вентилятор вы обратили внимание?

— Да, но мне кажется, что в этом маленьком отверстии между двумя комнатами нет ничего необычного. Оно так мало, что даже мышь едва ли может пролезть сквозь него.

— Я знал об этом вентиляторе прежде, чем мы приехали в Сток-Морон.

— Дорогой мой Холмс!

— Да, знал. Помните, мисс Стоунер сказала, что ее сестра чувствовала запах сигар, которые курит доктор Ройлотт? А это доказывает, что между двумя комнатами есть отверстие, и, конечно, оно очень мало, иначе его заметил бы следователь при осмотре комнаты. Я решил, что тут должен быть вентилятор.

— Но какую опасность может таить в себе вентилятор?

— А посмотрите, какое странное совпадение: над кроватью устраивают вентилятор, вешают шнур, и леди, спящая на кровати, умирает. Разве это не поражает вас?

— Я до сих пор не могу связать эти обстоятельства.

— А в кровати вы не заметили ничего особенного?

— Нет.

— Она привинчена к полу. Вы когда-нибудь видели, чтобы кровати привинчивали к полу?

— Пожалуй, не видел.

— Леди не могла передвинуть свою кровать, ее кровать всегда оставалась в одном и том же положении по отношению к вентилятору и шнуру. Этот звонок приходится называть просто шнуром, так как он не звонит.

— Холмс! — вскричал я. — Кажется, я начинаю понимать, на что вы намекаете. Значит, мы явились как раз вовремя, чтобы предотвратить ужасное и утонченное преступление.

— Да, утонченное и ужасное. Когда врач совершает преступление, он опаснее всех прочих преступников. У него крепкие нервы и большие знания. Палмер и Причард[1] были лучшими специалистами в своей области. Этот человек очень хитер, но я надеюсь, Уотсон, что нам удастся перехитрить его. Сегодня ночью нам предстоит пережить немало страшного, и потому, прошу вас, давайте пока спокойно закурим трубки и проведем эти несколько часов, разговаривая о чем-нибудь более веселом.

Часов около девяти свет, видневшийся между деревьями, погас, и усадьба погрузилась во тьму. Так прошло часа два, и вдруг ровно в одиннадцать одинокий яркий огонек засиял прямо против нашего окна.

— Это сигнал для нас, — сказал Холмс, вскакивая. — Свет горит в среднем окне.

Выходя, он сказал хозяину гостиницы, что мы идем в гости к одному знакомому и, возможно, там и переночуем. Через минуту мы вышли на темную дорогу. Свежий ветер дул нам в лицо, желтый свет, мерцая перед нами во мраке, указывал путь.

---

[1] Палмер, Уильям — английский врач, отравивший стрихнином своего приятеля; казнен в 1856 году.

Причард, Эдуард Уильям — английский врач, отравивший свою жену и тещу; казнен в 1865 году.

Попасть к дому было нетрудно, потому что старая парковая ограда обрушилась во многих местах. Пробираясь между деревьями, мы достигли лужайки, пересекли ее и уже собирались влезть в окно, как вдруг какое-то существо, похожее на отвратительного урода-ребенка, выскочило из лавровых кустов, бросилось, корчась, на траву, а потом промчалось через лужайку и скрылось в темноте.

— Боже! — прошептал я. — Вы видели?

В первое мгновение Холмс испугался не меньше меня. Он схватил мою руку и сжал ее, словно тисками. Потом тихо рассмеялся и, приблизив губы к моему уху, пробормотал еле слышно:

— Милая семейка! Ведь это павиан.

Я совсем забыл о любимцах доктора. А гепард, который каждую минуту может оказаться у нас на плечах? Признаться, я почувствовал себя значительно лучше, когда, следуя примеру Холмса, сбросил ботинки, влез в окно и очутился в спальне. Мой друг бесшумно закрыл ставни, переставил лампу на стол и быстро оглядел комнату. Здесь было все как днем. Он приблизился ко мне и, сложив руку трубкой, прошептал так тихо, что я едва понял его:

— Малейший звук погубит нас.

Я кивнул головой, показывая, что слышу.

— Нам придется сидеть без огня. Сквозь вентилятор он может заметить свет.

Я кивнул еще раз.

— Не засните — от этого зависит ваша жизнь. Держите револьвер наготове. Я сяду на край кровати, а вы на стул.

Я вытащил револьвер и положил его на угол стола. Холмс принес с собой длинную, тонкую трость и поместил ее возле себя на кровать вместе с коробкой спичек и огарком свечи. Потом задул лампу, и мы остались в полной темноте.

Забуду ли я когда-нибудь эту страшную бессонную ночь! Ни один звук не доносился до меня. Я не слышал даже дыхания своего друга, а между тем знал, что он сидит в двух шагах от меня с открытыми глазами, в таком же напряженном, нервном состоянии, как и я.

Ставни не пропускали ни малейшего луча света, мы сидели в абсолютной тьме. Изредка снаружи доносился крик ночной птицы, а раз у самого нашего окна раздался протяжный вой, похожий на кошачье мяуканье: гепард, видимо, гулял на свободе. Слышно было, как вдалеке церковные часы гулко отбивали четверти. Какими долгими они казались нам, эти каждые пятнадцать минут! Пробило двенадцать, час, два, три, а мы все сидели молча, ожидая чего-то неизбежного.

Внезапно у вентилятора мелькнул свет и сразу же исчез, но тотчас мы почувствовали сильный запах горелого масла и накаленного металла. Кто-то в соседней комнате зажег потайной фонарь. Я услышал, как что-то двинулось, потом все смолкло, и только запах стал еще сильнее. С полчаса я сидел, напряженно вглядываясь в темноту. Внезапно послышался какой-то новый звук, нежный и тихий, словно вырывалась из котла тонкая струйка пара. И в то же мгновение Холмс вскочил с кровати, чиркнул спичкой и яростно хлестнул своей тростью по шнуру.

— Вы видите ее, Уотсон? — проревел он. — Видите?

Но я ничего не видел. Пока Холмс чиркал спичкой, я слышал тихий отчетливый свист, но внезапный яркий свет так ослепил мои утомленные глаза, что я не мог ничего разглядеть и не понял, почему Холмс так яростно хлещет тростью. Однако я успел заметить выражение ужаса и отвращения на его мертвенно-бледном лице.

Holmes lashed furiously.

Холмс перестал хлестать и начал пристально разглядывать вентилятор, как вдруг тишину ночи прорезал такой ужасный крик, какого я не слышал никогда в жизни. Этот хриплый крик, в котором смешались страдание, страх и ярость, становился все громче и громче. Рассказывали потом, что не только в деревне, но даже в отдаленном домике священника крик этот разбудил всех спящих. Похолодевшие от ужаса, мы глядели друг на друга, пока последний вопль не замер в тишине.

— Что это значит? — спросил я, задыхаясь.

— Это значит, что все кончено, — ответил Холмс. — И в сущности, это к лучшему. Возьмите револьвер, и пойдем в комнату доктора Ройлотта.

Лицо его было сурово. Он зажег лампу и пошел по коридору. Дважды он стукнул в дверь комнаты доктора, но изнутри никто не ответил. Тогда он повернул ручку и вошел в комнату. Я шел следом за ним, держа в руке заряженный револьвер.

Необычайное зрелище представилось нашим взорам. На столе стоял фонарь, бросая яркий луч света на железный несгораемый шкаф, дверца которого была полуоткрыта. У стола на соломенном стуле сидел доктор Гримиби Ройлотт в длинном сером халате, из-под которого виднелись голые лодыжки. Ноги его были в красных турецких туфлях без задников. На коленях лежала та самая плеть, которую мы еще днем заметили в его комнате. Он сидел, задрав подбородок кверху, неподвижно устремив глаза в потолок; в глазах застыло выражение страха. Вокруг его головы туго обвилась какая-то необыкновенная, желтая с коричневыми крапинками лента. При нашем появлении доктор не шевельнулся и не издал ни звука.

— Лента! Пестрая лента! — прошептал Холмс.

He made neither sound nor motion.

Я сделал шаг вперед. В то же мгновение странный головной убор зашевелился, и из волос доктора Ройлотта поднялась граненая головка и раздувшаяся шея ужасной змеи.

— Болотная гадюка! — вскричал Холмс. — Самая смертоносная индийская змея! Он умер через девять секунд после укуса. «Поднявший меч от меча и погибнет», и тот, кто роет другому яму, сам в нее попадет. Посадим эту тварь в ее логово, отправим мисс Стоунер в какое-нибудь спокойное место и дадим знать полиции о том, что случилось.

Он схватил плеть с колен мертвого, накинул петлю на голову змеи, стащил ее с ужасного насеста, швырнул внутрь несгораемого шкафа и захлопнул дверцу.

Таковы истинные обстоятельства смерти доктора Гримсби Ройлотта из Сток-Морона. Не стану подробно рассказывать, как мы сообщили печальную новость испуганной девушке, как утренним поездом мы препроводили ее на попечение тетки в Харроу и как туповатое полицейское следствие пришло к заключению, что доктор погиб от собственной неосторожности, забавляясь со своей любимицей — ядовитой змеей. Остальное Шерлок Холмс рассказал мне, когда мы на следующий день ехали обратно.

— В начале я пришел к совершенно неправильным выводам, мой дорогой Уотсон, — сказал он, — и это доказывает, как опасно опираться на неточные данные. Присутствие цыган, восклицание несчастной девушки, пытавшейся объяснить, что она увидела, чиркнув спичкой, — всего этого было достаточно, чтобы навести меня на ложный след. Но когда мне стало ясно, что в комнату невозможно проникнуть ни через дверь, ни через окно, что не оттуда грозит опасность обитателю этой комнаты, я понял свою ошибку, и это может послужить мне оправданием. Я уже говорил вам, внимание мое сразу привлекли вентилятор и шнур от звонка, висящий над кроватью. Когда обнаружилось, что звонок фальшивый, а кровать прикреплена к полу, у меня зародилось подозрение, что шнур служит лишь мостом, соединяющим вентилятор с кроватью. Мне сразу же пришла мысль о змее, а зная, как доктор любит окружать себя всевозможными индийскими тварями, я понял, что, пожалуй, угадал. Только такому хитрому, жестокому злодею, прожившему много лет на Востоке могло прийти в голову прибегнуть к яду, который нельзя обнаружить химическим путем. В пользу этого яда, с его точки зрения, говорило и то, что он действует мгновенно. Следователь должен был бы обладать поистине необыкновенно острым зрением, чтобы разглядеть два крошечных темных пятнышка, оставленных зубами змеи. Потом я вспомнил о свисте. Свистом доктор звал змею обратно, чтобы ее не увидели на рассвете рядом с мертвой. Вероятно, давая ей молоко, он приучил ее возвращаться к нему. Змею он пропускал через вентилятор в самый глухой час ночи и знал наверняка, что она поползет по шнуру и спустится на кровать. Рано или поздно девушка должна была стать жертвой ужасного замысла, змея ужалила бы ее, если не сейчас, то через неделю. Я пришел к этим выводам еще до того, как посетил комнату доктора Ройлотта. Когда же я исследовал сиденье его стула, я понял, что у доктора была привычка становиться на стул, чтобы достать до вентилятора. А когда я увидел несгораемый шкаф, блюдце с молоком и плеть, мои последние сомнения окончательно рассеялись. Металлический лязг, который слышала мисс Стоунер, был, очевидно, стуком дверцы несгораемого шкафа, куда доктор прятал змею. Вам известно, что я предпринял, убедившись в правильности своих выводов. Как только я услышал шипение змеи — вы, конечно, тоже слыхали его, — я немедленно зажег свет и начал стегать ее тростью.

— Вы прогнали ее назад в вентилятор…

— …и тем самым заставил напасть на хозяина. Удары моей трости разозлили ее, в ней проснулась змеиная злоба, и она напала на первого попавшегося ей человека. Таким образом, я косвенно виновен в смерти доктора Гримеби Ройлотта, но не могу сказать, чтобы эта вина тяжким бременем легла на мою совесть.

ПАЛЕЦ ИНЖЕНЕРА

Из всех задач, какие приходилось решать моему другу мистеру Шерлоку Холмсу, мною его вниманию было предложено лишь две, а именно: случай, когда мистер Хэдерли лишился большого пальца, и происшествие с обезумевшим полковником Уорбэртоном. Последняя представляла собой обширное поле деятельности для тонкого и самобытного наблюдателя, зато первая оказалась столь своеобразной и столь драматичной по своим подробностям, что скорее заслуживает изложения в моих записках, хотя и не позволила моему приятелю применить те дедуктивные методы мышления, благодаря которым он неоднократно добивался таких примечательных результатов. Об этой истории, мне помнится, не раз писали газеты, но, как и все подобные события, втиснутая в газетный столбец, она казалась значительно менее увлекательной, нежели тогда, когда ее рассказывал участник событий, и действие как бы медленно развертывалось перед нашими глазами, и мы шаг за шагом проникали в тайну и приближались к истине. В свое время обстоятельства этого дела произвели на меня глубокое впечатление, и прошедшие с тех пор два года ничуть не ослабили этот эффект.

События, о которых я хочу рассказать, произошли летом 1889 года, вскоре после моей женитьбы. Я снова занялся врачебной практикой и навсегда распрощался с квартирой на Бейкер-стрит, хотя часто навещал Холмса и время от времени даже убеждал отказаться от богемных привычек и почаще приходить к нам. Практика моя неуклонно росла, а поскольку я жил неподалеку от Паддингтона, то среди пациентов у меня было несколько служащих этого вокзала. Один из них, которого мне удалось вылечить от тяжелой, изнурительной болезни, без устали рекламировал мои достоинства и посылал ко мне каждого страждущего, кого он был способен уговорить обратиться к врачу.

Однажды утром, часов около семи, меня разбудила, постучав в дверь, наша служанка. Она сказала, что с Паддингтона пришли двое мужчин и ждут меня в кабинете. Я быстро оделся, зная по опыту, что несчастные случаи на железной дороге редко бывают пустячными, и сбежал вниз. Из приемной, плотно прикрыв за собой дверь, вышел мой старый пациент — кондуктор.

— Он здесь, — прошептал он, указывая на дверь. — Все в порядке.

— Кто? — не понял я. По его шепоту можно было подумать, что он запер у меня в кабинете какое-то необыкновенное существо.

— Новый пациент, — так же шепотом продолжал он. — Я решил, что лучше сам приведу его, тогда ему не сбежать. Он там, все в порядке. А мне пора. У меня, доктор, как и у вас, свои обязанности.

И он ушел, мой верный поклонник, не дав мне даже возможности поблагодарить его.

Я вошел в приемную; возле стола сидел человек. Он был одет в недорогой костюм из пестротканого твида; кепка его лежала на моих книгах. Одна рука у него была обвязана носовым платком сплошь в пятнах крови. Он был молод, лет двадцати пяти, не больше, с выразительным мужественным лицом, но страшно бледен и словно чем-то потрясен — он был совершенно не в силах овладеть собою.

— Извините, что так рано потревожил вас, доктор, — сказал он, — но со мной нынче ночью произошло нечто серьезное. Я приехал в Лондон утренним поездом, и, когда начал узнавать в Паддингтоне, где найти врача, этот добрый человек любезно проводил меня к вам. Я дал служанке свою карточку, но, вижу, она оставила ее на столе.

Я взял карточку и прочел имя, род занятий и адрес моего посетителя: «Мистер Виктор Хэдерли, инженер-гидравлик. Виктория-стрит, 16-а (4-й этаж)».

— Очень сожалею, что заставил вас ждать, — сказал я, усаживаясь в кресло у письменного стола. — Вы ведь всю ночь ехали — занятие само по себе не из веселых.

— О, эту ночь скучной я никак не могу назвать, — ответил он и расхохотался.

Откинувшись на спинку стула, он весь трясся от смеха, и в его смехе звучала какая-то высокая, звенящая нота. Мне, как медику, его смех не понравился.

— Прекратите! Возьмите себя в руки! — крикнул я и налил ему воды из графина.

Но и это не помогло. Им овладел один из тех истерических припадков, которые случаются у сильных натур, когда переживания уже позади. Наконец смех утомил его, и он несколько успокоился.

— Я веду себя крайне глупо, — задыхаясь, вымолвил он.

— Вовсе нет. Выпейте это! — Я плеснул в воду немного коньяку, и его бледные щеки порозовели.

— Спасибо, — поблагодарил он. — А теперь, доктор, будьте добры посмотреть мой палец, или, лучше сказать, то место, где он когда-то был.

Он снял платок и протянул руку. Даже я, привычный к такого рода зрелищам, содрогнулся. На руке торчало только четыре пальца, а на месте большого было страшное красное вздутие. Палец был оторван или отрублен у самого основания.

He unwound the handkerchief and held out his hand.

— Боже мой! — воскликнул я. — Какая ужасная рана! Крови, наверное, вытекло предостаточно.

— Да. После удара я упал в обморок и, наверное, был без сознания очень долго. Очнувшись, я увидел, что кровь все еще идет, тогда я туго завязал платок вокруг запястья и закрутил узел щепкой.

— Превосходно! Из вас вышел бы хороший хирург.

— Да нет, просто я разбираюсь в том, что имеет отношение к гидравлике.

— Рана нанесена тяжелым и острым инструментом, — сказал я, осматривая руку.

— Похожим на нож мясника, — добавил он.

— Надеюсь, случайно?

— Никоим образом.

— Неужели покушение?

— Вот именно.

— Не пугайте меня.

Я промыл и обработал рану, а затем укутал руку ватой и перевязал пропитанными корболкой бинтами. Он сидел, откинувшись на спинку стула, и ни разу не поморщился, хотя время от времени закусывал губы.

— Ну, как? — закончив, спросил я.

— Превосходно! После вашего коньяка и перевязки я словно заново родился. Я очень ослабел, ведь мне пришлось немало испытать.

— Может, лучше не говорить о случившемся? Вы будете волноваться.

— О нет. Сейчас уже нет. Все равно придется выкладывать всю историю в полиции. Но, между нами говоря, только моя рана может заставить их поверить моему заявлению. История эта совершенно необычная, а я ничем подтвердить ее не могу. Даже если мне поверят, доводы, которые я способен представить в доказательство ее, настолько неопределенны, что вряд ли здесь восторжествует правосудие.

— Значит, это загадка, которую нужно разрешить, — воскликнул я. — Тогда я настоятельно рекомендую вам, прежде чем обращаться в полицию, пойти к моему другу мистеру Шерлоку Холмсу.

— Я слышал об этом человеке, — ответил мой пациент, — и был бы очень рад, если бы он взял это дело на себя, хотя, разумеется, все равно придется заявить в полицию. Может, вы порекомендуете меня ему?

— Больше того, я сам отвезу вас к нему.

— Премного буду вам обязан.

— Давайте вызовем экипаж и поедем. Мы как раз поспеем к завтраку. Вы в состоянии ехать?

— Да. На душе у меня будет неспокойно до тех пор, пока я не расскажу мою историю.

— Тогда я попрошу служанку вызвать кэб и через минуту буду готов.

Я побежал наверх, в нескольких словах рассказал о случившемся жене и через пять минут вместе с моим новым знакомым уже ехал по направлению к Бейкер-стрит.

Как я и предполагал, Шерлок Холмс — еще в халате — сидел в гостиной, читал ту колонку из «Таймса», в которой публикуются сведения о розыске различных лиц, и курил трубку. Эту трубку он обычно выкуривал до завтрака, набивая всякими остатками всех табаков — они с особой тщательностью собирались и сушились на каминной доске. Он принял нас с присущим ему спокойствием и радушием, заказал для нас яичницу с ветчиной, и мы на славу позавтракали. Когда с едой было покончено, он усадил нашего нового знакомого на диван, подложил ему под спину подушку, а рядом поставил стакан воды с коньяком.

He settled our new acquaintance on the sofa.

— Вам, видно, пришлось пережить нечто необычное, мистер Хэдерли, — сказал он. — Прошу вас прилечь на диван и чувствовать себя как дома. Рассказывайте, пока сможете, но, если почувствуете себя плохо, помолчите и попробуйте восстановить силы при помощи вот этого легкого средства.

— Благодарю вас, — ответил мой пациент, — но я чувствую себя другим человеком после того, как доктор перевязал мне руку, а ваш завтрак, по-видимому, завершил курс лечения. Я постараюсь недолго занимать у вас драгоценное время и поэтому тотчас же приступаю к рассказу о моих удивительных приключениях.

Опустив тяжелые веки, будто от усталости — что на самом деле лишь скрывало присущее ему жадное любопытство, — Холмс поудобнее уселся в кресло, я пристроился напротив, и мы принялись слушать действительно невероятную историю, которую наш посетитель изложил во всех подробностях.

— Должен сказать вам, — начал он, — что родители мои умерли, я не женат и потому живу совершенно один в своей лондонской квартире. По профессии я инженер-гидравлик и приобрел немалый опыт в течение тех семи лет, что пробыл в подручных в известной гринвичской фирме «Веннер и Мейтсон». Два года назад, унаследовав солидную сумму денег после смерти отца, я решил завести собственное дело и открыл контору на Виктория-стрит.

Наверное, каждому, кто открывает собственное дело, сначала приходится туго. Во всяком случае, так было со мной. В течение двух лет мне довелось дать всего три консультации и выполнить одну небольшую работу — вот и все, что дала мне моя специальность. Весь мой доход составляет на сегодняшний день двадцать семь фунтов десять шиллингов. Ежедневно с девяти утра до четырех я сидел в своей захудалой конторе и наконец с тяжелым сердцем начал понимать, что у меня не будет настоящей работы.

Но вот вчера, когда я собрался было уходить, вошел мой клерк, доложил, что меня желает видеть по делу какой-то джентльмен, и подал мне визитную карточку: «Полковник Лизандер Старк». А следом в комнату вошел и сам полковник, человек роста выше среднего, но чрезвычайно худой. До сих пор мне не доводилось встречать таких худых людей. Кожа так обтягивала выпирающие скулы, что лицо его, казалось, состояло лишь из носа и подбородка. Тем не менее худым он был по природе, а не от какой-либо болезни, ибо взгляд у него сверкал, двигался он проворно и держался уверенно. Он был просто, но аккуратно одет, а по возрасту, решил я, ему под сорок.

Colonel Lysander Stark.

— Мистер Хэдерли? — спросил он с немецким акцентом. — Вас порекомендовали мне как человека не только опытного, но и скромного, умеющего хранить тайну.

Я поклонился, чувствуя себя польщенным, как и всякий молодой человек при обращении подобного рода.

— Разрешите узнать, кто дал мне такую лестную характеристику? — полюбопытствовал я.

— Я предпочитаю пока умолчать об этом. Из того же источника мне стало известно, что родители ваши умерли, вы холосты и живете в Лондоне один.

— Совершенно правильно, — ответил я, — но простите, я не совсем понимаю, какое это имеет отношение к моей деятельности. Вы ведь желали увидеть меня по делу?

— Именно так. Вы сейчас убедитесь, что все, о чем я говорю, имеет непосредственное отношение к делу. Я хочу поручить вам одну работу, но при этом должна сохраняться полная тайна, полная тайна, понятно? Чего, разумеется, можно скорее ожидать от человека одинокого, нежели от человека, который живет в кругу семьи.

— Если я дам слово хранить тайну, — сказал я, — можете быть уверены, я его не нарушу.

Он пристально посмотрел на меня, и я подумал, что ни разу не видел столь подозрительного и недоверчивого взгляда.

— Итак, вы обещаете? — спросил он.

— Да, обещаю.

— Обещаете хранить полное молчание до, во время и после работы? Никогда не упоминать об этом деле ни устно, ни письменно?

— Я уже дал вам слово.

— Очень хорошо.

Вдруг он вскочил и, молнией метнувшись по комнате, распахнул дверь настежь. За дверью никого не было.

— Все в порядке, — заметил он, возвращаясь на место. — Известно, как клерки порой интересуются делами своих хозяев. Теперь можем поговорить спокойно.

Он подвинул свой стул вплотную к моему и уставился на меня тем же недоверчиво-пронзительным взглядом.

Чувство отвращения и что-то похожее на страх начало расти во мне при столь странном поведении этого чересчур худого человека. Даже боязнь потерять клиента не могла заставить меня терпеливо ждать, пока он заговорит.

— Прошу вас, сэр, изложить дело, я дорожу своим временем.

Да простит мне небо эти слова, но они сами сорвались с моих уст.

— Вас устроят пятьдесят гиней за одну ночь работы? — спросил он.

— Вполне.

— Я сказал — за ночь работы, но правильнее сказать — за час. Мне просто нужно ваше мнение по поводу гидравлического пресса, который вышел из строя. Если вы подскажете, в чем дело, мы сумеем сами устранить неисправность. Что скажете?

— Дело несложное, плата хороша.

— Именно так. Нам хотелось бы, чтобы вы приехали сегодня вечером последним поездом.

— Куда?

— В Айфорд. Это небольшая деревушка в Брекшире, на границе с Оксфордширом, в семи милях от Рединга. От Паддингтона есть поезд, который прибывает туда примерно в одиннадцать пятнадцать.

— Превосходно.

— Я приеду в экипаже встретить вас.

— Значит, придется добираться на лошадях?

— Да, наш дом находится в стороне от железной дороги. От Айфорд до него добрых семь миль.

— Значит, вряд ли мы доберемся до места к полуночи. И обратного поезда уже не будет. Мне придется провести у вас всю ночь.

— Что же, это не проблема.

— Но не очень-то удобно. А не мог бы я приехать в какое-нибудь другое, более подходящее время?

— Самое лучшее, считаем мы, если вы приедете поздно вечером. Именно за неудобства мы и платим вам, никому не известному молодому человеку, сумму, за которую можем получить совет самых крупных специалистов по вашей профессии. Конечно, если предложение вам не по душе, еще есть время от него отказаться.

Я подумал, как мне пригодятся пятьдесят гиней.

— Нет, нет, — заспешил я, — я готов сделать так, как вы считаете нужным. Однако мне хотелось бы более четко представить себе, что именно от меня требуется.

— Совершенно справедливо. Обещание хранить тайну, которое мы взяли с вас, вполне естественно, возбудило ваше любопытство. Я отнюдь не хочу, чтобы вы брали какие-то обязательства, не ознакомившись предварительно со всеми деталями. Надеюсь, нас никто не подслушивает?

— Никто.

— Дело обстоит следующим образом. Вам, вероятно известно, что сукновальная глина — довольно ценное сыры и что залежи ее в Англии встречаются в одном-двух местах.

— Я слышал об этом.

— Некоторое время назад я купил маленький участок земли, совсем крохотный, в десяти милях от Рединга. И вдруг оказалось, что мне повезло: я обнаружил на одном поле пласт сукновальной глины. Я исследовал его и выяснил, что он составляет лишь небольшую перемычку, соединяющую два очень мощных пласта слева и справа, расположенных на участках моих соседей. В их земле хранится сырье не менее ценное, чем золото, а эти добрые люди пребывают в полном неведении. Мне, естественно, было бы выгодно купить у них землю, прежде чем они узнают ее истинную стоимость, но, к сожалению, я не располагаю для этого достаточным капиталом. Поэтому я посвятил в тайну нескольких своих приятелей, и они предложили потихоньку, не говоря никому ни слова, разрабатывать наш собственный небольшой пласт, чтобы заработать деньги, а впоследствии купить землю у соседей. Этим мы и заняты вот уже некоторое время и в помощь установили гидравлический пресс. Но пресс, как я уже сказал, вышел из строя, и нам нужен ваш совет. Мы ревностно храним наш секрет, и если станет известно, что к нам приезжал гидравлик, то тотчас же начнутся расспросы, факты выплывут наружу, и тогда прощай соседские поля, а с ними и наши планы. Вот почему я взял с вас слово никому не рассказывать, что вы сегодня вечером едете в Айфорд. Надеюсь, теперь все ясно?

— Единственное, что мне не совсем ясно, — ответил я, — это зачем вам гидравлический пресс. Сукновальную глину, насколько я знаю, вычерпывают, как песок из карьера.

— А, — небрежно махнул он рукой, — у нас свои методы работы. Чтобы соседи ничего не заметили, мы прессуем глину в кирпичи. Но это деталь. Я доверяю вам, мистер Хэдерли, и рассказал все. — Он встал. — Итак, жду вас в Айфорде в 23:15.

— Я обязательно приеду.

— И помните: никому ни слова.

Он еще раз посмотрел на меня долгим вопросительным взглядом и, пожав мне руку своей холодной, влажной рукой, поспешно вышел.

«Not a word to a soul!»

Хладнокровно поразмыслив, я, как вы представляете, не мог все-таки отделаться от удивления по поводу этого странного поручения. С одной стороны, я, разумеется, был рад, ибо плату мне предложили в десять раз большую, чем та, которую запросил бы я сам. Кроме того, есть надежда, что за этим поручением последуют и другие. С другой стороны, облик и манеры моего клиента произвели на меня такое гнетущее впечатление, что я не мог отвязаться от мысли, что вся эта история с сукновальной глиной не вполне объясняет необходимость приехать непременно в полночь и избежать огласки. Однако я отбросил от себя страхи, на славу поужинал, доехал до Паддингтона и отправился в путь.

В Рединге мне пришлось сделать пересадку. Но я успел на последний поезд в Айфорд и в начале двенадцатого прибыл на маленькую, тускло освещенную станцию. Я оказался единственным, кто там сошел, на платформе не было ни души, кроме заспанного носильщика с фонарем в руках. За станционной оградой я увидел моего утреннего знакомого — он стоял в тени на противоположной стороне. Не сказав ни слова, он схватил меня за руку и втащил в экипаж, дверца которого предусмотрительно оказалась открытой. Опустив с обеих сторон окошки, полковник постучал кучеру, и лошадь рванулась вперед.

— Одна лошадь? — перебил Холмс.

— Да одна.

— Вы не заметили масть?

— Заметил при свете фонаря, когда садился в экипаж. Лошадь рыжей масти.

— Усталая или свежая?

— Свежая, шерсть у нее лоснилась.

— Благодарю. Извините, что перебил. Прошу продолжать ваше весьма интересное повествование.

— Итак, мы тронулись в путь и ехали по меньшей мере с час. Полковник Лизандер Старк сказал, что до места всего семь миль, но, если принять во внимание скорость, с какой мы мчались, и время, что нам потребовалось, мне показалось, что расстояние там, должно быть, миль в двенадцать. Он молча сидел рядом, и я чувствовал, когда поглядывал на него, что он не спускает с меня глаз. Проселочные дороги в тех местах, по-видимому, в неважном состоянии, и нас ужасно кидало из стороны в сторону. Я попытался было в окошко разглядеть, где мы едем, но сквозь матовое стекло мог различить только мелькавшие кое-где световые пятна. Несколько раз я хотел завести разговор — уж очень монотонным было наше путешествие, но полковник отвечал односложно, и разговор быстро затухал. Наконец ямы и ухабы закончились, колеса захрустели по посыпанной гравием дорожке, и экипаж остановился. Полковник Лизандер Старк спрыгнул на землю, я последовал за ним, и он тут же потащил меня на крыльцо, где зияла отворенная дверь. Таким образом, прямо из экипажа я очутился в прихожей и не сумел даже краем глаза разглядеть фасад дома. Едва я переступил порог, дверь тяжело захлопнулась за нами, и я услышал слабый стук отъезжающего экипажа.

В доме царил полный мрак, и полковник, что-то бормоча себе под нос, принялся шарить по карманам в поисках спичек. Внезапно в дальнем конце коридора дверь отворилась, и в коридор упал длинный луч золотистого света. Луч становился шире и шире, и в дверях, держа высоко над головой лампу, появилась женщина; вытянув шею, она вглядывалась в нас. Я заметил, что она очень красивая, а блеск, которым отливало ее темное платье, свидетельствовал о том, что оно из дорогого материала. Она произнесла несколько слов на каком-то языке, и по тону я догадался, что она о чем-то спросила моего попутчика, но тот лишь сердито буркнул в ответ, и она так вздрогнула, что чуть не выронила лампу. Полковник Старк подошел к ней, шепнул что-то на ухо и, проводив обратно в комнату, вернулся ко мне с лампой в руках.

— Будьте добры подождать несколько минут здесь, — сказал он, отворяя другую дверь в незатейливо убранную комнатку с круглым столом посредине, на котором лежало несколько немецких книг. Полковник Старк поставил лампу на крышку фисгармонии рядом с дверью. — Я постараюсь не задержать вас, — добавил он и исчез в темноте.

Я посмотрел книги на столе и, хотя не знаю немецкого, все же понял, что две из них были научные, а остальные — сборники поэзии. Затем я подошел к окну в надежде разглядеть, где нахожусь, но оно было плотно прикрыто дубовыми ставнями. Удивительно молчаливый дом! Кругом царила мертвая тишина, лишь где-то в коридоре громко тикали часы.

Смутное чувство тревоги овладевало мною. Кто эти немцы и что они делают в этом странном, уединенном доме? И где находится сам дом? Милях в десяти от Айфорда — вот и все, что мне было известно, но к северу, югу, востоку или западу от него, я и представления не имел. Однако неподалеку от Айфорда находится и Рединг и, наверное, другие города, так что место это не может быть очень уж уединенным. Все же царившая вокруг полная тишина ясно давала понять, что мы в деревне. Я ходил взад и вперед по комнате, мурлыкая что-то себе под нос, чтобы окончательно не упасть духом, и размышляя, что недаром получу обещанные пятьдесят гиней.

И вдруг беззвучно и медленно отворилась дверь, и в темном проеме появилась та женщина. Желтый свет от моей лампы упал на ее красивое лицо. Я понял, что она чего-то боится, и мне самому стало страшно. Дрожащим пальцем она подала мне знак хранить молчание и прошептала что-то на ломаном английском языке, то и дело косясь назад во мрак, словно напуганная лошадь.

— Я уйду, — сказала она, очевидно, изо всех сил стараясь говорить спокойно. — Я уйду. Я не могу оставаться здесь. И вам здесь тоже нечего делать.

— Сударыня, — возразил я, — я ведь еще не выполнил того, ради чего приехал. Я не могу уехать, пока не осмотрю пресс.

— Не нужно медлить, — настаивала она. — Уходите в эту дверь. Там никого нет. — Видя, что я лишь улыбаюсь и качаю головой, она вдруг отбросила всю свою сдержанность и, стиснув руки, шагнула ко мне. — Во имя неба, — прошептала она, — уходите отсюда, пока не поздно.

«Get away from here before it is too late!»

Но я довольно упрям по характеру, и, когда на пути у меня возникает какое-нибудь препятствие, я загораюсь еще больше и хочу довести дело до конца. Я подумал об обещанных пятидесяти гинеях, об утомительном путешествии и о тех неудобствах, что меня ожидают, если мне придется провести ночь на станции. Значит, все впустую? Почему я должен уехать, не выполнив работы и не получив тех денег, которые мне должны? Может, эта женщина — ведь я ничего о ней не знаю — помешанная? С самым независимым видом, хотя, признаться, ее поведение напугало меня больше, чем хотелось бы показать, я снова покачал головой и заявил о своем намерении остаться. Она было принялась уговаривать меня, но где-то наверху стукнула дверь, и послышались шаги на лестнице. На мгновение она прислушалась, а потом, заломив в отчаянии руки, исчезла так же внезапно и бесшумно, как и появилась.

В комнату вошли полковник Лизандер Старк и маленький толстый человек с седой бородой, торчащей из складок его двойного подбородка. Его представили мне как мистера Фергюсона.

— Это мой секретарь и управляющий, — сказал полковник.

— Между прочим, мне казалось, что, уходя, я закрыл эту дверь. Вас не просквозило?

— Наоборот, — возразил я, — это я приоткрыл дверь, в комнате душновато.

Полковник вновь нацелился на меня подозрительным взглядом.

— Пора перейти к делу, — сказал он. — Мы с мистером Фергюсоном покажем вам, где стоит пресс.

— Я, пожалуй, надену шляпу.

— Зачем? Пресс находится в доме.

— Что? Разве залежи сукновальной глины здесь в доме?

— Нет-нет! Мы только прессуем здесь. Да, собственно, какая разница? Нам нужно, чтобы вы посмотрели машину и сказали, в чем неисправность.

Мы поднялись наверх, впереди полковник с лампой, за ним толстяк-управляющий, а потом я. Это был не дом, а настоящий лабиринт — с бесчисленными коридорами, галереями, узкими винтовыми лестницами и низкими дверцами, пороги которых были истоптаны ногами многих поколений. На первом этаже не было ни ковров, ни мебели, со стен сыпалась штукатурка, и зелеными пятнами проступала сырость. Я старался сделать вид, что все это меня мало трогает, но отнюдь не забывал предостережения женщины — хоть и пренебрег им — и зорко следил за своими спутниками. Фергюсон был угрюм и молчалив, но по тем нескольким словам, что он произнес, я понял, что он по крайней мере уроженец Англии.

Наконец полковник Лизандер Старк остановился и отпер какую-то дверь. Она вела в маленькую квадратную комнату, в которой мы трое вряд ли могли поместиться. Фергюсон остался в коридоре, а мы с полковником вошли в комнату.

— Мы находимся сейчас, — сказал он, — внутри гидравлического пресса, и если бы кто-нибудь включил его, нам не сдобровать. Потолок этой камеры в действительности — плоскость рабочего поршня, который с силой, равной весу нескольких тонн, опускается на металлический пол. Снаружи установлены боковые цилиндры, в которые поступает вода, она действует на поршень... Впрочем, с механикой вы знакомы. Пресс работает, но что-то заедает, и он не развивает полную мощность. Будьте добры осмотреть его и подсказать нам, что следует исправить.

Я взял у него лампу и внимательно осмотрел пресс. Это была машина гигантских размеров, способная создавать огромное давление. Когда я вышел из камеры я включил рычаги управления, где-то зашипело, и я понял, что в боковом цилиндре имеется небольшая утечка. Осмотр показал, что резиновая прокладка в одном месте потеряла эластичность и сквозь нее просачивается вода. Именно это было причиной падения мощности. Мои спутники весьма внимательно выслушали меня и задали несколько практических вопросов насчет того, как устранить неисправность. Объяснив им все подробно, я возвратился в главную камеру и из любопытства принялся ее осматривать. С первого же взгляда было ясно, что история с сукновальной глиной — сплошная выдумка, ибо глупо было даже предположить, что столь мощный механизм предназначен для столь ничтожной цели. Стены камеры были деревянные, но основание из железа, и я увидел на нем металлическую накипь. Я наклонился и попытался соскоблить кусочек, чтобы получше его рассмотреть, как услышал приглушенное восклицание по-немецки и увидел мертвенно-бледное лицо полковника.

— Что вы тут делаете? — спросил он.

Я разозлился, когда понял, как был обманут той искусно придуманной историей, которую он мне поведал.

— Любуюсь вашей сукновальной глиной, — ответил я. — Думается, я мог бы дать вам лучший совет, если бы знал истинное назначение этого пресса.

Едва я произнес эти слова, как тут же пожалел о своей несдержанности. Лицо его окаменело, в серых глазах вспыхнул зловещий огонек.

— Ну что ж, — прошипел он, — сейчас вы узнаете все подробности.

Он сделал шаг назад, захлопнул дверцу и повернул ключ в замке. Я бросился к двери, стал дергать за ручку, колотить, но дверь оказалась весьма надежной и никак не поддавалась.

— Эй, полковник! — закричал я. — Выпустите меня.

I rushed to the door.

И вдруг в тишине раздался звук, от которого душа у меня ушла в пятки. Он включил пресс. Лампа стояла на полу, где я ее поставил, когда рассматривал накипь, и при свете ее я увидел, что черный потолок начал двигаться на меня, медленно, толчками, но с такой силой, что через минуту — и я понимал это лучше, чем кто-либо другой — от меня останется мокрое место. Я снова с криком бросился к двери, ногтями пытался сорвать замок. Я умолял полковника выпустить меня, но беспощадный лязг рычагов заглушал мои крики. Потолок уже находился на расстоянии одного-двух футов от меня, и, подняв руку, я мог дотронуться до его твердой и неровной поверхности. И в тот же момент в голове у меня сверкнула мысль о том, что смерть моя может показаться менее болезненной в зависимости от положения, в каком я ее приму. Если лечь на живот, то вся тяжесть придется на позвоночник, и я содрогнулся, представив себе, как он захрустит. Лучше, конечно, лечь на спину, но достанет ли у меня духу смотреть, как неумолимо надвигается черная тень? Я уже не мог стоять в полный рост, но тут я увидел нечто такое, от чего в душе моей затрепетала надежда.

Я уже сказал, что пол и потолок были железными, а стены камеры обшиты деревянной панелью. И вот в ту минуту, когда я в последний раз лихорадочно озирался вокруг, я заметил тонкую щель желтого света между двумя досками, которая ширилась и ширилась по мере того, как потолок опускался. На мгновение я даже не поверил, что это выход, который может спасти меня от смерти. В следующую секунду я бросился вперед и в полуобморочном состоянии свалился с другой стороны. Отверстие закрылось. Хруст лампы, а затем и стук металлических плит поведали о том, что я был на волосок от гибели.

Я пришел в себя оттого, что кто-то отчаянно дергал меня за руку, и увидел, что лежу на каменном полу в узком коридоре, надо мной склонилась женщина, одной рукой она тянет меня, а другой — держит свечу. Это была та самая моя благожелательница, чьим предупреждением я по глупости пренебрег.

— Идемте! Идемте! — задыхаясь, вскричала она. — Они сейчас будут здесь. Они увидят, что вас там нет. О, не теряйте драгоценного времени, идемте!

На этот раз я внял ее совету. Кое-как поднявшись на ноги, я вместе с ней бросился по коридору, а потом вниз по винтовой лестнице. Лестница привела нас в более широкий коридор, и тут же мы услышали топот и крики: кто-то, находящийся на том этаже, с которого мы только что спустились, отвечал на возгласы снизу. Моя провожатая остановилась и огляделась вокруг, не зная, что предпринять. Затем она распахнула дверь в спальню, где в окно полным светом светила луна.

— Это единственная возможность, — сказала она. — Окно высоко, но, может, вам удастся спрыгнуть.

В это время в дальнем конце коридора появился свет, и я увидел полковника Лизандера Старка: он бежал, держа в одной руке фонарь, а в другой что-то похожее на нож мясника. Я бросился в комнату к окну, распахнул его и выглянул. Каким тихим, приветливыми и спокойным казался сад, залитый лунным светом; окно было не более тридцати футов над землей. Я взобрался на подоконник, но медлил: мне хотелось узнать, что станется с моей спасительницей. Я решил, несмотря ни на что, прийти ей на помощь, если ей придется плохо. Едва я подумал об этом, как этот негодяй ворвался в комнату и бросился ко мне. Она обхватила его обеими руками и пыталась удержать.

— Фриц! Фриц! Вспомни свое обещание после прошлого раза, — кричала она на английском языке. — Ты обещал, что этого не повторится. Он будет молчать! Он будет молчать!

— Ты сошла с ума, Эльза! — гремел он, стараясь вырваться от нее. — Ты нас погубишь. Он видел слишком много. Пусти меня, говорю я тебе!

Он отбросил ее в сторону, метнулся к окну и замахнулся своим оружием. Я успел соскользнуть с подоконника и висел, держась за раму, когда он нанес мне удар. Я почувствовал тупую боль, руки мои разжались, и я упал в сад под окном.

He cut at me.

Падение меня оглушило, но и только. Я вскочил и со всех ног бросился в кусты, понимая, что не ушел еще от опасности. На бегу меня вдруг охватила страшная слабость и тошнота. Руку дергало от боли, и только тогда я заметил, что у меня нет большого пальца и из раны хлещет кровь. Я попытался было обвязать руку носовым платком, но в этот момент в висках у меня застучало, и я свалился в тяжелом обмороке среди кустов роз.

Сколько я был без сознания, сказать не могу. Наверное, очень долго, потому что, когда я пришел в себя, луна уже зашла и занимался день. Одежда моя промокла до нитки от выпавшей ночью росы, а рукав пиджака был насквозь пропитан кровью. Жгучая боль напомнила мне о событиях минувшей ночи, и я вскочил на ноги, сознавая, что не могу считать себя в полной безопасности. Но каково же было мое удивление, когда, оглядевшись вокруг, я не увидел ни дома, ни сада. Я лежал у изгороди возле дороги, а немного подальше виднелось длинное строение; когда я подошел к нему, оно оказалось той самой станцией, куда я и прибыл накануне вечером. И если бы не страшная рана на руке, все происшедшее могло бы показаться просто ночным кошмаром. Ничего не понимая, я вошел в здание и спросил, скоро ли будет утренний поезд. Менее чем через час будет поезд на Рединг, ответили мне. Дежурил тот самый носильщик, что и накануне. Я спросил у него, не знает ли он полковника Лизандера Старка. Нет, имя это ему незнакомо. Не видел ли он экипаж у станции вчера вечером? Нет, не видел. Есть ли поблизости полицейский участок? Да, милях в трех от станции.

Я совсем ослабел, а рука у меня так болела, что нечего было и думать туда дойти. Я решил сначала вернуться в город, а потом уж пойти в полицию. Я приехал в Лондон в начале седьмого, прежде всего отправился перевязывать рану, и доктор оказался настолько любезен, что сам привез меня к вам. Целиком полагаюсь на вас и готов следовать любому вашему совету.

Он закончил свое удивительное повествование, и некоторое время мы сидели молча. Затем Шерлок Холмс взял с полки один из увесистых альбомов, в которых хранил вырезки из газет.

— Вот заметка, которая может вас заинтересовать, — сказал он. — Она появилась в газетах около года назад. Послушайте: «9-го числа этого месяца пропал без вести мистер Джереми Хейлинг, двадцати шести лет, по профессии инженер-гидравлик. Он ушел из дома в десять часов вечера, и с тех пор о нем ничего не известно. Был одет…» и так далее и так далее. Это и был, по-видимому, именно тот «прошлый раз», когда полковнику понадобилось ремонтировать свой пресс.

— Боже мой! — воскликнул мой пациент. — Так вот что означали слова женщины.

— Несомненно! Совершенно ясно, что полковник — человек хладнокровный и отчаянный и, подобно головорезам, которые не оставляли в живых ни одного человека на захваченном судне, сметает любые препятствия на своем пути. Однако нельзя терять ни минуты, и если вы в состоянии двигаться, мы немедленно отправимся в Скотланд-Ярд, а потом поедем в Айфорд.

Через каких-нибудь три часа или около того мы все сидели в поезде, направлявшемся из Рединга в маленькую беркширскую деревню. Мы — это Шерлок Холмс, гидротехник, инспектор Бродстрит из Скотланд-Ярда, агент в штатском и я. Бродстрит расстелил на скамейке подробную карту Англии и циркулем вычертил на ней окружность с центром в Айфорде.

— Смотрите, эта окружность имеет радиус в десять миль, — сказал он. — Нужное нам место находится где-то внутри этого круга. Вы, кажется, сказали, десять миль, сэр?

— Да, мы ехали около часа.

— И вы предполагаете, что они отвезли вас обратно, пока вы были без сознания?

— По-видимому, так. Мне смутно помнится, что меня поднимали и куда-то несли.

— Не понимаю, — вмешался я, — почему они сохранили вам жизнь, когда нашли вас без сознания в саду. Может, женщина умолила этого негодяя пощадить вас?

— Вряд ли. За всю мою жизнь не видел более зверской физиономии.

— Все это мы скоро выясним, — сказал Бродстрит. — Итак, окружность готова, сейчас остается узнать только, в какой точке находятся те люди, которых мы ищем.

— Мне думается, я могу вам показать, — спокойно ответил Холмс.

— Вот как? — воскликнул инспектор. — Значит, у вас уже есть определенное мнение. Посмотрим, что думают остальные. Я утверждаю, что это произошло на юге, ибо там местность менее населенная.

— А я говорю, на востоке, — возразил мой пациент.

— Я стою за запад, — заметил человек в штатском. — Там расположено несколько тихих деревушек.

— А я — за север, — сказал я. — На севере нет холмов, а наш друг утверждает, что не заметил, чтобы дорога шла в гору.

— Ну и ну! Неплохой букет мнений, — смеясь подытожил инспектор. — Мы назвали все румбы компаса. Кого же вы поддерживаете, мистер Холмс?

— Вы все ошибаетесь.

— Как же могут все ошибаться?

— Могут. Я считаю, что это произошло здесь. — И Холмс ткнул пальцем в центр окружности. — Тут мы их и найдем.

— А двенадцатимильная поездка? — удивился Хэдерли.

— Нет ничего проще: шесть миль туда и шесть обратно. Вы сами сказали, что когда вы садились в экипаж, лошадь была свежей и шерсть у нее лоснилась. Могло ли это быть, если она прошла двенадцать миль по плохой дороге?

— Они в самом деле могли использовать такую уловку, — задумчиво заметил Бродстрит и добавил: — Дела этой шайки, конечно, сомнений не вызывают.

— Разумеется, нет, — ответил Холмс. — Они фальшивомонетчики, причем крупного масштаба, пресс они используют для чеканки амальгамы, которая заменяет серебро.

— Нам уже некоторое время известно о существовании очень ловкой шайки, которая в огромном количестве выпускает полукроны, — сказал инспектор. — Мы даже выследили их до Рединга, но потом застряли. Они так умело замели следы, что сразу видно: стреляные воробьи. И все-таки на этот раз благодаря счастливой случайности их, пожалуй, накроем.

Но инспектор ошибся: преступникам не суждено было попасть в руки правосудия. Подъехав к Айфорду, мы увидели огромный столб дыма, который гигантским страусовым пером висел над деревьями.

«A house on fire!»

— Пожар? — спросил Бродстрит у начальника станции, когда поезд, пыхтя, двинулся дальше.

— Да, сэр, — ответил тот.

— Когда начался?

— Говорят ночью, сэр, но сейчас усилился, весь дом в огне.

— А чей это дом?

— Доктора Бичерта.

— Скажите, — вмешался Холмс, — доктор Бичер — это тощий немец с длинным острым носом?

Начальник станции громко рассмеялся.

— Нет, сэр, доктор Бичер — самый настоящий англичанин. Но у него в доме живет какой-то джентльмен, его пациент, говорят, вот он иностранец, и вид у него такой, что ему не помешало бы отведать нашей доброй беркширской говядины.

Не успел начальник станции договорить, как мы все были уже на пути к горящему дому. Дорога поднималась на невысокий холм, на вершине которого стояло большое приземистое, выбеленное известкой строение; из окон и дверей его вырывался огонь, а три пожарные машины тщетно пытались прибить пламя.

— Ну конечно же! — воскликнул Хэдерли в крайнем волнении. — Вон дорожка, посыпанная гравием, а вон розовые кусты, где я лежал. А вот это окно, второе с краю, — то самое, из которого я прыгнул.

— Что ж, — заметил Холмс, — вы по крайней мере сумели им отомстить. Огонь из вашей керосиновой лампы, когда ее сплющило, перекинулся на стены, а преступники, увлекшись погоней, этого не заметили. Смотрите-ка внимательнее, нет ли в этой толпе ваших вчерашних приятелей, думается мне, они сейчас уже в доброй сотне миль отсюда.

Предположение Холмса оправдалось, ибо с тех пор мы ни слова не слышали ни о красивой женщине, ни о злом немце, ни о мрачном англичанине. Правда, утром в тот день один крестьянин встретил повозку с людьми, доверху набитую какими-то громоздкими ящиками. Повозка направлялась в сторону Рединга, но затем следы беглецов терялись, и даже Холмс при всей его проницательности оказался не в состоянии установить хотя бы приблизительно их местонахождение.

Пожарники были немало озадачены тем странным устройством, которое они обнаружили внутри дома, и еще более тем, что на подоконнике окна на третьем этаже они нашли отрубленный большой палец. На заходе солнца их усилия увенчались наконец успехом, огонь погас, хотя к тому времени крыша уже провалилась и весь дом превратился в руины; от машины, осмотр которой так дорого обошелся нашему незадачливому знакомому, ничего не осталось, если не считать помятых труб и цилиндров. В сарае обнаружили большие запасы никеля и жести, но ни единой монеты не нашли — их, по-видимому, увезли в тех громоздких ящиках, о которых уже говорилось.

Мы оба так никогда бы и не узнали, каким образом наш гидравлик очутился на том месте, где он пришел в себя, если бы не мягкая почва, поведавшая нам весьма простую историю. Его, очевидно, несли двое, у одного из них были удивительно маленькие ноги, а у второго — необыкновенно большие. В общем, весьма вероятно, что молчаливый англичанин, более трусливый или менее жестокий, чем его компаньон, помог женщине избавить потерявшего сознание человека от грозившей ему опасности.

— Да, для меня это хороший урок, — уныло заметил Хэдерли, когда мы сели в поезд, направлявшийся обратно, в Лондон. — Я лишился пальца и пятидесяти гиней, а что я приобрел?

— Опыт, — смеясь, ответил Холмс. — Может, он вам и пригодится. Нужно только облечь его в слова, чтобы всю жизнь слыть отличным рассказчиком.

Знатный холостяк

Женитьба лорда Сент-Саймона, закончившаяся таким удивительным образом, давно перестала занимать те круги великосветского общества, где вращается злополучный жених. Новые скандальные истории своими более пикантными подробностями затмили эту драму и отвлекли от нее внимание салонных болтунов, тем более что с тех пор прошло уже четыре года. Но так как я имею основание думать, что многие факты так и не дошли до широкой публики, и так как это дело прояснилось главным образом благодаря моему другу Шерлоку Холмсу, я считаю, что мои воспоминания о нем были бы неполны без краткого очерка об этом любопытном эпизоде.

Как-то днем, за несколько недель до моей собственной свадьбы, когда я еще жил вместе с Холмсом на Бейкер-стрит, на его имя пришло письмо. Холмса не было дома, он где-то бродил после обеда, я же весь день сидел в комнате, потому что погода внезапно испортилась, поднялся сильный осенний ветер, пошел дождь, и застрявшая в ноге пуля, которую я привез с собой на память об афганском походе, напоминала о себе тупой непрерывной болью. Удобно усевшись в одном кресле и положив ноги на другое, я занялся чтением газет, но потом, пресыщенный злободневными новостями, отшвырнул весь этот бумажный ворох в сторону и от нечего делать стал разглядывать лежавшее на столе письмо. Огромный герб и монограмма красовались на конверте, и я лениво размышлял о том, какая же это важная особа состоит в переписке с моим другом.

Elliot lifted the lid as Bat Girl came up behind her and looked over her shoulder. Together they peered inside.

"Elliot," Professor Snyder hissed. She snapped her fingers to get Elliot's attention.

Elliot smiled apologetically at her professor. "We won't touch anything else."

Jaime Sullivan's story had been reduced to items stored in a box, items collected in her final moments of life. A journal, a collection of newspaper articles clipped together, random pieces of mail, seven index cards with a date written on each one—not one date the same—and a stack of crime scene photos.

Horrible photos too. Jaime naked and left discarded without a care. Images of the room, a broken lamp on the floor. A chair overturned.

But Elliot knew that wasn't Jaime Sullivan. All her research told her Jaime Sullivan was a girl who had defied the odds. She'd spent half her life bouncing between shelters and homelessness, and yet she managed to graduate high school with honors and go to college on a full scholarship. By all accounts, Jaime had been a positive person who looked for the silver lining.

Eventually, though, Jaime would be forgotten, and from the way things were going, her case left unsolved. A fact that made Elliot both angry and sad.

"Is this what I think it is? Is this evidence?" Elliot asked Bat Girl.

Bat Girl said, "This looks like the actual evidence that is stored in the property room at the police station, but I can't be sure. It's not properly bagged and tagged. So maybe it's not actual cataloged evidence?"

She pointed to a clear sealed bag that held the journal.

Professor Snyder shrugged. "Hard to say. The quality of the call was bad." She looked at Bat Girl. "I almost ignored it."

The athlete asked, "So now what?"

Professor Snyder jerked her head to the hallway. "Let's go to my office."

They followed her down the hallway, not in a line but each of them moving in the same direction while keeping their distance.

Professor Snyder slid a key into the lock and twisted the knob, swinging the door open with a kick. She leaned in slightly to switch on her light, not fully entering the room. Elliot had seen her do this before. In class, the professor had told them about a time when, on assignment, she'd returned to her motel only to find a stranger with a knife waiting in the room to silence her. She had a four-inch scar running from her scalp, across her forehead, and to her right eye as a daily reminder of that night.

Professor Snyder's shoulders stiffened, and Elliot sensed something or someone was waiting in the room. She moved around her teacher to look inside. On Professor Snyder's desk was a box. The kind reams of paper came in. Taped to the side of the box was a large manila envelope, and written on it in bold black strokes was CAMPUS MURDER CLUB Case #1.

Elliot scanned the room before entering, wanting to make sure it was empty.

Professor Snyder moved into the room toward her desk. "I'm calling security. Don't touch anything, Elliot."

But Elliot couldn't help herself. At home she had a similar box and wondered if like items were inside. Case files. Pictures of evidence. Police reports.

Elliot looked away quickly. She continued, "And am I correct in assuming that no one here sent the note?"

They all nodded.

"Bullshit," Bat Girl said.

Elliot had to agree.

The front door hummed then clicked to disengage, and Professor Libby Whitehorse Snyder entered. She shook out an umbrella before putting it in the stand next to the door. Life in the Pacific Northwest was all about umbrellas and rain gear. Professor Snyder was a tall, middle-aged woman with short gray bobbed hair and a no-nonsense demeanor.

Surprise crossed her face as she took in the students. "Elliot?"

"Hello, Professor. We... ah..." Elliot had no excuse for why she was there or why these students, who weren't supposed to be in the journalism building at night, were, in fact, in the building.

"We're being pranked," Bat Girl said. "Someone sent us a note telling us to be here at this time on this day. Saying we were being called on to solve the Jaime Sullivan case. I stupidly let curiosity get the best of me." Arms crossed, she rolled her eyes.

Professor Snyder said, "Jaime Sullivan, you say?"

Elliot nodded and handed the note to her professor. "It's weird, right?"

Professor Snyder slid on a pair of reading glasses, glanced at the note, then looked over their rims at Elliot. "Not as weird as getting a phone call from an unidentified caller saying I had to get here right away, that Jaime Sullivan's killer was getting away with murder, and I needed to stop them."

"Was the caller a man or a woman?" Elliot asked.

The rhinestones on Ball Cap Girl's hat winked as she nodded adamantly in agreement.

Elliot shook her head. "I didn't send any letter. And to be clear, we're talking about this?" From her messenger bag, she pulled out the note.

Bat Girl pointed at the letter. "Yeah, that's it."

Elliot pointed to Ball Cap Girl. "You got one too?"

She tapped her front pant pocket as if to say that was where her letter was.

"So did I," the jock said. He moved in a little closer while digging his note from his front pocket. He handed it to Elliot. The letters were identical.

They all looked at the last person to join them.

"What about you?" Bat Girl asked.

He wiped his forearm across the top of his head and cleared his throat. "Same letter."

"If you didn't send it, then who did?" Bat Girl said to Elliot with skepticism.

Elliot shrugged and looked at the others.

"I didn't," Ball Cap Girl said. "I don't even know any of you."

"I don't know any of you either," Bat Girl said. "And I don't think this is a funny joke. Frankly, I don't see the purpose of this."

Yet she didn't turn to leave. And she'd come in, hadn't she?

Elliot asked, "Does anyone here know anyone else?"

The athlete jerked his head toward Elliot. "I wouldn't say I know ya, but I know who you are.'" His accent was subtle, southern. Probably at the University on a scholarship. And yet, he still knew who she was.

— Вас ждет великосветское послание, — сообщил я Холмсу, когда он вошел в комнату. — А с утренней почтой вы, если не ошибаюсь, получили письма от торговца рыбой и таможенного чиновника?

— Вся прелесть моей корреспонденции именно в ее разнообразии, — ответил он улыбаясь, — и в большинстве случаев, чем скромнее автор письма, тем интереснее письмо. А вот это, мне кажется, одно из тех несносных официальных приглашений, которые либо нагоняют на вас скуку, либо заставляют прибегнуть ко лжи.

He broak the seal and glanced over the contents.

Он сломал печать и быстро пробежал письмо.

— Э, нет! Тут, пожалуй, может оказаться кое-что интересное.

— Значит, это не приглашение?

— Нет, письмо сугубо деловое.

— И от знатного клиента?

— От одного из самых знатных в Англии.

— Поздравляю вас, милый друг.

— Даю вам слово, Уотсон, — и поверьте, я не рисуюсь, — что общественное положение моего клиента значит для меня гораздо меньше, чем его дело. Однако этот случай может оказаться любопытным. Вы, кажется, довольно усердно читали газеты в последнее время?

— Как видите! — ответил я уныло, показывая на груду газет в углу. — Больше мне ничего было делать.

— Это очень кстати. В таком случае вы сможете информировать меня. Я ведь ничего не читаю, кроме уголовной хроники и объявлений о розыске пропавших родственников. Там бывают поучительные вещи. Ну, а если вы следили за происшествиями, то, вероятно, читали о лорде Сент-Саймоне и его свадьбе?

— О да! С большим интересом.

— Отлично. Так вот, в руке у меня письмо от лорда Сент-Саймона. Сейчас я прочитаю его вам, а вы за это время еще раз просмотрите газеты и расскажете все, что имеет отношение к этой истории. Вот что он пишет:

«Уважаемый мистер Шерлок Холмс!

Лорд Бэкуотер сказал мне, что я вполне могу довериться Вашему чутью и Вашему умению хранить тайну. Поэтому я решил обратиться к Вам за советом по поводу прискорбного события, которое произошло в связи с моей свадьбой. Мистер Лестрейд из Скотланд-Ярда уже ведет расследование по этому делу, но он ничего не имеет против Вашего сотрудничества, и даже считает, что оно может оказаться полезным. Я буду у Вас сегодня в четыре часа дня и надеюсь, что ввиду первостепенной важности моего дела Вы отложите все другие встречи, если они назначены Вами на это время.

Уважающий вас Роберт Сент-Саймон».

— Письмо отправлено из особняка в Гровнере и написано гусиным пером, причем благородный лорд имел несчастье испачкать чернилами тыльную сторону правого мизинца, — сказал Холмс, складывая послание.

— Он пишет, что приедет в четыре часа. Сейчас три. Через час он будет здесь.

— Значит, я как раз успею с вашей помощью выяснить кое-какие обстоятельства. Просмотрите газеты и подберите заметки в хронологическом порядке, а я, покамест, взгляну, что представляет собой наш клиент.

Он взял с полки толстую книгу в красном переплете, стоявшую в ряду с другими справочниками.

— Вот он! — сказал Холмс, усевшись в кресло и раскрыв книгу у себя на коленях. — «Роберт Уолсингэм де Вир Сент-Саймон, второй сын герцога Балморалского». Гм!.. «Герб: голубое поле, три звездочки чертополоха над полоской собольего меха. Родился в 1846». Значит, ему сорок один год — достаточно зрелый возраст для женитьбы. Был товарищем министра колоний в прежнем составе Кабинета. Герцог, его отец, был одно время министром иностранных дел. Потомки Плантагенетов по мужской линии и Тюдоров — по женской. Так... Все это ничего нам не дает. Надеюсь, что вы, Уотсон, приготовили что-нибудь более существенное?

— Мне было совсем нетрудно найти нужный материал, — сказал я. — Ведь события эти произошли совсем недавно и сразу привлекли мое внимание. Я только потому не рассказывал вам о них, что вы были заняты каким-то расследованием, а мне известно, как вы не любите, когда вас отвлекают.

— А, вы имеете в виду ту пустячную историю с фургоном для перевозки мебели по Гровнер-сквер? Она уже совершенно выяснена, да, впрочем, там все было ясно с самого начала. Ну, расскажите же, что вы там откопали.

— Вот первая заметка. Она помещена несколько недель назад в «Морнинг пост», в разделе «Хроника светской жизни»: «Состоялась помолвка, и, если верить слухам, в скором времени состоится бракосочетание лорда Роберта Сент-Саймона, второго сына герцога Балморалского, и мисс Хетти Доран, единственной дочери эсквайра Алоизиеса Дорана, из Сан-Франциско, Калифорния, США».

— Коротко и ясно, — заметил Холмс, протягивая поближе к огню свои длинные, тонкие ноги.

— На той же самой неделе в какой-то газете, в светской хронике, был столбец, в котором более подробно говорилось об этой происшествии. Ага, вот он:

«В скором времени понадобится издание закона об охране нашего брачного рынка, ибо принцип свободной торговли, господствующий ныне, весьма вредно отражается на нашей отечественной продукции. Власть над отпрысками благороднейших фамилий Великобритании постепенно переходит в ручки наших прелестных заатлантических кузин. Список трофеев, захваченных очаровательными завоевательницами, пополнился на прошлой неделе весьма ценным приобретением. Лорд Сент-Саймон, который в течение двадцати с лишним лет был неуязвим для стрел Амура, недавно объявил о своем намерении вступить в брак с мисс Хетти Доран, пленительной дочерью калифорнийского миллионера. Мисс Доран, чья грациозная фигура и прелестное лицо произвели фурор на всех празднествах в Вестбери-Хаус, является единственной дочерью, и, по слухам, ее приданое приближается к миллиону, не говоря уже о видах на будущее. Так как ни для кого не секрет, что герцог Балморалский был вынужден за последние годы распродать свою коллекцию картин, а у лорда Сент-Саймона нет собственного состояния, если не считать небольшого поместья в Берчмуре, ясно, что от этого союза, который с легкостью превратит гражданку республики в титулованную английскую леди, выиграет не только калифорнийская наследница».

— Что-нибудь еще? — спросил Холмс, зевая.

— О да, и очень много. Вот другая заметка. В ней говорится, что свадьба будет самая скромная, что венчание состоится в церкви святого Георгия, на Ганновер-сквер, и приглашены будут только пять-шесть самых близких друзей, а потом все общество отправится в меблированный особняк на Ланкастер-гейт, нанятый мистером Алоизиесом Дораном. Два дня спустя, то есть в прошлую среду, появилось краткое сообщение о том, что венчание состоялось и что медовый месяц молодые проведут в поместье лорда Бэкуотера, близ Питерсфилда. Вот и все, что было в газетах до исчезновения невесты.

— Как вы сказали? — спросил Холмс, вскакивая с места.

— До исчезновения новобрачной, — повторил я.

— Когда же она исчезла?

— Во время свадебного обеда.

difference. "Forget this shit," she said. "Some dumbass is playing a prank." Her annoyance was clear in the bite of her words.

Elliot beelined for the digital lock and ran her card. Don't get her started on how the university tracked all activity through their keycards. The front door gave a hum followed by a loud click, and the lock disengaged.

Bat Girl studied Elliot with a narrowed gaze. Ball Cap Girl pulled open the door, rushed in, and held the door open with a back-stretched arm. Elliot and the dude with the basketball hurried into the large foyer.

Elliot took over holding the door and looked back at the girl with the bat. "You coming in?"

Following a moment of hesitation, the girl entered, and they stepped away from the door, letting it go to swing shut. But right before it could latch again, it was jerked open, and in stepped a tall, lanky guy with reddish-brown hair and a scruffy beard. He seemed slightly older than everyone else, with dark circles under his eyes and chewed fingernails. Grad student, maybe? Elliot glanced at his shoes. Black monochrome Chuck Taylors. Not the something in the trees she'd thought she'd seen.

This time the door did click shut. They stood around each other, more than six feet apart. Maybe part habit, maybe part protective instinct. The athlete held his basketball but shifted awkwardly from one foot to the other. He cleared his throat, his gaze bouncing between them.

Bat Girl crossed her arms and glared at Elliot. The bat hung from her hand. "Who are you, and why did you send me this letter? I mean, if we can call it a letter?" Her eyes narrowed farther.

From the corner of Elliot's eye, she caught movement in the trees behind where Bat Girl sat. A flash of white near the ground. Sneakers, maybe? She strained to see more.

The clock tower chimed nine times just as the skies opened up and lightly tossed rain down on them. They were all cutting it close to curfew.

"Crap." Elliot pulled up her hood. She dreaded biking home in the rain. The main road to her apartment had steady traffic, a poorly designated bike path, and no sidewalk. Rain would make it harder for drivers to see her. Not checking the forecast before setting out had been stupid on her part. It wasn't like rain was unexpected in the Pacific Northwest. She'd been so distracted by the letter she'd made a safety error. She would likely have to splurge on an Uber.

Elliot pulled out the lanyard with her student keycard as she scanned the trees once more for whatever had caught her eye. But it was gone. She headed for the front doors.

"Freaking awesome," the athlete said as he looked around, likely for cover.

Ball Cap Girl raced to the front door and pulled repeatedly on the handle. The door didn't budge.

Bat Girl rushed to the front door as well. "Try this." She swiped her keycard through the digital lock.

Ball Cap Girl tugged again. Nothing.

Elliot surveyed the area around them one last time, looking for something to stand out, for more people. There was no telling how many had received the letter. Could one of the three before her be the sender? Only time would tell.

The rain increased, and Elliot fast walked to the front door. Ball Cap Girl had her hands pressed to the glass, trying to look in.

Bat Girl was knocking, as if that was going to make a

— Вот как! Дело становится куда интереснее. Весьма драматично.

— Да, мне тоже показалось, что тут что-то не совсем заурядное.

— Женщины нередко исчезают до брачной церемонии, порою во время медового месяца, но я не могу припомнить ни одного случая, когда бы исчезновение произошло столь скоропалительно. Расскажите мне, пожалуйста, подробности.

— Предупреждаю, что они далеко не полны.

— Ну, может быть, нам самим удастся их пополнить.

— Вчера появилась статья в утренней газете, и это все. Сейчас я прочту вам ее. Заголовок: «Удивительное происшествие на великосветской свадьбе».

«Семья лорда Роберта Сент-Саймона потрясена загадочными и в высшей степени прискорбными событиями, связанными с его женитьбой. Венчание действительно состоялось вчера утром, как об этом коротко сообщалось во вчерашних газетах, но только сегодня мы можем подтвердить странные слухи, упорно циркулирующие в публике. Несмотря на попытки друзей замять происшествие, оно привлекло к себе всеобщее внимание, и теперь уже нет смысла замалчивать то, что сделалось достоянием толпы.

Свадьба была очень скромная и происходила в церкви святого Георгия. Присутствовали только отец невесты — мистер Алоизиес Доран, герцогиня Балморалская, лорд Бэкуотер, лорд Юсташ и леди Клара Сент-Саймон (младшие брат и сестра жениха), а также леди Алисия Уитингтон. После венчания все общество отправилось на Ланкастер-гейт, где в доме мистера Алоизиеса Дорана их ждал обед. По слухам, там имел место небольшой инцидент: неизвестная женщина — ее имя так и не было установлено — пыталась проникнуть в дом вслед за гостями, утверждая, будто у нее есть какие-то права на лорда Сент-Саймона. И только после продолжительной и тяжелой сцены дворецкому и лакею удалось выпроводить эту особу. Невеста, к счастью, вошла в дом до этого неприятного вторжения. Она села за стол вместе с остальными, но вскоре пожаловалась на внезапное недомогание и ушла в свою комнату. Так как она долго не возвращалась, гости начали выражать недоумение. Мистер Алоизиес Доран отправился за дочерью, но ее горничная сообщила, что мисс Хетти заходила в комнату только на минутку, что она накинула длинное дорожное пальто, надела шляпу и быстро пошла к выходу. Один из лакеев подтвердил, что какая-то дама в пальто и в шляпке действительно вышла из дому, но он никак не мог признать в ней свою госпожу, так как был уверен, что та в это время сидит за столом с гостями. Убедившись, что дочь исчезла, мистер Алоизиес Доран немедленно отправился с новобрачным в полицию, и начались энергичные поиски, которые, вероятно, очень скоро прольют свет на это удивительное происшествие. Однако пока что местопребывание исчезнувшей леди не выяснено. Ходят слухи, что тут имеет место шантаж и что женщина, которая разыскивала лорда Сент-Саймона, арестована, ибо полиция предполагает, что из ревности или из иных побуждений она могла быть причастна к таинственному исчезновению новобрачной».

She was ejected by the butler and the footman.

— И это все?

— Есть еще одна заметка в другой утренней газете. Пожалуй, она даст вам кое-что.

— О чем же она?

— О том, что мисс Флора Миллар, виновница скандала, и в самом деле арестована. Кажется, она была прежде танцовщицей в «Аллегро» и встречалась с лордом Сент-Саймоном в течение нескольких лет. Других подробностей нет, так что теперь вам известно все, что напечатано об этом случае в газетах.

— Дело представляется мне чрезвычайно интересным. Я был бы крайне огорчен, если бы оно прошло мимо меня. Но кто-то звонит, Уотсон. Пятый час. Не сомневаюсь, что это идет наш высокородный клиент. Только не вздумайте уходить: мне может понадобиться свидетель, хотя бы на тот случай, если я что-нибудь забуду.

— Лорд Роберт Сент-Саймон! — объявил наш юный слуга, распахивая дверь.

Lord Robert St. Simon.

Вошел джентльмен с приятными тонкими чертами лица, бледный, с крупным носом, с чуть надменным ртом и твердым, открытым взглядом — взглядом человека, которому выпал счастливый жребий повелевать и встречать повиновение. Движения у него были легкие и живые, но из-за некоторой сутулости и манеры сгибать колени при ходьбе он казался старше своих лет. Волосы на висках у него поседели, а когда он снял шляпу с загнутыми полями, обнаружилось, что они, кроме того, сильно поредели на макушке. Его костюм представлял верх изящества, граничившего с фатовством: высокий крахмальный воротничок, черный сюртук с белым жилетом, желтые перчатки, лакированные ботинки и светлые гетры. Он медленно вошел в комнату и огляделся по сторонам, нервно вертя в руке шнурок от золотого лорнета.

— Добрый день, лорд Сент-Саймон, — любезно сказал Холмс, поднимаясь навстречу посетителю. — Садитесь, пожалуйста, сюда, в плетеное кресло. Это мой друг и коллега, доктор Уотсон. Придвиньтесь поближе к огню, и потолкуем о вашем деле…

— … как нельзя более мучительном для меня, мистер Холмс! Я потрясен. Разумеется, вам не раз приходилось вести дела щекотливого свойства, сэр, но вряд ли ваши клиенты принадлежали к такому классу общества, к которому принадлежу я.

— Да, вы правы, это для меня ступень вниз.

— Простите?

— Последним моим клиентом по делу такого рода был король.

— Вот как! Я не знал. Какой же это король?

— Король Скандинавии.

— Как, у него тоже пропала жена?

— Надеюсь, вы понимаете, — самым учтивым тоном произнес Холмс, — что в отношении всех моих клиентов я соблюдаю такую же тайну, какую обещаю и вам.

— О, конечно, конечно! Вы совершенно правы, прошу меня извинить. Что касается моего случая, я готов сообщить вам любые сведения, какие могут помочь вам составить мнение по поводу происшедшего.

— Благодарю вас. Я уже ознакомился с тем, что было в газетах, но не знаю ничего больше. Надо полагать, что можно считать их сообщения верными? Хотя бы вот эту заметку — об исчезновении невесты?

Лорд Сент-Саймон наскоро пробежал заметку.

— Да, это более или менее верно.

— Но для того, чтобы я мог прийти к определеному заключению, мне понадобится ряд дополнительных данных. Пожалуй, лучше будет, если я задам вам несколько вопросов.

— Я к вашим услугам.

— Когда вы познакомились с мисс Хетти Доран?

— Год назад, в Сан-Франциско.

— Вы путешествовали по Соединенным Штатам?

— Да.

— Вы еще там обручились с нею?

— Нет.

— Но вы ухаживали за ней?

— Мне было приятно ее общество, и я этого не скрывал.

— Отец ее очень богат?

— Он считается самым богатым человеком на всем Тихоокеанском побережье.

— А где и как он разбогател?

— На золотых приисках. Еще несколько лет назад у него ничего не было. Потом ему посчастливилось напасть на богатую золотоносную жилу, он удачно поместил капитал и быстро пошел в гору.

— А не могли бы вы обрисовать мне характер молодой леди — вашей супруги? Что она за человек?

Лорд Сент-Саймон начал быстро раскачивать лорнет и посмотрел в огонь.

— Видите ли, мистер Холмс, — сказал он, — моей жене было уже двадцать лет, когда ее отец стал богатым человеком. До того она свободно носилась по прииску и бродила по лесам и горам, так что ее воспитанием занималась скорее природа, чем школа. Настоящая «сорви-голова», как мы называем таких девушек в Англии, натура сильная и свободолюбивая, не скованная никакими традициями. У нее порывистый, я бы даже сказал, бурный характер. Быстро принимает решения и бесстрашно доводит до конца то, что задумала. С другой стороны, я не дал бы ей имени, которое имею честь носить, — тут он с достоинством откашлялся, — если бы не был уверен, что, в сущности, это благороднейшее создание. Я твердо знаю, что она способна на героическое самопожертвование и что все бесчестное ее отталкивает.

— Есть у вас ее фотография?

— Я принес с собой вот это.

Он открыл медальон и показал нам прелестное женское лицо. Это была не фотография, а миниатюра на слоновой кости. Художнику удалось передать прелесть блестящих черных волос, больших темных глаз, изящно очерченного рта. Холмс долго и внимательно рассматривал миниатюру, потом закрыл медальон и вернул его лорду Сент-Саймону.

— А потом молодая девушка приехала в Лондон и вы возобновили знакомство с нею?

— Да, на этот сезон отец привез ее в Лондон, мы начали встречаться, обручились, и вот теперь я женился на ней.

— За ней дали, должно быть, порядочное приданое?

— Прекрасное приданое, но такова традиция в нашей семье.

— И поскольку ваш брак — уже совершившийся факт, оно конечно, останется в вашем распоряжении?

— Право, не знаю. Я не наводил никаких справок на этот счет.

— Ну, понятно. Скажите, виделись вы с мисс Доран накануне свадьбы?

— Да.

— И в каком она была настроении?

— В отличном. Все время строила планы нашей будущей совместной жизни.

— Вот как? Это чрезвычайно любопытно. А утром в день свадьбы?

— Она была очень весела — по крайней мере до конца церемонии.

— А потом вы, стало быть, заметили в ней какую-то перемену?

— Да, по правде говоря, я тогда впервые имел случай убедиться в некоторой неровности ее характера. Впрочем, этот эпизод настолько незначителен, что не стоит о нем и рассказывать. Он не имеет ни малейшего значения.

— Все-таки расскажите, прошу вас.

— Хорошо, но это такое ребячество... Когда мы с ней шли от алтаря, она уронила букет. В этот момент мы как раз поравнялись с передней скамьей, и букет упал под скамью. Произошло минутное замешательство, но какой-то джентльмен, сидевший на скамье, тут же нагнулся и подал ей букет, который ничуть не пострадал. И все-таки, когда я заговорил с ней об этом, она ответила какой-то резкостью и потом, сидя в карете, когда мы ехали домой, казалась до нелепости взволнованной этой ерундой.

The gentleman in the pew handed it up to her.

— Ах вот что! Значит, на скамье сидел какой-то джентльмен? Стало быть, в церкви все-таки была посторонняя публика?

— Ну конечно. Это неизбежно, раз церковь открыта.

— И этот джентльмен не принадлежал к числу знакомых вашей жены?

— О нет! Я только из вежливости назвал его «джентльменом»: судя по виду, это человек не нашего круга. Впрочем, я даже не разглядел его хорошенько. Но, право же, мы отвлекаемся от темы.

— Итак, возвратясь из церкви, леди Сент-Саймон была уже не в таком хорошем расположении духа? Чем она занялась, когда вошла в дом отца?

— Начала что-то рассказывать своей горничной.

— А что представляет собой ее горничная?

— Ее зовут Алиса. Она американка и приехала вместе со своей госпожой из Калифорнии.

— Вероятно она пользуется доверием вашей жены?

— Пожалуй, даже чересчур большим доверием. Мне всегда казалось, что мисс Хетти слишком много ей позволяет. Впрочем, в Америке иначе смотрят на эти вещи.

— Сколько времени продолжался их разговор?

— Кажется, несколько минут. Не знаю, право, я был слишком занят.

— И вы не слышали о чем они говорили?

— Леди Сент-Саймон сказала что-то о «захвате чужого участка». Она постоянно употребляет такого рода жаргонные словечки. Понятия не имею, что она имела в виду.

— Американский жаргон иногда очень выразителен. А что делала ваша жена после разговора со служанкой?

— Пошла в столовую.

— Под руку с вами?

— Нет, одна. Она чрезвычайно независима в таких мелочах. Минут через десять она поспешно встала из-за стола, пробормотала какие-то извинения и вышла из комнаты. Больше я не видел ее.

— Если не ошибаюсь, горничная Алиса показала на допросе, что ее госпожа вошла в свою комнату, накинула на подвенечное платье длинное дорожное пальто, надела шляпку и ушла.

— Совершенно верно. И потом ее видели в Гайд-парке. Она там была с Флорой Миллар — женщиной, которая утром того же дня устроила скандал в доме мистера Дорана. Сейчас она арестована.

— Ах да, расскажите, пожалуйста, об этой молодой особе и о характере ваших отношений.

Лорд Сент-Саймон пожал плечами и поднял брови.

— В течение нескольких лет мы были с ней в дружеских, я бы даже сказал, в очень дружеских отношениях. Она танцевала в «Аллегро». Я обошелся с ней, как подобает благородному человеку, и она не может иметь ко мне никаких претензий, но вы же знаете женщин, мистер Холмс, Флора — очаровательное существо, но она чересчур импульсивна я до безумия влюблена в меня. Узнав, что я собираюсь жениться, она начала писать мне ужасные письма, и, говоря откровенно, я только потому и устроил такую скромную свадьбу, что боялся скандала в церкви. Едва мы успели приехать после венчания, как она прибежала к дому мистера Дорана и сделала попытку проникнуть туда, выкрикивая при этом оскорбления и даже угрозы по адресу моей жены. Однако, предвидя возможность чего-либо в этом роде, я заранее пригласил двух полицейских в штатском, и те быстро выпроводили ее. Как только Флора поняла, что скандалом тут не поможешь, она сразу успокоилась.

— Слышала все это ваша жена?

— К счастью, нет.

— А потом с этой самой женщиной ее видели на улице?

— Да. И вот этот-то факт мистер Лестрейд из Скотланд-Ярда считает тревожным. Он думает, что Флора выманила мою жену из дому и устроила ей какую-нибудь ужасную ловушку.

— Что ж, это не лишено вероятия.

— Значит, и вы того же мнения?

— Вот этого я не сказал. Ну, а сами вы допускаете такую возможность?

— Я убежден, что Флора не способна обидеть и муху.

— Однако ревность иногда совершенно меняет характер человека. Скажите, а каким образом объясняете то, что произошло, вы сами?

— Я пришел сюда не для того, чтобы объяснять что-либо, а чтобы получить объяснение от вас. Я сообщил вам все факты, какими располагал. Впрочем, если вас интересует моя точка зрения, извольте: я допускаю, что возбуждение, которое испытала моя жена в связи с огромной переменой, происшедшей в ее судьбе, в ее общественном положении, могло вызвать у нее легкое нервное расстройство.

— Короче говоря, вы полагаете, что она внезапно потеряла рассудок?

— Если хотите, да. Когда я думаю, что она могла отказаться... не от меня, нет, но от всего того, о чем тщетно мечтали многие другие женщины, мне трудно найти иное объяснение.

— Что же, и это тоже вполне приемлемая гипотеза, — ответил Холмс улыбаясь. — Теперь, лорд Сент-Саймон, у меня, пожалуй, есть почти все нужные сведения. Скажите только одно: могли вы, сидя за свадебном столом, видеть в окно то, что происходило на улице?

— Нам виден был противоположный тротуар и парк.

— Отлично. Итак, у меня, пожалуй, больше нет необходимости вас задерживать. Я напишу вам.

— Только бы вам посчастливилось разрешить эту загадку! — сказал наш клиент, поднимаясь с места.

— Я уже разрешил ее.

— Что? Я, кажется, ослышался.

— Я сказал, что разрешил эту загадку.

— В таком случае, где же моя жена?

— Очень скоро я отвечу вам и на этот вопрос.

Лорд Сент-Саймон нахмурился.

— Боюсь, что над этим делом еще немало помучаются и более мудрые головы, чем у нас с вами, — заметил он и, церемонно поклонившись, с достоинством удалился.

Шерлок Холмс засмеялся:

— Лорд Сент-Саймон оказал моей голове большую честь, поставив ее на один уровень со своей!.. Знаете что, я не прочь бы выпить виски с содовой и выкурить сигару после этого длительного допроса. А заключение по данному делу сложилось у меня еще до того, как наш клиент вошел в комнату.

— Полноте, Холмс!

— В моих заметках есть несколько аналогичных случаев, хотя, как я уже говорил вам, ни одно из тех исчезновений не было столь скоропалительным. Беседа же с лордом Сент-Саймоном превратила мои предположения в уверенность. Побочные обстоятельства бывают иногда так же красноречивы, как муха в молоке, — если вспомнить Торо.[1]

— Однако, Холмс, ведь я присутствовал при разговоре и слышал то же, что слышали и вы.

— Да, но вы не знаете тех случаев, которые уже имели место и которые сослужили мне отличную службу. Почти такая же история произошла несколько лет назад в Абердине и нечто очень похожее — в Мюнжене, на следующий год после франко-прусской войны. Данный случай… А, вот и Лестрейд! Здравствуйте, Лестрейд! Вон там, на буфете, вино, а здесь, в ящике, сигары.

Официальный сыщик Скотланд-Ярда был облачен в куртку и носил на шее шарф, что делало его похожим на моряка. В руке он держал черный парусиновый саквояж. Отрывисто поздоровавшись, он опустился на стул и закурил предложенную сигару.

— Ну, выкладывайте, что случилось? — спросил Холмс с лукавым огоньком в глазах. — У вас недовольный вид.

— И я действительно недоволен. Черт бы побрал этого Сент-Саймона с его свадьбой! Ничего не могу понять.

— Неужели? Вы удивляете меня.

---

[1] Цитата взята из дневника американского писателя Генри Давида Торо (1817-1862).

— В жизни не встречал более запутанной истории. Не найти никаких концов. Сегодня я провозился с ней весь день.

— И, кажется, при этом изрядно промокли, — сказал Холмс, дотрагиваясь до рукава куртки.

— Да, я обшаривал дно Серпентайна.[1]

— О, Господи! Да зачем вам это понадобилось?

— Чтобы найти тело леди Сент-Саймон.

«There,» said he.

Шерлок Холмс откинулся на спинку кресла и от души расхохотался.

— А бассейн фонтана на Трафальгард-сквер вы не забыли обшарить? — спросил он.

— На Трафальгард-сквер? Что вы хотите этим сказать?

— Да то, что у вас точно такие же шансы найти леди Сент-Саймон здесь, как и там.

Лестрейд бросил сердитый взгляд на моего друга.

— Как видно, вы уже разобрались в этом деле? — насмешливо спросил он.

---

[1] Серпентайн (Змейка) — пруд в Гайд-парке, в Лондоне.

— Мне только что рассказали о нем, но я уже пришел к определенному выводу.

— Неужели! Так вы считаете, что Серпентайн тут ни при чем?

— Полагаю, что так.

— В таком случае, прошу объяснить, каким образом мы могли найти в пруду вот это.

Он открыл саквояж и выбросил на пол шелковое подвенечное платье, пару белых атласных туфелек и веночек с вуалью — все грязное и совершенно мокрое.

— Извольте! — сказал Лестрейд, кладя на эту кучу новенькое обручальное кольцо. — Раскусите-ка этот орешек, мистер Холмс!

— Вот оно что! — сказал Холмс, выпуская сизые кольца дыма. — И все эти вещи вы выудили в пруду?

— Они плавали у самого берега, их нашел сторож парка. Родственники леди Сент— Саймон опознали и платье и все остальное. По-моему, если там была одежда, то где— нибудь поблизости найдется и тело.

— Если исходить из этой остроумной теории, тело каждого человека должно быть найдено рядом с его одеждой. Так чего же вы надеетесь добиться с помощью вещей леди Сент-Саймон, хотел бы я знать?

— Какой-нибудь улики, доказывающей, что в ее исчезновении замешана Флора Миллар.

— Боюсь, это будет нелегко.

— Боитесь? — с горечью вскричал Лестрейд. — А я, Холмс, боюсь, что вы совсем оторвались от жизни с вашими вечными теориями и умозаключениями. За несколько минут вы сделали две грубые ошибки. Вот это самое платье, несомненно, уличает мисс Флору Миллар.

— Каким же образом?

— В платье есть карман. В кармане нашелся футляр для визитных карточек. А в футляре — записка. Вот она. — Он расправил записку на столе. — Сейчас я прочту ее вам: «Увидимся, когда все будет готово.

Выходите немедленно. Ф. Х. М.». Я с самого начала предполагал, что Флора Миллар под каким-нибудь предлогом выманила леди Сент-Саймон из дому и, разумеется, вместе с сообщниками является виновницей ее исчезновения. И вот перед нами записка — записка с ее инициалами, которую она, несомненно сунула леди Сент-Саймон у дверей дома, чтобы завлечь ее в свои сети.

— Отлично, Лестрейд, — со смехом сказал Холмс. — Право же, вы очень ловко все это придумали. Покажите-ка записку.

Он небрежно взял в руку бумажку, но что-то в ней вдруг приковало его внимание.

— Да, это действительно очень важно! — сказал он с довольным видом.

— Ага! Теперь убедились?

— Чрезвычайно важно! Сердечно поздравляю вас, Лестрейд.

Торжествующий Лестрейд вскочил и наклонился над запиской.

— Что это? — изумился он. — Ведь вы смотрите не на ту сторону?

— Нет, я смотрю именно туда, куда нужно.

— Да вы с ума сошли! Переверните бумажку. Записка-то ведь написана карандашом на обороте!

— Зато здесь я вижу обрывок счета гостиницы, который весьма интересует меня.

— Ничего в нем нет особенного! Я уже видел его: «Окт. 4-го. Комната — 8 шил. Завтрак — 2 шил.6 пенс. Коктейль — 1 шил. Ленч — 2 шил. 6 пенс. Стакан хереса — 8 пенс». Вот и все. Не вижу ничего интересного.

— Вполне возможно, что не видите. А между тем этот счет имеет большое значение. Что касается записки, она тоже имеет значение, во всяком случае, ее инициалы. Так что поздравляю вас еще раз, Лестрейд.

— Ну, хватит терять время! — сказал тот, поднимаясь с места. — Я, знаете ли, считаю, что надо работать, а не сидеть у камина и разводить разные там теории. До свидания, мистер Холмс. Посмотрим, кто первым доберется до сути этого дела.

Он собрал принесенную одежду, сунул ее в саквояж и направился к двери.

— Два слова, Лестрейд, — медленно произнес Холмс, обращаясь к спине своего уходящего соперника. — Я могу вам открыть разгадку вашего дела. Леди Сент-Саймон — миф. Ее нет и никогда не было.

Лестрейд обернулся и с грустью взглянул на моего друга. Потом он посмотрел на меня, трижды постучал пальцем по лбу, многозначительно покачал головой и поспешно вышел.

Как только за ним закрылась дверь, Холмс встал и надел пальто.

— В том, что сказал этот субъект, есть доля истины, — заметил он. — Нельзя все время сидеть дома, надо работать. Поэтому, Уотсон, я должен ненадолго оставить вас наедине с вашими газетами.

Шерлок Холмс покинул меня в половине шестого, но я недолго оставался в одиночестве, ибо не прошло и часа, как к нам явился посыльный из гастрономического магазина с большущей коробкой. С помощью мальчика, пришедшего с ним вместе, он распаковал ее, и, к моему великому удивлению, на скромном обеденном столе нашей квартирки появился роскошный холодный ужин. Здесь была парочка холодных вальдшнепов, фазан, паштет из гусиной печенки и несколько пыльных, покрытых паутиной бутылок старого вина. Расставив все эти лакомые блюда, оба посетителя исчезли, подобно духами из «Тысячи и одной ночи», успев сказать только, что за все уплачено и велено доставить по этому адресу.

Около девяти в комнату бодрыми шагами вошел Холмс. Лицо его было серьезно, но в глазах блестел огонек, по которому я сразу угадал, что он не обманулся в своих догадках.

— А, ужин уже на столе! — сказал он, потирая руки.

— Вы, значит, ждете гостей? Они накрыли на пять персон.

— Да, я думаю, что к нам может кое-кто зайти, — ответил он. — Странно, что лорда Сент-Саймона еще нет… Ага! Кажется, я слышу на лестнице его шаги.

Он не ошибся. В комнату быстро вошел наш утренний посетитель, еще сильнее прежнего раскачивая висевший на шнурке лорнет. На его аристократическом лице отражалось сильнейшее смятение.

— Стало быть, мой посыльный застал вас дома? — спросил Холмс.

— Да, но признаюсь, содержание письма поразило меня сверх всякой меры. Есть ли у вас доказательства того, что вы сообщили?

— Есть, и самые веские.

Лорд Сент-Саймон опустился в кресло и провел рукой по лбу.

— Что скажет герцог! — прошептал он. — Что он скажет, когда услышит об унижении, которому подвергся один из членов его семьи!

— Но ведь тут чистейшая случайность. Я никак не могу согласиться, что в этом есть что-нибудь унизительное.

— Ах, вы смотрите на такие вещи с другой точки зрения!

— Я решительно не вижу здесь ничьей вины. Мне кажется, эта леди просто не могла поступить иначе. Конечно, она действовала чересчур стремительно, но ведь у нее нет матери — ей не с кем было посоветоваться в критическую минуту.

— Это оскорбление, сэр, публичное оскорбление! — сказал лорд Сент-Саймон, барабаня пальцами по столу.

— Однако вы должны принять в расчет то исключительно положение, в котором оказалась бедная молодая девушка.

— Я не собираюсь принимать в расчет что бы то ни было. Со мной поступили бесчестно. Я просто вне себя.

— Кажется, звонят, — заметил Холмс. — Да, я слышу шаги на площадке… Что ж, если я не в силах убедить, вас, лорд Сент-Саймон, более снисходительно отнестись ко всему случившемуся, то, может быть, это скорее удастся адвокату, которого я пригласил.

Холмс распахнул дверь и впустил в комнату даму и господина.

— Лорд Сент-Саймон, — сказал он, — позвольте представить вас мистеру и миссис Фрэнсис Хей Маултон. С миссис Маултон вы, кажется, уже знакомы.

При виде новых посетителей наш клиент вскочил с места. Он стоял выпрямившись, опустив глаза, заложив руку за борт сюртука, — воплощение оскорбленного достоинства. Дама подбежала к нему и протянула руку, но он упорно не поднимал глаз. Так было, пожалуй, лучше для него, если он хотел остаться непреклонным: вряд ли кто-нибудь мог бы устоять перед ее умоляющим взглядом.

A picture of offended dignity.

— Вы сердитесь, Роберт? — сказала она. — Что ж, я понимаю, вы не можете не сердиться.

— Сделайте одолжение, не оправдывайтесь, — с горечью произнес лорд Сент-Саймон.

— Да, да, я знаю, я виновата, мне надо было поговорить с вами перед тем, как уйти, но я словно обезумела и с той самой минуты, как вдруг увидела Фрэнка, уже не сознавала, что делаю и что говорю. Удивительно еще, как это я не упала в обморок перед алтарем!

— Быть может, сударыня, вам угодно, чтобы мы — я и мой друг удалились на то время, пока вы будете объясняться с лордом Сент-Саймоном? — спросил Холмс.

— Если мне будет позволено высказать мое мнение, — вмешался мистер Маултон, — я скажу, что хватит делать тайну из этой истории. Что до меня, так я бы хотел, чтобы вся Европа и вся Америка услышали наконец правду.

Маултон был крепкий, загорелый молодой человек небольшого роста, с резкими чертами лица и быстрыми движениями.

— Ну хорошо, тогда я расскажу, как было дело, — сказала его спутница. — Мы с Фрэнком познакомились в 1881 году на прииске Мак-Квайра, близ Скалистых гор, где папа разрабатывал участок. Мы дали друг другу слово. Но вот однажды папа напал на богатую золотоносную жилу и разбогател, а участок бедного Фрэнка все истощался и в конце концов совсем перестал что-либо давать. Чем богаче становился папа, тем беднее становился Фрэнк. Папа теперь и слышать не хотел о нашем обручении и увез меня во Фриско. Но Фрэнк не сдавался. Он поехал за мной во Фриско, и мы продолжали видеться без ведома папы. Папа страшно рассердился бы, если б узнал об этом, поэтому мы и решили все сами. Фрэнк сказал, что он уедет и тоже наживет состояние и что приедет за мной только тогда, когда у него будет столько же денег, сколько у папы. А я пообещала, что буду ждать его, сколько бы ни понадобилось, и не выйду замуж за другого, пока он жив. «Если так, — сказал мне Фрэнк, — почему бы нам не обвенчаться теперь же? Я буду уверен в тебе, а твоим мужем стану лишь тогда, когда вернусь». Так мы и решили. Он отлично все устроил, священник обвенчал нас, и Фрэнк уехал искать счастья, а я вернулась к папе.

Через некоторое время я узнала, что Френк в Монтане. Потом он уехал искать золото в Аризону, а следующее известие о нем я получила уже из Нью-Мексико. Потом появилась длинная газетная статья о нападении на прииски индейцев-апачей, и в списке убитых было имя моего Фрэнка. Я потеряла сознание и потом несколько месяцев была тяжело больна. Папа уже думал, что у меня чахотка, и водил меня по всем докторам Фриско. Больше года я ни слова не слыхала о Фрэнке и была совершенно уверена, что он умер. Тут во Фриско приехал лорд Сент-Саймон, потом мы с папой поехали в Лондон, была решена свадьба, и папа был очень доволен, но я все время чувствовала, что ни один мужчина в мире не может занять в моем сердце то место, какое я отдала моему Фрэнку.

И все-таки, если бы я вышла замуж за лорда Сент-Саймона, я была бы ему верной женой. Мы не вольны в нашей любви, но управлять своими поступками в нашей власти. Я шла с ним к алтарю с твердым намерением исполнить свой долг, насколько это было в моих силах. Но вообразите себе, что я почувствовала, когда, подойдя к алтарю и оглянувшись, вдруг увидела Фрэнка. Он стоял возле первой скамьи и смотрел прямо на меня. Сначала я подумала, что это призрак. Но когда я оглянулась снова, он по-прежнему стоял там и взглядом словно спрашивал, рада я, что вижу его, или нет. Удивляюсь, как я не упала в обморок. Все кружилось передо мной, и слова священника доносились до меня, точно жужжание пчелы. Я не знала, как быть. Остановить брачную церемонию, решиться на скандал в церкви? Я снова взглянула на него и, должно быть, он прочитал мои мысли, потому что приложил палец к губам, как бы советуя молчать. Потом я увидела, как он торопливо пишет что-то на клочке бумаги, и поняла, что эта записка предназначалась мне. Проходя мимо него я уронила букет, и он, возвращая цветы, успел сунуть мне в руку записку. В ней было всего несколько слов: он просил, чтобы я вышла к нему, как только он подаст знак. У меня, конечно, не было и тени сомнения, что теперь мой главный долг — повиноваться ему и делать все, что он скажет.

Придя домой, я все рассказала моей служанке, которая знала Фрэнка еще в Калифорнии и очень любила его. Я велела ей молчать обо всем, сложить кое-что из самых необходимых вещей и приготовить мне пальто. Я знаю, мне следовало бы поговорить с лордом Сент-Саймоном, но это было так трудно в присутствии его матери и всех этих важных гостей! И я решила, что сначала убегу, а потом уже объяснюсь с ним. Мы просидели за столом минут десять, не больше, я вот, глядя в окно, я увидела Фрэнка, стоявшего на противоположном тротуаре. Он кивнул мне и зашагал по направлению к парку. Я вышла из столовой, накинула пальто и пошла вслед за ним. На улице ко мне подошла какая-то женщина и начала рассказывать что-то о лорде Сент-Саймоне. Я почти не слушала ее, но все же уловила, что у него тоже была какая-то тайна до нашей женитьбы. Вскоре мне удалось отделаться от этой женщины, и я нагнала Фрэнка. Мы сели в кэб и поехали на Гордон-сквер, где он успел снять квартиру, и это была моя настоящая свадьба после стольких лет ожидания. Фрэнк, оказывается, попал в плен к апачам, бежал, приехал во Фриско, узнал, что я, считая его умершим, уехала в Англию, поспешил вслед за мной сюда и наконец разыскал меня как раз в день моей второй свадьбы.

Some woman came talking about Lord St. Simon.

— Я прочитал о венчании в газетах, — пояснил американец. — Там было указано название церкви и имя невесты, но не было ее адреса.

— Потом мы начали советоваться, как нам поступить. Фрэнк с самого начала стоял за то, чтобы ничего не скрывать, но мне было так стыдно, что захотелось исчезнуть и никогда больше не встречать никого из этих людей, разве только написать несколько слов папе, чтоб он знал, что я жива и здорова. Я с ужасом представляла себе, как все эти лорды и леди сидят за свадебным столом и ждут моего возвращения. Итак, Фрэнк взял мое подвенечное платье и остальные вещи, связал их в узел, чтобы никто не мог выследить меня, и отнес в такое место, где никто не мог бы их найти. По всей вероятности, мы завтра же уехали бы в Париж, если бы сегодня к нам не пришел этот милый джентльмен, мистер Холмс, хотя каким чудом он нас нашел, просто уму непостижимо. Он доказал нам — очень убедительно и мягко, — что я была не права, а Фрэнк прав и что мы сами себе повредим, если будем скрываться. Потом он сказал, что может предоставить нам возможность поговорить с лордом Сент-Саймоном без свидетелей, и вот мы здесь. Теперь, Роберт, вы знаете все. Мне очень, очень жаль, если я причинила вам горе, но я надеюсь, что вы будете думать обо мне не так уж плохо.

Лорд Сент-Саймон слушал этот длинный рассказ все с тем же напряженным и холодным видом. Брови его были нахмурены, а губы сжаты.

— Прошу извинить меня, — сказал он, — но не в моих правилах обсуждать самые интимные свои дела в присутствии посторонних.

— Так вы не хотите простить меня? Не хотите пожать мне руку на прощание?

— Нет, почему же, если это может доставить вам удовольствие.

И он холодно пожал протянутую ему руку.

— Я полагал, — начал было Холмс, — что вы не откажетесь поужинать с нами.

— Право, вы требуете от меня слишком многого, — возразил достойный лорд. — Я вынужден примириться с обстоятельствами, но вряд ли можно ожидать, чтобы я стал радоваться тому, что произошло. С вашего позволения, я пожелаю вам приятного вечера.

Он сделал общий поклон и торжественно удалился.

«I will wish you all very good-night.»

— Но вы-то, надеюсь, удостоите меня своим обществом, — сказал Шерлок Холмс. — Мне, мистер Маултон, всегда приятно видеть американца, ибо я из тех, кто верит, что недомыслие монарха и ошибки министра,[1] имевшего место в давно минувшие годы, не помешают нашим детям превратиться когда-нибудь в граждан некой огромной страны, у которой будет единый флаг — англо-американский.

— Интересный выдался случай, — заметил Холмс, когда гости ушли. — Он с очевидностью доказывает, как просто можно иной раз объяснить факты, которые на первый взгляд представляются почти необъяснимыми. Что может быть проще и естественнее ряда событий, о которых нам рассказала молодая леди? И что может быть удивительнее тех выводов, которые легко сделать, если смотреть на вещи, скажем, с точки зрения мистера Лестрейда из Скотланд-Ярда!

— Так вы, значит, были на правильном пути с самого начала?

— Для меня с самого начала были очевидны два факта: первый — что невеста шла к венцу совершенно добровольно и второй — что

---

[1] Холмс имеет в виду английского короля Георга III (1738-1820) и премьер-министра Фредерика-Норта (1732-1792). Политика Георга III и Норта привела к конфликту, а затем к войне с американскими колониями.

place and got cozy with those they were forced to quarantine with.

The Thompson Building stood three stories tall and ran the length of a football field. Elliot knew this because the football stadium was directly behind the building. Large double doors were at the center and seemed to welcome anyone with a curious mind. Though, as with any building on campus, a person had to have the proper keycard to swipe if they wanted to enter.

Staying within the glow of the streetlights, Elliot approached the building and surveyed the three people lingering. One was a girl leaning against the building by the doors, her attention on her phone. She was shorter than Elliot's five feet five, dressed in baggy sweatpants and an oversized hoodie with her hair pulled back into a rhinestone-covered ball cap.

The second, a guy, was a multisport athlete. A message he broadcasted in both his dress and actions. He wore a school baseball jersey and spun a basketball on his finger, stopping to occasionally dribble it between his legs. His attention jumped between the building and the seven-story clock tower that stood at the center of campus, half a block away.

Sitting on a bench talking on her phone was a dark-haired girl. She lightly tapped a worn, sticker-covered baseball bat against the concrete next to her feet. She was the third person. Not an athlete; the bat was for protection. Elliot figured the girl had walked to the Thompson Building, which meant she likely lived in one of the sororities a few blocks away.

Elliot debated if she should approach them or wait to see if someone else took charge.

didn't strike Elliot as odd. She didn't know who sent the letter, but she figured it had to be another journalism student. Someone studying investigative journalism, like herself. Maybe a senior like Joe Lennox, looking to finish their senior project and using this clever and intriguing letter to rope in subjects. Sending an anonymous letter was totally something he would do. To what end? Elliot didn't know.

She hurried to lock her bike, wishing the bike rack was closer to the building's entrance, not off to the side in a hard-to-see area under a cluster of trees. Ever since Jaime Sullivan's murder, the campus had a restless, uneasy vibe, resulting in a person often looking over their shoulder and quickening their steps, even in broad daylight. Whether due to the violent nature of Jaime's death, the unnerving reality that a killer had gained access to one of the most secure dorms on campus without being detected, or because crime on campus in general had escalated wasn't clear. But campus life had changed after that night. An undebatable fact.

Tonight marked six months to the day of Jaime's death, which only added to the campus edginess. South Washington University administration continued its chokehold on campus life, restricting the return to normal with ongoing ten p.m. curfews and closing the late-night study halls at dusk, rendering their name an oxymoron. Weekend evening campus activities were quashed except for sporting events that were allowed because they could afford to pay for security. A growing number of students were objecting to the restrictions, mostly guys. The violent nature of Sullivan's death tended to leave the students, female ones for sure, nervous about venturing out. Instead, gatherings happened in dorms and the backyards of sororities and fraternities. Like when the pandemic hit, people hunkered down in немедленно после венчания она уже раскаивалась о своем поступке. Ясно как день, что за это время произошло нечто, вызвавшее в ней такую перемену. Что же это могло быть? Разговаривать с кем-либо вне дома у нее не было возможности, потому что жених ни на секунду не расставался с нею. Но, может быть, она встретила кого-нибудь? Если так, это мог быть только какой-нибудь американец: ведь в Англии она совсем недавно и вряд ли кто-нибудь здесь успел приобрести над ней такое огромное влияние, чтобы одним своим появлением заставить ее изменить все планы. Итак, методом исключения мы уже пришли к выводу, что она встретила какого-то американца. Но кто же он был, этот американец, и почему встреча с ним так подействовала на нее? По-видимому, это был либо возлюбленный, либо муж. Юность девушки прошла, как известно, среди суровых людей в весьма своеобразной обстановке. Все это я понял еще до рассказа лорда Сент-Саймона. А когда он сообщил нам о мужчине, оказавшемся в церкви, о том, как невеста переменила свое обращение с ним самим, как она уронила букет — испытанный способ получения записок, — о разговоре леди Сент-Саймон с любимой горничной и о ее многозначительном намеке на «захват чужого участка» (а на языке золотопромышленников это означает посягательство на то, чем уже завладел другой), все стало для меня совершенно ясно. Она сбежала с мужчиной, и этот мужчина был либо ее возлюбленным, либо мужем, причем последнее казалось более вероятным.

— Но каким чудом вам удалось разыскать их?

— Это, пожалуй, было бы трудновато, но мой друг Лестрейд, сам того не понимая, оказался обладателем ценнейшей информации. Инициалы, разумеется, тоже имели большое значение, но еще важнее было узнать, что на этой неделе человек с такими инициалами останавливался в одной из лучших лондонских гостиниц.

— А как вы установили, что это была одна из лучших?

— Очень просто: по ценам. Восемь шиллингов за номер и восемь пенсов за стакан хереса берут только в первоклассных гостиницах, а их в Лондоне не так много. Уже во второй гостинице, которую я посетил, на Нортумберленд-авеню, я узнал из книги для приезжающих, что некто мистер Фрэнсис X. Маултон, из Америки, выехал оттуда как раз накануне. А просмотрев его счета, я нашел те самые цифры, которые видел в копии счета. Свою корреспонденцию он распорядился пересылать по адресу: Гордон-сквер, 226, куда я и направился. Мне посчастливилось застать влюбленную пару дома, и я отважился дать молодым несколько отеческих советов. Мне удалось доказать им, что они только выиграют, если разъяснят широкой публике и особенно лорду Сент-Саймону, создавшееся положения Я пригласил их сюда, пообещав им встречу с лордом, и, как видите, мне удалось убедить его явиться на это свидание

— Но результаты не блестящи, — заметил я. — Он бы не слишком любезен.

— Ах, Уотсон, — с улыбкой возразил мне Холмс, — пожалуй, вы тоже были бы не слишком любезны, если бы после всех хлопот, связанных с ухаживанием и со свадьбой, оказались вдруг и без жены, и без состояния. По-моему, мы должны быть крайне снисходительны к лорду Сент-Саймону и благодарить судьбу за то, что, по всей видимости, никогда не окажемся в его положении... Передайте мне скрипку и садитесь поближе. Ведь теперь у нас осталась неразгаданной только одна проблема — как мы будем убивать время в эти темные осенние вечера.

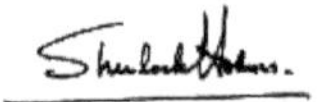

БЕРИЛЛОВАЯ ДИАДЕМА

— Посмотрите-ка, Холмс, — сказал я. — Какой-то сумасшедший бежит. Не понимаю, как родные отпускают такого без присмотра.

Я стоял у сводчатого окна нашей комнаты и глядел вниз, на Бейкер-стрит.

Холмс лениво поднялся с кресла, встал у меня за спиной и, засунув руки в карманы халата, взглянул в окно.

Было ясное февральское утро. Выпавший вчера снег лежал плотным слоем, сверкая в лучах зимнего солнца. На середине улицы снег превратился в бурую грязную массу, но по обочинам он оставался белым, как будто только что выпал. Хотя тротуары уже очистили, было все же очень скользко, и пешеходов на улице было меньше, чем обычно. Сейчас на улице на всем протяжении от станции подземки до нашего дома находился только один человек. Его эксцентричное поведение и привлекло мое внимание.

Это был мужчина лет пятидесяти, высокий, солидный, с широким энергичным лицом и представительной фигурой. Одет он был богато, но не броско: блестящий цилиндр, темный сюртук из дорогого материала, хорошо сшитые светло-серые брюки и коричневые гетры. Однако все его поведение решительно не соответствовало его внешности и одежде. Он бежал, то и дело подскакивая, как человек, не привыкший к физическим упражнениям, размахивал руками, вертел головой, лицо его искажалось гримасами.

— Что с ним? — недоумевал я. — Он, кажется, ищет какой-то дом.

— Я думаю, что он спешит сюда, — сказал Холмс, потирая руки.

— Сюда?

— Да. Полагаю, ему нужно посоветоваться со мной. Все признаки налицо. Ну, прав я был или нет?

В это время незнакомец, тяжело дыша, кинулся к нашей двери и принялся судорожно дергать колокольчик, огласив звоном весь дом.

Через минуту он вбежал в комнату, едва переводя дух и жестикулируя. В глазах у него затаилось такое горе и отчаяние, что наши улыбки погасли и насмешка уступила место глубокому сочувствию и жалости. Сначала он не мог вымолвить ни слова, только раскачивался взад и вперед и хватал себя за голову, как человек, доведенный до грани сумасшествия. Вдруг он бросился к стене и ударился о нее головой. Мы кинулись к нашему посетителю и оттащили его на середину комнаты. Холмс усадил несчастного в кресло, сам сел напротив и, похлопав его по руке, заговорил так мягко и успокаивающе, как никто, кроме него, не умел.

With look of grief and despair.

— Вы пришли ко мне, чтобы рассказать, что с вами случилось? — сказал он. — Вы утомились от быстрой ходьбы. Успокойтесь, придите в себя, и я с радостью выслушаю вас, что вы имеете сказать.

Незнакомцу потребовалась минута или больше того, чтобы отдышаться и побороть волнение. Наконец он провел платком по лбу, решительно сжал губы и повернулся к нам.

Is There a *Killer* Among Us?

Do you feel safe on campus? In your dorm?

Nursing student Jaime Sullivan was raped then strangled in her dorm. The campus police responded by adding a few extra patrols at night. The Sheriff's Department has moved on. Jaime Sullivan is an unsolved case. Soon to be cold and forgotten. How does that make you feel?

Who out there cares enough about those who no longer have a voice? You?

But do you care enough to make a difference?

Come Thursday the 13th Journalism Building 9 p.m.

Elliot Long knew she had to go. The thought of one more unsolved case made her blood boil. Sure, the last two years of therapy had helped her cope with her loss, but there was no reconciling the lack of justice. Besides, she had the perfect cover. She would show up at the Thompson Journalism Building at nine p.m. Thursday to check things out. If she got a bad vibe from who was gathered there, if the scene felt sketchy, she'd continue into the building like that had been her plan all along. She had every right to be in the building. She was, after all, a journalism major, and the building was literally her home away from home. Not that her tiny studio apartment could be called home. It was simply where she stored her stuff, microwaved an occasional meal, and slept. The Thompson Journalism Building was her happy place. Each Wednesday, she produced a podcast called *Ask Why* with a handful of her classmates and was often in the building long into the night. So she totally knew how the building should feel at nine p.m.

Using the Thompson Building as the meeting place

1

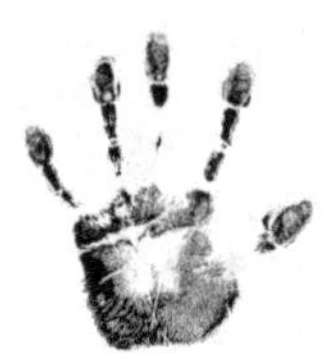

The challenge came as a letter, stuffed among the magazines and flyers in their mailboxes. There was no postage. No address for the sender or recipient. Just their names scrawled across the front in a thin, jagged cursive. Inside was a single sheet of paper. At the top was an image of a red splatter, the word *murder,* and a magnifying glass. The paper could easily have been mistaken for a cheap advertising flyer, an old-school practice gone the way of the dinosaur as smartphones and tablets became the primary source for information and advertising.

— Вы, конечно, сочли меня за сумасшедшего? — спросил он.

— Нет, но я вижу, что с вами стряслась беда, — ответил Холмс.

— Да, видит Бог! Беда такая неожиданная и страшная, что можно сойти с ума. Я вынес бы бесчестье, хотя на моей совести нет ни единого пятнышка. Личное несчастье — это случается с каждым. Но одновременно и то и другое, да еще в такой ужасной форме! Кроме того, это касается не только меня. Если не будет немедленно найден выход из моего бедственного положения, может пострадать одна из знатнейших персон нашей страны.

— Успокойтесь, сэр, прошу вас, — сказал Холмс. — Расскажите, кто вы и что с вами случилось.

— Мое имя, возможно, известно вам, — проговорил посетитель. — Я Александр Холдер из банкирского дома «Холдер и Стивенсон» на Тренидл-стрит.

Действительно, имя было хорошо знакомо нам; оно принадлежало старшему компаньону второй по значению банкирской фирмы в Лондоне. Что же привело в такое жалкое состояние одного из виднейших граждан столицы? Мы с нетерпением ждали ответа на этот вопрос. Огромным усилием воли Холдер взял себя в руки и приступил к рассказу.

— Я понимаю, что нельзя терять ни минуты. Как только полицейский инспектор порекомендовал мне обратиться к вам, я немедленно поспешил сюда. Я добрался до Бейкер-стрит подземкой и всю дорогу от станции бежал: по такому снегу кэбы движутся очень медленно. Я вообще мало двигаюсь и потому так запыхался. Но сейчас мне стало лучше, и я постараюсь изложить все факты как можно короче и яснее.

Вам, конечно, известно, что в банковском деле очень многое зависит от умения удачно вкладывать средства и в то же время расширять клиентуру. Один из наиболее выгодных способов инвестирования средств — выдача ссуд под солидное обеспечение. За последние годы мы немало успели в этом отношении. Мы ссужаем крупными суммами знатные семейства под обеспечение картинами, фамильными библиотеками, сервизами.

Вчера утром я сидел в своем кабинете в банке, и кто-то из клерков принес мне визитную карточку. Я вздрогнул, прочитав имя, потому что это был не кто иной, как... Впрочем, пожалуй, даже вам я не решусь его назвать. Это имя известно всему миру; имя одной из самых высокопоставленных и знатных особ Англии. Я был ошеломлен оказанной мне честью, и когда он вошел, хотел было выразить свои чувства высокому посетителю. Но он прервал меня: ему, видно, хотелось как можно быстрее уладить неприятное для него дело.

— Мистер Холдер, я слышал, что вы предоставляете ссуды.

— Да. Фирма дает ссуды под надежные гарантии, — отвечал я.

— Мне совершенно необходимы пятьдесят тысяч фунтов стерлингов, и притом немедленно, — заявил он. — Конечно, такую небольшую сумму я мог бы одолжить у своих друзей, но я предпочитаю сделать этот заем в деловом порядке. И я вынужден сам заниматься этим. Вы, конечно, понимаете, что человеку моего положения неудобно вмешивать в это дело посторонних.

— Позвольте узнать, на какой срок вам нужны деньги? — осведомился я.

— В будущий понедельник мне вернут крупную сумму денег, и я погашу вашу ссуду с уплатой любого процента. Но мне крайне важно получить деньги сразу.

— Я был бы счастлив безоговорочно дать вам деньги из своих личных средств, но это довольно крупная сумма, так что придется сделать это от имени фирмы. Элементарная справедливость по отношению к моему компаньону требует, чтобы я принял меры деловой предосторожности.

— Иначе и быть не может, — сказал он и взял в руки квадратный футляр черного сафьяна, который перед тем положил на стол возле себя. — Вы, конечно, слышали о знаменитой берилловой диадеме?

— Разумеется. Это — национальное достояние.

— Совершенно верно. — Он открыл футляр — на мягком розовом бархате красовалось великолепнейшее произведение ювелирного искусства.

— В диадеме тридцать девять крупных бериллов, — сказал он. — Ценность золотой оправы не поддается исчислению. Самая минимальная ее стоимость вдвое выше нужной мне суммы. Я готов оставить диадему у вас.

Я взял в руки футляр с драгоценной диадемой и с некоторым колебанием поднял глаза на своего именитого посетителя.

— Вы сомневаетесь в ценности диадемы? — улыбнулся он.

— О, что вы, я сомневаюсь лишь…

— …удобно ли мне оставить эту диадему вам? Можете не беспокоиться. Мне эта мысль и в голову не пришла, не будь я абсолютно убежден, что через четыре дня получу диадему обратно. Пустая формальность! Ну, а само обеспечение вы считаете удовлетворительным?

— Вполне.

— Вы, разумеется, понимаете, мистер Холдер, что мой поступок — свидетельство глубочайшего доверия, которое я питаю к вам. Это доверие основано на том, что я знаю о вас. Я рассчитываю на вашу скромность, на то, что вы воздержитесь от каких-либо разговоров о диадеме. Прошу вас также беречь ее особенно тщательно, так как любое повреждение вызовет скандал. Оно повлечет почти такие же катастрофические последствия, как и пропажа диадемы. В мире больше нет таких бериллов, и, если потеряется хоть один, возместить его будет нечем. Но я доверяю вам и со спокойной душой оставляю у вас диадему. Я вернусь за нею лично в понедельник утром.

Видя, что мой клиент спешит, я без дальнейших разговоров вызвал кассира и распорядился выдать пятьдесят банковских билетов по тысяче фунтов стерлингов.

«I took the precious case.»

Оставшись один и разглядывая драгоценность, лежащую на моем письменном столе, я подумал об огромной ответственности, которую принял на себя. В случае пропажи диадемы, несомненно, разразится невероятный скандал: ведь она достояние нации! Я даже начал сожалеть, что впутался в это дело. Но сейчас уже ничего нельзя было изменить. Я запер диадему в свой личный сейф и вернулся к работе.

Когда настал вечер, я подумал, что было бы опрометчиво оставлять в банке такую драгоценность. Кому не известны случаи взлома сейфов? А вдруг взломают и мой? В каком ужасном положении я окажусь, случись такая беда! И я решил держать диадему при себе. Затем я вызвал кэб и поехал домой в Стритем с футляром в кармане. Я не мог успокоиться, пока не поднялся к себе наверх и не запер диадему в бюро в комнате, смежной с моей спальней.

А теперь два слова о людях, живущих в моем доме. Я хочу, чтобы вы, мистер Холмс, полностью ознакомились с положением дел. Мой конюх и мальчик-слуга — приходящие работники, поэтому о них можно не говорить. У меня три горничные, работающие уже много лет, и их абсолютная честность не вызывает ни малейшего сомнения. Четвертая — Люси Парр, официантка, живет у нас только несколько месяцев. Она поступила с прекрасной рекомендацией и вполне справляется со своей работой. Люси — хорошенькая девушка, у нее есть поклонники, которые слоняются возле дома. Это — единственное, что мне не нравится. Впрочем, я считаю ее вполне порядочной девушкой во всех отношениях.

Вот и все, что касается слуг. Моя собственная семья так немногочисленна, что мне не придется много о ней говорить. Я вдовец и имею единственного сына Артура. К великому моему огорчению, он обманул мои надежды. Нет ни малейшего сомнения, что виноват я сам. Говорят, я избаловал его. Очень может быть. Когда скончалась жена, я понял, что теперь сын — моя единственная привязанность. Я не мог ему отказать ни в чем, я совершенно не мог выносить даже малейшего его неудовольствия. Может быть, для нас обоих было бы лучше, будь я с ним хоть чуточку построже. Но в то время я думал иначе.

Естественно, я мечтал, что Артур когда-нибудь сменит меня в моем деле. Однако у него не оказалось никакой склонности к этому. Он стал необузданным, своенравным, и, говоря по совести, я не мог доверить ему большие деньги. Юношей он вступил в аристократический клуб, а позже благодаря обаятельным манерам стал своим человеком в кругу самых богатых и расточительных людей. Он пристрастился к крупной игре в карты, проматывал деньги на скачках и поэтому все чаще и чаще обращался ко мне с просьбой дать ему денег — в счет будущих карманных расходов. Деньги нужны были для того, чтобы расплатиться с карточными долгами. Правда, Артур неоднократно пытался отойти от этой компании, но каждый раз влияние его друга сэра Джорджа Бэрнвелла возвращало его на прежний путь.

Собственно говоря, меня не очень удивляет, что сэр Джордж Бэрнвелл оказывал такое влияние на моего сына. Артур нередко приглашал его к нам, и должен сказать, что даже я подпадал под обаяние сэра Джорджа. Он старше Артура, светский человек до мозга костей, интереснейший собеседник, много поездивший и повидавший на своем веку, к тому же человек исключительно привлекательной внешности. Но все же, думая о нем спокойно, отвлекаясь от его личного обаяния и вспоминая его циничные высказывания и взгляды, я сознавал, что сэру Джорджу нельзя доверять.

Так думал не только я — того же взгляда придерживалась и Мэри, обладающая тонкой женской интуицией.

Теперь остается рассказать лишь о Мэри, моей племяннице. Когда лет пять тому назад умер брат и она осталась одна на всем свете, я взял ее к себе. С тех пор она для меня словно родная дочь. Мэри — солнечный луч в моем доме — такая ласковая, чуткая, милая, какой только может быть женщина, и к тому же превосходная хозяйка. Мэри — моя правая рука, я не могу себе представить, что я делал бы без нее. И только в одном она шла против моей воли. Мой сын Артур любит ее и дважды просил ее руки, но она каждый раз отказывала ему. Я глубоко убежден, что если хоть кто-нибудь способен направить моего сына на путь истинный, так это только она. Брак с ней мог бы изменить всю его жизнь... но сейчас, увы, слишком поздно. Все погибло!

Ну вот, мистер Холмс, теперь вы знаете людей, которые живут под моей крышей, и я продолжу свою печальную повесть.

Когда в тот вечер после обеда мы пили кофе в гостиной, я рассказал Артуру и Мэри, какое сокровище находится у нас в доме. Я, конечно, не назвал имени клиента. Люси Парр, подававшая нам кофе, к тому времени уже вышла из комнаты. Я твердо уверен в этом, хотя не берусь утверждать, что дверь за ней была плотно закрыта. Мэри и Артур, заинтригованные моим рассказом, хотели посмотреть знаменитую диадему, но я почел за благо не прикасаться к ней.

— Куда же ты ее положил? — спросил Артур.

— В бюро.

— Будем надеяться, что сегодня ночью к нам не вломятся грабители, — сказал он.

— Бюро заперто на ключ, — возразил я.

— Пустяки! К нему подойдет любой ключ. В детстве я сам открывал его ключом от буфета.

Он часто нес всякий вздор, и я не придал значения его словам.

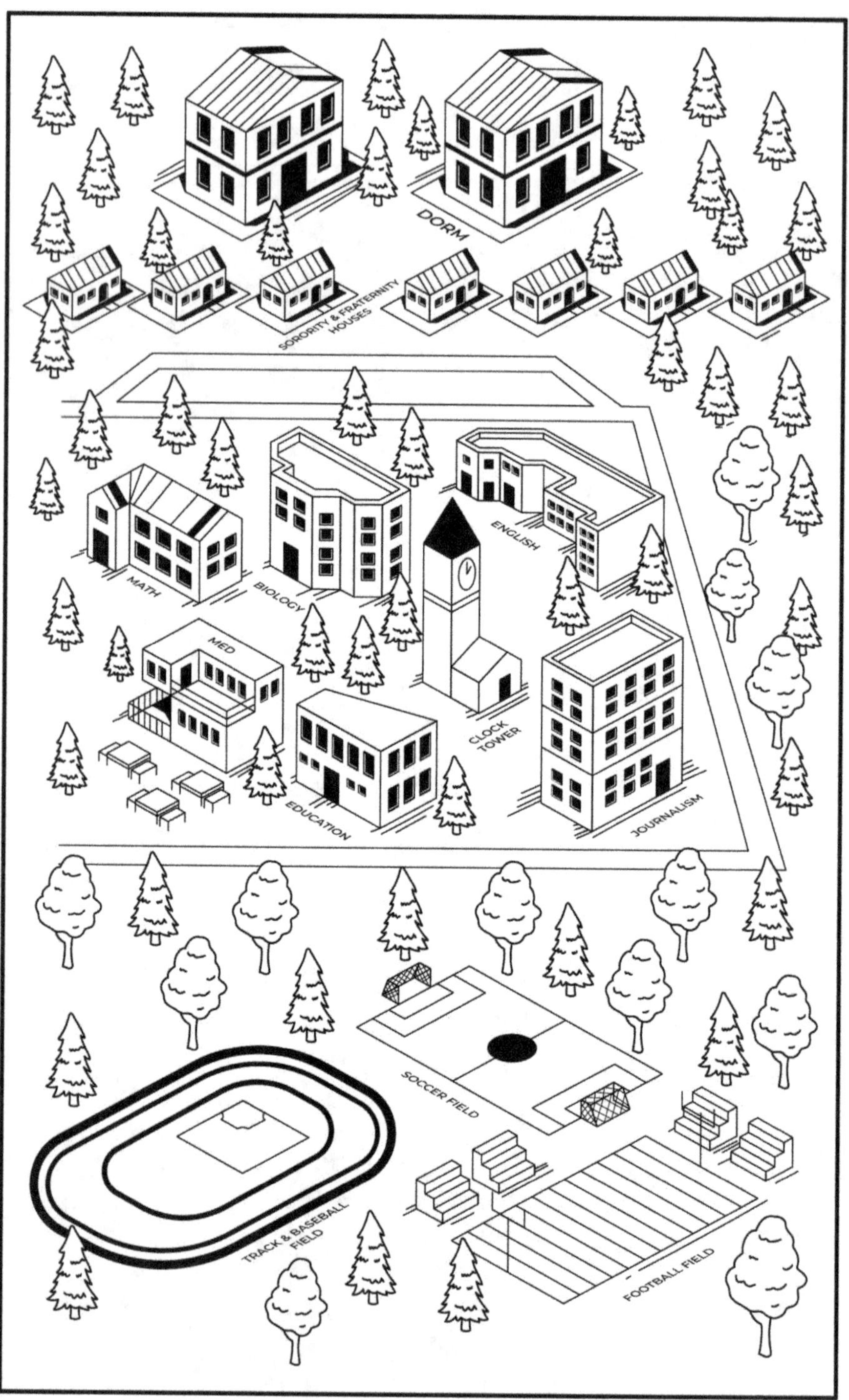
DORM
SORORITY & FRATERNITY HOUSES
ENGLISH
MATH
BIOLOGY
MED
CLOCK TOWER
EDUCATION
JOURNALISM
SOCCER FIELD
TRACK & BASEBALL FIELD
FOOTBALL FIELD

Vintage Housewife Books

PO BOX 842

Ridgefield, Wa 98642

www.kristirose.net

Publisher's Note: This is a work of fiction. Names, characters, places, and incidents are a product of the author's imagination. Locales and public names are sometimes used for atmospheric purposes. Any resemblance to actual people, living or dead, or to businesses, companies, events, institutions, or locales is completely coincidental.

Book Layout © 2023 Vellum

Cover Design © 2023 Damonza

Edited by: Red Adept Editing

Campus Murder Club. ***-- 1st edition. Special Edition cover with images included.***

Open your phone's camera to scan the QR code and SAVE

Link will take you to KristiRoseBooks.com Buying from me means a deal for you.

Campus Murder Club

Special Edition

Kristi Rose

«Oh, any old key will fit that bureau.»

После кофе Артур с мрачным видом последовал в мою комнату.

— Послушай, папа, — сказал он, опустив глаза. — Не мог бы ты одолжить мне двести фунтов?

— Ни в коем случае, — ответил я резко. — Я и так слишком распустил тебя в денежных делах.

— Да, ты всегда щедр, — сказал он. — Но сейчас мне крайне нужна эта сумма, иначе я не смогу показаться в клубе.

— Тем лучше! — воскликнул я.

— Но меня же могут посчитать за нечестного человека! Я не вынесу такого позора. Так или иначе я должен достать деньги. Если ты не дашь мне двести фунтов, я буду вынужден раздобыть их иным способом.

Я возмутился: за последний месяц он третий раз обращался ко мне с подобной просьбой.

— Ты не получишь ни фартинга! — закричал я.

Он поклонился и вышел из комнаты, не сказав ни слова. После ухода Артура я заглянул в бюро, убедился, что драгоценность на месте, и снова запер его на ключ.

Затем я решил обойти комнаты и посмотреть, все ли в порядке. Обычно эту обязанность берет на себя Мэри, но сегодня я решил, что лучше сделать это самому. Спускаясь с лестницы, я увидел свою племянницу — она закрывала окно в гостиной.

— Скажите, папа, вы разрешили Люси отлучиться? — Мне показалось, что Мэри немножко встревожена. — Об этом и речи не было.

— Она только что вошла через черный ход. Думаю, что она выходила к калитке повидаться с кем-нибудь. Мне кажется, это ни к чему, и пора это прекратить.

— Непременно поговори с ней завтра, или, если хочешь, я сам это сделаю. Ты проверила, все хорошо заперто?

— Да, папа.

— Тогда спокойной ночи, дитя мое. — Я поцеловал ее отправился к себе в спальню и вскоре уснул.

— Я подробно говорю обо всем, что может иметь хоть какое-нибудь отношение к делу, мистер Холмс. Но, если что-либо покажется вам неясным, спрашивайте, не стесняйтесь.

— Нет, нет, вы рассказываете вполне ясно, — ответил Холмс.

— Сейчас я перехожу к той части рассказа, которую хотел бы изложить особенно детально. Обычно я сплю не очень крепко, а беспокойство в тот раз отнюдь не способствовало крепкому сну. Около двух часов ночи я проснулся от какого-то слабого шума. Шум прекратился прежде, чем я сообразил, в чем дело, но у меня создалось впечатление, что где-то осторожно закрыли окно. Я весь обратился в слух. Вдруг до меня донеслись легкие шаги в комнате рядом с моей спальней. Я выскользнул из постели и, дрожа от страха, выглянул за дверь.

— Артур! — закричал я. — Негодяй! Вор! Как ты посмел притронуться к диадеме!

Газ был притушен, и при его свете я увидел своего несчастного сына — на нем была только рубашка и брюки. Он стоял около газовой горелки и держал в руках диадему. Мне показалось, что он старался согнуть ее или сломать. Услышав меня, Артур выронил диадему и повернулся ко мне, бледный как смерть. Я схватил сокровище: не хватало золотого зубца с тремя бериллами.

At my cry he dropped it.

— Подлец! — закричал я вне себя от ярости. — Сломать такую вещь! Ты обесчестил меня, понимаешь? Куда ты дел камни, которые украл?

— Украл? — попятился он.

— Да, украл! Ты вор! — кричал я, тряся его за плечи.

— Нет, не может быть, ничего не могло пропасть! — бормотал он.

— Тут недостает трех камней. Где они? Ты, оказывается, не только вор, но и лжец! Я же видел, как ты пытался отломить еще кусок.

— Хватит! Я больше не намерен терпеть оскорбления, — холодно сказал Артур. — Ты не услышишь от меня ни слова. Утром я ухожу из дому и буду сам устраиваться в жизни.

— Ты уйдешь из моего дома только в сопровождении полиции! — кричал я, обезумев от горя и гнева. — Я хочу знать все, абсолютно все!

— Я не скажу ни слова! — неожиданно взорвался он. — Если ты считаешь нужным вызвать полицию — пожалуйста, пусть ищут!

Я кричал так, что поднял на ноги весь дом. Мэри первой вбежала в комнату. Увидев диадему и растерянного Артура, она все поняла и, вскрикнув, упала без чувств. Я послал горничную за полицией. Когда прибыли полицейский инспектор и констебль, Артур, мрачно стоявший со скрещенными руками, спросил меня, неужели я действительно собираюсь предъявить ему обвинение в воровстве. Я ответил, что это дело отнюдь не частное, что диадема — собственность нации и что я твердо решил дать делу законный ход.

— Но ты по крайней мере не дашь им арестовать меня сейчас же, — сказал он. — Во имя наших общих интересов разреши мне отлучиться из дому хотя бы на пять минут.

— Для того, чтобы ты скрылся или получше припрятал краденое? — воскликнул я.

Я понимал весь ужас своего положения и заклинал его подумать о том, что на карту поставлено не только мое имя, но и честь гораздо более высокого лица, что исчезновение бериллов вызовет огромный скандал, который потрясет всю нацию. Всего можно избежать, если только он скажет, что он сделал с тремя камнями.

— Пойми, — говорил я. — Ты задержан на месте преступления. Признание не усугубит твою вину. Напротив, если ты вернешь бериллы, то поможешь исправить создавшееся положение и тебя простят.

— Приберегите свое прощение для тех, кто в нем нуждается, — сказал он высокомерно и отвернулся.

Я видел, что он крайне ожесточен, и понял, что дальнейшие уговоры бесполезны. Оставался один выход. Я пригласил инспектора, и тот взял Артура под стражу.

Полицейские немедленно обыскали Артура и его комнату, обшарили каждый закоулок в доме, но обнаружить драгоценные камни не удалось, а негодный мальчишка не раскрывал рта, несмотря на наши увещевания и угрозы. Сегодня утром его отправили в тюрьму. А я, закончив формальности, поспешил к вам. Умоляю вас применить все свое искусство, чтобы раскрыть это дело. В полиции мне откровенно сказали, что в настоящее время вряд ли смогут чем-нибудь помочь мне. Я не остановлюсь ни перед какими расходами. Я уже предложил вознаграждение в тысячу фунтов... Боже! Что же мне делать? Я потерял честь, состояние и сына в одну ночь... О, что мне делать?!

Он схватился за голову и, раскачиваясь из стороны в сторону, бормотал, как ребенок, который не в состоянии выразить свое горе.

Несколько минут Холмс сидел молча, нахмурив брови и устремив взгляд на огонь в камине.

— У вас часто бывают гости? — спросил он.

— Нет, у нас никого не бывает, иногда разве придет компаньон с женой да изредка кто-либо из друзей Артура. Недавно к нам несколько раз заглядывал сэр Джордж Бэрнвелл. Больше никого.

— А вы сами часто бываете в обществе?

— Артур — часто. А мы с Мэри всегда дома. Мы оба домоседы.

— Это необычно для молодой девушки.

— Она не очень общительная и к тому же не такая уж юная. Ей двадцать четыре года.

— Вы говорите, что случившееся явилось для нее ударом?

— О да! Она потрясена больше меня.

— А у вас не появлялось сомнения в виновности Артура?

— Какие же могут быть сомнения, когда я собственными глазами видел диадему в руках у Артура?

— Я не считаю это решающим доказательством вины. Скажите, кроме отломанного зубца, были какие-нибудь еще повреждения на диадеме?

— Она была погнута.

— А вам не приходила мысль, что ваш сын просто пытался распрямить ее?

— Что вы! Я понимаю, вы хотите оправдать его в моих глазах. Но это невозможно. Что он делал в моей комнате? Если он не имел преступных намерений, отчего он молчит?

— Все это верно. Но, с другой стороны, если он виновен, то почему бы ему не попытаться придумать какую-нибудь версию в свое оправдание? То обстоятельство, что он не хочет говорить, по-моему, исключает оба предположения. И вообще тут есть несколько неясных деталей. Что думает полиция о шуме, который вас разбудил?

— Они считают, что Артур, выходя из спальни, неосторожно стукнул дверью.

— Очень похоже! Человек, идущий на преступление, хлопает дверью, чтобы разбудить весь дом! А что они думают по поводу исчезнувших камней?

— Они и сейчас еще простукивают стены и обследуют мебель.

— А они не пытались искать вне дома?

— Они проявили исключительную энергию. Они прочесали весь сад.

— Ну, дорогой мистер Холдер, — сказал Холмс, — разве не очевидно, что все гораздо сложнее, чем предполагаете вы и полиция? Вы считаете дело ясным, а с моей точки зрения это очень запутанная история. Судите сами, по-вашему, ход событий таков: Артур поднимается с постели, пробирается с большим риском в ту комнату, открывает бюро и достает диадему, отламывает с большим трудом зубец, выходит и где-то прячет три берилла из тридцати девяти, причем с такой ловкостью, что никто не может их разыскать, затем вновь возвращается в вашу комнату, подвергая себя огромному риску: ведь его могут застать там. Неужели такая версия в самом деле кажется вам правдоподобной?

— Но тогда я ума не приложу, что могло случиться! — воскликнул банкир в отчаянии. — Если он не имел дурных намерений, почему он молчит?

— А вот это уже наше дело — разгадать загадку, — ответил Холмс. — Теперь, мистер Холдер, мы отправимся вместе с вами в Стритем и потратим часок-другой, чтобы на месте познакомиться с кое-какими обстоятельствами.

Мой друг настоял, чтобы я сопровождал его. И я охотно согласился: эта странная история вызвала у меня предельное любопытство и глубокую симпатию к несчастному мистеру Холдеру. Говоря откровенно, виновность Артура казалась мне, как и нашему клиенту, совершенно бесспорной, и все же я верил в чутье Холмса:

если мой друг не удовлетворился объяснениями Холдера, значит, есть какая-то надежда.

Пока мы ехали к южной окраине Лондона, Холмс не проронил ни слова. Погруженный в глубокое раздумье, он сидел, опустив голову на грудь и надвинув шляпу на самые глаза. Наш клиент, напротив, казалось, воспрянул духом от слабого проблеска надежды и даже пытался завести со мной разговор о своих банковских делах. В пути мы были недолго: непродолжительная поездка по железной дороге, краткая прогулка пешком — и вот мы уже в Фэрбенке, скромной резиденции богатого финансиста.

Фэрбенк — большой квадратный дом из белого камня, расположенный недалеко от шоссе, с которым его соединяет только дорога для экипажей. Сейчас эта дорога, упирающаяся в массивные железные ворота, была занесена снегом. Направо от нее — густые заросли кустарника, за ними — узкая тропинка, по обе стороны которой живая изгородь; тропинка ведет к кухне, и ею пользуются главным образом поставщики продуктов. Налево — дорожка к конюшне. Она, собственно говоря, не входит во владения Фэрбенка и является общественной собственностью. Впрочем, там очень редко можно встретить посторонних.

Холмс не вошел в дом вместе с нами; он медленно двинулся вдоль фасада, по дорожке, ведущей на кухню и дальше через сад, в сторону конюшни. Мистер Холдер и я так и не дождались Холмса; войдя в дом, мы молча расположились в столовой около камина. Внезапно дверь отворилась, и в комнату тихо вошла молодая девушка. Она была немного выше среднего роста, стройная, с темными волосами и глазами. Эти глаза казались еще темнее оттого, что в лице ее не было ни кровинки. Мне никогда еще не приходилось видеть такой мертвенной бледности. Губы тоже были совсем белые, глаза заплаканы. Казалось, что она сильнее потрясена горем, чем даже мистер Холдер. В то же время черты ее лица говорили о сильной воле и огромном самообладании.

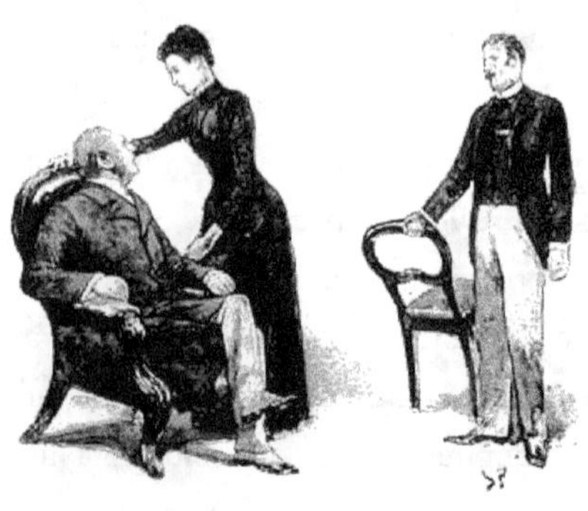

She went straight to her uncle.

Не обращая на меня внимания, она подошла к дяде и нежно провела рукой по его волосам.

— Вы распорядились, чтобы Артура освободили, папа? — спросила она.

— Нет, моя девочка, дело надо расследовать до конца.

— Я глубоко убеждена, что он не виновен. Мне сердце подсказывает это. Он не мог сделать ничего дурного. Вы потом сами пожалеете, что обошлись с ним так сурово.

— Но почему же он молчит, если не виновен?

— Возможно, он обиделся, что вы подозреваете его в краже.

— Как же не подозревать, если я застал его с диадемой в руках?

— Он взял диадему в руки, чтобы посмотреть. Поверьте, папа, он не виновен. Пожалуйста, прекратите это дело. Как ужасно, что наш дорогой Артур в тюрьме!

— Я не прекращу дела, пока не будут найдены бериллы. Ты настолько привязана к Артуру, что забываешь об ужасных последствиях. Нет, Мэри, я не отступлюсь, напротив, я пригласил джентльмена из Лондона для самого тщательного расследования.

— Это вы? — Мэри повернулась ко мне.

— Нет, это его друг. Тот джентльмен попросил, чтобы мы оставили его одного. Он хотел пройти по дорожке, которая ведет к конюшне.

— К конюшне? — Ее темные брови удивленно поднялись. — Что он думает там найти? А вот, очевидно, и он сам. Я надеюсь, сэр, что вам удастся доказать непричастность моего кузена к этому преступлению. Я убеждена в этом.

— Я полностью разделяю ваше мнение, — сказал Холмс, стряхивая у половика снег с ботинок. — Полагаю, я имею честь говорить с мисс Холдер? Вы позволите задать вам несколько вопросов?

— Ради Бога, сэр! Если б только мои ответы помогли распутать это ужасное дело!

— Вы ничего не слышали сегодня ночью?

— Ничего, пока до меня не донесся громкий голос дяди, и тогда я спустилась вниз.

— Накануне вечером вы закрывали окна и двери. Хорошо ли вы их заперли?

— Да.

— И они были заперты сегодня утром?

— Да.

— У вашей горничной есть поклонник. Вчера вечером вы говорили дяде, что она выходила к нему?

— Да, она подавала нам вчера кофе. Она могла слышать, как дядя рассказывал о диадеме.

— Понимаю. Отсюда вы делаете вывод, что она могла что-то сообщить своему поклоннику и они вместе замыслили кражу.

— Ну какой прок от всех этих туманных предположений? — нетерпеливо воскликнул мистер Холдер. — Ведь я же сказал, что застал Артура с диадемой в руках.

— Не надо спешить, мистер Холдер. К этому мы еще вернемся. Теперь относительно вашей прислуги. Мисс Холдер, она вошла в дом через кухню?

— Да. Я спустилась посмотреть, заперта ли дверь, и увидела Люси у порога. Заметила в темноте и ее поклонника.

— Вы знаете его?

— Да, он зеленщик, приносит нам овощи. Его зовут Фрэнсис Проспер.

— И он стоял немного в стороне, не у самой двери?

— Да.

— И у него деревянная нога?

Что-то вроде испуга промелькнуло в выразительных черных глазах девушки.

— Вы волшебник, — сказала она. — Как вы это узнали? — Она улыбнулась, но на худощавом энергичном лице Холмса не появилось ответной улыбки.

— Я хотел бы подняться наверх, — сказал он. — Впрочем, сначала я посмотрю окна.

Something like fear sprang up in the young lady's eyes.

Он быстро обошел первый этаж, переходя от одного окна к другому, затем остановился у большого окна, которое выходило на дорожку, ведущую к конюшне. Он открыл окно и тщательно, с помощью сильной лупы осмотрел подоконник. — Что ж, теперь пойдемте наверх, — сказал он наконец.

Комната, расположенная рядом со спальней банкира, выглядела очень скромно: серый ковер, большое бюро и высокое зеркало. Холмс первым делом подошел к бюро и тщательно осмотрел замочную скважину.

— Каким ключом отперли его? — спросил он.

— Тем самым, о котором говорил мой сын, — от буфета в чулане.

— Где ключ?

— Вон он, на туалетном столике.

Холмс взял ключ и открыл бюро.

— Замок бесшумный, — сказал он. — Не удивительно, что вы не проснулись. В этом футляре, я полагаю, и находится диадема? Посмотрим... — Он открыл футляр, извлек диадему и положил на стол. Это было чудесное произведение ювелирного искусства. Таких изумительных камней мне никогда не приходилось видеть. Один зубец диадемы был отломан.

— Вот этот зубец соответствует отломанному, — сказал Холмс. — Будьте любезны, мистер Холдер, попробуйте отломить его.

— Боже меня сохрани! — воскликнул банкир, в ужасе отшатнувшись от Холмса.

— Ну, так попробую я. — Холмс напряг все силы, но попытка оказалась безуспешной. — Немного поддается, но мне, пожалуй, пришлось бы долго повозиться, чтоб отломить зубец, хотя руки у меня очень сильные. Человеку с обычным физическим развитием это вообще не под силу. Но допустим, что я все же сломал диадему. Раздался бы треск, как выстрел из пистолета. Неужели вы полагаете, мистер Холдер, что это произошло чуть ли не над вашим ухом и вы ничего не услышали?

— Уж не знаю, что и думать. Мне все это совершенно непонятно.

— Как знать, может быть все разъяснится. А что вы думаете, мисс Холдер?

— Признаюсь, я разделяю недоумение моего дяди.

— Скажите, мистер Холдер, были ли в тот момент на ногах вашего сына ботинки или туфли?

— Нет, он был босой, на нем были только брюки и рубашка.

— Благодарю вас. Ну что ж, нам просто везет, и если мы не раскроем тайну, то только по нашей собственной вине. С вашего разрешения, мистер Холдер, я еще раз обойду вокруг дома.

Холмс вышел один: лишние следы, по его словам, только затрудняют работу.

Он пропадал около часу, а когда вернулся, ноги у него были все в снегу, а лицо непроницаемо, как обычно.

— Мне кажется, я осмотрел все, что нужно, — сказал он, — и могу отправиться домой.

— Ну, а как же камни, мистер Холмс, где они? — воскликнул банкир.

— Этого я сказать не могу.

Банкир в отчаянии заломил руки.

— Неужели они безвозвратно пропали? — простонал он. — А как же Артур? Дайте хоть самую маленькую надежду!

— Мое мнение о вашем сыне не изменилось.

— Ради всего святого, что же произошло в моем доме?

— Если вы посетите меня на Бейкер-стрит завтра утром между девятью и десятью, я думаю, что смогу дать более подробные объяснения. Надеюсь, вы предоставите мне свободу действий при условии, разумеется, что камни будут возвращены, и не постоите за расходами?

— Я отдал бы все свое состояние!

— Прекрасно. Я подумаю над этой историей. До свидания. Возможно, я еще загляну сегодня сюда.

Было совершенно ясно, что Холмс уже что-то надумал, но я даже приблизительно не мог представить себе, к каким выводам он пришел. По дороге в Лондон я несколько раз пытался навести беседу на эту тему, но Холмс всякий раз уходил от ответа. Наконец, отчаявшись, я прекратил свои попытки. Не было еще и трех часов, когда мы возвратились домой. Холмс поспешно ушел в свою комнату и через несколько минут снова появился. Он успел переодеться. Потрепанное пальто с поднятым воротником, небрежно повязанный красный шарф и стоптанные башмаки придавали ему вид типичного бродяги.

Dressed as a common loafer.

— Ну, так, я думаю, сойдет, — сказал он, взглянув в зеркало над камином. — Хотелось бы взять с собою и вас, Уотсон, но это невозможно. На верном пути я или нет, скоро узнаем. Думаю, что вернусь через несколько часов. — Он открыл буфет, отрезал кусок говядины, положил его между двумя кусками хлеба и, засунув сверток в карман, ушел.

Я только что закончил пить чай, когда Холмс возвратился в прекрасном настроении, размахивая каким-то старым ботинком. Он швырнул его в угол и налил себе чашку.

— Я заглянул на минутку, сейчас отправлюсь дальше.

— Куда же?

— На другой конец Вест-Энда. Вернусь, возможно, не скоро. Не ждите меня, если я запоздаю.

— Как успехи?

— Ничего, пожаловаться не могу. Я был в Стритеме, но в дом не заходил. Интересное дельце, не хотелось бы упустить его. Хватит, однако, болтать, надо сбросить это тряпье и снова стать приличным человеком.

По поведению моего друга я видел, что он доволен результатами. Глаза у него блестели, на бледных щеках, даже появился слабый румянец. Он поднялся к себе в комнату, и через несколько минут я услышал, как стукнула входная дверь. Холмс снова отправился на «охоту».

Я ждал до полуночи, но, видя, что его все нет и нет, отправился спать. Холмс имел обыкновение исчезать на долгое время, когда нападал на след, так что меня ничуть не удивило его опоздание. Не знаю, в котором часу он вернулся, но, когда на следующее утро я вышел к завтраку, Холмс сидел за столом с чашкой кофе в одной руке и газетой в другой. Как всегда, он был бодр и подтянут.

— Простите, Уотсон, что я начал завтрак без вас, — сказал он. — Но вот-вот явится наш клиент.

— Да, уже десятый час, — ответил я. — Кажется, звонят? Наверное, это он.

И в самом деле это был мистер Холдер. Меня поразила перемена, происшедшая в нем. Обычно массивное и энергичное лицо его осунулось и как-то сморщилось, волосы, казалось, побелели еще больше. Он вошел усталой походкой, вялый, измученный, что представляло еще более тягостное зрелище, чем его бурное отчаяние вчерашним утром. Тяжело опустившись в придвинутое мною кресло, он проговорил:

— Не знаю, за что такая кара! Два дня назад я был счастливым, процветающим человеком, а сейчас опозорен и обречен на одинокую старость. Беда не приходит одна. Исчезла Мэри.

— Исчезла?

— Да. Постель ее не тронута, комната пуста, а на столе вот эта записка. Вчера я сказал ей, что, выйди она замуж за Артура, с ним ничего не случилось бы. Я говорил без тени гнева, просто был убит горем. Вероятно, так не нужно было говорить. В записке она немекает на эти слова.

«Дорогой дядя!

Я знаю, что причинила вам много горя и что поступи я иначе, не произошло бы это ужасное несчастье. С этой мыслью я не смогу быть счастливой под вашей крышей и покидаю вас навсегда. Не беспокойтесь о моем будущем и, самое главное, не ищите меня, потому что это бесцельно и может только повредить мне.

Всю жизнь до самой смерти любящая вас Мэри».

— Что означает эта записка, мистер Холмс? Уж не хочет ли она покончить самоубийством?

— О нет, ничего подобного. Может быть, это наилучшим образом решает все проблемы. Я уверен, мистер Холдер, что ваши испытания близятся к концу.

— Да, вы так думаете? Вы узнали что-нибудь новое, мистер Холмс? Узнали, где бериллы?

— Тысячу фунтов за каждый камень вы не сочтете чересчур высокой платой?

— Я заплатил бы все десять!

— В этом нет необходимости. Трех тысяч вполне достаточно, если не считать некоторого вознаграждения мне. Чековая книжка при вас? Вот перо. Выпишите чек на четыре тысячи фунтов.

Банкир в изумлении подписал чек. Холмс подошел к письменному столу, достал маленький треугольный кусок золота с тремя бериллами и положил на стол. Мистер Холдер с радостным криком схватил свое сокровище.

— Я спасен, спасен! — повторял он, задыхаясь. — Вы нашли их!

Радость его была столь же бурной, как и вчерашнее отчаяние. Он крепко прижимал к груди найденное сокровище.

— За вами еще один долг, мистер Холдер, — сказал Холмс сурово.

— Долг? — Банкир схватил перо. — Назовите сумму, и я выплачу вам ее немедленно.

— Нет, не мне. Вы должны попросить прощения у вашего сына. Он держал себя мужественно и благородно. Имей я такого сына, я гордился бы им.

— Значит, не Артур взял камни?

— Да, не он. Я говорил это вчера и повторяю сегодня.

— В таком случае поспешим к нему и сообщим, что правда восторжествовала.

— Он все знает. Я беседовал с ним, когда распутал дело. Поняв, что он не хочет говорить, я сам изложил ему всю историю, и он признал, что я прав, и, в свою очередь, рассказал о некоторых подробностях, которые были неясны мне. Новость, которую вы нам только что сообщили, возможно, заставит его быть вполне откровенным.

— Так раскройте же, ради Бога, эту невероятную тайну!

— Сейчас я расскажу, каким путем мне удалось добраться до истины. Но сначала разрешите сообщить вам тяжелую весть: ваша племянница Мэри была в сговоре с сэром Джорджем Бэрнвеллом. Сейчас они оба скрылись.

— Мэри? Это невозможно!

— К сожалению, это факт! Принимая в своем доме сэра Джорджа Бэрнвелла, ни вы, ни ваш сын не знали его как следует. А между тем он один из опаснейших субъектов, игрок, отъявленный негодяй, человек без сердца и совести. Ваша племянница и понятия не имела, что бывают такие люди. Слушая его признания и клятвы, она думала, что завоевала его любовь. А он говорил то же самое многим до нее. Одному дьяволу известно, как он сумел поработить волю Мэри, но так или иначе она сделалась послушным орудием в его руках. Они виделись почти каждый вечер.

— Я не верю, не могу этому верить! — вскричал банкир. Его лицо стало пепельно-серым.

— А теперь я расскажу, что произошло в вашем доме вчера ночью. Когда ваша племянница убедилась, что вы ушли к себе, она спустилась вниз и, приоткрыв окно над дорожкой, которая ведет в конюшню, сообщила своему возлюбленному о диадеме. Следы сэра Джорджа ясно отпечатались на снегу под окном. Жажда наживы охватила сэра Джорджа, он буквально подчинил Мэри своей воле. Я не сомневаюсь, что Мэри любит вас, но есть категория женщин, у которых любовь к мужчине преодолевает все другие чувства. Мэри из их числа. Едва она успела договориться с ним о похищении драгоценности, как услышала, что вы спускаетесь по лестнице. Тогда, быстро закрыв окно, она сказала вам, что к горничной приходил ее зеленщик. И он в самом деле приходил…

В ту ночь Артуру не спалось: его тревожили клубные долги. Вдруг он услышал, как мимо его комнаты прошуршали осторожные шаги. Он встал, выглянул за дверь и с изумлением увидел двоюродную сестру — та крадучись пробиралась по коридору и исчезла в вашей комнате. Ошеломленный Артур наскоро оделся и стал ждать, что произойдет дальше. Скоро Мэри вышла; при свете лампы в коридоре ваш сын заметил у нее в руках драгоценную диадему. Мэри спустилась вниз по лестнице. Трепеща от ужаса, Артур проскользнул за портьеру около вашей двери: оттуда видно все, что происходит в гостиной. Мэри потихоньку открыла окно, передала кому-то в темноте диадему, а затем, закрыв окно, поспешила в свою комнату, пройдя совсем близко от Артура, застывшего за портьерой.

Боясь разоблачить любимую девушку, Артур ничего не мог предпринять, хотя понимал, каким ударом будет для вас пропажа диадемы и как важно вернуть драгоценность. Но едва Мэри скрылась за дверью своей комнаты, он бросился вниз полуодетый и босой, распахнул окно, выскочил в сад и помчался по дорожке; там, вдали, виднелся при свете луны чей-то темный силуэт.

Сэр Джордж Бэрнвелл попытался бежать, но Артур догнал его. Между ними завязалась борьба. Ваш сын тянул диадему за один конец, его противник — за другой. Ваш сын ударил сэра Джорджа и повредил ему бровь. Затем что-то неожиданно хрустнуло, и Артур почувствовал, что диадема у него в руках; он кинулся назад, закрыл окно и поднялся в вашу комнату. Только тут он заметил, что диадема погнута, и попытался распрямить ее. В это время вошли вы.

Arthur caught him.

— Боже мой! Боже мой! — задыхаясь, повторял банкир.

— Артур был потрясен вашим несправедливым обвинением. Ведь, напротив, вы должны были бы благодарить его. Он не мог рассказать вам правду, не предав Мэри, хотя она и не заслуживала снисхождения. Он вел себя как рыцарь и сохранил тайну.

— Так вот почему она упала в обморок, когда увидела диадему! — воскликнул мистер Холдер. — Бог мой, какой же я безумец! Ведь Артур просил отпустить его хотя бы на пять минут! Бедный мальчик думал отыскать отломанный кусок диадемы на месте схватки. Как я ошибался!

— Приехав к вам, — продолжал Холмс, — я в первую очередь внимательно осмотрел участок возле дома, надеясь что-нибудь обнаружить. Снега со вчерашнего вечера не выпадало, а сильный мороз должен был хорошо сохранить следы на снегу. Я прошел по дорожке, которой подвозят продукты, но она была утоптана. Но неподалеку от двери в кухню я заметил следы женских ботинок; рядом с женщиной стоял мужчина. Круглые отпечатки показывали, что одна нога у него деревянная. По-видимому, кто-то помешал их разговору, так как женщина побежала к двери: носки женских ботинок отпечатались глубже, чем каблуки. Человек с деревянной ногой подождал немного, а затем ушел. Я тут же подумал, что это должно быть, горничная и ее поклонник, о которых вы говорили. Так оно, и оказалось. Я обошел сад, но больше ничего не заметил, кроме беспорядочных следов, разбегавшихся во всех направлениях. Это ходили полицейские. Но когда я дошел до дорожки, которая вела к конюшне, вся сложная история этой ночи открылась мне, будто написанная на снегу.

Я увидел две линии следов: одна из них принадлежала человеку в ботинках, другая, как я с удовлетворением заметил, — человеку, бежавшему босиком. Я был уверен, что эта вторая линия — следы вашего сына. Впоследствии ваши слова подтвердили правильность моего предположения.

Первый человек спокойно шагал туда и обратно, второй бежал. Следы бежавшего отпечатались там же, где шел человек в ботинках. Из этого можно было сделать вывод, что второй человек преследовал первого. Я пошел по следам человека в ботинках. Они привели меня к окну вашей гостиной; здесь снег был весь истоптан, очевидно, этот человек кого-то долго поджидал. Тогда я направился по его следам в противоположную сторону. Они тянулись по дорожке примерно на сотню ярдов. Потом человек в ботинках обернулся — в этом месте снег был сильно истоптан, словно шла борьба. Капли крови на снегу свидетельствовали о том, что это так и было. Затем человек в ботинках бросился бежать. На некотором расстоянии я снова заметил кровь; значит, ранен был именно он. Я пошел по тропинке до самой дороги; там снег был счищен и следы обрывались.

Вы помните, что, войдя в дом, я осмотрел через лупу подоконник и раму окна гостиной и обнаружил, что кто-то вылезал из окна. Я заметил также очертание следа мокрой ноги, то есть человек залезал и обратно. После этого я уже был в состоянии представить себе все, что произошло. Кто-то стоял под окном, и кто-то подал ему диадему. Ваш сын видел это, бросился преследовать неизвестного, вступил с ним в борьбу. Каждый из них тянул сокровище к себе. Тогда-то и был отломан кусок диадемы. Артур поспешил с диадемой домой, не заметив, что у противника остался обломок. Пока все понятно. Но возникал вопрос: кто этот человек, боровшийся с вашим сыном, и кто подал ему диадему?

Мой старый принцип расследования состоит в том, чтобы исключить все явно невозможные предположения. Тогда то, что остается, является истиной, какой бы неправдоподобной она ни казалась.

Рассуждал я примерно так: естественно, не вы отдали диадему. Значит, оставались только ваша племянница или горничные. Но если в похищении замешаны горничные, то ради чего ваш сын согласился принять вину на себя? Для такого предположения нет оснований. Вы говорили, что Артур любит свою двоюродную сестру. И мне стала понятна причина его молчания: он не хотел выдавать Мэри. Тогда я вспомнил, что вы застали ее у окна и что она упала в обморок, увидав диадему в руках Артура. Мои предположения превратились в уверенность.

Но кто ее сообщник? Разумеется, это мог быть только ее возлюбленный. Лишь под его влиянием она могла так легко забыть, чем обязана вам. Я знал, что вы редко бываете в обществе и круг ваших знакомых ограничен. Но в их числе сэр Джордж Бэрнвелл. Я и прежде слышал о нем как о человеке крайне легкомысленном по отношению к женщинам. Очевидно, это он стоял под окном и только у него должны находиться пропавшие бериллы. Артур узнал его, и все же сэр Джордж считал себя в безопасности, ибо был уверен, что ваш сын не скажет ни слова, чтобы не скомпрометировать свою собственную семью.

Ну, а теперь элементарная логика подскажет вам, что я предпринял. Переодевшись бродягой, я отправился к сэру Джорджу. Мне удалось познакомиться с его лакеем, который сообщил, что его хозяин накануне где-то расшиб до крови голову. Мне удалось раздобыть у него за шесть шиллингов старые ботинки сэра Джорджа, с которыми я отправился в Стритем и убедился, что ботинки точно соответствуют следам на снегу.

— Вчера вечером я видел какого-то бродягу на тропинке, — сказал мистер Холдер.

— Совершенно верно, это был я. Я понял, что сэр Джордж в моих руках. Нужен был большой такт, чтобы успешно завершить дело и избежать огласки. Этот хитрый негодяй понимал, как связаны у нас руки.

Вернувшись домой, я переоделся и отправился к сэру Джорджу. Вначале он, разумеется, все отрицал, но когда я рассказал в подробностях, что произошло той ночью, он стал угрожать мне и даже схватил висевшую на стене трость. Я знал, с кем имею дело, и мигом приставил револьвер к его виску. Тогда он образумился. Я объявил ему, что мы согласны выкупить камни по тысяче фунтов за каждый. Тогда-то он впервые обнаружил признаки огорчения.

— Черт побери! Я уже отдал все три камня за шестьсот фунтов! — воскликнул он.

«I clapped a pistol to his head.»

Пообещав сэру Джорджу, что против него не будет возбуждено судебное расследование, я узнал адрес скупщика, поехал туда и после долгого торга выкупил у него камни по тысяче фунтов каждый. Затем я отправился к вашему сыну, объяснил ему, что все в порядке, и к двум часам ночи после тяжкого трудового дня добрался домой.

— Благодаря вам в Англии не разразился огромный скандал, — сказал банкир, поднимаясь с кресла. — Сэр, у меня нет слов, чтобы выразить свою признательность. Но вы убедитесь, что я не забуду того, что вы сделали для меня. Ваше искусство превосходит всякую фантазию. А сейчас я поспешу к моему дорогому мальчику и буду просить у него прощения за то, что так с ним обошелся. Что же касается бедняжки Мэри, то ее поступок глубоко поразил меня. Боюсь, что даже вы с вашим богатым опытом не сможете разыскать ее.

— Можно с уверенностью сказать, — возразил Холмс, — что она сейчас там же, где сэр Джордж Бэрнвелл. Несомненно также и то, что, как бы ни расценивать поступок вашей племянницы, она будет скоро наказана.

«МЕДНЫЕ БУКИ»

— Человек, который любит искусство ради искусства, — заговорил Шерлок Холмс, отбрасывая в сторону страницу с объявлениями из «Дейли телеграф», — самое большое удовольствие зачастую черпает из наименее значительных и ярких его проявлений. Отрадно заметить, что вы, Уотсон, хорошо усвоили эту истину при изложении наших скромных подвигов, которые по доброте своей вы решились увековечить и, вынужден констатировать, порой пытаетесь приукрашивать, уделяете внимание не столько громким делам и сенсационным процессам, в коих я имел честь принимать участие, сколько случаям самим по себе незначительным, но зато предоставляющим большие возможности для дедуктивных методов мышления и логического синтеза, что особенно меня интересует.

Talking up a glowing cinder with the tongs.

— Тем не менее, — улыбнулся я, — не смею утверждать, что в моих записках вовсе отсутствует стремление к сенсационности.

— Возможно, вы и ошибаетесь, — продолжал он, подхватив щипцами тлеющий уголек и раскуривая длинную трубку вишневого дерева, которая заменяла глиняную в те дни, когда он был настроен скорее спорить, нежели размышлять, — возможно, вы и ошибаетесь, стараясь приукрасить и оживить ваши записки вместо того, чтобы ограничиться сухим анализом причин и следствий, который единственно может вызывать интерес в том или ином деле.

— Мне кажется, в своих записках я отдаю вам должное, — несколько холодно возразил я, ибо меня раздражало самомнение моего друга, которое, как я неоднократно убеждался, было весьма приметной чертой в его своеобразном характере.

— Нет, это не эгоизм и не тщеславие, — сказал он, отвечая по привычке скорее моим мыслям, чем моим словам. — Если я прошу отдать должное моему искусству, то это не имеет никакого отношения ко мне лично, оно — вне меня. Преступление — вещь повседневная. Логика — редкая. Именно на логике, а не преступлении вам и следовало бы сосредоточиться. А у вас курс серьезных лекций превратился в сборник занимательных рассказов.

Было холодное утро начала весны; покончив с завтраком, мы сидели возле ярко пылавшего камина в нашей квартире на Бейкер-стрит. Густой туман повис между рядами сумрачных домов, и лишь окна напротив тусклыми, расплывшимися пятнами маячили в темно-желтой мгле. У нас горел свет, и блики его играли на белой скатерти и на посуде — со стола еще не убирали. Все утро Шерлок Холмс молчал, сосредоточенно просматривая газетные объявления, пока наконец, по-видимому, отказавшись от поисков и пребывая не в лучшем из настроений, не принялся читать мне нравоучения по поводу моих литературных занятий.

— В то же время, — после паузы продолжал он, попыхивая своей длинной трубкой и задумчиво глядя в огонь, — вас вряд ли можно обвинить в стремлении к сенсационности, ибо большинство тех

I07483б3

случаев, к которым вы столь любезно проявили интерес, вовсе не представляет собой преступления. Незначительное происшествие с королем Богемии, когда я пытался оказать ему помощь, странный случай с Мэри Сазерлэнд, история человека с рассеченной губой и случай со знатными холостяком — все это не может стать предметом судебного разбирательства. Боюсь, однако, что, избегая сенсационности, вы оказались в плену тривиальности.

— Может, в конце концов так и случилось, — ответил я, — но методы, о которых я рассказываю, своеобразны и не лишены новизны.

— Мой дорогой, какое дело публике, великой, но лишенной наблюдательности публике, едва ли способной по зубам узнать ткача или по большому пальцу левой руки — наборщика, до тончайших оттенков анализа и дедукции? И тем не менее, даже если вы банальны, я вас не виню, ибо дни великих дел сочтены. Человек, или по крайней мере преступник, утратил предприимчивость и самобытность. Что же касается моей скромной практики, то я, похоже, превращаюсь в агента по розыску утерянных карандашей и наставника молодых леди из пансиона для благородных девиц. Наконец-то я разобрался, на что гожусь. А полученное мною утром письмо означает, что мне пора приступить к новой деятельности. Прочтите его. — И он протянул мне помятый листок.

Письмо было отправлено из Монтегю-плейс накануне вечером.

«Дорогой мистер Холмс!

Мне очень хочется посоветоваться с вами по поводу предложения занять место гувернантки. Если разрешите, я зайду к вам завтра в половине одиннадцатого.

С уважением Вайолет Хантер».

— Вы знаете эту молодую леди? — спросил я.

— Нет.

— Сейчас половина одиннадцатого.

— Да, а вот, не сомневаюсь, она звонит.

— Это дело может оказаться более интересным, нежели вы предполагаете. Вспомните случай с голубым карбункулом, который сначала вы сочли просто недоразумением, а потом он потребовал серьезного расследования. Так может получиться и на этот раз.

— Что ж, будем надеяться! Наши сомнения очень скоро рассеются, ибо вот и особа, о которой идет речь.

Дверь отворилась, и в комнату вошла молодая женщина. Она была просто, но аккуратно одета, лицо у нее было смышленое, живое, все в веснушках, как яичко ржанки, а энергичность, которая чувствовалась в ее движениях, свидетельствовала о том, что ей самой приходится пробивать себе дорогу в жизни.

— Ради Бога, извините за беспокойство, — сказала она, когда мой друг поднялся ей навстречу, — но со мной произошло нечто настолько необычное, что я решила просить у вас совета. У меня нет ни родителей, ни родственников, к которым я могла бы обратиться.

— Прошу садиться, мисс Хантер. Буду счастлив помочь вам, чем могу.

Я понял, что речь и манеры клиентки произвели на Холмса благоприятное впечатление. Он испытующе оглядел ее с ног до головы, а затем, прикрыв глаза и сложив вместе кончики пальцев, приготовился слушать.

«Capital!»

— В течение пяти лет я была гувернанткой в семье полковника Спенса Манроу, но два месяца назад полковник получил назначение в Канаду и забрал с собой в Галифакс и детей. Я осталась без работы. Я давала объявления, сама ходила по объявлениям, но все безуспешно. Наконец та небольшая сумма денег, что мне удалось скопить, начала иссякать, и я просто ума не приложу, что делать.

В Вест-Энде есть агентство по найму «Вестэуэй» — его все знают, — и я взяла за правило заходить туда раз в неделю в поисках чего-либо подходящего. Вестэуэй — фамилия владельца этого агентства, в действительности же все дела вершит некая мисс Стопер. Она сидит у себя в кабинете, женщины, которые ищут работу, ожидают в приемной; их поочередно вызывают в кабинет, и она заглядывая в свой гроссбух, предлагает им те или иные вакансии.

По обыкновению и меня пригласили в кабинет, когда я зашла туда на прошлой неделе, но на этот раз мисс Стопер была не одна. Рядом с ней сидел толстый, претолстый человек с улыбчивым лицом и большим подбородком, тяжелыми складками спускавшимся на грудь, и сквозь очки внимательно разглядывал просительниц. Стоило лишь мне войти, как он подскочил на месте и обернулся к мисс Стопер.

— Подходит, — воскликнул он. — Лучшего и желать нельзя. Грандиозно! Грандиозно!

Он, по-видимому, был в восторге и от удовольствия потирал руки. На него приятно было смотреть: таким добродушным он казался.

— Ищете место, мисс? — спросил он.

— Да, сэр.

— Гувернантки?

— Да, сэр.

— А сколько вы хотите получать?

— Полковник Спенс Манроу, у которого я служила, платил мне четыре фунта в месяц.

— Вот это да! Самая что ни на есть настоящая эксплуатация! — вскричал он, яростно размахивая пухлыми кулаками. — Разве можно предлагать столь ничтожную сумму леди, наделенной такой внешностью и такими достоинствами?

— Мои достоинства, сэр, могут оказаться менее привлекательными, нежели вы полагаете, — сказала я. — Немного французский, немного немецкий, музыка и рисование…

— Вот это да! — снова вскричал он. — Значит и говорить не о чем. Кратко, в двух словах, вопрос вот в чем: обладаете ли вы манерами настоящей леди? Если нет, то вы нам не подходите, ибо речь идет о воспитании ребенка, который в один прекрасный день может сыграть значительную роль в истории Англии. Если да, то разве имеет джентльмен право предложить вам сумму, выраженную менее, чем трехзначной цифрой? У меня, сударыня, вы будете получать для начала сто фунтов в год.

Вы, конечно, представляете, мистер Холмс, что подобное предложение показалось мне просто невероятным — я ведь осталась совсем без средств. Однако джентльмен, прочитав недоверие на моем лице, вынул бумажник и достал оттуда деньги.

— В моих обычаях также ссужать юным леди половину жалованья вперед, — сказал он, улыбаясь на самый приятный манер, так что глаза его превратились в две сияющие щелочки среди белых складок лица, — дабы они могли оплатить мелкие расходы во время путешествия и приобрести нужный гардероб.

«Никогда еще я не встречала более очаровательного и внимательного человека», — подумалось мне. Ведь у меня уже появились кое-какие долги, аванс был очень кстати, и все-таки было что-то странное в этом деле, и, прежде чем дать согласие, я попыталась разузнать об этом человеке побольше.

— А где вы живете, сэр? — спросила я.

— В Хемпшире. Чудная сельская местность. «Медные буки», в пяти милях от Уинчестера. Место прекрасное, моя дорогая юная леди, и дом восхитительный — старинный загородный дом.

— А мои обязанности, сэр? Хотелось бы знать, в чем они состоят.

— Один ребенок, очаровательный маленький проказник, ему только что исполнилось шесть лет. Если бы вы видели, как он бьет комнатной туфлей тараканов! Шлеп! Шлеп! Шлеп! Не успеешь и глазом моргнуть, а трех как не бывало.

Расхохотавшись, он откинулся на спинку стула, и глаза его снова превратились в щелочки.

Меня несколько удивил характер детских забав, но отец смеялся — я решила, что он шутит.

— Значит, мои обязанности — присматривать за ребенком? — спросила я.

— Нет-нет, не только присматривать, не только, моя дорогая юная леди! — вскричал он. — Вам придется также — я уверен, вы и протестовать не будете, — выполнять кое-какие поручения моей жены при условии, разумеется, если эти поручения не будут унижать вашего достоинства. Немного, не правда ли?

— Буду рада оказаться вам полезной.

— Вот именно. Ну, например, речь пойдет о платье. Мы, знаете ли, люди чудаковатые, но сердце у нас доброе. Если мы попросим вас надеть платье, которое мы дадим, вы ведь не будете возражать против нашей маленькой прихоти, а?

— Нет, — ответила я в крайнем удивлении.

— Или сесть там, где нам захочется? Это ведь не покажется вам обидным?

— Да нет…

— Или остричь волосы перед приездом к нам?

Я едва поверила своим ушам. Вы видите, мистер Холмс, у меня густые волосы с особым каштановым отливом. Их считают красивыми. Зачем мне ни с того ни с сего жертвовать ими?

— Нет, это невозможно, — ответила я.

Он жадно глядел на меня своими глазками, и я заметила, что лицо у него помрачнело.

— Но это — обязательное условие, — сказал он. — Маленькая прихоть моей жены, а дамским капризам, как вам известно, сударыня, следует потакать. Значит, вам не угодно остричь волосы?

— Нет, сэр, не могу, — твердо ответила я.

— Что ж… Значит вопрос решен. Жаль, жаль, во всех остальных отношениях вы нам вполне подходите. Мисс Стопер, в таком случае мне придется познакомиться с другими юными леди.

Заведующая агентством все это время сидела, просматривая свои бумаги и не проронив ни слова, но теперь она глянула на меня с таким раздражением, что я поняла: из-за меня она потеряла немалое комиссионное вознаграждение.

— Вы хотите остаться в наши списках? — спросила она.

— Если можно, мисс Стопер.

— Мне это представляется бесполезным, поскольку вы отказались от очень интересного предложения, — резко заметила она. — Не будем же мы из кожи лезть вон, чтобы подобрать для вас такое место. Всего хорошего, мисс Хантер.

Она позвонила в колокольчик, и мальчик проводил меня обратно в приемную.

Вернувшись домой — в буфете у меня было пусто, а на столе — лишь новые счета, — я спросила себя, не поступила ли я неосмотрительно. Что из того, что у этих людей есть какие-то причуды и они хотят, чтобы исполнялись самые неожиданные их капризы? Они ведь готовы платить за это. Много ли в Англии гувернанток, получающих сотню в год? Кроме того, какой прок от моих волос? Некоторым даже идет короткая стрижка, может, пойдет и мне? На следующий день я подумала, что совершила ошибку, а еще через день перестала в этом сомневаться. Я уже собиралась, подавив чувство гордости, пойти снова в агентство, чтобы узнать, не занято ли еще это место, как вдруг получаю письмо от этого самого джентльмена. Вот оно, мистер Холмс, я прочту его.

«Медные буки», близ Винчестера.

Дорогая мисс Хантер!

Мисс Стопер любезно согласилась дать мне ваш адрес, и я пишу вам из дома, желая осведомиться, не переменили ли вы свое решение. Моя жена очень хочет, чтобы вы приехали к нам, — я описал ей вас, и вы ей страшно понравились. Мы готовы платить вам десять фунтов в месяц, то есть сто двадцать в год в качестве компенсации за те неудобства, которые могут причинить наши требования. Да они не так уж и суровы. Моя жена очень любит цвет электрик, и ей хотелось бы, чтобы вы надевали платье такого цвета по утрам. Вам совершенно незачем тратиться на подобную вещь, поскольку у нас есть платье моей дорогой дочери Алисы (ныне пребывающей в Филадельфии), думаю, оно будет вам впору. Полагаю, что и просьбу занять определенное место в комнате или выполнить какое-либо иное поручение вы не сочтете чересчур обременительной. Что же касается ваших волос, то их действительно очень жаль: даже во время нашей краткой беседы я успел заметить, как они хороши, но тем не менее я вынужден настаивать на этом условии. Надеюсь, что прибавка к жалованью вознаградит вас за эту жертву. Обязанности в отношении ребенка весьма несложны. Пожалуйста, приезжайте, я встречу вас в Винчестере. Сообщите каким поездом вы прибудете.

Искренне ваш Джефро Рукасл».

Вот какое письмо я получила, мистер Холмс, и твердо решила принять предложение. Однако, прежде чем сделать окончательный шаг, мне хотелось бы услышать ваше мнение.

— Что ж, мисс Хантер, коли вы решились, значит, дело сделано, — улыбнулся Холмс.

— А вы не советуете?

— Признаюсь, место это не из тех, что я пожелал бы для своей сестры.

— А что все-таки под этим кроется, мистер Холмс?

— Не знаю. Может, у вас есть какие-либо соображения?

— Я думаю, что мистер Рукасл — добрый, мягкосердечный человек. А его жена, наверное, немного сумасшедшая. Вот он и старается держать это в тайне, опасаясь, как бы ее не забрали в дом для умалишенных, и потворствует ее причудам, чтобы с ней не случился припадок.

— Может быть, может быть. На сегодняшний день это самое вероятное предположение. Тем не менее место это вовсе не для молодой леди.

— Но деньги, мистер Холмс, деньги!

— Да, конечно, жалованье хорошее, даже слишком хорошее. Вот это меня и тревожит. Почему они дают сто двадцать фунтов, когда легко найти человека и за сорок? Значит, есть какая-то веская причина.

— Вот я и подумала, что, если расскажу вам все обстоятельства дела, вы позволите мне в случае необходимости обратиться к вам за помощью. Я буду чувствовать себя гораздо спокойнее, зная, что у меня есть заступник.

— Можете вполне на меня рассчитывать. Уверяю вас, ваша маленькая проблема обещает оказаться наиболее интересной за последние месяцы. В деталях определенно есть нечто оригинальное. Если у вас появятся какие-либо подозрения или возникнет опасность…

— Опасность? Какая опасность?

— Если бы опасность можно было предвидеть, то ее не нужно было бы страшиться, — с самым серьезным видом пояснил Холмс.

— Во всяком случае, в любое время дня и ночи шлите телеграмму, и я приду вам на помощь.

— Тогда все в порядке. — Выражение озабоченности исчезло с ее лица, она проворно поднялась. — Сейчас же напишу мистеру Рукаслу, вечером остригу мои бедные волосы и завтра отправлюсь в Винчестер.

Скупо поблагодарив Холмса и попрощавшись, она поспешно ушла.

Holmes shook his head gravely.

— Во всяком случае, — сказал я, прислушиваясь к ее быстрым, твердым шагам на лестнице, — она производит впечатление человека, умеющего за себя постоять.

— Ей придется это сделать, — мрачно заметил Холмс. — Не сомневаюсь, через несколько дней мы получим от нее известие.

Предсказание моего друга, как всегда, сбылось. Прошла неделя, в течение которой я неоднократно возвращался мыслями к нашей посетительнице, задумываясь над тем, в какие дебри человеческих отношений может завести жизнь эту одинокую женщину. Большое жалованье, странные условия, легкие обязанности — во всем этом было что-то неестественное, хотя я абсолютно был не в состоянии решить, причуда это или какой-то замысел, филантроп этот человек или негодяй. Что касается Холмса, то он подолгу сидел, нахмурив лоб и рассеянно глядя вдаль, но когда я принимался его расспрашивать, он лишь махал в ответ рукой.

— Ничего не знаю, ничего! — раздраженно восклицал он. — Когда под рукой нет глины, из чего лепить кирпичи?

Телеграмма, которую мы получили, прибыла поздно вечером, когда я уже собирался лечь спать, а Холмс приступил к опытам, за которыми частенько проводил ночи напролет. Когда я уходил к себе, он стоял, наклонившись над ретортой и пробирками; утром, спустившись к завтраку, я застал его в том же положении. Он открыл желтый конверт и, пробежав взглядом листок, передал его мне.

— Посмотрите расписание поездов, — сказал он и повернулся к своим колбам.

Текст телеграммы был кратким и настойчивым:

«Прошу быть гостинице „Черный лебедь“ Винчестере завтра полдень. Приезжайте! Не знаю, что делать. Хантер».

— Поедете со мной? — спросил Холмс, на секунду отрываясь от своих колб.

— С удовольствием.

— Тогда посмотрите расписание.

— Есть поезд в половине десятого, — сказал я, изучая справочник. — Он прибывает в Винчестер в одиннадцать тридцать.

— Прекрасно. Тогда, пожалуй, я отложу анализ ацетона, завтра утром нам может понадобиться максимум энергии.

В одиннадцать утра на следующий день мы уже были на пути к древней столице Англии. Холмс всю дорогу не отрывался от газет, но после того как мы переехали границу Хампшира, он отбросил их принялся смотреть в окно. Стоял прекрасный весенний день, бледно-голубое небо было испещрено маленькими кудрявыми облаками, которые плыли с запада на восток. Солнце светило ярко, и в воздухе царило веселье и бодрость. На протяжении всего пути, вплоть до холмов Олдершота, среди яркой весенней листвы проглядывали красные и серые крыши ферм.

— До чего приятно на них смотреть! — воскликнул я с энтузиазмом человека, вырвавшегося из туманов Бейкер-стрит.

Но Холмс мрачно покачал головой.

— Знаете, Уотсон, — сказал он, — беда такого мышления, как у меня, в том, что я воспринимаю окружающее очень субъективно. Вот вы смотрите на эти рассеянные вдоль дороги дома и восхищаетесь их красотой. А я, когда вижу их, думаю только о том, как они уединенны и как безнаказанно здесь можно совершить преступление.

— О Господи! — воскликнул я. — Кому бы в голову пришло связывать эти милые сердцу старые домики с преступлением?

— Они внушают мне страх. Я уверен, Уотсон, — и уверенность эта проистекает из опыта, — что в самых отвратительных трущобах Лондона не свершается столько страшных грехов, сколько в этой восхитительной и веселой сельской местности.

— Вас прямо страшно слушать.

— И причина этому совершенно очевидна. То, чего не в состоянии совершить закон, в городе делает общественное мнение. В самой жалкой трущобе крик ребенка, которого бьют, или драка, которую затеял пьяница, тотчас же вызовет участие или гнев соседей, и правосудие близко, так что единое слово жалобы приводит его механизм в движение. Значит, от преступления до скамьи подсудимых — всего один шаг, А теперь взгляните на эти уединенные дома — каждый из них отстоит от соседнего на добрую милю, они населены в большинстве своем невежественным бедняками, которые мало что смыслят в законодательстве. Представьте, какие дьявольски жестокие помыслы и безнравственность тайком процветают здесь из года в год. Если бы эта дама, что обратилась к нам за помощью, поселилась в Винчестере, я не боялся бы за нее. Расстояние в пять миль от города — вот где опасность! И все-таки ясно, что опасность угрожает не ей лично.

— Понятно. Если она может приехать в Винчестер встретить нас, значит, она в состоянии вообще уехать.

— Совершенно справедливо. Ее свобода передвижения не ограничена.

— В чем же тогда дело? Вы нашли какое-нибудь объяснение?

— Я придумал семь разных версий, и каждая из них опирается на известные нам факты. Но какая из них правильная, покажут новые сведения, которые, не сомневаюсь, нас ждут. А вот и купол собора, скоро мы узнаем, что же хочет сообщить нам мисс Хантер.

«Черный лебедь» оказался уважаемой в городе гостиницей на Хайд-стрит, совсем близко от станции, там мы и нашли молодую женщину. Она сидела в гостиной, на столе нас ждал завтрак.

— Я рада, что вы приехали, — серьезно сказала она. — Большое спасибо. Я в самом деле не знаю, что делать. Мне страшно нужен ваш совет.

— Расскажите же, что случилось.

— Сейчас расскажу, я должна спешить, потому что обещала мистеру Рукаслу вернуться к трем. Он разрешил мне съездить в город нынче утром, хотя ему, конечно, неведомо зачем.

— Изложите все по порядку. — Холмс вытянул свои длинные ноги в сторону камина и приготовился слушать.

«I am so delighted that you have come.»

Прежде всего должна сказать, что, в общем, мистер и миссис Рукасл встретили меня довольно приветливо. Ради справедливости об этом следует упомянуть. Но понять их я не могу, и это не дает мне покоя.

— Что именно?

— Их поведение. Однако все по порядку. Когда я приехала, мистер Рукасл встретил меня на станции и повез в своем экипаже в «Медные буки». Поместье, как он и говорил, чудесно расположено, но вовсе не отличается красотой: большой квадратный дом, побеленный известкой, весь в пятнах и подтеках от дождя и сырости. С трех сторон его окружает лес, а с фасада — луг, который опускается к дороге на Саутгемптон, что проходит примерно ярдах в ста от парадного крыльца. Участок перед домом принадлежит мистеру Рукаслу, а леса вокруг — собственность лорда Саутертона. Прямо перед домом растет несколько медных буков, отсюда и название усадьбы.

Мой хозяин, сама любезность, встретил меня на станции и в тот же вечер познакомил со своей женой и сыном. Наша с вами догадка, мистер Холмс, оказалась неверной: миссис Рукасл не сумасшедшая. Молчаливая бледная женщина, она намного моложе своего мужа, на вид ей не больше тридцати, в то время как ему дашь все сорок пять. Из разговоров я поняла, что они женаты лет семь, что он остался вдовцом и что от первой жены у него одна дочь — та самая, которая в Филадельфии. Мистер Рукасл по секрету сообщил мне, что уехала она из-за того, что испытывала какую-то непонятную антипатию к мачехе. Поскольку дочери никак не менее двадцати лет, то я вполне представляю, как неловко она чувствовала себя рядом с молодой женой отца.

Миссис Рукасл показалась мне внутренне столь же бесцветным существом, сколь и внешне. Она не произвела на меня никакого впечатления. Пустое место. И сразу заметна ее страстная преданность мужу и сыну. Светло-серые глаза постоянно блуждают от одного к другому, подмечая их малейшее желание и по возможности предупреждая его. Мистер Рукасл тоже в присущей ему грубовато-добродушной манере неплохо к ней относится, и в целом они производят впечатление благополучной пары. Но у женщины есть какая-то тайна. Она часто погружается в глубокую задумчивость, и лицо ее становится печальным. Не раз я заставала ее в слезах. Порой мне кажется, что причиной этому — ребенок, ибо мне еще ни разу не доводилось видеть такое испорченное и злобное маленькое существо. Для своего возраста он мал, зато у него несоразмерно большая голова. Он то подвержен припадкам дикой ярости, то пребывает в состоянии мрачной угрюмости. Причинять боль любому слабому созданию — вот единственное его развлечение, и он выказывает недюжинный талант в ловле мышей, птиц и насекомых. Но о нем незачем распространяться, мистер Холмс, он не имеет отношения к нашей истории.

— Мне нужны все подробности, — сказал Холмс, — представляются они вам относящимися к делу или нет.

— Постараюсь ничего не пропустить. Что мне сразу не понравилось в этом доме, так это внешность и поведение слуг. Их всего двое, муж и жена. Толлер, так зовут слугу, — грубый, неотесанный человек с серой гривой и седыми бакенбардами, от него постоянно несет спиртным. Я дважды видела его совершенно пьяным, но мистер Рукасл, по-моему, не обращает на это внимания. Жена Толлера — высокая сильная женщина с сердитым лицом, она так же молчалива, как миссис Рукасл, но гораздо менее любезна. Удивительно неприятная пара! К счастью, большую часть времени я провожу в детской и в моей собственной комнате, они расположены рядом.

В первые дни после моего приезда в «Медные буки» все шло спокойно. На третий день сразу после завтрака миссис Рукасл что-то шепнула своему мужу.

— Мы очень обязаны вам, мисс Хантер, — поворачиваясь ко мне, сказал он, — за снисходительность к нашим капризам, вы ведь даже остригли волосы. Право же, это ничуть не испортило вашу внешность. А теперь посмотрим, как вам идет цвет электрик. У себя на кровати вы найдете платье, и мы будем очень благодарны, если вы согласитесь его надеть.

Платье, которое лежало у меня в комнате, весьма своеобразного оттенка синего цвета, сшито было из хорошей шерсти, но, сразу заметно, уже ношенное. Сидело оно безукоризненно, как будто его шили специально для меня. Когда я вошла, мистер и миссис Рукасл выразили восхищение, но мне их восторг показался несколько наигранным. Мы находились в гостиной, которая тянется по всему фасаду дома, с тремя огромными окнами, доходящими до самого пола. Возле среднего окна спинкой к нему стоял стул. Меня усадили на этот стул, а мистер Рукасл принялся ходить взад и вперед по комнате и рассказывать смешные истории. Вы представить себе не можете, как комично он рассказывал, и я хохотала до изнеможения. Миссис Рукасл чувство юмора, очевидно, чуждо, она сидела, сложив на коленях руки, с грустным и озабоченным выражением на лице, так ни разу и не улыбнувшись. Примерно через час мистер Рукасл вдруг объявил, что пора приступать к повседневным обязанностям и что я могу переодеться и пойти в детскую к маленькому Эдуарду.

Два дня спустя при совершенно таких же обстоятельствах вся эта сцена повторилась. Снова я должна была переодеться, сесть у окна и хохотать над теми забавными историями, неисчислимым запасом которых обладал мой хозяин. И рассказчиком он был неподражаемым. Затем он дал мне какой-то роман в желтой обложке и, подвинув мой стул так, чтобы моя тень не падала на страницу, попросил почитать ему вслух. Я читала минут десять, начав где-то в середине главы, а потом он вдруг перебил меня, не дав закончить фразы, и велел пойти переодеться.

«I read for about ten minutes.»

Вы, конечно, понимаете, мистер Холмс, как меня удивил этот спектакль. Я заметила, что они настойчиво усаживали меня, чтобы я оказалась спиной к окну, поэтому я решила во что бы то ни стало узнать, что происходит на улице. Сначала это не представлялось возможным, но потом мне пришла в голову счастливая мысль: у меня был осколок ручного зеркальца, и я спрятала его в носовой платок. В следующий раз, в самый разгар веселья, я приложила носовой платок к глазам и, чуть-чуть приспособившись, сумела рассмотреть все, что находилось позади. Признаться, я была разочарована. Там не было ничего.

По крайней мере так было на первый взгляд. Но, присмотревшись, я заметила на Саутгемптонской дороге невысокого бородатого человека в сером костюме. Он смотрел в нашу сторону. Дорога эта очень оживленная, на ней всегда полно народу. Но этот человек стоял, опершись на ограду, и пристально вглядывался в дом. Я опустила платок и увидела, что миссис Рукасл испытующе смотрит на меня. Она ничего не сказала, но, я уверена, поняла, что у меня зеркало и я видела, кто стоит перед домом. Она тотчас же поднялась.

— Джефри, — сказал она, — на дороге стоит какой-то мужчина и самым непозволительным образом разглядывает мисс Хантер.

— Может быть, ваш знакомый, мисс Хантер? — спросил он.

— Нет. Я никого здесь не знаю.

— Подумайте, какая наглость! Пожалуйста, повернитесь и помашите ему, чтобы он ушел.

— А не лучше ли просто не обращать внимания?

— Нет, нет, не то он все время будет здесь слоняться. Пожалуйста, повернитесь и помашите ему.

Я сделала, как меня просили, и в ту же секунду миссис Рукасл опустила занавеску. Это произошло неделю назад, с тех пор я не сидела у окна, не надевала синего платья и человека на дороге тоже не видела.

— Прошу вас, продолжайте, — сказал Холмс. — Все это очень интересно.

— Боюсь, мой рассказ довольно бессвязен. Не знаю, много ли общего между всеми этими событиями. Так вот, в первый же день моего приезда в «Медные буки» мистер Рукасл подвел меня к маленькому флигелю позади дома. Когда мы приблизились, я услышала звяканье цепи: внутри находилось какое-то большое животное.

— Загляните-ка сюда, — сказал мистер Рукасл, указывая на щель между досками. — Ну, разве это не красавец?

Я заглянула и увидела два горящих во тьме глаза и смутное очертание какого-то животного. Я вздрогнула.

— Не бойтесь, — засмеялся мой хозяин. — Это мой дог Карло. Я называю его моим, но в действительности только старик Толлер осмеливается подойти к нему, чтобы опустить с цепи на ночь, и да поможет Бог тому, в кого он вонзит свои клыки. Ни под каким видом не переступайте порога дома ночью, ибо тогда вам суждено распроститься с жизнью.

Предупредил он меня не зря. На третью ночь я случайно выглянула из окна спальни примерно часа в два. Стояла прекрасная лунная ночь, и лужайка перед домом вся сверкала серебром. Я стояла, захваченная мирной красотой пейзажа, как вдруг заметила, что в тени буков кто-то движется. Таинственное существо вышло на лужайку, и я увидела огромного, величиной с теленка, дога рыжевато-коричневой масти, с отвислым подгрудком, черной мордой и могучими мослами. Он медленно пересек лужайку и исчез в темноте на противоположной стороне. При виде этого страшного немого стража сердце у меня замерло так, как никогда не случалось при появлении грабителя.

А вот еще одно происшествие, о котором мне тоже хочется вам рассказать. Вы знаете, что я остригла волосы еще до отъезда из Лондона и отрезанную косу спрятала на дно чемодана. Однажды вечером, уложив мальчика спать, я принялась раскладывать свои вещи. В комнате стоит старый комод, два верхних ящика его открыты, и там ничего не было, но нижний заперт. Я положила свое белье в верхние ящики, места не хватило, и я, естественно, была недовольна тем, что нижний ящик заперт. Я решила, что его заперли по недоразумению, поэтому, достав ключи, я попыталась его открыть. Подошел первый же ключ, ящик открылся. Там лежала только одна вещь. И как вы думаете, что именно? Моя коса!

Я взяла ее и как следует рассмотрела. Такой же особый цвет, как у меня, такие же густые волосы. Но затем я сообразила, что это не мои волосы. Как они могли очутиться в запертом ящике комода? Дрожащими руками я раскрыла свой чемодан, выбросила из него вещи и на дне его увидела свою косу. Я положила две косы рядом, уверяю вас, они были совершенно одинаковыми. Ну, разве это не удивительно? Я была в полнейшем недоумении. Я положила чужую косу обратно в ящик и ничего не сказала об этом Рукаслам: я поступила дурно, чувствовала я, открыв запертый ящик.

«I took it up and examined it.»

Вы, мистер Холмс, наверное, заметили, что я наблюдательна, поэтому мне не составило труда освоиться с расположением комнат и коридоров в доме. Одно крыло его, по-видимому, было нежилым. Дверь, которая вела туда, находилась напротив комнат Толлеров, но была заперта. Однажды, поднимаясь по лестнице, я увидела, как оттуда с ключами в руках выходил мистер Рукасл. Лицо его в этот момент было совсем не таким, как всегда. Щеки его горели, лоб морщинился от гнева, а на висках набухли вены. Не взглянув на меня и не сказав ни слова, он запер дверь и поспешил вниз.

Это событие пробудило мое любопытство. Отправившись на прогулку с ребенком, я пошла туда, откуда хорошо видны окна той части дома. Окон было четыре, все они выходили на одну сторону, три просто грязные, а четвертое еще и загорожено ставнями. Там, по-видимому, никто не жил. Пока я ходила взад и вперед по саду, ко мне вышел снова веселый и жизнерадостный мистер Рукасл.

— Не сочтите за грубость, моя дорогая юная леди, — обратился ко мне он, — что я прошел мимо вас, не сказав ни слова привета. Я был очень озабочен своими делами.

Я уверила его, что ничуть не обиделась.

— Между прочим, — сказала я, — у вас наверху, по-видимому, никто не живет, потому что одно окно даже загорожено ставнями.

— Я увлекаюсь фотографией, — ответил он, — и устроил там темную комнату. Но до чего вы наблюдательны, моя дорогая юная леди! Кто бы мог подумать!

Так вот, мистер Холмс, как только я поняла, что от меня что-то скрывают, я загорелась желанием проникнуть в эти комнаты. Это было не просто любопытство, хоть и оно мне не чуждо. Это было чувство долга и уверенности, что если я туда проникну, я совершу добрый поступок. Говорят, что у женщин есть какое-то особое чутье. Быть может, именно оно поддерживало эту уверенность. Во всяком случае, я настойчиво искала возможность проникнуть за запретную дверь.

Возможность эта представилась только вчера. Должна сказать вам, что кроме мистера Рукасла в пустые комнаты зачем-то входили Толлер и его жена, а один раз я даже видела, как Толлер вынес оттуда большой черный мешок. Последние дни он много пьет и вчера вечером был совсем пьян. Поднявшись наверх, я заметила, что ключ от двери торчит в замке. Мистер и миссис Рукасл находились внизу, ребенок был с ними, поэтому я решила воспользоваться предоставившейся мне возможностью. Тихо повернув ключ, я отворила дверь и проскользнула внутрь.

Передо мной был небольшой коридор с голыми стенами и пол, не застланный ковром. В конце коридор сворачивал налево. За углом шли подряд три двери, первая и третья отворены и вели в пустые комнаты, запыленные и мрачные. В первой комнате было два окна, а во второй — одно, такое грязное, что сквозь него еле-еле проникал вечерний свет. Средняя дверь была закрыта и заложена снаружи широкой перекладиной от железной кровати; один конец перекладины был продет во вделанное в стену кольцо, а другой привязан толстой веревкой. Ключа в двери не оказалось. Эта забаррикадированная дверь вполне соответствовала закрытому ставнями окну, но по свету, что пробивался из-под нее, я поняла, что в комнате не совсем темно. По-видимому, свет проникал туда из люка, ведущего на чердак. Я стояла в коридоре, глядя на страшную дверь и раздумывая, что может таиться за нею, как вдруг услышала внутри шаги и увидела, как на узкую полоску тусклого света, проникающего из-под двери, то надвигалась какая-то тень, то удалялась от нее. Безумный страх охватил меня, мистер Холмс. Напряженные нервы не выдержали, я повернулась и бросилась бежать — так, будто сзади меня хватала какая-то страшная рука. Я промчалась по коридору, выбежала на площадку и очутилась прямо в объятиях мистера Рукасла.

— Значит, — улыбаясь, сказал он, — это были вы. Я так и подумал, когда увидел, что дверь открыта.

— Ох, как я перепугалась! — пролепетала я.

— Моя дорогая юная леди! Что же так напугало вас, моя дорогая юная леди?

Вы и представить себе не можете, как ласково и успокаивающе он это говорил.

Но голос его был чересчур добрым. Он переигрывал. Я снова была начеку.

— По глупости я забрела в нежилое крыло, — объяснила я. — Но там так пусто и такой мрак, что я испугалась и убежала. Ох, как там страшно!

— И это все? — спросил он, зорко вглядываясь в меня.

— Что же еще? — воскликнула я.

— Как вы думаете, почему я запер эту дверь?

— Откуда же мне знать?

— Чтобы посторонние не совали туда свой нос. Понятно?

Он продолжал улыбаться самой любезной улыбкой.

— Уверяю вас, если бы я знала…

— Что ж, теперь знайте. И если вы хоть раз снова переступите этот порог… — при этих словах улыбка его превратилась в гневную гримасу, словно дьявол глянул на меня своим свирепым оком, — я отдам вас на растерзание моему мастифу.

«Oh, I am so frightened!» I panted.

Я была так напугана, что не помню, как поступила в ту минуту. Наверное, я метнулась мимо него в свою комнату. Очнулась я, дрожа всем телом, уже у себя на постели. И тогда я подумала про вас, мистер Холмс. Я больше не могла там находиться, мне нужно было посоветоваться с вами. Этот дом, этот человек, его жена, его слуги, даже ребенок — все внушало мне страх. Если бы только вызвать вас сюда, тогда все было бы в порядке. Конечно, я могла бы бежать оттуда, но меня терзало любопытство, не менее сильное, чем страх. И я решила послать вам телеграмму. Я надела пальто и шляпу, сходила на почту, что в полу-миле от нас, и затем, испытывая некоторое облегчение, пошла назад. У самого дома мне пришла в голову мысль, не спустили ли они собаку, но тут же я вспомнила, что Толлер напился до бесчувствия, а без него никто не сумеет спустить с цепи эту злобную тварь. Я благополучно проскользнула внутрь и полночи не спала, радуясь, что увижу вас. Сегодня утром я без труда получила разрешение съездить в Винчестер. Правда, мне нужно вернуться к трем часам, так как мистер и миссис Рукасл едут к кому-то в гости, поэтому я весь вечер должна быть с ребенком. Теперь вам известны, мистер Холмс, все мои приключения, и я была бы очень рада, если бы вы объяснили мне, что все это значит, и прежде всего научили, как я должна поступить.

Холмс и я, затаив дыхание, слушали этот удивительный рассказ. Мой друг встал и, засунув руки в карманы, принялся ходить взад и вперед по комнате. Лицо его было чрезвычайно серьезным.

— Толлер все еще пьян? — спросил он.

— Да. Его жена утром говорила миссис Рукасл, что ничего не может с ним сделать.

— Хорошо. Так вы говорите, что Рукаслов нынче весь вечер не будет дома?

— Да.

— В доме есть какой-нибудь погреб, который закрывается на хороший, крепкий замок?

— Да, винный погреб.

— Мисс Хантер, вы вели себя очень отважно и разумно. Сумеете ли вы совершить еще один смелый поступок? Я бы не обратился с подобной просьбой, если бы не считал вас женщиной незаурядной.

— Попробую. А что я должна сделать?

— Мы, мой друг и я, приедем в «Медные буки» в семь часов. К этому времени Рукаслы уедут, а Толлер, надеюсь не проспится. Остается мисс Толлер. Если вы сумеете под каким-нибудь предлогом послать ее в погреб, а потом запереть там, вы облегчите нашу задачу.

— Я это сделаю.

— Прекрасно! Тогда нам удастся поподробнее расследовать эту историю, у которой только одно объяснение. Вас пригласили туда сыграть роль некоей молодой особы, которую они заточили в комнате наверху. Тут нет никаких сомнений. Кто она? Я уверен, что дочь мистера Рукасла, Алиса, которая, если я не запамятовал, уехала в Америку. Выбор пал на вас, вы похожи на нее ростом, фигурой и цветом волос. Во время болезни ей, наверное, остригли волосы, поэтому пришлось принести в жертву и ваши. Вы случайно нашли ее косу. Человек на дороге — это ее друг или жених, а так как вы похожи на нее — на вас было ее платье, — то видя, что вы смеетесь и даже машете, чтобы он ушел, он решил, что мисс Рукасл счастлива и более в нем не нуждается. Собаку спускали по ночам для того, чтобы помешать его попыткам увидеться с Алисой. Все это совершенно ясно. Самое существенное в этом деле — это ребенок.

— Он-то какое отношение имеет ко всей этой истории? — воскликнул я.

— Мой дорогой Уотсон, вы врач и должны знать, что поступки ребенка можно понять, изучив нрав его родителей. И наоборот. Я часто определял характер родителей, изучив нрав их детей. Этот ребенок аномален в своей жестокости, он наслаждается ею, и унаследовал ли он ее от своего улыбчивого отца или от матери, эта черта одинаково опасна для той девушки, что находится в их власти.

— Вы совершенно правы, мистер Холмс! — вскричала наша клиентка. — Мне приходят на память тысячи мелочей, которые свидетельствуют о том, как вы правы. О, давайте не будем терять ни минуты, поможем этой бедняжке.

— Надо быть осторожными, потому что мы имеем дело с очень хитрым человеком. До вечера мы ничего не можем предпринять. В семь мы будем у вас и сумеем разгадать эту тайну.

Мы сдержали слово и ровно в семь, оставив нашу двуколку у придорожного трактира, явились в «Медные буки». Даже если бы мисс Хантер с улыбкой на лице и не ждала нас на пороге, мы все равно узнали бы дом, увидев деревья с темными листьями, сверкающими, как начищенная медь, в лучах заходящего солнца.

— Удалось? — только и спросил Холмс.

Откуда-то снизу доносился глухой стук.

— Это миссис Толлер в погребе, — объяснила мисс Хантер.

— А ее муж храпит в кухне на полу. Вот ключи, кажется такие же, как у мистера Рукасла.

— Умница! — восхищенно вскричал Холмс. — А теперь ведите нас, через несколько минут преступление будет раскрыто.

Мы поднялись по лестнице, отперли дверь, прошли по коридору и очутились перед дверью, о которой рассказывала нам мисс Хантер. Холмс перерезал веревку и снял перекладину. Затем он хотел отпереть дверь, но ни один ключ не подходил к замку. Изнутри не доносилось ни звука, и Холмс нахмурился.

— Надеюсь, мы не опоздали, — сказал он. — Мне кажется, мисс Хантер, нам лучше войти туда без вас. Ну-ка, Уотсон, нажмите на дверь плечем, не удастся ли нам открыть ее силой.

Старая, обшарпанная дверь тотчас же уступила нашим объединенным усилиям, и мы ворвались в комнату. Она была пуста. В ней не было ничего, кроме маленькой жесткой постели, стола и корзины с бельем. Люк на чердак был распахнут, пленница бежала.

— Здесь что-то произошло, — сказал Холмс. — Этот красавчик, очевидно, догадался о намерениях мисс Хантер и уволок свою жертву.

— Но каким образом?

— Через люк. Сейчас посмотрим, как он это сделал. — Он влез на стол. — Правильно, вот и обрывок веревочной лестницы, привязанной к карнизу. Вот как он это сделал.

— Но это невозможно, — возразила мисс Хантер. — Когда Рукаслы уезжали, никакой лестницы не было.

— Он вернулся и проделал все, что надо. Говорю вам, это умный и опасный человек. Я не удивлюсь, если услышу на лестнице его шаги. Уотсон, вам лучше приготовить свой пистолет.

Едва он произнес эти слова, как на пороге появился очень полный, крупный мужчина с толстой палкой в руках. Мисс Хантер вскрикнула и прижалась к стене, но Шерлок Холмс решительно встал между ними.

— Негодяй! — сказал он. — Куда вы дели свою дочь?

«You villain!» said he, «where's your daughter!»

Толстяк обежал глазами комнату и затем бросил взгляд на люк.

— Это я у вас должен спросить! — закричал он. — Воры! Шпионы и воры! Я поймал вас! Вы в моей власти! Я вам покажу! — Он повернулся и бросился вниз по лестнице.

— Он пошел за собакой! — воскликнула мисс Хантер.

— У меня есть пистолет, — сказал я.

— Надо закрыть парадную дверь, — распорядился Холмс, и мы втроем побежали вниз.

Едва мы спустились, как раздался собачий лай, а затем ужасных вопль, сопровождаемый жутким рычанием. Из соседней двери, спотыкаясь, выскочил пожилой мужчина с красным лицом и дрожащими руками.

— Боже мой! — вскричал он. — Кто-то спустил собаку. Ее не кормили целых два дня. Быстрее, не то будет поздно!

Мы с Холмсом выбежали из дома и вслед за Толлером завернули за угол. Огромный зверь с черной мордой терзал за горло Рукасла, а тот корчился на земле и кричал. Подбежав к собаке, я выстрелив; она упала, но белые ее клыки так и остались в жирных складках шеи. С большим трудом мы оторвали собаку от Рукасла и понесли его, еще живого, но жестоко искалеченного, в дом. Мы положили его на диван в гостиной, послали протрезвевшего Толлера за его женой, а я попытался по мере сил и возможностей облегчить положение раненого. Мы все стояли вокруг него, когда дверь отворилась и в комнату вошла высокая худая женщина.

Running up, I blew its brains out.

— Миссис Толлер! — воскликнула мисс Хантер.

— Да, мисс, это я. Мистер Рукасл отпер погреб, когда вернулся, а потом уж пошел наверх к вам. Как жаль, мисс, что вы не рассказали мне о своих намерениях. Я бы убедила вас, что вы стараетесь напрасно.

— Так! — воскликнул Холмс, пристально глядя на нее. — Значит, мисс Толлер известно об этом деле больше, чем кому-либо другому.

— Да, сэр, и я готова рассказать, что знаю.

— Тогда, пожалуйста, садитесь, и мы послушаем, некоторые детали, признаюсь, я еще не совсем уяснил.

— Постараюсь прояснить их, — сказала она. — Я бы сделала это и раньше, если бы сумела выбраться из погреба. Коли вмешается полиция, прошу вас помнить, что я была на вашей стороне и помогла мисс Алисе.

У мисс Алисы не было счастья с тех пор, как ее отец женился вторично. На нее не обращали внимания, с ней не считались. Но совсем плохо стало, когда у своей подруги она познакомилась с молодым мистером Фаулером. Насколько мне известно, у мисс Алисы по завещанию были собственные деньги, но уж такой робкой и терпеливой она была, что и словом не заикнулась про них, а просто передала все в руки мистера Рукасла. Он знал, что в отношении денег ему беспокоиться не о чем. Однако перспектива замужества, когда супруг может потребовать все, что принадлежит ему по закону, заставила его призадуматься и решить, что пора действовать. Он хотел, чтобы она подписала бумагу о том, что он имеет право распоряжаться деньгами, независимо от того, выйдет она замуж или нет. Она отказалась это сделать, но он не отставал до тех пор, пока у нее не сделалось воспаление мозга, и шесть недель она находилась между жизнью и смертью. Потом она поправилась, но стала как тень, а ее прекрасные волосы пришлось остричь. Правда, молодого человека это ничуть не смутило — он по-прежнему оставался ей предан, как и полагается порядочному человеку.

— Ваш рассказ значительно прояснил дело, — заметил Холмс. — Остальное я, пожалуй, в состоянии домыслить сам. Значит, мистер Рукасл применил систему насильственной изоляции?

— Да, сэр.

— И привез миссис Хантер из Лондона, чтобы избавиться от настойчивости мистера Фаулера?

— Именно так, сэр.

— Но мистер Фаулер, будучи человеком упрямым, как и подобает настоящему моряку, осадил дом, а встретившись с вами, сумел звоном монет и другими способами убедить вас, что у вас с ним общие интересы.

— Мистер Фаулер умеет уговаривать, человек он щедрый, — безмятежно отозвалась миссис Толлер.

— Ему удалось сделать так, что ваш почтенный супруг не испытывал недостатка в спиртном и чтобы на тот случай, когда ваш хозяин уедет из дома, лестница была наготове.

— Именно так, сэр, все и произошло.

— Премного вам обязан, миссис Толлер, за то, что вы разъяснили нам кое-какие непонятные вещи, — сказал Холмс. — А вот и здешний доктор и с ним миссис Рукасл! Мне думается, Уотсон, нам пора взять мисс Хантер с собой в Винчестер, так как наш locus standi [1] представляется сейчас довольно сомнительным.

Так была раскрыта тайна страшного дома с медными буками у парадного крыльца. Мистер Рукасл остался жив, но превратился в полного инвалида, и существование его теперь целиком зависит от забот преданной жены. Они по-прежнему живут вместе со старыми слугами, которым, наверное, так много известно из прошлой жизни мистера Рукасла, что у него нет сил с ними расстаться. Мистер Фаулер и мисс Рукасл обвенчались в Саутгемптоне на следующий же день после побега, и сейчас он правительственный чиновник на острове святого Маврикия. Что же касается мисс Вайолет Хантер, то мой друг

---

[1] Положение (лат.)

Холмс, к крайнему моему неудовольствию, больше не проявлял к ней никакого интереса, поскольку она перестала быть центром занимающей его проблемы, и сейчас она трудится на посту директора частной школы в Уолсоле, делая это, не сомневаюсь, весьма успешно.

Примечания

1

Карлсбад (Карловы Вары) — курорт в Чехословакии.

2

Валленштейн — немецкий полководец XVII века.

3

Шесть футов и шесть дюймов — приблизительно 1 метр 90 сантиметров.

4

Грум — конюх.

5

Темпл — лондонский квартал, где сосредоточены конторы юристов.

6

Ландо — открытая коляска, запряженная парой лошадей.

7

Франкмасоны (сокр. — масоны) — члены тайного религиозно-философского общества.

8

Дуга и окружность — масонские знаки. Прежде они были тайными, но современные масоны, нарушая старинный устав, нередко носят их на брелоках и запонках.

9

«Все неведомое кажется нам великолепным» (лат.)

10

Сарасате (1844-1908) — знаменитый испанский скрипач и композитор.

11

В Итоне и Оксфорде находятся аристократические учебные заведения.

12

«Человек — ничто, дело — все» (фр.)

13

Цитата принадлежит, видимо, самому Конан Дойлю.

14

Джордж Мередит (1828-1909) — известный английский писатель.

15

Ярд — около 0,9 метра.

16

Фут — около 0,3 метра.

17

A rat (а рэт) — по-английски значит «крыса».

18

Гражданская война Южных и Северных штатов (1861 — 1865), окончившаяся победой северян над рабовладельческим Югом.

19

Генерал Ли командовал Южной армией.

Джексон и Гуд — генералы этой армии.

20

Кювье (1769-1832) — знаменитый французский ученый, положивший начало палеонтологии (наука об ископаемых животных).

21

Останки (лат.)

22

Палмер, Уильям — английский врач, отравивший стрихнином своего приятеля; казнен в 1856 году.

Причард, Эдуард Уильям — английский врач, отравивший свою жену и тещу; казнен в 1865 году.

23

Цитата взята из дневника американского писателя Генри Давида Торо (1817-1862).

24

Серпентайн (Змейка) — пруд в Гайд-парке, в Лондоне.

25

Холмс имеет в виду английского короля Георга III (1738-1820) и премьер-министра Фредерика-Норта (1732-1792). Политика Георга III и Норта привела к конфликту, а затем к войне с американскими колониями.

26

Положение (лат.)

www.ingramcontent.com/pod-product-compliance
Lightning Source LLC
Chambersburg PA
CBHW060616310726
48982CB00003B/575
* 9 7 8 1 7 6 3 7 4 7 9 8 2 *